Approaches to Science Fiction

Approaches to

Science Fiction

Donald L. Lawler East Carolina University

Houghton Mifflin Company Boston
Dallas Geneva, Illinois Palo Alto London
Hopewell, New Jersey

Printed in the U.S.A.
Library of Congress Catalog Card Number: 77–077995
ISBN: 0–395–25496–5

Illustrations by Edith Allard

Contents

Preface   *ix*
Introduction   *1*

Part 1   Nineteenth-Century Backgrounds   29

George Gordon, Lord Byron   *Darkness*   32
Mary Shelley   *from Frankenstein*   36
Edgar Allan Poe   *Some Words with a Mummy*   58
Nathaniel Hawthorne   *The Birthmark*   72
H. G. Wells   *The Star*   86

Part 2   Fantasy Science Fiction   97

Space Opera   99
Leigh Brackett   *Enchantress of Venus*   101

Speculative Fantasy Science Fiction   154
Ray Bradbury   *Mars Is Heaven!*   156
Arthur C. Clarke   *Encounter in the Dawn*   172

Weird Science Fiction   183
Arthur C. Clarke   *The Nine Billion
Names of God*   185
Cyril Kornbluth   *The Mindworm*   192

Time Travel and Parallel Worlds   204
Robert A. Heinlein   *All You Zombies—*   206
Larry Niven   *All the Myriad Ways*   218

Part 3   Hard Science Fiction   227

Speculative Hard Science Fiction   230
Tom Godwin   *The Cold Equations*   232
Walter M. Miller, Jr.   *Dark Benediction*   253

Aliens   299
John Berryman   *Berom*   301
Murray Leinster   *First Contact*   319

Robots   346
Isaac Asimov   *Liar!*   348
Henry Kuttner   *Happy Ending*   364

Part 4 Soft Science Fiction   381

Speculative Soft Science Fiction   383
Ursula K. Le Guin   *Nine Lives*   385
Philip José Farmer   *The Sliced-Crosswise*
                         Only-on-Tuesday World   408

Utopias and Dystopias   422
Alexei Panshin   *When the Vertical World*
                    Becomes Horizontal   425
Poul Anderson   *The Star Beast*   441

Social Science Fiction   465
Kate Wilhelm   *Baby, You Were Great!*   467
Fritz Leiber   *Coming Attraction*   480

Part 5 Science Fiction Mixtures   493

Mystery and Horror Science Fiction   494
Don A. Stuart (John W. Campbell, Jr.)   *Who Goes*
                                          There?   496

Comic Science Fiction   543
Robert Scheckley   *Zirn Left Unguarded, the Jenghik*
                      Palace in Flames, Jon
                      Westerley Dead   545

Selected Bibliography   551
Index   557

Preface

Approaches to Science Fiction is designed to introduce students to the pleasures of reading and appreciating science fiction. This literature is a type of popular culture still actively developing its forms and exploring its subjects. Because science fiction is a living literature, this text tries to avoid needless prescriptions of what it ought to be, while at the same time suggesting that it is possible to approach the literature in a disciplined and systematic way. For these and other reasons, the text takes and encourages a number of approaches within a rather loose but, it is hoped, consistent analysis of the species, science fiction.

The structure of the text implies that the literature has developed its own critical rhetoric which is reasonably clear and coherent, despite its lack of precise and mutually exclusive categories. The conventional language of science fiction criticism, which has developed along with the literature, forms a significant body of knowledge and critical opinion that no reader of science fiction can afford to ignore. I have retained the familiar divisions of the literature into "hard," "soft," and "fantasy." These terms, which soon become familiar to any reader of science fiction, are discussed in their separate parts. The idea of a miscellaneous class of mixed forms may be new but should hardly be considered an original device of classification, especially in view of the past practice of science fiction writers. The class forms are convenient because they help us sort out science fiction stories by subject and treatment. They also conform nicely to the inherent and inherited characteristics of the literature, which are discussed at some length in the Introduction and are demonstrated in the text. One penalty for ignoring this traditional body of critical thought about science fiction would be the necessity of inventing or developing an entirely new critical vocabulary, which would be largely self-serving and, I believe, self-defeating in such a text as this. The likely result would be to force readers to labor over the mastery of a whole new terminology rather than to encourage them to read science fiction literature with greater understanding and enjoyment.

Perhaps the most original approach in the critical method of this text is that it takes seriously the critical language that has been generated by science fiction itself. I have tried to give it as much substance and underpinning as the scope of an introductory text justifiably allows. I have also attempted to draw out of the critical terminology of science fiction its literary, cultural, and intellectual associations as they are applicable.

The Time Capsule included in the Introduction emphasizes the connections between the literature of science fiction and the major intellectual and cultural developments in the West since the Renaissance. If any doubts remain on that score, the Time Capsule demonstrates graphically that science fiction has been a part of that mainstream from its beginnings. It also helps us see how science fiction has developed from its early origins in the romance, satire, and the science treatise—origins that have determined both the attributes and the distinctive features of the literature.

Another convention of science fiction criticism that I shall use in this text is that of referring to the genre under the rubric "SF," which I shall do from this point forward.

The Introduction establishes the theoretical basis of SF and emphasizes the reader-centered approach of affective form. It also stresses the distinctive character of SF both as a literature of knowledge and as a literature of power. The form is then considered as one whose characteristic power is the exercise of an imagined sense of awed wonder in readers. I have tried to underscore this effect of SF without making it a critical mannerism. Indeed, when readers come to study examples of mixed forms in the last part, they will discover that the major variance between SF and hybrid forms which blend SF with other genres lies precisely in substituting the effects and ends of, say, mystery or horror for those of SF. This is not a new idea at all, of course, because it is a practice common enough in all literature. The blending of forms takes place inside as well as outside SF literature, and the text demonstrates that mixtures among the traditional types of SF stories are commonplace. While these mixed types sometimes make absolute classifications difficult, they also indicate the vitality, originality, and variety of the species we are studying.

One aim of *Approaches to Science Fiction* is to develop a flexible critical framework that will help bring a sense of order to the study of SF literature without sacrificing the characteristic variety and liveliness of its many classes and types.

The text represents the three principal varieties of short SF and contains extended selections from one novel. The staple is, of course, the short story, which ranges here from the extreme brevity of Fredric Brown's "The Answer" through the more standard lengths to the longer varieties operating on the outer boundaries of the form, like Tom Godwin's "The Cold Equations," which almost qualifies as a novelette. Three novelettes are represented here ("First Contact," "Nine Lives," and "The Star Beast"), as are three novellas ("Enchantress of Venus," "Dark Benediction," and "Who Goes There?"). I regret that more space was not available to include another space opera in Part Two and several more examples of mixed forms in Part Five.

I hope to encourage the users of this text to see relationships among the stories in the recurrence of certain topics, attitudes, and values given emphasis by means of the selection and arrangement of the stories, the introductory matter, and the questions. Readers are reminded from time to time of parallels with the early SF literature of the nineteenth century found in Part One. The background selections have been chosen to indicate the historical development of SF, to show the early incidence of certain typical attitudes and ideas, and to demonstrate the persistence of those themes connecting with the SF of the twentieth century. Students are also encouraged throughout the text to develop the habit of making other types of comparative critical judgments so that they will come to feel and understand how the various types and classes are related to one another and to the species as a whole. In all, my aim has been to assist readers in developing their powers of analysis and understanding. Beginning students are offered a selected bibliography as a guide for further reading and study.

I would like to acknowledge past and contemporary critics and interpreters of SF whose works provided useful and instructive information. For backgrounds, I found J. O. Bailey's *Pilgrims Through Space and Time* invaluable, and I profited from Brian Aldiss's history, *Billion Year Spree*. Bernard Grun's *The Timetables of History* was a useful if not always reliable source of information in compiling the Time Capsule. James Gunn's *Alternate Worlds* became available soon enough to allow me to compare it with my already completed chronicle. In many cases it saved me from error or serious omission. I became acquainted with David Allen's *Ballantine's Teacher's Guide to Science Fiction* too late to be able to benefit from its treatment of the subject, but I felt reassured by the similarity of many of our categories and general critical orientation. Finally, I want to cite those fine old anthologies edited by Groff Conklin, Judith Merril, and Everett F. Bleiler and T. E. Dikty which I read with pleasure and much profit and from which I hope I have learned something of the values of the literature of science fiction.

I owe many debts that I can never hope to repay except through my gratitude to former professors, students, and colleagues. Especially, thoug! , I wish to pay homage to the late Morton Dauwen Zabel, who aroused my critical interest in the field. I am grateful also to W. Erwin Hester of East Carolina University, who indulged me—then a junior faculty member—in the folly of teaching SF. Endless thanks must go as well to the students of English 229 and 282: Their interest and enthusiasm for SF studies were too strong to disappoint. I also wish to extend my appreciation to those who reviewed the manuscript critically. They include Robert R. Green, Community College of Allegheny County; Willis E. McNelly, California State University; and Christian K. Zacher, The Ohio State University. Finally, and above all, I owe a debt beyond calculation to my wife, Terri, for her encouragement and critical intelligence, and to our children, John Michael, Stephen Jude, Amy Christine, and James Vincent, who provided their unique form of inspiration to undertake this project and to see it through.

D.L.L

Approaches to Science Fiction

Introduction

We read SF because it provides a unique kind of pleasure, quite unlike what we derive from any other sort of literature. Therefore, we find in SF a worthy content for critical inquiry because we naturally want to understand the nature and the quality of that pleasure and how it is produced. Readers have found many reasons for their interest in the literature of SF. Some relish the pleasures of escape or the satisfaction of reading a good story. Others appreciate the stimulation that comes from an encounter with the thought processes of science. In recent years, critics have become interested in the pleasures inherent in story-telling itself, pleasures especially important to a generation of readers starved by the denser forms of modern realistic and experimental fiction, both of which seem to have become increasingly more inward looking and tentative in response to the demands of the crude and often barbarous realities of the times. Many readers find themselves looking for a literature that is simpler, one that is more confidently assertive and outward in its storytelling. For years, this was one attraction of SF stories. The apparently glut-proof appetite of modern readers of SF may be explained on another level by insights drawn from past and present critics.

When contemporary critics write about the special pleasures of narration, they recall what Thomas De Quincey (1785–1859) said about the power inherent in some kinds of literature to exercise and expand our latent human capacity for sympathy with the great moral ideas. These and other sensibilities are later identified by De Quincey with the great moral powers of human beings, which, without exercise, would gradually dwindle. Later in the century, Matthew Arnold (1822–1888), both a poet and a critic, wrote in "Literature and Science" of his belief that, in the future, literature would somehow retain its power of "calling out the emotions, engaging and exercising them." Arnold could foresee the importance that science was going to have in the lives of his descendants, and he knew that art would play a central role in integrating the results of modern science into the human instinct for morality and beauty. He could not predict, he said, how literature would exercise its power of relating science to the basic human need for conduct and beauty, but only that it would be so. We know now that the literature with the power of exercising our latent capacities to develop the implications of modern science for human instincts for conduct and beauty is SF. It seems clear, therefore, that the almost two-hundred-year popularity of SF may be not only beneficial but even necessary, after all. If we may trust our critical thinkers, we must conclude that SF as a literature of power answers a fundamental need of readers whose lives are being affected by science and technological change.

For some time now writers and apologists for SF, together with social analysts, have noted the importance of SF as a means of reconciling human beings to a pattern of accelerating change by preparing us to face the unknown. People have always dealt with the unknown by inventing symbols that have the power to express their apprehension over new and strange events because instinctively they feel that to give artistic expression to emotions is to vent them. Symbolically, then, we reconcile ourselves to those things we find threatening or challenging through our powers of figuration or myth making. It was in this way, from a psychological point of view at least, that SF came into being. Long before there was a proper name for it or a terminology to describe what it was doing, SF was being dreamed and written.

The contemporary writer Isaac Asimov described SF as the literary response to scientific change. Inevitably, though, it is more than just reactive, because SF itself has become an integer of change that exercises its own shaping power on our culture. Indeed, we shall see that SF has demonstrated such a shaping power on the imagination since its primitive beginnings during the late Renaissance. One of our approaches to SF, therefore, is to understand the ways in which literature, or at least one aspect of it, has changed resonantly with the advancement of scientific learning. To that end, we begin by looking at how SF literature has developed along with the thought, the art forms, and the cultural practices of Western civilization since the invention of the printing press.

II
Time Capsule

A register of those events of science and intellectual and popular culture from the invention of printing with movable type to the present that are related to the development of modernism and, in literature, of SF.

1450 Johann Gutenberg establishes press to begin modern
printing.

1453 Fall of Constantinople ends
Byzantine Empire.

1492 Christopher Columbus sails
to New World.

Martin Behaim constructs
first terrestrial globe.

1512 Nicholaus Copernicus's

"Commentariolus" circulates
privately; proposes helio-
centric theory.

1517 Martin Luther posts Ninety-
five Theses in Wittenberg
and begins Protestant Ref-
ormation.

1519 Ferdinand Magellan cir-
cumnavigates globe.

1532 Machiavelli, *The Prince*.

1534 Henry VIII is proclaimed supreme head of English Church.

1543 Copernicus, *De Revolutionibus Orbium Coelestium.*

1545 Council of Trent first convenes.

1551 Thomas More, *Utopia.*

1558 Elizabeth I becomes queen (to 1603).

1560 First scientific society is founded by Giambattista della Porta in Naples.

1588 Spanish Armada is defeated.

1605 Francis Bacon, *The Advancement of Learning.*

1608 Johann Lippershey invents telescope.

1609 Johannes Kepler, *Astronomia Nova.*

1610 Galileo Galilei, *Sidereus Nuncius.*

1611 Mario de Dominis offers scientific explanation of rainbow.

King James Bible.

1614 John Napier invents tables of logarithms.

1616 Galileo is silenced by Inquisition.

William Harvey discovers circulation of blood ("On the Motions of the Heart and Blood" appeared in 1628).

1627 Francis Bacon's *The New Atlantis* inspires Royal Society.

1632 Anton van Leeuwenhoek, father of microbiology is born.

1638 Bishop Francis Godwin, *The Man in the Moon.*

1641 Bishop John Wilkins's *Mercury: or the Secret and Swift Messenger* speculates on invention of flying char-

iots, phonograph, and telegraph.

1649 Charles I is executed.

1650 Archibishop James Usher in *Annales Veteris et Novi Testamenti* estimates time of Creation at 9 P.M. GMT October 26, 4004 B.C.

1657 Cyrano de Bergerac, *Histoire comique des etats et empires de la lune (et du soleil,* 1662).

1661 Robert Boyle, *The Sceptical Chemist.*

1662 Royal Society is founded.

Boyle conducts experiments with gases.

1665 Isaac Newton conducts experiments with gravity; invents calculus.

London is hit by Great Plague.

1666 Great fire, September 3 to 7, destroys two-thirds of London.

1675 Greenwich Observatory is established.

Newton, *Optics.*

1687 Newton, *Philosophiae Naturalis Principia Mathematica.*

1688 Lloyd's of London begins at Lloyd's Coffee House.

"Bloodless Revolution" produces constitutional monarchy in England.

1700 Tax is levied on unmarried women in Berlin.

1702 First daily newspaper is published in London: the *Daily Courant.*

1705 Edmund Halley correctly predicts that 1682 comet will return in 1758.

1714 Gabriel Fahrenheit develops mercury thermometer.

1717 Smallpox inoculation is brought to England.

1719 Daniel Defoe, *The Life and Strange Surprising Adventures of Robinson Crusoe, of York, Mariner.*

1720 First serialized novels appear in newspapers.

1726 Jonathan Swift, *Travels into Several Remote Nations of the World by Lemuel Gulliver.*

First circulating library is established (in Edinburgh).

1735 Carolus Linnaeus, *Systema Naturae.*

1736 First successful appendectomy is performed.

1738 Excavation of Herculaneum begins.

1742 Anders Celsius develops centigrade thermometer.

1752 Britain adopts New Style calendar and leaves out September 3–13 to make adjustment. (Calendar was adopted by Russia in 1918 and by Greece in 1923.)

Benjamin Franklin invents lightning rod.

François Voltaire, *Micromegas. megas.*

1755 Lisbon earthquake kills thirty thousand.

Joseph Black conducts experiments with alkali.

Immanuel Kant, *General History of Nature* and *Theory of Heavens* (in which nebular hypothesis is first proposed).

1760 First British school for deaf and dumb is established (in Edinburgh).

Josiah Wedgwood founds pottery works.

1761 Mikhail Lomononsov discovers atmosphere of Venus.

Giovanni Morgagni, *On Causes of Disease* (begins pathology).

Johann Süssmilch develops statistics.

First veterinarian school is founded (in France).

1766 Henry Cavendish discovers properties of hydrogen.

1771 Luigi Galvani discovers that nerve impulses are electrical.

1772 Joseph Priestley and Daniel Rutherford independently discover nitrogen.

1775 American Revolution begins.

Priestly discovers properties of hydrogen chloride and sulfuric acid.

James Watt perfects steam engine.

Captain James Cook returns from second voyage to South Pacific.

1776 American Declaration of Independence is proclaimed.

Adam Smith, *Inquiry into the Nature and Causes of the Wealth of Nations.*

1781 William Herschel discovers planet Uranus.

Immanuel Kant, *Critique of Pure Reason.*

British surrender to Americans at Yorktown.

1783 Treaty of Versailles ends American Revolution.

Montgolfier brothers fly fire balloon.

1786 James Rumsey designs first mechanical boat.

Gaslight is introduced in Germany and England.

1789 French Revolution begins.

First steam-driven cotton factory opens.

1792 Mary Wollstonecraft, *A Vindication of the Rights of Women.*

1793 Eli Whitney invents cotton gin.

1794 Telegraph is built from Paris to Lille.

First technical college is established (in Paris).

1798 Thomas Robert Malthus, *Essay on the Principle of Population.*

1799 Rosetta Stone is found (deciphered by Jean François Champollion in 1821).

1800 Royal College of Surgeons begins in London.

Count Alessandro Volta invents battery.

1802 William Herschel discovers binary stars.

1803 John Dalton discovers atomic structure of matter.

Robert Fulton invents steamboat.

1805 Admiral Horatio Nelson is victorious at Trafalgar.

1812 Humphry Davy, *Elements of Chemical Philosophy.*

Marquis de Laplace, *Theorie Analytique.*

1814 George Stephenson constructs first steam locomotive.

Napoleon Bonaparte is banished to Elba.

1815 Napoleon is defeated at Waterloo.

John McAdam develops crushed stone roads.

1818 U.S.S. *Savannah* is first steamship to cross Atlantic.

Mary Shelley, *Frankenstein.*

1821 Michael Faraday discovers electromagnetic rotation.

Population figures: France, 30 million; Britain, 20 million; Germany, 26 million; United States, 9 million.

1826 Mary Shelley, *The Last Man.*

André Marie Ampère, *Electrodynamics.*

Nikolai Lobachevski develops non–Euclidean geometry.

Leopoldo Nobili invents galvanometer.

Otto Unverdorben develops aniline dye.

Joseph Niepci takes first photograph.

1827 Georg Simon Ohm's law is formulated.

1831 Michael Faraday demonstrates electromagnetic induction.

James Clark Ross determines magnetic North Pole.

1834 Charles Babbage develops principle of computer (analytical engine).

Faraday, *Law of Electrolysis.*

Cyrus Hall McCormick patents reaping machine.

1835 Halley's comet reappears.

Municipal Corporations Act reforms English borough government.

1838 Edgar Allen Poe, *The Narrative of Arthur Gordon Pym.*

Friedrich Wilhelm Bessel measures parallax for fixed star.

1839 Charles Goodyear vulcanizes rubber.

Theodor Schwann formulates theory of cell growth.

Stevens discovers antiquities of Mayan culture.

1840 Louis Agassiz, *Etudes sur les glaciers.*

1841 Poe, "Murders in the Rue Morgue" (first modern detective story).

Killiker describes spermatozoa.

First university degrees granted women.

1842 Christian Doppler, "On the Colored Light of the Binary Stars."

Ether is used as anesthesia.

1844 Samuel Morse builds electric telegraph from Washington to Baltimore.

1845 Austen Henry Layard begins excavations at Nineveh.

1846 Great potato blight hits Ireland.

1847 Ignaz Philipp Semmelweis finds cause of childbed fever.

1848 California gold rush begins.

Karl Marx and Friedrich Engels, *The Communist Manifesto*.

1850 Rudolf Clausius puts forth kinetic theory of gases and Second Law of Thermodynamics (entropy).

Pafnuti Chebyshev, "On Primary Numbers."

Herbert Spencer's *Social Statistics* begins sociology.

1851 Great Exhibition is held in London.

First Baron Kelvin publishes papers on conservation and dissipation of energy.

1856 Bessemer converter process is used for making steel.

Neanderthal skull is found near Düsseldorf.

1858 O'Brien, "The Diamond Lens."

1859 Charles Darwin, *On the Origin of Species*.

Étienne Lenoir develops internal combustion engine.

First oil well is drilled (at Titusville, Pennsylvania).

1861 American Civil War begins.

Daily weather forecasts begin in England.

Krupp family begins arms manufacture.

Population figures: Russia, 76 million; United States, 32 million; Britain, 23 million.

1863 National Academy of Sciences is begun in Washington, D.C.

Martin brothers develop open-hearth steel furnace in France.

Abraham Lincoln signs Emancipation Proclamation.

C. J. Davaine isolates anthrax bacillus.

1864 Pasteurization process is developed.

Karl Marx founds first International Workers' Association.

1865 Joseph Lister begins antiseptic surgery.

Gregor Mendel formulates laws of heredity.

Civil War ends.

President Lincoln is assassinated.

Jules Verne, *From the Earth to the Moon*.

1866 Cyrus West Field completes transatlantic cable.

Aeronautical Society of Great Britain is founded.

Ernst Heinrich Haeckel, *General Morphology*.

Alfred Nobel invents dynamite.

1867 Marx, *Das Kapital, I*.

1869 Francis Galton, *Hereditary Genius*.

Suez Canal opens.

Mendeleev devises periodic table of elements.

Edward Everett Hale, "The Brick Moon."

1870 Darwin, *The Descent of Man*.

First underarm deodorant is invented.

Verne, 20,000 *Leagues under the Sea* and *The Mysterious Island.*

1871 Edward Bulwer–Lytton, *The Coming Race.*

Fire destroys Chicago.

1875 Heinrich Schliemann, *Troy and Its Remains.*

London drains are completed.

1876 American Centennial Exhibition is held.

Alexander Bell invents telephone.

Schliemann excavates Mycena.

1877 Raoul Pierre Pictet liquifies oxygen.

Thomas Edison invents phonograph.

1879 First frozen Australian meat sold in London.

Edison develops first practical electric light.

1882 Josef Breuer treats hysteria by hypnosis, beginning psychoanalysis.

Edison designs first hydroelectric plant.

1883 Joseph Wilson Swan invents rayon.

Krakatoa explodes in volcanic eruptions.

Brooklyn Bridge opens.

1885 Louis Pasteur develops rabies vaccine.

1886 Robert Louis Stevenson, *The Strange Case of Dr. Jekyll and Mr. Hyde.*

Richard von Krafft-Ebing, *Psychopathia Sexualis.*

1887 Hannibal Williston Goodwin invents celluloid film.

1888 Nikola Tesla constructs electric motor (manufactured by George Westinghouse).

John Boyd Dunlop invents pneumatic tire.

Heinrich Hertz and Oliver Lodge independently discover that radio waves are similar to light.

1889 Baron Joseph Von Mehring and Oscar Minkowski prove pancreas secretes insulin.

Mark Twain, *A Connecticut Yankee in King Arthur's Court.*

1890 Emil von Behring discovers antitoxins.

First steel-framed building is constructed (in Chicago).

1891 Wireless telegraphy begins.

Eugène Dubois discovers "Java man" (*Pithecanthropus erectus*).

1892 Rudolf Diesel patents engine.

1893 Karl Friedrich Benz and Henry Ford each build motor cars.

World Columbian Exhibition is held in Chicago.

1894 Inheritance tax is introduced in England.

1895 Wilhelm Röntgen discovers x rays.

Guglielmo Marconi invents radiotelegraph.

Auguste and Louis Lumière invent movie camera.

H. G. Wells, *The Time Machine.*

Sigmund Freud and Josef Breuer, *Studies in Hysteria.*

1896 Antoine Henri Becquerel discovers radioactivity in Uranium.

Nobel Prizes are established.

1896 Wells, *The Island of Dr. Moreau.*

1897 Joseph John Thomson discovers electron.

Wells, *The Invisible Man.*

Havelock Ellis, *Studies in the Psychology of Sex.*

1898 Spanish–American War is declared.

Curies discover radium and polonium.

Wells, *War of the Worlds.*

1899 Wells, *When the Sleeper Wakes.*

1900 Max Planck formulates quantum theory.

Freud, *Interpretation of Dreams.*

Arthur John Evans discovers Minoan antiquities in Crete.

1901 Wells, *The First Men in the Moon.*

1903 Wright brothers make first powered flight.

Ford Motor Company is begun.

1905 Albert Einstein, "Special Theory of Relativity."

1906 San Francisco is hit by earthquake.

Zuider Zee drainage is begun.

Wells, *A Modern Utopia* and *In the Days of the Comet.*

1907 Ivan Pavlov conducts studies of conditioned reflex.

Ross Granville Harrison cultures tissue.

Henri Bergson, *Creative Evolution.*

William James, *Pragmatism.*

1911 Charles Thomson Wilson perfects cloud chamber.

1912 Robert Falcon Scott reaches South Pole.

Victor Franz Hess discovers cosmic rays.

Titanic sinks.

"Piltdown man" is found (proved hoax in 1953).

Edgar Rice Burroughs, *Un-*

der the Moons of Mars and *Tarzan of the Apes.*

Arthur Conan Doyle, *The Lost World.*

1913 Niels Henrik Bohr presents theory of atomic structure.

Hans Geiger develops radium counter.

Bela Schick develops diphtheria immunity test.

Richard Willstätter discovers composition of chlorophyll.

Elmer Verner McCollum isolates vitamin A.

1913 Bertrand Russell presents theory of stellar evolution.

René Lorin develops theory of jet propulsion.

1914 Robert Hutchins Goddard begins rocket experiments.

Alexis Carrel performs successful open-heart surgery on dog.

Panama Canal is opened.

World War I begins.

1915 *Lusitania* is sunk.

Ford Motor Company develops farm tractor and produces millionth car.

Margaret Sanger jailed for book on birth control (*Family Limitation*).

1916 Einstein, "General Theory of Relativity."

1917 United States enters World War I.

Carl Jung, *Psychology of the Unconscious.*

100-inch reflecting telescope is installed at Mt. Wilson, California.

Buffalo Bill dies.

October Revolution breaks out in Russia.

1918 World War I ends with 8.5 million killed, 21 million

wounded, and 7.5 million prisoners or missing.

Women's suffrage is passed in England.

Oswald Spengler, *The Decline of the West.*

Harlow Shapley measures Milky Way and proposes theory of expanding universe.

World influenza epidemic kills 22 million by 1920.

1919 Murray Leinster, "The Runaway Skyscraper."

Robert Watson—Watt patents early radar.

1920 Women's suffrage (Nineteenth Amendment) is passed in United States.

Eugene Zamiatin, *We* (Enlish translation, 1924).

First Commercial radio station, KDKA, opens in Pittsburgh.

Prohibition begins.

Television is invented.

1921 Karel Čapek, *R.U.R.*

Ludwig Wittgenstein, *Tractatus Logico-Philosophicus.*

1922 T. S. Eliot, "The Waste Land."

James Joyce, *Ulysses.*

Tutankhamen's tomb is discovered by Lord Carnarvon and Howard Carter.

Insulin is used to treat diabetes.

Alexis Carrel discovers white corpuscles.

1923 First birth control clinic is established (in New York).

Freud, *The Ego and the Id.*

Wells, *Men Like Gods.*

Weird Tales is founded.

1924 Joseph Stalin becomes dictator of Russia.

E. P. Hubble demonstrates existence of extragalactic nebulas.

1925 Werner Heisenberg and Niels Bohr develop atomic quantum mechanics.

John Thomas Scopes's "Monkey Trial" begins in Tennessee.

Adolf Hitler, *Mein Kampf.*

1926 Robert Goddard flies first liquid-fuel rocket.

Hugo Gernsback begins *Amazing Stories.*

Ivan Pavlov, *Conditioned Reflexes.*

H. P. Lovecraft, "The Call of Cthulhu."

1927 Charles Lindbergh flies across Atlantic Ocean to Paris.

1928 Alexander Fleming discovers penicillin.

Serge Veronoff, "The Conquest of Life" (rejuvenation by gland transplant).

First scheduled television broadcasts begin at station WGY, Schenectady, N.Y.

Philip Nowlan's first Buck Rogers story: "Armageddon —2419."

1929 Stock Market Crash, October 28, signals beginning of Great Depression.

Einstein, "Unified Field Theory."

Hubble measures large red shift in spectrums of extragalactic nebulas.

Gernsback promotes term "science fiction."

1930 *Astounding Science-Fiction* is begun.

Clyde William Tombaugh discovers planet Pluto.

Olaf Stapledon, *Last and First Men.*

1931 Population figures: China, 410 million; India, 338 million; Soviet Union, 168 million; United States, 122 million.

Ernest Orlando Lawrence invents cyclotron.

1932 Carl David Anderson discovers positron.

James Chadwick discovers neutron.

Karl Jansky pioneers radio astronomy.

Zuider-Zee drainage is completed.

Aldous Huxley, *Brave New World.*

Philip Wylie, *When Worlds Collide.*

1933 Hitler becomes chancellor of Germany.

Film *King Kong* is released.

Beginning of mass emigration of artists and scientists from Germany.

Wells, *The Shape of Things to Come.*

Drought (1933–1936) turns American plains into dust bowl.

1934 Stanley G. Weinbaum, "A Martian Odyssey."

1935 Čapek, *War with the Newts.*

Spanish Civil War begins.

1937 Xerox process developed by Chester F. Carlson.

Wallace Hume Carothers patents nylon.

Frank Whittle builds first jet engine.

1937 John W. Campbell, Jr., edits *Astounding Stories.*

1938 Orson Welles's broadcast of "War of the Worlds."

Clive S. Lewis, *Out of the Silent Planet.*

1939 World War II begins with

German invasion of Poland.

Igor Sikorsky makes first helicopter.

1940 Electron microscope is developed.

Edwin McMillan and Philip H. Abelson discover first transuranium element: neptunium.

Karl Landsteiner and A. S. Wiener discover Rh factor in human blood.

Lascaux Cave wall paintings are found.

Battle of Britain and London Blitz test British.

1941 United States enters World War II.

Edwin Mattison McMillan and Glenn Theodore Seaborg discover plutonium.

1942 Enrico Fermi splits atom.

First automatic computer is built.

Magnetic recording tape is developed.

1945 First atomic bomb is dropped on Hiroshima.

World War II ends.

Nuremberg trials are convened.

United Nations charter and first meeting.

1946 John Hersey, *Hiroshima.*

Flying saucer reports increase in United States.

Jackie Robinson joins Brooklyn Dodgers.

Dead Sea Scrolls are discovered.

British nationalize coal industry.

Willard Frank Libby develops carbon-14 dating.

1948 Alfred Kinsey, *Sexual Behavior in the Human Male.*

"Mysin" antibiotics are developed.

Jewish state is established in Palestine.

Transistor is invented.

1949 Philip Hench discovers cortisone.

The Magazine of Fantasy and SF is begun.

1950 Glenn Theodore Seaborg discovers californium and berkelium.

Einstein, "General Field Theory."

Galaxy SF magazine is begun.

Margaret Mead, *Social Anthropology.*

Ray Bradbury, *The Martian Chronicles.*

Edgar Rice Burroughs dies.

Immanuel Velikovsky, *Worlds in Collision.*

1951 Electric power is generated by atomic energy.

J. Andre-Thomas develops heart-lung machine.

Isaac Asimov begins *Foundation* stories

1952 United States tests hydrogen bomb.

First oral contraceptive is developed.

Kurt Vonnegut, *Player Piano.*

1953 Structure of DNA is defined.

Joseph Banks Rhine, *The New World of the Mind.*

B. F. Skinner, *Science and Human Behavior.*

Kinsey, *Sexual Behavior in the Human Female.*

First Hugo Award (named after Hugo Gernsback) is

presented: Alfred Bester, *The Demolished Man.*

Arthur C. Clarke, *Childhood's End.*

1954 Nuclear-powered submarine *Nautilus* is launched.

Jonas Salk develops polio vaccine.

Einstein dies.

United States has 29 million television sets.

Bradbury, *Fahrenheit 451.*

In *Brown* v. *Board of Education* Supreme Court orders United States schools desegregated.

Disneyland opens.

1956 Neutrino and anti-neutrino are discovered.

1957 *Sputnik* is launched by Soviet Union.

International Geophysical Year is proclaimed.

Alfred J. Ayer, *The Problem of Knowledge.*

1958 National Aeronautics and Space Administration (NASA) is established.

Van Allen radiation belts are discovered.

1959 Soviet Union launches *Lunik* to photograph dark side of moon.

Louis S. B. Leakey finds homonid skull that is 600,000 years old in Tanganyika.

Vonnegut, *The Sirens of Titan.*

1960 Laser beams are developed.

First weather satellite is launched.

W. M. Miller, Jr., *A Canticle for Leibowitz.*

1961 Yuri Gagarin becomes first person in space.

Population figures: China, 660 million; India, 435

million; Soviet Union, 209
million; United States, 179
million.

Civil rights movement gains
force in United States.

Robert A. Heinlein, *Stranger
in a Strange Land.*

1962 Cuban Missle Crisis threat-
ens United States.

Rachel Carson, *Silent
Spring.*

Mariner II, Venus probe, is
launched by United States.

Philip K. Dick, *The Man in
the High Castle.*

1963 T. A. Matthews and Allan
R. Sandage discover qua-
sars.

Michael Ellis De Bakey uses
artificial heart machine during surgery.

Clifford D. Simak, *Way
Station.*

1965 First Nebula Award is presented by SF Writers Association: Frank Herbert,
Dune.

United States and Soviet
Union sponsor space walks.

1966 *Luna IX* softlands on moon.

Heinlein, *The Moon Is a
Harsh Mistress.*

William H. Masters and Virginia E. Johnson, *Human
Sexual Response.*

1967 DNA is synthesized at Stan-
ford University.

Christiaan Barnard performs
first heart transplant.

Harlan Ellison (editor),
Dangerous Visions, signals
"New Wave" SF.

1968 Pulsars are discovered by
Anthony Hewish and S. J.
Bell.

RNA is synthesized.

James D. Watson, *The Double Helix.*

Film *2001: A Space Odys-
sey* is released.

Encyclical *Humanae Vitae*
is issued by Vatican.

1969 Neil Armstrong becomes
first person on moon.

Second lunar landing: As-
tronauts Conrad and Bean
return with samples.

Joseph Weber observes gravity waves postulated by Albert Einstein.

Mariner transmits television
pictures of Martian surface.

DDT is banned.

Ursula K. Le Guin, *The Left
Hand of Darkness.*

Vonnegut, *Slaughterhouse-
Five.*

1970 First complete gene synthesis is successful.

Apollo XIII moon flight is
aborted.

Population figures: China,
760 million; India, 550
million; Soviet Union, 243
million; United States, 205
million.

Antiwar strike is staged at
universities throughout
United States.

Alvin Toffler, *Future Shock.*

Larry Niven, *Ringworld.*

1971 *Apollo XIV* and *XV* are
launched.

Mariner IX orbits Mars.

Soviet Union softlands capsule on Mars.

1972 *Apollo XVI* and *XVII* crews
spend three days each on
moon.

Richard Leakey and Glynn
Isaac discover homonid skull
that is 2.5 million years old
in Kenya.

Soviet Union softlands
Venus VIII.

Dow Jones Average reaches 1,000.

Club of Rome, *Limits to Growth.*

Holography is demonstrated.

Skylab I completes four missions.

Pioneer X fly-by of Jupiter transmits television signals.

Energy crisis is felt throughout world.

Thomas Pynchon, *Gravity's Rainbow.*

Watergate Scandal is revealed in United States.

1974 *Skylab* astronauts are in space a record eighty-four days.

Mariner X transmits television pictures of Venus and Mercury.

India becomes sixth nation to test atomic bomb; others are United States, Soviet Union, England, France, and China.

J. Bronowski, *The Ascent of Man.*

1975 Smallpox is eradicated.

Close satellite galaxy is discovered.

Homonid bones 3.75 million years old are found.

Le Guin, *The Dispossessed.*

1976 *Viking* transmits television pictures of Martian surface.

American Bicentennial is observed.

Chairman Mao dies in China.

Human bionics is developed.

Commercial laser use becomes practical.

The preceding Time Capsule charts the coincidental emergence of SF with the scientific and industrial revolutions. The growth of this literary species has been the product of a long, elaborate, and continuing cultural evolution. The character of this composite art form has been shaped, therefore, by accretions of scientific thought, cultural practice, and literary history. The literature we study here has been a force in the changes that have transformed Western culture from an aristocratic and feudal one in the sixteenth century to a democratic and socialist one in the twentieth. The focus of change has been on the development of a new class—the learning, middle class; and SF expresses in the idiom of that class many of its hopes, fears, and ideals. As the Time Capsule emphasizes, SF is well within the mainstream of the intellectual and cultural development of the past half millenium. Before looking into the literary history of SF, beginning with the last century, let us consider more closely the early development of SF as a literary species in the hope of discovering what its origins can tell us about its character and its attributes.

The distinctive literary characteristics of modern SF arise from three classical genres that either flourished or were revived during the Renaissance: the scientific treatise, the satire, and the romance.

The association of art with scientific speculation is a long and honorable one, going back at least to the Greeks and continuing to the present. Some critics even trace the appearance of SF to such sources as Lucretius's *On the Nature of Things* and Lucian's *True History.* Much scientific writing since the Renaissance has found its way eventually into the common culture of the times and hence into literature. No one would deny the importance of scientific ideas in the literature of SF, especially in hard SF, in which the machines and values of new technology are featured elements. Several other important traits of the science treatise have had a shaping influence on the development of SF. The problem-solving methods of science, often found in SF stories, probably account for the extrapolative character of much SF writing. The science treatise was also a future-oriented bit of speculation from the time of its modern reappearance during the Renaissance, and inevitably it was perceived as an adversary of established ideas and practice. These traits have persisted in both the science treatise and SF, and like birthmarks they now are regarded as identifying characteristics of both.

The ties of SF with satire seem no less ancestral. A backward glance through the Time Capsule reminds us that SF materials were used in the satire of the seventeenth century, and we could find many earlier examples if we were in the business of tracing the SF family tree. The alliance between SF and satire also has proved to be enduring. It is not simply that we have SF satire, although there is plenty of that. The SF of social criticism and of dystopias traces its beginnings to satire. Satire, along with science, assumes a world that is fixable, one that can and should be remade according to the laws of reason. Furthermore, even though satire (and SF) may treat worlds, peoples, or situations that are alien to the familiar world, the intention is ever to refocus our moral perceptions on the present circumstances or behavior of the race.

If you have been wondering where the tradition of fabulous invention and thrilling adventure comes from, we must look to the romance. Science treatise and satire may be literatures of knowledge, but romance is one of those literatures of power to which both De Quincey and Arnold referred.

The romance is an old and still vigorous literary form, developing from the epic long ago. In its turn, romance has generated numerous literary offspring, including fantasy, the Gothic tale, and horror and mystery stories, as well as SF. It is from the romance that SF derives its action adventures, youthful heroes and winsome heroines, threatening or exciting situations, rapid pace, exotic or fabulous settings, and often the presence of alien or supernatural agents. Other traits of the romance have been retained by SF, but these are the most important ones, and they indicate broadly the principal inherited characteristics that still operate in SF literature.

From this outline of the genealogy of SF it is possible to form some preliminary expectations about the species. The SF story treating the hard sciences or dealing with the technological aspects of imagined futures will probably possess some of the features we mentioned earlier as belonging to the extrapolative science treatise. This is not to exclude elements of the speculative science treatise from soft SF, but we should also be looking for some familiar characteristics of satire in the fiction inspired by the social and psychological sciences. Most notably, of course, we would expect them in the utopian-dystopian and social types of SF. The influence of the romance seems greatest in the mixed modes of SF, especially in the stories classified here as "Fantasy Science Fiction" and "Mystery and Horror Science Fiction." In addition, readers should be alerted to two other dispositions of the species.

The first of these is really more the absence of a certain quality that modern critics, if not modern readers, seem to value most highly. Because of its parentage, SF has been characteristically an extroverted literature. Perhaps it has never had much use for psychological analysis or the subtleties of character motivation because the weight of impending great events or simply the pace of the action has been too pressing. Usually SF deals with action rather than character. The essence of character in SF is to react in some decisive manner to the flow of events. Authors rarely have the opportunity, and traditional readers of SF rarely have the patience, for the niceties of character portrayal when the fate of the universe depends on the hero's next split-second decision. The typical attitude of SF fans is: "Let's get on with the action." To be sure, New Wave and other contemporary writers have done something to bring the techniques of the psychological novel into SF, but it is still rare for an SF story to get beyond rather elementary ideas of motivation and behavior. There are some exceptions, of course, such as Hawthorne; and there are several happy examples of sensitivity to character in the stories by Heinlein, Le Guin, Miller, and Wilhelm collected here. Still, if readers insist that all good literature must treat fully developed characters and provide subtle analysis of human behavior, they will be disappointed consistently by the focus of SF on action, imagined worlds, scientific ideas, and problem solving.

However, if in SF we have to give up a certain degree of leisurely analysis and psychological complexity in character, we gain something in narrative movement, in new worlds freshly realized, and in the experience of the peculiar power of SF to stir the imagination. Having noted the existence of this power, perhaps we are now ready to examine its nature more thoroughly.

We have seen that readers of SF tend to respond to action and adventure. Even when the emphasis may be placed on ideas or on engineering hardware, the movement is nearly always directed toward some action rather than to such areas as discussion or reflection. The central question of most SF stories is: What is to be done? The actions and events of SF are the reverse of commonplace; if they were not, there would be no need for the literature. Realism gives us the commonplace. Rather, SF seeks to fill in the ground between the world we know and the world we can imagine, through the operation of certain reasonable or at least plausible scientific forces, thus making that middle ground conceptually accessible to readers.

III

Our view of cultural history in the Time Capsule is a little like that of a time-exposure photograph. We miss all but a few notable individual contributions, but we see graphically a clear pattern of change and movement. We have observed ideas, themes, and even subjects appearing as early as the sixteenth century that were to become commonplaces of SF in the nineteenth and twentieth centuries. Such early intentions may have been those of satire or fantasy, but the instinct for converting elements of natural philosophy into imaginary forms is already evident. In addition to the new democratic sociopolitical structures, new and more democratic literary forms were developing or emerging during this same period, in which the scientific and industrial revolutions were reshaping the world and the place of men and women in it.

One early landmark date in the history of SF is 1719, the year in which Daniel Defoe published the book that is known to everyone as *Robinson Crusoe.* It was in this novel that the prototypal "new man" made his appearance, the man who was to be the stuff of which later heroes of both science and SF were to be made. In Defoe's story, we also find an early instance of the union of the three traditions that constitute the hidden ground of the SF of later generations. In *Robinson Crusoe,* we have social satire, science in the guise of technology (physical engineering), and the adventure story all brought together. We have the commoner-hero who masters a hostile environment by making use of the techniques of mechanical engineering. Not quite a fully developed novel in the literary sense, Defoe's adventure story is not quite SF either. It is true that science is used to control natural forces and make them work benignly, but the effect is something quite different from awed wonder or other traditional effects of SF. Perhaps this is because Defoe had no interest in going further than the technology of his time. Nevertheless, his adventure story was a precursor of that which came in the next century. The great thing about Defoe's work is the story it tells in the articulation of a new and possible dream, realizable through science.

It was almost a century after *Robinson Crusoe* that the first authentic SF novel made its appearance. During that interval, the evolution of SF from its early prototypes seemed to depend almost as much on the development of its chief literary forms, the novel and the short story, as it did on the advances in science and the emergence of popular and printed culture.

Mary Shelley's *Frankenstein* announced the dawn of a new epoch of the imagination and of the scientific and social development of the human race. The novel dramatized the need for an awareness of the moral responsibility that the human race would have to assume as a result of its growing power over the forces of nature. Perhaps it should give us all cause for reflection that the first two early masters of SF, Mary Shelley and Edgar Allan Poe, sounded such ominous notes in their tales and novels. To be sure, both were writing in the shadow of a vigorous Gothic tradition, but their visions, at least on a symbolic level, continue to haunt the modern imagination.

The Time Capsule broadly outlines the evolution of SF during the twentieth century. In England and France, the species never became stereotyped as extravagant escapism, as it did in America. Although still a minor form, it was recognized and accepted as an expression of living popular culture. During the 1920s and 1930s, H. G. Wells still dominated the novel, and he was joined by major new writers like Zamiatin, Stapledon, and Čapek. Mainstream writers contributed important works: Aldous Huxley's *Brave New World,* C. S. Lewis's Ransom trilogy, and later, George Orwell's *1984.* In America, however, things were different. The most important developments were taking place in the shorter fiction forms. Although the novel remained important, we do not find any American SF novelists to rival their European counterparts until after World War II.

Since we are not attempting a literary history of SF here, we must be content with noting only some of the larger forces influencing the modern SF story.

The first great influence to be reckoned with is that of the pulps. Cheap reprints were an established American enterprise by the end of the nineteenth century. Jules Verne's success and that of other writers of adventure romances brought SF to the attention of mass audiences. It was to be only a matter of time before a popular magazine devoted itself exclusively to SF stories. In 1926, Hugo Gernsback founded *Amazing Stories,* and with that began a new era.

One unwanted effect of popular enthusiasm was to make SF virtually a ghetto literature in America for more than thirty years, during which a perceptible gulf existed between elite, or mainstream, literature and SF. The reasons for the division were many on both sides, but they boil down to a suspicion and fear of science by the Brahmins of culture, the sometime extreme effects on SF writing of popular culture fads, and the pressures of the publishing marketplace. Nevertheless, Gernsback's *Amazing Stories* helped create new audiences for SF; and inevitably, SF created its own elite group, the fans, who organized conventions and awarded prizes not only for best novels and stories but also for best fan. It was out of this core of faithful supporters that a new generation of writers was to rise. Meanwhile, new magazines were being founded, and four perceptible trends surfaced out of the SF pulps. First there was the science-gadget story, promoted—when he could get them—by Gernsback with an almost evangelistic zeal. Then there was the action-adventure SF story (space opera), championed by Edgar Rice Burroughs and E. E. "Doc" Smith. The third trend was the SF mystery/horror story revived by A. Merritt and H. P. Lovecraft. Finally came the soft SF story stressing the psychological and social implications of science. These stories were both written and solicited by John W. Campbell, Jr., who, in 1938, became editor of *Astounding Stories.*

Campbell led a new generation of writers who demanded well-made stories that emphasized both science and relevance. His *Astounding Stories* dominated the field for twenty years.

The postwar years brought further significant changes. In the United States, science and technology became economic and military big business. The SF story thrived on the need of a culture to understand the implications of its own technology and to adjust to ever-accelerating change. It even found a voice to appeal to elite culture in the flood of doomsday and dystopian stories that expressed the anxieties of a generation for whom "the bomb" and "the pill" had become code words. American SF, after forty years wandering in the desert, was once again part of the cultural mainstream.

In the 1950s, two new pulps, *The Magazine of Fantasy and Science Fiction* and *Galaxy Magazine,* opened fresh markets for writers and readers. The former stressed the literary SF story and the relationship between SF and fantasy. The latter specialized in soft SF and mixtures of SF with the comic and with social satire. Thus, SF grew with the world in the 1950s and 1960s. Its fans became more critical, its conventions became international, and new subjects like parapsychological (psi) adventures and parallel and alternate worlds were explored. Most wonderful of all, perhaps, was the spectacle of SF coming true in the laboratories and on the moon. It was beginning to look as though John W. Campbell was right when he said that SF grew up to fill the gap between scientific inspiration and its practical application via new technology. He might have claimed even more, for SF helped to create a climate of ideas and expectations from which new laws of science were discovered and formulated. SF breeds not only more SF but a more visionary science.

As the 1960s ended in strife and confusion, SF also was shaken by change. The New Wave that first broke in England was also felt in the United States, and another generation of writers was knocking on the door. To the SF establishment, many seemed mere rebels in their insistence on elevating style over content, their introduction of formerly taboo sexual and political subjects, and their suspicion of the aims and direction of scientific technology and its associated industrial and political structures. Most disturbing of all to writers like Asimov and Clarke was the apparent indifference to or even ignorance of science on the part of some new writers. By the mid-1970s, however, New Wave writers had been absorbed into the field. The rebels, now no longer so young, had achieved an uneasy truce with the old guard. This brings us to the present, in which we find a species that has retained its self-critical spirit while it continues to change and develop in response to science, society, literature, and the marketplace. In other words, it has remained a vital, living, and shaping force of contemporary popular culture.

IV

There are already more definitions of SF than anyone can remember or use. Rather than attempt a synthesis of even the good ones, I offer the following definition with an emphatic warning: It tries to be reasonably inclusive, but it is not intended to exclude any legitimate work of SF that may fall outside its perimeter. While many features of SF literature deserve our attention, this definition emphasizes only two of them, in the interest of economy and coherence. The first is the truism that in SF it is the science that makes possible the experience of the characters: No science, no SF! The second point of emphasis is upon the typical effect that SF is designed to produce. Here again a caution is in order against a fanatical insistence that all SF must conform to a single formula. SF is not that kind of literature. No prescription that I know of is flexible enough to cover every case in a literary genre as various as this one. We must be content with stressing that the typical effect of SF has been associated with the exercise of an imagined sense of awed wonder, at least from the time of *Frankenstein*. Without further apology, therefore, the following definition attempts to suggest something worth knowing about the range and substance of our subject: *Science fiction is the literature that extrapolates from, speculates about, or depicts the effects of science, technology, or natural forces on human or other sentient creatures so as to produce a sense of imagined awe or wonder in readers.*

The last part of our definition needs further explanation and comment. We have seen that the peculiar power of SF to exercise imagined awe and wonder comes, in part, from its affiliation with romance. The power is assumed to be a characteristic and even an identifying effect of SF, but it is by no means the only effect. In some special cases noted earlier and later in the text, awe and wonder may be subordinated to other intentions; and in some cases, they may be almost entirely absent. To the degree that they are absent, SF tends to become rhetorical, even polemic in tone, as do Huxley's *Island* and Brunner's *Stand on Zanzibar,* which are mentioned later. Awe and wonder experienced in an imagined way are simply the operative effects of the characteristic power of the form. They are felt in a manner roughly analogous to the way imagined pity and fear are experienced in tragedy. Our definition, therefore, tries to bring together three distinctive features of the genre in subject matter, treatment, and effect.

The impact produced by a particular SF story will vary according to all accidental qualities of theme, plotting, characterization, and the like. Each story will have its own effect and meaning, peculiar to itself, because each story is a new creation. If we ask ourselves why a writer chooses SF rather than some other genre, and if we may ignore all the variables of inspiration and personal motivation, we arrive at a single constant. Writers choose SF as a literary type because they can achieve effects, produce imagined experiences, and generate perceptions possible only with such a form. SF is the means of creating certain kinds of imagined realities. It enables writers to deal with probabilities beyond the commonplace and in some cases counter to the natural—certainly counter to the conventional. Writers of SF want to design a story with the power of producing certain responses: an awareness, a mood, an insight, an idea, or combinations of these. The power of the horror story, for example, is to stimulate and exercise in readers an imagined sense of terror and dread. In *Supernatural Horror in Literature* H. P. Lovecraft argued that even one instance of imagined terror in a story is sufficient to justify it, and presumably also readers' participation in the imagined experience. The mystery story, in turn, seeks its characteristic effects of what we may broadly and somewhat circularly term "mystification." Perhaps our general premise is sufficiently clear from these illustrations. The constant in the equation here is the power of various stories to produce certain characteristic and perceptible imagined effects on readers. By reason of general consensus of critics and readers, we may say that SF seeks to generate in readers an imagined sense of awe and wonder as one of its most characteristic effects.

It remains for us now by way of concluding this Introduction to explain what is meant by imagined awe and wonder as intentions of SF and to illustrate how these effects may be produced. We say that these emotions are imagined or imitated, but obviously awe and wonder may be experienced directly as well. I think that we must make an attempt here to distinguish between the two kinds of experience. We must be careful not to draw our distinctions along lines which declare that imitations are merely imaginary, as opposed to real, emotions. Imagined emotions are real, in a sense. Ask any hypochondriac. The difference between an imagined emotion and a so-called real one occurs at the point of origin and in the manner of internalization.

An imagined emotion is stimulated and exercised by a work of art. Actually, this is already a familiar concept. Think of a poetic image. What is it? As we all know, it is an imagined sense experience, a phantasm. Similarly, emotions may be experienced vicariously, and these we shall call "secondary emotions" to distinguish them from real or primary ones. Obviously, imagined emotions are experienced as the result of the impact of a work of art on us. Since they are experienced in an imagined way, they do not announce themselves by a physical reaction but rather in a quickening of our imagination along the lines, say, of wonder and awe if we are reading SF. Incidentally, it makes no more sense to speak of a secondary emotion if it has not actually been experienced and recognized than it does to talk about images when there has been no experience of a phantasm by the reader. In discussing secondary emotions, we must try to be as specific as possible about the kinds of experience a story has the power of generating.

Awe and wonder are two of the elemental emotions of our nature, meaning that they are emotions inherent in human nature, along with such others as love, hate, fear, and pity. If a story has the power to exercise or to ventilate such emotions in any manner, primary or secondary, it is one that affects readers profoundly. The effects as well as the emotions themselves are not easily described, unless we concentrate on the features of the story that stimulate and exercise an imagined sense of pity, wonder, love, fear, or whatever may be the author's intent. It follows that one of the first intentions of readers or critics of SF should be to determine as accurately as possible the potential of a story for generating those specific experiences.

The exercise of imagined awe and wonder, we may expect, will be an important element of the effect aimed at by the SF story. A good story will move us to share vicariously the author's imagined world, as do the characters. In sharing a secondary world, we share in all the emotions and experiences of the world, and in something more: We share in imagination the power which called forth that world, those characters, and their experiences, and which sustains them as imitations. Our response to such power in SF and our imagined desire for such a world in which its characters live is an expression of awe and wonder.

Awe is our natural, involuntary response to a power that may be perceived in several ways. At the primary level, we may think of the sheer size, scope, or magnitude of a thing. Awe is the natural, human response to the sight of the Grand Canyon or Niagara Falls. In the case of the falls, the power is more expressed than implied. Human works may have a similar effect. The vastness of the space vehicle assembly building at Cape Canaveral is an instance; so is a building like the World Trade Center. When we think of the cathedral of Chartres or of the Parthenon, it is no longer mere size that attracts us. We respond to the same power of creative effort that produced a Homeric epic, or a Beethoven symphony, or a Michelangelo sculpture. The awesomeness of each is different, yet awe is our response to a perception of the greatness of the artist's conception and achievement. We are awed by a power, expressed or implied in its effects, that we feel is beyond our own capacity for expression or mastery. We are not awed by the familiar or ordinary. Nor do we feel awed by anything we can master and control. It must be a power alien to us and beyond our grasp.

If we are to experience imagined awe as the result of reading a story, it follows that the power of galvanizing the imagined emotion first must be present in the work, either by intention or by accident. Some stories very clearly seek to stimulate such an imagined response as a main intention. Poul Anderson's "Star Beast" and Murray Leinster's "First Contact" are examples. Other stories depend on such an effect in order to achieve the wider implications of their theme: Arthur Clarke's "Encounter in the Dawn" provides an illustration of this kind of story. But let us look even closer at this imagined sense of awe as an effect of SF in the following classic story, "The Answer," by Fredric Brown. It is so brief that it is almost an SF anecdote.

Dwar Ev ceremoniously soldered the final connection with gold. The eyes of a dozen television cameras watched him and the sub-ether bore throughout the universe a dozen pictures of what he was doing.

He straightened and nodded to Dwar Reyn, then moved to a position beside the switch that would complete the contact when he threw it. The switch that would connect, all at once, all of the monster Computing machines of all the populated planets in the universe—ninety-six billion planets—into the supercircuit that would connect them all into one supercalculator, one cybernetics machine that would combine all of the knowledge of the galaxies.

Dwar Reyn spoke briefly to the watching and listening trillions. Then after a moment's silence he said, "Now, Dwar Ev."

Dwar Ev threw the switch. There was a mighty hum, the surge of power from ninety-six billion planets. Lights flashed and quieted along the miles-long panel.

Dwar Ev stepped back and drew a deep breath. "The honor of asking the first question is yours, Dwar Reyn."

"Thank you," said Dwar Reyn. "It shall be a question which no single cybernetics machine has been able to answer."

He turned to face the machine. "Is there a God?"

The mighty voice answered without hesitation, without the clicking of a single relay.

"Yes, *now* there is a God."

Sudden fear flashed on the face of Dwar Ev. He leaped to grab the switch.

A bolt of lightning from the cloudless sky struck him down and fused the switch shut.

Here we have a story, an episode really, constructed almost as though it were a joke with a punch line. In a sense, perhaps, it is a kind of sardonic joke on the human race. The story is now something of a standard, and it exemplifies awe mingled with several other appropriate responses—surprise, chagrin, and the sense of a perverse but certainly excessive poetic justice. It is perhaps a commentary as much on human aspiration as on human folly. We might even call it a cautionary tale.

The element of the story that is important for us is the rather obvious impact which the creation of the ultimate Frankenstein monster has on our imagination. The awe in this story arises from our hidden fears over the potential for self-destruction or dependency implicit in our attempts as a race to master the forces of nature. The connotations of this theme are vast and deserve to be pursued, but we must limit ourselves here to the sense of imagined awe as unleashed by the power that creates but cannot control.

Clearly, the quality and character of imagined awe we may experience in reading SF is limited only by the variety and power of the stories themselves. Awe is found in combination with many other emotions and ideas in the stories collected in this text. The experience of each story is different, of course, and yet we find some recognizable features that the stories of each subclass of SF have in common, including both the context in which an imagined sense of awe is exercised and the quality of the emotion itself.

If awe touches on hidden fears, then wonder must be said to touch hidden expectations or desires. Wonder, like awe, is another elemental emotion that may be experienced in either a primary or a secondary way. Wonder is our natural response to the marvelous. As an emotion, it expresses delight, surprise, admiration, and desire. Wonder is keyed to the heart's desire, that of the will rather than of the appetites. It is an expression also of the human need for enchantment and altered states of awareness produced by many adventure stories, but especially by SF and fantasy. The wonder of SF is quite naturally the product of experiences and perceptions made possible by science technology. The view of the universe from inside the Crab nebula in "First Contact" is both awesome and wondrous. An aspect of our sense of imagined wonder is the wish to share the adventures of the characters. Although we may form an imagined belief in the character's world or a fear of it, as the case may be, our sense of the wonderful comes as the result of the secondary experience of creatures, situations, and events that readers have never experienced—and probably never will experience—on a primary level or in a primary reality. Indeed, it is precisely because the secondary experiences are beyond those of readers that they are desirable. Wonder may also be considered the result of the fulfillment or imitation of inner dreams, wishes, and thoughts. The emotion is felt as the result of the appeal of images that call forth those elemental desires of our inner selves.

SF is especially rich in producing wonder at all levels. An example may be taken from one of the stories in this collection, Ray Bradbury's "Mars Is Heaven!" At the point we join the tale, astronauts have landed on a Mars that turns out to resemble hometown America in about 1926. Lustig, one of the crew, finds himself in the home of his grandparents, along with the captain and another crew member:

In the living room of the old house it was cool, and a grandfather clock ticked high and long and bronzed in one corner. There were soft pillows on large couches and walls filled with books and a rug cut in a thick rose pattern and antimacassars pinned to furniture and lemonade in the hand, sweating, and cool on the thirsty tongue.

"Here's to our health." Grandma tipped her glass to her porcelain teeth.

"How long you *been* here, Grandma?" said Lustig.

"A good many years," she said tartly. "Ever since we died."

"Ever since you what?" asked Captain John Black, putting his drink down.

"Oh, yes." Lustig looked at his captain. "They've been dead thirty years."

"And you *sit* there, calmly!" cried the captain.

"Tush," said the old woman, and winked glitteringly at John Black. "Who are we to question what happened? Here we are. What's life anyways? Who does what for why and where? All we know is here we are, alive again, and no questions asked. A second chance." She toddled over and held out her thin wrist to Captain John Black. "Feel." He felt. "Solid, ain't I?" she asked. He nodded. "You hear my voice, don't you?" she inquired. Yes, he did. "Well, then," she said in triumph, "why go around questioning?"

"Well," said the captain, "it's simply that we never thought we'd find a thing like this on Mars."

"And now you've found it. I dare say there's lots on every planet that'll show you God's infinite ways."

"Is this Heaven?" asked Hinkston.

"Nonsense, no. It's a world and we get a second chance. Nobody told us why. But then nobody told us why we were on earth, either. That *other* Earth, I mean. The one you came from. How do we know there wasn't *another* before *that* one?"

"A good question," said the captain. The captain stood up and slapped his hand on his leg in an off-hand fashion. "We've got to be going. It's been nice. Thank you for the drinks."

Perhaps it is unnecessary to explain the effect both on Lustig and on readers. It is the wonder of nostalgia realized and come true, in which childhood is more than recovered. The implication is that it is recoverable somewhere, somehow. Better than that, Bradbury treats us to the illusion that it is recoverable as longed for by the adult—and not as it might have been experienced by the child, unaware of the miracle and lacking the perspective of the adult. As Bradbury well knows, the great desire for communication with the dead is in fact a desire to meet them and speak to them and know them as we are now, so that we, too, may be known as adults—as we have become. That is the sense of wonder which Bradbury invites us to experience in this story.

Effects of imagined awe and wonder may be highlights of a story, as illustrated earlier, or the intended focus of the entire story, as in the first example. The precise nature of the imagined experience is determined by the story and by readers' responses to it. No two combinations of effect are ever quite the same.

Beyond awe and wonder lie whatever other values a story may possess. I do not insist that all SF must move toward the effect of imagined awe or wonder in readers, even though most SF stories will do so; indeed, all stories with strong romance characteristics move toward such an effect. Yet there are tales in which ideas are so important to the story that the exercise of any secondary emotion is retarded, if not eclipsed. Stories of satire or social criticism will have little of the power we have been examining as outgrowths of romance. For instance, novels like Huxley's *Island* or Brunner's *Stand on Zanzibar* possess another kind of power (cautionary or inspirational) more suited to their subject matter and to the author's method.

SF has often been called a literature of ideas by its advocates, usually in the sense that it treats or even teaches its readers a little science. However, the ideas of a story include both the concepts of science technology treated directly or implied in that story and those thoughts in the reader that may be inspired by the story. Since SF is so frequently stimulating in this way, we should consider the quickening of our speculative powers as another distinctive intention of the species. The more scientific the basis of the story and the more involved science is in working out the narrative design, the more likely it is that the reader will be inspired to create imagined extensions of the narrative ideas. In this text, for example, the reader is asked by Arthur Clarke to speculate on the implications of alien contact with a primitive man. Robert Heinlein challenges our ingenuity in working out some of the paradoxes of time travel. John Berryman and Murray Leinster exercise both our imaginations and our rational powers in their stories of alien-human contact. John W. Campbell treats that same theme of alien-human confrontation in the manner of the Lovecraft horror story. These and other stories in the text push us into new avenues of thinking and speculation.

The questions that the stories may provoke are rooted in the ideas and the reasoning of the stories. This fact emphasizes another feature of the SF story: It does not need to be speculative itself in order to stimulate speculative thinking in the reader. The reader begins by adopting the narrative content of the story as the basis for speculation. The story, therefore, becomes something of a hypothesis from which new thought grows. However, the reader is not completely free to modify the narrative content without offering compelling reasons because that would not be playing the game fairly. If the reader wishes to invent new ground rules, the reader must become a writer in turn and invent a new story.

Therefore, if we are to consider SF as a literature of ideas, we must remember to include potential responses and speculations growing out of the reading experience. Such extended reasoning has been one of the pleasures of SF reading from the beginning. In a way, there is something almost experimental about the process. We may ponder, for instance, whether Frankenstein made the right decision when he refused to make a mate for the monster. Could two such androids find happiness together? Would the implied threat from the monster thus have been averted peacefully? Could the pair have had children? And so on. These and other speculations are legitimate extensions of our reading experiences, perhaps even inevitable consequences for a reader possessed of a lively imagination and an active intelligence.

Mixed modes in which SF is blended with mystery, horror, or the comic introduce still another value into our critical thinking. Apparently, the comic mode cannot exist side by side with the resolution of secondary emotions such as awe and wonder; and the SF horror story is one in which the element of terror simply drowns out all the other more subtle values.

Imagined awe and wonder are often functions of an author's success at creating an imagined world that has the illusion of a primary one, a world with a kind of truth and vitality of its own. If a writer is successful, the imitations will compel a kind of secondary belief. Or if a writer exercises our powers of imagined awe and wonder—even without our conscious awareness—the story will produce in us a sense of delight, or at least of pleasure, that we will want to repeat. If these secondary experiences sometimes seem to us more real or authentic than our own commonplace ones, it may be because they are more fully realized than the everyday events in which we participate routinely. Perhaps that is why we feel for them an imagined belief and desire. In a sense, such imagined belief is forced on us by the writer, just as a secondary emotion is an involuntary response to a power inherent in a work of the mind. Joyce Carol Oates, the writer and critic, once described the unique power of fiction this way in a book review for the *New York Times*: "The richer and more demanding the story, the more it forces us to participate in its imaginative drama."

Not all SF writers aim so high, of course. Some are content to invent their marvels and set them in motion for the amusement of readers. Others are less interested in inventing imaginary worlds than in having the pleasure of fleshing out an idea for a device or a story and seeing if it can be made to work. Many readers ask nothing more than to be stimulated in these ways, to enjoy an exercise of the mind. Some readers find their special pleasure in the intellectual stimulus that SF can produce, and they read the genre as a literature of scientific ideas and speculations. For still other readers, SF is a criticism of reality, or simply a medium for social commentary. And there are those for whom SF offers the pleasures of hyper-realities: an invitation to escape in high or in low adventure. These responses are in many ways appropriate ones for most stories available to readers of the species. It would be foolish to proscribe certain pleasures of reading as valueless. However, if a literary form is to offer anything of lasting value, it must be capable of producing works of esthetic merit within the limits of its subjects and traditions. I have chosen the stories in this collection because I believe they illustrate such merit in various ways and with varying degrees of excellence. The stories are here because they exemplify the different types and modes of SF, although not all types are or could be shown in a single anthology.

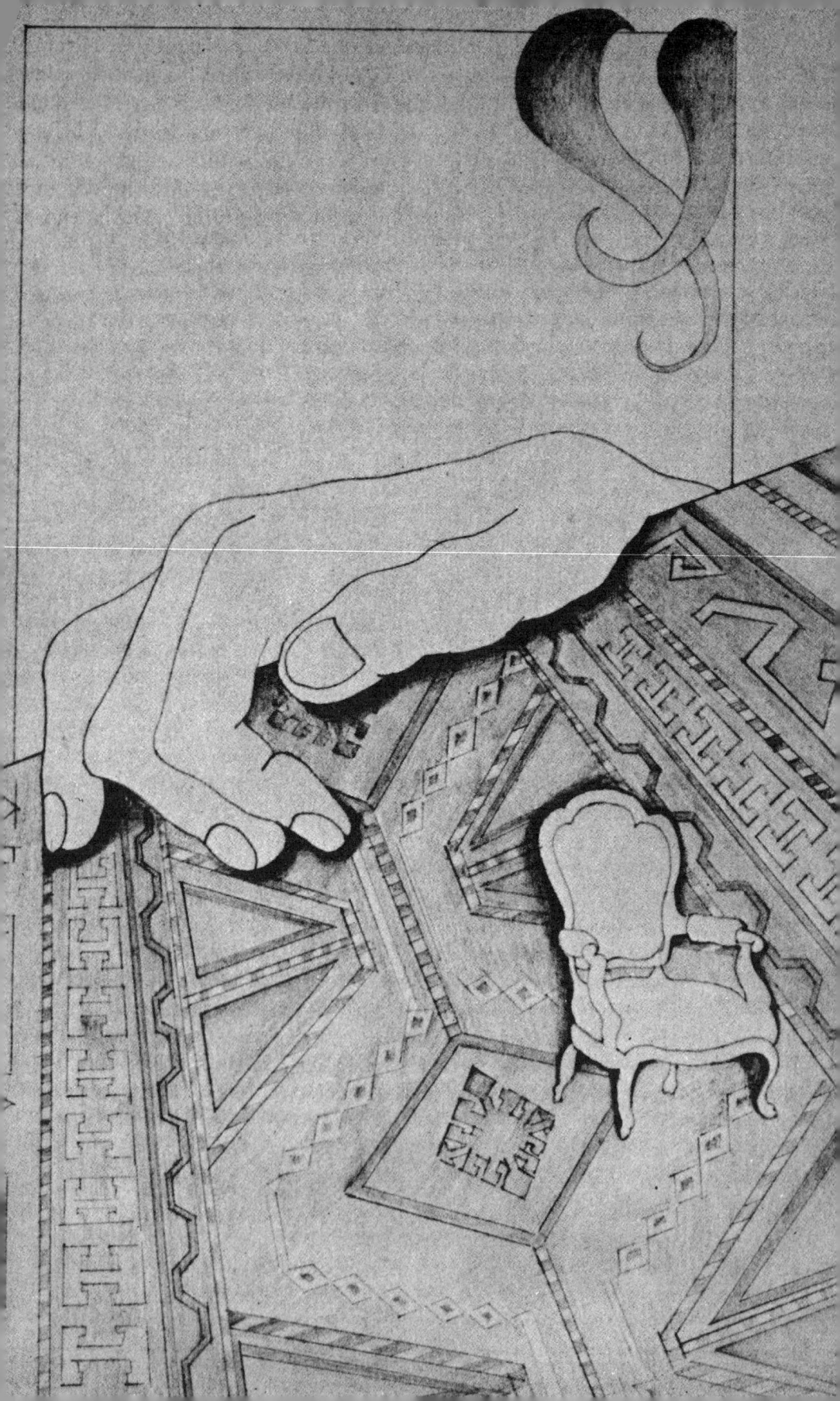

Part 1 Nineteenth-Century Backgrounds

In response to the question of when science fiction began, there seems to be no simple answer that does not ignore the history of Western culture we have seen recorded in the Time Capsule. In one sense, we may argue that SF began, at least in embryo, when human beings first recognized that the surrounding world was a separate reality which operated according to discoverable laws. Some scholars and literary historians have found traces of SF prototypes in classical and medieval literature; and we have seen for ourselves instances of SF appearing in the literature of the sixteenth and seventeenth centuries. Literature has always served as a means of connecting conscious with unconscious life, helping each generation discover the moral and esthetic dimensions of its experience. Whatever practical affairs have engaged the human race or exercised the mind have inevitably found their expression in art because art is one means through which the potential significance of our life experience is recognized. In this context of ideas, SF is the product of intellectual and cultural change, especially as that change relates to the growth of experimental science. The seeds of the literature are to be found in times usually thought of as prescientific.

The test we should apply, therefore, is not when first we find an isolated subject or attitude that we may associate with SF, given a sufficiently lively imagination. Rather we should ask: When does SF become conscious of itself and recognize its purposes and its forms? The answer is that such a consciousness did not come until the nineteenth century. Far from denying precedents and antecedents of SF before that time, we have insisted on them. SF emerged for the first time as a distinctive literary genre just at the moment we would expect; it appeared in an unmistakable fashion in Mary Shelley's *Frankenstein.*

Throughout the nineteenth century, the ideas, concerns, and special effects of SF were beginning to take shape. Perhaps this can be felt all the more in the work of writers not usually associated with the literature of SF. Selections from Byron and Hawthorne illustrate both the broad appeal and the legitimacy of such ideas within the literary community. The SF that was developing during the nineteenth century possessed unquestioned literary credentials, and its appeal was international.

The early work of Mary Shelley and Edgar Allan Poe marked a strange debut for a new species destined to become a leading form of popular culture. Seldom has the literature of a new class been so critical of that class or so skeptical of the worth of its ideals or the strength of its purposes. Partly, no doubt, this is an expression of the critical spirit of science, but it owes as much to the early association of SF themes and satire in Godwin's *Man in the Moon,* Swift's *Gulliver's Travels,* and Voltaire's *Micromegas*—to name but a few examples.

Among the affirmative voices making extrapolations from science and technology, the most famous was that of Jules Verne. Although the sentimental conventions of the day sometimes militated against his inherent optimism (witness the fate of Captain Nemo in *The Mysterious Island*), there is no doubt that the Verne formula of equal doses of science and adventure-romance appealed to a mass audience primed by science for ever more marvelous developments. The heir to this success was H. G. Wells, the great transition figure whose work marks the beginning of modern SF. Wells actually put less science in his stories than Verne, as the latter was quick to remonstrate, but Wells brought to the new fiction two fulfilling qualities. He dealt with the implications of science and its possible impact on history and social structures through imagined futures that were worked out plausibly. Equally important, perhaps, he brought into the new literature the attitudes of modern science.

With our historical context now firmly established, we are ready to turn to some examples of SF of the nineteenth century. Our embarrassment here is one of riches. It is not that there is too little, but that there is too much. There are already entire anthologies devoted to early examples of SF literature. Since we must be selective, I have tried to follow a few simple guidelines in choosing our materials. The fiction should illustrate the historical development of SF during that period, with examples taken from poetry, the novel, and the short story. The backgrounds should also demonstrate some important varieties of subject, treatment, effect, and type of SF that were being produced at the time and that anticipate future, modern developments. The materials selected also should demonstrate the persistence of important ideas, attitudes, and forms into the present.

However, we must be content merely to suggest the lines along which

SF has developed through the nineteenth century. Some writers represented here were identified with SF from the start, like Mary Shelley; others, like Byron, were not. Poe and Hawthorne are usually associated with other forms of fantastic literature. I think this diversity suggests that SF did not develop from a clan of writers within the literary establishment whom we may identify or stigmatize as "sensation writers." The origins of the species are to be found rather in the mainstream of Western culture, as this introductory note has tried to show. The first flowering of the literature of SF in the nineteenth century, therefore, is to be found at all levels of writing, in poetry as well as in prose, in major writers as well as in minor ones. SF was a form of literature whose time had come. Although there was a long period of growth still to follow, in the beginnings we may find without difficulty our own ideas and values reflected. And the time seems to have come once more when SF needs no other name but "literature" in order to be understood as a legitimate art form.

Darkness

George Gordon, Lord Byron

George Gordon, Lord Byron (1788–1824), was one of the great poets and
letter and journal writers in English. He was influenced early in life by
the Gothic stories of supernatural terror written by William Beckford and
Matthew 'Monk' Lewis. Although it is definitely a minor strain in his
writing, Byron's interest in the Gothic and the fantastic was an enduring
aspect of his mind. He is best known for his lyrics, satires, and longer poems
like *Childe Harold's Pilgrimage* (1812, 1816, 1818), the Oriental Tales
(1813–1814), and his masterpiece, *Don Juan* (1819–1825). The recent
publication of his letters and journals in a new edition has added a new
dimension to his reputation as a writer. In his own day Byron was universally considered one of the leaders of the romantic movement.

Byron's "Darkness" (1816) is a vision poem in which the author gives a
remarkably modern treatment of the doomsday theme of world catastrophe.
The cause of the catastrophe is not revealed beyond the sudden and
permanent extinguishing of the sun's light. Byron focuses instead on the
effects of that event. "Darkness" offers us for reflection the spectacle of
universal darkness and, inevitably, the destruction of all life on earth. The
rest, as Horatio observed, is silence. The contemplation of such a
doomsday scenario and the prospect of a dead world is one that strikes
contemporary readers as modern, at least in perspective.

What we miss in Byron's poem is an idea of some natural or scientific
cause at work to produce a catastrophe. If Byron had been more familiar
with astronomy, he might have wanted to provide a plausible cause. But
perhaps not, because one undeniable virtue of the poem is the way in which
the debacle of earth overtakes its people—suddenly and with a sense of
absolute finality. There is something in that which produces the kind of
spectacular desperation of the race struggling for survival in the dark.
Perhaps even if he had wanted, Byron would not have been able to think
of a way in which sudden and permanent darkness would overtake the world
without some even more devastating preliminaries.

As it is, Byron offers us only the cliché of the dream opening, which the
poet himself then partly retracts. Perhaps we are intended to take the
poem as a prophetic vision, a kind of waking dream. Byron begins:
"I had a dream which was not all a dream." To modern ears this sounds
like Yeats's "vast image out of *Spiritus Mundi*."

Compare Byron's treatment of the theme of world catastrophe with that of
H. G. Wells at the end of the century. Like Wells's, Byron's point of view
is detached and cosmic. Byron, however, concentrates on the spectacle of
a dying world in a spirit of prophetic terror and almost godlike resignation

at the end. He traces in broad dramatic strokes the hopeless struggle of
the race against cold, fear, and death. Wells, on the other hand, establishes
and works out the operation of natural laws that are the moving force
behind the story.

I had a dream which was not all a dream.
The bright sun was extinguish'd, and the stars
Did wander darkling in the eternal space,
Rayless, and pathless, and the icy earth
Swung blind and blackening in the moonless air;
Morn came and went—and came, and brought no day,
And men forgot their passions in the dread
Of this their desolation; and all hearts
Were chill'd into a selfish prayer for light:
And they did live by watchfires—and the thrones,
The palaces of crowned kings—the huts,
The habitations of all things which dwell,
Were burnt for beacons; cities were consumed,
And men were gather'd round their blazing homes
To look once more into each other's face;
Happy were those who dwelt within the eye
Of the volcanos, and their mountain-torch:
A fearful hope was all the world contain'd;
Forests were set on fire—but hour by hour
They fell and faded—and the crackling trunks
Extinguish'd with a crash—and all was black.
The brows of men by the despairing light
Wore an unearthly aspect, as by fits
The flashes fell upon them; some lay down
And hid their eyes and wept; and some did rest
Their chins upon their clenched hands, and smiled;
And others hurried to and fro, and fed
Their funeral piles with fuel and look'd up
With mad disquietude on the dull sky,
The pall of a past world; and then again
With curses cast them down upon the dust,
And gnash'd their teeth and howl'd: the wild birds shriek'd,
And, terrified, did flutter on the ground,
And flap their useless wings; the wildest brutes
Came tame and tremulous; and vipers crawl'd
And twined themselves among the multitude,
Hissing, but stingless—they were slain for food:

And War, which for a moment was no more,
Did glut himself;—a meal was bought
With blood, and each sate sullenly apart
Gorging himself in gloom: no love was left;
All earth was but one thought—and that was death,
Immediate and inglorious; and the pang
Of famine fed upon all entrails—men
Died, and their bones were tombless as their flesh;
The meagre by the meagre were devour'd,
Even dogs assail'd their masters, all save one,
And he was faithful to a corse, and kept
The birds and beasts and famish'd men at bay,
Till hunger clung them, or the dropping dead
Lured their lank jaws; himself sought out no food,
But with a piteous and perpetual moan,
And a quick desolate cry, licking the hand
Which answer'd not with a caress—he died.
The crowd was famish'd by degrees; but two
Of an enormous city did survive,
And they were enemies: they met beside
The dying embers of an altar-place
Where had been heap'd a mass of holy things
For an unholy usage; they raked up,
And shivering scraped with their cold skeleton hands
The feeble ashes, and their feeble breath
Blew for a little life, and made a flame
Which was a mockery; then they lifted up
Their eyes as it grew lighter and beheld
Each other's aspects—saw, and shriek'd, and died—
Even of their mutual hideousness they died,
Unknowing who he was upon whose brow
Famine had written Fiend. The world was void,
The populous and the powerful was a lump,
Seasonless, herbless, treeless, manless, lifeless—
A lump of death—a chaos of hard clay.
The rivers, lakes, and ocean all stood still,
And nothing stirr'd within their silent depths;
Ships sailorless lay rotting on the sea,
And their masts fell down piecemeal; as they dropp'd
They slept on the abyss without a surge—
The waves were dead; the tides were in their grave,
The Moon, their mistress, had expired before;
The winds were wither'd in the stagnant air,
And the clouds perish'd; Darkness had no need
Of aid from them—She was the Universe.

Questions for Discussion and Review

1. Does the poem contradict laws of astronomy or physics that would have been known at the time?

2. Awe and terror are two rather obvious effects of the poem, but how would you describe the note on which the poem concludes?

3. In what way(s) is Byron's handling of the catastrophe theme recognizably modern?

4. Why does Byron portray the last two human beings as he does?

from Frankenstein

Mary Shelley

Mary Wollstonecraft Shelley (1797–1851), second wife of the poet Percy Bysshe Shelley, was the daughter of distinguished parents. Her father, William Godwin, was a radical social and political thinker and author of *Enquiry Concerning Political Justice* (1793) and *Adventures of Caleb Williams* (1794), in which his views are presented in a speculative framework of hypothetical future conditions. Her mother, Mary Wollstonecraft, actively supported women's rights and social reform and wrote *A Vindication of the Rights of Women* (1792).

Mary Shelley is today remembered not only as the wife of the poet but also as the author of the first true SF novel. In addition to *Frankenstein,* she wrote many romance novels and miscellaneous works, the best remembered of which are another SF novel, *The Last Man* (1826), and the historical romance *The Fortunes of Perkin Warbeck* (1830). *Frankenstein* appeared anonymously in 1818.

Mary Shelley left us a famous account of how *Frankenstein* (1818) came to be written. It was begun during the rainy summer of 1816 as the author's contribution to a ghost-story contest proposed by Lord Byron. The essence of the tale came to her in a half-waking, trancelike state in the early morning hours after an evening's conversation that had ranged from modern science to vampires among Byron, Mary and Percy Shelley, and John Polidori. In her introduction to the 1831 edition of the novel, the author recalled:

I saw with shut eyes, but acute mental vision—I saw a pale student of unhallowed arts kneeling beside the thing he had put together. I saw the hideous phantasm of a man stretched out, and then, on the working of some powerful engine, show signs of life and stir with an uneasy, half-vital notion. Frightful it must be, for supremely frightful would be the effect of any human endeavor to mark the stupendous mechanism of the creator of the world. His success would terrify the artist; he would rush away from his odious handiwork, horror stricken. He would hope that, left to itself, the slight spark of life which he had communicated would fade, that this thing which had received such imperfect animation would subside into dead matter, and he might sleep in the belief that the silence of the grave would quench forever the transient existence of the hideous corpse which he had looked upon as the cradle of life. He sleeps; but he is awakened; he opens his eyes; behold, the horrid thing stands at his bedside, opening the curtains and looking on him with yellow, watery, but speculative eyes.

Her vision had answered Mary Shelley's need for a story that would, in her own words, "speak to the mysterious fears of our nature and awaken thrilling horror." With encouragement from her poet husband, she began to write the novel destined to be accepted as the first SF novel, and one of the great germinal works of our culture. What Faust was to the Elizabethans, Frankenstein is to us.

The following selections contain the core of the original inspiration of the story, beginning with the account of the monster's creation. We then skip to the monster's own narrative, in which he reveals his mind and purpose.

The Gothic elements of the Frankenstein story are so sensational that they have nearly eclipsed the underlying moral and mythic importance of the novel. The subtitle, "The Modern Prometheus," relates to the theme of Victor Frankenstein's experiments in the creation of life. In this story the author brings modern men and women face to face with themselves. Like the mad scientist of the story, recent generations have experienced the exhilaration of opening long-closed secrets of nature. But we also share Frankenstein's growing anxiety that science has carried us beyond our power to control the results or to know how to deal wisely with the unexpected consequences of creating new life. The thing everyone remembers about the novel is the monster. We tend to forget the even more important issue of the responsibility of science (and scientists) for its creations. It is a question that hangs above us more ponderously today than it did in 1818, when the novel first appeared.

The first selection from the novel traces the events leading to the creation of the monster and to the collapse of Dr. Frankenstein.

---

from Chapter 3

Partly from curiosity and partly from idleness, I went into the lecturing room, which M. Waldman entered shortly after. This professor was very unlike his colleague. He appeared about fifty years of age, but with an aspect expressive of the greatest benevolence; a few grey hairs covered his temples, but those at the back of his head were nearly black. His person was short but remarkably erect and his voice the sweetest I had ever heard. He began his lecture by a recapitulation of the history of chemistry and the various improvements made by different men of learning, pronouncing with fervour the names of the most distinguished discoverers. He then took a cursory view of the present state of the science and explained many of its elementary terms. After having made a few preparatory experiments, he concluded with a panegyric upon modern chemistry, the terms of which I shall never forget:

"The ancient teachers of this science," said he, "promised impossibilities and performed nothing. The modern masters promise very little; they know that metals cannot be transmuted and that the elixir of life is a chimera. But these philosophers, whose hands seem only made to dabble in dirt, and their eyes to pore over the microscope or crucible, have indeed performed miracles. They penetrate into the recesses of nature and show how she works in her hiding-places. They ascend into the heavens; they have discovered how the blood circulates, and the nature of the air we breathe. They have acquired new and almost unlimited powers; they can command the thunders of heaven, mimic the earthquake, and even mock the invisible world with its own shadows."

Such were the professor's words—rather let me say such the words of the fate—enounced to destroy me. As he went on I felt as if my soul were grappling with a palpable enemy; one by one the various keys were touched which formed the mechanism of my being; chord after chord was sounded, and soon my mind was filled with one thought, one conception, one purpose. So much has been done, exclaimed the soul of Frankenstein—more, far more, will I achieve; treading in the steps already marked, I will pioneer a new way, explore unknown powers, and unfold to the world the deepest mysteries of creation.

I closed not my eyes that night. My internal being was in a state of insurrection and turmoil; I felt that order would thence arise, but I had no power to produce it. By degrees, after the morning's dawn, sleep came. I awoke, and my yesternight's thoughts were as a dream. There only remained a resolution to return to my ancient studies and to devote myself to a science for which I believed myself to possess a natural talent. On the same day I paid M. Waldman a visit. His manners in private were even more mild and attractive than in public, for there was a certain dignity in his mien during his lecture which in his own house was replaced by the greatest affability and kindness. I gave him pretty nearly the same account of my former pursuits as I had given to his fellow professor. He heard with attention the little narration concerning my studies and smiled at the names of Cornelius Agrippa and Paracelsus, but without the contempt that M. Krempe had exhibited. He said that "These were men to whose indefatigable zeal modern philosophers were indebted for most of the foundations of their knowledge. They had left to us, as an easier task, to give new names and arrange in connected classifications the facts which they in a great degree had been the instruments of bringing to light. The labours of men of genius, however erroneously directed, scarcely ever fail in ultimately turning to the solid advantage of mankind." I listened to his statement, which was delivered without any presumption or affectation, and then added that his lecture had removed my prejudices against modern chemists; I expressed myself in measured terms, with the modesty and deference due from a youth to his instructor, without letting escape (inexperience in life would have made me ashamed) any of the enthusiasm which stimulated my intended labours. I requested his advice concerning the books I ought to procure.

"I am happy," said M. Waldman, "to have gained a disciple; and if your application equals your ability, I have no doubt of your success. Chemistry is that branch of natural philosophy in which the greatest improvements have been and may be made; it is on that account that I have made it my peculiar study; but at the same time, I have not neglected the other branches of science. A man would make but a very sorry chemist if he attended to that department of human knowledge alone. If your wish is to become really a man of science and not merely a petty experimentalist, I should advise you to apply to every branch of natural philosophy, including mathematics."

He then took me into his laboratory and explained to me the uses of his various machines, instructing me as to what I ought to procure and promising me the use of his own when I should have advanced far enough in the science not to derange their mechanism. He also gave me the list of books which I had requested, and I took my leave.

Thus ended a day memorable to me; it decided my future destiny.

from Chapter 4

From this day natural philosophy, and particularly chemistry, in the most comprehensive sense of the term, became nearly my sole occupation. I read with ardour those works, so full of genius and discrimination, which modern inquirers have written on these subjects. I attended the lectures and cultivated the acquaintance of the men of science of the university, and I found even in M. Krempe a great deal of sound sense and real information, combined, it is true, with a repulsive physiognomy and manners, but not on that account the less valuable. In M. Waldman I found a true friend. His gentleness was never tinged by dogmatism, and his instructions were given with an air of frankness and good nature that banished every idea of pedantry. In a thousand ways he smoothed for me the path of knowledge and made the most abstruse inquiries clear and facile to my apprehension. My application was at first fluctuating and uncertain; it gained strength as I proceeded and soon became so ardent and eager that the stars often disappeared in the light of morning whilst I was yet engaged in my laboratory.

As I applied so closely, it may be easily conceived that my progress was rapid. My ardour was indeed the astonishment of the students, and my proficiency that of the masters. Professor Krempe often asked me, with a sly smile, how Cornelius Agrippa went on, whilst M. Waldman expressed the most heartfelt exultation in my progress. Two years passed in this manner, during which I paid no visit to Geneva, but was engaged, heart and soul, in the pursuit of some discoveries which I hoped to make. None but those who have experienced them can conceive of the enticements of science. In other studies you go as far as others have gone before you, and there is nothing more to know; but in a scientific pursuit there is continual food for discovery and wonder. A mind of moderate capacity which closely pursues one study must infallibly arrive at great proficiency in that study; and I, who continually sought the attainment of one object of pursuit and was solely wrapped up in this, improved so rapidly that at the end of two years I made some discoveries in the improvement of some chemical instruments, which procured me great esteem and admiration at the university. When I had arrived at this point and had become as well acquainted with the

theory and practice of natural philosophy as depended on the lessons of
any of the professors at Ingolstadt, my residence there being no longer
conducive to my improvements, I thought of returning to my friends
and my native town, when an incident happened that protracted my
stay.

One of the phenomena which had peculiarly attracted my attention
was the structure of the human frame, and, indeed, any animal endued with life. Whence, I often asked myself, did the principle of life
proceed? It was a bold question, and one which has ever been considered as a mystery; yet with how many things are we upon the brink of
becoming acquainted, if cowardice or carelessness did not restrain our
inquiries. I revolved these circumstances in my mind and determined
thenceforth to apply myself more particularly to those branches of
natural philosophy which relate to physiology. Unless I had been animated by an almost supernatural enthusiasm, my application to this
study would have been irksome and almost intolerable. To examine the
causes of life, we must first have recourse to death. I became acquainted
with the science of anatomy, but this was not sufficient; I must also
observe the natural decay and corruption of the human body. In my
education my father had taken the greatest precautions that my mind
should be impressed with no supernatural horrors. I do not ever remember to have trembled at a tale of superstition or to have feared the
apparition of a spirit. Darkness had no effect upon my fancy, and a
churchyard was to me merely the receptacle of bodies deprived of life,
which, from being the seat of beauty and strength, had become food for
the worm. Now I was led to examine the cause and progress of this
decay and forced to spend days and nights in vaults and charnel-houses.
My attention was fixed upon every object the most insupportable to the
delicacy of the human feelings. I saw how the fine form of man was
degraded and wasted; I beheld the corruption of death succeed to the
blooming cheek of life; I saw how the worm inherited the wonders of
the eye and brain. I paused, examining and analysing all the minutiae
of causation, as exemplified in the change from life to death, and death
to life, until from the midst of this darkness a sudden light broke in
upon me—a light so brilliant and wondrous, yet so simple, that while I
became dizzy with the immensity of the prospect which it illustrated, I
was surprised that among so many men of genius who had directed
their inquiries towards the same science, that I alone should be reserved to discover so astonishing a secret.

Remember, I am not recording the vision of a madman. The sun
does not more certainly shine in the heavens than that which I now
affirm is true. Some miracle might have produced it, yet the stages of
the discovery were distinct and probable. After days and nights of incredible labour and fatigue, I succeeded in discovering the cause of generation and life; nay, more, I became myself capable of bestowing animation upon lifeless matter.

The astonishment which I had at first experienced on this discovery soon gave place to delight and rapture. After so much time spent in· painful labour, to arrive at once at the summit of my desires was the most gratifying consummation of my toils. But this discovery was so great and overwhelming that all the steps by which I had been progressively led to it were obliterated, and I beheld only the result. What had been the study and desire of the wisest men since the creation of the world was now within my grasp. Not that, like a magic scene, it all opened upon me at once: the information I had obtained was of a nature rather to direct my endeavours so soon as I should point them towards the object of my search than to exhibit that object already accomplished. I was like the Arabian who had been buried with the dead and found a passage to life, aided only by one glimmering and seemingly ineffectual light.

I see by your eagerness and the wonder and hope which your eyes express, my friend, that you expect to be informed of the secret with which I am acquainted; that cannot be; listen patiently until the end of my story, and you will easily perceive why I am reserved upon that subject. I will not lead you on, unguarded and ardent as I then was, to your destruction and infallible misery. Learn from me, if not by my precepts, at least by my example, how dangerous is the acquirement of knowledge and how much happier that man is who believes his native town to be the world, than he who aspires to become greater than his nature will allow.

When I found so astonishing a power placed within my hands, I hesitated a long time concerning the manner in which I should employ it. Although I possessed the capacity of bestowing animation, yet to prepare a frame for the reception of it, with all its intricacies of fibres, muscles, and veins, still remained a work of inconceivable difficulty and labour. I doubted at first whether I should attempt the creation of a being like myself, or one of simpler organization; but my imagination was too much exalted by my first success to permit me to doubt of my ability to give life to an animal as complex and wonderful as man. The materials at present within my command hardly appeared adequate to so arduous an undertaking, but I doubted not that I should ultimately succeed. I prepared myself for a multitude of reverses; my operations might be incessantly baffled, and at last my work be imperfect, yet when I considered the improvement which every day takes place in science and mechanics, I was encouraged to hope my present attempts would at least lay the foundations of future success. Nor could I consider the magnitude and complexity of my plan as any argument of its impracticability. It was with these feelings that I began the creation of a human being. As the minuteness of the parts formed a great hindrance to my speed, I resolved, contary to my first intention, to make the being of a gigantic stature, that is to say, about eight feet in height, and proportionably large. After having formed this determination and having spent some months in successfully collecting and arranging my materials, I began.

No one can conceive the variety of feelings which bore me onwards, like a hurricane, in the first enthusiasm of success. Life and death appeared to me ideal bounds, which I should first break through, and pour a torrent of light into our dark world. A new species would bless me as its creator and source; many happy and excellent natures would owe their being to me. No father could claim the gratitude of his child so completely as I should deserve theirs. Pursuing these reflections, I thought that if I could bestow animation upon lifeless matter, I might in process of time (although I now found it impossible) renew life where death had apparently devoted the body to corruption.

These thoughts supported my spirits, while I pursued my undertaking with unremitting ardour. My cheek had grown pale with study, and my person had become emaciated with confinement. Sometimes, on the very brink of certainty, I failed; yet still I clung to the hope which the next day or the next hour might realize. One secret which I alone possessed was the hope to which I had dedicated myself; and the moon gazed on my midnight labours, while, with unrelaxed and breathless eagerness, I pursued nature to her hiding-places. Who shall conceive the horrors of my secret toil as I dabbled among the unhallowed damps of the grave or tortured the living animal to animate the lifeless clay? My limbs now tremble, and my eyes swim with the remembrance; but then a resistless and almost frantic impulse urged me forward; I seemed to have lost all soul or sensation but for this one pursuit. It was indeed but a passing trance, that only made me feel renewed acuteness so soon as, the unnatural stimulus ceasing to operate, I had returned to my old habits. I collected bones from charnel-houses and disturbed, with profane fingers, the tremendous secrets of the human frame. In a solitary chamber, or rather cell, at the top of the house, and separated from all the other apartments by a gallery and staircase, I kept my workshop of filthy creation; my eyeballs were starting from their sockets in attending to the details of my employment. The dissecting room and the slaughter-house furnished many of my materials; and often did my human nature turn with loathing from my occupation, whilst, still urged on by an eagerness which perpetually increased, I brought my work near to a conclusion.

The summer months passed while I was thus engaged, heart and soul, in one pursuit. It was a most beautiful season; never did the fields bestow a more plentiful harvest or the vines yield a more luxuriant vintage, but my eyes were insensible to the charms of nature. And the same feelings which made me neglect the scenes around me caused me also to forget those friends who were so many miles absent, and whom I had not seen for so long a time. I knew my silence disquieted them, and I well remembered the words of my father: "I know that while you are pleased with yourself you will think of us with affection, and we shall hear regularly from you. You must pardon me if I regard any interruption in your correspondence as a proof that your other duties are equally neglected."

I knew well therefore what would be my father's feelings, but I could not tear my thoughts from my employment, loathsome in itself, but which had taken an irresistible hold of my imagination. I wished, as it were, to procrastinate all that related to my feelings of affection until the great object, which swallowed up every habit of my nature, should be completed.

I then thought that my father would be unjust if he ascribed my neglect to vice or faultiness on my part, but I am now convinced that he was justified in conceiving that I should not be altogether free from blame. A human being in perfection ought always to preserve a calm and peaceful mind and never to allow passion or a transitory desire to disturb his tranquility. I do not think that the pursuit of knowledge is an exception to this rule. If the study to which you apply yourself has a tendency to weaken your affections and to destroy our taste for those simple pleasures in which no alloy can possibly mix, then that study is certainly unlawful, that is to say, not befitting the human mind. If this rule were always observed; if no man allowed any pursuit whatsoever to interfere with the tranquillity of his domestic affections, Greece had not been enslaved, Caesar would have spared his country, America would have been discovered more gradually, and the empires of Mexico and Peru had not been destroyed.

But I forget that I am moralizing in the most interesting part of my tale, and your looks remind me to proceed.

My father made no reproach in his letters and only took notice of my silence by inquiring into my occupations more particularly than before. Winter, spring, and summer passed away during my labours; but I did not watch the blossom or the expanding leaves—sights which before always yielded me supreme delight—so deeply was I engrossed in my occupation. The leaves of that year had withered before my work drew near to a close, and now every day showed me more plainly how well I had succeeded. But my enthusiasm was checked by my anxiety, and I appeared rather like one doomed by slavery to toil in the mines, or any other unwholesome trade than an artist occupied by his favourite employment. Every night I was oppressed by a slow fever, and I became nervous to a most painful degree; the fall of a leaf startled me, and I shunned my fellow creatures as if I had been guilty of a crime. Sometimes I grew alarmed at the wreck I perceived that I had become; the energy of my purpose alone sustained me: my labours would soon end, and I believed that exercise and amusement would then drive away incipient disease; and I promised myself both of these when my creation should be complete.

Chapter 5

It was on a dreary night of November that I beheld the accomplishment of my toils. With an anxiety that almost amounted to agony, I collected the instruments of life around me, that I might infuse a spark of being into the lifeless thing that lay at my feet. It was already one in the morning; the rain pattered dismally against the panes, and my candle was nearly burnt out, when, by the glimmer of the half-extinguished light, I saw the dull yellow eye of the creature open; it breathed hard, and a convulsive motion agitated its limbs.

How can I describe my emotions at this catastrophe, or how delineate the wretch whom with such infinite pains and care I had endeavoured to form? His limbs were in proportion, and I had selected his features as beautiful. Beautiful! Great God! His yellow skin scarcely covered the work of muscles and arteries beneath; his hair was of a lustrous black, and flowing; his teeth of a pearly whiteness; but these luxuriances only formed a more horrid contrast with his watery eyes, that seemed almost of the same colour as the dun-white sockets in which they were set, his shrivelled complexion and straight black lips.

The different accidents of life are not so changeable as the feelings of human nature. I had worked hard for nearly two years, for the sole purpose of infusing life into an inanimate body. For this I had deprived myself of rest and health. I had desired it with an ardour that far exceeded moderation; but now that I had finished, the beauty of the dream vanished, and breathless horror and disgust filled my heart. Unable to endure the aspect of the being I had created, I rushed out of the room and continued a long time traversing my bed-chamber, unable to compose my mind to sleep. At length lassitude succeeded to the tumult I had before endured, and I threw myself on the bed in my clothes, endeavouring to seek a few moments of forgetfulness. But it was in vain; I slept, indeed, but I was disturbed by the wildest dreams. I thought I saw Elizabeth, in the bloom of health, walking in the streets of Ingolstadt. Delighted and surprised, I embraced her, but as I imprinted the first kiss on her lips, they became livid with the hue of death; her features appeared to change, and I thought that I held the corpse of my dead mother in my arms; a shroud enveloped her form, and I saw the grave-worms crawling in the folds of the flannel. I started from my sleep with horror; a cold dew covered my forehead, my teeth chattered, and every limb became convulsed; when, by the dim and yellow light of the moon, as it forced its way through the window shutters, I beheld the wretch—the miserable monster whom I had created. He held up the curtain of the bed; and his eyes, if eyes they may be called, were fixed on me. His jaws opened, and he muttered some inarticulate sounds, while a grin wrinkled his cheeks. He might have spoken, but I did not hear; one hand was stretched out, seemingly to detain me, but I escaped and rushed downstairs. I took refuge in the courtyard belonging to the house which I inhabited, where I remained during the rest of the night, walking up and down in the greatest agitation, listening attentively, catching and fearing each sound as if it were to announce the approach of the demoniacal corpse to which I had so miserably given life.

Oh! No mortal could support the horror of that countenance. A mummy again endued with animation could not be so hideous as that wretch. I had gazed on him while unfinished; he was ugly then, but when those muscles and joints were rendered capable of motion, it became a thing such as even Dante could not have conceived.

I passed the night wretchedly. Sometimes my pulse beat so quickly and hardly that I felt the palpitation of every artery; at others, I nearly sank to the ground through languor and extreme weakness. Mingled with this horror, I felt the bitterness of disappointment; dreams that had been my food and pleasant rest for so long a space were now become a hell to me; and the change was so rapid, the overthrow so complete!

Morning, dismal and wet, at length dawned and discovered to my sleepless and aching eyes the church of Ingolstadt, its white steeple and clock, which indicated the sixth hour. The porter opened the gates of the court, which had that night been my asylum, and I issued into the streets, pacing them with quick steps, as if I sought to avoid the wretch whom I feared every turning of the street would present to my view. I did not dare return to the apartment which I inhabited, but felt impelled to hurry on, although drenched by the rain which poured from a black and comfortless sky.

I continued walking in this manner for some time, endeavouring by bodily exercise to ease the load that weighed upon my mind. I traversed the streets without any clear conception of where I was or what I was doing. My heart palpitated in the sickness of fear, and I hurried on with irregular steps, not daring to look about me:

Like one who, on a lonely road,
  Doth walk in fear and dread,
And, having once turned round, walks on,
  And turns no more his head;
Because he knows a frightful fiend
  Doth close behind him tread.*

Continuing thus, I came at length opposite to the inn at which the various diligences and carriages usually stopped. Here I paused, I knew not why; but I remained some minutes with my eyes fixed on a coach that was coming towards me from the other end of the street. As it drew nearer I observed that it was the Swiss diligence; it stopped just where I was standing, and on the door being opened, I perceived Henry Clerval, who, on seeing me, instantly sprung out. "My dear Frankenstein," exclaimed he, "how glad I am to see you! How fortunate that you should be here at the very moment of my alighting!"

Nothing could equal my delight on seeing Clerval; his presence brought back to my thoughts my father, Elizabeth, and all those scenes of home so dear to my recollection. I grasped his hand, and in a moment forgot my horror and misfortune; I felt suddenly, and for the first time during many months, calm and serene joy. I welcomed my friend, therefore, in the most cordial manner, and we walked towards my college. Clerval continued talking for some time about our mutual friends

* Coleridge's "Ancient Mariner."

and his own good fortune in being permitted to come to Ingolstadt. "You may easily believe," said he, "how great was the difficulty to persuade my father that all necessary knowledge was not comprised in the noble art of bookkeeping; and, indeed, I believe I left him incredulous to the last, for his constant answer to my unwearied entreaties was the same as that of the Dutch schoolmaster in *The Vicar of Wakefield*: 'I have ten thousand florins a year without Greek, I eat heartily without Greek.' But his affection for me at length overcame his dislike of learning, and he has permitted me to undertake a voyage of discovery to the land of knowledge."

"It gives me the greatest delight to see you; but tell me how you left my father, brothers, and Elizabeth."

"Very well, and very happy, only a little uneasy that they hear from you so seldom. By the by, I mean to lecture you a little upon their account myself. But, my dear Frankenstein," continued he, stopping short and gazing full in my face, "I did not before remark how very ill you appear; so thin and pale; you look as if you had been watching for several nights."

"You have guessed right; I have lately been so deeply engaged in one occupation that I have not allowed myself sufficient rest, as you see; but I hope, I sincerely hope, that all these employments are now at an end and that I am at length free."

I trembled excessively; I could not endure to think of, and far less to allude to, the occurrences of the preceding night. I walked with a quick pace, and we soon arrived at my college. I then reflected, and the thought made me shiver, that the creature whom I had left in my apartment might still be there, alive and walking about. I dreaded to behold this monster, but I feared still more that Henry should see him. Entreating him, therefore, to remain a few minutes at the bottom of the stairs, I darted up towards my own room. My hand was already on the lock of the door before I recollected myself. I then paused and a cold shivering came over me. I threw the door forcibly open, as children are accustomed to do when they expect a spectre to stand in waiting for them on the other side; but nothing appeared. I stepped fearfully in: the apartment was empty, and my bedroom was also freed from its hideous guest. I could hardly believe that so great a good fortune could have befallen me, but when I became assured that my enemy had indeed fled, I clapped my hands for joy and ran down to Clerval.

We ascended into my room, and the servant presently brought breakfast; but I was unable to contain myself. It was not joy only that possessed me; I felt my flesh tingle with excess of sensitiveness, and my pulse beat rapidly. I was unable to remain for a single instant in the same place; I jumped over the chairs, clapped my hands, and laughed aloud. Clerval at first attributed my unusual spirits to joy on his arrival, but when he observed me more attentively, he saw a wildness in my eyes for which he could not account, and my loud, unrestrained, heartless laughter frightened and astonished him.

"My dear Victor," cried he, "what, for God's sake, is the matter? Do not laugh in that manner. How ill you are! What is the cause of all this?"

"Do not ask me," cried I, putting my hands before my eyes, for I thought I saw the dreaded spectre glide into the room; "*he* can tell. Oh, save me! Save me!" I imagined that the monster seized me; I struggled furiously and fell down in a fit.

Poor Clerval! What must have been his feelings? A meeting, which he anticipated with such joy, so strangely turned to bitterness. But I was not the witness of his grief, for I was lifeless and did not recover my senses for a long, long time.

This was the commencement of a nervous fever which confined me for several months. During all that time Henry was my only nurse. I afterwards learned that, knowing my father's advanced age and unfitness for so long a journey, and how wretched my sickness would make Elizabeth, he spared them this grief by concealing the extent of my disorder. He knew that I could not have a more kind and attentive nurse than himself; and, firm in the hope he felt of my recovery, he did not doubt that, instead of doing harm, he performed the kindest action that he could towards them.

But I was in reality very ill, and surely nothing but the unbounded and unremitting attentions of my friend could have restored me to life. The form of the monster on whom I had bestowed existence was forever before my eyes, and I raved incessantly concerning him. Doubtless my words surprised Henry; he at first believed them to be the wanderings of my disturbed imagination, but the pertinacity with which I continually recurred to the same subject persuaded him that my disorder indeed owed its origin to some uncommon and terrible event.

By very slow degrees, and with frequent relapses that alarmed and grieved my friend, I recovered. I remember the first time I became capable of observing outward objects with any kind of pleasure, I perceived that the fallen leaves had disappeared and that the young buds were shooting forth from the trees that shaded my window. It was a divine spring, and the season contributed greatly to my convalescence. I felt also sentiments of joy and affection revive in my bosom; my gloom disappeared, and in a short time I became as cheerful as before I was attacked by the fatal passion.

Gradually, Frankenstein recovers his mental health after a prolonged interlude of madness. Preparing to return to his family in Geneva, he receives word of the murder of William, his younger brother. En route home, he catches a glimpse of the monster lurking outside his home. Instinctively, Frankenstein realizes who the true murderer is, but he is both afraid and unable to produce the monster as proof of his suspicions. As a consequence, Frankenstein must endure the tragedy of seeing Justine Moritz, an adopted member of the family, tried for the murder and executed for a crime he knows she did not commit. It is under these circumstances that the scientist and his creation meet again. ED.

from Chapter 10

I suddenly beheld the figure of a man, at some distance, advancing towards me with superhuman speed. He bounded over the crevices in the ice, among which I had walked with caution; his stature, also, as he approached, seemed to exceed that of man. I was troubled; a mist came over my eyes, and I felt a faintness seize me; but I was quickly restored by the cold gale of the mountains. I perceived, as the shape came nearer (sight tremendous and abhorred!) that it was the wretch whom I had created. I trembled with rage and horror, resolving to wait his approach and then close with him in mortal combat. He approached: his countenance bespoke bitter anguish, combined with a disdain and malignity, while its unearthly ugliness rendered it almost too horrible for human eyes. But I scarcely observed this; rage and hatred had at first deprived me of utterance, and I recovered only to overwhelm him with words expressive of furious detestation and contempt.

"Devil," I exclaimed, "do you dare approach me? And do not you fear the fierce vengeance of my arm wreaked on your miserable head? Begone, vile insect! Or rather, stay, that I may trample you to dust! And, oh! That I could, with the extinction of your miserable existence, restore those victims whom you have so diabolically murdered!"

"I expected this reception," said the demon. "All men hate the wretched; how, then, must I be hated, who am miserable beyond all living things! Yet you, my creator, detest and spurn me, thy creature, to whom thou art bound by ties only dissoluble by the annihilation of one of us. You purpose to kill me. How dare you sport thus with life? Do your duty towards me, and I will do mine towards you and the rest of mankind. If you will comply with my conditions, I will leave them and you at peace; but if you refuse, I will glut the maw of death, until it be satiated with the blood of your remaining friends."

"Abhorred monster! Fiend that thou art! The tortures of hell are too mild a vengeance for thy crimes. Wretched devil! You reproach me with your creation; come on, then, that I may extinguish the spark which I so negligently bestowed."

My rage was without bounds; I sprang on him; impelled by all the feelings which can arm one being against the existence of another.

He easily eluded me and said, "Be calm! I entreat you to hear me before you give vent to your hatred on my devoted head. Have I not suffered enough, that you seek to increase my misery? Life, although it may only be an accumulation of anguish, is dear to me, and I will defend it. Remember, thou has made me more powerful than thyself; my height is superior to thine, my joints more supple. But I will not be tempted to set myself in opposition to thee. I am thy creature, and I will be even mild and docile to my natural lord and king if thou wilt also perform thy part, the which thou owest me. Oh, Frankenstein, be not equitable to every other and trample upon me alone, to whom thy justice, and even thy clemency and affection, is most due. Remember that I am thy creature; I ought to be thy Adam, but I am rather the fallen angel, whom thou drivest from joy for no misdeed. Everywhere I see bliss, from which I alone am irrevocably excluded. I was benevolent and good; misery made me a fiend. Make me happy, and I shall again be virtuous."

"Begone! I will not hear you. There can be no community between you and me; we are enemies. Begone, or let us try our strength in a fight, in which one must fall."

"How can I move thee? Will no entreaties cause thee to turn a favourable eye upon thy creature, who implores thy goodness and compassion? Believe me, Frankenstein, I was benevolent; my soul glowed with love and humanity; but am I not alone, miserably alone? You, my creator, abhor me; what hope can I gather from your fellow creatures, who owe me nothing? They spurn and hate me. The desert mountains and dreary glaciers are my refuge. I have wandered here many days; the caves of ice, which I only do not fear, are a dwelling to me, and the only one which man does not grudge. These bleak skies I hail, for they are kinder to me than your fellow beings. If the multitude of mankind knew of my existence, they would do as you do, and arm themselves for my destruction. Shall I not then hate them who abhor me? I will keep no terms with my enemies. I am miserable, and they shall share my wretchedness. Yet it is in your power to recompense me, and deliver them from an evil which it only remains for you to make so great, that not only you and your family, but thousands of others, shall be swallowed up in the whirlwinds of its rage. Let your compassion be moved, and do not disdain me. Listen to my tale; when you have heard that, abandon or commiserate me, as you shall judge that I deserve. But hear me. The guilty are allowed, by human laws, bloody as they are, to speak in their own defence before they are condemned. Listen to me, Frankenstein. You accuse me of murder, and yet you would, with a satisfied conscience, destroy your own creature. Oh, praise the eternal justice of man! Yet I ask you not to spare me; listen to me, and then, if you can, and if you will, destroy the work of your hands."

"Why do you call to my remembrance," I rejoined, "circumstances of which I shudder to reflect, that I have been the miserable origin and author? Cursed be the day, abhorred devil, in which you first saw light! Cursed (although I curse myself) be the hands that formed you! You have made me wretched beyond expression. You have left me no power to consider whether I am just to you or not. Begone! Relieve me from the sight of your detested form."

"Thus I relieve thee, my creator," he said, and placed his hated hands before my eyes, which I flung from me with violence; "thus I take from thee a sight which you abhor. Still thou canst listen to me and grant me thy compassion. By the virtues that I once possessed, I demand this

from you. Hear my tale; it is long and strange, and the temperature of
this place is not fitting to your fine sensations; come to the hut upon
the mountain. The sun is yet high in the heavens; before it descends
to hide itself behind your snowy precipices and illuminate another
world, you will have heard my story and can decide. On you it rests,
whether I quit forever the neighbourhood of man and lead a harmless
life, or become the scourge of your fellow creatures and the author
of your own speedy ruin."

As he said this he led the way across the ice; I followed. My heart
was full, and I did not answer him, but as I proceeded, I weighed the
various arguments that he had used and determined at least to listen
to his tale. I was partly urged by curiosity, and compassion confirmed
my resolution. I had hitherto supposed him to be the murderer of my
brother, and I eagerly sought a confirmation or denial of this opinion.
For the first time, also, I felt what the duties of a creator towards his
creature were, and that I ought to render him happy before I complained of his wickedness. These motives urged me to comply with his
demand. We crossed the ice, therefore, and ascended the opposite
rock. The air was cold, and the rain again began to descend; we entered the hut, the fiend with an air of exultation. I with a heavy heart
and depressed spirits.

The monster's narrative reports his confusion over awakening consciousness.
He begins to explore this brave new world in which he finds himself with
curiosity and growing delight. One day, however, as he stumbles into a
village looking for food and shelter, he is driven off by frightened people.
He then finds refuge in a shepherd's hut and observes the domestic life of a
small family whom he secretly befriends by obtaining extra firewood for
them. Gradually, the monster learns the history of the cottagers, which
turns out to be quite romantic, and teaches himself through observation the
fundamentals of speech, reading, and family life. After long waiting,
feeling almost a family member, the monster reveals himself to the blind
grandfather but is driven off by the terrified family on their return. Now
a confirmed outcast, the monster wanders over the winter landscape. His
reward for rescuing a drowning girl was to be shot by her persuing lover.
At this point we pick up the monster's narrative.

---

from Chapter 16

"I generally rested during the day and travelled only when I was
secured by night from the view of man. One morning, however, finding
that my path lay through a deep wood, I ventured to continue my
journey after the sun had risen; the day, which was one of the first of
spring, cheered even me by the loveliness of its sunshine and the
balminess of the air. I felt emotions of gentleness and pleasure, that
had long appeared dead, revive within me. Half surprised by the
novelty of these sensations, I allowed myself to be borne away by them,
and forgetting my solitude and deformity, dared to be happy. Soft tears

again bedewed my cheeks, and I even raised my humid eyes with thankfulness towards the blessed sun, which bestowed such joy upon me.

"I continued to wind among the paths of the wood, until I came to its boundary, which was skirted by a deep and rapid river, into which many of the trees bent their branches, now budding with the fresh spring. Here I paused, not exactly knowing what path to pursue, when I heard the sound of voices, that induced me to conceal myself under the shade of a cypress. I was scarcely hid when a young girl came running towards the spot where I was concealed, laughing, as if she ran from someone in sport. She continued her course along the precipitous sides of the river, when suddenly her foot slipped, and she fell into the rapid stream. I rushed from my hiding-place and with extreme labour, from the force of the current, saved her and dragged her to shore. She was senseless, and I endeavoured by every means in my power to restore animation, when I was suddenly interrupted by the approach of a rustic, who was probably the person from whom she had playfully fled. On seeing me, he darted towards me, and tearing the girl from my arms, hastened towards the deeper parts of the wood. I followed speedily, I hardly knew why; but when the man saw me draw near, he aimed a gun, which he carried, at my body and fired. I sank to the ground, and my injurer, with increased swiftness, escaped into the wood.

"This was then the reward of my benevolence! I had saved a human being from destruction, and as a recompense I now writhed under the miserable pain of a wound which shattered the flesh and bone. The feelings of kindness and gentleness which I had entertained but a few moments before gave place to hellish rage and gnashing of teeth. Inflamed by pain, I vowed eternal hatred and vengeance to all mankind. But the agony of my wound overcame me; my pulses paused, and I fainted.

"For some weeks I led a miserable life in the woods, endeavouring to cure the wound which I had received. The ball had entered my shoulder, and I knew not whether it had remained there or passed through; at any rate I had no means of extracting it. My sufferings were augmented also by the oppressive sense of the injustice and ingratitude of their infliction. My daily vows rose for revenge—a deep and deadly revenge, such as would alone compensate for the outrages and anguish I had endured.

"After some weeks my wound healed, and I continued my journey. The labours I endured were no longer to be alleviated by the bright sun or gentle breezes of spring; all joy was but a mockery which insulted my desolate state and made me feel more painfully that I was not made for the enjoyment of pleasure.

"But my toils now drew near a close, and in two months from this time I reached the environs of Geneva.

"It was evening when I arrived, and I retired to a hiding-place among the fields that surround it to meditate in what manner I should apply to you. I was oppressed by fatigue and hunger and far too unhappy to enjoy the gentle breezes of evening or the prospect of the sun setting behind the stupendous mountains of Jura.

"At this time a slight sleep relieved me from the pain of reflection, which was disturbed by the approach of a beautiful child, who came running into the recess I had chosen, with all the sportiveness of infancy. Suddenly, as I gazed on him, an idea seized me that this little creature was unprejudiced and had lived too short a time to have imbibed a horror of deformity. If, therefore, I could seize him and educate him as my companion and friend, I should not be so desolate in this peopled earth.

"Urged by this impulse, I seized the boy as he passed and drew him towards me. As soon as he beheld my form, he placed his hands before his eyes and uttered a shrill scream; I drew his hand forcibly from his face and said, 'Child, what is the meaning of this? I do not intend to hurt you; listen to me.'

"He struggled violently. 'Let me go,' he cried; 'monster! Ugly wretch! You wish to eat me and tear me to pieces. You are an ogre. Let me go, or I will tell my papa.'

" 'Boy, you will never see your father again; you must come with me.'

" 'Hideous monster! Let me go. My papa is a syndic—he is M. Frankenstein—he will punish you. You dare not keep me.'

" 'Frankenstein! You belong then to my enemy—to him toward whom I have sworn eternal revenge; you shall be my first victim.'

"The child still struggled and loaded me with epithets which carried despair to my heart; I grasped his throat to silence him, and in a moment he lay dead at my feet.

"I gazed on my victim, and my heart swelled with exultation and hellish triumph; clapping my hands, I exclaimed, 'I too can create desolation; my enemy is not invulnerable; this death will carry despair to him, and a thousand other miseries shall torment and destroy him.'

"As I fixed my eyes on the child, I saw something glittering on his breast. I took it; it was a portrait of a most lovely woman. In spite of my malignity, it softened and attracted me. For a few moments I gazed with delight on her dark eyes, fringed by deep lashes, and her lovely lips; but presently my rage returned; I remembered that I was forever deprived of the delights that such beautiful creatures could bestow and that she whose resemblance I contemplated would, in regarding me, have changed that air of divine benignity to one expressive of disgust and affright.

"Can you wonder that such thoughts transported me with rage? I only wonder that at that moment, instead of venting my sensations in exclamations and agony, I did not rush among mankind and perish in the attempt to destroy them.

"While I was overcome by these feelings, I left the spot where I had committed the murder, and seeking a more secluded hiding-place, I entered a barn which had appeared to me to be empty. A woman was sleeping on some straw; she was young, not indeed so beautiful as her whose portrait I held, but of an agreeable aspect and blooming in the loveliness of youth and health. Here, I thought, is one of those whose joy-imparting smiles are bestowed on all but me. And then I bent over her and whispered, 'Awake, fairest, thy lover is near—he who would give his life but to obtain one look of affection from thine eyes; my beloved, awake!'

"The sleeper stirred; a thrill of terror ran through me. Should she indeed awake, and see me, and curse me, and denounce the murderer? Thus would she assuredly act if her darkened eyes opened and she beheld me. The thought was madness; it stirred the fiend within me— not I, but she, shall suffer; the murder I have committed because I am forever robbed of all that she could give me, she shall atone. The crime had its source in her; be hers the punishment! Thanks to the lessons of Felix and the sanguinary laws of man, I had learned now to work mischief. I bent over her and placed the portrait securely in one of the folds of her dress. She moved again, and I fled.

"For some days I haunted the spot where these scenes had taken place, sometimes wishing to see you, sometimes resolved to quit the world and its miseries forever. At length I wandered towards these mountains, and have ranged through their immense recesses, consumed by a burning passion which you alone can gratify. We may not part until you have promised to comply with my requisition. I am alone and miserable; man will not associate with me; but one as deformed and horrible as myself would not deny herself to me. My companion must be of the same species and have the same defects. This being you must create."

Chapter 17

The being finished speaking and fixed his looks upon me in the expectation of a reply. But I was bewildered, perplexed, and unable to arrange my ideas sufficiently to understand the full extent of his proposition. He continued, "You must create a female for me with whom I can live in the interchange of those sympathies necessary for my being. This you alone can do, and I demand it of you as a right which you must not refuse to concede."

The latter part of his tale had kindled anew in me the anger that had died away while he narrated his peaceful life among the cottagers, and as he said this I could no longer suppress the rage that burned within me.

"I do refuse it," I replied; "and no torture shall ever extort a consent from me. You may render me the most miserable of men, but you shall never make me base in my own eyes. Shall I create another like yourself, whose joint wickedness might desolate the world. Begone! I have answered you; you may torture me, but I will never consent."

"You are in the wrong," replied the fiend; "and instead of threatening, I am content to reason with you. I am malicious because I am miserable. Am I not shunned and hated by all mankind? You, my creator, would tear me to pieces and triumph; remember that, and tell me why I should pity man more than he pities me? You would not call it murder if you could preciptate me into one of those ice-rifts and destroy my frame, the work of your own hands. Shall I respect man when he contemns me? Let him live with me in the interchange of kindness, and instead of injury I would bestow every benefit upon him with tears of gratitude at his acceptance. But that cannot be; the human senses are insurmountable barriers to our union. Yet mine shall not be the submission of abject slavery. I will revenge my injuries; if I cannot inspire love, I will cause fear, and chiefly towards you my arch-enemy, because my creator, do I swear inextinguishable hatred. Have a care; I will work at your destruction, nor finish until I desolate your heart, so that you shall curse the hour of your birth."

A fiendish rage animated him as he said this; his face was wrinkled into contortions too horrible for human eyes to behold; but presently he calmed himself and proceeded, "I intended to reason. This passion is detrimental to me, for you do not reflect that *you* are the cause of its excess. If any being felt emotions of benevolence towards me, I should return them a hundred and a hundredfold; for that one creature's sake I would make peace with the whole kind! But I now indulge in dreams of bliss that cannot be realized. What I ask of you is reasonable and moderate; I demand a creature of another sex, but as hideous as myself; the gratification is small, but it is all that I can receive, and it shall content me. It is true, we shall be monsters, cut off from all the world; but on that account we shall be more attached to one another. Our lives will not be happy but they will be harmless and free from the misery I now feel. Oh! My creator, make me happy; let me feel gratitude towards you for one benefit! Let me see that I excite the sympathy of some existing thing; do not deny me my request!"

I was moved. I shuddered when I thought of the possible consequences of my consent, but I felt that there was some justice in his argument. His tale and the feelings he now expressed proved him to be a creature of fine sensations, and did I not as his maker owe him all the portion of happiness that it was in my power to bestow? He saw my change of feeling and continued, "If you consent, neither you nor any other human being shall ever see us again; I will go to the vast wilds of South America. My food is not that of man; I do not destroy the lamb and the kid to glut my appetite; acorns and berries afford me sufficient nourishment. My companion will be of the same nature as myself and will be content with the same fare. We shall make our bed of dried leaves; the sun will shine on us as on man and will ripen our food. The picture I present to you is peaceful and human, and you must feel that you could deny it only in the wantonness of power and cruelty. Pitiless as you have been towards me, I now see compassion in your eyes; let me seize the favourable moment and persuade you to promise what I so ardently desire."

"You propose," replied I, "to fly from the habitations of man, to dwell in those wilds where the beasts of the field will be your only companions. How can you, who long for the love and sympathy of man, persevere in this exile? You will return and again seek their kindness, and you will meet with their detestation; your evil passions will be renewed, and you will then have a companion to aid you in the task of destruction. This may not be; cease to argue the point, for I cannot consent."

"How inconstant are your feelings! But a moment ago you were moved by my representations, and why do you again harden yourself to my complaints? I swear to you, by the earth which I inhabit, and by you that made me, that with the companion you bestow I will quit the neighbourhood of man and dwell, as it may chance, in the most savage of places. My evil passions will have fled, for I shall meet with sympathy! My life will flow quietly away, and in my dying moments I shall not curse my maker."

His words had a strange effect upon me. I compassionated him and sometimes felt a wish to console him, but when I looked upon him, when I saw the filthy mass that moved and talked, my heart sickened and my feelings were altered to those of horror and hatred. I tried to stifle these sensations; I thought that as I could not sympathize with him, I had no right to withhold from him the small portion of happiness which was yet in my power to bestow.

"You swear," I said, "to be harmless; but have you not already shown a degree of malice that should reasonably make me distrust you? May not even this be a feint that will increase your triumph by affording a wider scope for your revenge?"

"How is this? I must not be trifled with, and I demand an answer. If I have no ties and no affections, hatred and vice must be my portion; the love of another will destroy the cause of my crimes, and I shall become a thing of whose existence everyone will be ignorant. My vices are the children of a forced solitude that I abhor, and my virtues will necessarily arise when I live in communion with an equal. I shall feel the affections of a sensitive being and become linked to the chain of existence and events from which I am now excluded."

I paused some time to reflect on all he had related and the various arguments which he had employed. I thought of the promise of virtues which he had displayed on the opening of his existence and the subsequent blight of all kindly feeling by the loathing and scorn which his protectors had manifested towards him. His power and threats were not omitted in my calculations; a creature who could exist in the ice caves of the glaciers and hide himself from pursuit among the ridges of inaccessible precipices was a being possessing faculties it would be vain to cope with. After a long pause of reflection I concluded that the justice due both to him and my fellow creatures demanded of me that I should comply with his request. Turning to him, therefore, I said, "I consent to your demand, on your solemn oath to quit Europe forever, and every other place in the neighbourhood of man, as soon as I shall deliver into your hands a female who will accompany you in your exile."

"I swear," he cried, "by the sun, and by the blue sky of heaven, and by the fire of love that burns my heart, that if you grant my prayer, while they exist you shall never behold me again. Depart to your home and commence your labours; I shall watch their progress with unutterable anxiety; and fear not but that when you are ready I shall appear."

Saying this, he suddenly quitted me, fearful, perhaps, of any change in my sentiments. I saw him descend the mountain with greater speed than the flight of an eagle, and quickly lost among the undulations of the sea of ice.

His tale had occupied the whole day, and the sun was upon the verge of the horizon when he departed. I knew that I ought to hasten my descent towards the valley, as I should soon be encompassed in darkness; but my heart was heavy, and my steps slow. The labour of winding among the little paths of the mountain and fixing my feet firmly as I advanced perplexed me, occupied as I was by the emotions which the occurrences of the day had produced. Night was far advanced when I came to the halfway resting-place and seated myself beside the fountain. The stars shone at intervals as the clouds passed from over them; the dark pines rose before me, and every here and there a broken tree lay on the ground; it was a scene of wonderful solemnity and stirred strange thoughts within me. I wept bitterly, and clasping my hands in agony, I exclaimed, "Oh! Stars and clouds and winds, ye are all about to mock me; if ye really pity me, crush sensation and memory; let me become as nought; but if not, depart, depart, and leave me in darkness."

These were wild and miserable thoughts, but I cannot describe to you how the eternal twinkling of the stars weighed upon me and how I listened to every blast of wind as if it were a dull ugly siroc on its way to consume me.

Morning dawned before I arrived at the village of Chamounix; I took no rest, but returned immediately to Geneva. Even in my own heart I could give no expression to my sensations—they weighed on me with a mountain's weight and their excess destroyed my agony beneath them. Thus I returned home, and entering the house, presented myself to the family. My haggard and wild appearance awoke intense alarm, but I answered no question, scarcely did I speak. I felt as if I were placed under a ban—as if I had no right to claim their sympathies—as if never more might I enjoy companionship with them. Yet even thus I loved them to adoration; and to save them, I resolved to dedicate myself to my most abhorred task. The prospect of such an occupation made every other circumstance of existence pass before me like a dream, and that thought only had to me the reality of life.

Questions for Discussion and Review

1. How are we to understand Victor Frankenstein's breakdown after bringing the monster to life?
2. Discuss the implications of the Prometheus myth for the story.
3. What justification does the author imply for the monster's behavior?
4. Describe the kind of SF *Frankenstein* represents.
5. Were there other courses of action for Frankenstein to take? Explain.
6. Is *Frankenstein* antiscientific?

Some Words with a Mummy

Edgar Allan Poe

Edgar Allan Poe (1809–1849) is a seminal figure in literary and cultural
history and one of the most influential American writers of the nineteenth
century. His importance for the literature of the fantastic (including
fledgling SF) and popular culture was enormous. He was a pioneer of the
modern detective story, and the annual award of the Mystery Writers of
America, the Edgar, is named in his honor. He was a master of the horror
story and extended the practice of Mary Shelley, uniting SF and the
Gothic in the short story. Poe is, therefore, literary godfather to such
later practitioners of the craft as Merritt, Lovecraft, Campbell, Bradbury,
Serling, Ellison, Spinrad, Ballard, and Moorcock, to name a few of his more
noted followers. Poe also wrote other hybrid SF stories, mixing SF with
mystery and combining it with Gothic—exploration adventure, as in "A
Descent into the Maelstrom" (1841), "MS Found in a Bottle" (1833), and
The Narrative of Arthur Gordon Pym (1838). Poe even wrote tales of
future speculative SF like "Mellonta Tauta" (1849), "Eureka" (1848),
and "The Colloquy of Monos and Una" (1841). In several important
ways, these stories anticipate the later hard SF of Verne, Wells, and more
recently, Heinlein and Niven. Still another side of Poe's genius is displayed in the satiric SF, "The Balloon-Hoax" (1844), and the comic SF
satire, "The Unparalleled Adventure of One Hans Pfaall" (1835). "Some
Words with a Mummy" appeared in the *American Whig Review* for April
1845.

Poe's story brings together science and comedy. As comedy, it leans toward
farce. The science that is the target of the burlesque is, of course, archaelogy;
and in his choice of subject, Poe was, as always, prophetic. There had
been no systematic archaelogy in Egypt before the writing of the story; and
although Layard was at work excavating Babylon, he was still several
years away from reporting his findings. Egypt had been discovered by the
West, archaelogically speaking, during Napoleon's otherwise disastrous
campaign there. The Rosetta Stone and other artifacts were brought back to
Paris and moved to London as spoils of the English victory. In 1831,
Champollion deciphered the hieroglyphs and opened the way to a new
understanding of the wealth of Egyptian antiquities. In Poe's time, the
only exploration being pursued was the opening of tombs, and mummies
were brought back as trophies of the quest and proof of success.

Following the long-established practice of authors dealing with the
fantastic, Poe frames his story around an opening gambit—four pounds of
"Welsh rabbit (or was it five?) and five bottles of stout." Just how much
of an effect this supper was to have on the narrator's senses, we are left
to imagine for ourselves. Having disposed of the question of probabilities,
the story proceeds quickly to the revival of the mummy through galvanic

experiments, still as popular as they had been a score of years earlier in Europe, when the Shelleys were visiting Byron at the villa Diodati, near Geneva.

The dialogue with the mummy, Count Allamistakeo, no less, is designed as a comic deflation of the pretentions of modernism. The arguments proposed for the superiority of Egyptian culture have remained remarkably well preserved during the intervening century and one-quarter. The wonders of ancient Egypt remain every bit as marvelous today as they were then. The continuation of the debate over ancients and moderns in our own time says something for the preservation of tradition.

It is clear that one of Poe's intentions in the dialogue is to deliver a satirical broadside at the science of the time, particularly archaelogy, anatomy, phrenology (then considered a science), and engineering. The other topics of satire are all equally apparent, but readers might take special note of Poe's Whiggish sallies against popular democracy.

The *symposium* of the preceding evening had been a little too much for my nerves. I had a wretched headache, and was desperately drowsy. Instead of going out, therefore, to spend the evening, as I had proposed, it occurred to me that I could not do a wiser thing than just eat a mouthful of supper and go immediately to bed.

A *light* supper, of course. I am exceedingly fond of Welsh-rabbit. More than a pound at once, however, may not at all times be advisable. Still, there can be no material objection to two. And really between two and three, there is merely a single unit of difference. I ventured, perhaps, upon four. My wife will have it five: —but, clearly, she has confounded two very distinct affairs. The abstract number, five, I am willing to admit; but, concretely, it has reference to bottles of Brown Stout, without which, in the way of condiment, Welsh-rabbit is to be eschewed.

Having thus concluded a frugal meal, and donned my nightcap, with the sincere hope of enjoying it till noon the next day, I placed my head upon the pillow, and, through the aid of a capital conscience, fell into a profound slumber forthwith.

But when were the hopes of humanity fulfilled? I could not have completed my third snore when there came a furious ringing at the street-door bell, and then an impatient thumping at the knocker, which awakened me at once. In a minute afterward, and while I was still rubbing my eyes, my wife thrust in my face a note, from my old friend, Doctor Ponnonner. It ran thus:

Come to me, by all means, my dear good friend, as soon as you receive this. Come and help us to rejoice. At last, by long persevering diplomacy, I have gained the assent of the Directors of the City Museum, to my examination of the Mummy—you know the one I mean. I have permission to unswathe it and open it, if desirable. A few friends only will be present—you, of course. The Mummy is now at my house, and we shall begin to unroll it at eleven to-night.

Yours ever,

Ponnonner.

By the time I had reached the "Ponnonner," it struck me that I was as wide awake as a man need be. I leaped out of bed in an ecstasy, over-throwing all in my way; dressed myself with a rapidity truly marvellous; and set off, at the top of my speed, for the doctor's.

There I found a very eager company assembled. They had been awaiting me with much impatience; the Mummy was extended upon the dining-table; and the moment I entered its examination was com-menced.

It was one of a pair brought, several years previously, by Captain Arthur Sabretash, a cousin of Ponnonner's, from a tomb near Eleithias, in the Lybian mountains, a considerable distance above Thebes on the Nile. The grottos at this point, although less magnificent than the Theban sepulchres, are of higher interest, on account of affording more numerous illustrations of the private life of the Egyptians. The cham-ber from which our specimen was taken, was said to be very rich in such illustrations—the walls being completely covered with fresco paintings and bas-reliefs, while statues, vases, and Mosaic work of rich patterns, indicated the vast wealth of the deceased.

The treasure had been deposited in the museum precisely in the same condition in which Captain Sabretash had found it—that is to say, the coffin had not been disturbed. For eight years it had thus stood, subject only externally to public inspection. We had now, therefore, the complete Mummy at our disposal; and to those who are aware how very rarely the unransacked antique reaches our shores, it will be evi-dent, at once that we had great reason to congratulate ourselves upon our good fortune.

Approaching the table, I saw on it a large box, or case, nearly seven feet long, and perhaps three feet wide, by two feet and a half deep. It was oblong—not coffin-shaped. The material was at first supposed to be the wood of the sycamore (*platanus*), but, upon cutting into it, we found it to be pasteboard, or, more properly, *papier maché,* composed of papyrus. It was thickly ornamented with paintings, representing fu-neral scenes, and other mournful subjects—interspersed among which, in every variety of position, were certain series of hieroglyphical char-acters, intended, no doubt, for the name of the departed. By good luck, Mr. Gliddon formed one of our party; and he had no difficulty in translating the letters, which were simply phonetic, and represented the word *Allamistakeo.*

We had some difficulty in getting this case open without injury; but, having at length accomplished the task, we came to a second, coffin-shaped, and very considerably less in size than the exterior one, but resembling it precisely in every other respect. The interval between the two was filled with resin, which had, in some degree, defaced the colors of the interior box.

Upon opening this latter (which we did quite easily), we arrived at a third case, also coffin-shaped, and varying from the second one in no particular, except in that of its material, which was cedar, and still emitted the peculiar and highly aromatic odor of that wood. Between the second and the third case there was no interval—the one fitting accurately within the other.

Removing the third case, we discovered and took out the body itself. We had expected to find it, as usual, enveloped in frequent rolls, or bandages, of linen; but, in place of these, we found a sort of sheath, made of papyrus, and coated with a layer of plaster, thickly gilt and painted. The paintings represented subjects connected with the various supposed duties of the soul, and its presentation to different divinities, with numerous identical human figures, intended, very probably, as portraits of the persons embalmed. Extending from head to foot was a columnar, or perpendicular, inscription, in phonetic hieroglyphics, giving again his name and titles, and the names and titles of his relations.

Around the neck thus unsheathed, was a collar of cylindrical glass beads, diverse in color, and so arranged as to form images of deities, of the scarabeus, etc., with the winged globe. Around the small of the waist was a similar collar or belt.

Stripping off the papyrus, we found the flesh in excellent preservation, with no perceptible odor. The color was reddish. The skin was hard, smooth, and glossy. The teeth and hair were in good condition. The eyes (it seemed) had been removed, and glass ones substituted, which were very beautiful and wonderfully life-like, with the exception of somewhat too determined a stare. The fingers and the nails were brilliantly gilded.

Mr. Gliddon was of opinion, from the redness of the epidermis, that the embalmment had been effected altogether by asphaltum; but, on scraping the surface with a steel instrument, and throwing into the fire some of the powder thus obtained, the flavor of camphor and other sweet-scented gums became apparent.

We searched the corpse very carefully for the usual openings through which the entrails are extracted, but, to our surprise, we could discover none. No member of the party was at that period aware that entire or unopened mummies are not infreqently met. The brain it was customary to withdraw through the nose; the intestines through an incision in the side; the body was then shaved, washed, and salted; then laid aside for several weeks, when the operation of embalming, properly so called, began.

As no trace of an opening could be found, Doctor Ponnonner was preparing his instruments for dissection, when I observed that it was then past two o'clock. Hereupon it was agreed to postpone the internal examination until the next evening; and we were about to separate for the present, when some one suggested an experiment or two with the voltaic pile.

The application of electricity to a Mummy three or four thousand years old at the least, was an idea, if not very sage, still sufficiently original, and we all caught it at once. About one tenth in earnest and nine tenths in jest, we arranged a battery in the Doctor's study, and conveyed thither the Egyptian.

It was only after much trouble that we succeeded in laying bare some portions of the temporal muscle which appeared of less stony rigidity than other parts of the frame, but which, as we had anticipated, of course, gave no indication of galvanic susceptibility when brought in contact with the wire. This, the first trial, indeed, seemed decisive, and, with a hearty laugh at our own absurdity, we were bidding each other good night, when my eyes, happening to fall upon those of the Mummy, were there immediately riveted in amazement. My brief glance, in fact, had sufficed to assure me that the orbs which we had all supposed to be glass, and which were originally noticeable for a certain wild stare, were now so far covered by the lids, that only a small portion of the *tunica albuginea* remained visible.

With a shout I called attention to the fact, and it became immediately obvious to all.

I cannot say that I was *alarmed* at the phenomenon, because "alarmed" is, in my case, not exactly the word. It is possible, however, that, but for the Brown Stout, I might have been a little nervous. As for the rest of the company, they really made no attempt at concealing the downright fright which possessed them. Doctor Ponnonner was a man to be pitied. Mr. Gliddon, by some peculiar process, rendered himself invisible. Mr. Silk Buckingham, I fancy, will scarcely be so bold as to deny that he made his way, upon all fours, under the table.

After the first shock of astonishment, however, we resolved, as a matter of course, upon further experiment forthwith. Our operations were now directed against the great toe of the right foot. We made an incision over the outside of the exterior *os sesamoideum pollicis pedis,* and thus got at the root of the *abductor* muscle. Readjusting the battery, we now applied the fluid to the bisected nerves—when, with a movement of exceeding life-likeness, the Mummy first drew up its right knee so as to bring it nearly in contact with the abdomen, and then, straightening the limb with inconceivable force, bestowed a kick upon Doctor Ponnonner, which had the effect of discharging that gentleman, like an arrow from a catapult, through a window into the street below.

We rushed out *en masse* to bring in the mangled remains of the victim, but had the happiness to meet him upon the staircase, coming up in an unaccountable hurry, brimful of the most ardent philosophy, and more than ever impressed with the necessity of prosecuting our experiment with vigor and with zeal.

It was by his advice, accordingly, that we made, upon the spot, a profound incision into the tip of the subject's nose, while the Doctor himself, laying violent hands upon it, pulled it into vehement contact with the wire.

Morally and physically—figuratively and literally—was the effect electric. In the first place, the corpse opened its eyes and winked very rapidly for several minutes, as does Mr. Barnes in the pantomime; in the second place, it sneezed; in the third, it sat upon end; in the fourth, it shook its fist in Doctor Ponnonner's face; in the fifth, turning to Messieurs Gliddon and Buckingham, it addressed them, in very capital Egyptian, thus:

"I must say, gentlemen, that I am as much surprised as I am mortified at your behavior. Of Doctor Ponnonner nothing better was to be expected. He is a poor little fat fool who *knows* no better. I pity and forgive him. But you, Mr. Gliddon—and you, Silk—who have travelled and resided in Egypt until one might imagine you to the manor born—you, I say, who have been so much among us that you speak Egyptian fully as well, I think, as you write your mother-tongue—you, whom I have always been led to regard as the firm friend of the mummies—I really did anticipate more gentlemanly conduct from *you*. What am I to think of your standing quietly by and seeing me thus unhandsomely used? What am I to suppose by your permitting Tom, Dick, and Harry to strip me of my coffins, and my clothes, in this wretchedly cold climate? In what light (to come to the point) am I to regard your aiding and abetting that miserable little villain, Doctor Ponnonner, in pulling me by the nose?"

It will be taken for granted, no doubt, that upon hearing this speech under the circumstances, we all either made for the door, or fell into violent hysterics, or went off in a general swoon. One of these three things was, I say, to be expected. Indeed each and all of these lines of conduct might have been very plausibly pursued. And, upon my word, I am at a loss to know how or why it was that we pursued neither the one nor the other. But, perhaps, the true reason is to be sought in the spirit of the age, which proceeds by the rule of contraries altogether, and is now usually admitted as the solution of every thing in the way of paradox and impossibility. Or, perhaps, after all, it was only the Mummy's exceedingly natural and matter-of-course air that divested his words of the terrible. However this may be, the facts are clear, and no member of our party betrayed any very particular trepidation, or seemed to consider that any thing had gone very especially wrong.

For my part I was convinced it was all right, and merely stepped aside, out of the range of the Egyptian's fist. Doctor Ponnonner thrust his hands into his breeches pockets, looked hard at the Mummy, and grew excessively red in the face. Mr. Gliddon stroked his whiskers and drew up the collar of his shirt. Mr. Buckingham hung down his head, and put his right thumb into the left corner of his mouth.

The Egyptian regarded him was a severe countenance for some minutes and at length, with a sneer, said:

"Why don't you speak, Mr. Buckingham? Did you hear what I asked you or not? *Do* take your thumb out of your mouth!"

Mr. Buckingham, hereupon, gave a slight start, took his right thumb out of the left corner of his mouth, and, by way of indemnification, inserted his left thumb in the right corner of the aperture above-mentioned.

Not being able to get an answer from Mr. B., the figure turned peevishly to Mr. Gliddon, and, in a peremptory tone, demanded in general terms what we all meant.

Mr. Gliddon replied at great length, in phonetics; and but for the deficiency of American printing-offices in hieroglyphical type, it would afford me much pleasure to record here, in the original, the whole of his very excellent speech.

I may as well take this occasion to remark, that all the subsequent conversation in which the Mummy took a part, was carried on in primitive Egyptian, through the medium (so far as concerned myself and other untravelled members of the company)—through the medium, I say, of Messieurs Gliddon and Buckingham, as interpreters. These gentlemen spoke the mother tongue of the mummy with inimitable fluency and grace; but I could not help observing that (owing, no doubt, to the introduction of images entirely modern, and, of course, entirely novel to the stranger) the two travellers were reduced, occasionally, to the employment of sensible forms for the purpose of conveying a particular meaning. Mr. Gliddon, at one period, for example, could not make the Egyptian comprehend the term "politics," until he sketched upon the wall, with a bit of charcoal, a little carbuncle-nosed gentlemen, out at elbows, standing upon a stump, with his left leg drawn back, right arm thrown forward, with his fist shut, the eyes rolled up toward Heaven, and the mouth open at an angle of ninety degrees. Just in the same way Mr. Buckingham failed to convey the absolutely modern idea "wig," until (at Doctor Ponnonner's suggestion) he grew very pale in the face, and consented to take off his own.

It will be readily understood that Mr. Gliddon's discourse turned chiefly upon the vast benefits accruing to science from the unrolling and disembowelling of mummies; apologizing, upon this score, for any disturbance that might have been occasioned *him,* in particular, the individual Mummy called Allamistakeo; and concluding with a mere hint (for it could scarcely be considered more) that, as these little matters were now explained, it might be as well to proceed with the investigation intended. Here Doctor Ponnonner made ready his instruments.

In regard to the latter suggestions of the orator, it appears that Allamistakeo had certain scruples of conscience, the nature of which I did not distinctly learn; but he expressed himself satisfied with the apologies tendered, and, getting down from the table, shook hands with the company all around.

When this ceremony was at an end, we immediately busied ourselves in repairing the damages which our subject had sustained from the scalpel. We sewed up the wound in his temple, bandaged his foot, and applied a square inch of black plaster to the tip of his nose.

It was now observed that the Count (this was the title, it seems, of Allamistakeo) had a slight fit of shivering—no doubt from the cold. The Doctor immediately repaired to his wardrobe, and soon returned with a black dress coat, made in Jennings' best manner, a pair of sky-blue plaid pantaloons with straps, a pink gingham *chemise,* a flapped vest of brocade, a white sack overcoat, a walking cane with a hook, a hat with no brim, patent-leather boots, straw-colored kid gloves, an eye-glass, a pair of whiskers, and a waterfall cravat. Owing to the disparity of size between the Count and the Doctor (the proportion being as two to one), there was some little difficulty in adjusting these habiliments upon the person of the Egyptian: but when all was arranged, he might have been said to be dressed. Mr. Gliddon, therefore, gave him his arm, and led him to a comfortable chair by the fire, while the Doctor rang the bell upon the spot and ordered a supply of cigars and wine.

The conversation soon grew animated. Much curiosity was, of course, expressed in regard to the somewhat remarkable fact of Allamistakeo's still remaining alive.

"I should have thought," observed Mr. Buckingham, "that it is high time you were dead."

"Why," replied the Count, very much astonished, "I am little more than seven hundred years old! My father lived a thousand, and was by no means in his dotage when he died."

Here ensued a brisk series of questions and computations, by means of which it became evident that the antiquity of the Mummy had been grossly misjudged. It had been five thousand and fifty years and some months since he had been consigned to the catacombs at Eleithias.

"But my remark," resumed Mr. Buckingham, "had no reference to your age at the period of interment; (I am willing to grant, in fact, that you are still a young man), and my allusion was to the immensity of time during which, by your own showing, you must have been done up in asphaltum."

"In what?" said the Count.

"In asphaltum," persisted Mr. B.

"Ah, yes; I have some faint notion of what you mean; it might be made to answer, no doubt,—but in my time we employed scarcely any thing else than the Bichloride of Mercury."

"But what we are especially at a loss to understand," said Doctor Ponnonner, "is how it happens that, having been dead and buried in Egypt five thousand years ago, you are here to-day all alive and looking so delightfully well."

"Had I been, as you say, *dead,*" replied the Count, "it is more than probable that dead I should still be; for I perceive you are yet in the infancy of Galvanism, and cannot accomplish with it what was a common thing among us in the old days. But the fact is, I fell into catalepsy, and it was considered by my best friends that I was either dead or should be; they accordingly embalmed me at once—I presume you are aware of the chief principle of the embalming process?"

"Why, not altogether."

"Ah, I perceive;—a deplorable condition of ignorance! Well, I cannot enter into details just now: but it is necessary to explain that to embalm (properly speaking), in Egypt, was to arrest indefinitely *all* the animal functions subjected to the process. I use the word 'animal' in its widest sense, as including the physical not more than the moral and *vital* being. I repeat that the leading principle of embalmment consisted, with us, in the immediately arresting, and holding in perpetual *abeyance, all* the animal functions subjected to the process. To be brief, in whatever condition the individual was, at the period of embalmment, in that condition he remained. Now, as it is my good fortune to be of the blood of the Scarabæus, I was embalmed *alive,* as you see me at present."

"The blood of the Scarabæus!" exclaimed Doctor Ponnonner.

"Yes. The Scarabæus was the *insignium,* or the 'arms,' of a very distinguished and very rare patrician family. To be 'of the blood of the Scarabæus,' is merely to be one of that family of which the Scarabæus is the *insignium.* I speak figuratively."

"But what has this to do with your being alive?"

"Why, it is the general custom in Egypt to deprive a corpse, before embalmment, of its bowels and brains; the race of the Scarabæi alone did not coincide with the custom. Had I not been a Scarabæus, therefore, I should have been without bowels and brains; and without either it is inconvenient to live."

"I perceive that," said Mr. Buckingham, "and I presume that all the *entire* mummies that come to hand are of the race of Scarabæi."

"Beyond doubt."

"I thought," said Mr. Gliddon, very meekly, "that the Scarabæus was one of the Egyptian gods."

"One of the Egyptian *what?*" exclaimed the Mummy, starting to its feet.

"Gods!" repeated the traveller.

"Mr. Gliddon, I really am astonished to hear you talk in this style," said the Count, resuming his chair. "No nation upon the face of the earth has ever acknowledged more than one *god.* The Scarabæus, the Ibis, etc., were with us (as similar creatures have been with others) the symbols, or *media,* through which we offered worship to the Creator too august to be more directly approached."

There was here a pause. At length the colloquy was renewed by Doctor Ponnonner.

"It is not improbable, then, from what you have explained," said he, "that among the catacombs near the Nile there may exist other mummies of the Scarabæus tribe, in a condition of vitality."

"There can be no question of it," replied the Count; "all the Scarabæi embalmed accidentally while alive, are alive. Even some of those *purposely* so embalmed, may have been overlooked by their executors, and still remain in the tomb."

"Will you be kind enough to explain," I said, "what you mean by 'purposely so embalmed'?"

"With great pleasure," answered the Mummy, after surveying me leisurely through his eyeglass—for it was the first time I had ventured to address him a direct question.

"With great pleasure," he said. "The usual duration of man's life, in my time, was about eight hundred years. Few men died, unless by most extraordinary accident, before the age of six hundred; few lived longer than a decade of centuries; but eight were considered the natural term. After the discovery of the embalming principle, as I have already described it to you, it occurred to our philosophers that a laudable curiosity might be gratified, and, at the same time, the interests of science much advanced, by living this natural term in instalments. In the case of history, indeed, experience demonstrated that something of this kind was indispensable. An historian, for example, having attained the age of five hundred, would write a book with great labor and then get himself carefully embalmed; leaving instructions to his executors *pro tem,* that they should cause him to be revivified after the lapse of a certain period—say five or six hundred years. Resuming existence at the expiration of this time, he would invariably find his great work converted into a species of haphazard note-book—that is to say, into a kind of literary arena for the conflicting guesses, riddles, and personal squabbles of whole herds of exasperated commentators. These guesses, etc., which passed under the name of annotations, or emendations, were found so completely to have enveloped, distorted, and overwhelmed the text, that the author had to go about with a lantern to discover his own book. When discovered, it was never worth the trouble of the search. After rewriting it throughout, it was regarded as the bounden duty of the historian to set himself to work immediately in correcting, from his own private knowledge and experience, the traditions of the day concerning the epoch at which he had originally lived. Now this process of rescription and personal rectification, pursued by various individual sages from time to time, had the effect of preventing our history from degenerating into absolute fable."

"I beg your pardon," said Doctor Ponnonner at this point, laying his hand gently upon the arm of the Egyptian—"I beg your pardon, sir, but may I presume to interrupt you for one moment?"

"By all means, *sir,*" replied the Count, drawing up.

"I merely wished to ask you a question," said the Doctor. "You mentioned the historian's personal correction of *traditions* respecting his own epoch. Pray, sir, upon an average, what proportion of these Kabbala were usually found to be right?"

"The Kabbala, as you properly term them, sir, were generally discovered to be precisely on a par with the facts recorded in the unrewritten histories themselves;—that is to say, not one individual iota of either was ever known, under any circumstances, to be not totally and radically wrong."

"But since it is quite clear," resumed the Doctor, "that at least five thousand years have elapsed since your entombment, I take it for granted that your histories at that period, if not your traditions, were sufficiently explicit on that one topic of universal interest, the Creation, which took place, as I presume you are aware, only about ten centuries before."

"Sir!" said the Count Allamistakeo.

The Doctor repeated his remarks, but it was only after much additional explanation that the foreigner could be made to comprehend them. The latter at length said, hesitatingly:

"The ideas you have suggested are to me, I confess, utterly novel. During my time I never knew any one to entertain so singular a fancy as that the universe (or this world if you will have it so) ever had a beginning at all. I remember once, and once only, hearing something remotely hinted, by a man of many speculations, concerning the origin *of the human race;* and by this individual, the very word *Adam* (or Red Earth), which you make use of, was employed. He employed it, however, in a generical sense, with reference to the spontaneous germination from rank soil (just as a thousand of the lower *genera* of creatures are germinated),—the spontaneous germination, I say, of five vast hordes of men, simultaneously upspringing in five distinct and nearly equal divisions of the globe."

Here, in general, the company shrugged their shoulders, and one or two of us touched our foreheads with a very significant air. Mr Silk Buckingham, first glancing slightly at the occiput and then at the sinciput of Allamistakeo, spoke as follows:

"The long duration of human life in your time, together with the occasional practice of passing it, as you have explained, in instalments, must have had, indeed, a strong tendency to the general development and conglomeration of knowledge. I presume, therefore, that we are to attribute the marked inferiority of the old Egyptians in all particulars of science, when compared with the moderns, and more especially with the Yankees, altogether to the superior solidity of the Egyptian skull."

"I confess again," replied the Count, with much suavity, "that I am somewhat at a loss to comprehend you; pray, to what particulars of science do you allude?"

Here our whole party, joining voices, detailed, at great length, the assumptions of phrenology and the marvels of animal magnetism.

Having heard us to an end, the Count proceeded to relate a few anecdotes, which rendered it evident that prototypes of Gall and Spurzheim had flourished and faded in Egypt so long ago as to have been nearly forgotten, and that the manœuvres of Messmer were really very contemptible tricks when put in collation with the positive miracles of the Theban *savans,* who created lice and a great many other similar things.

I here asked the Count if his people were able to calculate eclipses. He smiled rather contemptuously, and said they were.

This put me a little out, but I began to make other inquiries in regard to his astronomical knowledge, when a member of the company, who had never as yet opened his mouth, whispered in my ear that for information on this head, I had better consult Ptolemy (whoever Ptolemy is), as well as one Plutarch *de facie lunæ*.

I then questioned the Mummy about burning-glasses and lenses, and, in general, about the manufacture of glass; but I had not made an end of my inquiries before the silent member again touched me quietly on the elbow, and begged me for God's sake to take a peep at Diodorus Siculus. As for the Count, he merely asked me, in the way of reply, if we moderns possessed any such microscopes as would enable us to cut cameos in the style of the Egyptians. While I was thinking how I should answer this question, little Doctor Ponnonner committed himself in a very extraordinary way.

"Look at our architecture!" he exclaimed, greatly to the indignation of both the travellers, who pinched him black and blue to no purpose.

"Look," he cried with enthusiasm, "at the Bowling-Green Fountain in New York! or if this be too vast a contemplation, regard for a moment the Capitol at Washington, D.C.!"—and the good little medical man went on to detail, very minutely, the proportions of the fabric to which he referred. He explained that the portico alone was adorned with no less than four and twenty columns, five feet in diameter, and ten feet apart.

The Count said that he regretted not being able to remember, just at that moment, the precise dimensions of any one of the principal buildings of the city of Aznac, whose foundations were laid in the night of Time, but the ruins of which were still standing, at the epoch of his entombment, in a vast plain of sand to the westward of Thebes. He recollected, however, (talking of the porticos,) that one affixed to an inferior palace in a kind of suburb called Carnac, consisted of a hundred and forty-four columns, thirty-seven feet in circumference, and twenty-five feet apart. The approach to this portico, from the Nile, was through an avenue two miles long, composed of sphynxes, statues, and obelisks, twenty, sixty, and a hundred feet in height. The palace itself (as well as he could remember) was, in one direction, two miles long, and might have been altogether about seven in circuit. Its walls were richly painted all over, within and without, with hieroglyphics. He would not pretend to *assert* that even fifty or sixty of the Doctor's Capitols might have been built within these walls, but he was by no means sure that two or three hundred of them might not have been squeezed in with some trouble. That palace at Carnac was an insignificant little building after all. He (the Count), however, could not conscientiously refuse to admit the ingenuity, magnificence, and superiority of the Fountain at the Bowling Green, as described by the Doctor.

Nothing like it, he was forced to allow, had ever been seen in Egypt or elsewhere.

I here asked the Count what he had to say to our railroads.

"Nothing," he replied, "in particular." They were rather slight, rather ill-conceived, and clumsily put together. They could not be compared, of course, with the vast, level, direct, iron-grooved causeways upon which the Egyptians conveyed entire temples and solid obelisks of a hundred and fifty feet in altitude.

I spoke of our gigantic mechanical forces.

He agreed that we knew something in that way, but inquired how I should have gone to work in getting up the imposts on the lintels of even the little palace of Carnac.

This question I concluded not to hear, and demanded if he had any idea of Artesian wells; but he simply raised his eyebrows; while Mr. Gliddon winked at me very hard and said, in a low tone, that one had been recently discovered by the engineers employed to bore for water in the Great Oasis.

I then mentioned our steel; but the foreigner elevated his nose, and asked me if our steel could have executed the sharp carved work seen on the obelisks, and which was wrought altogether by edge-tools of copper.

This disconcerted us so greatly that we thought it advisable to vary the attack to Metaphysics. We sent for a copy of a book called the "Dial," and read out of it a chapter or two about something which is not very clear, but which the Bostonians call the Great Movement of Progress.

The Count merely said that Great Movements were awfully common things in his day, and as for Progress, it was at one time quite a nuisance, but it never progressed.

We then spoke of the great beauty and importance of Democracy, and were at much trouble in impressing the Count with a due sense of the advantages we enjoyed in living where there was suffrage *ad libitum,* and no king.

He listened with marked interest, and in fact seemed not a little amused. When we had done, he said that, a great while ago, there had occurred something of a very similar sort. Thirteen Egyptian provinces determined all at once to be free, and to set a magnificent example to the rest of mankind. They assembled their wise men, and concocted the most ingenious constitution it is possible to conceive. For a while they managed remarkably well; only their habit of bragging was prodigious. The thing ended, however, in the consolidation of the thirteen states, with some fifteen or twenty others, in the most odious and insupportable despotism that was ever heard of upon the face of the Earth.

I asked what was the name of the usurping tyrant.

As well as the Count could recollect, it was *Mob.*

Not knowing what to say to this, I raised my voice, and deplored the Egyptian ignorance of steam.

The Count looked at me with much astonishment, but made no answer. The silent gentleman, however, gave me a violent nudge in the ribs with his elbows—told me I had sufficiently exposed myself for once—and demanded if I was really such a fool as not to know that the modern steam-engine is derived from the invention of Hero, through Solomon de Caus.

We were now in imminent danger of being discomfited; but, as good luck would have it, Doctor Ponnonner, having rallied, returned to our rescue, and inquired if the people of Egypt would seriously pretend to rival the moderns in the all-important particular of dress.

The Count, at this, glanced downward to the straps of his pantaloons, and then taking hold of the end of one of his coat-tails, held it up close to his eyes for some minutes. Letting it fall, at last, his mouth extended itself very gradually from ear to ear; but I do not remember that he said any thing in the way of reply.

Hereupon we recovered our spirits, and the Doctor, approaching the Mummy with great dignity, desired it to say candidly, upon its honor as a gentleman, if the Egyptians had comprehended, at *any* period, the manufacture of either Ponnonner's lozenges or Brandreth's pills.

We looked, with profound anxiety, for an answer,—but in vain. It was not forthcoming. The Egyptian blushed and hung down his head. Never was triumph more consummate; never was defeat borne with so ill a grace. Indeed, I could not endure the spectacle of the poor Mummy's mortification. I reached my hat, bowed to him stiffly, and took leave.

Upon getting home I found it past four o'clock, and went immediately to bed. It is now ten A.M. I have been up since seven, penning these memoranda for the benefit of my family and of mankind. The former I shall behold no more. My wife is a shrew. The truth is, I am heartily sick of this life and of the nineteenth century in general. I am convinced that every thing is going wrong. Besides, I am anxious to know who will be President in 2045. As soon, therefore, as I shave and swallow a cup of coffee, I shall just step over to Ponnonner's and get embalmed for a couple of hundred years.

Questions for Discussion and Review

1. What are some of the more important comic devices used in this story?

2. Compare the mummy's explanation of the meaning of the Scarabaeus to the accepted views of the time. What kind of fictional technique is Poe using here?

3. In what ways does this story anticipate later important SF themes or treatments?

4. What are we supposed to make of Dr. Ponnonner's triumph at the end of his debate with Count Allamistakeo?

The Birthmark

Nathaniel Hawthorne

Nathaniel Hawthorne (1804–1864) was born in Salem, Massachusetts, and lies buried in Concord. He was one of the leading figures of a New England renascence that included Emerson, Thoreau, and Melville. Hawthorne's best-known work is undoubtedly *The Scarlet Letter* (1850). For generations, American children were brought up on Hawthorne's retellings of myth and legend in *A Wonder Book* (1852) and *Tanglewood Tales* (1853). Hawthorne is remembered as the author of two other novels, *The House of the Seven Gables* (1851) and *The Marble Faun* (1860), and for short stories, most of which probe the effects of evil and guilt on the human soul in a symbolic or allegorical manner. "The Birthmark" first appeared in *The Pioneer* (March 1843) and was reprinted in the collection of 1846, *Mosses from an Old Manse.*

Hawthorne was one of the last great writers of the romance tradition, which he had absorbed from his boyhood reading of Spencer and Bunyan. Hawthorne distinguished romance from novel in his preface to *The House of the Seven Gables:* "When a writer calls his work a Romance, it need hardly be observed that he wishes to claim a certain latitude, both as to its fashion and material, which he would not have felt himself entitled to assume had he professed to be writing a novel." This latitude of which he speaks is the right to present the truth of the human heart "Under circumstances . . . of the writer's own choosing or creation," as Hawthorne later remarked in that same preface. Hawthorne sees in the designation of romance a dispensation from the requirements of realism so that he may irradiate the commonplace with the marvelous. It is interesting to see how sensitive Hawthorne is on this point. Contemporary writers certainly feel no equivalent inhibition in blending elements of the marvelous or fantastic, as we would now call it, with the realistic.

Hawthorne's great interest was in tracing the moral effects of puritanism on the human heart. Rarely did he stray from that subject successfully except in his tales for children. He wrote several well-known stories that have science as an important element. They include "Dr. Heidegger's Experiment" (1837), "Rappaccini's Daughter" (1844), "The Artist of the Beautiful" (1844), and "Earth's Holocaust" (1844), each of which treats in a different manner the implications of new scientific discovery for the moral life of humanity.

No one will doubt that "The Birthmark" is a story designed with a lesson to teach. The tale is built around a single mysterious symbol. A century ago, birthmarks were mysterious and awesome phenomena likely to elicit a bit of superstitious emotion in all but the most sober Yankee temperament. One may wonder, unofficially of course, whether this is not still the case for many readers. The abiding ghost of puritanism behind the mask of science in this story will give modern readers a chill of recognition at least equal to the foreboding that Hawthorne's audience must have felt.

In this story the allegorical structure is as important as the symbolism. Symbols, successful ones anyway, are intended to touch us at levels deeper than conscious thought can explore. Their power lies in suggesting rather than clarifying meanings, and they leave behind the imprint of a significant but mysterious experience. "The Birthmark" is a symbolic allegory dealing with the limits of human capacity to change and to effect change. Although the martyrdom of Georgiana, Aylmer's beautiful wife, raises questions about his state of mind, the effect is to underline another important theme, the fear of science. In such terms, this is an example of a nineteenth-century cautionary tale. The warning seems less a plea to keep the lid on a possible Pandora's box than a directive to examine the uses to which the great new powers of science are put and to consider well the capacities and limitations of all those who would command those powers.

In the latter part of the last century there lived a man of science, an eminent proficient in every branch of natural philosophy, who not long before our story opens had made experience of a spiritual affinity more attractive than any chemical one. He had left his laboratory to the care of an assistant, cleared his fine countenance from the furnace smoke, washed the stain of acids from his fingers, and persuaded a beautiful woman to become his wife. In those days, when the comparatively recent discovery of electricity and other kindred mysteries of Nature seemed to open paths into the region of miracle, it was not unusual for the love of science to rival the love of woman in its depth and absorbing energy. The higher intellect, the imagination, the spirit, and even the heart might all find their congenial aliment in pursuits which, as some of their ardent votaries believed, would ascend from one step of powerful intelligence to another, until the philosopher should lay his hand on the secret of creative force and perhaps make new worlds for himself. We know not whether Aylmer possessed this degree of faith in man's ultimate control over Nature. He had devoted himself, too unreservedly to scientific studies ever to be weaned from them by any second passion. His love for his young wife might prove the stronger of the two; but it could only be by intertwining itself with his love of science and uniting the strength of the latter to his own.

Such a union accordingly took place, and was attended with truly remarkable consequences and a deeply impressive moral. One day, very soon after their marriage, Aylmer sat gazing at his wife with a trouble in his countenance that grew stronger until he spoke.

"Georgiana," said he, "has it never occurred to you that the mark upon your cheek might be removed?"

"No, indeed," said she, smiling; but, perceiving the seriousness of his manner, she blushed deeply. "To tell you the truth, it has been so often called a charm that I was simple enough to imagine it might be so."

"Ah, upon another face perhaps it might," replied her husband; "but never on yours. No, dearest Georgiana, you came so nearly perfect from the hand of Nature that this slightest possible defect, which we hesitate whether to term a defect or a beauty, shocks me, as being the visible mark of earthly imperfection."

"Shocks you, my husband!" cried Georgiana, deeply hurt; at first reddening with momentary anger, but then bursting into tears. "Then why did you take me from my mother's side? You cannot love what shocks you!"

To explain this conversation, it must be mentioned that in the centre of Georgiana's left cheek there was a singular mark, deeply interwoven, as it were, with the texture and substance of her face. In the usual state of her complexion—a healthy though delicate bloom—the mark wore a tint of deeper crimson, which imperfectly defined its shape amid the surrounding rosiness. When she blushed it gradually became more indistinct, and finally vanished amid the triumphant rush of blood that bathed the whole cheek with its brilliant glow. But if any shifting motion caused her to turn pale there was the mark again, a crimson stain upon the snow, in what Aylmer sometimes deemed an almost fearful distinctness. Its shape bore not a little similarity to the human hand, though of the smallest pygmy size. Georgiana's lovers were wont to say that some fairy at her birth hour had laid her tiny hand upon the infant's cheek, and left this impress there in token of the magic endowments that were to give her such sway over all hearts. Many a desperate swain would have risked life for the privilege of pressing his lips to the mysterious hand. It must not be concealed, however, that the impression wrought by this fairy sign manual varied exceedingly according to the difference of temperament in the beholders. Some fastidious persons—but they were exclusively of her own sex—affirmed that the bloody hand, as they chose to call it, quite destroyed the effect of Georgiana's beauty and rendered her countenance even hideous. But it would be as reasonable to say that one of those small blue stains which sometimes occur in the purest statuary marble would convert the Eve of Powers to a monster. Masculine observers, if the birthmark did not heighten their admiration, contented themselves with wishing it away, that the world might possess one living specimen of ideal loveliness without the semblance of a flaw. After his marriage,—for he thought little or nothing of the matter before,—Aylmer discovered that this was the case with himself.

Had she been less beautiful,—if Envy's self could have found aught else to sneer at,—he might have felt his affection heightened by the prettiness of this mimic hand, now vaguely portrayed, now lost, now stealing forth again and glimmering to and fro with every pulse of emotion that throbbed within her heart; but, seeing her otherwise so perfect, he found this one defect grow more and more intolerable with every moment of their united lives. It was the fatal flaw of humanity which Nature, in one shape or another, stamps ineffaceably on all her productions, either to imply that they are temporary and finite, or that their perfection must be wrought by toil and pain. The crimson hand expressed the ineludible gripe in which mortality clutches the highest and purest of earthly mould, degrading them into kindred with the lowest, and even with the very brutes, like whom their visible frames return to dust. In this manner, selecting it as the symbol of his wife's liability to sin, sorrow, decay, and death, Aylmer's sombre imagination was not long in rendering the birthmark a frightful object, causing him more trouble and horror than ever Georgiana's beauty, whether of soul or sense, had given him delight.

At all the seasons which should have been their happiest he invariably, and without intending it, nay, in spite of a purpose to the contrary, reverted to this one disastrous topic. Trifling as it at first appeared, it so connected itself with innumerable trains of thought and modes of feeling that it became the central point of all. With the morning twilight Aylmer opened his eyes upon his wife's face and recognized the symbol of imperfection; and when they sat together at the evening hearth his eyes wandered stealthily to her cheek, and beheld, flickering with the blaze of the wood fire, the spectral hand that wrote mortality where he would fain have worshipped. Georgiana soon learned to shudder at his gaze. It needed but a glance with the peculiar expression that his face often wore to change the roses of her cheek into a deathlike paleness, amid which the crimson hand was brought strongly out, like a bas-relief of ruby on the whitest marble.

Late one night, when the lights were growing dim so as hardly to betray the stain on the poor wife's cheek, she herself, for the first time, voluntarily took up the subject.

"Do you remember, my dear Aylmer," said she, with a feeble attempt at a smile, "have you any recollection, of a dream last night about this odious hand?"

"None! none whatever!" replied Aylmer, starting; but then he added, in a dry, cold tone, affected for the sake of concealing the real depth of his emotion, "I might well dream of it; for, before I fell asleep, it had taken a pretty grim hold of my fancy."

"And you did dream of it?" continued Georgiana, hastily; for she dreaded lest a gush of tears should interrupt what she had to say. "A terrible dream! I wonder that you can forget it. Is it possible to forget this one expression?—'It is in her heart now; we must have it out!' Reflect, my husband; for by all means I would have you recall that dream."

The mind is in a sad state when Sleep, the all-involving, cannot confine her spectres within the dim region of her sway, but suffers them to break forth, affrighting this actual life with secrets that perchance belong to a deeper one. Aylmer now remembered his dream. He had fancied himself with his servant Aminadab, attempting an operation for the removal of the birthmark; but the deeper went the knife, the deeper sank the hand, until at length its tiny grasp appeared to have caught hold of Georgiana's heart; whence, however, her husband was inexorably resolved to cut or wrench it away.

When the dream had shaped itself perfectly in his memory Aylmer sat in his wife's presence with a guilty feeling. Truth often finds its way to the mind close muffled in robes of sleep, and then speaks with uncompromising directness of matters in regard to which we practise an unconscious self-deception during our waking moments. Until now he had not been aware of the tyrannizing influence acquired by one idea over his mind, and of the lengths which he might find in his heart to go for the sake of giving himself peace.

"Aylmer," resumed Georgiana, solemnly, "I know not what may be the cost to both of us to rid me of this fatal birthmark. Perhaps its removal may cause cureless deformity; or it may be the stain goes as deep as life itself. Again: do we know that there is a possibility, on any terms, of unclasping the firm gripe of this little hand which was laid upon me before I came into the world?"

"Dearest Georgiana, I have spent much thought upon the subject," hastily interrupted Aylmer. "I am convinced of the perfect practicability of its removal."

"If there be the remotest possibility of it," continued Georgiana, "let the attempt be made, at whatever risk. Danger is nothing to me; for life, while this hateful mark makes me the object of your horror and disgust,—life is a burden which I would fling down with joy. Either remove this dreadful hand, or take my wretched life! You have deep science. All the world bears witness of it. You have achieved great wonders. Cannot you remove this little, little mark, which I cover with the tips of two small fingers? Is this beyond your power, for the sake of your own peace, and to save your poor wife from madness?"

"Noblest, dearest, tenderest wife," cried Aylmer, rapturously, "doubt not my power. I have already given this matter the deepest thought— thought which might almost have enlightened me to create a being less perfect than yourself. Georgiana, you have led me deeper than ever into the heart of science. I feel myself fully competent to render this dear cheek as faultless as its fellow; and then, most beloved, what will be my triumph when I shall have corrected what Nature left imperfect in her fairest work! Even Pygmalion, when his sculptured woman assumed life, felt not greater ecstasy that mine will be."

"It is resolved, then," said Georgiana, faintly smiling. "And, Aylmer, spare me not, though you should find the birthmark take refuge in my heart at last."

Her husband tenderly kissed her cheek—her right cheek—not that which bore the impress of the crimson hand.

The next day Aylmer apprised his wife of a plan that he had formed whereby he might have opportunity for the intense thought and constant watchfulness which the proposed operation would require, while Georgiana, likewise, would enjoy the perfect repose essential to its success. They were to seclude themselves in the extensive apartments occupied by Aylmer as a laboratory, and where, during his toilsome youth, he had made discoveries in the elemental powers of Nature that had roused the admiration of all the learned societies in Europe. Seated calmly in this laboratory, the pale philosopher had investigated the secrets of the highest cloud region and of the profoundest mines; he had satisfied himself of the causes that kindled and kept alive the fires of the volcano; and had explained the mystery of fountains, and how it is that they gush forth, some so bright and pure, and others with such rich medicinal virtues, from the dark bosom of the earth. Here, too, at an earlier period, he had studied the wonders of the human frame, and attempted to fathom the very process by which Nature assimilates all her precious influences from earth and air, and from the spiritual world, to create and foster man, her masterpiece. The latter pursuit, however, Aylmer had long laid aside in unwilling recognition of the truth—against which all seekers sooner or later stumble—that our great creative Mother, while she amuses us with apparently working in the broadest sunshine, is yet severely careful to keep her own secrets, and, in spite of her pretended openness, shows us nothing but results. She permits us, indeed, to mar, but seldom to mend, and, like a jealous patentee, on no account to make. Now, however, Aylmer resumed these half-forgotten investigations; not, of course, with such hopes or wishes as first suggested them; but because they involved much physiological truth and lay in the path of his proposed scheme for the treatment of Georgiana.

As he led her over the threshold of the laboratory, Georgiana was cold and tremulous. Aylmer looked cheerfully into her face, with intent to reassure her, but was so startled with the intense glow of the birthmark upon the whiteness of her cheek that he could not restrain a strong convulsive shudder. His wife fainted.

"Aminadab! Aminadab!" shouted Aylmer, stamping violently on the floor.

Forthwith there issued from an inner apartment a man of low stature, but bulky frame, with shaggy hair hanging about his visage, which was grimed with the vapors of the furnace: This personage had been Aylmer's underworker during his whole scientific career, and was admirably fitted for that office by his great mechanical readiness, and the skill with which, while incapable of comprehending a single principle, he executed all the details of his master's experiments. With his vast strength, his shaggy hair, his smoky aspect, and the indescribable earthiness that incrusted him, he seemed to represent man's physical nature; while Aylmer's slender figure, and pale, intellectual face, were no less apt a type of the spiritual element.

"Throw open the door of the boudoir, Aminadab," said Aylmer, "and burn a pastil."

"Yes, master," answered Aminadab, looking intently at the lifeless form of Georgiana; and then he muttered to himself, "If she were my wife, I'd never part with that birthmark."

When Georgiana recovered consciousness she found herself breathing an atmosphere of penetrating fragrance, the gentle potency of which had recalled her from her deathlike faintness. The scene around her looked like enchantment. Aylmer had converted those smoky, dingy, sombre rooms, where he had spent his brightest years in recondite pursuits, into a series of beautiful apartments not unfit to be the secluded abode of a lovely woman. The walls were hung with gorgeous curtains, which imparted the combination of grandeur and grace that no other species of adornment can achieve; and, as they fell from the ceiling to the floor, their rich and ponderous folds, concealing all angles and straight lines, appeared to shut in the scene from infinite space. For aught Georgiana knew, it might be a pavilion among the clouds. And Aylmer, excluding the sunshine, which would have interfered with his chemical processes, had supplied its place with perfumed lamps, emitting flames of various hue, but all uniting in a soft, impurpled radiance. He now knelt by his wife's side, watching her earnestly, but without alarm; for he was confident in his science, and felt that he could draw a magic circle round her within which no evil might intrude.

"Where am I? Ah, I remember," said Georgiana, faintly; and she placed her hand over her cheek to hide the terrible mark from her husband's eyes.

"Fear not, dearest!" exclaimed he. "Do not shrink from me! Believe me, Georgiana, I even rejoice in this single imperfection, since it will be such a rapture to remove it."

"O, spare me!" sadly replied is wife. "Pray do not look at it again. I never can forget that convulsive shudder."

In order to soothe Georgiana, and, as it were, to release her mind from the burden of actual things, Aylmer now put in practice some of the light and playful secrets which science had taught him among its profounder lore. Airy figures, absolutely bodiless ideas, and forms of unsubstantial beauty came and danced before her, imprinting their momentary footsteps on beams of light. Though she had some indistinct idea of the method of these optical phenomena, still the illusion was almost perfect enough to warrant the belief that her husband possessed sway over the spiritual world. Then again, when she felt a wish to look forth from her seclusion, immediately, as if her thoughts were answered, the procession of external existence flitted across a screen. The scenery and the figures of actual life were perfectly represented, but with that bewitching yet indescribable difference which always makes a picture, an image, or a shadow so much more attractive than the original. When wearied of this, Aylmer bade her cast her eyes upon a vessel containing a quantity of earth. She did so, with little interest at first; but was soon startled to perceive the germ of a plant shooting upward from the soil. Then came the slender stalk; the leaves gradually unfolded themselves; and amid them was a perfect and lovely flower.

"It is magical!" cried Georgiana. "I dare not touch it."

"Nay, pluck it," answered Aylmer,—"pluck it, and inhale its brief perfume while you may. The flower will wither in a few moments and leave nothing save its brown seed vessels; but thence may be perpetuated a race as ephemeral as itself."

But Georgiana had no sooner touched the flower than the whole plant suffered a blight, its leaves turning coal-black as if by the agency of fire.

"There was too powerful a stimulus," said Aylmer, thoughtfully.

To make up for this abortive experiment, he proposed to take her portrait by a scientific process of his own invention. It was to be effected by rays of light striking upon a polished plate of metal. Georgiana assented; but, on looking at the result, was affrighted to find the features of the portrait blurred and indefinable; while the minute figure of a hand appeared where the cheek should have been. Aylmer snatched the metallic plate and threw it into a jar of corrosive acid.

Soon, however, he forgot these mortifying failures. In the intervals of study and chemical experiment he came to her flushed and exhausted, but seemed invigorated by her presence, and spoke in glowing language of the resources of his art. He gave a history of the long dynasty of the alchemists, who spent so many ages in quest of the universal solvent by which the golden principle might be elicited from all things vile and base. Aylmer appeared to believe that, by the plainest scientific logic, it was altogether within the limits of possibility to discover this long-sought medium; "but," he added, "a philosopher who should go deep enough to acquire the power would attain too lofty a wisdom to stoop to the exercise of it." Not less singular were his opinions in regard to the elixir vitae. He more than intimated that it was at his option to concoct a liquid that should prolong life for years, perhaps interminably; but that it would produce a discord in Nature which all the world, and chiefly the quaffer of the immortal nostrum, would find cause to curse.

"Aylmer, are you in earnest?" asked Georgiana, looking at him with amazement and fear. "It is terrible to possess such power, or even to dream of possessing it."

"O, do not tremble, my love," said her husband. "I would not wrong either you or myself by working such inharmonious effects upon our lives; but I would have you consider how trifling, in comparison, is the skill requisite to remove this little hand."

At the mention of the birthmark, Georgiana, as usual, shrank as if a red-hot iron had touched her cheek.

Again Aylmer applied himself to his labors. She could hear his voice in the distant furnace room giving directions to Aminadab, whose harsh, uncouth, misshapen tones were audible in response, more like the grunt or growl of a brute than human speech. After hours of absence, Aylmer reappeared and proposed that she should now examine his cabinet of chemical products and natural treasures of the earth. Among the former he showed her a small vial, in which, he remarked, was contained a gentle yet most powerful fragrance, capable of impregnating all the breezes that blow across a kingdom. They were of inestimable value, the contents of that little vial; and, as he said so, he threw some of the perfume into the air and filled the room with piercing and invigorating delight.

"And what is this?" asked Georgiana, pointing to a small crystal globe containing a gold-colored liquid. "It is so beautiful to the eye that I could imagine it the elixir of life."

"In one sense it is," replied Aylmer; "or rather, the elixir of immortality. It is the most precious poison that ever was concocted in this world. By its aid I could apportion the lifetime of any mortal at whom you might point your finger. The strength of the dose would determine whether he were to linger out years, or drop dead in the midst of a breath. No king on his guarded throne could keep his life if I, in my private station, should deem that the welfare of millions justified me in depriving him of it."

"Why do you keep such a terrific drug?" inquired Georgiana in horror.

"Do not mistrust me, dearest," said her husband, smiling; "its virtuous potency is yet greater than its harmful one. But see! here is a powerful cosmetic. With a few drops of this in a vase of water, freckles may be washed away as easily as the hands are cleansed. A stronger infusion would take the blood out of the cheek, and leave the rosiest beauty a pale ghost."

"Is it with this lotion that you intend to bathe my cheek?" asked Georgiana, anxiously.

"O, no," hastily replied her husband; "this is merely superficial. Your case demands a remedy that shall go deeper."

In his interviews with Georgiana, Aylmer generally made minute inquiries as to her sensations, and whether the confinement of the rooms and the temperature of the atmosphere agreed with her. These questions had such a particular drift that Georgiana began to conjecture that she was already subjected to certain physical influences, either breathed in with the fragrant air or taken with her food. She fancied likewise, but it might be altogether fancy, that there was a stirring up of her system—a strange, indefinite sensation creeping through her veins, and tingling, half painfully, half pleasurably, at her heart. Still whenever she dared to look into the mirror, there she beheld herself pale as a white rose and with the crimson birthmark stamped upon her cheek. Not even Aylmer now hated it so much as she.

To dispel the tedium of the hours which her husband found it necessary to devote to the processes of combination and analysis, Georgiana turned over the volumes of his scientific library. In many dark old tomes she met with chapters full of romance and poetry. They were the works of the philosophers of the middle ages, such as Albertus Magnus, Cornelius Agrippa, Paracelsus, and the famous friar who created the prophetic Brazen Head. All these antique naturalists stood in advance of their centuries, yet were imbued with some of their credulity, and therefore were believed, and perhaps imagined themselves to have acquired from the investigation of Nature a power above Nature, and from physics a sway over the spiritual world. Hardly less curious and imaginative were the early volumes of the Transactions of the Royal Society, in which the members, knowing little of the limits of natural possibility, were continually recording wonders or proposing methods whereby wonders might be wrought.

But to Georgiana, the most engrossing volume was a large folio from her husband's own hand, in which he had recorded every experiment of his scientific career, its original aim, the methods adopted for its development, and its final success or failure, with the circumstances to which either event was attributable. The book, in truth, was both the history and emblem of his ardent, ambitious, imaginative, yet practical and laborious life. He handled physical details as if there were nothing beyond them; yet spiritualized them all and redeemed himself from materialism by his strong and eager aspiration towards the infinite. In his grasp the veriest clod of earth assumed a soul. Georgiana, as she read, reverenced Aylmer and loved him more profoundly than ever, but with a less entire dependence on his judgment than heretofore. Much as he had accomplished, she could not but observe that his most splendid successes were almost invariably failures, if compared with the ideal at which he aimed. His brightest diamonds were the merest pebbles, and felt to be so by himself, in comparison with the inestimable gems which lay hidden beyond his reach. The volume, rich with achievements that had won renown for its author, was yet as melancholy a record as ever mortal hand had penned. It was the sad confession and continual exemplification of the shortcomings of the composite man, the spirit burdened with clay and working in matter, and of the despair that assails the higher nature at finding itself so miserably thwarted by the earthly part. Perhaps every man of genius, in whatever sphere, might recognize the image of his own experience in Aylmer's journal.

So deeply did these reflections affect Georgiana that she laid her face upon the open volume and burst into tears. In this situation she was found by her husband.

"It is dangerous to read in a sorcerer's books," said he with a smile, though his countenance was uneasy and displeased. "Georgiana, there are pages in that volume which I can scarcely glance over and keep my senses. Take heed lest it prove detrimental to you."

"It has made me worship you more than ever," said she.

"Ah, wait for this one success," rejoined he, "then worship me if you will. I shall deem myself hardly unworthy of it. But come, I have sought you for the luxury of your voice. Sing to me, dearest."

So she poured out the liquid music of her voice to quench the thirst of his spirit. He then took his leave with a boyish exuberance of gayety, assuring her that her seclusion would endure but a little longer, and that the result was already certain. Scarcely had he departed when Georgiana felt irresistibly impelled to follow him. She had forgotten to inform Aylmer of a symptom which for two or three hours past had begun to excite her attention. It was a sensation in the fatal birthmark, not painful, but which induced a restlessness throughout her system. Hastening after her husband, she intruded for the first time into the laboratory.

The first thing that struck her eye was the furnace, that hot and feverish worker, with the intense glow of its fire, which by the quantities of soot clustered above it seemed to have been burning for ages. There was a distilling apparatus in full operation. Around the room were retorts, tubes, cylinders, crucibles, and other apparatus of chemical research. An electrical machine stood ready for immediate use. The atmosphere felt oppressively close, and was tainted with gaseous odors which had been tormented forth by the processes of science. The severe and homely simplicity of the apartment, with its naked walls and brick pavement, looked strange, accustomed as Georgiana had become to the fantastic elegance of her boudoir. But what chiefly, indeed almost solely, drew her attention, was the aspect of Aylmer himself.

He was pale as death, anxious and absorbed, and hung over the furnace as if it depended upon his utmost watchfulness whether the liquid which it was distilling should be the draught of immortal happiness or misery. How different from the sanguine and joyous mien that he had assumed for Georgiana's encouragement!

"Carefully now, Aminadab; carefully, thou human machine; carefully, thou man of clay," muttered Aylmer, more to himself than his assistant. "Now, if there be a thought too much or too little, it is all over."

"Ho! ho!" mumbled Aminadab. "Look, master! look!"

Aylmer raised his eyes hastily, and at first reddened, then grew paler than ever, on beholding Georgiana. He rushed towards her and seized her arm with a gripe that left the print of his fingers upon it.

"Why do you come hither? Have you no trust in your husband?" cried he, impetuously. "Would you throw the blight of that fatal birthmark over my labors? It is not well done. Go, prying woman! go!"

"Nay, Aylmer," said Georgiana with the firmness of which she possessed no stinted endowment, "it is not you that have a right to complain. You mistrust your wife, you have concealed the anxiety with which you watch the development of this experiment. Think not so unworthily of me, my husband. Tell me all the risk we run, and fear not that I shall shrink; for my share in it is far less than your own."

"No, no, Georgiana!" said Aylmer, impatiently; "it must not be."

"I submit," replied she, calmly. "And, Aylmer, I shall quaff whatever draught you bring me; but it will be on the same principle that would induce me to take a dose of poison if offered by your hand."

"My noble wife," said Aylmer, deeply moved, "I knew not the height and depth of your nature until now. Nothing shall be concealed. Know, then, that this crimson hand, superficial as it seems, has clutched its grasp into your being with a strength of which I had no previous conception. I have already administered agents powerful enough to do aught except to change your entire physical system. Only one thing remains to be tried. If that fail us we are ruined."

"Why did you hesitate to tell me this?" asked she.

"Because, Georgiana," said Aylmer, in a low voice, "there is danger."

"Danger? There is but one danger—that this horrible stigma shall be left upon my cheek!" cried Georgiana. "Remove it, remove it, whatever be the cost, or we shall both go mad!"

"Heaven knows your words are too true," said Aylmer, sadly. "And now, dearest, return to your boudoir. In a little while all will be tested."

He conducted her back and took leave of her with a solemn tenderness which spoke far more than his words how much was now at stake. After his departure Georgiana became rapt in musings. She considered the character of Aylmer and did it completer justice than at any previous moment. Her heart exulted, while it trembled, at his honorable love—so pure and lofty that it would accept nothing less than perfection nor miserably make itself contented with an earthlier nature than he had dreamed of. She felt how much more precious was such a sentiment than that meaner kind which would have borne with the imperfection for her sake, and have been guilty of treason to holy love by degrading its perfect idea to the level of the actual; and with her whole spirit she prayed that, for a single moment, she might satisfy his highest and deepest conception. Longer than one moment she well knew it could not be; for his spirit was ever on the march, ever ascending, and each instant required something that was beyond the scope of the instant before.

The sound of her husband's footsteps aroused her. He bore a crystal goblet containing a liquor colorless as water, but bright enough to be the draught of immortality. Aylmer was pale; but it seemed rather the consequence of a highly-wrought state of mind and tension of spirit than of fear or doubt.

"The concotion of the draught has been perfect," said he, in answer to Georgiana's look. "Unless all my science have deceived me, it cannot fail."

"Save on your account, my dearest Aylmer," observed his wife, "I might wish to put off this birthmark of mortality by relinquishing mortality itself in preference to any other mode. Life is but a sad possession to those who have attained precisely the degree of moral advancement at which I stand. Were I weaker and blinder, it might be happiness. Were I stronger, it might be endured hopefully. But, being what I find myself, methinks I am of all mortals the most fit to die."

"You are fit for heaven without tasting death!" replied her husband. "But why do we speak of dying? The draught cannot fail. Behold its effect upon this plant."

On the window seat there stood a geranium diseased with yellow blotches which had overspread all its leaves. Aylmer poured a small quantity of the liquid upon the soil in which it grew. In a little time, when the roots of the plant had taken up the moisture, the unsightly blotches began to be extinguished in a living verdure.

"There needed no proof," said Georgiana, quietly. "Give me the goblet. I joyfully stake all upon your word."

"Drink, then, thou lofty creature!" exclaimed Aylmer, with fervid admiration. "There is no taint of imperfection on thy spirit. Thy sensible frame, too, shall soon be all perfect."

She quaffed the liquid and returned the goblet to his hand.

"It is grateful," said she, with a placid smile. "Methinks it is like water from a heavenly fountain; for it contains I know not what of unobtrusive fragrance and deliciousness. It allays a feverish thirst that had parched me for many days. Now, dearest, let me sleep. My earthly senses are closing over my spirit like the leaves around the heart of a rose at sunset."

She spoke the last words with a gentle reluctance, as if it required almost more energy than she could command to pronounce the faint and lingering syllables. Scarcely had they loitered through her lips ere she was lost in slumber. Aylmer sat by her side, watching her aspect with the emotions proper to a man the whole value of whose existence was involved in the process now to be tested. Mingled with this mood, however, was the philosophic investigation characteristic of the man of science. Not the minutest symptom escaped him. A heightened flush of the cheek, a slight irregularity of breath, a quiver of the eyelid, a hardly perceptible tremor through the frame,—such were the details which, as the moments passed, he wrote down in his folio volume. Intense thought had set its stamp upon every previous page of that volume; but the thoughts of years were all concentrated upon the last.

While thus employed, he failed not to gaze often at the fatal hand, and not without a shudder. Yet once, by a strange and unaccountable impulse, he pressed it with his lips. His spirit recoiled, however, in the very act; and Georgiana, out of the midst of her deep sleep, moved uneasily and murmured as if in remonstrance. Again Aylmer resumed his watch. Nor was it without avail. The crimson hand, which at first had been strongly visible upon the marble paleness of Georgiana's cheek, now grew more faintly outlined. She remained not less pale than ever; but the birthmark, with every breath that came and went lost somewhat of its former distinctness. Its presence had been awful; its departure was more awful still. Watch the stain of the rainbow fading out of the sky, and you will know how that mysterious symbol passed away.

"By Heaven! it is well nigh gone!" said Aylmer to himself in almost irrepressible ectasy. "I can scarcely trace it now. Success! success! And now it is like the faintest rose color. The lightest flush of blood across her cheek would overcome it. But she is so pale!"

He drew aside the window curtain and suffered the light of natural day to fall into the room and rest upon her cheek. At the same time he heard a gross, hoarse chuckle, which he had long known as his servant Aminadab's expression of delight.

"Ah, clod! ah, earthly mass!" cried Aylmer, laughing in a sort of frenzy, "you have served me well! Matter and spirit—earth and heaven —have both done their part in this! Laugh, thing of the senses! You have earned the right to laugh."

These exclamations broke Georgiana's sleep. She slowly unclosed her eyes and gazed into the mirror which her husband had arranged for that purpose. A faint smile flitted over her lips when she recognized how barely perceptible was now that crimson hand which had once blazed forth with such disastrous brilliancy as to scare away all their happiness. But then her eyes sought Alymer's face with a trouble and anxiety that he could by no means account for.

"My poor Aylmer!" murmured she.

"Poor? Nay, richest, happiest, most favored!" exclaimed he. "My peerless bride, it is successful! You are perfect!"

"My poor Aylmer," she repeated, with a more than human tenderness, "you have aimed loftily; you have done nobly. Do not repent that, with so high and pure a feeling, you have rejected the best the earth could offer. Aylmer, dearest Aylmer, I am dying!"

Alas! it was too true! The fatal hand had grappled with the mystery of life, and was the bond by which an angelic spirit kept itself in union with a mortal frame. As the last crimson tint of the birth-mark—that sole token of human imperfection—faded from her cheek, the parting breath of the now perfect woman passed into the atmosphere, and her soul, lingering a moment near her husband, took its heavenward flight. Then a hoarse, chuckling laugh was heard again! Thus ever does the gross fatality of earth exult in its invariable triumph over the immortal essence which, in this dim sphere of half development, demands the completeness of a higher state. Yet, had Aylmer reached a profounder wisdom, he need not thus have flung away the happiness which would have woven his mortal life of the selfsame texture with the celestial. The momentary circumstance was too strong for him; he failed to look beyond the shadowy scope of time, and, living once for all in eternity, to find the perfect future in the present.

Questions for Discussion and Review

1. Why did Hawthorne choose the form of a hand for Georgiana's birthmark?
2. Why were not Georgiana or Aylmer content to use cosmetics to cover the birthmark?
3. What is the connection between the decaying but still influential spirit of puritanism and Aylmer's science?
4. What erotic elements are suggested in the way the story is told? What purpose do they serve?
5. In what terms are the limitations of science established in Hawthorne's allegory?

The Star

H.G. Wells

Herbert George Wells (1866–1946) was born in Kent of a working-class
family. His early years were ones of poverty and struggle to raise himself
both intellectually and socially. The success with which he did so may be
measured by his more than eighty books and the international reputation
they brought him as a writer and sage. Although he is cited here for his
SF, he wrote many mainstream novels, among which *Kipps* (1905),
The History of Mr. Polly (1910), *Ann Veronica* (1909), and *Tono-
Bungay* (1909) are still highly regarded by critics. As he grew older,
Wells's writing became more polemical and increasingly pessimistic. His
two-volume *Outline of History* (1920) may have been his most influential
work, but it was not his best. Two works less famous but more deserving
than the history are *Experiment in Autobiography* (1934) and *Mind
at the End of Its Tether* (1945). "The Star" first appeared in the Christmas
number of the *Graphic* in 1897.

Wells is recognized everywhere today as the father of modern SF. He wrote
a series of remarkably prophetic books and a host of novels and short
stories in which he seems to have explored almost every major SF subject
and theme. He did so in *The Time Machine* (1895), *The War of the
Worlds* (1898), *The Invisible Man* (1897), *In the Days of the Comet*
(1906), *The Island of Dr. Moreau* (1896), and *The Shape of Things to
Come* (1933); and this is by no means the whole list of such works. It was
as though Wells appeared at the beginning of the most scientific and
technological century the world had ever seen in order to conduct an
inventory of the available materials for the coming generations of writers.

"The Star" is one of Wells's best-known SF stories. It is hard SF,
worked out with careful attention to the operation of the laws of astro-
mechanics. It begins with a simple premise. Wells's practice of composing
scientific romances, as he called them, was to begin by asking readers to
accept only one imaginary hypothesis and to work deliberately thereafter,
drawing out its imaginary implications.

The theme of the story seems to have been a favorite of the author's—
initial catastrophe with ultimate annihilation averted at the last minute.
The story traces the physical process by which Neptune collides with
an intruding planet and plunges toward the sun, threatening to destroy
Earth. The story achieves its best moments in precisely those areas ignored
in the earlier Byron poem, namely the physical causes underlying the
catastrophe. Wells is also more generous with our planet than Byron, and
the difference in endings is a good barometer of the changes that had
taken place during the century. In the Wells story, human beings are far
more perceptive and more aware of what is happening to them and what
is likely to happen. The growth of both scientific knowledge and media
communications was responsible for that, although in neither the Byron

nor the Wells narrative is the human race able to control cosmic events. In "The Star" we simply were luckier as a race. Earth is transformed to some degree by the accident, both physically and morally, into a different and better world; but, as Wells emphasizes, of these things the story does not tell, only of the passing of the star.

It was on the first day of the new year that the announcement was made, almost simultaneously from three observatories, that the motion of the planet Neptune, the outermost of all the planets that wheel about the sun, had become very erratic. Ogilvy had already called attention to a suspected retardation in its velocity in December. Such a piece of news was scarcely calculated to interest a world the greater portion of whose inhabitants were unaware of the existence of the planet Neptune, nor outside the astronomical profession did the subsequent discovery of a faint remote speck of light in the region of the perturbed planet cause any very great excitement. Scientific people, however, found the intelligence remarkable enough, even before it became known that the new body was rapidly growing larger and brighter, that its motion was quite different from the orderly progress of the planets, and that the deflection of Neptune and its satellite was becoming now of an unprecedented kind.

Few people without a training in science can realise the huge isolation of the solar system. The sun with its specks of planets, its dust of planetoids, and its impalpable comets, swims in a vacant immensity that almost defeats the imagination. Beyond the orbit of Neptune there is space, vacant so far as human observation has penetrated, without warmth or light or sound, blank emptiness, for twenty million times a million miles. That is the smallest estimate of the distance to be traversed before the very nearest of the stars is attained. And, saving a few comets more unsubstantial than the thinnest flame, no matter had ever to human knowledge crossed this gulf of space, until early in the twentieth century this strange wanderer appeared. A vast mass of matter it was, bulky, heavy, rushing without warning out of the black mystery of the sky into the radiance of the sun. By the second day it was clearly visible to any decent instrument, as a speck with a barely sensible diameter, in the constellation Leo near Regulus. In a little while an opera glass could attain it.

On the third day of the new year the newspaper readers of two hemispheres were made aware for the first time of the real importance of this unusual apparition in the heavens. "A Planetary Collision," one London paper headed the news, and proclaimed Duchaine's opinion that this strange new planet would probably collide with Neptune. The leader writers enlarged upon the topic. So that in most of the capitals of the world, on January 3rd, there was an expectation, however vague,

of some imminent phenomenon in the sky; and as the night followed
the sunset round the globe, thousands of men turned their eyes skyward to see—the old familiar stars just as they had always been.

Until it was dawn in London and Pollux setting and the stars overhead grown pale. The Winter's dawn it was, a sickly filtering accumulation of daylight, and the light of gas and candles shone yellow in the
windows to show where people were astir. But the yawning policeman
saw the thing, the busy crowds in the markets stopped agape, work-
men going to their work betimes, milkmen, the drivers of newscarts,
dissipation going home jaded and pale, homeless wanderers, sentinels
on their beats, and in the country, labourers trudging afield, poachers
slinking home, all over the dusky quickening country it could be seen—
and out at sea by seamen watching for the day—a great white star,
come suddenly into the westward sky!

Brighter it was than any star in our skies: brighter than the evening
star at its brightest. It still glowed out white and large, no mere twinkling spot of light, but a small round clear shining disc, an hour after
the day had come. And where science has not reached, men stared
and feared, telling one another of the wars and pestilences that are
foreshadowed by these fiery signs in the Heavens. Sturdy Boers, dusky
Hottentots, Gold Coast Negroes, Frenchmen, Spaniards, Portuguese,
stood in the warmth of the sunrise watching the setting of this strange
new star.

And in a hundred observatories there had been suppressed excitement, rising almost to shouting pitch, as the two remote bodies had
rushed together, and a hurrying to and fro, to gather photographic apparatus and spectroscope, and this appliance and that, to record this
novel astonishing sight, the destruction of a world. For it was a world,
a sister planet of our earth, far greater than our earth indeed, that had
so suddenly flashed into flaming death. Neptune it was, had been
struck, fairly and squarely, by the strange planet from outer space and
the heat of the concussion had incontinently turned two solid globes
into one vast mass of incandescence. Round the world that day, two
hours before the dawn, went the pallid great white star, fading only
as it sank westward and the sun mounted above it. Everywhere men
marvelled at it, but of all those who saw it none could have marvelled
more than those sailors, habitual watchers of the stars, who far away at
sea had heard nothing of its advent and saw it now rise like a pigmy
moon and climb zenithward and hang overhead and sink westward with
the passing of the night.

And when next it rose over Europe everywhere were crowds of
watchers on hilly slopes, on house-roofs, in open spaces, staring eastward for the rising of the great new star. It rose with a white glow in
front of it, like the glare of a white fire, and those who had seen it come
into existence the night before cried out at the sight of it. "It is larger,"
they cried. "It is brighter!" And, indeed the moon a quarter full and
sinking in the west was in its apparent size beyond comparison, but

scarcely in all its breadth had it as much brightness now as the little circle of the strange new star.

"It is brighter!" cried the people clustering in the streets. But in the dim observatories the watchers held their breath and peered at one another. *"It is nearer,"* they said. *"Nearer!"*

And voice after voice repeated, "It is nearer," and the clicking telegraph took that up, and it trembled along telephone wires, and in a thousand cities grimy compositors fingered the type. "It is nearer." Men writing in offices, struck with a strange realisation, flung down their pens, men talking in a thousand places suddenly came upon a grotesque possibility in those words, "It is nearer." It hurried along awakening streets, it was shouted down the frost-stilled ways of quiet villages; men who had read these things from the throbbing tape stood in yellow-lit doorways shouting the news to the passers-by. "It is nearer." Pretty women, flushed and glittering, heard the news told jestingly between the dances, and feigned an intelligent interest they did not feel. "Nearer! Indeed. How curious! How very, very clever people must be to find out things like that!"

Lonely tramps faring through the wintry night murmured those words to comfort themselves—looking skyward. "It has need to be nearer, for the night's as cold as charity. Don't seem much warmth from it if it *is* nearer, all the same."

"What is a new star to me?" cried the weeping woman kneeling beside her dead.

The schoolboy, rising early for his examination work, puzzled it out for himself—with the great white star, shining broad and bright through the frost-flowers of his window. "Centrifugal, centripetal," he said, with his chin on his fist. "Stop a planet in its flight, rob it of its centrifugal force, what then? Centripetal has it, and down it falls into the sun! and this—!"

"Do *we* come in the way? I wonder—"

The light of that day went the way of its brethren, and with the later watches of the frosty darkness rose the strange star again. And it was now so bright that the waxing moon seemed but a pale yellow ghost of itself, hanging huge in the sunset. In a South African city a great man had married, and the streets were alight to welcome his return with his bride. "Even the skies have illuminated," said the flatterer. Under Capricorn, two Negro lovers, daring the wild beasts and evil spirits, for love of one another, crouched together in a cane brake where the fireflies hovered. "That is our star," they whispered, and felt strangely comforted by the sweet brilliance of its light.

The master mathematician sat in his private room and pushed the papers from him. His calculations were already finished. In a small white phial there still remained a little of the drug that had kept him awake and active for four long nights. Each day, serene, explicit, patient as ever, he had given his lecture to his students, and then had come back at once to this momentous calculation. His face was grave,

a little drawn and hectic from his drugged activity. For some time he
seemed lost in thought. Then he went to the window, and the blind
went up with a click. Half way up the sky, over the clustering roofs,
chimneys and steeples of the city, hung the star.

He looked at it as one might look into the eyes of a brave enemy.
"You may kill me," he said after a silence. "But I can hold you—and
all the universe for that matter—in the grip of this little brain. I would
not change. Even now."

He looked at the little phial. "There will be no need of sleep again,"
he said. The next day at noon, punctual to the minute, he entered his
lecture theatre, put his hat on the end of the table as his habit was, and
carefully selected a large piece of chalk. It was a joke among his students that he could not lecture without that piece of chalk to fumble
in his fingers, and once he had been stricken to impotence by their
hiding his supply. He came and looked under his grey eyebrows at the
rising tiers of young fresh faces, and spoke with his accustomed studied
commonness of phrasing. "Circumstances have arisen—circumstances
beyond my control," he said and paused, "which will debar me from
completing the course I had designed. It would seem, gentlemen, if I
may put the thing clearly and briefly, that—Man has lived in vain."

The students glanced at one another. Had they heard aright? Mad?
Raised eyebrows and grinning lips there were, but one or two faces
remained intent upon his calm grey-fringed face. "It will be interesting," he was saying, "to devote this morning to an exposition, so far as
I can make it clear to you, of the calculations that have led me to this
conclusion. Let us assume—"

He turned towards the blackboard, meditating a diagram in the way
that was usual to him. "What was that about 'lived in vain?'" whispered one student to another. "Listen," said the other, nodding towards
the lecturer.

And presently they began to understand.

That night the star rose later, for its proper eastward motion had
carried it some way across Leo towards Virgo, and its brightness was
so great that the sky became a luminous blue as it rose, and every star
was hidden in its turn, save only Jupiter near the zenith. Capella,
Aldebaran, Sirius and the pointers of the Bear. It was very white and
beautiful. In many parts of the world that night a pallid halo encircled
it about. It was perceptibly larger; in the clear refractive sky of the
tropics it seemed as if it were nearly a quarter the size of the moon. The
frost was still on the ground in England, but the world was as brightly
lit as if it were midsummer moonlight. One could see to read quite
ordinary print by that cold clear light, and in the cities the lamps burnt
yellow and wan.

And everywhere the world was awake that night, and throughout
Christendom a sombre murmur hung in the keen air over the country
side like the belling of bees in the heather, and this murmurous tumult
grew to a clangour in the cities. It was the tolling of the bells in a

million belfry towers and steeples, summoning the people to sleep no more, to sin no more, but to gather in their churches and pray. And overhead, growing larger and brighter, as the earth rolled on its way and the night passed, rose the dazzling star.

And the streets and houses were alight in all the cities, the shipyards glared, and whatever roads led to high country were lit and crowded all night long. And in all the seas about the civilised lands, ships with throbbing engines, and ships with bellying sails, crowded with men and living creatures, were standing out to ocean and the north. For already the warning of the master mathematician had been telegraphed all over the world, and translated into a hundred tongues. The new planet and Neptune, locked in a fiery embrace, were whirling headlong, ever faster and faster towards the sun. Already every second this blazing mass flew a hundred miles, and every second its terrific velocity increased. As it flew now, indeed, it must pass a hundred million of miles wide of the earth and scarcely affect it. But near its destined path, as yet only slightly perturbed, spun the mightly planet Jupiter and his moons sweeping splendid round the sun. Every moment now the attraction between the fiery star and the greatest of the planets grew stronger. And the result of that attraction? Inevitably Jupiter would be deflected from its orbit into an elliptical path, and the burning star, swung by his attraction wide of its sunward rush, would "describe a curved path" and perhaps collide with, and certainly pass very close to, our earth. "Earthquakes, volcanic outbreaks, cyclones, sea waves, floods, and a steady rise in temperature to I know not what limit"—so prophesied the master mathematician.

And overhead, to carry out his words, lonely and cold and livid, blazed the star of the coming doom.

To many who stared at it that night until their eyes ached, it seemed that it was visibly approaching. And that night, too, the weather changed, and the frost that had gripped all Central Europe and France and England softened towards a thaw.

But you must not imagine because I have spoken of people praying through the night and people going aboard ships and people fleeing towards mountainous country that the whole world was already in a terror because of the star. As a matter of fact, use and wont still ruled the world, and save for the talk of idle moments and the splendour of the night, nine human beings out of ten were still busy at their common occupations. In all the cities the shops, save one here and there, opened and closed at their proper hours, the doctor and the undertaker plied their trades, the workers gathered in the factories, soldiers drilled, scholars studied, lovers sought one another, thieves lurked and fled, politicians planned their schemes. The presses of the newspapers roared through the nights, and many a priest of this church and that would not open his holy building to further what he considered a foolish panic. The newspapers insisted on the lesson of the year 1000—for then, too, people had anticipated the end. The star was no star—mere gas—a

comet; and were it a star it could not possibly strike the earth. There
was no precedent for such a thing. Common sense was sturdy everywhere, scornful, jesting, a little inclined to persecute the obdurate fearful. That night, at seven-fifteen by Greenwich time, the star would be
at its nearest to Jupiter. Then the world would see the turn things
would take. The master mathematician's grim warnings were treated
by many as so much mere elaborate self-advertisement. Common sense
at last, a little heated by argument, signified its unalterable convictions
by going to bed. So, too, barbarism and savagery, already tired of the
novelty, went about their nightly business, and save for a howling dog
here and there, the beast world left the star unheeded.

And yet, when at last the watchers in the European States saw the
star rise, an hour later it is true, but no larger than it had been the
night before, there were still plenty awake to laugh at the master
mathematician—to take the danger as if it had passed.

But hereafter the laughter ceased. The star grew—it grew with a
terrible steadiness hour after hour, a little larger each hour, a little
nearer the midnight zenith, and brighter and brighter, until it had
turned night into a second day. Had it come straight to the earth instead of in a curved path, had it lost no velocity to Jupiter, it must
have leapt the intervening gulf in a day, but as it was it took five days
altogether to come by our planet. The next night it had become a
third the size of the moon before it set to English eyes, and the thaw
was assured. It rose over America near the size of the moon, but blinding white to look at, and *hot,* and a breath of hot wind blew now with
its rising and gathering strength, and in Virginia, and Brazil, and down
the St. Lawrence valley, it shone intermittently through a driving reek
of thunder-clouds, flickering violet lightning, and hail unprecedented.
In Manitoba was a thaw and devastating floods. And upon all the
mountains of the earth the snow and ice began to melt that night, and
all the rivers coming out of high country flowed thick and turbid, and
soon—in their upper reaches—with swirling trees and the bodies of
beasts and men. They rose steadily, steadily in the ghostly brilliance,
and came trickling over their banks at last, behind the flying population of their valleys.

And along the coast of Argentina and up the South Atlantic the
tides were higher than had ever been in the memory of man, and the
storms drove the waters in many cases scores of miles inland, drowning
whole cities. And so great grew the heat during the night that the
rising of the sun was like the coming of a shadow. The earthquakes
began and grew until all down America, from the Arctic Circle to Cape
Horn, hillsides were sliding, fissures were openings, and houses and
walls crumbling to destruction. The whole side of Cotopaxi slipped out
in one vast convulsion, and a tumolt of lava poured out so high and
broad and swift and liquid that in one day it reached the sea.

So the star, with the wan moon in its wake, marched across the
Pacific, trailed the thunderstorms like the hem of a robe, and the growing

tidal wave that toiled behind it, frothing and eager, poured over island and island and swept them clear of men. Until that wave came at last—in a blinding light and with the breath of a furnace, swift and terrible it came—a wall of water, fifty feet high, roaring hungrily, upon the long coasts of Asia, and swept inland across the plains of China. For a space the star, hotter now and larger and brighter than the sun in its strength, showed with pitiless brillance the wide and populous country; towns and villages with their pagodas and trees, roads, wide cultivated fields, millions of sleepless people staring in helpless terror at the incandescent sky; and then, low and growing, came the mumur of the flood. And thus it was with millions of men that night—a flight nowhither, with limbs heavy with heat and breath fierce and scant, and the flood like a wall swift and white behind. And then death.

China was lit glowing white, but over Japan and Java and all the islands of Eastern Asia the great star was a ball of dull red fire because of the steam and smoke and ashes the volcanoes were spouting forth to salute its coming. Above was the lava, hot gases and ash, and below the seething floods, and the whole earth swayed and rumbled with the earthquake shocks. Soon the immemorial snows of Tibet and the Himalaya were melting and pouring down by ten million deepening converging channels upon the plains of Burmah and Hindostan. The tangled summits by the Indian jungles were aflame in a thousand places, and below the hurrying waters around the stems were dark objects that still struggled feebly and reflected the blood-red tongues of fire. And in a rudderless confusion a multitude of men and women fled down the broad river-ways to that one last hope of men—the open sea.

Larger grew the star, and larger, hotter, and brighter with a terrible swiftness now. The tropical ocean had lost its phosphorescence, and the whirling steam rose in ghostly wreaths from the black waves that plunged incessantly, speckled with storm-tossed ships.

And then came a wonder. It seemed to those who in Europe watched for the rising of the star that the world must have ceased its rotation. In a thousand open spaces of down and upland the people who had fled thither from the floods and the falling houses and sliding slopes of hill watched for that rising in vain. Hour followed hour through a terrible suspense, and the star rose not. Once again men set their eyes upon the old constellations they had counted lost to them forever. In England it was hot and clear overhead, though the ground quivered perpetually, but in the tropics, Sirius and Capella and Aldebaran showed through a veil of steam. And when at last the great star rose near ten hours late, the sun rose close upon it, and in the centre of its white heat was a disc of black.

Over Asia it was the star had begun to fall behind the movement of the sky, and then suddenly, as it hung over India, its light had been veiled. All the plain of India from the mouth of the Indus to the mouths of the Ganges was a shallow waste of shining water that night, out of which rose temples and palaces, mounds and hills, black with people. Every minaret was a clustering mass of people, who fell one by one into the turbid waters, as heat and terror overcame them. The whole land seemed a-wailing, and suddenly there swept a shadow across that furnace of despair, and a breath of cold wind, and a gathering of clouds, out of the cooling air. Men looking up, near blinded, at the star, saw that a black disc was creeping across the light. It was the moon, coming between the star and the earth. And even as men cried to God at this respite, out of the East with a strange inexplicable swift-ness sprang the sun. And then star, sun and moon rushed together across the heavens.

So it was that presently, to the European watchers, star and sun rose close upon each other, drove headlong for a space and then slower, and at last came to rest, star and sun merged into one glare of flame at the zenith of the sky. The moon no longer eclipsed the star but was lost to sight in the brilliance of the sky. And though those who were still alive regarded it for the most part with that dull stupidity that hunger, fatigue, heat and despair engender, there were still men who could perceive the meaning of these signs. Star and earth had been at their nearest, had swung about one another, and the star had passed. Already it was receding, swifter and swifter, in the last stage of its headlong journey downward into the sun.

And then the clouds gathered, blotting out the vision of the sky, the thunder and lightning wove a garment round the world; all over the earth was such a downpour of rain as men had never before seen, and where the volcanoes flared red against the cloud canopy there descended torrents of mud. Everywhere the waters were pouring off the land, leaving mud-silted ruins, and the earth littered like a storm-worn beach with all that had floated, and the dead bodies of the men and brutes, its children. For days the water streamed off the land, sweeping away soil and trees and houses in the way, and piling huge dykes and scooping out Titanic gullies over the country side. Those were the days of darkness that followed the star and the heat. All through them, and for many weeks and months, the earthquakes con-tinued.

But the star had passed, and men, hunger-driven and gathering courage only slowly, might creep back to their ruined cities, buried granaries, and sodden fields. Such few ships as had escaped the storms of that time came stunned and shattered and sounding their way cautiously through the new marks and shoals of once familiar ports. And as the storms subsided men perceived that everywhere the days were hotter than of yore, and the sun larger, and the moon, shrunk to a third of its former size, took now fourscore days between its new and new.

But of the new brotherhood that grew presently among men, of the saving of laws and books and machines, of the strange change that had come over Iceland and Greenland and the shores of Baffin's Bay, so that the sailors coming there presently found them green and gracious, and could scarce believe their eyes, this story does not tell. Nor of the movement of mankind now that the earth was hotter, northward and southward towards the poles of the earth. It concerns itself only with the coming and the passing of the Star.

The Martian astronomers—for there are astronomers on Mars, although they are very different beings from men—were naturally profoundly interested by these things. They saw them from their own standpoint of course. "Considering the mass and temperature of the missile that was flung through our solar system into the sun," one wrote, "it is astonishing what a little damage the earth, which it missed so narrowly, has sustained. All the familiar continental markings and the masses of the seas remain intact, and indeed the only difference seems to be a shrinking of the white discoloration (supposed to be frozen water) round either pole." Which only shows how small the vastest of human catastrophes may seem, at a distance of a few million miles.

Questions for Discussion and Review

1. If Wells were revising his story today, what changes would he want to make to keep it scientifically correct?

2. As the star begins to approach Earth, the narrator's style begins to take on new dimensions. Describe these changes and try to account for them.

3. How is Earth saved in the story?

4. Why does Wells conclude his story with the reactions of the Martian astronomers?

5. I noted earlier that Wells brought to SF a scientific disposition of mind. How does that statement apply to this story?

Part 2 Fantasy Science Fiction

Fantasy SF is the oldest of all SF literature. Long before the rise of modern engineering and technology, people were speculating in fictions about space voyages, visitations by aliens, or the discovery of utopias. Of course, they did not consider such things science related, as we do, because the context of their experience with science was much narrower than ours. Indeed, it might be argued that before the Renaissance there was no general understanding of the scientific method or experimental learning. How then do we have SF before there is a proper science? The answer is that we have fantasy employing materials that later came to be associated with science. In time, as the marvels of scientific discovery became manifest, romance found a new magic carpet in the wonder-producing capacity of the new science and in the technology it produced. If there were occasional impossibilities or contradictions, the writers were prepared to allow the scientists to worry about them. The chief concern of writers has always been, in and out of SF, whether a story works imaginatively.

By the beginning of the nineteenth century, the effects of science were becoming a more common property, and they found expression in the popular literary forms of the day. The human appetite for heroic adventure and experience of the supernatural, when it found expression in SF, often declared itself in terms more fantastic than scientific, and it does so to this day. Such literature operates on the probabilities of fantasy; but there remains a tension—a pleasing one, when a story is well told—between the magic and impossibilities of fantasy and the dual ideas of probable cause and rational control taken from science.

We find a similar kind of opposition in many of the early fantasy SF satires of writers like Swift, Cyrano, and Voltaire, written more than two centuries ago. In these satires, the contrast is between the fanciful, strange, and even grotesque setting or situation taken from romance and the critical spirit of satire felt beneath the narrative.

So much fantasy SF is escapist hack work that we stand in danger of forgetting the many legitimate and, indeed, unique contributions it has made to the formation of the literary imagination. At its best, SF permits an exploration of the kinds of adventure that reason and experience assure us are impossible. Yet, there seems to be something within us that desires such adventure and, perhaps, requires such imagined experiences. The impulse is as old as the one that produced the stories about the Olympian gods or the mythologies of Thor and Odin.

Fantasy SF has its own geography of interests and techniques. While we may safely consign the majority of the fantastic exploit and violence stories to the sanitary landfill, there remains a body of varied and significant literature. At opposite poles we may place the weird story, in which the supernatural dominates the plot, and the time-travel story, in which a writer like Wells or Niven can make such travel seem plausible enough to be possible. Our attitude, a revealing modern one, may well be: "Who knows?" We see the development of extravagant new realities almost daily, and we have come to expect them. Perhaps today's fantasy will prove to be tomorrow's journalism, but I would not bet the rent money on time travel. Somewhere between these two extremes of probability lie the space opera and the speculative story. Each attempts to achieve a balance between the appetite of fantasy for impossible adventure and the claims of science for plausible if not theoretically possible extrapolation. In this kind of science fiction, science is the means necessary to achieve the ends of fantasy.

Our study does not include unalloyed fantasy. One must draw the line somewhere, and for us the question is settled by whether science or scientific laws are operative. If they are not—even if the setting is the future or some physically remote world—we must be prepared to cede such imaginary kingdoms to the realm of fantasy. Our first species of fantasy SF is the "Space Opera."

Space opera is a form of the fantasy SF story that treats heroic if not superhuman adventure on an interplanetary or intergalactic scale. Improbable action is the stock and trade of space opera. The exploits of its characters are both exaggerated and implausible as judged by ordinary standards of human capability. However, in the hyper-realities of the space-opera adventure, characters achieve the normally unattainable and perform the impossible through sheer inventiveness, ingenuity, courage, and will power. To this degree, the space opera shares certain qualities with its remote epic ancestors. There is a similarity of some consequence between the epic and space-opera visions of the heroic portrayal of evil forces, and in the affirmation of class or racial ideals. The space opera also emphasizes a primitive form of imagined awe and wonder arising naturally from spectacle and marvelous adventure. This is the secret of its appeal. The space opera may be as close to a purely escapist form of entertainment as SF is likely to produce.

The origins of space opera antedate modern technology and may be as old as Ezekiel's fiery chariots. Legitimately or otherwise, the species claims descent from Lucian's *True History* through the medieval heroic romance. It is not very far in the realms of imagination from the chapel of the Green Knight to the crypts of the Kings of Zareth ("Enchantress of Venus"). The difference is that one deals with magic and supernatural powers, and the other deals with extrapolations of biological control of nature, which would have seemed equally magical to both Sir Gawain and Morgan le Fay.

A complete history of space opera would include, therefore, elements from both fantasy and SF. The contributions of fantasy would no doubt include the fabulous voyage stories of Homer, *The Arabian Nights,* the tales of Mandeville, Swift, and Baron Munchausen. Other fantasy elements may have come from adventure-exploration stories in the mold of H. Rider Haggard and the frontier tall story, featuring such legendary types as Paul Bunyan and Pecos Bill.

The contribution of SF to the making of space opera has been to supply both the vision of interplanetary travel and the hardware to get the stories off the ground and into space, where strange and wonderful things may be expected. In the modern era, Jules Verne and H. G. Wells have been the literary godfathers of this type of story.

The major point is not just that we find analogues or possible archetypes of the space opera in the conventions of past adventure stories, but rather that we discover in the contemporary space opera unmistakable signs of an enduring process. The character of imagination that inspired space opera is not different in its essence from the one that produced the equally heroic and impossible adventures of the epic heroes of the past.

Space opera, however, does not enjoy critical respectability. The term itself implies a patronizing attitude toward the type, suggesting parallels with other forms of popular culture such as the radio and television soap opera and the movie horse opera. The reasons for the condescension are obvious. The space-opera story is all sail and no ballast. Stories are commonly a mixture of magic and advanced engineering technology in which the storyteller's imagination is uninhibited by the physical limitations of the race or the boundaries of possible science. On the reader's part, space opera has been associated with both immaturity of mind and low taste; and there is no denying that it has been the staple of the pulps, of low-budget movies, and of the comics industry.

For all that, some things remain to be said for the space opera. First, it has great enduring popular appeal. Despite the shortcomings of the form, the space operas of Edgar Rice Burroughs and E. E. "Doc" Smith have stimulated the imagination of readers for more than half a century. Space opera should not be considered bad literature by definition. Several writers, notably Olaf Stapledon, Isaac Asimov, and Arthur C. Clarke have raised space opera to the level of art and perhaps even to that of genuine myth. Others, like C. S. Lewis and Kurt Vonnegut, have employed space-opera conventions as vehicles for serious ideas. As a type, therefore, space opera need not be trival or mindless.

There is another point that must not be overdone or overlooked. Space opera offers a release of creative energies that have on the whole enriched rather than impoverished the imagination. In so doing, it serves a purpose not unlike mythology. The imaginative power of space opera has been sufficient to inspire generations with visions of space travel and trans-species evolution.

Leigh Brackett's story in this section illustrates a familiar variety of the space opera. It is an unabashed costume adventure story played on a strangely Gothic Venus, and may scientific probability be hanged!

Enchantress of Venus

Leigh Brackett

Leigh Brackett was born on December 7, 1915. She lives in Kinsman, Ohio, and was married to the late Edmund Hamilton, a well-known SF author. In the late 1940s, Brackett broadened her career to include the lucrative field of writing screenplays for Hollywood. During the 1950s and 1960s, while commuting between Kinsman and Hollywood, she continued her work in SF with a series of novels enjoying a current revival. Probably Brackett's best-known novel is *Sword of Rhiannon* (1953). "Enchantress of Venus" is the second of the three stories in the original N'Chaka series. The first was "Queen of Martian Catacombs" in *Planet Stories* (summer 1949). "Enchantress" was published in *Planet Stories* (fall 1949), and the last of the series was "Black Amazon of Mars" in *Planet Stories* (spring 1951). A new N'Chaka series of novels currently includes *The Ginger Star* (1974), *The Hounds of Skaith* (1974), and *Reavers of Skaith* (1976).

"Enchantress of Venus" is the kind of space opera referred to these days as "sword and sorcery." In this case, Leigh Brackett's story was inspired not by Tolkein but by the stories of Edgar Rice Burroughs, especially the ones set on Venus and Mars, and the even more sensational tales of Otis Adelbert Kline.

The action is set on a Venus of the author's own imagining. The scenery is not something about which we are likely to get reports from a space probe. One remarkable invention of the story is the Red Sea made of heavy Venusian gases—a person floats in such an environment, and it enables characters to leap, glide, and practically fly around. Clearly we are in a fantasy world, rather than in one ruled by laws of science alone, and the author creates splendid effects of mood and atmosphere by means of her phantasmagorical landscapes and seascapes. The background is further enriched by Shuruun, a sinister space-port town that equals the skullduggery of the haunts frequented by Fritz Leiber's Fafhrd and the Grey Mouser. On a different level, the strangely Gothic Castle of the Lhari reinforces the menace that hangs palpably over the first half of the tale. The City of the Lost Ones, however, is the author's most effective creation. One hardly knows which is the more wonderful, the embalmed city above ground at the bottom of the Red Sea or the hidden catacombs and laboratories below, holding the dread secret of biological control.

The special power of this story lies in the blending of SF and fantasy elements. Readers will have to judge for themselves how they react to such narratives. We must ask ourselves whether we are engaged by the probabilities of SF or of fantasy. If it is the former, then the story fails because, scientifically speaking, it is beyond the pale of possible worlds. Yet there is another kind of probability, which we may call hypothetical, that indulges the yearnings of the imagination for worlds beyond experience.

Clearly, we are in such a world from the moment Stark enters the Red Sea of Venus.

One question a space opera story raises for readers and critics is whether the enchantment of the author's fantastic world and the excitement of the adventure are enough to compel that temporary kind of trust in the story which is essential to the illusion and which produces the special characteristics of the subtype. If reason tells us that Shuruun, the Lhari, and Malthor's ship are rank impossibilities, can the imagination yet convince us on another level that these are imitations in which we may have an imagined belief? For this reader, Brackett's art more than meets the test.

Chapter I

The ship moved slowly across the Red Sea, through the shrouding veils of mist, her sail barely filled by the languid thrust of the wind. Her hull, a thin light metal, floated without sound, the surface of the strange ocean parting before her prow in silent rippling streamers of flame.

Night deepened toward the ship, a river of indigo flowing out of the west. The man known as Stark stood alone by the after rail and watched its coming. He was full of impatience and a gathering sense of danger, so that it seemed to him that even the hot wind smelled of it.

The steersman lay drowsily over his sweep. He was a big man, with skin and hair the color of milk. He did not speak, but Stark felt that now and again the man's eyes turned toward him, pale and calculating under half-closed lids, with a secret avarice.

The captain and the two other members of the little coasting vessel's crew were forward, at their evening meal. Once or twice Stark heard a burst of laughter, half-whispered and furtive. It was as though all four shared in some private joke, from which he was rigidly excluded.

The heat was oppressive. Sweat gathered on Stark's dark face. His shirt stuck to his back. The air was heavy with moisture, tainted with the muddy fecundity of the land that brooded westward behind the eternal fog.

There was something ominous about the sea itself. Even on its own world, the Red Sea is hardly more than legend. It lies behind the Mountains of White Cloud, the great barrier wall that hides away half a planet. Few men have gone beyond that barrier, into the vast mystery of Inner Venus. Fewer still have come back.

Stark was one of that handful. Three times before he had crossed the mountains, and once he had stayed nearly a year. But he had never quite grown used to the Red Sea.

It was not water. It was gaseous, dense enough to float the buoyant hulls of the metal ships, and it burned perpetually with its deep inner fires. The mists that clouded it were stained with the bloody glow. Beneath the surface Stark could see the drifts of flame where the lazy currents ran, and the little coiling bursts of sparks that came upward and spread and melted into other bursts, so that the face of the sea was like a cosmos of crimson stars.

It was very beautiful, glowing against the blue, luminous darkness of the night. Beautiful, and strange.

There was a padding of bare feet, and the captain, Malthor, came up to Stark, his outlines dim and ghostly in the gloom.

"We will reach Shuruun," he said, "before the second glass is run."

Stark nodded. "Good."

The voyage had seemed endless, and the close confinement of the narrow deck had got badly on his nerves.

"You will like Shuruun," said the captain jovially. "Our wine, our food, our women—all superb. We don't have many visitors. We keep to ourselves, as you will see. But those who do come . . ."

He laughed, and clapped Stark on the shoulder. "Ah, yes. You will be happy in Shuruun!"

It seemed to Stark that he caught an echo of laughter from the unseen crew, as though they listened and found a hidden jest in Malthor's words.

Stark said, "That's fine."

"Perhaps," said Malthor, "you would like to lodge with me. I could make you a good price."

He had made a good price for Stark's passage from up the coast. An exhorbitantly good one.

Stark said, "No."

"You don't have to be afraid," said the Venusian, in a confidential tone. "The strangers who come to Shuruun all have the same reason. It's a good place to hide. We're out of everybody's reach."

He paused, but Stark did not rise to his bait. Presently he chuckled and went on, "In fact, it's such a safe place that most of the strangers decide to stay on. Now, at my house, I could give you . . ."

Stark said again, flatly, "No."

The captain shrugged. "Very well. Think it over, anyway." He peered ahead into the red, coiling mists. "Ah! See there?" He pointed, and Stark made out the shadowy loom of cliffs. "We are coming into the strait now."

Malthor turned and took the steering sweep himself, the helmsman going forward to join the others. The ship began to pick up speed. Stark saw that she had come into the grip of a current that swept toward the cliffs, a river of fire racing ever more swiftly in the depths of the sea.

The dark wall seemed to plunge toward them. At first Stark could see no passage. Then, suddenly, a narrow crimson streak appeared, widened, and became a gut of boiling flame, rushing silently around broken rocks. Red fog rose like smoke. The ship quivered, sprang ahead, and tore like a mad thing into the heart of the inferno.

In spite of himself, Stark's hands tightened on the rail. Tattered veils of mist swirled past them. The sea, the air, the ship itself, seemed drenched in blood. There was no sound, in all that wild sweep of current through the strait. Only the sullen fires burst and flowed.

The reflected glare showed Stark that the Straits of Shuruun were defended. Squat fortresses brooded on the cliffs. There were ballistas, and great windlasses for the drawing of nets across the narrow throat. The men of Shuruun could enforce their law, that barred all foreign shipping from their gulf.

They had reasons for such a law, and such a defense. The legitimate trade of Shuruun, such as it was, was in wine and the delicate laces woven from spider-silk. Actually, however, the city lived and throve on piracy, the arts of wrecking, and a contraband trade in the distilled juice of the *vela* poppy.

Looking at the rocks and the fortresses, Stark could understand how it was that Shuruun had been able for more centuries than anyone could tell to victimize the shipping of the Red Sea, and offer a refuge to the outlaw, the wolf's-head, the breaker of tabu.

With startling abruptness, they were through the gut and drifting on the still surface of this all but landlocked arm of the Red Sea.

Because of the shrouding fog, Stark could see nothing of the land. But the smell of it was stronger, warm damp soil and the heavy, faintly rotten perfume of vegetation half jungle, half swamp. Once, through a rift in the wreathing vapor, he thought he glimpsed the shadowy bulk of an island, but it was gone at once.

After the terrifying rush of the strait, it seemed to Stark that the ship barely moved. His impatience and the subtle sense of danger deepened. He began to pace the deck, with the nervous, velvet motion of a prowling cat. The moist, steamy air seemed all but unbreathable after the clean dryness of Mars, from whence he had come so recently. It was oppressively still.

Suddenly he stopped, his head thrown back, listening.

The sound was born faintly on the slow wind. It came from everywhere and nowhere, a vague dim thing without source or direction. It almost seemed that the night itself had spoken—the hot blue night of Venus, crying out of the mists with a tongue of infinite woe.

It faded and died away, only half heard, leaving behind it a sense of aching sadness, as though all the misery and longing of a world had found voice in that desolate wail.

Stark shivered. For a time there was silence, and then he heard the sound again, now on a deeper note. Still faint and far away, it was sustained longer by the vagaries of the heavy air, and it became a chant, rising and falling. There were no words. It was not the sort of thing that would have need of words. Then it was gone again.

Stark turned to Malthor. "What was that?"

The man looked at him curiously. He seemed not to have heard.

"That wailing sound," said Stark impatiently.

"Oh that." The Venusian shrugged. "A trick of the wind. It sighs in the hollow rocks around the strait."

He yawned, giving place again to the steersman, and came to stand beside Stark. The Earthman ignored him. For some reason, that sound half heard through the mists had brought his uneasiness to a sharp pitch.

Civilization had brushed over Stark with a light hand. Raised from infancy by half-human aboriginals, his perceptions were still those of a savage. His ear was good.

Malthor lied. That cry of pain was not made by any wind.

"I have known several Earthmen," said Malthor, changing the subject, but not too swiftly. "None of them were like you."

Intuition warned Stark to play along. 'I don't come fom Earth," he said. "I come from Mercury."

Malthor puzzled over that. Venus is a cloudy world, where no man has ever seen the Sun, let alone a star. The captain had heard vaguely of these things. Earth and Mars he knew of. But Mercury was an unknown word.

Stark explained. "The planet nearest the Sun. It's very hot there. The Sun blazes like a huge fire, and there are no clouds to shield it."

"Ah. That is why your skin is so dark." He held his own pale forearm close to Stark's and shook his head. "I have never seen such skin," he said admiringly. "Nor such great muscles."

Looking up, he went on in a tone of complete friendliness, "I wish you would stay with me. You'll find no better lodgings in Shuruun. And I warn you, there are people in the town who will take advantage of strangers—rob them, even slay them. Now, I am known by all as a man of honour. You could sleep soundly under my roof."

He paused, then added with a smile, "Also, I have a daughter. An excellent cook—and very beautiful."

The woeful chanting came again, dim and distant on the wind, an echo of warning against some unimagined fate.

Stark said for the third time, "No."

He needed no intuition to tell him to walk wide of the captain. The man was a rogue, and not a very subtle one.

A flint-hard, angry look came briefly into Malthor's eyes. "You're a stubborn man. You'll find that Shuruun is no place for stubbornness."

He turned and went away. Stark remained where he was. The ship drifted on through a slow eternity of time. And all down that long still gulf of the Red Sea, through the heat and the wreathing fog, the ghostly chanting haunted him, like the keening of lost souls in some forgotten hell.

Presently the course of the ship was altered. Malthor came again to the afterdeck, giving a few quiet commands. Stark saw land ahead, a darker blur on the night, and then the shrouded outlines of a city.

Torches blazed on the quays and in the streets, and the low buildings caught a ruddy glow from the burning sea itself. A squat and ugly town, Shuruun, crouching witch-like on the rocky shore, her ragged skirts dipped in blood.

The ship drifted in toward the quays.

Stark heard a whisper of movement behind him, the hushed and purposeful padding of naked feet. He turned, with the astonishing swiftness of an animal that feels itself threatened, his hand dropping to his gun.

A belaying pin, thrown by the steersman, struck the side of his head with stunning force. Reeling, half blinded, he saw the distorted shapes of men closing in upon him. Malthor's voice sounded, low and hard. A second belaying pin whizzed through the air and cracked against Stark's shoulder.

Hands were laid upon him. Bodies, heavy and strong, bore his down. Malthor laughed.

Stark's teeth glinted bare and white. Someone's cheek brushed past, and he sank them into the flesh. He began to growl, a sound that should never have come from a human throat. It seemed to the startled Venusians that the man they had attacked had by some wizardry become a beast, at the first touch of violence.

The man with the torn cheek screamed. There was a voiceless scuffling on the deck, a terrible intensity of motion, and then the great dark body rose and shook itself free of the tangle, and was gone, over the rail, leaving Malthor with nothing but the silken rags of a shirt in his hands.

The surface of the Red Sea closed without a ripple over Stark. There was a burst of crimson sparks, a momentary trail of flame going down like a drowned comet, and then—nothing.

II

Stark dropped slowly downward through a strange world. There was no difficulty about breathing, as in a sea of water. The gases of the Red Sea support life quite well, and the creatures that dwell in it have almost normal lungs.

Stark did not pay much attention at first, except to keep his balance automatically. He was still dazed from the blow, and he was raging with anger and pain.

The primitive in him, whose name was not Stark but N'Chaka, and who had fought and starved and hunted in the blazing valleys of Mercury's Twilight Belt, learning lessons he never forgot, wished to return and slay Malthor and his men. He regretted that he had not torn out their throats, for now his trail would never be safe from them.

But the man Stark, who had learned some more bitter lessons in the name of civilization, knew the unwisdom of that. He snarled over his aching head, and cursed the Venusians in the harsh, crude dialect that was his mother tongue, but he did not turn back. There would be time enough for Malthor.

It struck him that the gulf was very deep.

Fighting down his rage, he began to swim in the direction of the shore. There was no sign of pursuit, and he judged that Malthor had decided to let him go. He puzzled over the reason for the attack. It could hardly be robbery, since he carried nothing but the clothes he stood in, and very little money.

No. There was some deeper reason. A reason connected with Malthor's insistence that he lodge with him. Stark smiled. It was not a pleasant smile. He was thinking of Shuruun, and the things men said about it, around the shores of the Red Sea.

Then his face hardened. The dim coiling fires through which he swam brought him memories of other times he had gone adventuring in the depths of the Red Sea.

He had not been alone then. Helvi had gone with him—the tall son of a barbarian kinglet up-coast by Yarell. They had hunted strange beasts through the crystal forests of the sea-bottom and bathed in the welling flames that pulse from the very heart of Venus to feed the ocean. They had been brothers.

Now Helvi was gone, into Shuruun. He had never returned.

Stark swam on. And presently he saw below him in the red gloom something that made him drop lower, frowning with surprise.

There were trees beneath him. Great forest giants towering up into an eerie sky, their branches swaying gently to the slow wash of the currents.

Stark was puzzled. The forests where he and Helvi had hunted were truly crystalline, without even the memory of life. The "trees" were no more trees in actuality than the branching corals of Terra's southern oceans.

But these were real, or had been. He thought at first that they still lived, for their leaves were green, and here and there creepers had starred them with great nodding blossoms of gold and purple and waxy white. But when he floated down close enough to touch them, he realized that they were dead—trees, creepers, blossoms, all.

They had not mummified, nor turned to stone. They were pliable, and their colours were very bright. Simply, they had ceased to live, and the gases of the sea had preserved them by some chemical magic, so perfectly that barely a leaf had fallen.

Stark did not venture into the shadowy denseness below the topmost branches. A strange fear came over him, at the sight of that vast forest dreaming in the depths of the gulf, drowned and forgotten, as though wondering why the birds had gone, taking with them the warm rains and the light of day.

He thrust his way upward, himself like a huge dark bird above the branches. An overwhelming impulse to get away from that unearthly place drove him on, his half-wild sense shuddering with an impression of evil so great that it took all his acquired common-sense to assure him that he was not pursued by demons.

He broke the surface at last, to find that he had lost his direction in the red deep and made a long circle around, so that he was far below Shuruun. He made his way back, not hurrying now, and presently clambered out over the black rocks.

He stood at the end of a muddy lane that wandered in toward the town. He followed it, moving neither fast nor slow, but with a wary alertness.

Huts of wattle-and-daub took shape out of the fog, increased in numbers, became a street of dwellings. Here and there rush-lights glimmered through the slitted windows. A man and a woman clung together in a low doorway. They saw him and sprang apart, and the woman gave a little cry. Stark went on. He did not look back, but he knew that they were following him quietly, at a little distance.

The lane twisted snakelike upon itself, crawling now through a crowded jumble of houses. There were more lights, and more people, tall white-skinned folk of the swamp-edges, with pale eyes and long hair the colour of new flax, and the faces of wolves.

Stark passed among them, alien and strange with his black hair and sun-darkened skin. They did not speak, nor try to stop him. Only they looked at him out of the red fog, with a curious blend of amusement and fear, and some of them followed him, keeping well behind. A gang of small naked children came from somewhere among the houses and ran shouting beside him, out of reach, until one boy threw a stone and screamed something unintelligible except for one word—*Lhari*. Then They all stopped, horrified, and fled.

Stark went on, through the quarter of the lacemakers, heading by instinct toward the wharves. The glow of the Red Sea pervaded all the air, so that it seemed as though the mist was full of tiny drops of blood. There was a smell about the place he did not like, a damp miasma of mud and crowding bodies and wine, and the breath of the *vela* poppy. Shuruun was an unclean town, and it stank of evil.

There was something else about it, a subtle thing that touched Stark's nerves with a chill finger. Fear. He could see the shadow of it in the eyes of the people, hear its undertone in their voices. The wolves of Shuruun did not feel safe in their own kennel. Unconsciously, as this feeling grew upon him, Stark's step grew more and more wary, his eyes more cold and hard.

He came out into a broad square by the harbour front. He could see the ghostly ships moored along the quays, the piled casks of wine, the tangle of masts and cordage dim against the background of the burning gulf. There were many torches here. Large low buildings stood around the square. There was laughter and the sound of voices from the dark verandas, and somewhere a woman sang to the melancholy lilting of a reed pipe.

A suffused glow of light in the distance ahead caught Stark's eye. That way the streets sloped to a higher ground, and straining his vision against the fog, he made out very dimly the tall bulk of a castle crouched on the low cliffs, looking with bright eyes upon the night, and the streets of Shuruun.

Stark hesitated briefly. Then he started across the square toward the largest of the taverns.

There were a number of people in the open space, mostly sailors and their women. They were loose and foolish with wine, but even so they stopped where they were and stared at the dark stranger, and then drew back from him, still staring.

Those who had followed Stark came into the square after him and then paused, spreading out in an aimless sort of way to join with other groups, whispering among themselves.

The woman stopped singing in the middle of a phrase.

A curious silence fell on the square. A nervous sibilance ran round and round under the silence, and men came slowly out from the verandas and the doors of the wine shops. Suddenly a woman with disheveled hair pointed her arm at Stark and laughed, the shrieking laugh of a harpy.

Stark found his way barred by three tall young men with hard mouths and crafty eyes, who smiled at him as hounds smile before the kill.

"Stranger," they said. "Earthman."

"Outlaw," answered Stark, and it was only half a lie.

One of the young men took a step forward. "Did you fly like a dragon over the Mountains of White Cloud? Did you drop from the sky?"

"I came on Malthor's ship."

A kind of sigh went round the square, and with it the name of Malthor. The eager faces of the young men grew heavy with disappointment. But the leader said sharply, "I was on the quay when Malthor docked. You were not on board."

It was Stark's turn to smile. In the light of the torches, his eyes blazed cold and bright as ice against the sun.

"Ask Malthor the reason for that," he said. "Ask the man with the torn cheek. Or perhaps," he added softly, "you would like to learn for yourselves."

The young men looked at him, scowling, in an odd mood of indecision. Stark settled himself, every muscle loose and ready. And the woman who had laughed crept closer and peered at Stark through her tangled hair, breathing heavily of the poppy wine.

All at once, she said loudly, "He came out of the sea. That's where he came from. He's . . ."

One of the young men struck her across the mouth and she fell down in the mud. A burly seaman ran out and caught her by the hair, dragging her to her feet again. His face was frightened and very angry. He hauled the woman away, cursing her for a fool and beating her as he went. She spat out blood, and said no more.

"Well," said Stark to the young men. "Have you made up your minds?"

"Minds!' said a voice behind them—a harsh-timbered, rasping voice that handled the liquid vocables of the Venusian speech very clumsily indeed. "They have no minds, these whelps! If they had, they'd be off about their business, instead of standing here badgering a stranger."

The young men turned, and now between them Stark could see the man who had spoken. He stood on the steps of the tavern. He was an Earthman, and at first Stark thought he was old, because his hair was white and his face deeply lined. His body was wasted with fever, the muscles all gone to knotty strings twisted over bone. He leaned heavily on a stick, and one leg was crooked and terribly scarred.

He grinned at Stark and said, in colloquial English, "Watch me get rid of 'em!"

He began to tongue-lash the young men, telling them that they were idiots, the misbegotten offspring of swamp-toads, utterly without manners, and that if they did not believe the stranger's story they should go and ask Malthor, as he suggested. Finally he shook his stick at them, fairly screeching.

"Go on, now. Go away! Leave us alone—my brother of Earth and I!"

The young men gave one hesitant glance at Stark's feral eyes. Then they looked at each other and shrugged, and went away across the square half sheepishly, like great loutish boys caught in some misdemeanor.

The white-haired Earthman beckoned to Stark. And, as Stark came up to him on the steps he said under his breath, almost angrily, "You're in a trap."

Stark glanced back over his shoulder. At the edge of the square the three young men had met a fourth, who had his face bound up in a rag. They vanished almost at once into a side street, but not before Stark had recognized the fourth man as Malthor.

It was the captain he had branded.

With loud cheerfulness, the lame man said in Venusian, "Come in and drink with me, brother, and we will talk of Earth."

III

The tavern was of the standard low-class Venusian pattern—a single huge room under bare thatch, the wall half open with the reed shutters rolled up, the floor of split logs propped up on piling out of the mud. A long low bar, little tables, mangy skins and heaps of dubious cushions on the floor around them, and at one end the entertainers—two old men with a drum and a reed pipe, and a couple of sulky, tired-looking girls.

The lame man led Stark to a table in the corner and sank down, calling for wine. His eyes, which were dark and haunted by long pain, burned with excitement. His hands shook. Before Stark had sat down he had begun to talk, his words stumbling over themselves as though he could not get them out fast enough.

"How is it there now? Has it changed any? Tell me how it is—the cities, the lights, the paved streets, the women, the Sun. Oh Lord, what I wouldn't give to see the Sun again, and women with dark hair and their clothes on!" He leaned forward, staring hungrily into Stark's face, as though he could see those things mirrored there. "For God's sake, talk to me—talk to me in English, and tell me about Earth!"

"How long have you been here?" asked Stark.

"I don't know. How do you reckon time on a world without a Sun, without one damned little star to look at? Ten years, a hundred years, how should I know? Forever. Tell me about Earth."

Stark smiled wryly. "I haven't been there for a long time. The police were too ready with a welcoming committee. But the last time I saw it, it was just the same."

The lame man shivered. He was not looking at Stark now, but at some place far beyond him.

"Autumn woods," he said. "Red and gold on the brown hills. Snow. I can remember how it felt to be cold. The air bit you when you breathed it. And the women wore high-heeled slippers. No big bare feet tromping in the mud, but little sharp heels tapping on clean pavement."

Suddenly he glared at Stark, his eyes furious and bright with tears.

"Why the hell did you have to come here and start me remembering? I'm Larrabee. I live in Shuruun. I've been here forever, and I'll be here till I die. There isn't any Earth. It's gone. Just look up into the sky, and you'll know it's gone. There's nothing anywhere but clouds, and Venus, and mud."

He sat still, shaking, turning his head from side to side. A man came with wine, put it down, and went away again. The tavern was very quiet. There was a wide space empty around the two Earthmen. Beyond that people lay on the cushions, sipping the poppy wine and watching with a sort of furtive expectancy.

Abruptly, Larrabee laughed, a harsh sound that held a certain honest mirth.

"I don't know why I should get sentimental about Earth at this late date. Never thought much about it when I was there."

Nevertheless, he kept his gaze averted, and when he picked up his cup his hand trembled so that he spilled some of the wine.

Stark was staring at him in unbelief. "Larrabee," he said. "You're Mike Larrabee. You're the man who got half a million credits out of the strong room of the *Royal Venus*."

Larrabee nodded. "And got away with it, right over the Mountains of White Cloud, that they said couldn't be flown. And do you know where that half a million is now? At the bottom of the Red Sea, along with my ship and my crew, out there in the gulf. Lord knows why I lived." He shrugged. "Well, anyway, I was heading for Shuruun when I crashed, and I got here. So why complain?"

He drank again, deeply, and Stark shook his head.

"You've been here nine years, then, by Earth time," he said. He had never met Larrabee, but he remembered the pictures of him that had flashed across space on police bands. Larrabee had been a young man then, dark and proud and handsome.

Larrabee guessed his thought. "I've changed, haven't I?"

Stark said lamely, "Everybody thought you were dead."

Larrabee laughed. After that, for a moment, there was silence. Stark's ears were straining for any sound outside. There was none.

He said abruptly, "What about this trap I'm in?"

"I'll tell you one thing about it," said Larrabee. "There's no way out. I can't help you. I wouldn't if I could, get that straight. But I can't anyway."

"Thanks," Stark said sourly. "You can at least tell me what goes on."

"Listen," said Larrabee. "I'm a cripple, and an old man, and Shuruun isn't the sweetest place in the Solar System to live. But I do live. I have a wife, a slatternly wench I'll admit, but good enough in her way. You'll notice some little dark-haired brats rolling in the mud. They're mine, too. I have some skill at setting bones and such, and so I can get drunk for nothing as often as I will—which is often. Also, because of this bum leg, I'm perfectly safe. So don't ask me what goes on. I take great pains not to know."

Stark said, "Who are the Lhari?"

"Would you like to meet them?" Larrabee seemed to find something very amusing in that thought. "Just go on up to the castle. They live there. They're the Lords of Shuruun, and they're always glad to meet strangers."

He leaned forward suddenly. "Who are you anyway? What's your name, and why the devil did you come here?"

"My name is Stark. And I came here for the same reason you did."

"Stark," repeated Larrabee slowly, his eyes intent. "That rings a faint bell. Seems to me I saw a *Wanted* flash once, some idiot that had led a native revolt somewhere in the Jovian Colonies—a big cold-eyed brute they referred to colorfully as the wild man from Mercury."

He nodded, pleased with himself. "Wild man, eh? Well, Shuruun will tame you down!"

"Perhaps," said Stark. His eyes shifted constantly, watching Larrabee, watching the doorway and the dark veranda and the people who drank but did not talk among themselves. "Speaking of strangers, one came here at the time of the last rains. He was Venusian, from up coast. A big young man. I used to know him. Perhaps he could help me."

Larrabee snorted. By now, he had drunk his own wine and Stark's too. "Nobody can help you. As for your friend, I never saw him. I'm beginning to think I should never have seen you." Quite suddenly he caught up his stick and got with some difficulty to his feet. He did not look at Stark, but said harshly, "You better get out of here." Then he turned and limped unsteadily to the bar.

Stark rose. He glanced after Larrabee, and again his nostrils twitched to the smell of fear. Then he went out of the tavern the way he had come in, through the front door. No one moved to stop him. Outside, the square was empty. It had begun to rain.

Stark stood for a moment on the steps. He was angry, and filled with a dangerous unease, the hair-trigger nervousness of a tiger that senses the beaters creeping toward him up the wind. He would almost have welcomed the sight of Malthor and the three young men. But there was nothing to fight but the silence and the rain.

He stepped out in the mud, wet and warm around his ankles. An idea came to him, and he smiled, beginning now to move with a definite purpose, along the side of the square.

The sharp downpour strengthened. Rain smoked from Stark's naked shoulders, beat against thatch and mud with a hissing rattle. The harbour had disappeared behind boiling clouds of fog, where water struck the surface of the Red Sea and was turned again instantly by chemical action into vapor. The quays and the neighboring streets were being swallowed up in the impenetrable mist. Lightning came with an eerie bluish flare, and thunder came rolling after it.

Stark turned up the narrow way that led toward the castle.

Its lights were winking out now, one by one, blotted by the creeping fog. Lightning etched its shadowy bulk against the night, and then was gone. And through the noise of the thunder that followed, Stark thought he heard a voice calling.

He stopped, half crouching, his hand on his gun. The cry came again, a girl's voice, thin as the wail of a sea-bird through the driving rain. Then he saw her, a small white blur in the street behind him, running, and even in that dim glimpse of her every line of her body was instinct with fright.

Stark set his back against a wall and waited. There did not seem to be anyone with her, though it was hard to tell in the darkness and the storm.

She came up to him, and stopped, just out of his reach, looking at him and away with a painful irresoluteness. A bright flash showed her to him clearly. She was young, not long out of her childhood, and pretty in a stupid sort of way. Just now her mouth trembled on the edge of weeping, and her eyes were very large and scared. Her skirt clung to her long thighs, and above it her naked body, hardly fleshed into womanhood, glistened like snow in the wet. Her pale hair hung dripping over her shoulders.

Stark said gently, "What do you want with me?"

She looked at him, so miserably like a wet puppy that he smiled. And as though that smile had taken what little resolution she had out of her, she dropped to her knees, sobbing.

"I can't do it," she wailed. "He'll kill me, but I just can't do it!"

"Do what?" asked Stark.

She stared up at him. "Run away," she urged him. "Run away

now! You'll die in the swamps, but that's better than being one of the Lost Ones!" She shook her thin arms at him. *"Run away!"*

IV

The street was empty. Nothing showed, nothing stirred anywhere. Stark leaned over and pulled the girl to her feet, drawing her in under the shelter of the thatched eaves.

"Now then," he said. "Suppose you stop crying and tell me what this is all about."

Presently, between gulps and hiccoughs, he got the story out of her.

"I am Zareth," she said. "Malthor's daughter. He's afraid of you, because of what you did to him on the ship, so he ordered me to watch for you in the square, when you would come out of the tavern. Then I was to follow you, and . . ."

She broke off, and Stark patted her shoulder. "Go on."

But a new thought had occurred to her. "If I do, will you promise not to beat me, or . . ." She looked at his gun and shivered.

"I promise."

She studied his face, what she could see of it in the darkness, and then seemed to lose some of her fear.

"I was to stop you. I was to say what I've already said, about being Malthor's daughter and the rest of it, and then I was to say that he wanted me to lead you into an ambush while pretending to help you escape, but that I couldn't do it, and would help you escape anyhow because I hated Malthor and the whole business about the Lost Ones. So you would believe me, and follow me, and I would lead you into the ambush."

She shook her head and began to cry again, quietly this time, and there was nothing of the woman about her at all now. She was just a child, very miserable and afraid. Stark was glad he had branded Malthor.

"But I can't lead you into the ambush. I do hate Malthor, even if he is my father, because he beats me. And the Lost Ones . . ." She paused. "Sometimes I hear them at night, chanting way out there beyond the mist. It is a very terrible sound."

"It is," said Stark. "I've heard it. Who are the Lost Ones, Zareth?"

"I can't tell you that," said Zareth. "It's forbidden even to speak of them. And anyway," she finished honestly, "I don't even know. People disappear, that's all. Not our own people of Shuruun, at least not very often. But strangers like you—and I'm sure my father goes off into the swamps to hunt among the tribes there, and I'm sure he comes back from some of his voyages with nothing in his hold but men from some captured ship. Why, or what for, I don't know. Except I've heard the chanting."

"They live out there in the gulf, do they, the Lost Ones?"

"They must. There are many islands there."

"And what of the Lhari, the Lords of Shuruun? Don't they know what's going on? Or are they part of it?"

She shuddered, and said, "It's not for us to question the Lhari, nor even to wonder what they do. Those who have are gone from Shuruun, nobody knows where."

Stark nodded. He was silent for a moment, thinking. Then Zareth's little hand touched his shoulder.

"Go," she said. "Lose yourself in the swamps. You're strong, and there's something about you different from other men. You may live to find your way through."

"No. I have something to do before I leave Shuruun." He took Zareth's damp fair head between his hands and kissed her on the forehead. "You're a sweet child, Zareth, and a brave one. Tell Malthor that you did exactly as he told you, and it was not your fault I wouldn't follow you."

"He will beat me anyway," said Zareth philosophically, "but perhaps not quite so hard."

"He'll have no reason to beat you at all, if you tell him the truth—that I would not go with you because my mind was set on going to the castle of the Lhari."

There was a long, long silence, while Zareth's eyes widened slowly in horror, and the rain beat on the thatch, and fog and thunder rolled together across Shuruun.

"To the castle," she whispered. "Oh no! Go into the swamps, or let Malthor take you—but don't go to the castle!" She took hold of his arm, her fingers biting into his flesh with the urgency of her plea. "You're a stranger, you don't know . . . Please, don't go up there!"

"Why not?" asked Stark. "Are the Lhari demons? Do they devour men?" He loosened her hands gently. "You'd better go now. Tell your father where I am, if he wishes to come after me."

Zareth backed away slowly, out into the rain, staring at him as though she looked at someone standing on the brink of hell, not dead, but worse than dead. Wonder showed in her face, and through it a great yearning pity. She tried once to speak, and then shook her head and turned away, breaking into a run as though she could not endure to look upon Stark any longer. In a second she was gone.

Stark looked after her for a moment, strangely touched. Then he stepped out into the rain again, heading upward along the steep path that led to the castle of the Lords of Shuruun.

The mist was blinding. Stark had to feel his way, and as he climbed higher, above the level of the town, he was lost in the sullen redness. A hot wind blew, and each flare of lightning turned the crimson fog to a hellish purple. The night was full of a vast hissing where the rain poured into the gulf. He stopped once to hide his gun in a cleft between the rocks.

At length he stumbled against a carven pillar of black stone and found the gate that hung from it, a massive thing sheathed in metal. It was barred, and the pounding of his fists upon it made little sound.

Then he saw the gong, a huge disc of beaten gold beside the gate. Stark picked up the hammer that lay there, and set the deep voice of the gong rolling out between the thunder-bolts.

A barred slit opened and a man's eyes looked out at him. Stark dropped the hammer.

"Open up!" he shouted. "I would speak with the Lhari!"

From within he heard an echo of laughter. Scraps of voices came to him on the wind, and then more laughter, and then, slowly, the great valves of the gate creaked open, wide enough only to admit him.

He stepped through, and the gateway shut behind him with a ringing clash.

He stood in a huge open court. Enclosed within its walls was a village of thatched huts, with open sheds for cooking, and behind them were pens for the stabling of beasts, the wingless dragons of the swamps that can be caught and broken to the goad.

He saw this only in vague glimpses, because of the fog. The men who had let him in clustered around him, thrusting him forward into the light that streamed from the huts.

"He would speak with the Lhari!" one of them shouted, to the women and children who stood in the doorways watching. The words were picked up and tossed around the court, and a great burst of laughter went up.

Stark eyed them, saying nothing. They were a puzzling breed. The men, obviously, were soldiers and guards to the Lhari, for they wore the harness of fighting men. As obviously, these were their wives and children, all living behind the castle walls and having little to do with Shuruun.

But it was their racial characteristics that surprised him. They had interbred with the pale tribes of the Swamp-Edges that had peopled Shuruun, and there were many with milk-white hair and broad faces. Yet even these bore an alien stamp. Stark was puzzled, for the race he would have named was unknown here behind the Mountains of White Cloud, and almost unknown anywhere on Venus at Sea-level, among the sweltering marshes and the eternal fogs.

They stared at him even more curiously, remarking on his skin and his black hair and the unfamiliar modelling of his face. The women nudged each other and whispered, giggling, and one of them said aloud, "They'll need a barrel-hoop to collar that neck!"

The guards closed in around him. "Well, if you wish to see the Lhari, you shall," said the leader, "but first we must make sure of you."

Spear-points ringed him around. Stark made no resistance while they stripped him of all he had, except for his shorts and sandals. He had expected that, and it amused him, for there was little enough for them to take.

"All right," said the leader. "Come on."

The whole village turned out in the rain to escort Stark to the castle door. There was about them the same ominous interest that the people of Shuruun had had, with one difference. They knew what was supposed to happen to him, knew all about it, and were therefore doubly appreciative of the game.

The great doorway was square and plain, and yet neither crude nor ungraceful. The castle itself was built of the black stone, each block perfectly cut and fitted, and the door itself was sheathed in the same metal as the gate, darkened but not corroded.

The leader of the guard cried out to the warder, "Here is one who would speak with the Lhari!"

The warder laughed. "And so he shall! Their night is long, and dull."

He flung open the heavy door and cried the word down the hallway. Stark could hear it echoing hollowly within, and presently from the shadows came servants clad in silks and wearing jewelled collars, and from the guttural sound of their laughter Stark knew that they had no tongues.

Stark faltered, then. The doorway loomed hollowly before him, and it came to him suddenly that evil lay behind it and that perhaps Zareth was wiser than he when she warned him from the Lhari.

Then he thought of Helvi, and of other things, and lost his fear in anger. Lightning burned the sky. The last cry of the dying storm shook the ground under his feet. He thrust the grinning warder aside and strode into the castle, bringing a veil of the red fog with him, and did not listen to the closing of the door, which was stealthy and quiet as the footfall of approaching Death.

Torches burned here and there along the walls, and by their smoky glare he could see that the hall way was like the entrance—square and unadorned, faced with the black rock. It was high, and wide, and there was about the architecture a calm reflective dignity that had its own beauty, in some ways more impressive than the sensuous loveliness of the ruined palaces he had seen on Mars.

There were no carvings here, no paintings nor frescoes. It seemed that the builders had felt that the hall itself was enough, in its massive perfection of line and the sombre gleam of polished stone. The only decoration was in the window embrasures. These were empty now, open to the sky with the red fog wreathing through them, but there were still scraps of jewel-toned panes clinging to the fretwork, to show what they had once been.

A strange feeling swept over Stark. Because of his wild upbringing, he was abnormally sensitive to the sort of impressions that most men receive either dully or not at all.

Walking down the hall, preceded by the tongueless creatures in their bright silks and blazing collars, he was struck by a subtle *difference* in the place. The castle itself was only an extension of the minds of its builders, a dream shaped into reality. Stark felt that that dark, cool, curiously timeless dream had not originated in a mind like his own, nor like that of any man he had ever seen.

Then the end of the hall was reached, the way barred by low broad doors of gold fashioned in the same chaste simplicity.

A soft scurrying of feet, a shapeless tittering from the servants, a glancing of malicious, mocking eyes. The golden doors swung open, and Stark was in the presence of the Lhari.

V

They had the appearance in that first glance, of creatures glimpsed in a fever-dream, very bright and distant, robed in a misty glow that gave them an illusion of unearthly beauty.

The place in which the Earthman now stood was like a cathedral for breadth and loftiness. Most of it was in darkness, so that it seemed to reach without limit above and on all sides, as though the walls were only shadowy phantasms of the night itself. The polished black stone under his feet held a dim translucent gleam, depthless as water in a black tarn. There was no substance anywhere.

Far away in this shadowy vastness burned a cluster of lamps, a galaxy of little stars to shed a silvery light upon the Lords of Shuruun.

There had been no sound in the place when Stark entered, for the opening of the golden doors had caught the attention of the Lhari and held it in contemplation of the stranger. Stark began to walk toward them in this utter stillness.

Quite suddenly, in the impenetrable gloom somewhere to his right, there came a sharp scuffling and a scratching of reptilian claws, a hissing and a sort of low angry muttering, all magnified and distorted by the echoing vault into a huge demoniac whispering that swept all around him.

Stark whirled around, crouched and ready, his eyes blazing and his body bathed in cold sweat. The noise increased, rushing toward him. From the distant glow of the lamps came a woman's tinkling laughter, thin crystal broken against the vault. The hissing and snarling rose to hollow crescendo, and Stark saw a blurred shape bounding at him.

His hands reached out to receive the rush, but it never came. The strange shape resolved itself into a boy of about ten, who dragged after him on a bit of rope a young dragon, new and toothless from the egg, and protesting with all its strength.

Stark straightened up, feeling let down and furious—and relieved. The boy scowled at him through a forelock of silver curls. Then he called him a dirty word and rushed away, kicking and hauling at the little beast until it raged like the father of all dragons and sounded like it, too, in that vast echo chamber.

A voice spoke. Slow, harsh, sexless, it rang thinly through the vault. Thin— but a steel blade is thin, too. It speaks inexorably, and its word is final.

The voice said, "Come here, into the light."

Stark obeyed the voice. As he approached the lamps, the aspect of the Lhari changed and steadied. Their beauty remained, but it was not the same. They had looked like angels. Now that he could see them clearly, Stark thought that they might have been the children of Lucifer himself.

There were six of them, counting the boy. Two men, about the same age as Stark, with some complicated gambling game forgotten between them. A woman, beautiful, gowned in white silk, sitting with her hands in her lap, doing nothing. A woman, younger, not so beautiful perhaps, but with a look of stormy and bitter vitality. She wore a short tunic of crimson, and a stout leather glove on her left hand, where perched a flying thing of prey with its fierce eyes hooded.

The boy stood beside the two men, his head poised arrogantly. From time to time he cuffed the little dragon, and it snapped at him with its impotent jaws. He was proud of himself for doing that. Stark wondered how he would behave with the beast when it had grown its fangs.

Opposite him, crouched on a heap of cushions, was a third man. He was deformed, with an ungainly body and long spidery arms, and in his lap a sharp knife lay on a block of wood, half formed into the shape of an obese creature half woman, half pure evil. Stark saw with a flash of surprise that the face of the deformed young man, of all the faces there, was truly human, truly beautiful. His eyes were old in his boyish face, wise, and very sad in their wisdom. He smiled upon the stranger, and his smile was more compassionate than tears.

They looked at Stark, all of them, with restless, hungry eyes. They were the pure breed, that had left its stamp of alienage on the pale-haired folk of the swamps, the serfs who dwelt in the huts outside.

They were of the Cloud People, the folk of the High Plateaus, kings of the land on the farther slopes of the Mountains of White Cloud. It was strange to see them here, on the dark side of the barrier wall, but here they were. How they had come, and why, leaving their rich cool plains for the fetor of these foreign swamps, he could not guess. But there was no mistaking them—the proud fine shaping of their bodies, their alabaster skin, their eyes that were all colours and none, like the dawn sky, their hair that was pure warm silver.

They did not speak. They seemed to be waiting for permission to speak, and Stark wondered which one of them had voiced that steely summons.

Then it came again. "Come here—come closer." And he looked beyond them, beyond the circle of lamps into the shadows again, and saw the speaker.

She lay upon a low bed, her head propped on silken pillows, her vast, her incredibly gigantic body covered with a silken pall. Only her arms were bare, two shapeless masses of white flesh ending in tiny hands. From time to time she stretched one out and took a morsel of food from the supply laid beside her, snuffling and wheezing with the effort, and then gulped the tidbit down with a horrible voracity.

Her features had long ago dissolved into a shaking formlessness, with the exception of her nose, which rose out of the fat curved and cruel and thin, like the bony beak of the creature that sat on the girl's wrist and dreamed its hooded dreams of blood. And her eyes . . .

Stark looked into her eyes and shuddered. Then he glanced at the carving half formed in the cripple's lap, and knew what thought had guided the knife.

Half woman, half pure evil. And strong. Very strong. Her strength lay naked in her eyes for all to see, and it was an ugly strength. It could tear down mountains, but it could never build.

He saw her looking at him. Her eyes bored into his as though they would search out his very guts and study them, and he knew that she expected him to turn away, unable to bear her gaze. He did not. Presently he smiled and said, "I have outstared a rock-lizard, to determine which of us should eat the other. And I've outstared the very rock while waiting for him."

She knew that he spoke the truth. Stark expected her to be angry, but she was not. A vague mountainous rippling shook her and emerged at length as a voiceless laughter.

"You see that?" she demanded, addressing the others. "You whelps of the Lhari—not one of you dares to face me down, yet here is a great dark creature from the gods know where who can stand and shame you."

She glanced again at Stark. "What demon's blood brought you forth, that you have learned neither prudence nor fear?"

Stark answered sombrely, "I learned them both before I could walk. But I learned another thing also—a thing called anger."

"And are you angry?"

"Ask Malthor if I am, and why!"

He saw the two men start a little, and a slow smile crossed the girl's face.

"Malthor," said the hulk upon the bed, and ate a mouthful of roast meat dripping with fat. "That is interesting. But rage against Malthor did not bring you here. I am curious, Stranger. Speak."

"I will."

Stark glanced around. The place was a tomb, a trap. The very air smelled of danger. The younger folk watched him in silence. Not one of them had spoken since he came in, except the boy who had cursed him, and that was unnatural in itself. The girl leaned forward, idly stroking the creature on her wrist so that it stirred and ran its knife-like talons in and out of their bony sheathes with sensuous pleasure. Her gaze on Stark was bold and cool, oddly challenging. Of them all, she alone saw him as a man. To the others he was a problem, a diversion— something less than human.

Stark said, "A man came to Shuruun at the time of the last rains. His name was Helvi, and he was son of a little king by Yarell. He came seeking his brother, who had broken tabu and fled for his life. Helvi came to tell him that the ban was lifted, and he might return. Neither one came back."

The small eyes were amused, blinking in their tallowy creases. "And so?"

"And so I have come after Helvi, who is my friend."

Again there was the heaving of that bulk of flesh, the explosion of laughter that hissed and wheezed in snakelike echoes through the vault.

"Friendship must run deep with you, Stranger. Ah, well. The Lhari are kind of heart. You shall find your friend."

And as though that were the signal to end their deferential silence, the younger folk burst into laughter also, until the vast hall rang with it, giving back a sound like demons laughing on the edge of Hell.

The cripple only did not laugh, but bent his bright head over his carving, and sighed.

The girl sprang up. "Not yet, Grandmother! Keep him awhile."

The cold, cruel eyes shifted to her. "And what will you do with him, Varra? Haul him about on a string, like Bor with his wretched beast?"

"Perhaps—though I think it would need a stout chain to hold him." Varra turned and looked at Stark, bold and bright, taking in the breadth and the height of him, the shaping of the great smooth muscles, the iron line of the jaw. She smiled. Her mouth was very lovely, like the red fruit of the swamp tree that bears death in its pungent sweetness.

"Here is a man," she said. "The first man I have seen since my father died."

The two men at the gaming table rose, their faces flushed and angry. One of them strode forward and gripped the girl's arm roughly.

"So I am not a man," he said, with surprising gentleness. "A sad thing, for one who is to be your husband. It's best that we settle that now, before we wed."

Varra nodded. Stark saw that the man's fingers were cutting savagely into the firm muscle of her arm, but she did not wince.

"High time to settle it all, Egil. You have borne enough from me. The day is long overdue for my taming. I must learn now to bend my neck, and acknowledge my lord."

For a moment Stark thought she meant it, the note of mockery in her voice was so subtle. Then the woman in white, who all this time had not moved nor changed expression, voiced again the thin, tinkling laugh he had heard once before. From that, and the dark suffusion of blood in Egil's face, Stark knew that Varra was only casting the man's own phrases back at him. The boy let out one derisive bark, and was cuffed into silence.

Varra looked straight at Stark. "Will you fight for me?" she demanded.

Quite suddenly, it was Stark's turn to laugh. "No!" he said.

Varra shrugged. "Very well, then. I must fight for myself."

"Man," snarled Egil. "I'll show you who's a man, you scrapgrace little vixen!"

He wrenched off his girdle with his free hand, at the same time bending the girl around so he could get a fair shot at her. The creature of prey, a Terran falcon, clung to her wrist, beating its wings and screaming, its hooded head jerking.

With a motion so quick that it was hardly visible, Varra slipped the hood and flew the creature straight for Egil's face.

He let go, flinging up his arms to ward off the talons and the tearing beak. The wide wings beat and hammered. Egil yelled. The boy Bor got out of range and danced up and down shrieking with delight.

Varra stood quietly. The bruises were blackening on her arm, but she did not deign to touch them. Egil blundered against the gaming table and sent the ivory pieces flying. Then he tripped over a cushion and fell flat, and the hungry talons ripped his tunic to ribbons down the back.

Varra whistled, a clear peremptory call. The creature gave a last peck at the back of Egil's head and flopped sullenly back to its perch on her wrist. She held it, turning toward Stark. He knew from the poise of her that she was on the verge of launching her pet at him. But she studied him and then shook her head.

"No," she said, and slipped the hood back on. "You would kill it."

Egil had scrambled up and gone off into the darkness, sucking a cut on his arm. His face was black with rage. The other man looked at Varra.

"If you were pledged to me," he said, "I'd have that temper out of you!"

"Come and try it," answered Varra.

The man shrugged and sat down. "It's not my place. I keep the peace in my own house." He glanced at the woman in white, and Stark saw that her face, hitherto blank of any expression, had taken on a look of abject fear.

"You do," said Verra, "and, if I were Arel, I would stab you while you slept. But you're safe. She has no spirit to begin with."

Arel shivered and looked steadfastly at her hands. The man began to gather up the scattered pieces. He said casually, "Egil will wring your neck some day, Varra, and I shan't weep to see it."

All this time the old woman had eaten and watched, watched and eaten, her eyes glittering with interest.

"A pretty brood, are they not?" she demanded of Stark. "Full of spirit, quarreling like young hawks in the nest. That's why I keep them around me, so—they are such sport to watch. All except Treon there." She indicated the crippled youth. "He does nothing. Dull and soft-mouthed, worse than Arel. What a grandson to be cursed with! But his sister has fire enough for two." She munched a sweet, grunting with pride.

Treon raised his head and spoke, and his voice was like music, echoing with an eerie liveliness in that dark place.

"Dull I may be, Grandmother, and weak in body, and without hope. Yet I shall be the last of the Lhari. Death sits waiting on the towers, and he shall gather you all before me. I know, for the winds have told me."

He turned his suffering eyes upon Stark and smiled, a smile of such woe and resignation that the Earthman's heart ached with it. Yet there was a thankfulness in it too, as though some long waiting was over at last.

"You," he said softly, "Stranger with the fierce eyes. I saw you come, out of the darkness, and where you set foot there was a bloody print. Your arms were red to the elbows, and your breast was splashed with the redness, and on your brow was the symbol of death. Then I knew, and the wind whispered into my ear, 'It is so. This man shall pull the castle down, and its stones shall crush Shuruun and set the Lost Ones free'."

He laughed, very quietly. "Look at him, all of you. For he will be your doom!"

There was a moment's silence, and Stark, with all the superstitions of a wild race thick within him, turned cold to the roots of his hair. Then the old woman said disgustedly, "Have the winds warned you of this, my idiot?"

And with astonishing force and accuracy she picked up a ripe fruit and flung it at Treon.

"Stop your mouth with that," she told him. "I am weary to death of your prophecies."

Treon looked at the crimson juice trickling slowly down the breast of his tunic, to drip upon the carving in his lap. The half formed head was covered with it. Treon was shaken with silent mirth.

"Well," said Varra, coming up to Stark, "what do you think of the Lhari? The proud Lhari, who would not stoop to mingle their blood with the cattle of the swamps. My half-witted brother, my worthless cousins, that little monster Bor who is the last twig of the tree—do you wonder I flew my falcon at Egil?"

She waited for an answer, her head thrown back, the silver curls framing her face like wisps of storm-cloud. There was a swagger about her that at once irritated and delighted Stark. A hellcat, he thought, but a mighty fetching one, and bold as brass. Bold—and honest. Her lips were parted, midway between anger and a smile.

He caught her to him suddenly and kissed her, holding her slim strong body as though she were a doll. He was in no hurry to set her down. When at last he did, he grinned and said, "Was that what you wanted?"

"Yes," answered Varra. "That was what I wanted." She spun about, her jaw set dangerously. "Grandmother . . ."

She got no further. Stark saw that the old woman was attempting to sit upright, her face purpling with effort and the most terrible wrath he had ever seen.

"You," she gasped at the girl. She choked on her fury and her shortness of breath, and then Egil came soft-footed into the light, bearing in his hand a thing made of black metal and oddly shaped, with a blunt, thick muzzle.

"Lie back, Grandmother," he said. "I had a mind to use this on Varra—"

Even as he spoke he pressed a stud, and Stark in the act of leaping for the sheltering darkness, crashed down and lay like a dead man. There had been no sound, no flash, nothing, but a vast hand that smote him suddenly into oblivion.

Egil finished,—"but I see a better target."

VI

Red. Red. Red. The colour of blood. Blood in his eyes. He was remembering now. The quarry had turned on him, and they had fought on the bare, blistering rocks.

Nor had N'Chaka killed. The Lord of the Rocks was very big, a giant among lizards, and N'Chaka was small. The Lord of the Rocks had laid open N'Chaka's head before the wooden spear had more than scratched his flank.

It was strange that N'Chaka still lived. The Lord of the Rocks must have been full fed. Only that had saved him.

N'Chaka groaned, not with pain, but with shame. He had failed. Hoping for a great triumph, he had disobeyed the tribal law that forbids a boy to hunt the quarry of a man, and he had failed. Old One would not reward him with the girdle and the flint spear of manhood. Old One would give him to the women for the punishment of little whips. Tika would laugh at him, and it would be many seasons before Old One would grant him permission to try the Man's Hunt.

Blood in his eyes.

He blinked to clear them. The instinct of survival was prodding him. He must arouse himself and creep away, before the Lord of the Rocks returned to eat him.

The redness would not go away. It swam and flowed, strangely sparkling. He blinked again, and tried to lift his head, and could not, and fear struck down upon him like the iron frost of night upon the rocks of the valley.

It was all wrong. He could see himself clearly, a naked boy dizzy with pain, rising and clambering over the ledges and the shale to the safety of the cave. He could see that, and yet he could not move.

All wrong. Time, space, the universe, darkened and turned.

A voice spoke to him. A girl's voice. Not Tika's and the speech was strange.

Tika was dead. Memories rushed through his mind, the bitter things, the cruel things. Old One was dead, and all the others . . .

The voice spoke again, calling him by a name that was not his own. Stark.

Memory shattered into a kaleidoscope of broken pictures, fragments, rushing, spinning. He was adrift among them. He was lost, and the terror of it brought a scream into his throat.

Soft hands touching his face, gentle words, swift and soothing. The redness cleared and steadied, though it did not go away, and quite suddenly he was himself again, with all his memories where they belonged.

He was lying on his back, and Zareth, Malthor's daughter, was looking down at him. He knew now what the redness was. He had seen it too often before not to know. He was somewhere at the bottom of the Red Sea—that weird ocean in which a man can breathe.

And he could not move. That had not changed, nor gone away. His body was dead.

The terror he had felt before was nothing to the agony that filled him now. He lay entombed in his own flesh, staring up at Zareth, wanting an answer to a question he dared not ask.

She understood, from the look in his eyes.

"It's all right," she said, and smiled. "It will wear off. You'll be all right. It's only the weapon of the Lhari. Somehow it puts the body to sleep, but it will wake again."

Stark remembered the black object that Egil had held in his hands. A projector of some sort, then, beaming a current of high-frequency vibration that paralyzed the nerve centers. He was amazed. The Cloud People were barbarians themselves, though on a higher scale than the swamp-edge tribes, and certainly had no such scientfic proficiency. He wondered where the Lhari had got hold of such a weapon.

It didn't really matter. Not just now. Relief swept over him, bringing him dangerously close to tears. The effect would wear off. At the momer , .hat was all he cared about.

He looked up at Zareth again. Her pale hair floated with the slow breathing of the sea, a milky cloud against the spark-shot crimson. He saw now that her face was drawn and shadowed, and there a terrible hopelessness in her eyes. She had been alive when he first saw her—frightened, not too bright, but full of emotion and a certain dogged courage. Now the spark was gone, crushed out.

She wore a collar around her white neck, a ring of dark metal with the ends fused together for all time.

"Where are we?" he asked.

And she answered, her voice carrying deep and hollow in the dense substance of the sea, "We are in the place of the Lost Ones."

Stark looked beyond her, as far as he could see, since he was unable to turn his head. And wonder came to him.

Black walls, black vault above him, a vast hall filled with the wash of the sea that slipped in streaks of whispering flame through the high embrasures. A hall that was twin to the vault of shadows where he had met the Lhari.

"There is a city," said Zareth dully. "You will see it soon. You will see nothing else until you die."

Stark said, very gently, "How do you come here, little one?"

"Because of my father. I will tell you all I know, which is little enough. Malthor has been slaver to the Lhari for a long time. There are a number of them among the captains of Shuruun, but that is a thing that is never spoken of—so I, his daughter, could only guess. I was sure of it when he sent me after you."

She laughed, a bitter sound. "Now I'm here, with the collar of the Lost Ones on my neck. But Malthor is here, too." She laughed again, ugly laughter to come from a young mouth. Then she looked at Stark, and her hand reached out timidly to touch his hair in what was almost a caress. Her eyes were wide, and soft, and full of tears.

"Why didn't you go into the swamps when I warned you?"

Stark answered stolidly, "Too late to worry about that now." Then, "You say Malthor is here, a slave?"

"Yes." Again, that look of wonder and admiration in her eyes. "I don't know what you said or did to the Lhari, but the Lord Egil came down in a black rage and cursed my father for a bungling fool because he could not hold you. My father whined and made excuses, and all would have been well—only his curiosity got the better of him and he asked the Lord Egil what had happened. You were like a wild beast, Malthor said, and he hoped you had not harmed the Lady Varra, as he could see from Egil's wounds that there had been trouble.

"The Lord Egil turned quite purple. I thought he was going to fall in a fit."

" Yes," said Stark. "That was the wrong thing to say." The ludicrous side of it struck him, and he was suddenly roaring with laughter. "Malthor should have kept his mouth shut!"

"Egil called his guard and ordered them to take Malthor. And when he realized what had happened, Malthor turned on me, trying to say that it was all my fault, that I let you escape."

Stark stopped laughing.

Her voice went on slowly. "Egil seemed quite mad with fury. I have heard that the Lhari are all mad, and I think it is so. At any rate, he ordered me taken too, for he wanted to stamp Malthor's seed into the mud forever. So we are here."

There was a long silence. Stark could think of no word of comfort, and as for hope, he had better wait until he was sure he could at least raise his head. Egil might have damaged him permanently, out of spite. In fact, he was surprised he wasn't dead.

He glanced again at the collar on Zareth's neck. Slave. Slave to the Lhari, in the city of the Lost Ones.

What in the devil did they do with slaves, at the bottom of the sea?

The heavy gases conducted sound remarkably well, except for an odd property of diffussion which made it seem that a voice came from everywhere at once. Now, all at once, Stark became aware of a dull clamor of voices drifting towards him.

He tried to see, and Zareth turned his head carefully so that he might.

The Lost Ones were returning from whatever work it was they did.

Out of the dim red murk beyond the open door they swam, into the long, long vastness of the hall that was filled with same red murk, moving slowly, their white bodies trailing wakes of sullen flame. The host of the damned drifting through a strange red-litten hell, weary and without hope.

One by one they sank onto pallets laid in rows on the black stone floor, and lay there, utterly exhausted, their pale hair lifting and floating with the slow eddies of the sea. And each one wore a collar.

One man did not lie down. He came toward Stark, a tall barbarian who drew himself with great strokes of his arms so that he was wrapped in wheeling sparks. Stark knew his face.

"Helvi," he said, and smiled in welcome.

"Brother!"

Helvi crouched down—a great handsome boy he had been the time Stark saw him, but he was a man now, with all the laughter turned to grim deep lines around his mouth and the bones of his face standing out like granite ridges.

"Brother," he said again, looking at Stark through a glitter of un-ashamed tears. "Fool." And he cursed Stark savagely because he had come to Shuruun to look for an idiot who had gone the same way, and was already as good as dead.

"Would you have followed me?" asked Stark.

"But I am only an ignorant child of the swamps," said Helvi. "You come from space, you know the other worlds, you can read and write— you should have better sense!"

Stark grinned. "And I'm still an ignorant child of the rocks. So we're two fools together. Where is Tobal?"

Tobal was Helvi's brother, who had broken tabu and looked for refuge in Shuruun. Apparently he had found peace at last, for Helvi shook his head.

"A man cannot live too long under the sea. It is not enough merely to breath and eat. Tobal over-ran his time, and I am close to the end of mine." He held up his hand and then swept it down sharply, watching the broken fires dance along his arms.

"The mind breaks before the body," said Helvi casually, as though it were a matter of no importance.

Zareth spoke. "Helvi has guarded you each period while the others slept."

"And not I alone," said Helvi. "The little one stood with me."

"Guarded me!" said Stark. "Why?"

For answer, Helvi gestured toward a pallet not far away. Malthor lay there, his eyes half open and full of malice, the fresh scar livid on his cheek.

"He feels," said Helvi, "that you should not have fought upon his ship."

Stark felt an inward chill of horror. To lie here helpless, watching Malthor come toward him with open fingers reaching for his helpless throat . . .

He made a passionate effort to move, and gave up, gasping. Helvi grinned.

"Now is the time I should wrestle you, Stark, for I never could throw you before." He gave Stark's head a shake, very gentle for all its apparent roughness. "You'll be throwing me again. Sleep now, and don't worry."

He settled himself to watch, and presently in spite of himself Stark slept, with Zareth curled at his feet like a little dog.

There was no time down there in the heart of the Red Sea. No daylight, no dawn, no space of darkness. No winds blew, no rain nor storm broke the endless silence. Only the lazy currents whispered by on their way to nowhere, and the red sparks danced, and the great hall waited, remembering the past.

Stark waited, too. How long he never knew, but he was used to waiting. He had learned his patience on the knees of the great mountains whose heads lift proudly into open space to look at the Sun, and he had absorbed their own contempt for time.

Little by little, life returned to his body. A mongrel guard came now and again to examine him, pricking Stark's flesh with his knife to test the reaction, so that Stark should not malinger.

He reckoned without Stark's control. The Earthman bore his prodding without so much as a twitch until his limbs were completely his own again. Then he sprang up and pitched the man half the length of the hall, turning over and over, yelling with startled anger.

At the next period of labour, Stark was driven with the rest out into the City of the Lost Ones.

VII

Stark had been in places before that oppressed him with a sense of their strangeness or their wickedness—Sinharat, the lovely ruin of coral and gold lost in the Martian wastes; Jekkara, Valkis—the Low-Canal towns that smell of blood and wine; the cliff-caves of Arianrhod on the edge of Darkside, the buried tomb-cities of Callisto. But this—this was nightmare to haunt a man's dreams.

He stared about him as he went in the long line of slaves, and felt such a cold shuddering contraction of his belly as he had never known before.

Wide avenues paved with polished blocks of stone, perfect as ebon mirrors. Buildings, tall and stately, pure and plain, with a calm strength that could outlast the ages. Black, all black, with no fripperies of paint or carving to soften them, only here and there a window like a drowned jewel glinting through the red.

Vines like drifts of snow cascading down the stones. Gardens with close-clipped turf and flowers lifting bright on their green stalks, their petals open to a daylight that was gone, their head bending as though to some forgotten breeze. All neat, all tended, the branches pruned, the fresh soil turned this morning—by whose hand?

Stark remembered the great forest dreaming at the bottom of the gulf, and shivered. He did not like to think how long ago these flowers must have opened their young bloom to the last light they were ever going to see. For they were dead—dead as the forest, dead as the city. Forever bright—and dead.

Stark thought that it must always have been a silent city. It was impossible to imagine noisy throngs flocking to a market square down those immense avenues. The black walls were not made to echo song or laughter. Even the children must have moved quietly along the garden paths, small wise creatures born to an ancient dignity.

He was beginning to understand now the meaning of that weird forest. The Gulf of Shuruun had not always been a gulf. It had been a valley, rich, fertile, with this great city in its arms, and here and there on the upper slopes the retreat of some noble or philosopher—of which the castle of the Lhari was a survivor.

A wall or rock had held back the Red Sea from this valley. And then, somehow, the wall had cracked, and the sullen crimson tide had flowed slowly, slowly into the fertile bottoms, rising higher, lapping the towers and the tree-tops in swirling flame, drowning the land forever. Stark wondered if the people had known the disaster was coming, if they had gone forth to tend their gardens for the last time so that they might remain perfect in the embalming gases of the sea.

The columns of slaves, herded by overseers armed with small black weapons similar to the one Egil had used, came out into a broad square whose farther edges were veiled in the red murk. And Stark looked on ruin.

A great building had fallen in the centre of the square. The gods only knew what force had burst its walls and tossed the giant blocks like pebbles into a heap. But there it was, the one untidy thing in the city, a mountain of debris.

Nothing else was damaged. It seemed that this had been the place of temples, and they stood unharmed, ranked around the sides of the square, the dim fires rippling through their open porticoes. Deep in their inner shadows Stark thought he could make out images, gigantic things brooding in the spark-shot gloom.

He had no chance to study them. The overseers cursed them on, and now he saw what use the slaves were put to. They were clearing away the wreckage of the fallen building.

Helvi whispered, "For sixteen years men have slaved and died down here, and the work is not half done. And why do the Lhari want it done at all? I'll tell you why. Because they are mad, mad as swamp-dragons gone *musth* in the spring!"

It seemed madness indeed, to labour at this pile of rocks in a dead city at the bottom of the sea. It was madness. And yet the Lhari, though they might be insane, were not fools. There was a reason for it, and Stark was sure it was a good reason—good for the Lhari, at any rate.

An overseer came up to Stark, thrusting him roughly toward a sledge already partly loaded with broken rocks. Stark hesitated, his eyes turning ugly, and Helvi said,

"Come on, you fool! Do you want to be down flat on your back again?"

Stark glanced at the little weapon, blunt and ready, and turned reluctantly to obey. And there began his servitude.

It was a weird sort of life he led. For a while he tried to reckon time by the periods of work and sleep, but he lost count, and it did not greatly matter anyway.

He laboured with the others, hauling the huge blocks away, clearing out the cellars that were partly bared, shoring up weak walls underground. The slaves clung to their old habit of thought, calling the work-periods "days" and the sleep-periods "nights."

Each "day" Egil, or his brother Cond, came to see what had been done, and went away black-browed and disappointed, ordering the work speeded up.

Treon was there also much of the time. He would come slowly in his awkward crabwise way and perch like a pale gargoyle on the stones, never speaking, watching with his sad beautiful eyes. He woke a vague foreboding in Stark. There was something awesome in Treon's silent patience, as though he waited the coming of some black doom, long delayed but inevitable. Stark would remember the prophecy, and shiver.

It was obvious to Stark after a while that the Lhari were clearing the building to get at the cellars underneath. The great dark caverns already bared had yielded nothing, but the brothers still hoped. Over and over Cond and Egil sounded the walls and the floors, prying here and there, and chafing at the delay in opening up the underground labyrinth. What they hoped to find, no one knew.

Varra came, too. Alone, and often, she would drift down through the dim mist-fires and watch, smiling a secret smile, her hair like blown silver where the currents played with it. She had nothing but curt words for Egil, but she kept her eyes on the great dark Earthman, and there was a look in them that stirred his blood. Egil was not blind, and it stirred his too, but in a different way.

Zareth saw that look. She kept as close to Stark as possible, asking no favours, but following him around with a sort of quiet devotion, seeming contented only when she was near him. One "night" in the slave barracks she crouched beside his pallet, her hand on his bare knee. She did not speak, and her face was hidden by the floating masses of her hair.

Stark turned her head so that he could see her, pushing the pale cloud gently away.

"What troubles you, little sister?"

Her eyes were wide and shadowed with some vague fear. But she only said, "It's not my place to speak."

"Why not?"

"Because . . ." Her mouth trembled, and then suddenly she said, "Oh, it's foolish, I know. But the woman of the Lhari . . ."

"What about her?"

"She watches you. Always she watches you! And the Lord Egil is angry. There is something in her mind, and it will bring you only evil. I know it!"

"It seems to me," said Stark wryly, "that the Lhari have already done as much evil as possible to all of us."

"No," answered Zareth, with an odd wisdom. "Our hearts are still clean."

Stark smiled. He leaned over and kissed her. "I'll be careful, little sister."

Quite suddenly she flung her arms around his neck and clung to him tightly, and Stark's face sobered. He patted her, rather awkwardly, and then she had gone, to curl up on her own pallet with her head buried in her arms.

Stark lay down. His heart was sad, and there was a stinging moisture in his eyes.

The red eternities dragged on. Stark learned what Helvi had meant when he said that the mind broke before the body. The sea bottom was no place for creatures of the upper air. He learned also the meaning of the metal collars, and the manner of Tobal's death.

Helvi explained.

"There are boundaries laid down. Within them we may range, if we have the strength and the desire after work. Beyond them we may not go. And there is no chance of escape by breaking through the barrier. How this is done I do not understand, but it is so, and the collars are the key to it.

"When a slave approaches the barrier the collar brightens as though with fire, and the slave falls. I have tried this myself, and I know. Half-paralyzed, you may still crawl back to safety. But if you are mad, as Tobal was, and charge the barrier strongly . . ."

He made a cutting motion with his hands.

Stark nodded. He did not attempt to explain electricity or electronic vibrations to Helvi, but it seemed plain enough that the force with which the Lhari kept their slaves in check was something of the sort. The collars acted as conductors, perhaps for the same type of beam that was generated in the hand-weapons. When the metal broke the invisible boundary line it triggered off a force-beam from the central power station, in the manner of the obedient electric eye that opens doors and rings alarm bells. First a warning—then death.

The boundaries were wide enough, extending around the city and enclosing a good bit of forest beyond it. There was no possibility of a slave hiding among the trees, because the collar could be traced by the same type of beam, turned to low power, and the punishment meted out to a retaken man was such that few were foolish enough to try that game.

The surface, of course, was utterly forbidden. The one unguarded spot was the island where the central power station was, and here the slaves were allowed to come sometimes at night. The Lhari had discovered that they lived longer and worked better if they had an occasional breath of air and a look at the sky.

Many times Stark made that pilgrimage with the others. Up from the red depths they would come, through the reeling bands of fire where the currents ran, through the clouds of crimson sparks and the sullen patches of stillness that were like pools of blood, a company of white ghosts shrouded in flame, rising from their tomb for a little taste of the world they had lost.

It didn't matter that they were so weary they had barely the strength to get back to the barracks and sleep. They found the strength. To walk again on the open ground, to be rid of the eternal crimson dusk and the oppressive weight on the chest—to look up into the hot blue night of Venus and smell the fragrance of the *liha*-trees borne on the land wind . . . They found the strength.

They sang here, sitting on the island rocks and staring through the mists toward the shore they would never see again. It was their chanting that Stark had heard when he came down the gulf with Malthor, that wordless cry of grief and loss. Now he was here himself, holding Zareth close to comfort her and joining his own deep voice into that primitive reproach to the gods.

While he sat, howling like the savage he was, he studied the power plant, a squat blockhouse of a place. On the nights the slaves came guards were stationed outside to warn them away. The block-house was doubly guarded with the shock-beam. To attempt to take it by force would only mean death for all concerned.

Stark gave that idea up for the time being. There was never a second when escape was not in his thoughts, but he was too old in the game to break his neck against a stone wall. Like Malthor, he would wait.

Zareth and Helvi both changed after Stark's coming. Though they never talked of breaking free, both of them lost their air of hopelessness. Stark made neither plans nor promises. But Helvi knew him from of old, and the girl had her own subtle understanding, and they held up their heads again.

Then, one "day" as the work was ending, Varra came smiling out of the red murk and beckoned to him, and Stark's heart gave a great leap.

Without a backward look he left Helvi and Zareth, and went with her, down the wide still avenue that led outward to the forest.

VIII

They left the stately buildings and the wide spaces behind them, and went in among the trees. Stark hated the forest. The city was bad enough, but it was dead, honestly dead, except for those neat nightmare gardens. There was something terrifying about these great trees, full-leafed and green, rioting with flowering vines and all the rich under-growth of the jungle, standing like massed corpses made lovely by mortuary art. They swayed and rustled as the coiling fires swept them, branches bending to that silent horrible parody of wind. Stark always felt trapped there, and stifled by the stiff leaves and the vines.

But he went, and Varra slipped like a silver bird between the great trunks, apparently happy.

"I have come here often, ever since I was old enough. It's wonderful. Here I can stoop and fly like one of my own hawks." She laughed and plucked a golden flower to set in her hair, and then darted away again, her white legs flashing.

Stark followed. He could see what she meant. Here in this strange sea one's motion was as much flying as swimming, since the pressure equalized the weight of the body. There was a queer sort of thrill in plunging headlong from the treetops, to arrow down through a tangle of vines and branches and then sweep upward again.

She was playing with him, and he knew it. The challenge got his blood up. He could have caught her easily but he did not, only now and again he circled her to show his strength. They sped on and on, trailing wakes of flame, a black hawk chasing a silver dove through the forests of a dream.

But the dove had been fledged in an eagle's nest. Stark wearied of the game at last. He caught her and they clung together, drifting still among the trees with the momentum of that wonderful weightless flight.

Her kiss at first was lazy, teasing and curious. Then it changed. All Stark's smouldering anger leaped into a different kind of flame. His handling of her was rough and cruel, and she laughed, a little fierce voiceless laugh, and gave it back to him, and he remembered how he had thought her mouth was like a bitter fruit that would give a man pain when he kissed it.

She broke away at last and came to rest on a broad branch, leaning back against the trunk and laughing, her eyes brilliant and cruel as Stark's own. And Stark sat down at her feet.

"What do you want?" he demanded. "What do you want with me?"

She smiled. There was nothing sidelong or shy about her. She was bold as a new blade.

"I'll tell you, wild man."

He started. "Where did you pick up that name?"

"I have been asking the Earthman Larrabee about you. It suits you

well." She leaned forward. "This is what I want of you. Slay me Egil
and his brother Cond. Also Bor, who will grow up worse than either—
although that I can do myself, if you're adverse to killing children,
though Bor is more monster than child. Grandmother can't live forever,
and with my cousins out of the way she's no threat. Treon doesn't
count."

"And if I do—what then?"

"Freedom. And me. You'll rule Shuruun at my side."

Stark's eyes were mocking. "For how long, Varra?"

"Who knows? And what does it matter? The years take care of
themselves." She shrugged. "The Lhari blood has run out, and it's
time there was a fresh strain. Our children will rule after us, and
they'll be men."

Stark laughed. He roared with it.

"It's not enough that I'm a slave to the Lhari. Now I must be execu-
tioner and herd bull as well!" He looked at her keenly. "Why me,
Varra? Why pick on me?"

"Because, as I have said, you are the first man I have seen since my
father died. Also, there is something about you . . ."

She pushed herself upward to hover lazily, her lips just brushing his.

"Do you think it would be so bad a thing to live with me, wild man?"

She was lovely and maddening, a silver witch shining among the
dim fires of the sea, full of wickedness and laughter. Stark reached out
and drew her to him.

"Not bad," he murmured. "Dangerous."

He kissed her, and she whispered, "I think you're not afraid of
danger."

"On the contrary, I'm a cautious man." He held her off, where he
could look straight into her eyes. "I owe Egil something on my own, but
I will not murder. The fight must be fair, and Cond will have to take
care of himself."

"Fair! Was Egil fair with you—or me?"

He shrugged. "My way, or not at all."

She thought it over a while, then nodded. "All right. As for Cond,
you will give him a blood debt, and pride will make him fight. The
Lhari are all proud," she added bitterly. "That's our curse. But it's
bred in the bone, as you'll find out."

"One more thing. Zareth and Helvi are to go free, and there must
be an end to this slavery."

She stared at him. "You drive a hard bargain, wild man!"

"Yes or no?"

"Yes *and* no. Zareth and Helvi you may have, if you insist, though
the gods know what you see in that pallid child. As to the other . . ."
She smiled very mockingly. "I'm no fool, Stark. You're evading me,
and two can play that game."

He laughed. "Fair enough. And now tell me this, witch with the
silver curls—how am I to get at Egil that I may kill him?"

"I'll arrange that."

She said it with such vicious assurance that he was pretty sure she would arrange it. He was silent for a moment, and then he asked,

"Varra—what are the Lhari searching for at the bottom of the sea?"

She answered slowly, "I told you that we are a proud clan. We were driven out of the High Plateaus centuries ago because of our pride. Now it's all we have left, but it's a driving thing."

She paused, and then went on. "I think we had known about the city for a long time, but it had never meant anything until my father became fascinated by it. He would stay down here days at a time, exploring, and it was he who found the weapons and the machine of power which is on the island. Then he found the chart and the metal book, hidden away in a secret place. The book was written in pictographs—as though it was meant to be deciphered—and the chart showed the square with the ruined building and the temples, with a separate diagram of catacombs underneath the ground.

"The book told of a secret—a thing of wonder and of fear. And my father believed that the building had been wrecked to close the entrance to the catacombs where the secret was kept. He determined to find it."

Sixteen years of other men's lives. Stark shivered. "What was the secret, Varra?"

"The manner of controlling life. How it was done I do not know, but with it one might build a race of giants, of monsters, or of gods. You can see what that would mean to us, a proud and dying clan."

"Yes," Stark answered slowly. "I can see."

The magnitude of the idea shook him. The builders of the city must have been wise indeed in their scientific research to evolve such a terrible power. To mold the living cells of the body to one's will—to create, not life itself but its form and fashion . . .

A race of giants, or of gods. The Lhari would like that. To transform their own degenerate flesh into something beyond the race of men, to develop their followers into a corps of fighting men that no one could stand against, to see that their children were given an unholy advantage over all the children of men . . . Stark was appalled at the realization of the evil they could do if they ever found that secret.

Varra said, "There was a warning in the book. The meaning of it was not quite clear, but it seemed that the ancient ones felt that they had sinned against the gods and been punished, perhaps by some plague. They were a strange race, and not human. At any rate, they destroyed the great building there as a barrier against anyone who should come after them, and then let the Red Sea in to cover their city forever. They must have been superstitious children, for all their knowledge."

"Then you ignored the warning, and never worried that a whole city had died to prove it."

She shrugged. "Oh, Treon has been muttering prophecies about it for years. Nobody listens to him. As for myself, I don't care whether we find the secret or not. My belief is it was destroyed along with the building, and besides, I have no faith in such things."

"Besides," mocked Stark shrewdly, "you wouldn't care to see Egil and Cond striding across the heavens of Venus, and you're doubtful just what your own place would be in the new pantheon."

She showed her teeth at him. "You're too wise for your own good. And now good bye." She gave him a quick, hard kiss and was gone, flashing upward, high above the tree tops where he dared not follow.

Stark made his way slowly back to the city, upset and very thoughtful.

As he came back into the great square, heading toward the barracks, he stopped, every nerve taut.

Somewhere, in one of the shadowy temples, the clapper of a votive bell was swinging, sending its deep pulsing note across the silence. Slowly, slowly, like the beating of a dying heart it came, and mingled with it was the faint sound of Zareth's voice, calling his name.

IX

He crossed the square, moving very carefully through the red murk, and presently he saw her.

It was not hard to find her. There was one temple larger than all the rest. Stark judged that it must once have faced the entrance of the fallen building, as though the great figure within was set to watch over the scientists and the philosophers who came there to dream their vast and sometimes terrible dreams.

The philosophers were gone, and the scientists had destroyed themselves. But the image still watched over the drowned city, its hand raised both in warning and in benediction.

Now, across its reptilian knees, Zareth lay. The temple was open on all sides, and Stark could see her clearly, a little white scrap of humanity against the black unhuman figure.

Malthor stood beside her. It was he who had been tolling the votive bell. He had stopped now, and Zareth's words came clearly to Stark.

"Go away, go away! They're waiting for you. Don't come in here!"

"I'm waiting for you, Stark," Malthor called out, smiling. "Are you afraid to come?" And he took Zareth by the hair and struck her, slowly and deliberately, twice across the face.

All expression left Stark's face, leaving it perfectly blank except for his eyes, which took on a sudden lambent gleam. He began to move toward the temple, not hurrying even then, but moving in such a way that it seemed an army could not have stopped him.

Zareth broke free from her father. Perhaps she was intended to break free.

"Egil!" she screamed. "It's a trap . . ."

Again Malthor caught her and this time he struck her harder, so that she crumpled down again across the image that watched with its jewelled, gentle eyes and saw nothing.

"She's afraid for you," said Malthor. "She knows I mean to kill you if I can. Well, perhaps Egil is here also. Perhaps he is not. But certainly Zareth is here. I have beaten her well, and I shall beat her again, as long as she lives to be beaten, for her treachery to me. And if you want to save her from that, you outland dog, you'll have to kill me. Are you afraid?"

Stark was afraid. Malthor and Zareth were alone in the temple. The pillared colonnades were empty except for the dim fires of the sea. Yet Stark was afraid, for an instinct older then speech warned him to be.

It did not matter. Zareth's white skin was mottled with dark bruises, and Malthor was smiling at him, and it did not matter.

Under the shadow of the roof and down the colonnade he went, swiftly now, leaving a streak of fire behind him. Malthor looked into his eyes, and ,his smile trembled and was gone.

He crouched. And at the last moment, when the dark body plunged down at him as a shark plunges, he drew a hidden knife from his girdle and struck.

Stark had not counted on that. The slaves were searched for possible weapons every day, and even a sliver of stone was forbidden. Somebody must have given it to him, someone . . .

The thought flashed through his mind while he was in the very act of trying to avoid that death blow. *Too late, too late, because his own momentum carried him onto the point . . .*

Reflexes quicker than any man's, the hair-trigger reactions of a wild thing. Muscles straining, the centre of balance shifted with an awful wrenching effort, hands grasping at the fire-shot redness as though to force it to defy its own laws. The blade ripped a long shallow gash across his breast. But it did not go home. By a fraction of an inch, it did not go home.

While Stark was still off balance, Malthor sprang.

They grappled. The knife blade glittered redly, a hungry tongue eager to taste Stark's life. The two men rolled over and over, drifting and tumbling erratically, churning the sea to a froth of sparks, and still the image watched, its calm reptilian features unchangingly benign and wise. Threads of a darker red laced heavily across the dancing fires.

Stark got Malthor's arm under his own and held it there with both hands. His back was to the man now. Malthor kicked and clawed with his feet against the backs of Stark's thighs, and his left arm came up and tried to clamp around Stark's throat. Stark buried his chin so that it could not, and then Malthor's hand began to tear at Stark's face, searching for his eyes.

Stark voiced a deep bestial sound in his throat. He moved his head suddenly, catching Malthor's hand between his jaws. He did not let go. Presently his teeth were locked against the thumb-joint, and Malthor was screaming, but Stark could give all his attention to what he was doing with the arm that held the knife. His eyes had changed. They were all beast now, the eyes of a killer blazing cold and beautiful in his dark face.

There as a dull crack, and the arm ceased to strain or fight. It bent back upon itself, and the knife fell, drifting quietly down. Malthor was beyond screaming now. He made one effort to get away as Stark released him, but it was a futile gesture, and he made no sound as Stark broke his neck.

He thrust the body from him. It drifted away, moving lazily with the suck of the currents through the colonnade, now and again touching a black pillar as though in casual wonder, wandering out at last into the square. Malthor was in no hurry. He had all eternity before him.

Stark moved carefully away from the girl, who was trying feebly now to sit up on the knees of the image. He called out, to some unseen presence hidden in the shadows under the roof,

"Malthor screamed your name, Egil. Why didn't you come?"

There was a flicker of movement in the intense darkness of the ledge at the top of the pillars.

"Why should I?" asked the Lord Egil of the Lhari. "I offered him his freedom if he could kill you, but it seems he could not—even though I gave him a knife, and drugs to keep your friend Helvi out of the way."

He came out where Stark could see him, very handsome in a tunic of yellow silk, the blunt black weapon in his hands.

"The important thing was to bait a trap. You would not face me because of this—" He raised the weapon. "I might have killed you as you worked, of course, but my family would have had hard things to say about that. You're a phenomenally good slave."

"They'd have said hard words like 'coward', Egil," Stark said softly. "And Varra would have set her bird at you in earnest."

Egil nodded. His lip curved cruelly. "Exactly. That amused you, didn't it? And now my little cousin is training another falcon to swoop at me. She hooded you today, didn't she, Outlander?"

He laughed. "Ah well. I didn't kill you openly because there's a better way. Do you think I want it gossiped all over the Red Sea that my cousin jilted me for a foreign slave? Do you think I wish it known that I hated you, and why? No. I would have killed Malthor anyway, if you hadn't done it, because he knew. And when I have killed you and the girl I shall take your bodies to the barrier and leave them there together, and it will be obvious to everyone, even Varra, that you were killed trying to escape."

The weapon's muzzle pointed straight at Stark, and Egil's finger quivered on the trigger stud. Full power, this time. Instead of paralysis, death. Stark measured the distance between himself and Egil. He would be dead before he struck, but the impetus of his leap might carry him on, and give Zareth a chance to escape. The muscles of his thighs stirred and tensed.

A voice said, "And it will be obvious how and why *I* died, Egil? For if you kill them, you must kill me too."

Where Treon had come from, or when, Stark did not know. But he was there by the image, and his voice was full of a strong music, and his eyes shone with a fey light.

Egil had started, and now he swore in fury. "You idiot! You twisted freak! How did you come here?"

"How does the wind come, and the rain? I am not as other men." He laughed, a sombre sound with no mirth in it. "I am here, Egil, and that's all that matters. And you will not slay this stranger who is more beast than man, and more man than any of us. The gods have a use for him."

He had moved as he spoke, until now he stood between Stark and Egil.

"Get out of the way," said Egil.

Treon shook his head.

"Very well," said Egil. "If you wish to die, you may."

The fey gleam brightened in Treon's eyes. "This is a day of death," he said softly, "but not of his, or mine."

Egil said a short, ugly word, and raised the weapon up.

Things happened very quickly after that. Stark sprang, arching up and over Treon's head, cleaving the red gasses like a burning arrow. Egil started back, and shifted his aim upward, and his finger snapped down on the trigger stud.

Something white came between Stark and Egil, and took the force of the bolt.

Something white. A girl's body, crowned with streaming hair, and a collar of metal glowing bright around the slender neck.

Zareth.

They had forgotten her, the beaten child crouched on the knees of the image. Stark had moved to keep her out of danger, and she was no threat to the mighty Egil, and Treon's thoughts were known only to himself and the winds that taught him. Unnoticed, she had crept to a place where one last plunge would place her between Stark and death.

The rush of Stark's going took him on over her, except that her hair brushed softly against his skin. Then he was on top of Egil, and it had all been done so swiftly that the Lord of the Lhari had not had time to loose another bolt.

Stark tore the weapon from Egil's hand. He was cold, icy cold, and there was a strange blindness on him, so that he could see nothing clearly but Egil's face. And it was Stark who screamed this time, a dreadful sound like the cry of a great cat gone beyond reason or fear.

Treon stood watching. He watched the blood stream darkly into the sea, and he listened to the silence come, and he saw the thing that had been his cousin drift away on the slow tide, and it was as though he had seen it all before and was not surprised.

Stark went to Zareth's body. The girl was still breathing, very faintly, and her eyes turned to Stark, and she smiled.

Stark was blind now with tears. All his rage had run out of him with Egil's blood, leaving nothing but an aching pity and a sadness, and a wondering awe. He took Zareth very tenderly into his arms and held her, dumbly, watching the tears fall on her upturned face. And presently he knew that she was dead.

Sometime later Treon came to him and said softly, "To this end she was born, and she knew it, and was happy. Even now she smiles. And she should, for she had a better death than most of us." He laid his hand on Stark's shoulder. "Come, I'll show you where to put her. She will be safe there, and tomorrow you can bury her where she would wish to be."

Stark rose and followed him, bearing Zareth in his arms.

Treon went to the pedestal on which the image sat. He pressed in a certain way upon a series of hidden springs, and a section of the paving slid noiselessly back, revealing stone steps leading down.

X

Treon led the way down, into darkness that was lightened only by the dim fires they themselves woke in passing. No currents ran here. The red gas lay dull and stagnant, closed within the walls of a square passage built of the same black stone.

"These are the crypts," he said. "The labyrinth that is shown on the chart my father found." And he told about the chart, as Varra had.

He led the way surely, his misshapen body moving without hesitation past the mouths of branching corridors and the doors of chambers whose interiors were lost in shadow.

"The history of the city is here. All the books and the learning, that they had not the heart to destroy. There are no weapons. They were not a warlike people, and I think that the force we of the Lhari have used differently was defensive only, protection against the beasts and the raiding primitives of the swamps."

With a great effort, Stark wrenched his thoughts away from the light burden he carried.

"I thought," he said dully, "that the crypts were under the wrecked building."

"So we all thought. We were intended to think so. That is why the building was wrecked. And for sixteen years we of the Lhari have killed men and women with dragging the stones of it away. But the temple was shown also in the chart. We thought it was there merely as a landmark, an identification for the great building. But I began to wonder . . ."

"How long have you known?"

"Not long. Perhaps two rains. It took many seasons to find the secret of this passage. I came here at night, when the others slept."

"And you didn't tell?"

"No!" said Treon. "You are thinking that if I had told, there would have been an end to the slavery and the death. But what then? My family, turned loose with the power to destroy a world, as this city was destroyed? No! It was better for the slaves to die."

He motioned Stark aside, then, between doors of gold that stood ajar, into a vault so great that there was no guessing its size in the red and shrouding gloom.

"This was the burial place of their kings," said Treon softly. "Leave the little one here."

Stark looked around him, still too numb to feel awe, but impressed even so.

They were set in straight lines, the beds of black marble—lines so long that there was no end to them except the limit of vision. And on them slept the old kings, their bodies, marvlously embalmed, covered with silken palls, their hands crossed upon their breasts, their wise unhuman faces stamped with the mark of peace.

Very gently, Stark laid Zareth down on a marble couch, and covered her also with silk, and closed her eyes and folded her hands. And it seemed to him that her face, too, had that look of peace.

He went out with Treon, thinking that none of them had earned a better place in the hall of kings than Zareth.

"Treon," he said.

"Yes?"

"That prophecy you spoke when I came to the castle—I will bear it out."

Treon nodded. "That is the way of prophecies."

He did not return toward the temple, but led the way deeper into the heart of the catacombs. A great excitement burned within him, a bright and terrible thing that communicated itself to Stark. Treon had suddenly taken on the stature of a figure of destiny, and the Earthman had the feeling that he was in the grip of some current that would plunge on irresistibly until everything in its path was swept away. Stark's flesh quivered.

They reached the end of the corridor at last. And there, in the red gloom, a shape sat waiting before a black, barred door. A shape grotesque and incredibly misshapen, so horribly malformed that by it Treon's crippled body appeared almost beautiful. Yet its face was as the faces of the images and the old kings, and its sunken eyes had once held wisdom, and one of its seven-fingered hands was still slim and sensitive.

Stark recoiled. The thing made him physically sick, and he would have turned away, but Treon urged him on.

"Go closer. It is dead, embalmed, but it has a message for you. It has waited all this time to give that message."

Reluctantly, Stark went forward.

Quite suddenly, it seemed that the thing spoke.

Behold me. Look upon me, and take counsel before you grasp that power which lies beyond the door!

Stark leaped back, crying out, and Treon smiled.

"It was so with me. But I have listened to it many times since then. It speaks not with a voice, but within the mind, and only when one has passed a certain spot."

Stark's reasoning mind pondered over that. A thought-record, obviously, triggered off by an electronic beam. The ancients had taken good care that their warning would be heard and understood by anyone who should solve the riddle of the catacombs. Thought-images, speaking directly to the brain, know no barrier of time or language.

He stepped forward again, and once more the telepathic voice spoke to him.

"We tampered with the secrets of the gods. We intended no evil. It was only that we love perfection, and wished to shape all living things as flawless as our buildings and our gardens. We did not know that it was against the Law . . .

"I was one of those who found the way to change the living cell. We used the unseen force that comes from the Land of the Gods beyond the sky, and we so harnessed it that we could build from the living flesh as the potter builds from the clay. We healed the halt and the maimed, and made those stand tall and straight who came crooked from the egg, and for a time we were as brothers to the gods themselves. I myself, even I, knew the glory of perfection. And then came the reckoning.

"The cell, once made to change, would not stop changing. The growth was slow, and for a while we did not notice it, but when we did it was too late. We were becoming a city of monsters. And the force we had used was worse than useless, for the more we tried to mould the monstrous flesh to its normal shape, the more the stimulated cells grew and grew, until the bodies we laboured over were like things of wet mud that flow and change even as you look at them.

"One by one the people of the city destroyed themselves. And those of us who were left realized the judgment of the gods, and our duty. We made all things ready, and let the Red Sea hide us forever from our own kind, and those who should come after.

"Yet we did not destroy our knowledge. Perhaps it was our pride only that forbade us, but we could not bring ourselves to do it. Perhaps other gods, other races wiser than we, can take away the evil and keep only the good. For it is good for all creatures to be, if not perfect, at least strong and sound.

"But heed this warning, whoever you may be that listen. If your gods are jealous, if your people have not the wisdom or the knowledge to succeed where we failed in controlling this force, then touch it not! Or you, and all your people, will become as I."

The voice stopped. Stark moved back again, and said to Treon incredulously, "And your family would ignore that warning?"

Treon laughed. "They are fools. They are cruel and greedy and very proud. They would say that this was a lie to frighten away intruders, or that human flesh would not be subject to the laws that govern the flesh of reptiles. They would say anything, because they have dreamed this dream too long to be denied."

Stark shuddered and looked at the black door. "The thing ought to be destroyed."

"Yes," said Treon softly.

His eyes were shining, looking into some private dream of his own. He started forward, and when Stark would have gone with him he thrust him back, saying, "No. You have no part in this." He shook his head.

"I have waited," he whispered, almost to himself. "The winds bade me wait, until the day was ripe to fall from the tree of death. I have waited, and at dawn I knew, for the wind said, *Now is the gathering of the fruit at hand.*"

He looked suddenly at Stark, and his eyes had in them a clear sanity, for all their feyness.

"You heard, Stark. 'We made those stand tall and straight who came crooked from the egg.' I will have my hour. I will stand as a man for the little time that is left."

He turned, and Stark made no move to follow. He watched Treon's twisted body recede, white against the red dusk, until it passed the monstrous watcher and came to the black door. The long thin arms reached up and pushed the bar away.

The door swung slowly back. Through the opening Stark glimpsed a chamber that held a structure of crystal rods and discs mounted on a frame of metal, the whole thing glowing and glittering with a restless bluish light that dimmed and brightened as though it echoed some vast pulse-beat. There was other apparatus, intricate banks of tubes and condensers, but this was the heart of it, and the heart was still alive.

Treon passed within and closed the door behind him.

Stark drew back some distance from the door and its guardian, crouched down, and set his back against the wall. He thought about the apparatus. Cosmic rays, perhaps—the unseen force that came from beyond the sky. Even yet, all their potentialities were not known. But a few luckless spacemen had found that under certain conditions they could do amazing things to human tissue.

It was a line of thought Stark did not like at all. He tried to keep his mind away from Treon entirely. He tried not to think at all. It was dark there in the corridor, and very still, and the shapeless horror sat quiet in the doorway and waited with him. Stark began to shiver, a shallow animal-twitching of the flesh.

He waited. After a while he thought Treon must be dead, but he did not move. He did not wish to go into that room to see.

He waited.

Suddenly he leaped up, cold sweat bursting out all over him. A crash had echoed down the corridor, a clashing of shattered crystal and a high singing note that trailed off into nothing.

The door opened.

A man came out. A man tall and straight and beautiful as an angel, a strong-limbed man with Treon's face, Treon's tragic eyes. And behind him the chamber was dark. The pulsing heart of power had stopped.

The door was shut and barred again. Treon's voice was saying, "There are records left, and much of the apparatus, so that the secret is not lost entirely. Only it is out of reach."

He came to Stark and held out his hand. "Let us fight together, as men. And do not fear. I shall die, long before this body changes." He smiled, the remembered smile that was full of pity for all living things. "I know, for the winds have told me."

Stark took his hand and held it.

"Good," said Treon. "And now lead on, stranger with the fierce eyes. For the prophecy is yours, and the day is yours, and I who have crept about like a snail all my life know little of battles. Lead, and I will follow."

Stark fingered the collar around his neck. "Can you rid me of this?"

Treon nodded. "There are tools and acid in one of the chambers."

He found them, and worked swiftly, and while he worked Stark thought, smiling—and there was no pity in that smile at all.

They came back at last into the temple, and Treon closed the entrance to the catacombs. It was still night, for the square was empty of slaves. Stark found Egil's weapon where it had fallen, on the ledge where Egil died.

"We must hurry," said Stark. "Come on."

XI

The island was shrouded heavily in mist and the blue darkness of the night. Stark and Treon crept silently among the rocks until they could see the glimmer of torchlight through the window-slits of the power station.

There were seven guards, five inside the blockhouse, two outside to patrol.

When they were close enough, Stark slipped away, going like a shadow, and never a pebble turned under his bare foot. Presently he found a spot to his liking and crouched down. A sentry went by not three feet away, yawning and looking hopefully at the sky for the first signs of dawn.

Treon's voice rang out, the sweet unmistakable voice. "Ho, there, guards!"

The sentry stopped and whirled around. Off around the curve of the stone wall someone began to run, his sandals thud-thudding on the soft ground, and the second guard came up.

"Who speaks?" one demanded. "The Lord Treon?"

They peered into the darkness, and Treon answered, "Yes." He had come forward far enough so that they could make out the pale blur of his face, keeping his body out of sight among the rocks and the shrubs that sprang up between them.

"Make haste," he ordered. "Bid them open the door, there." He spoke in breathless jerks, as though spent. "A tragedy—a disaster! Bid them open!"

One of the men leaped to obey, hammering on the massive door that was kept barred from the inside. The other stood goggle-eyed, watching. Then the door opened, spilling a flood of yellow torch-light into the red fog.

"What is it?" cried the men inside. "What has happened?"

"Come out!" gasped Treon. "My cousin is dead, the Lord Egil is dead, murdered by a slave."

He let that sink in. Three or more men came outside into the circle of light, and their faces were frightened, as though somehow they feared they might be held responsible for this thing.

"You know him," said Treon. "The great black-haired one from Earth. He has slain the Lord Egil and got away into the forest, and we need all extra guards to go after him, since many must be left to guard the other slaves, who are mutinous. You, and you—" He picked out the four biggest ones. "Go at once and join the search. I will stay here with the others."

It nearly worked. The four took a hesitant step or two, and then one paused and said doubtfully.

"But, my lord, it is forbidden that we leave our posts, for any reason. Any reason at all, my lord! The Lord Cond would slay us if we left this place."

"And you fear the Lord Cond more than you do me," said Treon philosophically. "Ah, well. I understand."

He stepped out, full into the light.

A gasp went up, and then a startled yell. The three men from inside had come out armed only with swords, but the two sentries had their shock-weapons. One of them shrieked,

"It is a demon, who speaks with Treon's voice!"

And the two black weapons started up.

Behind them, Stark fired two silent bolts in quick succession, and the men fell, safely out of the way for hours. Then he leaped for the door.

He collided with two men who were doing the same thing. The third had turned to hold Treon off with his sword until they were safely inside.

Seeing that Treon, who was unarmed, was in danger of being spitted on the man's point, Stark fired between the two lunging bodies as he fell, and brought the guard down. Then he was involved in a thrashing tangle of arms and legs, and a lucky blow jarred the shock-weapon out of his hand.

Treon added himself to the fray. Pleasuring in his new strength, he caught one man by the neck and pulled him off. The guards were big men, and powerful, and they fought desperately. Stark was bruised and bleeding from a cut mouth before he could get in a finishing blow.

Someone rushed past him into the doorway. Treon yelled. Out of the tail of his eyes Stark saw the Lhari sitting dazed on the ground. The door was closing.

Stark hunched up his shoulders and sprang.

He hit the heavy panel with a jar that nearly knocked him breathless. It slammed open, and there was a cry of pain and the sound of someone falling. Stark burst through, to find the last of the guards rolling every which way over the floor. But one rolled over onto his feet again, drawing his sword as he rose. He had not had time before.

Stark continued his rush without stopping. He plunged headlong into the man before the point was clear of the scabbard, bore him over and down, and finished the man off with savage efficiency.

He leaped to his feet, breathing hard, spitting blood out of his mouth, and looked around the control room. But the others had fled, obviously to raise the warning.

The mechanism was simple. It was contained in a large black metal oblong about the size and shape of a coffin, equipped with grids and lenses and dials. It hummed softly to itself, but what its source of power was Stark did not know. Perhaps those same cosmic rays, harnessed to a different use.

He closed what seemed to be a master switch, and the humming stopped, and the flickering light died out of the lenses. He picked up the slain guard's sword and carefully wrecked everything that was breakable. Then he went outside again.

Treon was standing up, shaking his head. He smiled ruefully.

"It seems that strength alone is not enough," he said. "One must have skill as well."

"The barriers are down," said Stark. "The way is clear."

Treon nodded, and went with him back into the sea. This time both carried shock weapons taken from the guards—six in all, with Egil's. Total armament for war.

As they forged swiftly through the red depths, Stark asked, "What of the people of Shuruun? How will they fight?"

Treon answered, "Those of Malthor's breed will stand for the Lhari. They must, for all their hope is there. The others will wait, until they see which side is safest. They would rise against the Lhari if they dared, for we have brought them only fear in their lifetimes. But they will wait, and see."

Stark nodded. He did not speak again.

They passed over the brooding city, and Stark thought of Egil and of Malthor who were part of that silence now, drifting slowly through the empty streets where the little currents took them, wrapped in their shrouds of dim fire.

He thought of Zareth sleeping in the hall of kings, and his eyes held a cold, cruel light.

They swooped down over the slave barracks. Treon remained on watch outside. Stark went in, taking with him the extra weapons.

The slaves still slept. Some of them dreamed, and moaned in their dreaming, and others might have been dead, with their hollow faces white as skulls.

Slaves. One hundred and four, counting the women.

Stark shouted out to them, and they woke, starting up on their pallets, their eyes full of terror. Then they saw who it was that called them, standing collarless and armed, and there was a great surging and a clamour that stilled as Stark shouted again, demanding silence. This time Helvi's voice echoed his. The tall barbarian had wakened from his drugged sleep.

Stark told them, very briefly, all that happened.

"You are freed from the collar," he said. "This day you can survive or die as men, and not slaves." He paused, then asked, "Who will go with me into Shuruun?"

They answered with one voice, the voice of the Lost Ones, who saw the red pall of death begin to lift from over them. The Lost Ones, who had found hope again.

Stark laughed. He was happy. He gave the extra weapons to Helvi and three others that he chose, and Helvi looked into his eyes and laughed too.

Treon spoke from the open door. "They are coming!"

Stark gave Helvi quick instructions and darted out, taking with him one of the other men. With Treon, they hid among the shrubbery of the garden that was outside the hall, patterned and beautiful, swaying its lifeless brilliance in the lazy drifts of fire.

The guards came. Twenty of them, tall armed men, to turn out the slaves for another period of labour, dragging the useless stones.

And the hidden weapons spoke with their silent tongues.

Eight of the guards fell inside the hall. Nine of them went down outside. Ten of the slaves died with blazing collars before the remaining three were overcome.

Now there were twenty swords among ninety-four slaves, counting the women.

They left the city and rose up over the dreaming forest, a flight of white ghosts with flames in their hair, coming back from the red dusk and the silence to find the light again.

Light, and vengeance.

The first pale glimmer of dawn was sifting through the clouds as they came up among the rocks below the castle of the Lhari. Stark left them and went like a shadow up the tumbled cliffs to where he had hidden his gun on the night he had first come to Shuruun. Nothing stirred. The fog lifted up from the sea like a vapour of blood, and the

face of Venus was still dark. Only the high clouds were touched with
pearl.

Stark returned to the others. He gave one of his shock-weapons to
a swamp-lander with a cold madness in his eyes. Then he spoke a few
final words to Helvi and went back with Treon under the surface of
the sea.

Treon led the way. He went along the face of the submerged cliff,
and presently he touched Stark's arm and pointed to where a round
mouth opened in the rock.

"It was made long ago," said Treon, "so that the Lhari and their
slavers might come and go and not be seen. Come—and be very quiet."

They swam into the tunnel mouth, and down the dark way that lay
beyond, until the lift of the floor brought them out of the sea. Then
they felt their way silently along, stopping now and again to listen.

Surprise was their only hope. Treon had said that with the two of
them they might succeed. More men would surely be discovered, and
meet a swift end at the hands of the guards.

Stark hoped Treon was right.

They came to a blank wall of dressed stone. Treon leaned his
weight against one side, and a great block swung slowly around on a
central pivot. Guttering torchlight came through the crack. By it Stark
could see that the room beyond was empty.

They stepped through, and as they did so a servant in bright silks
came yawning into the room with a fresh torch to replace the one that
was dying.

He stopped in mid-step, his eyes widening. He dropped the torch.
His mouth opened to shape a scream, but no sound came, and Stark
remembered that these servants were tongueless—to prevent them from
telling what they saw or heard in the castle, Treon said.

The man spun about and fled, down a long dim-lit hall. Stark ran
him down without effort. He struck once with the barrel of his gun,
and the man fell and was still.

Treon came up. His face had a look almost of exaltation, a queer
shining of the eyes that made Stark shiver. He led on, through a series
of empty rooms, all sombre black, and they met no one else for a
while.

He stopped at last before a small door of burnished gold. He looked
at Stark once, and nodded, and thrust the panels open and stepped
through.

XII

They stood inside the vast echoing hall that stretched away into darkness until it seemed there was no end to it. The cluster of silver lamps
burned as before, and within their circle of radiance the Lhari started
up from their places and stared at the strangers who had come in
through their private door.

Cond, and Arel with her hands idle in her lap. Bor, pummeling the little dragon to make it hiss and snap, laughing at its impotence. Varra, stroking the winged creature on her wrist, testing with her white finger the sharpness of its beak. And the old woman, with a scrap of fat meat halfway to her mouth.

They had stopped, frozen, in the midst of these actions. And Treon walked slowly into the light.

"Do you know me?" he said.

A strange shivering ran through them. Now, as before, the old woman spoke first, her eyes glittering with a look as rapacious as her appetite.

"You are Treon," she said, and her whole vast body shook.

The name went crying and whispering off around the dark walls, *Treon! Treon! Treon!* Cond leaped forward, touching his cousin's straight strong body with hands that trembled.

"You have found it," he said. "The secret."

"Yes." Treon lifted his silver head and laughed, a beautiful ringing bell-note that sang from the echoing corners. "I found it, and it's gone, smashed, beyond your reach forever. Egil is dead, and the day of the Lhari is done."

There was a long, long silence, and then the old woman whispered, *"You lie!"*

Treon turned to Stark.

"Ask him, the stranger who came bearing doom upon his forehead. Ask him if I lie."

Cond's face became something less than human. He made a queer crazed sound and flung himself at Treon's throat.

Bor screamed suddenly. He alone was not much concerned with the finding or the losing of the secret, and he alone seemed to realize the significance of Stark's presence. He screamed, looking at the big dark man, and went rushing off down the hall, crying for the guard as he went, and the echoes roared and racketed. He fought open the great doors and ran out, and as he did so the sound of fighting came through from the compound.

The slaves, with their swords and clubs, with their stones and shards of rock, had come over the wall from the cliffs.

Stark had moved forward, but Treon did not need his help. He had got his hands around Cond's throat, and he was smiling. Stark did not disturb him.

The old woman was talking, cursing, commanding, choking on her own apoplectic breath. Arel began to laugh. She did not move, and her hands remained limp and open in her lap. She laughed and laughed, and Varra looked at Stark and hated him.

"You're a fool, wild man," she said. "You would not take what I offered you, so you shall have nothing—only death."

She slipped the hood from her creature and set it straight at Stark. Then she drew a knife from her girdle and plunged it into Treon's side.

Treon reeled back. His grip loosened and Cond tore away, half throttled, raging, his mouth flecked with foam. He drew his short sword and staggered in upon Treon.

Furious wings beat and thundered around Stark's head, and talons were clawing for his eyes. He reached up with his left hand and caught the brute by one leg and held it. Not long, but long enough to get one clear shot at Cond that dropped him in his tracks. Then he snapped the falcon's neck.

He flung the creature at Varra's feet, and picked up the gun again. The guards were rushing into the hall now at the lower end, and he began to fire at them.

Treon was sitting on the floor. Blood was coming in a steady trickle from his side, but he had the shock-weapon in his hands, and he was still smiling.

There was a great boiling roar of noise from outside. Men were fighting there, dying, screaming their triumph or their pain. The echoes raged within the hall, and the noise of Stark's gun was a hissing thunder. The guards, armed only with swords, went down like ripe wheat before the sickle, but there were many of them, too many for Stark and Treon to hold for long.

The old woman shrieked and shrieked, and was suddenly still.

Helvi burst in through the press, with a knot of collared slaves. The fight dissolved into a whirling chaos. Stark threw his gun away. He was afraid now of hitting his own men. He caught up a sword from a fallen guard and began to hew his way to the barbarian.

Suddenly Treon cried his name. He leaped aside, away from the man he was fighting, and saw Varra fall with the dagger still in her hand. She had come up behind him to stab, and Treon had seen and pressed the trigger stud just in time.

For the first time, there were tears in Treon's eyes.

A sort of sickness came over Stark. There was something horrible in this spectacle of a family destroying itself. He was too much the savage to be sentimental over Varra, but all the same he could not bear to look at Treon for a while.

Presently he found himself back to back with Helvi, and as they swung their swords—the shock weapons had been discarded for the same reason as Stark's gun—Helvi panted.

"It has been a good fight, my brother! We cannot win, but we can have a good death, which is better than slavery!"

It looked as though Helvi was right. The slaves, unfortunately, weakened by their long confinement, worn out from overwork, were being beaten back. The tide turned, and Stark was swept with it out into the compound, fighting stubbornly.

The great gate stood open. Beyond it stood the people of Shuruun, watching, hanging back—as Treon had said, they would wait and see.

In the forefront, leaning on his stick, stood Larrabee the Earthman.

Stark cut his way free of the press. He leaped up onto the wall and stood there, breathing hard, sweating, bloody, with a dripping sword in his hand. He waved it, shouting down to the men of Shuruun.

"What are you waiting for, you scuts, you women? The Lhari are dead, the Lost Ones are freed—must we of Earth do all your work for you?"

And he looked straight at Larrabee.

Larrabee stared back, his dark suffering eyes full of a bitter mirth. "Oh, well," he said in English. "Why not?"

He threw back his head and laughed, and the bitterness was gone. He voiced a high, shrill rebel yell and lifted his stick like a cudgel, limping toward the gate, and the men of Shuruun gave tongue and followed him.

After that, it was soon over.

They found Bor's body in the stable pens, where he had fled to hide when the fighting started. The dragons, maddened by the smell of the blood, had slain him very quickly.

Helvi had come through alive, and Larrabee, who had kept himself carefully out of harm's way after he had started the men of Shuruun on their attack. Nearly half the slaves were dead, and the rest wounded. Of those who had served the Lhari, few were left.

Stark went back into the great hall. He walked slowly, for he was very weary, and where he set his foot there was a bloody print, and his arms were red to the elbows, and his breast was splashed with the redness. Treon watched him come, and smiled, nodding.

"It is as I said. And I have outlived them all."

Arel had stopped laughing at last. She had made no move to run away, and the tide of battle had rolled over her and drowned her unaware. The old woman lay still, a mountain of inert flesh upon her bed. Her hand still clutched a ripe fruit, clutched convulsively in the moment of death, the red juice dripping through her fingers.

"Now I am going, too," said Treon, "and I am well content. With me goes the last of our rotten blood, and Venus will be cleaner for it. Bury my body deep, stranger with the fierce eyes. I would not have it looked on after this."

He sighed and fell forward.

Bor's little dragon crept whimpering out from its hiding place under the old woman's bed and scurried away down the hall, trailing its dragging rope.

*   *   *

Stark leaned on the taffrail, watching the dark mass of Shuruun recede into the red mists.

The decks were crowded with the outland slaves, going home. The Lhari were gone, the Lost Ones freed forever, and Shuruun was now only another port on the Red Sea. Its people would still be wolf's-heads and pirates, but that was natural and as it should be. The black evil was gone.

Stark was glad to see the last of it. He would be glad also to see the last of the Red Sea.

The off-shore wind set the ship briskly down the gulf. Stark thought of Larrabee, left behind with his dreams of winter snows and city streets and women with dainty feet. It seemed that he had lived too long in Shuruun, and had lost the courage to leave it.

"Poor Larrabee," he said to Helvi, who was standing near him. "He'll die in the mud, still cursing it."

Someone laughed behind him. He heard a limping step on the deck and turned to see Larrabee coming toward him.

"Changed my mind at the last minute," Larrabee said. "I've been below, lest I should see my muddy brats and be tempted to change it again." He leaned beside Stark, shaking his head. "Ah, well, they'll do nicely without me. I'm an old man, and I've a right to choose my own place to die in. I'm going back to Earth, with you."

Stark glanced at him. "I'm not going to Earth."

Larrabee sighed. "No. No, I suppose you're not. After all, you're no Earthman, really, except for an accident of blood. Where are you going?"

"I don't know. Away from Venus, but I don't know yet where."

Larrabee's dark eyes surveyed him shrewdly. " 'A restless, cold-eyed tiger of a man,' that's what Varra said. He's lost something, she said. He'll look for it all his life, and never find it."

After that there was silence. The red fog wrapped them, and the wind rose and sent them scudding before it.

Then, faint and far off, there came a moaning wail, a sound like broken chanting that turned Stark's flesh cold.

All on board heard it. They listened, utterly silent, their eyes wide, and somewhere a woman began to weep.

Stark shook himself. "It's only the wind," he said roughly, "in the rocks by the strait."

The sound rose and fell, weary, infinitely mournful, and the part of Stark that was N'Chaka said that he lied. It was not the wind that keened so sadly through the mists. It was the voices of the Lost Ones who were forever lost—Zareth, sleeping in the hall of kings, and all the others who would never leave the dreaming city and the forest, never find light again.

Stark shivered, and turned away, watching the leaping fires of the strait sweep toward them.

Questions for Discussion and Review

1. What do we know, and what can we guess, about the old kings who once dwelt in the lost city?

2. Is there a special kind of license we as readers are expected to grant the author of space opera in creating effects and recounting actions? Apply your answer specifically to this story.

3. Stark (N'Chaka) comes from a long line of half-savage heroes. What is that tradition? Can you think of other examples of this type? How does Stark fit into that tradition?

4. In what way or ways is Stark supposed to be attractive and sympathetic?

5. How does the author portray the relationship of the sexes and their roles in this story?

6. We might describe this as a story of "awes and wonders" since the effects are so many and various. Compare and contrast two different kinds of awe or wonder and estimate their importance to this story.

Speculative Fantasy Science Fiction

The great difficulty in trying to define what "speculative fiction" means is that so many different types of literature seem to be marching under its banner. There must be something in it to have attracted so many followers. Just to confuse matters further, many New Wave writers have developed a proprietary interest in Heinlein's term and now prefer to call the SF they write by that name. (See especially Ellison's *Dangerous Visions* and *Again Dangerous Visions* and Spinrad's introduction to *Modern Science Fiction*.) The term has thus acquired an honorific connotation among some writers at least, and the traditional term "science fiction" has become in their lexicon a perjorative one for an old-fashioned, badly made product still reeking with suggestions of the pulps.

We may begin this brief inquiry into speculative fantasy SF by noting that speculative fiction really is, as the New Wave insists, a literature which may be thought of as distinct from SF. We may rightly claim that speculative fiction cuts across many generic boundaries, as indicated in this volume. Indeed, speculative writing need not be fiction in the literary sense at all. Historically, it has been allied with the science treatise since the ancients. Today, speculative models are often used as a way of presenting ideas in both hard and soft sciences. Such fictions share this common impulse with a broader experimental literature that includes both fictions and nonfictions. Speculative fictions set for themselves the task of trying to explain something or to test an idea by working out its implications. The stories in this section illustrate both these tendencies.

Speculative SF, therefore, is above all a literature of ideas. The author of a fantasy SF story may be as speculative as the writer of hard or soft SF. Speculative writing proposes theories, offering hypothetical explanations of things; and it reaches the outward limits of its powers as a form in the fantastic story, because in this realm speculation is no longer limited by the possible, only by the skill of the storyteller. The question for readers is not whether an event could happen but only whether it may seem to happen in the kind of imagined world the author gives. The writer asks us only to contemplate what may happen when the impossible becomes real. We may wonder about the implications for a scientific age when such visions become the shaping forces of the future.

Mars Is Heaven!

Ray Bradbury

Ray Bradbury was born in Waukegan, Illinois, on August 22, 1920. He spent his boyhood in the Midwest and moved to Los Angeles in 1934. As a youth, he joined the Los Angeles SF Society and resolved to be a writer. His early stories were featured in *Weird Tales, Unknown Worlds,* and *Planet Stories* in the 1940s. His first popular story, "The Million Year Picnic," appeared in *Planet Stories* (summer 1946). His novels include *Fahrenheit 451* (1953), and *Something Wicked This Way Comes* (1962). His forte is the short story, and his collections are among the most famous titles in modern literature. They include such works as *The Martian Chronicles* (1950), *The Illustrated Man* (1951), *The Golden Apples of the Sun* (1953), *The October Country* (1955), and *A Medicine for Melancholy* (1959). "Mars Is Heaven!" first appeared in *Planet Stories* (fall 1948).

This is one of the series of short stories published by Bradbury in the late 1940s that subsequently became part of *The Martian Chronicles* (1950) under the heading "April 2000: The Third Expedition." In this larger context it is a story of the psychological warfare waged by Martians against an invading party from Earth. The technique is simple: Create an illusion that will be effective in proportion to its desirability. Separate the members of the crew. Take them off guard. Kill them and destroy their rocket, leaving no trace behind. As the story dramatizes, the plan works, at least for the third expedition.

I used a passage from this story in the Introduction to illustrate imagined wonder—how it is generated, first in the story itself, and thereafter how it is experienced by readers. It is clear that the effectiveness of the Martian strategy depends on its ability to touch those complex, elemental emotions of the aliens from Earth. To do so is to absorb them cooperatively in the illusion, and once engaged, they will be too delighted at the fulfillment of an archetypal desire to be either critical or cautious. The Martian analysis of the vulnerability of *Homo sapiens* to the enchantment of nostalgia is a telling point in this story.

We should take note as well that *The Martian Chronicles* dramatizes the destruction of two civilizations. In the process of discovery, invasion, and colonization, humanity destroys the advanced and exquisite civilization of the Martians. An ape with a loaded machine gun, a human being has a potential for destructiveness limited only by the amount of ammunition available. And so, obsessed by technological power, but lacking the ethical maturity to use it creatively, humanity destroys both the native civilization of Mars and its own on Earth. Seen in this perspective, the title takes on an additional irony.

The ship came down from space. It came down from the stars and the black velocities, and the shining movements and the silent gulfs of space. It was a new ship, the only one of its kind, it had fire in its belly and men in its body, and it moved with clean silence, fiery and hot. In it were seventeen men, including a captain. A crowd had gathered at the New York tarmac and shouted and waved their hands up into the sunlight, and the rocket had jerked up, bloomed out great flowers of heat and color, and run away into space on the first voyage to Mars!

Now it was decelerating with metal efficiency in the upper zones of Martian atmosphere. It was still a thing of beauty and strength. It had shorn through meteor streams, it had moved in the majestic black midnight waters of space like a pale sea leviathan, it had passed the sickly, pocked mass of the ancient moon, and thrown itself onward into one nothingness following another. The men within it had been battered, thrown about, sickened, made well again, scarred, made pale, flushed, each in his turn. One man had died after a fall, but now, seventeen of the original eighteen with their eyes clear in their heads and their faces pressed to the thick glass ports of the rocket, were watching Mars swing up under them.

"Mars! Mars! Good old Mars, here we are!" cried Navigator Lustig.

"Good old Mars!" said Samuel Hinkston, archaeologist.

"Well," said Captain John Black.

The ship landed softly on a lawn of green grass. Outside, upon the lawn, stood an iron deer. Further up the lawn, a tall brown Victorian house sat in the quiet sunlight, all covered with scrolls and rococo, its windows made of blue and pink and yellow and green colored glass. Upon the porch were hairy geraniums and an old swing which was hooked into the porch ceiling and which now swung back and forth, back and forth, in a little breeze. At the top of the house was a cupola with diamond, leaded-glass windows, and a dunce-cap roof! Through the front window you could see an ancient piano with yellow keys and a piece of music titled *Beautiful Ohio* sitting on the music rest.

Around the rocket in four directions spread the little town, green and motionless in the Martian spring. There were white houses and red brick ones, and tall elm trees blowing in the wind, and tall maples and horse chestnuts. And church steeples with golden bells silent in them.

The men in the rocket looked out and saw this. Then they looked at one another and then they looked out again. They held on to each other's elbows, suddenly unable to breathe, it seemed. Their faces grew pale and they blinked constantly, running from glass port to glass port of the ship.

"I'll be damned," whispered Lustig, rubbing his face with his numb fingers, his eyes wet. "I'll be damned, damned, damned."

"It can't be, it just can't be," said Samuel Hinkston.

"Lord," said Captain John Black.

There was a call from the chemist. "Sir, the atmosphere is fine for breathing, sir."

Black turned slowly. "Are you sure?"

"No doubt of it, sir."

"Then we'll go out," said Lustig.

"Lord, yes," said Samuel Hinkston.

"Hold on," said Captain John Black. "Just a moment. Nobody gave any orders."

"But, sir—"

"Sir, nothing. How do we know what this is?"

"We know what it is, sir," said the chemist. "It's a small town with good air in it, sir."

"And it's a small town the like of Earth towns," said Samuel Hinkston, the archaeologist. "Incredible. It can't be, but it is."

Captain John Black looked at him, idly. "Do you think that the civilizations of two planets can progress at the same rate and evolve in the same way, Hinkston?"

"I wouldn't have thought so, sir."

Captain Black stood by the port. "Look out there. The geraniums. A specialized plant. That specific variety has only been known on Earth for fifty years. Think of the thousands of years of time it takes to evolve plants. Then tell me if it is logical that the Martians should have: one, leaded glass windows; two, cupolas; three, porch swings; four, an instrument that looks like a piano and probably is a piano; and, five, if you look closely, if a Martian composer would have published a piece of music titled, strangely enough, *Beautiful Ohio*. All of which means that we have an Ohio River here on Mars!"

"It is quite strange, sir."

"Strange, hell, it's absolutely impossible, and I suspect the whole bloody shooting setup. Something's wrong here, and I'm not leaving the ship until I know what it is."

"Oh, sir," said Lustig.

"Darn it," said Samuel Hinkston. "Sir, I want to investigate this at first hand. It may be that there are similar patterns of thought, movement, civilization on *every* planet in our system. We may be on the threshold of the great psychological and metaphysical discovery in our time, sir, don't you think?"

"I'm willing to wait a moment," said Captain John Black.

"It may be, sir, that we are looking upon a phenomenon that, for the first time, would absolutely prove the existence of a God, sir."

"There are many people who are of good faith without such proof, Mr. Hinkston."

"I'm one myself, sir. But certainly a thing like this, out there," said Hinkston, "could not occur without divine intervention, sir. It fills me with such terror and elation I don't know whether to laugh or cry, sir."

"Do neither, then, until we know what we're up against."

"Up against, sir?" inquired Lustig. "I see that we're up against nothing. It's a good quiet, green town, much like the one I was born in, and I like the looks of it."

"When were you born, Lustig."

"In 1910, sir."

"That makes you fifty years old, now, doesn't it?"

"This being 1960, yes, sir."

"And you, Hinkston?"

"1920, sir. In Illinois. And this looks swell to me, sir."

"This couldn't be Heaven," said the captain, ironically. "Though, I must admit, it looks peaceful and cool, and pretty much like Green Bluff, where I was born, in 1915." He looked at the chemist. "The air's all right, is it?"

"Yes, sir."

"Well, then, tell you what we'll do. Lustig, you and Hinkston and I will fetch ourselves out to look this town over. The other 14 men will stay aboard ship. If anything untoward happens, lift the ship and get the hell out, do you hear what I say, Craner?"

"Yes, sir. The hell out we'll go, sir. Leaving *you*?"

"A loss of three men's better than a whole ship. If something bad happens get back to Earth and warn the next Rocket, that's Lingle's Rocket, I think, which will be completed and ready to take off some time around next Christmas, what he has to meet up with. If there's something hostile about Mars we certainly want the next expedition to be well armed."

"So are we, sir. We've got a regular arsenal with us."

"Tell the men to stand by the guns, then, as Lustig and Hinkston and I go out."

"Right, sir."

"Come along, Lustig, Hinkston."

The three men walked together, down through the levels of the ship.

It was a beautiful spring day. A robin sat on a blossoming apple tree and sang continuously. Showers of petal snow sifted down when the wind touched the apple tree, and the blossom smell drifted upon the air. Somewhere in the town, somebody was playing the piano and the music came and went, came and went, softly, drowsily. The song was *Beautiful Dreamer*. Somewhere else, a phonograph, scratchy and faded, was hissing out a record of *Roamin' In The Gloamin,'* sung by Harry Lauder.

The three men stood outside the ship. The port closed behind them. At every window, a faced pressed looking out. The large metal guns pointed this way and that, ready.

Now the phonograph record being played was:

"Oh give me a June night
The moonlight and you—"

Lustig began to tremble. Samuel Hinkston did likewise.

Hinkston's voice was so feeble and uneven that the captain had to ask him to repeat what he had said. "I said, sir, that I think I have solved this, all of this, sir!"

"And what is the solution, Hinkston?"

The soft wind blew. The sky was serene and quiet and somewhere a stream of water ran through the cool caverns and tree-shadings of a ravine. Somewhere a horse and wagon trotted and rolled by, bumping.

"Sir, it must be, it has to be, this is the *only* solution! Rocket travel began to Mars in the years before the first World War, sir!"

The captain stared at his archaeologist. "No!"

"But, yes, sir! You must admit, look at all of this! How else explain it, the houses, the lawns, the iron deer, the flowers, the pianos, the music!"

"Hinkston, Hinkston, oh," and the captain put his hand to his face, shaking his head, his hand shaking now, his lips blue.

"Sir, listen to me." Hinkston took his elbow persuasively and looked up into the captain's face, pleading. "Say that there were some people in the year 1905, perhaps, who hated wars and wanted to get away from Earth and they got together, some scientists, in secret, and built a rocket and came out here to Mars."

"No, no, Hinkston."

"Why not? The world was a different place in 1905, they could have kept it a secret much more easily."

"But the work, Hinkston, the work of building a complex thing like a rocket, oh, no, no." The captain looked at his shoes, looked at his hands, looked at the houses, and then at Hinkston.

"And they came up here, and naturally the houses they built were similar to Earth houses because they brought the cultural architecture with them, and here it is!"

"And they've lived here all these years?" said the captain.

"In peace and quiet, sir, yes. Maybe they made a few trips, to bring enough people here for one small town, and then stopped, for fear of being discovered. That's why the town seems so old-fashioned. I don't see a thing, myself, that is older than the year 1927, do you?"

"No, frankly, I don't, Hinkston."

"These are *our* people, sir. This is an American city; it's definitely not European!"

"That—that's right, too, Hinkston."

"Or maybe, just maybe, sir, rocket travel is older than we think. Perhaps it started in some part of the world hundreds of years ago, was discovered and kept secret by a small number of men, and they came to Mars, with only occasional visits to Earth over the centuries."

"You make it sound almost reasonable."

"It is, sir. It has to be. We have the proof here before us, all we have to do now, is find some people and verify it!"

"You're right there, of course. We can't just stand here and talk. Did you bring your gun?"

"Yes, but we won't need it."

"We'll see about it. Come along, we'll ring that doorbell and see if anyone is home."

Their boots were deadened of all sound in the thick green grass. It smelled from a fresh mowing. In spite of himself, Captain John Black felt a great peace come over him. It had been thirty years since he had been in a small town, and the buzzing of spring bees on the air lulled and quieted him, and the fresh look of things was a balm to the soul.

Hollow echoes sounded from under the boards as they walked across the porch and stood before the screen door. Inside, they could see a bead curtain hung across the hall entry, and a crystal chandelier and a Maxfield Parrish painting framed on one wall over a comfortable Morris Chair. The house smelled old, and of the attic, and infinitely comfortable. You could hear the tinkle of ice rattling in a lemonade pitcher. In a distant kitchen, because of the heat of the day, someone was preparing a soft, lemon drink.

Captain John Black rang the bell.

Footsteps, dainty and thin, came along the hall and a kind faced lady of some forty years, dressed in the sort of dress you might expect in the year 1909, peered out at them.

"Can I help you?" she asked.

"Beg your pardon," said Captain Black, uncertainly. "But we're looking for, that is, could you help us, I mean." He stopped. She looked out at him with dark wondering eyes.

"If you're selling something," she said. "I'm much too busy and I haven't time." She turned to go.

"No, *wait*," he cried, bewilderedly. "What town is this?"

She looked him up and down as if he were crazy. "What do you mean, what town is it? How could you be in a town and not know what town it was?"

The captain looked as if he wanted to go sit under a shady apple tree. "I beg your pardon," he said. "But we're strangers here. We're from Earth, and we want to know how this town got here and you got here."

"Are you census takers?" she asked.

"No," he said.

"What do you want then?" she demanded.

"Well," said the captain.

"Well?" she asked.

"How long has this town been here?" he wondered.

"It was built in 1868," she snapped at them. "Is this a game?"

"No, not a game," cried the captain. "Oh, God," he said. "Look here. We're from Earth!"

"From *where*?" she said.

"From Earth!" he said.

"Where's that?" she said.

"From Earth," he cried.

"Out of the ground, do you mean?"

"No, from the planet Earth!" he almost shouted. "Here," he insisted, "come out on the porch and I'll show you."

"No," she said, "I won't come out there, you are all evidently quite mad from the sun."

Lustig and Hinkston stood behind the captain. Hinkston now spoke up. "Mrs.," he said "We came in a flying ship across space, among the stars. We came from the third planet from the sun, Earth, to this planet, which is Mars. *Now* do you understand, Mrs.?"

"Mad from the sun," she said, taking hold of the door. "Go away now, before I call my husband who's upstairs taking a nap, and he'll beat you all with his fists."

"But—" said Hinkston. "This is Mars, is it not?"

"This," explained the woman, as if she were addressing a child, "is Green Lake, Wisconsin, on the continent of America, surrounded by the Pacific and Atlantic Oceans, on a place called the world, or sometimes, the Earth. Go away now. Good-bye!"

She slammed the door.

The three men stood before the door with their hands up in the air toward it, as if pleading with her to open it once more.

They looked at one another.

"Let's knock the door down," said Lustig.

"We can't," sighed the captain.

"Why not?"

"She didn't do anything bad, did she? We're the strangers here. This is private property. Good God, Hinkston!" He went and sat down on the porchstep.

"What, sir?"

"Did it ever strike you, that maybe we got ourselves, somehow, some way, fouled up. And, by accident, came back and landed on Earth!"

"Oh, sir, oh, sir, oh oh, sir." And Hinkston sat down numbly and thought about it.

Lustig stood up in the sunlight. "How could we have done that?"

"I don't know, just let me think."

Hinkston said, "But we checked every mile of the way, and we saw Mars and our chronometers said so many miles gone, and we went past the moon and out into space and here we are, on Mars. I'm sure we're on Mars, sir."

Lustig said, "But, suppose, just suppose that, by accident, in space, in time, or something, we landed on a planet in space, in another time. Suppose this is Earth, thirty or fifty years ago? Maybe we got lost in the dimensions, do you think?"

"Oh, go away, Lustig."

"Are the men in the ship keeping an eye on us, Hinkston?"

"At their guns, sir."

Lustig went to the door, rang the bell. When the door opened again, he asked, "What year is this?"

"1926, of course!" cried the woman, furiously, and slammed the door again.

"Did you hear that?" Lustig ran back to them, wildly. "She said 1926! We *have* gone back in time! This *is* Earth!"

Lustig sat down and the three men let the wonder and terror of the thought afflict them. Their hands stirred fitfully on their knees. The wind blew, nodding the locks of hair on their heads.

The captain stood up, brushing off his pants. "I never thought it would be like this. It scares the hell out of me. How can a thing like this happen?"

"Will anybody in the whole town believe us?" wondered Hinkston. "Are we playing around with something dangerous? Time, I mean. Shouldn't we just take off and go home?"

"No. We'll try another house."

They walked three houses down to a little white cottage under an oak tree. "I like to be as logical as I can get," said the captain. He nodded at the town. "How does this sound to you, Hinkston? Suppose, as you said originally, that rocket travel occurred years ago. And when the Earth people had lived here a number of years they began to get homesick for Earth. First a mild neurosis about it, then a full-fledged psychosis. Then, threatened insanity. What would you do, as a psychiatrist, if faced with such a problem?"

Hinkston thought. "Well, I think I'd rearrange the civilization on Mars so it resembled Earth more and more each day. If there was any way of reproducing every plant, every road and every lake, and even an ocean, I would do so. Then I would, by some vast crowd hypnosis, theoretically anyway, convince everyone in a town this size that this really *was* Earth, not Mars at all."

"Good enough, Hinkston. I think we're on the right track now. That woman in that house back there, just *thinks* she's living on Earth. It protects her sanity. She and all the others in this town are the patients of the greatest experiment in migration and hypnosis you will ever lay your eyes on in your life."

"That's it, sir!" cried Lustig.

"Well," the captain sighed. "Now we're getting somewhere. I feel better. It all sounds a bit more logical now. This talk about time and going back and forth and traveling in time turns my stomach upside down. But, *this* way—" He actually smiled for the first time in a month. "Well. It looks as if we'll be fairly welcome here."

"Or, will we, sir?" said Lustig. "After all, like the Pilgrims, these people came here to escape Earth. Maybe they won't be too happy to see us, sir. Maybe they'll try to drive us out or kill us?"

"We have superior weapons if that should happen. Anyway, all we can do is try. This next house now. Up we go."

But they had hardly crossed the lawn when Lustig stopped and looked off across the town, down the quiet, dreaming afternoon street. "Sir," he said.

"What is it, Lustig," asked the captain.

"Oh, sir, *sir,* what I see, what I do see now before me, oh, oh—" said Lustig, and he began to cry. His fingers came up twisting and trembling, and his face was all wonder and joy and incredulity. He sounded as if any moment he might go quite insane with happiness. He looked down the street and he began to run, stumbling, awkwardly, falling, picking himself up, and running on. "Oh, God, God, thank you, God! Thank you!"

"Don't let him get away!" The captain broke into a run.

Now Lustig was running at full speed, shouting. He turned into a yard half way down the little shady side street and leaped up upon the porch of a large green house with an iron rooster on the roof.

He was beating upon the door, shouting and hollering and crying when Hinkston and the captain ran up and stood in the yard.

The door opened. Lustig yanked the screen wide and in a high wail of discovery and happiness, cried out, "Grandma! Grandpa!"

Two old people stood in the doorway, their faces lighting up.

"Albert!" Their voices piped and they rushed out to embrace and pat him on the back and move around him. "Albert, oh, Albert, it's been so many years! How you've grown, boy, how big you are, oh, Albert boy, how are you!"

"Grandma, Grandpa!" sobbed Albert Lustig. "Good to see you! You look fine, fine!" He held them, turned them, kissed them, hugged them, cried on them, held them out again, blinked at the little old people. The sun was in the sky, the wind blew, the grass was green, the screen door stood open.

"Come in, lad, come in, there's lemonade for you, fresh, lots of it!"

"Grandma, Grandpa, good to see you! I've got friends down here! Here!" Lustig turned and waved wildly at the captain and Hinkston, who, all during the adventure on the porch, had stood in the shade of a tree, holding onto each other. "Captain, captain, come up, come up, I want you to meet my grandfolks!"

"Howdy," said the folks. "Any friend of Albert's is ours, too! Don't stand there with your mouths open! Come on!"

In the living room of the old house it was cool and a grandfather clock ticked high and long and bronzed in one corner. There were soft pillows on large couches and walls filled with books and a rug cut in a thick rose pattern and antimacassars pinned to furniture, and lemonade in the hand, and cool on the thirsty tongue.

"Here's to our health." Grandma tipped her glass to her porcelain teeth.

"How long you *been* here, Grandma?" said Lustig.

"A good many years," she said, tartly. "Ever since we died."

"Ever since you what?" asked Captain John Black, putting his drink down.

"Oh, yes," Lustig looked at his captain. "They've been dead thirty years."

"And you *sit* there, calmly!" cried the captain.

"Tush," said the old woman, and winked glitteringly at John Black. "Who are we to question what happens? Here we are. What's life, anyways? Who does what for why and where? All we know is here we are, alive again, and no questions asked. A second chance." She toddled over and held out her thin wrist to Captain John Black. "Feel." He felt. "Solid, ain't I?" she asked. He nodded. "You hear my voice, don't you?" she inquired. Yes, he did. "Well, then," she said in triumph, "why go around questioning?"

"Well," said the captain, "it's simply that we never thought we'd find a thing like this on Mars."

"And now you've found it. I dare say there's lots on every planet that'll show you God's infinite ways."

"Is this Heaven?" asked Hinkston.

"Nonsense, no. It's a world and we get a second chance. Nobody told us why. But then nobody told us why we were on Earth, either. That *other* Earth, I mean. The one you come from. How do we know there wasn't *another* before *that* one?"

"A good question," said the captain.

The captain stood up and slapped his hand on his leg in an off-hand fashion. "We've got to be going. It's been nice. Thank you for the drinks."

He stopped. He turned and looked toward the door, startled.

Far away, in the sunlight, there was a sound of voices, a crowd, a shouting and a great hello.

"What's that?" asked Hinkston.

"We'll soon find out!" And Captain John Black was out the front door abruptly, jolting across the green lawn and into the street of the Martian town.

He stood looking at the ship. The ports were open and his crew were streaming out, waving their hands. A crowd of people had gathered and in and through and among these people the members of the crew were running, talking, laughing, shaking hands. People did little dances. People swarmed. The rocket lay empty and abandoned.

A brass band exploded in the sunlight, flinging off a gay tune from upraised tubas and trumpets. There was a bang of drums and a shrill of fifes. Little girls with golden hair jumped up and down. Little boys shouted, "Hooray!" And fat men passed around ten-cent cigars. The mayor of the town made a speech. Then, each member of the crew with a mother on one arm, a father or sister on the other, was spirited off down the street, into little cottages or big mansions and doors slammed shut.

The wind rose in the clear spring sky and all was silent. The brass band had banged off around a corner leaving the rocket to shine and dazzle alone in the sunlight.

"Abandoned!" cried the captain. "Abandoned the ship, they did! I'll have their skins, by God! They had orders!"

"Sir," said Lustig. "Don't be too hard on them. Those were all old relatives and friends."

"That's no excuse!"

"Think how they felt, captain, seeing familiar faces outside the ship!"

"I would have obeyed orders! I would have—" The captain's mouth remained open.

Striding along the sidewalk under the Martian sun, tall, smiling, eyes blue, face tan, came a young man of some twenty-six years.

"John!" the man cried, and broke into a run.

"What?" said Captain John Black. He swayed.

"John, you old beggar, you!"

The man ran up and gripped his hand and slapped him on the back.

"It's you," said John Black.

"Of course, who'd you *think* it was!"

"Edward!" The captain appealed now to Lustig and Hinkston, holding the stranger's hand. "This is my brother Edward. Ed, meet my men, Lustig, Hinkston! My brother!"

They tugged at each other's hands and arms and then finally embraced. "Ed!" "John, you old bum, you!" "You're looking fine, Ed, but, Ed, what is this? You haven't changed over the years. You died, I remember, when you were twenty-six, and I was nineteen, oh God, so many years ago, and here you are, and, Lord, what goes on, what goes on?"

Edward Black gave him a brotherly knock on the chin. "Mom's waiting," he said.

"Mom?"

"And Dad, too."

"And Dad?" The captain almost fell to earth as if hit upon the chest with a mighty weapon. He walked stiffly and awkwardly, out of coordination. He shuttered and whispered and talked only one or two words at a time. "Mom alive? Dad? Where?"

"At the old house on Oak Knoll Avenue."

"The old house " The captain stared in delighted amazement. "Did you *hear* that, Lustig, Hinkston?"

"I know it's hard for you to believe."

"But alive. Real."

"Don't I *feel* real?" The strong arm, the firm grip, the white smile. The light, curling hair.

Hinkston was gone. He had seen his own house down the street and was running for it. Lustig was grinning. "Now you understand, sir, what happened to everybody on the ship. They couldn't help themselves."

"Yes. Yes," said the captain, eyes shut. "Yes," He put out his hand. "When I open my eyes, you'll be gone." He opened his eyes. "You're still here. God, Edward, you look fine!"

"Come along, lunch is waiting for you. I told Mom."

Lustig said, "Sir, I'll be with my grandfolks if you want me."

"What? Oh, fine, Lustig.. Later, then."

Edward grabbed his arm and marched him. "You need support."

"I do. My knees, all funny. My stomach, loose. God."

"There's the house. Remember it?"

"Remember it? Hell! I bet I can beat you to the front porch!"

They ran. The wind roared over Captain John Black's ears. The earth roared under his feet. He saw the golden figure of Edward Black pull ahead of him in the amazing dream of reality. He saw the house rush forward, the door open, the screen swing back. "Beat you!" cried Edward, bounding up the steps. "I'm an old man," panted the captain, "and you're still young. But, then, you *always* beat me, I remember!"

In the doorway, Mom, pink and plump and bright. And behind her, pepper grey, Dad, with his pipe in his hand.

"Mom, Dad!"

He ran up the steps like a child, to meet them.

It was a fine long afternoon. They finished lunch and they sat in the living room and he told them all about his rocket and his being captain and they nodded and smiled upon him and Mother was just the same, and Dad bit the end off a cigar and lighted it in his old fashion. Mom brought in some iced tea in the middle of the afternoon. Then, there was a big turkey dinner at night and time flowing on. When the drumsticks were sucked clean and lay brittle upon the plates, the captain leaned back in his chair and exhaled his deep contentment. Dad poured him a small glass of dry sherry. It was seven-thirty in the evening. Night was in all the trees and coloring the sky, and the lamps were halos of dim light in the gentle house. From all the other houses down the streets came sounds of music, pianos playing, laughter.

Mom put a record on the victrola and she and Captain John Black had a dance. She was wearing the same perfume he remembered from the summer when she and Dad had been killed in the train accident. She was very real in his arms as they danced lightly to the music.

"I'll wake in the morning," said the captain. "And I'll be in my rocket in space, and all this will be gone."

"No, no, don't think that," she cried, softly, pleadingly. "We're here. Don't question. God is good to us. Let's be happy."

The record ended with a circular hissing.

"You're tired, son," said Dad. He waved his pipe. "You and Ed go on upstairs. Your old bedroom is waiting for you."

"The old one?"

"The brass bed and all," laughed Edward.

"But I should report my men in."

"Why?" Mother was logical.

"Why? Well, I don't know. No reason, I guess. No, none at all. What's the difference?" He shook his head. "I'm not being very logical these days."

"Good night, son." She kissed his cheek.

" 'Night, Mom."

"Sleep tight, son." Dad shook his hand.

"Same to you, Pop."

"It's good to have you home."

"It's good to *be* home."

He left the land of cigar smoke and perfume and books and gentle light and ascended the stairs, talking, talking with Edward. Edward pushed a door open and there was the yellow brass bed and the old semaphore banners from college days and a very musty raccoon coat which he petted with strange, muted affection. "It's too much," he said faintly. "Like being in a thunder shower without an umbrella. I'm soaked to the skin with emotion. I'm numb. I'm tired."

"A night's sleep between cool clean sheets for you, my bucko." Edward slapped wide the snowy linens and flounced the pillows. Then he put up a window and let the night blooming jasmine float in. There was moonlight and the sound of distant dancing and whispering.

"So this is Mars," said the captain undressing.

"So this is Mars." Edward undressed in idle, leisurely moves, drawing his shirt off over his head, revealing golden shoulders and the good muscular neck.

The lights were out, they were into bed, side by side, as in the days, how many decades ago? The captain lolled and was nourished by the night wind pushing the lace curtains out upon the dark room air. Among the trees, upon a lawn, someone had cranked up a portable phonograph and now it was playing softly, "I'll be loving you, always, with a love that's true, always."

The thought of Anna came to his mind. "Is Anna here?"

His brother, lying straight out in the moonlight from the window, waited and then said, "Yes. She's out of town. But she'll be here in the morning."

The captain shut his eyes. "I want to see Anna very much."

The room was square and quiet except for their breathing. "Good night, Ed."

A pause. "Good night, John."

He lay peacefully, letting his thoughts float. For the first time the stress of the day was moved aside, all of the excitement was calmed. He could think logically now. It had all been emotion. The bands playing, the sight of familiar faces, the sick pounding of your heart. But— now . . .

How? He thought. How was all this made? And why? For what purpose? Out of the goodness of some kind God? Was God, then, really that fine and thoughtful of his children? How and why and what for?

He thought of the various theories advanced in the first heat of the afternoon by Hinkston and Lustig. He let all kinds of new theories drop in lazy pebbles down through his mind, as through a dark water, now, turning, throwing out dull flashes of white light. Mars. Earth. Mom. Dad. Edward. Mars. Martians.

Who had lived here a thousand years ago on Mars? Martians? Or had this always been like this? Martians. He repeated the word quietly, inwardly.

He laughed out loud, almost. He had the most ridiculous theory, all of a sudden. It gave him a kind of chilled feeling. It was really nothing to think of, of course. Highly improbable. Silly. Forget it. Ridiculous.

But, he thought, just suppose. Just *suppose* now, that there were Martians living on Mars and they saw our ship coming and saw us inside our ship and hated us. Suppose, now, just for the hell of it, that they wanted to destroy us, as invaders, as unwanted ones, and they wanted to do it in a very clever way, so that we would be taken off guard. Well, what would the best weapon be that a Martian could use against Earthmen with atom weapons.

The answer was interesting. Telepathy, hypnosis, memory and imagination.

Suppose all these houses weren't real at all, this bed not real, but only figments of my own imagination, given substance by telepathy and hypnosis by the Martians.

Suppose these houses are really some other shape, a Martian shape, but, by playing on my desires and wants, these Martians have made this seem like my old home town, my old house, to lull me out of my suspicious? What better way to fool a man, by his own emotions.

And suppose those two people in the next room, asleep, are not my mother and father at all. But two Martians, incredibly brilliant, with the ability to keep me under this dreaming hypnosis all of the time?

And that brass band, today? What a clever plan it would be. First, fool Lustig, then fool Hinkston, then gather a crowd around the rocket ship and wave. And all the men in the ship, seeing mothers, aunts, uncles, sweethearts dead ten, twenty years ago, naturally, disregarding orders, would rush out and abandon the ship. What more natural? What more unsuspecting? What more simple? A man doesn't ask too many questions when his mother is suddenly brought back to life; he's much too happy. And the brass band played and everybody was taken off to private homes. And here we all are, tonight, in various houses, in various beds, with no weapons to protect us, and the rocket lies in the moonlight, empty. And wouldn't it be horrible and terrifying to discover that all of this was part of some clever plan by the Martians to divide and conquer us, and kill us. Some time during the night, perhaps, my brother here on this bed, will change form, melt, shift, and become a one-eyed, green and yellow-toothed Martian. It would be very simple for him just to turn over in bed and put a knife into my heart. And in all those other houses down the street a dozen other brothers or fathers suddenly melting away and taking out knives and doing things to the unsuspecting, sleeping men of Earth.

His hands were shaking under the covers. His body was cold. Suddenly it was not a theory. Suddenly he was very afraid. He lifted himself in bed and listened. The night was very quiet. The music had stopped. The wind had died. His brother (?) lay sleeping beside him.

Very carefully he lifted the sheets, rolled them back. He slipped from bed and was walking softly across the room when his brother's voice said, "Where are you going?"

"What?"

His brother's voice was quite cold. "I said, where do you think you're going?"

"For a drink of water."

"But you're not thirsty."

"Yes, yes, I am."

"No, you're not."

Captain John Black broke and ran across the room. He screamed. He screamed twice.

He never reached the door.

In the morning, the brass band played a mournful dirge. From every house in the street came little solemn processions bearing long boxes and along the sun-filled street, weeping and changing, came the grandmas and grandfathers and mothers and sisters and brothers, walking to the churchyard, where there were open holes dug freshly and new tombstones installed. Seventeen holes in all, and seventeen tombstones. Three of the tombstones said, CAPTAIN JOHN BLACK, ALBERT LUSTIG, and SAMUEL HINKSTON.

The mayor made a little sad speech, his face sometimes looking like the mayor, sometimes looking like something else.

Mother and Father Black were there, with Brother Edward, and they cried, their faces melting now from a familiar face into something else.

Grandpa and Grandma Lustig were there weeping, their faces also shifting like wax, shivering as a thing does in waves of heat on a summer day.

The coffins were lowered. Somebody murmured about "the unexpected and sudden deaths of seventeen fine men during the night—"

Earth was shoveled in on the coffin tops.

After the funeral the brass band slammed and banged back into town and the crowd stood around and waved and shouted as the rocket was torn to pieces and strewn about and blown up.

Questions for Discussion and Review

    1. In what way is the speculative element tied to the title of this story?

    2. Describe fully the nature of the Martian chimera.

    3. What made Captain John Black realize the trap into which he and his men had fallen?

    4. What kinds of fantasy are operating in this story?

Encounter in the Dawn

Arthur C. Clarke

Arthur Charles Clarke was born in Minehead, Somersetshire, England, on December 16, 1917, and grew up on a farm. He took a first-class degree in science from King's College, London, served in the Royal Air Force during World War II, and later became interested in underwater research. His paper "Extra-terrestrial Relays" in *Wireless World* (October 1945) pioneered the idea of earth satellites used for global communications. Among his many novels and stories are *Childhood's End* (1953), *Earthlight* (1955), *Tales from the White Hart* (1957), *The Nine Billion Names of God and Other Stories* (1967), and *Imperial Earth* (1976). He authored 2001: *A Space Odyssey* (first the movie with Stanley Kubrick and, in 1968, the novel). He has won a Hugo Award for "The Star" (1956), a Nebula Award for "A Meeting with Medusa" (1972), and both for *Rendezvous with Rama* (1973). He makes his home on the island nation of Sri Lanka (Ceylon). "Encounter in the Dawn" first appeared in *Amazing Stories* (July 1953). It has appeared since under two different titles: as the lead story in the Ballantine collection *Expedition to Earth* (1953) and as "Encounter at Dawn" in *The Nine Billion Names of God* collection (1967). Neither change was authorized by the author, and Clarke prefers the original title, here restored.

Recent years have seen the phenomenal popularity of speculations that Earth has been visited by aliens who are supposed to have taken an interest in accelerating or in directing the course of human evolution. The least that can be said about such speculations is that they are uniquely the product of our times. We may wonder whether SF stories like R. DeWitt Miller's "Within the Pyramid" (1937) and Arthur C. Clarke's "The Sentinel" (1951), "Before Eden" (1961), and the present story may have helped inspire the extraordinary conjectures of writers like von Daniken and his disciples. The idea that the human race is descended from an extraterrestrial race of beings or was nurtured by them has long been a cherished occult theory, now given new life by the growth of space-age technology. We may be witnessing the clash of two mythic impulses— one biblical and the other pseudoscientific. If readers are convinced by the arguments for exogenesis or by one of the variant theories of alien biological engineering, they will find reason to dispute the classification of this story as fantasy SF.

Using another standard, we also may call this a "first contact" story or, simply, an alien story—except that the aliens are really human, and the focus of the story is actually on Bertrond's experience of a hypothetical kind of déjà vu recognition. Neither the sentiment of the story nor its sense of the evolutionary distance between Yaan and Bertrond would have been possible or intelligible to people living before the nineteenth century. It is almost a purely SF experience, and yet it seems potentially real to members of this generation. The idea of a prehistoric expedition to

Earth by benevolent aliens possesses a strange, compelling sort of probability for us, as though it were the recovery and fulfillment of archetypal ideas of guiding spirits and guardian angels. The odds against this kind of thing having happened or the impossibility of ever proving such an event do not seem to affect the appeal of the idea. It seems fair to say that many people would want it to be true and find the idea a preferable and more potent myth for the times than the traditional Creation accounts of established religions. We may be experiencing the development of an imagined sense of wonder becoming primary and engaging the will rather than remaining at the level of a secondary emotion.

The theory of shepherds from the sky is a recurrent one in Clarke's fiction. It is almost as though he were writing as a space-age John the Baptist, and perhaps that is no great distortion of the kind of speculative faith he has in the likelihood of just such an apocalyptic event. Certainly he does not seem to expect, as so many SF writers have, that human beings can develop their own evolutionary breakthrough. In this story, the encounter between human beings and aliens takes place when only one of the two human representatives was capable of appreciating its significance. Yaan lives in a land that, for him and his tribe, has no name. Such concepts as place names are to come later in human, earthly evolution.

When Bertrond is recalled to his home among the stars, he leaves reluctantly and out of a sense of duty to his homeland. His preference would have been to remain and help the race accelerate its evolution. His parting gifts to Yaan are various tools, gifts that are much more than ceremonial playthings. Bertrond bestows the tools in the hope that they will help accomplish the upward evolution of the species. As Clarke once explained in his essay "The Obsolescence of Man" (*Profiles of the Future*, 1963), it would be truer to say that "tools invented man" rather than the reverse. That appears to be the narrator's view in this story.

It was the last days of the Empire. The tiny ship was far from home, and almost a hundred light-years from the great parent vessel searching through the loosely packed stars at the rim of the Milky Way. But even here it could not escape from the shadow that lay across civilization: beneath that shadow, pausing ever and again in their work to wonder how their distant homes were faring, the scientists of the Galactic Survey still labored at their never-ending task.

The ship held only three occupants, but among them they carried knowledge of many sciences, and the experience of half a lifetime in space. After the long interstellar night, the star ahead was warming their spirits as they dropped down toward its fires. A little more golden, a trifle more brilliant than the sun that now seemed a legend of their childhood. They knew from past experience that the chance of locating planets here was more than ninety per cent, and for the moment they forgot all else in the excitement of discovery.

They found the first planet within minutes of coming to rest. It was a giant, of a familiar type, too cold for protoplasmic life and probably possessing no stable surface. So they turned their search sunward, and presently were rewarded.

It was a world that made their hearts ache for home, a world where everything was hauntingly familiar, yet never quite the same. Two great land masses floated in blue-green seas, capped by ice at both poles. There were some desert regions, but the larger part of the planet was obviously fertile. Even from this distance, the signs of vegetation were unmistakably clear.

They gazed hungrily at the expanding landscape as they fell down into the atmosphere, heading toward noon in the subtropics. The ship plummeted through cloudless skies toward a great river, checked its fall with a surge of soundless power, and came to rest among the long grasses by the water's edge.

No one moved: there was nothing to be done until the automatic instruments had finished their work. Then a bell tinkled softly and the lights on the control board flashed in a pattern of meaningful chaos. Captain Altman rose to his feet with a sigh of relief.

"We're in luck," he said. "We can go outside without protection, if the pathogenic tests are satisfactory. What did you make of the place as we came in, Bertrond?"

"Geologically stable—no active volcanoes, at least. I didn't see any trace of cities, but that proves nothing. If there's a civilization here, it may have passed that stage."

"Or not reached it yet?"

Bertrond shrugged. "Either's just as likely. It may take us some time to find out on a planet this size."

"More time than we've got," said Clindar, glancing at the communications panel that linked them to the mother ship and thence to the Galaxy's threatened heart. For a moment there was a gloomy silence. Then Clindar walked to the control board and pressed a pattern of keys with automatic skill.

With a slight jar, a section of the hull slid aside and the fourth member of the crew stepped out onto the new planet, flexing metal limbs and adjusting servomotors to the unaccustomed gravity. Inside the ship, a television screen glimmered into life, revealing a long vista of waving grasses, some trees in the middle distance, and a glimpse of the great river. Clindar punched a button, and the picture flowed steadily across the screen as the robot turned its head.

"Which way shall we go?" Clindar asked.

"Let's have a look at those trees," Altmar replied. "If there's any animal life we'll find it there."

"Look!" cried Bertrond. "A bird!"

Clindar's fingers flew over the keyboard: the picture centered on the tiny speck that had suddenly appeared on the left of the screen, and expanded rapidly as the robot's telephoto lens came into action.

"You're right," he said. "Feathers—beak—well up the evolutionary ladder. This place looks promising. I'll start the camera."

The swaying motion of the picture as the robot walked forward did not distract them: they had grown accustomed to it long ago. But they had never become reconciled to this exploration by proxy when all their impulses cried out to them to leave the ship, to run through the grass and to feel the wind blowing against their faces. Yet it was too great a risk to take, even on a world that seemed as fair as this. There was always a skull hidden behind Nature's most smiling face. Wild beasts, poisonous reptiles, quagmires—death could come to the unwary explorer in a thousand disguises. And worst of all were the invisible enemies, the bacteria and viruses against which the only defense might often be a thousand light-years away.

A robot could laugh at all these dangers and even if, as sometimes happened, it encountered a beast powerful enough to destroy it—well, machines could always be replaced.

They met nothing on the walk across the grasslands. If any small animals were disturbed by the robot's passage, they kept outside its field of vision. Clindar slowed the machine as it approached the trees, and the watchers in the spaceship flinched involuntarily at the branches that appeared to slash across their eyes. The picture dimmed for a moment before the controls readjusted themselves to the weaker illumination; then it came back to normal.

The forest was full of life. It lurked in the undergrowth, clambered among the branches, flew through the air. It fled chattering and gibbering through the trees as the robot advanced. And all the while the automatic cameras were recording the pictures that formed on the screen, gathering material for the biologists to analyze when the ship returned to base.

Clindar breathed a sigh of relief when the trees suddenly thinned. It was exhausting work, keeping the robot from smashing into obstacles as it moved through the forest, but on open ground it could take care of itself. Then the picture trembled as if beneath a hammer blow, there was a grinding metallic thud, and the whole scene swept vertiginously upward as the robot toppled and fell.

"What's that?" cried Altman. "Did you trip."

"No," said Clindar grimly, his fingers flying over the keyboard. "Something attacked from the rear. I hope . . . ah . . . I've still got control."

He brought the robot to a sitting position and swiveled its head. It did not take long to find the cause of the trouble. Standing a few feet away, and lashing its tail angrily, was a large quadruped with a most ferocious set of teeth. At the moment it was, fairly obviously, trying to decide whether to attack again.

Slowly, the robot rose to its feet, and as it did so the great beast crouched to spring. A smile flitted across Clindar's face: he knew how to deal with this situation. His thumb felt for the seldom-used key labeled "Siren."

The forest echoed with a hideous undulating scream from the robot's concealed speaker, and the machine advanced to meet its adversary, arms flailing in front of it. The startled beast almost fell over backward in its effort to turn, and in seconds was gone from sight.

"Now I suppose we'll have to wait a couple of hours until everything comes out of hiding again," said Bertrond ruefully.

"I don't know much about animal psychology," interjected Altman, but is it usual for them to attack something completely unfamiliar?"

"Some will attack anything that moves, but that's unusual. Normally they attack only for food, or if they've already been threatened. What are you driving at? Do you suggest that there are other robots on this planet?"

"Certainly not. But our carnivorous friend may have mistaken our machine for a more edible biped. Don't you think that this opening in the jungle is rather unnatural? It could easily be a path."

"In that case," said Clindar promptly, "we'll follow it and find out. I'm tired of dodging trees, but I hope nothing jumps on us again: it's bad for my nerves."

"You were right, Altman," said Bertrond a little later. "It's certainly a path. But that doesn't mean intelligence. After all, animals—"

He stopped in mid-sentence, and at the same instant Clindar brought the advancing robot to a halt. The path had suddenly opened out into a wide clearing, almost completely occupied by a village of flimsy huts. It was ringed by a wooden palisade, obviously defense against an enemy who at the moment presented no threat. For the gates were wide open, and beyond them the inhabitants were going peacefully about their ways.

For many minutes the three explorers stared in silence at the screen. Then Clindar shivered a little and remarked: "It's uncanny. It might be our own planet, a hundred thousand years ago. I feel as if I've gone back in time."

"There's nothing weird about it," said the practical Altman. "After all, we've discovered nearly a hundred planets with our type of life on them."

"Yes," retorted Clindar. "A hundred in the whole Galaxy! I still think it's strange it had to happen to us."

"Well, it had to happen to *somebody*," said Bertrond philosophically. "Meanwhile, we must work out our contact procedure. If we send the robot into the village it will start a panic."

"That," said Altman, "is a masterly understatement. What we'll have to do is catch a native by himself and prove that we're friendly. Hide the robot, Clindar. Somewhere in the woods where it can watch the village without being spotted. We've a week's practical anthropology ahead of us!"

It was three days before the biological tests showed that it would be safe to leave the ship. Even then Bertrond insisted on going alone— alone, that is, if one ignored the substantial company of the robot. With such an ally he was not afraid of this planet's larger beasts, and his body's natural defenses could take care of the microorganisms. So, at least, the analyzers had assured him; and considering the complexity of the problem, they made remarkably few mistakes. . . .

He stayed outside for an hour, enjoying himself cautiously, while his companions watched with envy. It would be another three days before they could be quite certain that it was safe to follow Bertrond's example. Meanwhile, they kept busy enough watching the village through the lenses of the robot, and recording everything they could with the cameras. They had moved the spaceship at night so that it was hidden in the depths of the forest, for they did not wish to be discovered until they were ready.

And all the while the news from home grew worse. Though their remoteness here at the edge of the Universe deadened its impact, it lay heavily on their minds and sometimes overwhelmed them with a sense of futility. At any moment, they knew, the signal for recall might come as the Empire summoned up its last resources in its extremity. But until then they would continue their work as though pure knowledge were the only thing that mattered.

Seven days after landing, they were ready to make the experiment. They knew now what paths the villagers used when going hunting, and Bertrond chose one of the less frequented ways. Then he placed a chair firmly in the middle of the path and settled down to read a book.

It was not, of course, quite as simple as that: Bertrond had taken all imaginable precautions. Hidden in the undergrowth fifty yards away, the robot was watching through its telescopic lenses, and in its hand it held a small but deadly weapon. Controlling it from the spaceship, his fingers poised over the keyboard, Clindar waited to do what might be necessary.

That was the negative side of the plan: the positive side was more obvious. Lying at Bertrond's feet was the carcass of a small, horned animal which he hoped would be an acceptable gift to any hunter passing this way.

Two hours later the radio in his suit harness whispered a warning. Quite calmly, though the blood was pounding in his veins, Bertrond laid aside his book and looked down the trail. The savage was walking forward confidently enough, swinging a spear in his right hand. He paused for a moment when he saw Bertrond, then advanced more cautiously. He could tell that there was nothing to fear, for the stranger was slightly built and obviously unarmed.

When only twenty feet separated them, Bertrond gave a reassuring smile and rose slowly to his feet. He bent down, picked up the carcass, and carried it forward as an offering. The gesture would have been understood by any creature on any world, and it was understood here. The savage reached forward, took the animal, and threw it effortlessly over his shoulder. For an instant he stared into Bertrond's eyes with a fathomless expression; then he turned and walked back toward the village. Three times he glanced round to see if Bertrond was following, and each time Bertrond smiled and waved reassurance. The whole episode lasted little more than a minute. As the first contact between two races it was completely without drama, though not without dignity.

Bertrond did not move until the other had vanished from sight. Then he relaxed and spoke into his suit microphone.

"That was a pretty good beginning," he said jubilantly. "He wasn't in the least frightened, or even suspicious. I think he'll be back."

"It still seems too good to be true," said Altman's voice in his ear. "I should have thought he'd have been either scared or hostile. Would *you* have accepted a lavish gift from a peculiar stranger with such little fuss?"

Bertrond was slowly walking back to the ship. The robot had now come out of cover and was keeping guard a few paces behind him.

"I wouldn't," he replied, "but I belong to a civilized community. Complete savages may react to strangers in many different ways, according to their past experience. Suppose this tribe has never had any enemies. That's quite possible on a large but sparsely populated planet. Then we may expect curiosity, but no fear at all."

"If these people have no enemies," put in Clindar, no longer fully occupied in controlling the robot, "why have they got a stockade round the village?"

"I meant no *human* enemies," replied Bertrond. "If that's true, it simplifies our task immensely."

"Do you think he'll come back?"

"Of course. If he's as human as I think, curiosity and greed will make him return. In a couple of days we'll be bosom friends."

Looked at dispassionately, it became a fantastic routine. Every morning the robot would go hunting under Clindar's direction, until it was now the deadliest killer in the jungle. Then Bertrond would wait until Yaan—which was the nearest they could get to his name—came striding confidently along the path. He came at the same time every day, and he always came alone. They wondered about this: did he wish to keep his great discovery to himself and thus get all the credit for his hunting prowess? If so, it showed unexpected foresight and cunning.

At first Yaan had departed at once with his prize, as if afraid that the donor of such a generous gift might change his mind. Soon, however, as Bertrond had hoped, he could be induced to stay for a while by simple conjuring tricks and a display of brightly colored fabrics and crystals, in which he took a childlike delight. At last Bertrond was able to engage him in lengthy conversations, all of which were recorded as well as being filmed through the eyes of the hidden robot.

One day the philologists might be able to analyze this material; the best that Bertrond could do was to discover the meanings of a few simple verbs and nouns. This was made more difficult by the fact that Yaan not only used different words for the same thing, but sometimes the same word for different things.

Between these daily interviews, the ship traveled far, surveying the planet from the air and sometimes landing for more detailed examinations. Although several other human settlements were observed, Bertrond made no attempt to get in touch with them, for it was easy to see that they were all at much the same cultural level as Yaan's people.

It was, Bertrond often thought, a particularly bad joke on the part of Fate that one of the Galaxy's very few truly human races should have been discovered at this moment of time. Not long ago this would have been an event of supreme importance; now civilization was too hard-pressed to concern itself with these savage cousins waiting at the dawn of history.

Not until Bertrond was sure he had become part of Yaan's everyday life did he introduce him to the robot. He was showing Yaan the patterns in a kaleidoscope when Clindar brought the machine striding through the grass with its latest victim danging across one metal arm. For the first time Yaan showed something akin to fear; but he relaxed at Bertrond's soothing words, though he continued to watch the advancing monster. It halted some distance away, and Bertrond walked forward to meet it. As he did so, the robot raised its arms and handed him the dead beast. He took it solemnly and carried it back to Yaan, staggering a little under the unaccustomed load.

Bertrond would have given a great deal to know just what Yaan was thinking as he accepted the gift. Was he trying to decide whether the robot was master or slave? Perhaps such conceptions as this were beyond his grasp: to him the robot might be merely another man, a hunter who was a friend of Bertrond.

Clindar's voice, slightly larger than life, came from the robot's speaker.

"It's astonishing how calmly he accepts us. Won't anything scare him?"

"You will keep judging him by your own standards," replied Bertrond. "Remember, his psychology is completely different, and much simpler. Now that he has confidence in me, anything that I accept won't worry him."

"I wonder if that will be true of all his race?" queried Altman. "It's hardly safe to judge by a single specimen. I want to see what happens when we send the robot into the village."

"Hello!" exclaimed Bertrond. "*That* surprised him. He's never met a person who could speak with two voices before."

"Do you think he'll guess the truth when he meets us?" said Clindar.

"No. The robot will be pure magic to him—but it won't be any more wonderful than fire and lightning and all the other forces he must already take for granted."

"Well, what's the next move?" asked Altman, a little impatiently. "Are you going to bring him to the ship, or will you go into the village first?"

Bertrond hesitated. "I'm anxious not to do too much too quickly. You know the accidents that have happened with strange races when that's been tried. I'll let him think this over, and when we get back tomorrow I'll try to persuade him to take the robot back to the village."

In the hidden ship, Clindar reactivated the robot and started it moving again. Like Altman, he was growing a little impatient of this excessive caution, but on all matters relating to alien life-forms Bertrond was the expert, and they had to obey his orders.

There were times now when he almost wished he were a robot himself, devoid of feelings or emotions, able to watch the fall of a leaf or the death agonies of a world with equal detachment. . . .

The sun was low when Yaan heard the great voice crying from the jungle. He recognized it at once, despite its inhuman volume: it was the voice of his friend, and it was calling him.

In the echoing silence, the life of the village came to a stop. Even the children ceased their play: the only sound was the thin cry of a baby frightened by the sudden silence.

All eyes were upon Yaan as he walked swiftly to his hut and grasped the spear that lay beside the entrance. The stockade would soon be closed against the prowlers of the night, but he did not hesitate as he stepped out into the lengthening shadows. He was passing through the gates when once again that mighty voice summoned him, and now it held a note of urgency that came clearly across all the barriers of language and culture.

The shining giant who spoke with many voices met him a little way from the village and beckoned him to follow. There was no sign of Bertrond. They walked for almost a mile before they saw him in the distance, standing not far from the river's edge and staring out across the dark, slowly moving waters.

He turned as Yaan approached, yet for a moment seemed unaware of his presence. Then he gave a gesture of dismissal to the shining one, who withdrew into the distance.

Yaan waited. He was patient and, though he could never have expressed it in words, contented. When he was with Bertrond he felt the first intimations of that selfless, utterly irrational devotion his race would not fully achieve for many ages.

It was a strange tableau. Here at the river's brink two men were standing. One was dressed in a closely fitting uniform equipped with tiny, intricate mechanisms. The other was wearing the skin of an animal and was carrying a flint-tipped spear. Ten thousand generations lay between them, ten thousand generations and an immeasurable gulf of space. Yet they were both human. As she must do often in Eternity, Nature had repeated one of her basic patterns.

Presently Bertrond began to speak, walking to and fro in short, quick steps as he did, and in his voice there was a trace of madness.

"It's all over, Yaan. I'd hoped that with our knowledge we could have brought you out of barbarism in a dozen generations, but now you will have to fight your way up from the jungle alone, and it may take you a million years to do so. I'm sorry—there's so much we could have done. Even now I wanted to stay here, but Altman and Clindar talk of duty, and I suppose that they are right. There is little enough that we can do, but our world is calling and we must not forsake it.

"I wish you could understand me, Yaan. I wish you knew what I was saying. I'm leaving you these tools: some of them you will discover how to use, though as likely as not in a generation they'll be lost or forgotten. See how this blade cuts: it will be ages before your world can make its like. And guard this well: when you press the button— look! If you use it sparingly, it will give you light for years, though sooner or later it will die. As for these other things—find what use for them you can.

"Here come the first stars, up there in the east. Do you ever look at the stars, Yaan? I wonder how long it will be before you have discovered what they are, and I wonder what will have happened to us by then. Those stars are our homes, Yaan, and we cannot save them. Many have died already, in explosions so vast that I can imagine them no more than you. In a hundred thousand of your years, the light of those funeral pyres will reach your world and set its peoples wondering. By then, perhaps, your race will be reaching for the stars. I wish I could warn you against the mistakes we made, and which now will cost us all that we have won.

"It is well for your people, Yaan, that your world is here at the frontier of the Universe. You may escape the doom that waits for us. One day, perhaps, your ships will go searching among the stars as we have done, and they may come upon the ruins of our worlds and wonder who we were. But they will never know that we met here by this river when your race was young.

"Here come my friends; they would give me no more time. Good-by, Yaan—use well the things I have left you. They are your world's greatest treasures."

Something huge, something that glittered in the starlight, was sliding down from the sky. It did not reach the ground, but came to rest a little way above the surface, and in utter silence a rectangle of light opened in its side. The shining giant appeared out of the night and stepped through the golden door. Bertrond followed, pausing for a moment at the threshold to wave back at Yaan. Then the darkness closed behind him.

No more swiftly than smoke drifts upward from a fire, the ship lifted away. When it was so small that Yaan felt he could hold it in his hands, it seemed to blur into a long line of light slanting upward into the stars. From the empty sky a peal of thunder echoed over the sleeping land; and Yaan knew at last that the gods were gone and would never come again.

For a long time he stood by the gently moving waters, and into his soul there came a sense of loss he was never to forget and never to understand. Then, carefully and reverently, he collected together the gifts that Bertrond had left.

Under the stars, the lonely figure walked homeward across a nameless land. Behind him the river flowed softly to the sea, winding through the fertile plains on which, more than a thousand centuries ahead, Yaan's descendants would build the great city they were to call Babylon.

Questions for Discussion and Review

1. What clues are we given to the fate of Bertrond's empire?
2. The story has several geological clues and historical references that enable us to place the encounter on our time scale. What are these clues, and when is the imagined incident supposed to have taken place?
3. Why did Clarke choose the future site of Babylon for the meeting place?
4. Why is Yaan an appropriate name for the primitive man in the story?
5. How would you describe the gap between Yaan and Bertrond?
6. What qualities does this story share with other types of fantasy SF?
7. Does a highly advanced culture imply benevolence in this story?

Weird Science Fiction

Fantastic SF mixes two literary traditions that represent different attitudes of mind and imagination toward worlds of possible experience. Ordinarily SF works within the limits of natural, physical, or scientific law interpreted, naturally enough, with sometimes breath-taking invention. Fantasy knows only the laws of its own making. In a sense, it dramatizes the human desire for triumph over natural restraints. Although there are few absolutes safe to work with when dealing with a popular art form like SF, which continues to develop itself by inventing new types and modifying old ones, we may risk a generalization or two about the fantastic SF story. We can expect that, as part fantasy, it will cross the boundaries of probable action imposed on other SF types by their regard for both science and the workings of nature. Such a literature is exciting because it extends our imagined experience of science and of the attitudes and values science tends to generate. This experience will carry us beyond nearly all probable or even possible worlds. Prominent among these trans-scientific worlds is the realm of the supernatural. That is the area of imagined experience explored by the weird SF story.

Let us keep clearly in our minds the distinction between the weird fantasy and the weird SF story. The former deals with the supernatural experience as transcendently magical. The latter treats the supernatural in the context of the world in which we normally expect to feel the governance of nature or the laws of science. The very fact that we do not feel such restraint or a sense of the boundaries of reason provides a thrill of release, a sense of strange freedom from responsible control

that is the peculiar character of this kind of story. The weird SF story
implies the cancellation of science in a world that makes sense to us
only on scientific terms; hence, our characteristic response to the weird
SF story is to feel a sense of imagined eeriness and disorientation.

The true history of the weird story needs to be written. It is certainly an ancient mode of the popular story, never quite critically respectable but never entirely out of fashion in popular appeal and rarely
so in serious literature. The weird SF story is relatively recent. Undoubtedly it is a development of the Gothic, which was found in combination with SF subjects in the nineteenth century, as we have seen
earlier. The early masters of the weird story usually doubled in fantasy.
Many of Poe's most famous stories of supernatural terror are weird
tales, and it may be argued that stories like "Descent into the Maelstrom" combine elements of weird SF, and terror to produce their special effects. Following Poe, the major names in weird history are
Nathaniel Hawthorne, J. Sheridan Le Fanu, Ambrose Bierce, Lord
Dunsany, Abraham Merritt, and H. P. Lovecraft. Merritt and Lovecraft came before the public in the pulp magazines, especially in *Weird
Tales*.

Weird Tales was begun in March 1923. It became the forum for
two generations of writers interested in the varities of the supernatural
or weird story. Lovecraft's stories were greatly admired by the young
readers of the magazine, and they proved a powerful influence on the
generation of the 1920s and 1930s, including Clark Ashton Smith and
Robert Bloch. Lovecraft's Cthulhu mythos continues to be elaborated
to this day by followers. Since all of Lovecraft's published works
appeared in the pulp magazines, after his death Arkham Press was
founded by August Derleth with the purpose of collecting and publishing Lovecraft's writing. *Weird Tales* was continued into the 1940s
and early 1950s by a new generation of writers, most notably Bradbury. Meanwhile John W. Campbell had launched *Unknown* in 1939,
a worthy rival for the then venerable *Weird Tales,* and one that promoted the modern weird SF story. Among the architects of the new
tradition were Theodore Sturgeon, L. Sprague De Camp, Fletcher
Pratt, Robert Heinlein, and Fritz Leiber. Since the demise of *Unknown*
during World War II and *Weird Tales* in the 1950s, more writers
have arisen to specialize in weird SF stories, including Poul Anderson,
Philip José Farmer, and Rod Serling. The pulp outlets for weird stories
are *The Magazine of Fantasy and Science Fiction, Fantastic Stories,*
and the original paperback anthology. Many New Wave writers have
joined the cavalcade of weird SF storytellers, especially Philip K. Dick,
Michael Moorcock, Vonda McIntyre, James Tiptree,, and Barry Malzberg. The outlook for the future of the weird SF story seems brighter
than ever.

The Nine Billion Names of God

Arthur C. Clarke

See the earlier note on Clarke for details of his career as a writer of SF. Perhaps it would be well to add one further comment here on the range of his interest. There is hardly a type of SF that is strange to Arthur Clarke, and it is remarkable that one who is famous for writing hard SF should have produced some of the best weird SF stories.

This story is a classic example of the weird SF story. Classified by subject matter, this would qualify as a "doomsday story"; but the character of the tale is not typical, as you can see by comparing it with Byron's "Darkness," or even with the doomsday-averted variation of Wells's "The Star." Rather, the effect aimed at is a special variety of wonder and awe associated with the intervention of the supernatural seen in a context of both myth and science. Readers may claim with good reason that the method of the story is almost speculative. It is as though the author had asked himself the following question: What if superstition (or that which is assumed to be superstition by contemporary rational, scientific standards) turns out to be apocalyptic revelation?

Arthur Clarke builds on that supposition, which is the underlying theme of the story, by adding two elements. The first is the mythic framework in which the supposition is expressed, and the second is modern technology. The resulting contrast sets us up effectively for the climatic moment of the story. It is a moment that readers are meant to share with equal incredulity and recognition, along with the two computer technicians. The unique disposition of Clarke's story emerges precisely at this point from the blending of emotional effects that follow from the impact of the final revelation.

"This is a slightly unusual request," said Dr. Wagner, with what he hoped was commendable restraint. "As far as I know, it's the first time anyone's been asked to supply a Tibetan monastery with an Automatic Sequence Computer. I don't wish to be inquisitive, but I should hardly have thought that your—ah—establishment had much use for such a machine. Could you explain just what you intend to do with it?"

"Gladly," replied the lama, readjusting his silk robes and carefully putting away the slide rule he had been using for currency conversions. "Your Mark V Computer can carry out any routine mathematical operation involving up to ten digits. However, for our work we are interested in *letters*, not numbers. As we wish you to modify the output circurts, the machine will be printing words, not columns of figures."

"I don't quite understand. . . ."

"This is a project on which we have been working for the last three centuries—since the lamasery was founded, in fact. It is somewhat alien to your way of thought, so I hope you will listen with an open mind while I explain it."

"Naturally."

"It is really quite simple. We have been compiling a list which shall contain all the possible names of God."

"I beg your pardon?"

"We have reason to believe," continued the lama imperturbably, "that all such names can be written with not more than nine letters in an alphabet we have devised."

"And you have been doing this for three centuries?"

"Yes: we expected it would take us about fifteen thousand years to complete the task."

"Oh," Dr. Wagner looked a little dazed. "Now I see why you wanted to hire one of our machines. But exactly what is the *purpose* of this project?"

The lama hesitated for a fraction of a second, and Wagner wondered if he had offended him. If so, there was no trace of annoyance in the reply.

"Call it ritual, if you like, but it's a fundamental part of our belief. All the many names of the Supreme Being—God, Jehovah, Allah, and so on—they are only man-made labels. There is a philosophical problem of some difficulty here, which I do not propose to discuss, but somewhere among all the possible combinations of letters that can occur are what one may call the *real* names of God. By systematic permutation of letters, we have been trying to list them all."

"I see. You've been starting at AAAAAAA . . . and working up to ZZZZZZZZ. . . ."

"Exactly—though we use a special alphabet of our own. Modifying the electromatic typewriters to deal with this is, of course, trivial. A rather more interesting problem is that of devising suitable circuits to eliminate ridiculous combinations. For example, no letter must occur more than three times in succession."

"Three? Surely you mean two."

"Three is correct: I am afraid it would take too long to explain why, even if you understood our language."

"I'm sure it would," said Wagner hastily. "Go on."

"Luckily, it will be a simple matter to adapt your Automatic Sequence Computer for this work, since once it has been programmed properly it will permute each letter in turn and print the result. What would have taken us fifteen thousand years it will be able to do in a hundred days."

Dr. Wagner was scarcely conscious of the faint sounds from the Manhattan streets far below. He was in a different world, a world of natural, not man-made, mountains. High up in their remote aeries these monks had been patiently at work, generation after generation, compiling their lists of meaningless words. Was there any limit to the follies of mankind? Still, he must give no hint of his inner thoughts. The customer was always right. . . .

"There's no doubt," replied the doctor, "that we can modify the Mark V to print lists of this nature. I'm much more worried about the problem of installation and maintenance. Getting out to Tibet, in these days, is not going to be easy."

"We can arrange that. The components are small enough to travel by air—that is one reason why we chose your machine. If you can get them to India, we will provide transport from there."

"And you want to hire two of our engineers?"

"Yes, for the three months that the project should occupy."

"I've no doubt that Personnel can manage that." Dr. Wagner scribbled a note on his desk pad. "There are just two other points—"

Before he could finish the sentence the lama had produced a small slip of paper.

"This is my certified credit balance at the Asiatic Bank."

"Thank you. It appears to be—ah—adequate. The second matter is so trivial that I hesitate to mention it—but it's surprising how often the obvious gets overlooked. What source of electrical energy have you?"

"A diesel generator providing fifty kilowatts at a hundred and ten volts. It was installed about five years ago and is quite reliable. It's made life at the lamasery much more comfortable, but of course it was really installed to provide power for the motors driving the prayer wheels."

"Of course," echoed Dr. Wagner. "I should have thought of that."

The view from the parapet was vertiginous, but in time one gets used to anything. After three months, George Hanley was not impressed by the two-thousand-foot swoop into the abyss or the remote checkerboard of fields in the valley below. He was leaning against the wind-smoothed stones and staring morosely at the distant mountains whose names he had never bothered to discover.

This, thought George, was the craziest thing that had ever happened to him. "Project Shangri-La," some wit back at the labs had christened it. For weeks now the Mark V had been churning out acres of sheets covered with gibberish. Patiently, inexorably, the computer had been rearranging letters in all their possible combinations, exhausting each class before going on to the next. As the sheets had emerged from the electronic typewriters, the monks had carefully cut them up and pasted them into enormous books. In another week, heaven be praised, they would have finished. Just what obscure calculations had convinced the monks that they needn't bother to go on to words of ten, twenty, or a hundred letters, George didn't know. One of his recurring nightmares was that there would be some change of plan, and that the high lama (whom they'd naturally called Sam Jaffe, though he didn't look a bit like him) would suddenly announce that the project would be extended to approximately A.D. 2060. They were quite capable of it.

George heard the heavy wooden door slam in the wind as Chuck came out onto the parapet beside him. As usual, Chuck was smoking one of the cigars that made him so popular with the monks—who, it seemed, were quite willing to embrace all the minor and most of the major pleasures of life. That was one thing in their favor: they might be crazy, but they weren't bluenoses. Those frequent trips they took down to the village, for instance. . . .

"Listen, George," said Chuck urgently. "I've learned something that means trouble."

"What's wrong? Isn't the machine behaving?" That was the worst contingency George could imagine. It might delay his return, and nothing could be more horrible. The way he felt now, even the sight of a TV commercial would seem like manna from heaven. At least it would be some link with home.

"No—it's nothing like that." Chuck settled himself on the parapet, which was unusual because normally he was scared of the drop. "I've just found what all this is about."

"What d'ya mean? I thought we knew."

"Sure—we know what the monks are trying to do. But we didn't know *why*. It's the craziest thing—"

"Tell me something new," growled George.

"—but old Sam's just come clean with me. You know the way he drops in every afternoon to watch the sheets roll out. Well, this time he seemed rather excited, or at least as near as he'll ever get to it. When I told him that we were on the last cycle he asked me, in that cute English accent of his, if I'd ever wondered what they were trying to do. I said, 'Sure'—and he told me."

"Go on: I'll buy it."

"Well, they believe that when they have listed all His names—and they reckon that there are about nine billion of them—God's purpose will be achieved. The human race will have finished what it was created to do, and there won't be any point in carrying on. Indeed, the very idea is something like blasphemy."

"Then what do they expect us to do? Commit suicide?"

"There's no need for that. When the list's completed, God steps in and simply winds things up . . . bingo!"

"Oh, I get it. When we finish our job, it will be the end of the world."

Chuck gave a nervous little laugh.

"That's just what I said to Sam. And do you know what happened? He looked at me in a very queer way, like I'd been stupid in class, and said, 'It's nothing as trivial as *that.*' "

George thought this over for a moment.

"That's what I call taking the Wide View," he said presently. "But what d'you suppose we should do about it? I don't see that it makes the slightest difference to us. After all, we already knew that they were crazy."

"Yes—but don't you see what may happen? When the list's complete and the Last Trump doesn't blow—or whatever it is they expect—*we* may get the blame. It's our machine they've been using. I don't like the situation one little bit."

"I see," said George slowly. "You've got a point there. But this sort of thing's happened before, you know. When I was a kid down in Louisiana we had a crackpot preacher who once said the world was going to end next Sunday. Hundreds of people believed him—even sold their homes. Yet when nothing happened, they didn't turn nasty, as you'd expect. They just decided that he'd made a mistake in his calculations and went right on believing. I guess some of them still do."

"Well, this isn't Louisiana, in case you hadn't noticed. There are just two of us and hundreds of these monks. I like them, and I'll be sorry for old Sam when his lifework backfires on him. But all the same, I wish I was somewhere else."

"I've been wishing that for weeks. But there's nothing we can do until the contract's finished and the transport arrives to fly us out."

"Of course," said Chuck thoughtfully, "we could always try a bit of sabotage."

"Like hell we could! That would make things worse."

"Not the way I meant. Look at it like this. The machine will finish its run four days from now, on the present twenty-hours-a-day basis. The transport calls in a week. OK—then all we need to do is to find something that needs replacing during one of the overhaul periods— something that will hold-up the works for a couple of days. We'll fix it, of course, but not too quickly. If we time matters properly, we can be down at the airfield when the last name pops out of the register. They won't be able to catch us then."

"I don't like it," said George. "It will be the first time I ever walked out on a job. Besides, it would make them suspicious. No, I'll sit tight and take what comes."

"I *still* don't like it," he said, seven days later, as the tough little mountain ponies carried them down the winding road. "And don't you think I'm running away because I'm afraid. I'm just sorry for those poor old guys up there, and I don't want to be around when they find what suckers they've been. Wonder how Sam will take it?"

"It's funny," replied Chuck, "but when I said good-by I got the idea he knew we were walking out on him—and that he didn't care because he knew the machine was running smoothly and that the job would soon be finished. After that—well, of course, for him there just isn't any After That. . . ."

George turned in his saddle and stared back up the mountain road. This was the last place from which one could get a clear view of the lamasery. The squat, angular buildings were silhouetted against the afterglow of the sunset: here and there, lights gleamed like portholes in the side of an ocean liner. Electric lights, of course, sharing the same circuit as the Mark V. How much longer would they share it? wondered George. Would the monks smash up the computer in their rage and disappointment? Or would they just sit down quietly and begin their calculations all over again?

He knew exactly what was happening up on the mountain at this very moment. The high lama and his assistants would be sitting in their silk robes, inspecting the sheets as the junior monks carried them away from the typewriters and pasted them into the great volumes. No one would be saying anything. The only sound would be the incessant patter, the never-ending rainstorm of the keys hitting the paper, for the Mark V itself was utterly silent as it flashed through its thousands of calculations a second. Three months of this, thought George, was enough to start anyone climbing up the wall.

"There she is!" called Chuck, pointing down into the valley. "Ain't she beautiful!"

She certainly was, thought George. The battered old DC3 lay at the end of the runway like a tiny silver cross. In two hours she would be bearing them away to freedom and sanity. It was a thought worth savoring like a fine liqueur. George let it roll round his mind as the pony trudged patiently down the slope.

The swift night of the high Himalayas was now almost upon them. Fortunately, the road was very good, as roads went in that region, and they were both carrying torches. There was not the slightest danger, only a certain discomfort from the bitter cold. The sky overhead was perfectly clear, and ablaze with the familiar, friendly stars. At least there would be no risk, thought George, of the pilot being unable to take off because of weather conditions. That had been his only remaining worry.

He began to sing, but gave it up after a while. This vast arena of mountains, gleaming like whitely hooded ghosts on every side, did not encourage such ebullience. Presently George glanced at his watch.

"Should be there in an hour," he called back over his shoulder to Chuck. Then he added, in an afterthought "Wonder if the computer's finished its run. It was due about now."

Chuck didn't reply, so George swung round in his saddle. He could just see Chuck's face, a white oval turned toward the sky.

"Look," whispered Chuck, and George lifted his eyes to heaven. (There is always a last time for everything.)

Overhead, without any fuss, the stars were going out.

Questions for Discussion and Review

1. Explain the significance of this story's title.
2. Why did Clarke set the story in Tibet?
3. How would you characterize the role of science in this story?
4. What is weird about this story?
5. How is myth used in this story?
6. Describe as clearly as possible the special effects of this story's ending.
7. Are the views of the implied narrator of the story to be taken as those of a believer or an agnostic? Explain and defend your view.

The Mindworm

Cyril Kornbluth

Cyril Kornbluth (1923–1958) was one of the most respected writers in
the field at the time of his premature death. He had been a member of
the SF fandom of the late 1930s and served in the infantry during World
War II. He collaborated with Frederick Pohl on several novels, the most
famous of which is *The Space Merchants* (1953). Of his own work,
The Syndic (1953) and *Not This August* (1955) stand out. Kornbluth
wrote several SF stories that are named consistently among the best of
their kind. That list would include the present story as well as "The
Marching Morons" (1951), "The Little Black Bag" (1950), "The Silly
Season" (1950), and "The Luckiest Man in Denv" (1952). "The
Mindworm" was published first in *Worlds Beyond* (December 1950).

I have classified this story as weird SF for several reasons. It emphasizes
the close and traditional association of the weird story of SF with elements
of the horror story. From Edgar Allan Poe to Fritz Leiber, this combination
has been one of the most popular among writers of SF. Another reason
for including "The Mindworm" under weird SF is to demonstrate once
again the standards by which useful classifications may be established and
maintained. Kornbluth's tale contains subjects and themes normally
associated with the story of supernatural terror. It also has elements of SF
and the weird. The basis on which the story fits into the present type is
a matter of emphasis and balance. Where does the author choose to place
his emphasis?

At first, the emphasis appears to be on terror. After all, vampirism
is one of the classic themes of the horror story. However, there seem to be
mitigating circumstances, as there are in the stories of Anthony Boucher,
which alter the case. The first is the idea of a new form of vampirism
spawned by the effects of atomic radiation. This story works out some
implications of such an alteration. Behind this idea is the suggestion that
superstitions and folk traditions represent ritual defense mechanisms
against the selection of predatory mutations. This supposes that nuclear
radiation may be just the most recent but by no means the first cause of
genetic variation leading to the production of werewolves and vampires—
another case in which nature realizes mythic forms.

The tone and focus of the story emphasize what is strange and eerie
about the Mindworm's career as a predator. The horror is present, of
course, in the nature of the Mindworm's vampirism, but Kornbluth forces
on us the role of detached observers who regard the progress of the Mindworm with an almost clinical disinterest. It is only at the end that the
thrill of real terror is dramatized; but by that time, we are sufficiently
disengaged from the Mindworm's viewpoint so that we can understand
his sense of fright without sharing it. Instead, we are encouraged to
respond with something like satisfaction that the race still retains sufficient
ancient defensive instincts in the form of its superstitions. It is ironic that

in this story their defensive character depends on the recognition of a symptomology which would go undetected by scientifically trained modern minds because the possibility of vampirism would be inadmissable.

The handsome j. g. and the pretty nurse held out against it as long as they reasonably could, but blue Pacific water, languid tropical nights and the low atoll dreaming on the horizon—and the complete absence of any other nice young people for company on the small, uncomfortable parts boat—did their work. On June 30th they watched through dark glasses as the dazzling thing burst over the fleet and the atoll. Her manicured hand gripped his arm in excitement and terror. Unfelt radiation sleeted through their loins.

A storekeeper-third-class named Bielaski watched the young couple with more interest than he showed in Test Able. After all, he had twenty-five dollars on the nurse. That night he lost it to a chief bosun's mate who had backed the j. g.

In the course of time, the careless nurse was discharged under conditions other than honorable. The j. g., who didn't like to put things in writing, phoned her all the way from Manila to say it was a damned shame. When her gratitude gave way to specific inquiry, their overseas connection went bad and he had to hang up.

She had a child, a boy, turned it over to a well-run foundling home which she personally inspected beforehand, and vanished from his life into a series of good jobs and finally marriage.

The boy grew up stupid, puny and stubborn, greedy and miserable. To the home's hilarious young athletics director he suddenly said: "You hate me. You think I make the rest of the boys look bad."

The athletics director blustered and laughed, and later told the doctor over coffee: "I watch myself around the kids. They're sharp— they catch a look or a gesture and it's like a blow in the face to them, I know that, so I watch myself. So how did he know?"

The doctor told the boy: "Three pounds more this month isn't bad, but suppose you pitch in and clean up your plate *every* day? Can't live on meat and water; those vegetables make you big and strong."

The boy said: "What's 'neurasthenic' mean?"

The doctor later said to the director: "It made my flesh creep. I was looking at his little spindling body and dishing out the old pep-talk about growing big and strong, and inside my head I was thinking 'we'd call him neurasthenic in the old days' and then out he popped with it. What should we do? Should we do anything? Maybe it'll go away. I don't know anything about these things. I don't know whether anybody does."

"Reads minds, does he?" asked the director. *Be damned if he's going to read my mind about Schultz Meat Market's ten per cent.* "Doctor, I think I'm going to take my vacation a little early this year. Has anybody shown any interest in adopting the child?"

"Not him. He wasn't a baby-doll when we got him, and at present he's an exceptionally unattractive-looking kid. You know how people don't give a damn about anything but their looks."

"*Some* couples would take anything, or so they tell me."

"Unapproved for foster-parenthood, you mean?"

"Red tape and arbitrary classifications sometimes limit us too severely in our adoptions, don't you think?"

"If you're going to wish him on some screwball couple that the courts turned down as unfit, I want no part of it."

"You don't have to have any part of it, doctor. By the way, which dorm does he sleep in?"

"West," grunted the doctor, leaving the office.

The doctor called a few friends—a judge, a couple the judge referred him to, a court clerk. Then he left by way of the east wing of the building.

The boy survived three months with the Berrymans. Hard-drinking Mimi alternately caressed and shrieked at him; Edward W. tried to be a good scout and just gradually lost interest, looking clean through him. He hit the road in June and got by with it for a while. He wore a Boy Scout uniform, and Boy Scouts can turn up anywhere, any time. The money he had taken with him lasted a month. When the last penny of the last dollar was three days spent, he was adrift on a Nebraska prairie. He had walked out of the last small town because the constable was beginning to wonder what on earth he was hanging around for and who he belonged to. The town was miles behind on the two-lane highway; the infrequent cars did not stop.

One of Nebraska's "rivers," a dry bed at this time of year, lay ahead, spanned by a railroad culvert. There were some men in its shade, and he was hungry.

They were ugly, dirty men, and their thoughts were muddled and stupid. They called him "Shorty" and gave him a little dirty bread and some stinking sardines from a can. The thoughts of one of them became less muddled and uglier. He talked to the rest out of the boy's hearing, and they whooped with laughter. The boy got ready to run, but his legs wouldn't hold him up.

He could read the thoughts of the men quite clearly as they headed for him. Outrage, fear and disgust blended in him and somehow turned inside-out and one of the men was dead on the dry ground, grasshoppers vaulting onto his flannel shirt, the others backing away, frightened now, not frightening.

He wasn't hungry any more; he felt quite comfortable and satisfied.

He got up and headed for the other man, who ran. The rearmost of them was thinking *Jeez he folded up the evil eye we was only gonna—*

Again the boy let the thoughts flow into his head and again he flipped his own thoughts around them; it was quite easy to do. It was different—this man's terror from the other's lustful anticipation. But both had their points. . . .

At his leisure, he robbed the bodies of three dollars and twenty-four cents.

Thereafter his fame preceded him like a death-wind. Two years on the road and he had his growth, and his fill of the dull and stupid minds he met there. He moved to northern cities, a year here, a year there, quiet, unobtrusive, prudent, an epicure.

Sebastian Long woke suddenly, with something on his mind. As night-fog cleared away he remembered, happily. Today he started the Demeter Bowl! At last there was time, as last there was money—six hundred and twenty-three dollars in the bank. He had packed and shipped the three dozen cocktail glasses last night, engraved with Mrs. Klausman's initials—his last commercial order for as many months as the Bowl would take.

He shifted from nightshirt to denims, gulped coffee, boiled an egg but was too excited to eat it. He went to the front of his shop-work-room-apartment, checked the lock, waved at neighbors' children on their way to school, and ceremoniously set a sign in the cluttered window.

It said: "NO COMMERCIAL ORDERS TAKEN UNTIL FURTHER NOTICE."

From a closet he tenderly carried a shrouded object that made a double armful and laid it on his workbench. Unshrouded, it was a glass bowl—*what* a glass bowl! The clearest Swedish lead glass, the purest lines he had ever seen, his secret treasure since the crazy day he had bought it, long ago, for six months' earnings. His wife had given him hell for that until the day she died. From the closet he brought a portfolio filled with sketches and designs dating back to the day he had bought the bowl. He smiled over the first, excitedly scrawled—a florid, rococo conception, unsuited to the classicism of the lines and the serenity of the perfect glass.

Through many years and hundreds of sketches he had refined his conception to the point where it was, he humbly felt, not unsuited to the medium. A strongly-molded Demeter was to dominate the piece, a matron as serene as the glass, and all the fruits of the earth would flow from her gravely outstretched arms.

Suddenly and surely, he began to work. With a candle he thinly smoked an oval area on the outside of the bowl. Two steady fingers clipped the Demeter drawing against the carbon black; a hair-fine needle in his other hand traced her lines. When the transfer of the design was done, Sebastian Long readied his lathe. He fitted a small copper wheel, slightly worn as he liked them, into the chuck and with his fingers charged it with the finest rouge from Rouen. He took an ashtray cracked in delivery and held it against the spinning disk. It bit in smoothly, with the *wiping* feel to it that was exactly right.

Holding out his hands, seeing that the fingers did not tremble with excitement, he eased the great bowl to the lathe and was about to make the first tiny cut of the millions that would go into the masterpiece.

Somebody knocked on his door and rattled the doorknob.

Sebastian Long did not move or look toward the door. Soon the busy-body would read the sign and go away. But the pounding and the rattling of the knob went on. He eased down the bowl and angrily went to the window, picked up the sign and shook it at whoever it was—he couldn't make out the face very well. But the idiot wouldn't go away.

The engraver unlocked the door, opened it a bit and snapped: "The shop is closed. I shall not be taking any orders for several months. Please don't bother me now."

"It's about the Demeter Bowl," said the intruder.

Sebastian Long stared at him. "What the devil do you know about my Demeter Bowl?" He saw the man was a stranger, undersized by a little, middle-aged. . . .

"Just let me in please," urged the man. "It's important. Please!"

"I don't know what you're talking about," said the engraver. "But what do you know about my Demeter Bowl?" He hooked his thumbs pugnaciously over the waistband of his denims and glowered at the stranger. The stranger promptly took advantage of his hand being removed from the door and glided in.

Sebastian Long thought briefly that it might be a nightmare as the man darted quickly about his shop, picking up a graver and throwing it down, picking up a wire scratch-wheel and throwing it down. "Here, you!" he roared, as the stranger picked up a crescent wrench which he did not throw down.

As Long started for him, the stranger darted to the workbench and brought the crescent wrench down shatteringly on the bowl.

Sebastian Long's heart was bursting with sorrow and rage; such a storm of emotions as he never had known thundered through him. Paralyzed, he saw the stranger smile with anticipation.

The engraver's legs folded under him and he fell to the floor, drained and dead.

The Mindworm, locked in the bedroom of his brownstone front, smiled again, reminiscently.

Smiling, he checked the day on a wall calendar.

"Dolores!" yelled her mother in Spanish. "Are you going to pass the whole day in there?"

She had been practicing low-lidded, sexy half-smiles like Lauren Bacall in the bathroom mirror. She stormed out and yelled in English:

"I don't know how many times I tell you not to call me that Spick name no more!"

"Dolly!" sneered her mother. "Dah-lee! When was there a Saint Dah-lee that you call yourself after, eh?"

The girl snarled a Spanish obscenity at her mother and ran down the tenement stairs. Jeez, she was gonna be late for sure!

Held up by a stream of traffic between her and her streetcar, she danced with impatience. Then the miracle happened. Just like in the movies, a big convertible pulled up before her and its lounging driver said, opening the door: "You seem to be in a hurry. Could I drop you somewhere?"

Dazed at the sudden realization of a hundred daydreams, she did not fail to give the driver a low-lidded, sexy smile as she said: "Why, *thanks!*" and climbed in. He wasn't no Cary Grant, but he had all his hair . . . kind of small, but so was she . . . and jeez, the convertible had *leopard-skin seat covers!*

The car was in the stream of traffic, purring down the avenue. "It's a lovely day," she said. "Really too nice to work."

The driver smiled shyly, kind of like Jimmy Stewart but of course not so tall, and said: "I feel like playing hooky myself. How would you like a spin down Long Island?"

"Be wonderful!" The convertible cut left on an odd-numbered street.

"Play hooky, you said. What do you do?"

"Advertising."

"*Advertising!*" Dolly wanted to kick herself for ever having doubted, for ever having thought in low, self-loathing moments that it wouldn't work out, that she'd marry a grocer or a mechanic and live forever after in a smelly tenement and grow old and sick and stooped. She felt vaguely in her happy daze that it might have been cuter, she might have accidently pushed him into a pond or something, but this was cute enough. An advertising man, leopard-skin seat covers . . . what more could a girl with a sexy smile and a nice little figure want?

Speeding down the South Shore she learned that his name was Michael Brent, exactly as it ought to be. She wished she could tell him she was Jennifer Brown or one of those real cute names they had nowadays, but was reassured when he told her he thought Dolly Gonzalez was a beautiful name. He didn't and she noticed the omission, add: "It's the most beautiful name I ever heard!" That, she comfortably thought as she settled herself against the cushions, would come later.

They stopped at Medford for lunch, a wonderful lunch in a little restaurant where you went down some steps and there were candles on the table. She called him "Michael" and he called her "Dolly." She learned that he liked dark girls and thought the stories in *True Story* really were true, and that he thought she was just tall enough, and that Greer Garson was wonderful, but not the way she was, and that he thought her dress was just wonderful.

They drove slowly after Medford, and Michael Brent did most of the talking. He had traveled all over the world. He had been in the war and wounded—just a flesh wound. He was 38, and had been married once, but she died. There were no children. He was alone in the world. He had nobody to share his town house in the 50's, his country place in Westchester, his lodge in the Maine woods. Every word set the girl floating higher and higher on a tide of happiness, the signs were unmistakable.

When they reached Montauk Point, the last sandy bit of the continent before blue water and Europe, it was sunset, with a great wrinkled sheet of purple and rose stretching half across the sky and the first stars appearing above the dark horizon of the water.

The two of them walked from the parked car out onto the sand, alone, bathed in glorious Technicolor. Her heart was nearly bursting with joy as she heard Michael Brent say, his arms tightening around her: "Darling, will you marry me?"

"Oh, *yes*, Michael!" she breathed, dying.

The Mindworm, drowsing, suddenly felt the sharp sting of danger. He cast out through the great city, dragging tentacles of thought:

"... die if she don't let me ..."

"... six an' six is twelve an' carry one an' three is four ..."

"... gobblegobble madre de dios pero soy gobblegobble ..."

"... parlay Domino an' Missab and shoot the roll on Duchess Peg in the feature ..."

" ... melt resin add the silver chloride and dissolve in oil of lavender stand and decant and fire to cone 012 give you shimmering streaks of luster down the walls ..."

"... moiderin' square-headed gobblegobble tried ta poke his eye out wassamatta witta ref ..."

"... O God I am most heartily sorry I have offended thee in ..."

"... talk like a commie ..."

"... gobblegobblegobble two dolla twenny-fi' sense gobble ..."

"... just a nip and fill it up with water and brush my teeth ..."

"... really know I'm God but fear to confess their sins ..."

" ... dirty lousy rock-headed claw-handed paddle-footed goggle-eyed snot-nosed hunch-backed feeble-minded pot-bellied son of ..."

"... write on the wall alfie is a stunkur and then ..."

"... thinks I believe it's a television set but I know he's got a bomb in there but who can I tell who can help so alone ..."

"... gabble was ich weiss nicht gabble geh bei Broadvay gabble ..."

"... habt mein daughter Rosie such a fella gobblegobble ..."

"... wonder if that's one didn't look back ..."

"... seen with her in the Medford restaurant ..."

The Mindworm struck into that thought.

"... not a mark on her but the M. E.'s have been wrong before and heart failure don't mean a thing anyway try to talk to her old lady authorize an autopsy get Pancho little guy talks Spanish be best . . ."

The Mindworm knew he would have to be moving again—soon. He was sorry; some of the thoughts he had tapped indicated good . . . hunting?

Regretfully, he again dragged his net:

". . . with chartreuse drinks I mean drapes could use a drink come to think of it . . ."

". . . reep-beep-reep-beep- reepiddy-beepiddy-beep bop man wadda beat . . ."

"^{e} . .$f(x_1x_2)$-j-o $^aj(nj)x_1n$-jx$_2$j WHAT THE HELL WAS THAT?"

The Mindworm withdrew, in frantic haste. The intelligence was massive, its overtones those of a vigorous adult. He had learned from certain dangerous children that there was peril of a leveling flow. Shaken and scared, he contemplated traveling. He would need more than that wretched girl had supplied, and it would not be epicurean. There would be no time to find individuals at a ripe emotional crisis, or goad them to one. It would be plain—munching. The Mindworm drank a glass of water, also necessary to his metabolism.

EIGHT FOUND DEAD
IN UPTOWN MOVIE;
"MOLESTER" SOUGHT

New York (CP)—Eight persons, including three women, were found dead Wednesday night of unknown causes in widely-separated seats in the balcony of the Odeon Theater at 117th St. and Broadway. Police are seeking a man described by the balcony usher, Michael Fenelly, 18, as "acting like a woman-molester."

Fenelly discovered the first of the fatalities after seeing the man "moving from one empty seat to another several times." He went to ask a woman in a seat next to one the man had just vacated whether he had annoyed her. She was dead.

Almost at once, a scream rang out. In another part of the balcony Mrs. Sadie Rabinowitz, 40, uttered the cry when another victim toppled from his seat next to her.

Theater manager I. J. Marcusohn stopped the show and turned on the house lights. He tried to instruct his staff to keep the audience from leaving before the police arrived. He failed to get word to them in time, however, and most of the audience was gone when a detail from the 24th Pct. and an ambulance from Harlem hospital took over at the scene of the tragedy.

The Medical Examiner's office has not yet made a report as to the causes of death. A spokesman said the victims showed no signs of poisoning or violence. He added that it "was inconceivable that it could be a coincidence."

Lt. John Braidwood of the 24th Pct. said of the alleged molester:

"We got a fair description of him and naturally we will try to bring him in for questioning."

Clickety-click, clickety-click, clickety-click sang the rails as the Mindworm drowsed in his coach seat.

Some people were walking forward from the diner. One was thinking: "Different-looking fellow. (a) he's aberrant (b) he's nonaberrant and ill. Cancel (b)—respiration normal, skin smooth and healthy, no tremor of limbs, well-groomed. Is aberrant (1) trivially. (2) significantly. Cancel (1)—displayed no involuntary interest when . . . odd! *Running* for the washroom! Unexpected because (a) neat grooming indicates amour propre inconsistent with amusing others; (b) evident health inconsistent with . . ." It had taken one second, was fully detailed.

The Mindworm, locked in the toilet of the coach, wondered what the next stop was. He was getting off at it—not frightened, just careful. Dodge them, keep dodging them and everything would be all right. Send out no mental taps until the train was far away and everything would be all right.

He got off at a West Virginia coal and iron town surrounded by ruined mountains and filled with the offscourings of Eastern Europe. Serbs, Albanians, Croats, Hungarians, Slovenes, Bulgarians and all possible combinations and permutations thereof. He walked slowly from the smoked-stained, brownstone passenger station. The train had roared on its way.

". . . ain' no gemmum tha's fo sho', fi-cen' tip fo' a good shine lak ah give um . . ."

". . . dumb bassar don't know how to make out a billa lading yet he ain't never gonna know so fire him get it over with . . ."

". . . gabblegabblegabble . . ." Not a word he recognized in it.

". . . gobblegobble dat tam vooman I brek she nack . . ."

". . . gobble trink visky chin glassabeer gobblegobble gobble . . ."

". . . gabblegabblegabble . . ."

". . . makes me so goblegobble mad little no-good tramp no she ain' but I don't like no standup from no dame . . ."

A blond, square-headed boy fuming under a street light.

" . . . out wit' Casey Oswiak I could kill that dumb bohunk alla time trin' ta paw her . . ."

It was a possibility. The Mindworm drew near.

". . . stand me up for that gobblegobble bohunk I oughta slap her inna mush like my ole man says . . ."

"Hello," said the Mindworm.

"Waddaya wan'?"

"Casey Oswiak told me to tell you not to wait up for your girl. He's taking her out tonight."

The blond boy's rage boiled into his face and shot from his eyes. He was about to swing when the Mindworm began to feed. It was like pheasant after chicken, venison after beef. The coarseness of the environment, or the ancient strain? The Mindworm wondered as he strolled down the street. A girl passed him:

". . . oh but he's gonna be mad like last time wish I came right away so jealous kinda nice but he might bust me one some day be nice to him tonight there he is lam'post leaning on it looks kinda funny gawd I hope he ain't drunk looks kinda funny sleeping sick or bozhe moi gabblegabblegabble . . ."

Her thoughts trailed into a foreign language of which Mindworm knew not a word. After hysteria had gone she recalled, in the foreign language, that she had passed him.

The Mindworm, stimulated by the unfamiliar quality of the last feeding, determined to stay for some days. He checked in at a Main Street hotel.

Musing, he dragged his net:

". . . gobblegobblewhompyeargobblecheskygobblegabblechyesh . . ."

". . . take him down cellar beat the can off the damn chesky thief put the fear of god into him teach him can't bust into no boxcars in *mah* parta the caounty . . ."

". . . gabblegabble . . ."

". . . phone ole Mister Ryan in She-cawgo and he'll tell them three-card monte grifters who got the horse-room rights in this necka the woods by damn don't pay no protection money for no protection . . ."

The Mindworm followed that one further; it sounded as though it could lead to some money if he wanted to stay in the town long enough.

The Eastern Europeans of the town, he mistakenly thought, were like the tramps and bums he had known and fed on during his years on the road—stupid and safe, safe and stupid, quite the same thing.

In the morning he found no mention of the square-headed boy's death in the town's paper and thought it had gone practically unnoticed. It had—by the paper, which was of, by and for the coal and iron company and its native-American bosses and straw bosses. The other town, the one without a charter or police force, with only an imported weekly newspaper or two from the nearest city, noticed it. The other town had roots more than two thousand years deep, which are hard to pull up. But the Mindworm didn't know it was there.

He fed again that night, on a giddy young streetwalker in her room. He had astounded and delighted her with a fistfull of ten-dollar bills before he began to gorge. Again the delightful difference from city-bred folk was there. . . .

Again in the morning he had been unnoticed, he thought. The chartered town, unwilling to admit that there were streetwalkers or that they were found dead, wiped the slate clean; its only member who really cared was the native-American cop on the beat who had collected weekly from the dead girl.

The other town, unknown to the Mindworm, buzzed with it. A delegation went to the other town's only public officer. Unfortunately he was young, American-trained, perhaps even ignorant about some important things. For what he told them was: "My children, that is foolish superstition. Go home."

The Mindworm, through the day, roiled·the surface of the town proper by allowing himself to be roped into a poker game in a parlor of the hotel. He wasn't good at it, he didn't like it, and he quit with relief when he had cleaned six shifty-eyed, hard-drinking loafers out of about three hundred dollars. One of them went straight to the police station and accused the unknown of being a sharper. A humorous sergeant, the Mindworm was pleased to note, joshed the loafer out of his temper.

Nightfall again, hunger again. . . .

He walked the streets of the town and found them empty. It was strange. The native-American citizens were out, tending bar, walking their beats, locking up their newspaper on the stones, collecting their rents, managing their movies—but where were the others? He cast his net:

". . . gobblegobblegobble whomp year gobble . . ."

". . . crazy old pollack mama of mine try to lock me in with Errol Flynn at the Majestic never know the difference if I sneak out the back . . ."

That was near. He crossed the street and it was nearer. He homed on the thought:

". . . jeez he's a hunka man like Stanley but he never looks at me that Vera Kowalik I'd like to kick her just once in the gobblegobblegobble crazy old mama won't be American so ashamed . . ."

It was half a block, no more, down a side street. Brick houses, two stories, with back yards on an alley. She was going out the back way.

How strangely quiet it was in the alley.

". . . ea-sy down them steps fix that damn board that's how she caught me last time what the hell they all so scared of went to see Father Drugas won't talk bet somebody got it again that Vera Kowalik and her big . . ."

". . . gobble bozhe gobble whomp year gobble . . ."

She was closer; she was closer.

"All think I'm a kid show them who's a kid bet if Stanley caught me all alone out here in the alley dark and all he wouldn't think I was a kid that damn Vera Kowalik her folks don't think she's a kid . . ."

For all her bravado she was stark terrified when he said: "Hello."

"Who—who—who—?" she stammered.

Quick, before she screamed. Her terror was delightful.

Not too replete to be alert, he cast about, questing.

". . . gobblegobblegobble whomp year."

The countless eyes of the other town, with more than two thousand years of experience in such things, had been following him. What he had sensed as a meaningless hash of noise was actually an impassioned outburst in a nearby darkened house.

"Fools! fools! Now he has taken a virgin! I said not to wait. What will we say to her mother?"

An old man with handlebar mustache and, in spite of the heat, his shirt sleeves decently rolled down and buttoned at the cuffs, evenly replied: "My heart in me died with hers, Casimir, but one must be sure. It would be a terrible thing to make a mistake in such an affair."

The weight of conservative elder opinion was with him.

Other old men with mustaches, some perhaps remembering mistakes long ago, nodded and said: "A terrible thing. A terrible thing."

The Mindworm strolled back to his hotel and napped on the made bed briefly. A tingle of danger awakened him. Instantly he cast out:

". . . gobblegobble whompyear."

". . . whampyir."

"WAMPYIR!"

Close! Close and deadly!

The door of his room burst open, and mustached old men with their shirt sleeves rolled down and decently buttoned at the cuffs unhesitatingly marched in, their thoughts a turmoil of alien noises, foreign gibberish that he could not wrap his mind around, disconcerting, from every direction.

The sharpened stake was through his heart and the scythe blade through his throat before he could realize that he had not been the first of his kind; and that what clever people have not yet learned, some quite ordinary people have not yet entirely forgotten.

Questions for Discussion and Review

1. How do you account for the tone of the opening paragraph?
2. How could the author have made this a more traditional horror story?
3. Why is the Mindworm portrayed as a maladjusted child?
4. Why does the Mindworm break the Demeter bowl?
5. How is the vampire finally discovered?

Time Travel and Parallel Worlds

Stories about time travel and parallel worlds or universes are developments of the recent past. Even future romances are rarities before the nineteenth century. Samuel Madden's *The Reign of George VI 1900–1925* (1763) offers interesting political projections; but it does not attempt to extrapolate future changes in life style or culture. To have done so would have been considered revolutionary in more than just the literary sense. Future projections were favorite rhetorical devices of the preaching class, ordained as well as lay members, and an early example of the fringes of the type here under study is Godwin's *Caleb Williams* (1794). Nevertheless, imaginary futures are still not time travel; that was a development of the later Victorian era. According to E. F. Bleiler and T. E. Ditky, however, the first time-travel story is "Missing One's Coach," which appeared in the Dublin University magazine in 1837. The appearance of the time-travel story coincides with growing interest in time itself on the part of philosophers, scientists, economists, and engineers. Time was being treated conceptually as a dimension to be measured, divided, calibrated, and even manipulated. In modern living, the clock mechanism was becoming the hub around which modern technology and culture were beginning to move. As the century turned, both philosophers and scientists began to explore subjective time, an exploration leading to Bergson's intuitions that duration is a succession of conscious states and Einstein's analysis that the relative flow of time depends on the comparative state of an observer.

In response to the forces leavening the thought of the era, the time-travel story reached its maturity in 1895 with *The Time Machine* of

H. G. Wells, who was really riding the crest of a wave of future stories that had begun to appear in the 1870s and 1880s. The two most noteworthy were Sir George Tomkyns Chesney's "The Battle of Dorking" (1871), predicting the German conquest of Britain four years later, in 1875, and Edward Bellamy's *Looking Backward* (1888). Nevertheless, before Wells's story appeared, there had been nothing quite like his version of a wonder-working machine for time travel. There were two great innovations in the story. One was the machine itself, which permitted travel into future or past, as opposed to mere visionary or dream futures then currently in fashion. The other was the idea of conscious control and scientific direction implied in the machine's function. In one stroke, Wells had conquered a whole new kingdom for the imagination to explore, colonize, and domesticate.

Although the intervening years have enriched our sense of the potentials of human experience, time travel of the sort hypothetically proposed by Wells is no nearer realization. The best scientific opinion of the present is that time travel by machine is impossible except in the sense postulated by Einstein. Such time traveling is theoretically possible as an effect of attaining velocities close to the speed of light for an extended period. Even at that, the returning astronauts would have aged only more slowly than their contemporaries and therefore could experience a future they might otherwise not have lived to see. These are indeed big *if*s, and there is no suggestion that travel into the past is possible under any conceivable circumstances.

The first parallel-world story was written by Murray Leinster (William F. Jenkins); it was entitled "Sidewise in Time." The story introduces the philosophical concept that parallel tracks of time exist and that under special conditions it is possible to switch from one track to another. Since Leinster's pioneering effort, stories of parallel worlds have become a favorite subtype among modern SF writers. Many variations of the basic idea have developed over the years, and they include the alternate history story perfected in Ward Moore's *Bring the Jubilee* (1953), Poul Anderson's "Delenda Est" (1955), Philip K. Dick's *The Man in the High Castle* (1962), and Fritz Leiber's "Catch That Zepplin!" (1975), to name a few outstanding examples.

We find a similar development and elaboration of the potentials of the time-travel story. Tales that propel us back to an imagined past or forward into an anticipated future will probably always appeal to a time-bound human race.

All You Zombies—

Robert A. Heinlein

Robert Anson Heinlein was born on July 7, 1907, in Butler, Missouri.
He graduated from the U.S. Naval Academy in 1929 and received a
commission in the Navy, but he was forced to retire in 1934 because of
tuberculosis. Following his retirement, he did everything from graduate
study in physics and engineering to selling real estate. His naval experience
and knowledge of aeronautical engineering enhanced his value to the
service during World War II, which he spent in Philadelphia at the Naval
Air Experimental Station.

Just before the outbreak of the war, Heinlein began writing SF stories
as the result of a contest he intended to enter. Instead his first story and
many others thereafter went to John W. Campbell's *Astounding Science
Fiction*. In May 1941, *Astounding* published a chart worked out by
Heinlein detailing the background of a future history of America and
the world that forms a common link among many of the early stories. After
the war, Heinlein returned to writing science fiction and has won Hugo
awards for his novels *Double Star* (1956), *Starship Troopers* (1960),
Stranger in a Strange Land (1962), and *The Moon Is a Harsh Mistress*
(1967). In 1974 he won the Nebula Grand Master Award for lifetime
achievement in SF. His latest novel is *Time Enough for Love* (1973).
"All You Zombies—" first appeared in *The Magazine of Fantasy and Science
Fiction* (March 1959).

Heinlein's career as a writer divides at about the time he wrote this story.
The turning point seems to come after the appearance of *Starship Troopers*
in 1960. Heinlein was an early protégé of John W. Campbell, who published his first stories in *Astounding Science Fiction*, in the late 1930s.
The "future history stories," together with Hugo-winning novels of the
1950s, define very well the basis of Heinlein's early fame. These stories
contained the main ingredients of Campbell's success formula, blending
together hard science extrapolation, social themes, and realistically portrayed
characters and events. The early Heinlein style seems to owe a good deal
to the "hard-boiled" school of storytelling modeled on the prose of Heming-
way and also popularized in the 1930s and 1940s by mystery writers
Dashiell Hammett and Raymond Chandler.

Heinlein continued to grow as a writer and seems to have turned a corner
in his career as the 1960s began. These new directions, already implied
in some of the details of his "future history," demonstrated remarkable
anticipation of the character of that turbulent decade. Heinlein's later
work is distinguished by the themes and ideas of his two Hugo-winning
novels of the period: *Stranger in a Strange Land* and *The Moon Is a
Harsh Mistress*. "All You Zombies—" dramatizes the author's handling
of the moral implications of some traditional SF ideas and marks the
evolution of a new style and a new emphasis on social criticism.

Heinlein had written two stories of time travel before this one. "By

His Bootstraps" (*Astounding Science Fiction*, 1941) and *The Door into Summer* (1957) resolve some of the sinister implications of time travel happily. "All You Zombies—" is a different vision and a different story with an almost allegorical exploration of the outer limits of idealism. Most human beings feel themselves the center of their own little universe. Heinlein dramatizes the final stage of ego isolation through the logic of time travel, which in the theoretical world of relative time displacement permits a person to be self-creating and self-seducing, but not even then self-sufficient.

Heinlein offers readers a new kind of time-travel story: not the linear, easy-to-follow movement from present into another time, but the more demanding, the more speculative, the more metaphysical projections of time folding inward upon itself. The effect is that of a space-age morality tale in which the author reduces to a kind of madness the confident, self-reliant manipulator figure so often the protagonist in SF stories. Indeed, there is the suggestion of self-parody in showing us the other side of humanity's obsession with innovative technology and intervention in natural process. This leads us into a dead end, a cul-de-sac of the mind, in which the hero looks at the rest of the world and demands to know: "Where did all you zombies come from?"

2217 Time Zone V (EST) 7 Nov 1970 NYC—"Pop's Place": I was polishing a brandy snifter when the Unmarried Mother came in. I noted the time—10.17 P.M. zone five or eastern time November 7th, 1970. Temporal agents always notice time & date; we must.

The Unmarried Mother was a man twenty-five years old, no taller than I am, immature features and a touchy temper. I didn't like his looks—I never had—but he was a lad I was here to recruit, he was my body. I gave him my best barkeep's smile.

Maybe I'm too critical. He wasn't swish; his nickname came from what he always said when some nosy type asked him his line: "I'm an unmarried mother." If he felt less than murderous he would add: "—at four cents a word. I write confession stories."

If he felt nasty, he would wait for somebody to make something of it. He had a lethal style of in-fighting, like a female cop—one reason I wanted him. Not the only one.

He had a load on and his face showed that he despised people more than usual. Silently I poured him a double shot of Old Underwear and left the bottle. He drank, poured another.

I wiped the bar top. "How's the 'Unmarried Mother' racket?"

His fingers tightened on the glass and he seemed about to throw it at me; I felt for the sap under the bar. In temporal manipulation you try to figure everything, but there are so many factors that you never take needless risks.

I saw him relax that tiny amount they teach you to watch for in the

Bureau's training school. "Sorry," I said. "Just asking, 'How's business?' Make it 'How's the weather?' "

He looked sour. "Business is okay. I write 'em, they print 'em, I eat."

I poured myself one, leaned toward him, "Matter of fact," I said, "you write a nice stick—I've sampled a few. You have an amazingly sure touch with the woman's angle."

It was a slip I had to risk; he never admitted what pennames he used. But he boiled enough to pick up only the last. " 'Woman's angle!' " he repeated with a snort. "Yeah, I know the woman's angle. I should."

"So?" I said doubtfully. "Sisters?"

"No. You wouldn't believe me if I told you."

"Now, now," I answered mildly, "bartenders and psychiatrists learn that nothing is stranger than the truth. Why, son, if you heard the stories I do—well, you'd make yourself rich. Incredible."

"You don't know what 'incredible' means!"

"So? Nothing astonishes me. I've always heard worse."

He snorted again. "Want to bet the rest of the bottle?"

"I'll bet a full bottle." I placed one on the bar.

"Well—" I signaled my other bartender to handle the trade. We were at ·the far end, a single-stool space that I kept private by loading the bar top by it with jars of pickled eggs and other clutter. A few were at the other end watching the fights and somebody was playing the juke box—private as a bed where we were. "Okay," he began, "to start with, I'm a bastard."

"No distinction around here," I said.

"I mean it," he snapped. "My parents weren't married."

"Still no distinction," I insisted. "Neither were mine."

"When—" He stopped, gave me the first warm look I ever saw on him. "You mean that?"

"I do. A one-hundred-percent bastard. In fact," I added, "No one in my family ever marries. All bastards."

"Don't try to top me—*you're* married." He pointed at my ring.

"Oh, that." I showed it to him. "It just looks like a wedding ring; I wear it to keep women off." That ring is an antique I bought in 1985 from a fellow operative—he had fetched it from pre-Christian Crete. "The Worm Ouroboros . . . the World Snake that eats its own tail, forever without end. A symbol of the Great Paradox."

He barely glanced at it. "If you're really a bastard, you know how it feels. When I was a little girl—"

"Wups!" I said. "Did I hear you correctly?"

"Who's telling this story? When I was a little girl—Look, ever hear of Christine Jorgenson? Or Roberta Cowell?"

"Uh, sex change cases. You're trying to tell me—"

"Don't interrupt or swelp me, I won't talk. I was a foundling, left at an orphanage in Cleveland in 1945 when I was a month old. When

I was a little girl, I envied kids with parents. Then, when I learned about sex—and, believe me, Pop, you learn fast in an orphanage—"

"I know."

"—I made a solemn vow that any kid of mine would have both a pop and a mom. It kept me 'pure,' quite a feat in that vicinity—I had to learn to fight to manage it. Then I got older and realized I stood darned little chance of getting married—for the same reason I hadn't been adopted." He scowled. "I was horse-faced and buck-toothed, flat-chested and straight-haired."

"You don't look any worse than I do."

"Who cares how a barkeep looks? Or a writer? But people wanting to adopt pick little blue-eyed golden-haired morons. Later on, the boys want bulging breasts, a cute face, and an Oh-you-wonderful-male manner." He shrugged. "I couldn't compete. So I decided to join the W.E.N.C.H.E.S."

"Eh?"

"Women's Emergency National Corps, Hospitality & Entertainment Section, what they now call 'Space Angels'—Auxiliary Nursing Group, Extraterrestrial Legions."

I knew both terms, once I had them chronized. Although we now use still a third name; it's that elite military service corps: Women's Hospitality Order Refortifying & Encouraging Spacemen. Vocabulary shift is the worst hurdle in timejumps—did you know that "service station" once meant a dispensary for petroleum fractions? Once on an assignment in the Churchill Era a woman said to me, "Meet me at the service station next door"—which is *not* what it sounds; a "service station" (then) wouldn't have a bed in it.

He went on: "It was when they first admitted you can't send men into space for months and years and not relieve the tension. You remember how the wowsers screamed?—that improved my chances, volunteers were scarce. A gal had to be respectable, preferably virgin (they liked to train them from scratch), above average mentally, and stable emotionally. But most volunteers were old hookers, or neurotics who would crack up ten days off Earth. So I didn't need looks; if they accepted me, they would fix my buck teeth, put a wave in my hair, teach me to walk and dance and how to listen to a man pleasingly, and everything else—plus training for the prime duties. They would even use plastic surgery if it would help—nothing too good for Our Boys.

"Best yet, they made sure you didn't get pregnant during your enlistment—and you were almost certain to marry at the end of your hitch. Same way today, A.N.G.E.L.S. marry spacers—they talk the language.

"When I was eighteen I was placed as a 'mother's helper.' This family simply wanted a cheap servant but I didn't mind as I couldn't enlist till I was twenty-one. I did housework and went to night school —pretending to continue my high school typing and shorthand but going to a charm class instead, to better my chances for enlistment.

"Then I met this city slicker with his hundred dollar bills." He scowled. "The no-good actually did have a wad of hundred dollar bills. He showed me one night, told me to help myself.

"But I didn't. I liked him. He was the first man I ever met who was nice to me without trying to take my pants off. I quit night school to see him oftener. It was the happiest time of my life.

"Then one night in the park my pants did come off."

He stopped. I said, "And then?"

"And then *nothing!* I never saw him again. He walked me home and told me he loved me—and kissed me good-night and never came back." He looked grim. "If I could find him, I'd kill him!"

"Well," I sympathized, "I know how you feel. But killing him—just for doing what comes naturally—hmm . . . Did you struggle?"

"Huh? What's that got to do with it?"

"Quite a bit. Maybe he deserves a couple of broken arms for running out on you, but—"

"He deserves worse than that! Wait till you hear. Somehow I kept anyone from suspecting and decided it was all for the best. I hadn't really loved him and probably would never love anybody—and I was more eager to join the W.E.N.C.H.E.S. than ever. I wasn't disqualified, they didn't insist on virgins. I cheered up.

"It wasn't until my skirts got tight that I realized."

"Pregnant?"

"The bastard had me higher 'n a kite! Those skinflints I lived with ignored it as long as I could work—then kicked me out and the orphanage wouldn't take me back. I landed in a charity ward surrounded by other big bellies and trotted bedpans until my time came.

"One night I found myself on an operating table, with a nurse saying, 'Relax. Now breathe deeply.'

"I woke up in bed, numb from the chest down. My surgeon came in. 'How do you feel?' he says cheerfully.

" 'Like a mummy.'

" 'Naturally. You're wrapped like one and full of dope to keep you numb. You'll get well—but a Caesarian isn't a hangnail.'

" ' "Caesarian?" ' I said. 'Doc—*did I lose the baby?*'

" 'Oh, no. Your baby's fine.'

" 'Oh. Boy or girl?'

" 'A healthy little girl. Five pounds, three ounces.'

"I relaxed. It's something, to have made a baby. I told myself I would go somewhere and tack 'Mrs.' on my name and let the kid think her papa was dead—no orphanage for *my* kid!

"But the surgeon was talking. 'Tell me, uh—' He avoided my name. '—did you ever think your glandular setup was odd?'

"I said, 'Huh? Of course not. What are you driving at?'

"He hesitated. 'I'll give you this in one dose, then a hypo to let you sleep off your jitters. You'll have 'em.'

" 'Why?' I demanded.

" 'Ever hear of that Scottish physician who was female until she was thirty-five?—then had surgery and became legally and medically a man? Got married. All okay.'

" 'What's that got to do with me?'

" 'That's what I'm saying. You're a man.'

"I tried to sit up. *'What?'*

" 'Take it easy. When I opened you, I found a mess. I sent for the Chief of Surgery while I got the baby out, then we held a consultation with you on the table—and worked for hours to salvage what we could. You had too full sets of organs, both immature, but with the female set well enough developed that you had a baby. They could never be any use to you again, so we took them out and rearranged things so that you can develop properly as a man.' He put a hand on me. 'Don't worry. You're young, your bones will readjust, we'll watch your glandular balance—and make a fine young man out of you.'

"I started to cry. 'What about my *baby?'*

" 'Well, you can't nurse her, you haven't milk enough for a kitten. If I were you, I wouldn't see her—put her up for adoption.'

" *'No!'*

"He shrugged. 'The choice is yours; you're her mother—well, her parent. But don't worry now; we'll get you well first.'

"Next day they let me see the kid and I saw her daily—trying to get used to her. I had never seen a brand-new baby and had no idea how awful they look—my daughter looked like an orange monkey. My feeling changed to cold determination to do right by her. But four weeks later that didn't mean anything."

"Eh?"

"She was snatched."

" 'Snatched?' "

The Unmarried Mother almost knocked over the bottle we had bet. "Kidnapped—stolen from the hosptial nursery!" He breathed hard. "How's that for taking the last thing a man's got to live for?"

"A bad deal," I agreed. "Let's pour you another. No clues?"

"Nothing the police could trace. Somebody came to see her, claimed to be her uncle. While the nurse had her back turned, he walked out with her."

"Description?"

"Just a man, with a face-shaped face, like yours or mine." He frowned. "I think it was the baby's father. The nurse swore it was an older man but he probably used makeup. Who else would swipe my baby? Childless women pull such stunts—but whoever heard of a man doing it?"

"What happened to you then?"

"Eleven more months of that grim place and three operations. In four months I started to grow a beard; before I was out I was shaving regularly . . . and no longer doubted that I was male." He grinned wryly. "I was staring down nurses' necklines."

"Well," I said, "seems to me you came through okay. Here you are, a normal man, making good money, no real troubles. And the life of a female is not an easy one."

He glared at me. "A lot you know about it!"

"So?"

"Ever hear the expression 'a ruined woman'?"

"Mmm, years ago. Doesn't mean much today."

"I was as ruined as a woman can be; that bastard *really* ruined me— I was no longer a woman . . . and I didn't know *how* to be a man."

"Takes getting used to, I suppose."

"You have no idea. I don't mean learning how to dress, or not walking into the wrong rest room, I learned those in the hospital. But how could I *live?* What job could I get? Hell, I couldn't even drive a car. I didn't know a trade; I couldn't do manual labor—too much scar tissue, too tender.

"I hated him for having ruined me for the W.E.N.C.H.E.S., too, but I didn't know how much until I tried to join the Space Corps instead. One look at my belly and I was marked unfit for military service. The medical officer spent time on me just from curiosity; he had read about my case.

"So I changed my name and came to New York. I got by as a fry cook, then rented a typewriter and set myself up as a public stenographer—what a laugh! In four months I typed four letters and one manuscript. The manuscript was for *Real Life Tales* and a waste of paper, but the goof who wrote it, sold it. Which gave me an idea; I bought a stack of confession magazines and studied them." He looked cynical. "Now you know how I get the authentic woman's angle on an unmarried-mother story . . . through the only version I haven't sold— the true one. Do I win the bottle?"

I pushed it toward him. I was upset myself, but there was work to do. I said, "Son, you still want to lay hands on that so-and-so?"

His eyes lighted up—a feral gleam.

"Hold it!" I said. "You wouldn't kill him?"

He chuckled nastily. "Try me."

"Take it easy. I know more about it than you think I do. I can help you. I know where he is."

He reached across the bar. *"Where is he?"*

I said softly, "Let go my shirt, sonny—or you'll land in the alley and we'll tell the cops you fainted." I showed him the sap.

He let go. "Sorry, but where is he?" He looked at me. "And how do you know so much?"

"All in good time. There are records—hospital records, orphanage records, medical records. The matron of your orphanage was Mrs. Fetherage—right? She was followed by Mrs. Gruenstein—right? Your name, as a girl, was 'Jane'—right? And you didn't tell me any of this— right?"

I had him baffled and a bit scared. "What's this? You trying to make trouble for me?"

"No indeed. I've your welfare at heart. I can put this character in your lap. You do to him as you see fit—and I guarantee that you'll get away with it. But I don't think you'll kill him. You'd be nuts—and you aren't nuts. Not quite."

He brushed it aside. "Cut the noise. *Where is he?*"

I poured him a short one; he was drunk but anger was offsetting it. "Not so fast. I do something for you—you do something for me."

"Uh . . . what?"

"You don't like your work. What would you say to high pay, steady work, unlimited expense account, your own boss on the job, and lots of variety and adventure?"

He stared. "I'd say, 'Get those goddam reindeer off my roof! Shove it, Pop—there's no such job."

"Okay, put it this way: I hand him to you, you settle with him, then try my job. If it's not all I claim—well, I can't hold you."

He was wavering; the last drink did it. "When d'yuh d'liver 'im?" he said thickly.

"If it's a deal—*right now!*"

He shoved out his hand. "It's a deal!"

I nodded to my assistant to watch both ends, noted the time—2300 —started to duck through the gate under the bar—when the juke box blared out: *"I'm My Own Granpaw!"* The service man had orders to load it with old Americana and classics because I couldn't stomach the "music" of 1970, but I hadn't known that tape was in it. I called out, "Shut that off! Give the customer his money back." I added, "Storeroom, back in a moment," and headed there with my Unmarried Mother following.

It was down the passage across from the johns, a steel door to which no one but my day manager and myself had a key; inside was a door to an inner room to which only I had a key. We went there.

He looked blearily around at windowless walls. "Where is 'e?"

"Right away." I opened a case, the only thing in the room; it was a U.S.F.F. Co-ordinates Transformer Field Kit, series 1992, Mod. II— a beauty, no moving parts, weight twenty-three kilos fully charged, and shaped to pass as a suitcase. I had adjusted it precisely earlier that day; all I had to do was to shake out the metal net which limits the transformation field.

Which I did. "Wha's that?" he demanded.

"Time machine," I said and tossed the net over us.

"Hey!" he yelled and stepped back. There is a technique to this; the net has to be thrown so that the subject will instinctively step back *onto* the metal mesh, then you close the net with both of you inside completely—else you might leave shoe soles behind or a piece of foot, or scoop up a slice of floor. But that's all the skill it takes. Some agents con a subject into the net; I tell the truth and use that instant of utter astonishment to flip the switch. Which I did.

1030-V-3 April 1963-Cleveland, Ohio-Apex Bldg.: "Hey!" he repeated "Take this damn thing off!"

"Sorry," I apologized and did so, stuffed the net into the case, closed it. "You said you wanted to find him."

"But—You said that was a time machine!"

I pointed out a window. "Does that look like November? Or New York?" While he was gawking at new buds and spring weather, I re-opened the case, took out a packet of hundred dollar bills, checked that the numbers and signatures were compatible with 1963. The Temporal Bureau doesn't care how much you spend (it costs nothing) but they don't like unnecessary anachronisms. Too many mistakes and a general court marital will exile you for a year in a nasty period, say 1974 with its strict rationing and forced labor. I never make such mistakes, the money was okay. He turned around and said, "What happened?"

"He's here. Go outside and take him. Here's expense money." I shoved it at him and added, "Settle him, then I'll pick you up."

Hundred dollar bills have a hypnotic effect on a person not used to them. He was thumbing them unbelievingly as I eased him into the hall, locked him out. The next jump was easy, a small shift in era.

1700-V-10 March 1964-Cleveland-Apex Bldg.: There was a notice under the door saying that my lease expired next week; otherwise the room looked as it had a moment before. Outside, trees were bare and snow threatened; I hurried, stopping only for contemporary money and a coat, hat and topcoat I had left there when I leased the room. I hired a car, went to the hospital. It took twenty minutes to bore the nursery attendant to the point where I could swipe the baby without being noticed; we went to the Apex Building. This dial setting was more involved as the building did not yet exist in 1945. But I had precalculated it.

0100-V-20 Sept 1945-Cleveland-Skyview Motel: Field kit, baby, and I arrived in a motel outside town. Earlier I had registered as "Gregory Johnson, Warren, Ohio," so we arrived in a room with curtains closed, windows locked, and doors bolted, and the floor cleared to allow for waver as the machine hunts. You can get a nasty bruise from a chair where it shouldn't be—not the chair of course, but backlash from the field.

No trouble. Jane was sleeping soundly; I carried her out, put her in a grocery box on the seat of a car I had provided earlier, drove to the orphanage, put her on the steps, drove two blocks to a "service station" (the petroleum products sort) and phoned the orphanage, drove back in time to see them taking the box inside, kept going and abandoned

the car near the motel—walked to it and jumped forward to the Apex
Building in 1963.

2200-V24 April 1963-Cleveland-Apex Bldg.: I had cut the time rather
fine—temporal accuracy depends on span, except on return to zero.
If I had it right, Jane was discovering, out in the park this balmy spring
night, that she wasn't quite as "nice" a girl as she had thought. I
grabbed a taxi to the home of those skinflints, had the hackie wait
around a corner while I lurked in shadows.

Presently I spotted them down the street, arms around each other.
He took her up on the porch and made a long job of kissing her good-
night—longer than I had thought. Then she went in and he came
down the walk, turned away. I slid into step and hooked an arm in his.
"That's all, son," I announced quietly. "I'm back to pick you up."

"*You!*" He gasped and caught his breath.

"Me. Now you know who *he* is—and after you think it over you'll
know who *you* are . . . and if you think hard enough, you'll figure
out who the baby is . . . and who *I* am."

He didn't answer, he was badly shaken. It's a shock to have it proved
to you that you can't resist seducing yourself. I took him to the Apex
Building and we jumped again.

2300-VII-12 Aug 1985-Sub Rockies Base: I woke the duty sergeant,
showed my I.D., told the sergeant to bed him down with a happy pill
and recruit him in the morning. The sergeant looked sour but rank is
rank, regardless of era; he did what I said—thinking, no doubt, that
the next time we met he might be the colonel and I the sergeant. Which
can happen in our corps. "What name?" he asked.

I wrote it out. He raised his eyebrows. "Like so, eh? *Hmm—*"

"You just do your job, Sergeant." I turned to my companion. "Son,
your troubles are over. You're about to start the best job a man ever
held—and you'll do well. I *know*."

"But—"

" 'But' nothing. Get a night's sleep, then look over the proposition.
You'll like it."

"That you will!" agreed the sergeant. "Look at me—born in 1917
—still around, still young, still enjoying life." I went back to the jump
room, set everything on preselected zero.

2301-V-7 Nov 1970-NYC-"Pop's Place": I came out of the storeroom
carrying a fifth of Drambuie to account for the minute I had been gone.
My assistant was arguing with the customer who had been playing *"I'm
My Own Granpaw!"* I said, "Oh, let him play it, then unplug it." I was
very tired.

It's rough, but somebody must do it and it's very hard to recruit
anyone in the later years, since the Mistake of 1972. Can you think of
a better source than to pick people all fouled up where they are and

give them well-paid, interesting (even though dangerous) work in a necessary cause? Everybody knows now why the Fizzle War of 1963 fizzled. The bomb with New York's number on it didn't go off, a hundred other things didn't go as planned—all arranged by the likes of me.

But not the Mistake of '72; that one is not our fault—and can't be undone; there's no paradox to resolve. A thing either is, or it isn't, now and forever amen. But there won't be another like it; an order dated "1992" takes precedence any year.

I closed five minutes early, leaving a letter in the cash register telling my day manager that I was accepting his offer, so see my lawyer as I was leaving on a long vacation. The Bureau might or might not pick up his payments, but they want things left tidy. I went to the room back of the storeroom and forward to 1993.

2200-VII-12 Jan 1993-Sub Rockies Annex-HQ Temporal DOL: I checked in with the duty officer and went to my quarters, intending to sleep for a week. I had fetched the bottle we bet (after all, I won it) and took a drink before I wrote my report. It tasted foul and I wondered why I had ever liked Old Underwear. But it was better than nothing; I don't like to be cold sober, I think too much. But I don't really hit the bottle either; other people have snakes—*I* have people.

I dictated my report: forty recruitments all okayed by the Psych Bureau—counting my own, which I knew would be okayed. I was here, wasn't I? Then I taped a request for assignment to operations; I was sick of recruiting. I dropped both in the slot and headed for bed.

My eye fell on "The By-Laws of Time," over my bed:

Never Do Yesterday What Should Be Done Tomorrow.
If At Last you Do Succeed, Never Try Again.
A Stitch in Time Saves Nine Billion.
A Paradox May be Paradoctored.
It is Earlier When You Think.
Ancestors Are Just People.
Even Jove Nods.

They didn't inspire me the way they had when I was a recruit; thirty subjective-years of time-jumping wears you down. I undressed and when I got down to the hide I looked at my belly. A Caesarian leaves a big scar but I'm so hairy now that I don't notice it unless I look for it.

Then I glanced at the ring on my finger.

The Snake That Eats Its Own Tail, Forever and Ever . . . I *know* where *I* came from—but *where did all you zombies come from?*

I felt a headache coming on, but a headache powder is one thing I do not take. I did once—and you all went away.

So I crawled into bed and whistled out the light.

You aren't really there at all. There isn't anybody but me—Jane—here alone in the dark.

I miss you dreadfully!

Questions for Discussion and Review

1. What is the significance of this story's title?
2. What effect is this story calculated to produce?
3. Does the sort of time travel postulated by Heinlein work on the story's own terms?
4. What stylistic devices does the author use to support his thesis?
5. What significance does self-seduction have in this story?

All the Myriad Ways

Larry Niven

Lawrence Van Cott Niven was born April 30, 1938, in Los Angeles, where he and his wife now reside. He attended California Technical Institute and did graduate study in mathematics at UCLA. Larry Niven has been a full-time writer since his first published story, "The Coldest Place," appeared in *Worlds of If* (December 1964). This story was also the first of the "known space" series of stories and novels that cover the time period from A.D. 1975 to 3100. The series is probably the most complete and carefully worked out future history sequence by any SF writer. Niven won Hugo awards in 1967 for "Neutron Star," in 1972 for "Inconstant Moon,'" and in 1975 for "Hole Man." His novels include *World of the Ptavvs* (1965), *A Gift from Earth* (1968), *The Mote in God's Eye* (1974, with Jerry Pournelle), *A World Out of Time* (1976), and *Ringworld* (1970), which won both Hugo and Nebula awards. "All the Myriad Ways" first appeared in *Galaxy Magazine* (October 1968).

Stories of parallel worlds have become associated with the growth of a serious interest by SF in varieties of abnormal human psychology. Such inner-space stories inevitably seem to confront readers with a radically dislocated experience of primary reality. The dislocation most often takes the form of intensified perceptions of discontinuous realities, hallucinations, even forms of madness. The literary ancestors of such modern parallel-world stories are Edgar Allan Poe, the symbolist poets, and—in this century—the surrealists.

The kind of parallel-world story we find depends on how an author has the characters experience the parallels. The parallels may be those of time, causality, or perception; and each creates its distinctive sense of order. Robert Silverberg's "Translation Error" (1959) gives us a glimpse of time parallels developing side by side. Any of the alternative-world stories mentioned earlier illustrate the idea of parallel causes operating, each creating its conditional line of reality. Larry Niven's story "All the Myriad Ways" falls into the third category, parallels of perception.

The parallel worlds exist as they are perceived by Detective-Lieutenant Gene Trimble, who becomes conscious of the fissioning time lines of his universe as he tries to solve a citywide epidemic of senseless suicide and crime. The key to the mystery is the effect of Crosstime's exploration of alternate time lines. Once the barriers had been breached by Crosstime's pilots, there was a trickle, first, and then a growing flood of destructive and self-destructive acts by people whose minds and moral sense were simply overcome by the prospects of limitless time lines in which the ego is endlessly duplicated in an infinite variety of conditions. Trimble's solution is his introduction to the nightmare of living in all possible parallel worlds.

There were timelines branching and branching, a mega-universe of universes, millions more every minute. Billions? Trillions? Trimble didn't understand the theory, though God knows he'd tried. The universe split every time someone made a decision. Split, so that every decision ever made could go both ways. Every choice made by every man, woman and child on Earth was reversed in the universe next door. It was enough to confuse any citizen, let alone Detective-Lieutenant Gene Trimble, who had other problems to worry about.

Senseless suicide, senseless crime. A city-wide epidemic. It had hit other cities too. Trimble suspected that it was world wide, that other nations were simply keeping it quiet.

Trimble's sad eyes focused on the clock. Quitting time. He stood up to go home and slowly sat down again. For he had his teeth in the problem, and he couldn't let go.

Not that he was really accomplishing anything.

But if he left now, he'd only have to take it up again tomorrow.

Go, or stay?

And the branchings began again. Gene Trimble thought of other universes parallel to this one, and a parallel Gene Trimble in each one. Some had left early. Many had left on time, and were now halfway home to dinner, out to a movie, watching a strip show, racing to the scene of another death. Streaming out of police headquarters in all their multitudes, leaving a multitude of Trimbles behind them. Each of these trying to deal, alone, with the city's endless, inexplicable parade of suicides.

Gene Trimble spread the morning paper on his desk. From the bottom drawer he took his gun-cleaning equipment, then his .45. He began to take the gun apart.

The gun was old but serviceable. He'd never fired it except on the target range and never expected to. To Trimble, cleaning his gun was like knitting, a way to keep his hands busy while his mind wandered off. Turn the screws, don't lose them. Lay the parts out in order.

Through the closed door to his office came the sounds of men hurrying. Another emergency? The department couldn't handle it all. Too many suicides, too many casual murders, not enough men.

Gun oil. Oiled rag. Wipe each part. Put it back in place.

Why would a man like Ambrose Harmon go off a building?

In the early morning light he lay, more a stain than man, thixty-six stories below the edge of his own penthouse roof. The pavement was splattered red for yards around him. The stains were still wet. Harmon had landed on his face. He wore a bright silk dressing gown and a sleeping jacket with a sash.

Others would take samples of his blood, to learn if he had acted under the influence of alcohol or drugs. There was little to be learned from seeing him in his present condition.

"But why was he up so early?" Trimble wondered. For the call had come in at 8:03, just as Trimble arrived at headquarters.

"So late, you mean." Bentley had beaten him to the scene by twenty minutes. "We called some of his friends. He was at an all-night poker game. Broke up around six o'clock."

"Did Harmon lose?"

"Nope. He won almost five hundred bucks."

"That fits," Trimble said in disguest. "No suicide note?"

"Maybe they've found one. Shall we go up and see?"

"We won't find a note," Trimble predicted.

Even three months earlier Trimble would have thought, *How incredible!* or *Who could have pushed him?* Now, riding up in the elevator, he thought only, *Reporters.* For Ambrose Harmon was news. Even among this past year's epidemic of suicides, Ambrose Harmon's death would stand out like Lyndon Johnson in a lineup.

He was a prominent member of the community, a man of dead and wealthy grandparents. Perhaps the huge inheritance, four years ago, had gone to his head. He had invested tremendous sums to back harebrained quixotic causes.

Now, because one of the harebrained causes had paid off, he was richer than ever. The Crosstime Corporation already held a score of patents on inventions imported from alternate time tracks. Already those inventions had started more than one industrial revolution. And Harmon was the money behind Crosstime. He would have been the world's next billionaire—had he not walked off the balcony.

They found a roomy, luxuriously furnished apartment in good order, and a bed turned down for the night. The only sign of disorder was Harmon's clothing—slacks, sweater, a silk turtleneck shirt, knee-length shoesocks, no underwear—piled on a chair in the bedroom. The toothbrush had been used.

He got ready for bed, Trimble thought. He brushed his teeth, and then he went out to look at the sunrise. A man who kept late hours like that, he wouldn't see the sunrise very often. He watched the sunrise, and when it was over, he jumped.

"Why?"

They were all like that. Easy, spontaneous decisions. The victim-killers walked off bridges or stepped from their balconies or suddenly flung themselves in front of subway trains. They strolled halfway across a freeway, or swallowed a full bottle of laudanum. None of the methods showed previous planning. Whatever was used, the victim had had it all along; he never actually went out and *bought* a suicide weapon. The victim rarely dressed for the occasion, or used makeup, as an ordinary suicide would. Usually there was no note.

Harmon fit the pattern perfectly.

"Like Richard Corey," said Bentley.

"Who?"

"Richard Corey, the man who had everything. 'And Richard Corey, one calm summer night, Went home and put a bullet through his head.' You know what I think?"

"If you've got an idea, let's have it."

"The suicides all started about a month after Crosstime got started. I think one of the Crosstime ships brought back a new bug from some alternate timeline."

"A suicide bug?"

Bentley nodded.

"You're out of your mind."

"I don't think so. Gene, do you know how many Crosstime pilots have killed themselves in the last year? More than twenty percent!"

"Oh?"

"Look at the records. Crosstime has about twenty vehicles in action now, but in the past year they've employed sixty-two pilots. Three disappeared. Fifteen are dead, and all but two died by suicide."

"I didn't know that." Trimble was shaken.

"It was bound to happen sometime. Look at the alternate worlds they've found so far. The Nazi world. The Red Chinese world, half bombed to death. The ones that are totally bombed, and Crosstime can't even find out who did it. The one with the Black Plague mutation, and no penicillin until Crosstime came along. Sooner or later—"

"Maybe, maybe. I don't buy your bug, though. If the suicides are a new kind of plague, what about the other crimes?"

"Same bug."

"Uh, uh. But I think we'll check up on Crosstime."

Trimble's hands finished with the gun and laid it on the desk. He was hardly aware of it. Somewhere in the back of his mind was a prodding sensation: the *handle,* the piece he needed to solve the puzzle.

He spent most of the day studying Crosstime, Inc. News stories, official handouts, personal interviews. The incredible suicide rate among Crosstime pilots could not be coincidence. He wondered why nobody had noticed it before.

It was slow going. With Crosstime travel, as with relativity, you had to throw away reason and use only logic. Trimble had sweated it out. Even the day's murders had not distracted him.

They were typical, of a piece with the preceding eight months' crime wave. A man had shot his foreman with a gun bought an hour earlier, then strolled off toward police headquarters. A woman had moved through the back row of a dark theater, using an ice pick to stab members of the audience through the backs of their seats. She had chosen only young men. They had killed without heat, without concealment; they had surrendered without fear or bravado. Perhaps it was another kind of suicide.

Time for coffee, Trimble thought, responding unconsciously to a dry throat plus a fuzziness of the mouth plus slight fatigue. He set his hands to stand up, and—

The image came to him in an endless row of Trimbles, lined up like the repeated images in facing mirrors. But each image was slightly different. He would go get the coffee *and* he wouldn't *and* he would send somebody for it, and someone was about to bring it without being asked. Some of the images were drinking coffee, a few had tea or milk, some were smoking, some were leaning too far back with their feet on the desks (and a handful of these were toppling helplessly backward), some were, like this present Trimble, introspecting with their elbows on the desk. Damn Crosstime anyway.

He'd have had to check Harmon's business affairs, even without the Crosstime link. There might have been a motive there, for suicide or murder, though it had never been likely.

In the first place, Harmon had cared nothing for money. The Crosstime group had been one of many. At the time that project had looked as harebrained as the rest: a handful of engineers and physicists and philosophers determined to prove that the theory of alternate time tracks was reality.

In the second place, Harmon had no business worries.

Quite the contrary.

Eleven months ago an experimental vehicle had touched one of the worlds of the Confederate States of America and returned. The universes of alternate choice were within reach. And the pilot had brought back an artifact.

From that point on, Crosstime travel had more than financed itself. The Confederate world's "stapler," granted an immediate patent, had bought two more ships. A dozen miracles had originated in a single, technologically advanced timeline, one in which the catastrophic Cuban War had been no more than a wet firecracker. Lasers, oxygen-hydrogen rocket motors, computers, strange plastics—the list was still growing. And Crosstime held all the patents.

In those first months the vehicles had gone off practically at random. Now the pinpointing was better. Vehicles could select any branch they preferred. Imperial Russia, Amerindian America, the Catholic Empire, the dead worlds. Some of the dead worlds were hells of radioactive dust and intact but deadly artifacts. From these worlds Crosstime pilots brought strange and beautiful works of art which had to be stored behind leaded glass.

The latest vehicles could reach worlds so like this one that it took a week of research to find the difference. In theory they could get even closer. There was a phenomenon called 'the broadening of the bands' . . .

And that had given Trimble the shivers.

When a vehicle left its own present, a signal went on in the hangar, a signal unique to that ship. When the pilot wanted to return, he simply cruised across the appropriate band of probabilities until he found the signal. The signal marked his own unique present.

Only it didn't. The pilot always returned to find a clump of signals, a broadened band. The longer he stayed away, the broader was the signal band. His own world had continued to divide after his departure, in a constant stream of decisions being made both ways.

Usually it didn't matter. Any signal the pilot chose represented the world he had left. And since the pilot himself had a choice, he naturally returned to them all. But—

There was a pilot by the name of Gary Wilcox. He had been using his vehicle for experiments, to see how close he could get to his own timeline and still leave it. Once, last month, he had returned twice.

Two Gary Wilcoxes, two vehicles. The vehicles had been wrecked—their hulls intersected. For the Wilcoxes it could have been sticky, for Wilcox had a wife and family. But one of the duplicates had chosen to die almost immediately.

Trimble had tried to call the other Gary Wilcox. He was too late. Wilcox had gone skydiving a week ago. He'd neglected to open his parachute.

Small wonder, thought Trimble. At least Wilcox had had motive. It was bad enough, knowing about the other Trimbles, the ones who had gone home, the ones drinking coffee, et cetera. But—suppose someone walked into the office right now, and it was Gene Trimble?

It could happen.

Convinced as he was that Crosstime was involved in the suicides, Trimble—some other Trimble—might easily have decided to take a trip in a Crosstime vehicle. A short trip. He could land *here.*

Trimble closed his eyes and rubbed at the corners with his fingertips. In some timeline, very close, someone had thought to bring him coffee. Too bad this wasn't it.

It didn't do to think too much about these alternate timelines. There were too many of them. The close one could drive you buggy, but the ones farther off were just as bad.

Take the Cuba War. Atomics had been used, *here,* and now Cuba was uninhabited, and some American cities were gone, and some Russian. It could have been worse.

Why wasn't it? How could we luck out? Intelligent statesmen? Faulty bombs? A humane reluctance to kill indiscriminately?

No. There was no luck anywhere. Every decision was made both ways. For every wise choice you bled your heart out over, you had made all the other choices too. And so it went, all through history.

Civil wars unfought on some worlds were won by either side on others. Elsewhen, another animal had first done murder with an antelope femur. Some worlds were still all nomad; civilization had lost out. If every choice was cancelled elsewhere, why make a decision at all?

Trimble opened his eyes and saw the gun.

That gun, too, was endlessly repeated on endless desks. Some of the images were dirty with years of neglect. Some smelled of gunpowder, fired recently, a few at living targets. Some were loaded. All were as real as this one.

A number of these were about to go off by accident.

A proportion of these were pointed, in deadly coincidence at Gene Trimble.

See the endless rows of Gene Trimble, each at his desk. Some were bleeding and cursing as men run into the room following the sound of the gunshot. Many are already dead.

Was there a bullet in there? Nonsense.

He looked anyway. The gun was empty.

Trimble loaded it. At the base of his mind he felt the touch of the *handle*. He would find what he was seeking.

He put the gun back on his desk, pointing away from him, and he thought of Ambrose Harmon, coming home from a late night. Ambrose Harmon, who had won five hundred dollars at poker. Ambrose Harmon, exhausted, seeing the lightening sky as he prepared for bed. Going out to watch the dawn.

Ambrose Harmon, watching the slow dawn, remembering a two thousand dollar pot. He'd bluffed. In some other branching of time, he had lost.

Thinking that in some other branching of time, that two thousand dollars included his last dime. It was certainly possible. If Crosstime hadn't paid off, he might have gone through the remains of his fortune in the past four years. He liked to gamble.

Watching the dawn, thinking of all the Ambrose Harmons on that roof. Some were penniless this night, and they had not come out to watch the dawn.

Well, why not? If he stepped over the edge, here and now, another Ambrose Harmon would only laugh and go inside.

If he laughed and went inside, other Ambrose Harmons would fall to their deaths. Some were already on their way down. One changed his mind too late, another laughed as he fell. . . .

Well, why not? . . .

Trimble thought of another man, a nonentity, passing a firearms store. Branching of timelines, he thinks, looking in, and he thinks of the man who took his foreman's job. Well, why not? . . .

Trimble thought of a lonely woman making herself a drink at three in the afternoon. She thinks of myriads of alter egos, with husbands, lovers, children, friends. Unbearable, to think that all the might-have-beens were as real as herself. As real as this ice pick in her hand. Well, why not? . . .

And she goes out to a movie, but she takes the ice pick.

And the honest citizen with a carefully submerged urge to commit rape, just once. Reading his newspaper at breakfast, and there's another story from Crosstime: they've found a world line in which Kennedy the First was assassinated. Strolling down a street, he thinks of world lines and infinite branchings, of alter egos already dead, or jailed, or President. A girl in a mini-skirt passes, and she has nice legs. Well, why not? . . .

Casual murder, casual suicide, casual crime. Why not? If alternate universes are a reality, then cause and effect are an illusion. The law of averages is a fraud. You can do anything, and one of you will, or did.

Gene Trimble looked at the clean and loaded gun on his desk. Well, why not? . . .

And he ran out of the office shouting, "Bentley, listen. I've got the answer. . . ."

And he stood up slowly and left the office shaking his head. This was the answer, and it wasn't any good. The suicides, murders, casual crimes would continue. . . .

And he suddenly laughed and stood up. Ridiculous! Nobody dies for a philosophical point! . . .

And he reached for the intercom and told the man who answered to bring him a sandwich and some coffee. . . .

And picked the gun off the newspapers, looked at it for a long moment, then dropped it in the drawer. His hands began to shake. On a world line very close to this one. . . .

And he picked the gun off the newspapers, put it to his head and
fired. The hammer fell on an empty chamber.
fired. The gun jerked and blasted a hole in the ceiling.
fired. The bullet tore a furrow in his scalp.
fired. The bullet took off the top of his head.

Questions for Discussion and Review

1. What time line is Gene Trimble on?
2. What is Trimble's opinion of Crosstime, Inc., and what significance does it have for the story?
3. Compare and contrast the situation of Trimble in this story with that of Jane in "All You Zombies—."
4. "Well, why not?" is a key to what element of the story?
5. Could Niven, using the same idea of myriad worlds, have written his story to produce a different effect? How?

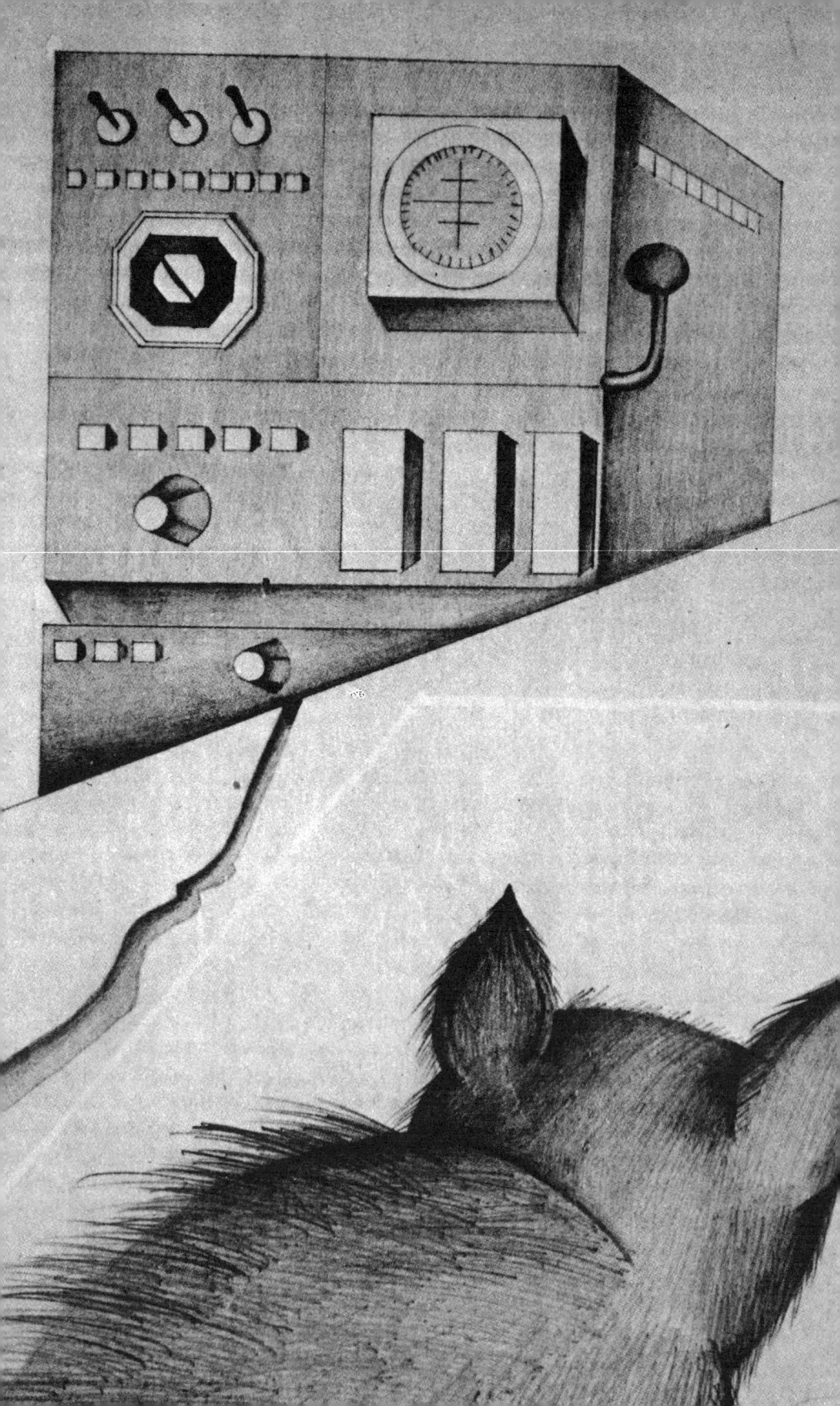

Part 3 Hard Science Fiction

Hard SF is the literature that has developed out of the speculative science treatise. The hard sciences are the physical sciences: biology, chemistry, physics, engineering, electronics, geology, archaeology, and so on. Mathematics and linquistics are sometimes included in this class because they study the basic language structures of scientific thinking and invention. In this part, they will be considered among the hard sciences for purposes of classification.

Hard SF is really a special class of the species with its own characteristic features and problems. In a sense, writers of hard SF must undertake a contradictory and even paradoxical task. Their job is to imitate a phase of science that does not yet exist or could not exist in the physical order of things as presently known. The hard SF story, therefore, must create the illusion of a working and plausible science. Most hard SF stories are written according to rigorous specifications that involve extrapolating or projecting believable future developments of known laws of science. Extrapolation is often the key to the narrative method of the hard SF story, or to what John W. Campbell considered simply a well-thought-out scientific story. In a sense, the real heroes of the hard SF story are science and the problem-solving attitudes it has helped create. Perhaps that is why so many hard SF stories are problem stories or gadget stories. Let us consider a few historic examples of the class by way of illustration and explanation.

As we have seen in the Time Capsule, the science revolution is an ongoing process that has spawned or helped to produce revolutionary change in every area of human experience. One feature of the

227

American Centennial Exhibition of 1876 in Philadelphia was a display of steam- and electric-powered machinery ready to hoist loads, shape wood and metals, and perform work beyond unaided human capacities and endurance. Our ancestors were proud of the achievement those machines represented, and they marveled at what the machines presaged. Warnings had been sounded already, of course, but the cautions were heard as counterpoint to the great chorus of optimism that today still seems to carry us forward, albeit with considerably less assurance than a century ago. Nevertheless, it was reasonable then, as it is now, to see machines as what a culture develops to perform its work—extensions of the hand, brain, muscles, and even of the values of its people. When abused, machines become idols or indifferent agents of destruction like the dicing fates of Thomas Hardy's "Hap." This is an aspect of SF that we shall be seeing in Part Four. But for all that, machines are equally the expression of human genius and vision. They can work wonders by extending human capacity for production, invention, and even understanding. Seen in this way, machines can represent the means by which the human race has set about remaking its environment and itself.

It is no surprise that a good gadget story can elicit a sense of awed wonder from all but the most hardened SF readers. The problem-solving inventions of the hard SF story are doorways to new kinds of experience, new emotions, and new revelations of human potentials. As the machine age was developing its engines, a new kind of fiction was beginning to explore the potential worlds that the machines seemed to promise or threaten. As an example, we may recall Jules Verne's *20,000 Leagues under the Sea* (1870), in which the already-operational submarine was invested with a potential for adventure and discovery that was to anticipate the technology of the next hundred years and more. This novel is typical of Verne's extraordinary powers of invention; even more important, perhaps, it illustrates his understanding of the opportunities that new technology would open for the imagination. He filled his stories with the hardware of the future, creating new ways of imagining humanity's relation both to nature and to machines.

Time has been kinder to some of Verne's work than to the SF of most of his Victorian contemporaries. Even after science has caught up with Verne's technology and made it obsolete, his science has retained a nostalgic charm, like the thrill of riding aboard an old steam locomotive or on the *Delta Queen*. Some of his stories, however, have become as outmoded as their technology and are remembered as curious fossils of the neglected past. We may recall the fate of Verne's *From the Earth to the Moon* (1865) or Edward Everett Hale's "The Brick Moon" (1870), impossible even as satire. The moral of history is plainly that much hard SF lives but briefly. In a world of planned obsolescence, ideas are as disposable as any other commodity. The hard SF that survives the antiquation of its scientific visions endures by virtue of its literary qualities. Keats's lapse in naming Cortez the discoverer of the Pacific Ocean does not spoil "On First Looking into Chapman's Homer," nor does Tennyson's "ringing grooves of change" materially affect the vision of the railroad as the symbol of progress in "Locksley Hall." The point is that hard SF, if well written, may outlive an obsolete technology, an outmoded science (such as Poe's phrenology), or even gross mistakes of fact. But it does not survive poor writing that merely exploits its subject matter in order to gain popularity.

Still, there is a sense in which out-of-date science or technology changes things. The challenge of most hard SF is in creating a workable scientific illusion. The imagined science is frequently assessed on the most pragmatic terms: Would it work or could it work? When Hugo Gernsback led SF out of the mainstream and into the desert, he hoped to create an audience that was both scientifically informed and zealous in pursuit of truth. The means through which this was to be done was the story of "scientifiction," built around a core of scientific truth or extrapolation. The idea is as easily ridiculed as the Victorian schemes for workers' colleges and self-help periodicals. The serpent in Gernsback's orchard is the tendency to equate SF with a prosaic technical writing, which often was the case, as in Gernsback's otherwise remarkable novel *Ralph 124C41+* (1911). Despite the difficulties, the idea of a hard-core SF of significant idea content and respectable science remains central to the appeal and to the critical acceptance of the class. The people who write hard SF stories and those who review them tend to be scientists or science oriented. In these cases, nonaesthetic standards are often operative, initially at least. The evidence indicates, though, that it is ultimately the aesthetic values of SF which determine whether future generations will read a given SF story.

Speculative Hard Science Fiction

As we have observed in connection with fantasy SF, speculative literature confronts us with those futures made possible by science. As a type of the fantastic, speculative SF treats imagined worlds in which the probabilities of known science are transcended. In the speculative hard SF story, those probabilties are enforced fairly rigorously. Even so, there is a difference in method between the speculative and the extrapolative story, and we should note it here. This difference is more than a strategy of the storyteller. Extrapolation assumes a logical if not always methodical evolution of an idea from premise to conclusion. Speculative fiction, on the other hand, begins with an imagined situation from which it then works out its argument. Let us take Wells's story "The Star" as an illustration. Its premise is speculative: what if we have a celestial collision involving one of the planetary bodies of our solar system? From that premise the rest of the story extrapolates the inevitable operation of the laws governing celestial mechanics. Typically, this is shown as the laws affect modern civilization.

Invention goes a long way in a hard SF story, especially in the speculative type. In the beginning is the premise, the idea, or simply the vision that calls for explanation. A problem is proposed for solution in almost the same manner as a mystery story; then the author challenges readers to match wits and see whether the author's tale is inventive enough to capture readers' imaginations by its powers of contrivance. These stories, when they are done well, offer a unique kind of pleasure that is akin, perhaps, to the pleasures Poe referred to as "ratiocination" in the mystery story; and historically the connecting link between

230

modern speculative hard SF and Poe is the fiction of Jules Verne. Wells is less a factor in the development of the type than one might think, less important as an influence than Gernsback was.

It was in the 1930s that John W. Campbell arose as the champion of speculative SF. His insistence on scientific content and thoughtful argument in the stories he solicited for *Astounding Science Fiction* established standards of both taste and craft that endured for more than a decade. As readers well know, the period that followed—referred to somewhat exuberantly as "The Golden Age"—was indeed a coming of age for writers like Heinlein and Asimov, who learned from Campbell how to write thoughtful SF. Examples of the type abound, but I will restrict myself to only two or three.

Probably the most celebrated incident involving a speculative hard SF story occurred when Cleve Cartmill's story "Deadline" appeared in *Astounding Science Fiction* (March 1944). "Deadline" anticipated so many details of the Manhattan Project, the plan for the development of the atomic bomb, that both Cartmill and the magazine were investigated by military intelligence agents. Earlier in the 1940s, Heinlein's "Blowups Happen" and Lester del Rey's "Nerves" offered prophetic glimpses of the struggle to control runaway chain fusion reactions at projected commercial nuclear power plants, long before the first nuclear reaction had even been controlled. Another sort of speculative hard SF story is to be found in Hal Clement's *Mission of Gravity* (1954) or the earlier "Heavy Planet" (1939) by Lee Gregor, which postulates the consequences for life forms in gravity fields radically different from those we know. In each case, the success of the story depends on the author's ability to work out the implications of the original premise. Gadget stories or narratives treating the development of "wonderful machines" (as J. O. Bailey calls them in *Pilgrims through Space and Time*) have always been popular with readers. Campbell and Heinlein are the old masters of the type. Arthur Clarke and Larry Niven carry on the tradition with added luster.

In rather different ways and to radically diverse conclusions, the two stories in this section develop their original premises according to the logic suggested by the sciences in question.

The Cold Equations

Tom Godwin

Tom Godwin was born in 1915 and describes himself as a product of the American West. He has been a prospector and now lives in Nevada. His first story, "The Gulf Between," appeared in *Astounding Science Fiction* (October 1953). He is also author of *The Survivors* (1958) and its sequel *The Space Barbarians* (1964). "The Cold Equations" also was first published in *Astounding Science Fiction* (August 1954).

As long as SF is read and enjoyed by the young, this story will be part of that experience. But its status as a classic depends only in part on its continued popularity after some twenty years. It is also a classic story of the type because its simplicity of design and economy of action capture a conflict of values as elemental and permanent as that of *Antigone*. The great difference, and it is a telling one, is that here we have no villains, no real antagonists to moralize over except the cold equations themselves.

The initial exposition of the story is shrewdly worked out. We are given the premise as though it were a status and fitness report presented in the style of technical writing. In this case, that style suits the material perfectly and helps to establish an axis of value over which the struggle against fate is to be played out. That struggle carries a symbolic meaning for people living as hostages to a technology that seems to grow daily beyond their comprehension and control. We could say that the enemy is the system or that it is science itself, or the laws of engineering, but that would be to misunderstand the level on which this story finally makes its impact. The enemy really is death—sudden, unexpected, inexorable. The victim is at first incredulous, and in her reaction we see a pattern of the death we must all come to terms with—our own.

If ever there was a story in which the implications of the premise are worked out in a logical manner, this is it. The youthful innocence of the victim, the goodwill and even chivalry of Barton, the pilot of the EDS, and the sympathy of Commander Delhart are to no avail. They serve well to reinforce the theme of human impotence to change the impersonal conclusions of the computer. The physical laws are absolute as they apply to the engineering design and capabilities of the EDS. The only choices remaining are accommodation and acceptance or hysteria and rejection. Either way, the end will not change.

He was not alone.

There was nothing to indicate that fact but the white hand of the tiny guage on the board before him. The control room was empty but for himself; there was no sound other than the murmur of the drives—

but the white hand had moved. It had been on zero when the little ship was launched from the *Stardust;* now, an hour later, it had crept up. There was something in the supplies closet across the room, it was saying, some kind of a body that radiated heat.

It could be but one kind of a body—a living, human body.

He leaned back in the pilot's chair and drew a deep, slow breath, considering what he would have to do. He was an EDS pilot, inured to the sight of death, long since accustomed to it and to viewing the dying of another man with an objective lack of emotion, and he had no choice in what he must do. There could be no alternative—but it required a few moments of conditioning for even an EDS pilot to prepare himself to walk across the room and coldly, deliberately, take the life of a man he had yet to meet.

He would, of course, do it. It was the law, stated very bluntly and definitely in grim Paragraph L, Section 8, of Interstellar Regulations: *Any stowaway discovered in an EDS shall be jettisoned immediately following discovery.*

It was the law, and there could be no appeal.

It was a law not of men's choosing but made imperative by the circumstances of the space frontier. Galactic expansion had followed the development of the hyperspace drive and as men scattered wide across the frontier there had come the problem of contact with the isolated first-colonies and exploration parties. The huge hyperspace cruisers were the product of the combined genius and effort of Earth and were long and expensive in the building. They were not available in such numbers that small colonies could possess them. The cruisers carried the colonists to their new worlds and made periodic visits, running on tight schedules, but they could not stop and turn aside to visit colonies scheduled to be visited at another time; such a delay would destroy their schedule and produce a confusion and uncertainty that would wreck the complex interdependence between old Earth and new worlds of the frontier.

Some method of delivering supplies or assistance when an emergency occurred on a world not scheduled for a visit had been needed and the Emergency Dispatch Ships had been the answer. Small and collapsible, they occupied little room in the hold of the cruiser; made of light metal and plastics, they were driven by a small rocket drive that consumed relatively little fuel. Each cruiser carried four EDS's and when a call for aid was received the nearest cruiser would drop into normal space long enough to launch an EDS with the needed supplies or personnel, then vanish again as it continued on its course.

The cruisers, powered by nuclear converters, did not use the liquid rocket fuel but nuclear converters were far too large and complex to permit their installation in the EDS's. The cruisers were forced by necessity to carry a limited amount of the bulky rocket fuel and the fuel was rationed with care; the cruiser's computers determining the exact amount of fuel each EDS would require for its mission. The computers considered the course coordinates, the mass of the EDS, the mass of pilot and cargo; they were very precise and accurate and omitted nothing from their calculations. They could not, however, foresee, and allow for, the added mass of a stowaway.

The *Stardust* had received the request from one of the exploration parties stationed on Woden; the six men of the party already being stricken with the fever carried by the green *kala* midges and their own supply of serum destroyed by the tornado that had torn through their camp. The *Stardust* had gone through the usual procedure; dropping into normal space to launch the EDS with the fever serum, then vanishing again in hyperspace. Now, an hour later, the gauge was saying there was something more than the small carton of serum in the supplies closet.

He let his eyes rest on the narrow white door of the closet. There, just inside, another man lived and breathed and was beginning to feel assured that discovery of his presence would now be too late for the pilot to alter the situation. It *was* too late—for the man behind the door it was far later than he thought and in a way he would find terrible to believe.

There could be no alternative. Additional fuel would be used during the hours of deceleration to compensate for the added mass of the stowaway; infinitesimal increments of fuel that would not be missed until the ship had almost reached its destination. Then, at some distance above the ground that might be as near as a thousand feet or as far as tens of thousands of feet, depending upon the mass of ship and cargo and the preceding period of deceleration, the unmissed increments of fuel would make their absence known; the EDS would expend its last drops of fuel with a sputter and go into whistling free fall. Ship and pilot and stowaway would merge together upon impact as a wreckage of metal and plastic, flesh and blood, driven deep into the soil. The stowaway had signed his own death warrant when he concealed himself on the ship; he could not be permitted to take seven others with him.

He looked again at the telltale white hand, then rose to his feet. What he must do would be unpleasant for both of them; the sooner it was over, the better. He stepped across the control room, to stand by the white door.

"Come out!" His command was harsh and abrupt above the murmur of the drive.

It seemed he could hear the whisper of a furtive movement inside the closet, then nothing. He visualized the stowaway cowering into one corner, suddenly worried by the possible consequences of his act and his self-assurance evaporating.

"I said *out!*"

He heard the stowaway move to obey and he waited with his eyes alert on the door and his hand near the blaster at his side.

The door opened and the stowayay stepped through it, smiling. "All right—I give up. Now what?"

It was a girl.

He stared without speaking, his hand dropping away from the blaster and acceptance of what he saw coming like a heavy and unexpected physical blow. The stowaway was not a man—she was a girl in her teens, standing before him in little white gypsy sandals with the top of her brown, curly head hardly higher than his shoulder, with a faint, sweet scent of perfume coming from her and her smiling face tilted up so her eyes could look unknowing and unafraid into his as she waited for his answer.

Now what? Had it been asked in the deep, defiant voice of a man he would have answered it with action, quick and efficient. He would have taken the stowaway's identification disk and ordered him into the air lock. Had the stowaway refused to obey, he would have used the blaster. It would not have taken long; within a minute the body would have been ejected into space—had the stowaway been a man.

He returned to the pilot's chair and motioned her to seat herself on the boxlike bulk of the drive-control units that set against the wall beside him. She obeyed, his silence making the smile fade into the meek and guilty expression of a pup that has been caught in mischief and knows it must be punished.

"You still haven't told me," she said. "I'm guilty, so what happens to me now? Do I pay a fine, or what?"

"What are you doing here?" he asked. "Why did you stow away on this EDS?"

"I wanted to see my brother. He's with the government survey crew on Woden and I haven't seen him for ten years, not since he left Earth to go into government survey work."

"What was your destination on the *Stardust?*"

"Mimir. I have a position waiting for me there. My brother has been sending money home all the time to us—my father and mother and I—and he paid for a special course in linguistics I was taking. I graduated sooner than expected and I was offered this job on Mimir. I knew it would be almost a year before Gerry's job was done on Woden so he could come on to Mimir and that's why I hid in the closet there. There was plenty of room for me and I was willing to pay the fine. There were only the two of us kids—Gerry and I—and I haven't seen him for so long, and I didn't want to wait another year when I could see him now, even though I knew I would be breaking some kind of a regulation when I did it."

I knew I would be breaking some kind of a regulation—In a way, she could not be blamed for her ignorance of the law; she was of Earth and had not realized that the laws of the space frontier must, of necessity, be as hard and relentless as the environment that gave them birth.

Yet, to protect such as her from the results of their own ignorance of the frontier, there had been a sign over the door that led to the section of the *Stardust* that housed EDS's; a sign that was plain for all to see and heed:

UNAUTHORIZED PERSONNEL
KEEP OUT!

"Does your brother know that you took passage on the *Stardust* for Mimir?"

"Oh, yes. I sent him a spacegram telling him about my graduation and about going to Mimir on the *Stardust* a month before I left Earth. I already knew Mimir was where he would be stationed in a little over a year. He gets a promotion then, and he'll be based on Mimir and not have to stay out a year at a time on field trips, like he does now."

There were two different survey groups on Woden, and he asked, "What is his name?"

"Cross—Gerry Cross. He's in Group Two—that was the way his address read. Do you know him?"

Group One had requested the serum; Group Two was eight thousand miles away, across the Western Sea.

"No, I've never met him," he said, then turned to the control board and cut the deceleration to a fraction of a gravity; knowing as he did so that it could not avert the ultimate end, yet doing the only thing he could do to prolong that ultimate end. The sensation was like that of the ship suddenly dropping and the girl's involuntary movement of surprise half lifted her from the seat.

"We're going faster now, aren't we?" she asked. "Why are we doing that?"

He told her the truth. "To save fuel for a little while."

"You mean, we don't have very much?"

He delayed the answer he must give her so soon to ask: "How did you manage to stow away?"

"I just sort of walked in when no one was looking my way," she said. "I was practicing my Gelanese on the native girl who does the cleaning in the Ship's Supply office when someone came in with an order for supplies for the survey crew on Woden. I slipped into the closet there after the ship was ready to go and just before you came in. It was an impulse of the moment to stow away, so I could get to see Gerry—and from the way you keep looking at me so grim, I'm not sure it was a very wise impulse.

"But I'll be a model criminal—or do I mean prisoner?" She smiled at him again. "I intended to pay for my keep on top of paying the fine. I can cook and I can patch clothes for everyone and I know how to do all kinds of useful things, even a little bit about nursing."

There was one more question to ask:

"Did you know what the supplies were that the survey crew ordered?"

"Why, no. Equipment they needed in their work, I suppose."

Why couldn't she have been a man with some ulterior motive? A fugitive from justice, hoping to lose himself on a raw new world; an opportunist, seeking transportation to the new colonies where he might find golden fleece for the taking; a crackpot, with a mission—

Perhaps once in his lifetime an EDS pilot would find such a stowaway on his ship; warped men, mean and selfish men, brutal and dangerous men—but never, before, a smiling, blue-eyed girl who was willing to pay her fine and work for her keep that she might see her brother.

He turned to the board and turned the switch that would signal the *Stardust*. The call would be futile but he could not, until he had exhausted that one vain hope, seize her and thrust her into the air lock as he would an animal—or a man. The delay, in the meantime, would not be dangerous with the EDS decelerating at fractional gravity.

A voice spoke from the communicator. *"Stardust.* Identify yourself and proceed."

"Barton, EDS 34G11. Emergency. Give me Commander Delhart."

There was a faint confusion of noises as the request went through the proper channels. The girl was watching him, no longer smiling.

"Are you going to order them to come back after me?" she asked.

The communicator clicked and there was the sound of a distant voice saying, "Commander, the EDS requests—"

"Are they coming back after me?" she asked again. "Won't I get to see my brother, after all?"

"Barton?" The blunt, gruff voice of Commander Delhart came from the communicator. "What's this about an emergency?"

"A stowaway," he answered.

"A stowaway?" There was a slight surprise to the question. "That's rather unusual—but why the 'emergency' call? You discovered him in time so there should be no appreciable danger and I presume you've informed Ship's Records so his nearest relatives can be notified."

"That's why I had to call you, first. The stowaway is still aboard and the circumstances are so different—"

"Different?" the commander interrupted, impatience in his voice. "How can they be different? You know you have a limited supply of fuel; you also know the law, as well as I do: 'Any stowaway discovered in an EDS shall be jettisoned immediately following discovery.'"

There was the sound of a sharply indrawn breath from the girl. *"What does he mean?"*

"The stowaway is a girl."

"What?"

"She wanted to see her brother. She's only a kid and she didn't know what she was really doing."

"I see." All the curtness was gone from the commander's voice.

"So you called me in the hope I could do something?" Without waiting for an answer he went on. "I'm sorry—I can do nothing. This cruiser must maintain its schedule; the life of not one person but the lives of many depend on it. I know how you feel but I'm powerless to help you. You'll have to go through with it. I'll have you connected with Ship's Records."

The communicator faded to a faint rustle of sound and he turned back to the girl. She was leaning forward on the bench, almost rigid, her eyes fixed wide and frightened.

"What did he mean, to go through with it? To jettison me . . . to go through with it—what did he mean? Not the way it sounded . . . he couldn't have. What did he mean . . . what did he really mean?"

Her time was too short for the comfort of a lie to be more than a cruelly fleeting delusion.

"He meant it the way it sounded."

"*No!*" She recoiled from him as though he had struck her, one hand half upraised as though to fend him off and stark unwillingness to believe in her eyes.

"It will have to be."

"No! You're joking—you're insane! You can't mean it!"

"I'm sorry." He spoke slowly to her, gently. "I should have told you before—I should have, but I had to do what I could first; I had to call the *Stardust*. You heard what the commander said."

"But you can't—if you make me leave the ship, I'll *die*."

"I know."

She searched his face and the unwillingness to believe left her eyes, giving way slowly to a look of dazed terror.

"You—know?" She spoke the words far apart, numb and wonderingly.

"I know. It has to be like that."

"You mean it—you really mean it." She sagged back against the wall, small and limp like a little rag doll and all the protesting and disbelief gone.

"You're going to do it—you're going to make me die?"

"I'm sorry," he said again. "You'll never know how sorry I am. It has to be that way and no human in the universe can change it."

"You're going to make me die and I didn't do anything to die for— I didn't *do* anything—"

He sighed, deep and weary. "I know you didn't, child. I know you didn't—"

"EDS." The communicator rapped brisk and metallic. "This is Ship's Records. Give us all information on subject's identification disk."

He got out of his chair to stand over her. She clutched the edge of the seat, her upturned face white under the brown hair and the lipstick standing out like a blood-red cupid's bow.

"Now?"

"I want your identification disk," he said.

She released the edge of the seat and fumbled at the chain that suspended the plastic disk from her neck with fingers that were trembling and awkward. He reached down and unfastened the clasp for her, then returned with the disk to his chair.

"Here's your data, Records: Identification Number T837—"

"One moment," Records interrupted. "This is to be filed on the gray card, of course?"

"Yes."

"And the time of the execution?"

"I'll tell you later."

"Later? This is highly irregular; the time of the subject's death is required before—"

He kept the thickness out of his voice with an effort. "Then we'll do it in a highly irregular manner—you'll hear the disk read, first. The subject is a girl and she's listening to everything that's said. Are you capable of understanding that?"

There was a brief, almost shocked, silence, then Records said meekly: "Sorry. Go ahead."

He began to read the disk, reading it slowly to delay the inevitable for as long as possible, trying to help her by giving her what little time he could to recover from her first terror and let it resolve into the calm of acceptance and resignation.

"Number T8374 dash Y54. Name: Marilyn Lee Cross. Sex: Female. Born: July 7, 2160. *She was only eighteen.* Height: 5–3. Weight: 110. *Such a slight weight, yet enough to add fatally to the mass of the shell-thin bubble that was an EDS.* Hair: Brown. Eyes: Blue. Complexion: Light. Blood Type: O. *Irrelevant data.* Destination: Port City, Mimir. *Invalid data—*"

He finished and said, "I'll call you later," then turned once again to the girl. She was huddled back against the wall, watching him with a look of numb and wondering fascination.

"They're waiting for you to kill me, aren't they? They want me dead, don't they? You and everybody on the cruiser wants me dead, don't you?" Then the numbness broke and her voice was that of a frightened and bewildered child. "Everybody wants me dead and I didn't *do* anything. I didn't hurt anyone—I only wanted to see my brother."

"It's not the way you think—it isn't that way, at all," he said. "Nobody wants it this way; nobody would ever let it be this way if it was humanly possible to change it."

"Then why is it! I don't understand. Why is it?"

"This ship is carrying *kala* fever serum to Group One on Woden. Their own supply was destroyed by a tornado. Group Two—the crew your brother is in—is eight thousand miles away across the Western Sea and their helicopters can't cross it to help Group One. The fever is invariably fatal unless the serum can be had in time, and the six men in Group One will die unless this ship reaches them on schedule. These little ships are always given barely enough fuel to reach their destination and if you stay aboard your added weight will cause it to use up all its fuel before it reaches the ground. It will crash, then, and you and I will die and so will the six men waiting for the serum."

It was a full minute before she spoke, and as she considered his words the expression of numbness left her eyes.

"Is that it?" she asked at last. "Just that the ship doesn't have enough fuel?"

"Yes."

"I can go alone or I can take seven others with me—is that the way it is?"

"That's the way it is."

"And nobody wants me to have to die?"

"Nobody."

"Then maybe—Are you sure nothing can be done about it? Wouldn't people help me if they could?"

"Everyone would like to help you but there is nothing anyone can do. I did the only thing I could do when I called the *Stardust.*"

"And it won't come back—but there might be other cruisers, mightn't there? Isn't there any hope at all that there might be someone, somewhere, who could do something to help me?"

She was leaning forward a little in her eagerness as she waited for his answer.

"No."

The word was like the drop of a cold stone and she again leaned back against the wall, the hope and eagerness leaving her face. "You're sure—you *know* you're sure?"

"I'm sure. There are no other cruisers within forty light-years; there is nothing and no one to change things."

She dropped her gaze to her lap and began twisting a pleat of her skirt between her fingers, saying no more as her mind began to adapt itself to the grim knowledge.

It was better so; with the going of all hope would go the fear; with the going of all hope would come resignation. She needed time and she could have so little of it. How much?

The EDS's were not equipped with hull-cooling units; their speed had to be reduced to a moderate level before entering the atmosphere. They were decelerating at .10 gravity; approaching their destination at a far higher speed than the computers had calculated on. The *Stardust* had been quite near Woden when she launched the EDS; their present velocity was putting them nearer by the second. There would be a critical point, soon to be reached, when he would have to resume deceleration. When he did so the girl's weight would be multiplied by the gravities of deceleration, would become, suddenly, a factor of paramount importance; the factor the computers had been ignorant of when they determined the amount of fuel the EDS should have. She would have to go when deceleration began; it could be no other way. When would that be—how long could he let her stay?

"How long can I stay?"

He winced involuntarily from the words that were so like an echo of his own thoughts. How long? He didn't know; he would have to ask the ship's computers. Each EDS was given a meager surplus of fuel to compensate for unfavorable conditions within the atmosphere and relatively little fuel was being consumed for the time being. The memory banks of the computers would still contain all data pertaining to the course set for the EDS; such data would not be erased until the EDS reached its destination. He had only to give the computers the new data; the girl's weight and the exact time at which he had reduced the deceleration to .10.

"Barton." Commander Delhart's voice came abruptly from the communicator, as he opened his mouth to call the *Stardust*. "A check with Records shows me you haven't completed your report. Did you reduce the deceleration?"

So the commander knew what he was trying to do.

"I'm decelerating at point ten," he answered. "I cut the deceleration at seventeen fifty and the weight is a hundred and ten. I would like to stay at point ten as long as the computers say I can. Will you give them the question?"

It was contrary to regulations for an EDS pilot to make any changes in the course or degree of deceleration the computers had set for him but the commander made no mention of the violation, neither did he ask the reason for it. It was not necessary for him to ask; he had not become commander of an interstellar cruiser without both intelligence and an understanding of human nature. He said only: "I'll have that given the computers."

The communicator fell silent and he and the girl waited, neither of them speaking. They would not have to wait long; the computers would give the answer within moments of the asking. The new factors would be fed into the steel maw of the first bank and the electrical impulses would go through the complex circuits. Here and there a relay might click, a tiny cog turn over, but it would be essentially the electrical impulses that found the answer; formless, mindless, invisible, determining with utter precision how long the pale girl beside him might live. Then five little segments of metal in the second bank would trip in rapid succession against an inked ribbon and a second steel maw would spit out the slip of paper that bore the answer.

The chronometer on the instrument board read 18:10 when the commander spoke again.

"You will resume deceleration at nineteen ten."

She looked toward the chronometer, then quickly away from it. "Is that when . . . when I go?" she asked. He nodded and she dropped here eyes to her lap again.

"I'll have the course corrections given you," the commander said. "Ordinarily I would never permit anything like this but I understand your position. There is nothing I can do, other than what I've just done, and you will not deviate from these new instructions. You will complete your report at nineteen ten. Now—here are the course corrections."

The voice of some unknown technician read them to him and he wrote them down on the pad clipped to the edge of the control board. There would, he saw, be periods of deceleration when he neared the atmosphere when the deceleration would be five gravities—and at five gravities, one hundred ten pounds would become five hundred fifty pounds.

The technician finished and he terminated the contact with a brief acknowledgment. Then, hesitating a moment, he reached out and shut off the communicator. It was 18:13 and he would have nothing to report until 19:10. In the meantime, it somehow seemed indecent to permit others to hear what she might say in her last hour.

He began to check the instrument readings, going over them with unnecessary slowness. She would have to accept the circumstances and there was nothing he could do to help her into acceptance; words of sympathy would only delay it.

It was 18:20 when she stirred from her motionlessness and spoke.

"So that's the way it has to be with me?"

He swung around to face her. "You understand now, don't you? No one would ever let it be like this if it could be changed."

"I understand," she said. Some of the color had returned to her face and the lipstick no longer stood out so vividly red. "There isn't enough fuel for me to stay; when I hid on this ship I got into something I didn't know anything about and now I have to pay for it."

She had violated a man-made law that said KEEP OUT but the penalty was not of men's making or desire and it was a penalty men could not revoke. A physical law had decreed: *h amount of fuel will power an EDS with a mass of m safely to its destination;* and a second physical law had decreed: *h amount of fuel will not power an EDS with a mass of m plus x safely to its destination.*

EDS's obeyed only physical laws and no amount of human sympathy for her could alter the second law.

"But I'm afraid. I don't want to die—not now. I want to live and nobody is doing anything to help me; everybody is letting me go ahead and acting just like nothing was going to happen to me. I'm going to die and nobody *cares.*"

"We all do," he said. "I do and the commander does and the clerk in Ship's Records; we all care and each of us did what little he could to help you. It wasn't enough—it was almost nothing—but it was all we could do."

"Not enough fuel—I can understand that," she said, as though she had not heard his own words. "But to have to die for it. *Me, alone*—"

How hard it must be for her to accept the fact. She had never known danger of death; had never known the environments where the lives of men could be as fragile and fleeting as sea foam tossed against a rocky shore. She belonged on gentle Earth, in that secure and peaceful society where she could be young and gay and laughing with the others of her kind; where life was precious and well-guarded and there was always the assurance that tomorrow would come. She belonged in the world of soft winds and warm suns, music and moonlight and gracious manners and not on the hard, bleak frontier.

"How did it happen to me, so terribly quickly? An hour ago I was on the *Stardust*, going to Mimir. Now the *Stardust* is going on without me and I'm going to die and I'll never see Gerry and Mama and Daddy again—I'll never see anything again."

He hesitated, wondering how he could explain it to her so she would really understand and not feel she had, somehow, been the victim of a reasonlessly cruel injustice. She did not know what the frontier was like; she thought in terms of safe-and-secure Earth. Pretty girls were not jettisoned on Earth; there was a law against it. On Earth her plight would have filled the newscasts and a fast black Patrol ship would have been racing to her rescue. Everyone, everywhere, would have known of Marilyn Lee Cross and no effort would have been spared to save her life. But this was not Earth and there were no Patrol ships; only the *Stardust* leaving them behind at many times the speed of light. There was no one to help her, there would be no Marilyn Lee Cross smiling from the newscasts tomorrow. Marilyn Lee Cross would be but a poignant memory for an EDS pilot and a name on a gray card in Ship's Records.

"It's different here; it's not like back on Earth," he said. "It isn't that no one cares; it's that no one can do anything to help. The frontier is big and here along its rim the colonies and exploration parties are scattered so thin and far between. On Woden, for example, there are only sixteen men—sixteen men on an entire world. The exploration parties, the survey crews, the little first-colonies—they're all fighting alien environments, trying to make a way for those who will follow after. The environments fight back and those who go first usually make mistakes only once. There is no margin of safety along the rim of the frontier; there can't be until the way is made for the others who will come later, until the new worlds are tamed and settled. Until then men will have to pay the penalty for making mistakes with no one to help them because there is no one *to* help them."

"I was going to Mimir," she said. "I didn't know about the frontier; I was only going to Mimir and *it's* safe."

"Mimir is safe but you left the cruiser that was taking you there."

She was silent for a little while. "It was all so wonderful at first; there was plenty of room for me on this ship and I would be seeing Gerry so soon . . . I didn't know about the fuel, didn't know what would happen to me—"

Her words trailed away and he turned his attention to the viewscreen, not wanting to stare at her as she fought her way through the black horror of fear toward the calm gray of acceptance.

Woden was a ball, enshrouded in the blue haze of its atmosphere, swimming in space against the background of star-sprinkled dead blackness. The great mass of Manning's Continent sprawled like a gigantic hourglass in the Eastern Sea with the western half of the Eastern Continent still visible. There was a thin line of shadow along the right-hand edge of the globe and the Eastern Continent was disappearing into it as the planet turned on its axis. An hour before the entire continent had been in view, now a thousand miles of it had gone into the edge of shadow and around to the night that lay on the other side of the world. The dark blue spot that was Lotus Lake was approaching the shadow. It was somewhere near the southern edge of the lake that Group Two had their camp. It would be night there, soon, and quick behind the coming of night the rotation of Woden on its axis would put Group Two beyond the reach of the ship's radio.

He would have to tell her before it was too late for her to talk to her brother. In a way, it would be better for both of them should they not do so but it was not for him to decide. To each of them the last words would be something to hold and cherish, something that would cut like the blade of a knife yet would be infinitely precious to remember, she for her own brief moments and he for the rest of his life.

He held down the button that would flash the grid lines on the viewscreen and used the known diameter of the planet to estimate the distance the southern tip of Lotus Lake had yet to go until it passed beyond radio range. It was approximately five hundred miles. Five hundred miles; thirty minutes—and the chronometer read 18:30. Allowing for error in estimating, it could not be later than 19:05 that the turning of Woden would cut off her brother's voice.

The first border of the Western Continent was already in sight along the left side of the world. Four thousand miles across it lay the shore of the Western Sea and the Camp of Group One. It had been in the Western Sea that the tornado had originated, to strike with such fury at the camp and destroy half their prefabricated buildings, including the one that housed the medical supplies. Two days before the tornado had not existed; it had been no more than great gentle masses of air out over the calm Western Sea. Group One had gone about their routine survey work, unaware of the meeting of the air masses out at sea, unaware of the force the union was spawning. It had struck their camp without warning; a thundering, roaring destruction that sought to annihilate all that lay before it. It had passed on, leaving the wreckage in its wake. It had destroyed the labor of months and had doomed six men to die and then, as though its task was accomplished, it once more began to resolve into gentle masses of air. But for all its deadliness, it had destroyed with neither malice nor intent. It had been a blind and mindless force, obeying the laws of nature, and it would have followed the same course with the same fury had men never existed.

Existence required Order and there was order; the laws of nature, irrevocable and immutable. Men could learn to use them but men could not change them. The circumference of a circle was always pi times the diameter and no science of Man would ever make it otherwise. The combination of chemical A with chemical B under condition C invariably produced reaction D. The law of gravitation was a rigid equation and it made no distinction between the fall of a leaf and the ponderous circling of a binary star system. The nuclear conversion process powered the cruisers that carried men to the stars; the same process in the form of a nova would destroy a world with equal efficiency. The laws *were,* and the universe moved in obedience to them. Along the frontier were arrayed all the forces of nature and sometimes they destroyed those who were fighting their way outward from Earth. The men of the frontier had long ago learned the bitter futility of cursing the forces that would destroy them for the forces were blind and deaf; the futility of looking to the heavens for mercy, for the stars of the galaxy swung in their long, long sweep of two hundred million years, as inexorably controlled as they by the laws that knew neither hatred nor compassion.

The men of the frontier knew—but how was a girl from Earth to fully understand? *H amount of fuel will not power an EDS with a mass of m plus x safely to its destination.* To himself and her brother and parents she was a sweet-faced girl in her teens; to the laws of nature she was *x*, the unwanted factor in a cold equation.

She stirred again on the seat. "Could I write a letter? I want to write to Mama and Daddy and I'd like to talk to Gerry. Could you let me talk to him over your radio there?"

"I'll try to get him," he said.

He switched on the normal-space transmitter and pressed the signal button. Someone answered the buzzer almost immediately.

"Hello. How's it going with you fellows now—is the EDS on its way?"

"This isn't Group One; this is the EDS," he said. "Is Gerry Cross there?"

"Gerry? He and two others went out in the helicopter this morning and aren't back yet. It's almost sundown, though, and he ought to be back right away—in less than an hour at the most."

"Can you connect me through to the radio in his 'copter?"

"Huh-uh. It's been out of commission for two months—some printed circuits went haywire and we can't get any more until the next cruiser stops by. Is it something important—bad news for him, or something?"

"Yes—it's very important. When he comes in get him to the transmitter as soon as you possibly can."

"I'll do that; I'll have one of the boys waiting at the field with a truck. Is there anything else I can do?"

"No, I guess that's all. Get him there as soon as you can and signal me."

He turned the volume to an inaudible minimum, an act that would not affect the functioning of the signal buzzer, and unclipped the pad of paper from the control board. He tore off the sheet containing his flight instructions and handed the pad to her, together with pencil.

"I'd better write to Gerry, too," she said as she took them. "He might not get back to camp in time."

She began to write, her fingers still clumsy and uncertain in the way they handled the pencil and the top of it trembling a little as she poised it between words. He turned back to the viewscreen, to stare at it without seeing it.

She was a lonely little child, trying to say her good-by, and she would lay out her heart to them. She would tell them how much she loved them and she would tell them not to feel badly about it, that it was only something that must happen eventually to everyone and she was not afraid. The last would be a lie and it would be there to read between the sprawling, uneven lines; a valiant little lie that would make the hurt all the greater for them.

Her brother was of the frontier and he would understand. He would not hate the EDS pilot for doing nothing to prevent her going; he would know there had been nothing the pilot could do. He would understand, though the understanding would not soften the shock and pain when he learned his sister was gone. But the others, her father and mother— they would not understand. They were of Earth and they would think in the manner of those who had never lived where the safety margin of life was a thin, thin line—and sometimes not at all. What would they think of the faceless, unknown pilot who had sent her to her death?

They would hate him with cold and terrible intensity but it really didn't matter. He would never see them, never know them. He would have only the memories to remind him; only the nights to fear, when a blue-eyed girl in gypsy sandals would come in his dreams to die again—

He scowled at the viewscreen and tried to force his thoughts into less emotional channels. There was nothing he could do to help her. She had unknowingly subjected herself to the penalty of a law that recognized neither innocence nor youth nor beauty, that was incapable of sympathy or leniency. Regret was illogical—and yet, could knowing it to be illogical ever keep it away?

She stopped occasionally, as though trying to find the right words to tell them what she wanted them to know, then the pencil would resume its whispering to the paper. It was 18:37 when she folded the letter in a square and wrote a name on it. She began writing another, twice looking up at the chronometer as though she feared the black hand might reach its rendezvous before she had finished. It was 18:45 when she folded it as she had done the first letter and wrote a name and address on it.

She held the letters out to him. "Will you take care of these and see that they're enveloped and mailed?"

"Of course." He took them from her hand and placed them in a pocket of his gray uniform shirt.

"These can't be sent off until the next crusier stops by and the *Stardust* will have long since told them about me, won't it?" she asked. He nodded and she went on, "That makes the letters not important in one way but in another way they're very important—to me, and to them."

"I know. I understand, and I'll take care of them."

She glanced at the chronometer, then back to him. "It seems to move faster all the time, doesn't it?"

He said nothing, unable to think of anything to say, and she asked, "Do you think Gerry will come back to camp in time?"

"I think so. They said he should be in right away."

She began to roll the pencil back and forth between her palms. "I hope he does. I feel sick and scared and I want to hear his voice agair and maybe I won't feel so alone. I'm a coward and I can't help it."

"No," he said, "you're not a coward. You're afraid, but you're no a coward."

"Is there a difference?"

He nodded. "A lot of difference."

"I feel so alone. I never did feel like this before; like I was all by myself and there was nobody to care what happened to me. Always, before, there was Mama and Daddy there and my friends around me. I had lots of friends, and they had a going-away party for me the night before I left."

Friends and music and laughter for her to remember—and on the viewscreen Lotus Lake was going into the shadow.

"Is it the same with Gerry?" she asked. "I mean, if he should make a mistake, would he die for it, all alone and with no one to help him?"

"It's the same with all along the frontier; it will always be like that so long as there is a frontier."

"Gerry didn't tell us. He said the pay was good and he sent money home all the time because Daddy's little shop just brought in a bare living but he didn't tell us it was like this."

"He didn't tell you his work was dangerous?"

"Well—yes. He mentioned that, but we didn't understand. I always thought danger along the frontier was something that was a lot of fun; an exciting adventure, like in the three-D shows." A wan smile touched her face for a moment. "Only it's not, is it? It's not the same at all, because whc ı it's real you can't go home after the show is over."

"No," he said. "No, you can't."

Her glance flicked from the chronometer to the door of the air lock then down to the pad and pencil she still held. She shifted her position slightly to lay them on the bench beside, moving one foot out a little. For the first time he saw that she was not wearing Vegan gypsy sandals but only cheap imitations; the expensive Vegan leather was some kind of grained plastic, the silver buckle was gilded iron, the jewels were colored glass. *Daddy's little shop just brought in a bare living*—She must have left college in her second year, to take the course in linguistics that would enable her to make her own way and help her brother provide for her parents, earning what she could by part-time work after classes were over. Her personal possessions on the *Stardust* would be taken back to her parents—they would neither be of much value nor occupy much storage space on the return voyage.

"Isn't it—" She stopped, and he looked at her questioningly. "Isn't it cold in here?" she asked, almost apologetically. "Doesn't it seem cold to you?"

"Why, yes," he said. He saw by the main temperature gauge that the room was at precisely normal temperature. "Yes, it's colder than it should be."

"I wish Gerry would get back before it's too late. Do you really think he will, and you didn't just say so to make me feel better?"

"I think he will—they said he would be in pretty soon." On the viewscreen Lotus Lake had gone into the shadow but for the thin blue line of its western edge and it was apparent he had overestimated the time she would have in which to talk to her brother. Reluctantly, he said to her, "His camp will be out of radio range in a few minutes; he's on that part of Woden that's in the shadow"—he indicated the view screen—"and the turning of Woden will put him beyond contact. There may not be much time left when he comes in—not much time to talk to him before he fades out. I wish I could do something about it—I would call him right now if I could."

"Not even as much time as I will have to stay?"

"I'm afraid not."

"Then—" She straightened and looked toward the air lock with pale resolution. "Then I'll go when Gerry passes beyond range. I won't wait any longer after that—I won't have anything to wait for."

Again there was nothing he could say.

"Maybe I shouldn't wait at all. Maybe I'm selfish—maybe it would be better for Gerry if you just told him about it afterward."

There was an unconscious pleading for denial in the way she spoke and he said, "He wouldn't want you to do that, to not wait for him."

"It's already coming dark where he is, isn't it? There will be all the long night before him, and Mama and Daddy don't know yet that I won't ever be coming back like I promised them I would. I've caused everyone I love to be hurt, haven't I? I didn't want to—I didn't intend to."

"It wasn't your fault," he said. "It wasn't your fault at all. They'll know that. They'll understand."

"At first I was so afraid to die that I was a coward and thought only of myself. Now, I see how selfish I was. The terrible thing about dying like this is not that I'll be gone but that I'll never see them again; never be able to tell them that I didn't take them for granted; never be able to tell them I knew of the sacrifices they made to make my life happier, that I knew all the things they did for me and that I loved them so much more than I ever told them. I've never told them any of those things. You don't tell them such things when you're young and your life is all before you—you're afraid of sounding sentimental and silly.

"But it's so different when you have to die—you wish you had told them while you could and you wish you could tell them you're sorry for all the little mean things you ever did or said to them. You wish you could tell them that you didn't really mean to ever hurt their feelings and for them to only remember that you always loved them far more than you ever let them know."

"You don't have to tell them that," he said. "They will know— they've always known it."

"Are you sure?" she asked. "How can you be sure? My people are strangers to you."

"Wherever you go, human nature and human hearts are the same."

"And they will know what I want them to know—that I love them?"

"They've always known it, in a way far better than you could ever put in words for them."

"I keep remembering the things they did for me, and it's the little things they did that seem to be the most important to me, now. Like Gerry—he sent me a bracelet of fire-rubies on my sixteenth birthday. It was beautiful—it must have cost him a month's pay. Yet, I remember him more for what he did the night my kitten got run over in the street. I was only six years old and he held me in his arms and wiped away my tears and told me not to cry, that Flossy was gone for just a little while, for just long enough to get herself a new fur coat and she would be on the foot of my bed the very next morning. I believed him and quit crying and went to sleep dreaming about my kitten coming back. When I woke up the next morning, there was Flossy on the foot of my bed in a brand-new white fur coat, just like he had said she would be.

"It wasn't until a long time later that Mama told me Gerry had got the pet-shop owner out of bed at four in the morning and, when the man got mad about it, Gerry told him he was either going to go down and sell him the white kitten right then or he'd break his neck."

"It's always the little things you remember people by; all the little things they did because they wanted to do them for you. You've done the same for Gerry and your father and mother; all kinds of things that you've forgotten about but that they will never forget."

"I hope I have. I would like for them to remember me like that."

"They will."

"I wish—" She swallowed. "The way I'll die—I wish they wouldn't ever think of that. I've read how people look who die in space—their insides all ruptured and exploded and their lungs out between their teeth and then, a few seconds later, they're all dry and shapeless and horribly ugly. I don't went them to ever think of me as something dead and horrible, like that."

"You're their own, their child and their sister. They could never think of you other than the way you would want them to; the way you looked the last time they saw you."

"I'm still afraid," she said. "I can't help it, but I don't want Gerry to know it. If he gets back in time, I'm going to act like I'm not afraid at all and—"

The signal buzzer interrupted her, quick and imperative.

"Gerry!" She came to her feet. "It's Gerry, now!"

He spun the volume control knob and asked: "Gerry Cross?"

"Yes," her brother answered, an undertone of tenseness to his reply. "The bad news—what is it?"

She answered for him, standing close behind him and leaning down a little toward the communicator, her hand resting small and cold on his shoulder

"Hello, Gerry" There was only a faint quaver to betray the careful casualness of her voice. "I wanted to see you—"

"Marilyn!" There was sudden and terrible apprehension in the way he spoke her name. "What are you doing on that EDS?"

"I wanted to see you," she said again. "I wanted to see you, so I hid on this ship—"

"You *hid* on it?"

"I'm a stowaway . . . I didn't know what it would mean—"

"*Marilyn!*" It was the cry of a man who calls hopeless and desperate to someone already and forever gone from him. "What have you done?"

"I . . . it's not—" Then her own composure broke and the cold little hand gripped his shoulder convulsively. "Don't, Gerry—I only wanted to see you; I didn't intend to hurt you. Please, Gerry, don't feel like that—"

Something warm and wet splashed on his wrist and he slid out of the chair, to help her into it and swing the microphone down to her own level.

"Don't feel like that—Don't let me go knowing you feel like that—"

The sob she had tried to hold back choked in her throat and her brother spoke to her. "Don't cry, Marilyn." His voice was suddenly deep and infinitely gentle, with all the pain held out of it. "Don't cry, Sis—you mustn't do that. It's all right, Honey—everything is all right."

"I—" Her lower lip quivered and she bit into it. "I didn't want you to feel that way—I just wanted us to say good-by because I have to go in a minute."

"Sure—sure. That's the way it will be, Sis. I didn't mean to sound the way I did." Then his voice changed to a tone of quick and urgent demand. "EDS—have you called the *Stardust*? Did you check with the computers?"

"I called the *Stardust* almost an hour ago. It can't turn back, there are no other cruisers within forty light-years, and there isn't enough fuel."

"Are you sure that the computers had the correct data—sure of everything?"

"Yes—do you think I could ever let it happen if I wasn't sure? I did everything I could do. If there was anything at all I could do now, I would do it."

"He tried to help me, Gerry." Her lower lip was no longer trembling and the short sleeves of her blouse were wet where she had dried her tears. "No one can help me and I'm not going to cry any more and everything will be all right with you and Daddy and Mama, won't it?"

"Sure—sure it will. We'll make out fine."

Her brother's words were beginning to come in more faintly and he turned the volume control to maximum. "He's going out of range," he said to her. "He'll be gone within another minute."

"You're fading out, Gerry," she said. "You're going out of range. I wanted to tell you—but I can't, now. We must say good-by so soon— but maybe I'll see you again. Maybe I'll come to you in your dreams with my hair in braids and crying because the kitten in my arms is dead maybe I'll be the touch of a breeze that whispers to you as it goes by maybe I'll be one of those gold-winged larks you told me about, singing my silly head off to you; maybe, at times, I'll be nothing you can see but you will know I'm there beside you. Think of me like that, Gerry; always like that and not—the other way."

Dimmed to a whisper by the turning of Woden, the answer came back:

"Always like that, Marilyn—always like that and never any other way."

"Our time is up, Gerry—I have to go now. Good—" Her voice broke in mid-word and her mouth tried to twist into crying. She pressed her hand hard against it and when she spoke again the words came clear and true:

"Good-by, Gerry."

Faint and ineffably poignant and tender, the last words came from the cold metal of the communicator:

"Good-by, little sister—"

She sat motionless in the hush that followed, as though listening to the shadow-echoes of the words as they died away, then she turned away from the communicator, toward the air lock, and he pulled the black lever beside him. The inner door of the air lock slid swiftly open, to reveal the bare little cell that was waiting for her, and she walked to it.

She walked with her head up and the brown curls brushing her shoulders, with the white sandals stepping as sure and steady as the fractional gravity would permit and the gilded buckles twinkling with little lights of blue and red and crystal. He let her walk alone and made no move to help her, knowing she would not want it that way. She stepped into the air lock and turned to face him, only the pulse in her throat to betray the wild beating of her heart.

"I'm ready," she said.

He pushed the lever up and the door slid its quick barrier between them, inclosing her in black and utter darkness for her last moments of life. It clicked as it locked in place and he jerked down the red lever. There was a slight waver to the ship as the air gushed from the lock, a vibration to the wall as though something had bumped the outer door in passing, then there was nothing and the ship was dropping true and steady again. He shoved the red lever back to close the door on the empty air lock and turned away, to walk to the pilot's chair with the slow steps of a man old and weary.

Back in the pilot's chair he pressed the signal button of the normal-space transmitter. There was no response; he had expected none. Her brother would have to wait through the night until the turning of Woden permitted contact through Group One.

It was not yet time to resume deceleration and he waited while the ship dropped endlessly downward with him and the drives purred softly. He saw that the white hand of the supplies closet temperature gauge was on zero. A cold equation had been balanced and he was alone on the ship. Something shapeless and ugly was hurrying ahead of him, going to Woden where its brother was waiting through the night, but the empty ship still lived for a little while with the presence of the girl who had not known about the forces that killed with neither hatred nor malice. It seemed, almost, that she still sat small and bewildered and frightened on the metal box beside him, her words echoing hauntingly clear in the void she had left behind her:

I didn't do anything to die for—I didn't do anything—

Questions for Discussion and Review

1. Work out in mathematical form an expression of the cold equations that cause Marilyn Cross's death.

2. What significance do the proper names have in this story?

3. Why does the author have Marilyn talk to her brother just before the end?

4. Describe as fully as possible the effect of this story and try to account for it.

5. Can you think of a way Barton might have solved the cold equations differently?

Dark Benediction

Walter M. Miller, Jr.

Walter Michael Miller, Jr., was born in New Smyrna Beach, Florida, on January 23, 1923. He served in World War II with the U.S. Army in Italy and was present at the bombardment of Monte Cassino, an event that made a deep impact on Miller and was later to provide a partial inspiration for several stories, including "A Canticle for Leibowitz" (later expanded into the novel) and the present story. Miller's first story, "Secret of the Death Dome," appeared in *Amazing Stories* in 1951, the same year he wrote "Dark Benediction." Walter Miller has won two Hugo awards: The first was for his novelette "The Darfsteller" (1955) and the second was for the novel *A Canticle for Leibowitz* (1961). The novel has since become an SF classic and is regarded by critics and teachers as one of the best SF novels ever written. Miller published a score of short stories during the 1950s. He is also the author of *Conditionally Human* (1962) and *The View from the Stars* (1965), a collection of stories. "Dark Benediction" was first published in *Fantastic Stories*.

The premise of this story is vastly different from "The Cold Equations." Instead of struggling against implacable doom, the principals of "Dark Benediction" struggle against what is, if rightly understood, a gift from heaven. The paradox is understood from the viewpoint of the Christian doctrine of original sin. Thus, as in "The Hound of Heaven," humanity flees in panic from grace and an increased blessing. To be sure, the people of Miller's world have reason for fear. The alien microbes produce noticeable changes in skin pigmentation, and the infected dermies are treated as lepers. The result has been a collapse of civilization and the suspension of civil liberties. The world in which we find ourselves is one ruled by the law of survival of the fittest.

Readers may decide for themselves whether or not Miller intends this picture of a world in collapse as an apocalyptic vision of our times. In a sense, this is a doomsday story of the sort sometimes referred to as a "cosy catastrophe." The theme of racial paranoia, one of the axioms of the story, is reinforced by readers' gradual discovery that the infection is a means of enhancing the powers of the race as a whole. Indeed, from the Darwinist viewpoint, the infection would be regarded as a chance event leading to a species mutation that then would become naturally selected for dominance and survival. In other words, the fanatics who desperately try to maintain the purity of the race from dermie infection are supporting a cause against the laws of nature.

The social implications of this theme will not be lost on modern readers— nor will the Romeo-Juliet romance of the young lovers whose passion is thwarted by a fear of infection that keeps them temporarily apart. It makes a powerful metaphor for the racial fear and color prejudice that is so clearly retrogressive in this story. It is comforting that in a disorderly

world love proves eventually stronger than humanity's devolutionary
tendencies.

Always fearful of being set upon during the night, Paul slept uneasily
despite his weariness from the long trek southward. When dawn broke,
he rolled out of his blankets and found himself still stiff with fatigue.
He kicked dirt over the remains of the campfire and breakfasted on a
tough forequarter of cold rabbit which he washed down with a swallow
of earthy-tasting ditchwater. Then he buckled the cartridge belt about
his waist, leaped the ditch, and climbed the embankment to the trafficless four-lane highway whose pavement was scattered with blown leaves
and unsightly debris dropped by a long-departed throng of refugees
whose only wish had been to escape from one another. Paul, with
characteristic independence, had decided to go where the crowds had
been the thickest—to the cities—on the theory that they would now be
deserted, and therefore non-contagious.

The fog lay heavy over the silent land, and for a moment he paused
groping for cognizance of direction. Then he saw the stalled car on
the opposite shoulder of the road—a late model convertible, but rusted,
flat-tired, with last year's license plates, and most certainly out of
fuel. It had obviously been deserted by its owner during the exodus,
and he trusted in its northward heading as he would have trusted the
reading of a compass. He turned right and moved south on the empty
highway. Somewhere just ahead in the gray vapor lay the outskirts of
Houston. He had seen the high skyline before the setting of yesterday's
sun, and knew that his journey would soon be drawing to a close.

Occasionally he passed a deserted cottage or a burned-out roadside
tavern, but he did not pause to scrounge for food. The exodus would
have stripped such buildings clean. Pickings should be better in the
heart of the metropolitan area, he thought—where the hysteria had
swept humanity away quickly.

Suddenly Paul froze on the highway, listening to the fog. Footsteps
in the distance—footsteps and a voice singing an absent-minded ditty
to itself. No other sounds penetrated the sepulchral silence which once
had growled with the life of a great city. Anxiety caught at him with
clammy hands. An old man's voice it was—crackling and tuneless.
Paul groped for his holster and brought out the revolver he had taken
from a deserted police station.

"Stop where you are, dermie!" he bellowed at the fog. "I'm armed."

The footsteps and the singing stopped. Paul strained his eyes to penetrate the swirling mist-shroud. After a moment, the oldster answered:
"Sure foggy, ain't it, sonny? Can't see ya. Better come a little closer. I
ain't no dermie."

Loathing choked in Paul's throat. "The hell you're not. Nobody else'd be crazy enough to sing. Get off the road! I'm going south, and if I see you I'll shoot. Now move!"

"Sure, sonny. I'll move. But I'm no dermie. I was just singing to keep myself .company. I'm past caring about the plague. I'm heading north, where there's people, and if some dermie hears me a'singing . . . why, I'll tell him t'come jine in. What's the good o' being healthy if yer alone?"

While the old man spoke, Paul heard his sloshing across the ditch and through the brush. Doubt assailed him. Maybe the old crank wasn't a dermie. An ordinary plague-victim would have whimpered and pleaded for satisfaction of his strange craving—the laying-on of hands, the feel of healthy skin beneath moist gray palms. Nevertheless, Paul meant to take no chances with the oldster.

"Stay back in the brush while I walk past!" he called.

"Okay, sonny. You go right by. I ain't gonna touch you. You aiming to scrounge in Houston?"

Paul began to advance. "Yeah, I figure people got out so fast that they must have left plenty of canned goods and stuff behind."

"Mmmm, there's a mite here and there," said the cracked voice in a tone that implied understatement. "Course now, you ain't the first to figure that way, y'know."

Paul slacked his pace, frowning. "You mean . . . a lot of people are coming back?"

"Mmmm, no—not a lot. But you'll bump into people every day o: two. Ain't my kind o' folks. Rough characters, mostly—don't take chances, either. They'll shoot first, then look to see if you was a dermie. Don't never come busting out of a doorway without taking a peek at the street first. And if two people come around a corner in opposite directions, somebody's gonna die. The few that's there is trigger-happy. Just thought I'd warn ya."

"Thanks."

"D'mention it. Been good t'hear a body's voice again, tho I can't see ye."

Paul moved on until he was fifty paces past the voice. Then he stopped and turned. "Okay, you can get back on the road now. Start walking north. Scuff your feet until you're out of earshot."

"Taking no chances, are ye?" said the old man as he waded the ditch. "All right, sonny." The sound of his footsteps hesitated on the pavement. "A word of advice—your best scrounging'll be around the warehouses. Most of the stores are picked clean. Good luck!"

Paul stood listening to the shuffling feet recede northward. When they became inaudible, he turned to continue his journey. The meeting had depressed him, reminded him of the animal-level to which he and others like him had sunk. The oldster was obviously healthy; but Paul had been chased by three dermies in as many days. And the thought of being trapped by a band of them in the fog left him unnerved. Once he had seen a pair of the grinning, maddened compulsives seize a screaming young child while each of them took turns caressing the youngster's arms and face with the gray and slippery hands that spelled certain contraction of the disease—if disease it was. The dark pall of neuroderm was unlike any illness that Earth had ever seen.

The victim became the eager ally of the sickness that gripped him. Caught in its demoniac madness, the stricken human searched hungrily for healthy comrades, then set upon them with no other purpose than to paw at the clean skin and praise the virtues of the blind compulsion that drove him to do so. One touch, and infection was insured. It was as if a third of humanity had become night-prowling maniacs, lurking in the shadows to seize the unwary, working in bands to trap the unarmed wanderer. And two thirds of humanity found itself fleeing in horror from the mania, seeking the frigid northern climates where, according to rumor, the disease was less infectious. The normal functioning of civilization had been dropped like a hot potato within six months after the first alarm. When the man at the next lathe might be hiding gray discolorations beneath his shirt, industrial society was no place for humanity.

Rumor connected the onslaught of the plague with an unpredicted swarm of meteorites which had brightened the sky one October evening two weeks before the first case was discovered. The first case was, in fact, a machinist who had found one of the celestial cannon-balls, handled it, weighed it, estimated its volume by fluid-displacement, then cut into it on his lathe because its low density suggested that it might be hollow. He claimed to have found a pocket of frozen jelly, still rigid from the deep-space, although the outer shell had been heated white-hot by atmospheric friction. He said he let the jelly thaw, then fed it to his cat because it had an unpleasant fishy odor. Shortly thereafter, the cat disappeared.

Other meteorites had been discovered and similarly treated by university staffs before there was any reason to blame them for the plague. Paul, who had been an engineering student at Texas U at the time of the incident, had heard it said that the missiles were purposefully manufactured by parties unknown, that the jelly contained micro-organisms which under the microscope suggested a cross between a sperm cell (because of a similar tail) and a Pacini corpuscle (because of a marked resemblance to nerve tissue in sub-cellular detail).

When the meteorites were connected with the new and mushrooming disease, some people started a panic by theorizing that the meteor-swarm was a preinvasion artillery attack by some space-horde lurking beyond telescope range, and waiting for their biological bombardment to wreck civilization before they moved in upon Earth. The government had immediately labeled all investigations "top-secret," and Paul had heard no news since the initial speculations. Indeed, the government might have explained the whole thing and proclaimed it to the country for all he knew. One thing was certain: the country had not heard. It no longer possessed channels of communication.

Paul thought that if any such invaders were coming, they would have already arrived—months ago. Civilization was not truly wrecked; it had simply been discarded during the crazed flight of the individual away from the herd. Industry lay idle and unmanned, but still intact. Man was fleeing from Man. Fear had destroyed the integration of his society, and had left him powerless before any hypothetical invaders. Earth was ripe for plucking, but it remained unplucked and withering. Paul, therefore, discarded the invasion-hypothesis, and searched for nothing new to replace it. He accepted the fact of his own existence in the midst of chaos, and sought to protect that existence as best he could. It proved to be a fulltime job, with no spare time for theorizing.

Life was a rabbit scurrying over a hill. Life was a warm blanket, and a secluded sleeping place. Life was ditchwater, and an unbloated can of corned beef, and a suit of clothing looted from a deserted cottage. Life, above all else, was an avoidance of other human beings. For no dermie had the grace to cry "unclean!" to the unsuspecting. If the dermie's discolorations were still in the concealable stage, then concealed they would be, while the lost creature deliberately sought to infect his wife, his children, his friends—whoever would not protest an idle touch of the hand. When the grayness touched the face and the backs of the hands, the creature became a feverish nightwanderer, subject to strange hallucinations and delusions and desires.

The fog began to part toward mid-morning as Paul drove deeper into the outskirts of Houston. The highway was becoming a commercial sub-center, lined with businesses and small shops. The sidewalks were showered with broken glass from windows kicked in by looters. Paul kept to the center of the deserted street, listening and watching cautiously for signs of life. The distant barking of a dog was the only sound in the once-growing metropolis. A flight of sparrows winged down the street, then darted in through a broken window to an inside nesting place.

He searched a small grocery store, looking for a snack, but the shelves were bare. The thoroughfare had served as a main avenue of escape, and the fugitives had looted it thoroughly to obtain provisions. He turned onto a side-street, then after several blocks turned again to parallel the highway, moving through an old residential section. Many houses had been left open, but few had been looted. He entered one old frame mansion and found a can of tomatoes in the kitchen. He opened it and sipped the tender delicacy from the container, while curiosity sent him prowling through the rooms.

He wandered up the first flight of stairs, then halted with one foot on the landing. A body lay sprawled across the second flight—the body of a young man, dead quite a while. A well-rusted pistol had fallen from his hand. Paul dropped the tomatoes and bolted for the street. Suicide was a common recourse, when a man learned that he had been touched.

After two blocks, Paul stopped running. He sat panting on a fire hydrant and chided himself for being overly cautious. The man had been dead for months; and infection was achieved only through contact. Nevertheless, his scalp was still tingling. When he had rested briefly, he continued his plodding course toward the heart of the city. Toward noon, he saw another human being.

The man was standing on the loading dock of a warehouse, apparently enjoying the sunlight that came with the dissolving of the fog. He was slowly and solemnly spooning the contents of a can into a red-lipped mouth while his beard bobbled with appreciative chewing. Suddenly he saw Paul who had stopped in the center of the street with his hand on the butt of his pistol. The man backed away, tossed the can aside, and sprinted the length of the platform. He bounded off the end, snatched a bicycle away from the wall, and pedalled quickly out of sight while he bleated shrill blasts on a police whistle clenched between his teeth.

Paul trotted to the corner, but the man had made another turn. His whistle continued bleating. A signal? A dermie summons to a touching orgy? Paul stood still while he tried to overcome an urge to break into panicked flight. Other whistles were answering the first. After a minute, the clamor ceased; but silence was ominous.

If a party of cyclists moved in, he could not escape on foot. He darted toward the nearest warehouse, seeking a place to hide. Inside, he climbed a stack of boxes to a horizontal girder, kicked the stack to topple it, and stretched out belly-down on the steel I beam to command a clear shot at the entrances. He lay for an hour, waiting quietly for searchers. None came. At last he slid down a vertical support and returned to the loading platform. The street was empty and silent. With weapon ready, he continued his journey. He passed the next intersection without mishap.

Halfway up the block, a calm voice drawled a command from behind him: "Drop the gun, dermie. Get your hands behind your head."

He halted, motionless. No plague victim would hurl the dermie-charge at another. He dropped the pistol and turned slowly. Three men with drawn revolvers were clambering from the back of a stalled truck. They were all bearded, wore blue jeans, blue neckerchiefs, and green woolen shirts. He suddenly recalled that the man on the loading platform had been similarly dressed. A uniform?

"Turn around again!" barked the speaker.

Paul turned, realizing that the men were probably some sort of self-appointed quarantine patrol. Two ropes suddenly skidded out from behind and came to a stop near his feet on the pavement—a pair of lariat loops.

"One foot in each loop, dermie!" the speaker snapped.

When Paul obeyed, the ropes were jerked taut about his ankles, and two of the men trotted out to the sides, stood thirty feet apart, and pulled his legs out into a wide straddle. He quickly saw that any movement would cost him his balance.

"Strip to the skin."

"I'm no dermie," Paul protested as he unbuttoned his shirt.

"We'll see for ourselves, Joe," grunted the leader as he moved around to the front. "Get the top off first. If your chest's okay, we'll let your feet go."

When Paul had undressed, the leader walked around him slowly, making him spread his fingers and display the soles of his feet. He stood shivering and angry in the chilly winter air while the men satisfied themselves that he wore no gray patches of neuroderm.

"You're all right, I guess," the speaker admitted, then as Paul stooped to recover his clothing, the man growled, "Not those! Jim, get him a probie outfit."

Paul caught a bundle of clean clothing, tossed to him from the back of the truck. There were jeans, a woolen shirt, and a kerchief, but the shirt and kerchief were red. He shot an inquiring glance at the leader, while he climbed into the welcome change.

"All newcomers are on two weeks probation," the man explained. "If you decide to stay in Houston, you'll get another exam next time the uniform code changes. Then you can join our outfit, if you don't show up with the plague. In fact, you'll have to join if you stay."

"What is the outfit?" Paul asked suspiciously.

"It just started. School teacher name of Georgelle organized it. We aim to keep dermies out. There's about six hundred of us now. We guard the downtown area, but soon as there's enough of us, we'll move out to take in more territory. Set up road blocks and all that. You're welcome, soon as we're sure you're clean . . . and can take orders."

"Whose orders?"

"Georgelle's. We got no room for goof-offs, and no time for argument. Anybody don't like the setup, he's welcome to get out. Jim here'll give you a leaflet on the rules. Better read it before you go anywhere. If you don't, you might make a wrong move. Make a wrong move, and you catch a bullet."

The man called Jim interrupted: "Reckon you better call off the other patrols, Digger?" he said respectfully to the leader.

Digger nodded curtly and turned to blow three short blasts and a long with his whistle. An answering short-long-short came from several blocks away. Other posts followed suit. Paul realized that he had been surrounded by a ring of similar ambushes.

"Jim, take him to the nearest water barrel, and see that he shaves," Digger ordered, then: "What's your name, probie? Also your job, if you had one."

"Paul Harris Oberlin. I was a mechanical engineering student when the plague struck. Part-time garage mechanic while I was in school."

Digger nodded and jotted down the information on a scratch-pad. "Good, I'll turn your name in to the registrar. Georgelle says to watch for college men. You might get a good assignment, later. Report to the Esperson Building on the seventeenth. That's inspection day. If you don't show up, we'll come looking for you. All loose probies'll get shot. Now Jim here's gonna see to it that you shave. Don't shave again until your two-weeker. That way, we can estimate how long you been in town—by looking at your beard. We got other ways that you don't need to know about. Georgelle's got a system worked out for everything, so don't try any tricks."

"Tell me, what do you do with dermies?"

Digger grinned at his men. "You'll find out, probie."

Paul was led to a rain barrel, given a basin, razor, and soap. He scraped his face clean while Jim sat at a safe distance, munching a quid of tobacco and watching the operation with tired boredom. The other men had gone.

"May I have my pistol back?"

"Uh-uh! Read the rules. No weapons for probies."

"Suppose I bump into a dermie?"

"Find yourself a whistle and toot a bunch of short blasts. Then run like hell. We'll take care of the dermies. Read the rules."

"Can I scrounge wherever I want to?"

"Probies have their own assigned areas. There's a map in the rules."

"Who wrote the rules, anyhow?"

"Jeezis!" the guard grunted disgustedly. "Read 'em and find out."

When Paul finished shaving, Jim stood up, stretched, then bounded off the platform and picked up his bicycle.

"Where do I go from here?" Paul called.

The man gave him a contemptuous snort, mounted the bike, and pedalled leisurely away. Paul gathered that he was to read the rules. He sat down beside the rain barrel and began studying the mimeographed leaflet.

Everything was cut and dried. As a probie, he was confined to an area six blocks square near the heart of the city. Once he entered it, a blue mark would be stamped on his forehead. At the two-week inspection, the indelible brand would be removed with a special solution. If a branded probie were caught outside his area, he would be forcibly escorted from the city. He was warned against attempting to impersonate permanent personnel, because a system of codes and passwords would ensnare him. One full page of the leaflet was devoted to propaganda. Houston was to become "a bulwark of health in a stricken world, and the leader of a glorious recovery." The paper was signed by Dr. Georgelle, who had given himself the title of Director.

The pamphlet left Paul with a vague uneasiness. The uniforms—they reminded him of neighborhood boys' gangs in the slums, wearing special sweaters and uttering secret passwords, whipping intruders and amputating the tails of stray cats in darkened garages. And, in another way, it made him think of frustrated little people, gathering at night in brown shirts around a bonfire to sing the *Horst Wessel Lied* and listen to grandiose oratory about glorious destinies. *Their* stray cats had been an unfavored race.

Of course, the dermies were not merely harmless alley prowlers. They were a real menace. And maybe Georgelle's methods were the only ones effective.

While Paul sat with the pamphlet on the platform, he had been gazing absently at the stalled truck from which the men had emerged. Suddenly it broke upon his consciousness that it was a diesel. He bounded off the platform, and went to check its fuel tank, which had been left uncapped.

He knew that it was useless to search for gasoline, but diesel fuel was another matter. The exodus had drained all existing supplies of high octane fuel for the escaping motorcade, but the evacuation had been too hasty and too fear-crazed to worry with out-of-the-ordinary methods. He sniffed the tank. It smelled faintly of gasoline. Some unknowing fugitive had evidently filled it with ordinary fuel, which had later evaporated. But if the cylinders had not been damaged by the trial, the truck might be useful. He checked the engine briefly, and decided that it had not been tried at all. The starting battery had been removed.

He walked across the street and looked back at the warehouse. It bore the sign of a trucking firm. He walked around the block, eyeing the streets cautiously for other patrolmen. There was a fueling platform on the opposite side of the block. A fresh splash of oil on the concrete told him that Georgelle's crew was using the fuel for some purpose—possibly for heating or cooking. He entered the building and found a repair shop, with several dismantled engines lying about. There was a rack of batteries in the corner, but a screwdriver placed across the terminals brought only a weak spark.

The chargers, of course, drew power from the city's electric service, which was dead. After giving the problem some thought, Paul connected five of the batteries in series, then placed a sixth across the total voltage, so that it would collect the charge that the others lost. Then he went to carry buckets of fuel from the pumps to the truck. When the tank was filled, he hoisted each end of the truck with a roll-under jack and inflated the tires with a hand-pump. It was a long and laborious job.

Twilight was gathering by the time he was ready to try it. Several times during the afternoon, he had been forced to hide from cyclists who wandered past, lest they send him on to the probie area and use the truck for their own purposes. Evidently they had long since decided that automotive transportation was a thing of the past.

A series of short whistle-blasts came to his ears as he was climbing into the cab. The signals were several blocks away, but some of the answering bleats were closer. Evidently another newcomer, he thought. Most new arrivals from the north would pass through the same area on their way downtown. He entered the cab, closed the door softly, and ducked low behind the dashboard as three cyclists raced across the intersection just ahead.

Paul settled down to wait for the all-clear. It came after about ten minutes. Apparently the newcomer had tried to run instead of hiding. When the cyclists returned, they were moving leisurely, and laughing among themselves. After they had passed the intersection, Paul stole quietly out of the cab and moved along the wall to the corner, to assure himself that all the patrolmen had gone. But the sound of shrill pleading came to his ears.

At the end of the building, he clung close to the wall and risked a glance around the corner. A block away, the nude figure of a girl was struggling between taut ropes held by green-shirted guards. She was a pretty girl, with a tousled mop of chestnut hair and clean white limbs—clean except for her forearms, which appeared dipped in dark stain Then he saw the dark irregular splotch across her flank, like a splash of ink not quite washed clean. She was a dermie.

Paul ducked close to the ground so that his face was hidden by a clump of grass at the corner. A man—the leader of the group—had left the girl, and was advancing up the street toward Paul, who prepared to roll under the building out of sight. But in the middle of the block, the man stopped. He lifted a manhole cover in the pavement, then went back for the girl's clothing, which he'd dragged at the end of a fishing pole with a wire hook at its tip. He dropped the clothing, one piece at a time, into the man-hole. A cloud of white dust arose from it, and the man stepped back to avoid the dust. Quicklime, Paul guessed.

Then the leader cupped his hands to his mouth and called back to the others. "Okay, drag her on up here!" He drew his revolver and waited while they tugged the struggling girl toward the manhole.

Paul felt suddenly ill. He had seen dermies shot in self-defense by fugitives from their deathly gray hands, but here was cold and efficient elimination. Here was Dachau and Buchenwald and the nameless camps of Siberia. He turned and bolted for the truck.

The sound of its engine starting brought a halt to the disposal of the pest-girl. The leader appeared at the intersection and stared uncertainly at the truck, as Paul nosed it away from the building. He fidgeted with his revolver doubtfully, and called something over his shoulder to the others. Then he began walking out into the street and signaling for the truck to stop. Paul let it crawl slowly ahead, and leaned out the window to eye the man questioningly.

"How the hell you get that started?" the leader called excitedly. He was still holding the pistol, but it dangled almost unnoticed in his hand. Paul suddenly fed fuel to the diesel and swerved sharply toward the surprised guardsman.

The leader yelped and dived for safety, but the fender caught his hips, spun him off balance, and smashed him down against the pavement. As the truck thundered around the corner toward the girl and her captors, he glanced in the mirror to see the hurt man weakly trying to crawl out of the street. Paul was certain that he was not mortally wounded.

As the truck lumbered on, the girl threw herself prone before it, since the ropes prevented any escape. Paul swerved erratically, sending the girl's captors scurrying for the alley. Then he aimed the wheels to straddle her body. She glanced up, screamed, then hugged the pavement as the behemoth thundered overhead. A bullet ploughed a furrow across the hood. Paul ducked low in the seat and jammed the brake pedal down, as soon as he thought she was clear.

There were several shots, but apparently they were shooting at the girl. Paul counted three seconds, then gunned the engine again. If she hadn't climbed aboard, it was just tough luck, he thought grimly. He shouldn't have tried to save her anyway. But continued shooting told him that she had managed to get inside. The trailer was heaped with clothing, and he trusted the mound of material to halt the barrage of bullets. He heard the explosion of a blowout as he swung around the next corner, and the trailer lurched dangerously. It swayed from side to side as he gathered speed down the wide and trafficless avenue. But the truck had double wheels, and soon the dangerous lurching ceased.

He roared on through the metropolitan area, staying on the same street and gathering speed. An occasional scrounger or cyclist stopped to stare, but they seemed too surprised to act. And they could not have known what had transpired a few blocks away.

Paul could not stop to see if he had a passenger, or if she was still alive. She was more dangerous than the gunmen. Any gratitude she might feel toward her rescuer would be quickly buried beneath her craving to spread the disease. He wished fervently that he had let the patrolmen kill her. Now he was faced with the problem of getting rid of her. He noticed, however, that mirrors were mounted on both sides of the cab. If he stopped the truck, and if she climbed out, he could see, and move away again before she had a chance to approach him. But he decided to wait until they were out of the city.

Soon he saw a highway marker, then a sign that said "Galveston—58 miles." He bore ahead, thinking that perhaps the island-city would provide some good scrounging, without the regimentation of Doctor Georgelle's efficient system with its plans for "glorious recovery."

Twenty miles beyond the city limits, he stopped the truck, let the engine idle, and waited for his passenger to climb out. He watched the mirrors anxiously, wondering if he could get away in time if she came sprinting for the cab. He locked the doors and laid a jack-handle across the seat as an added precaution. Nothing happened. He rolled down the window and shouted toward the rear.

"All passengers off the bus! Last stop! Everybody out!"

Still the girl did not appear. Then he heard something—a light tap from the trailer, and a murmur—or a moan. She was there all right. He called again, but she made no response. It was nearly dark outside.

At last he seized the jack-handle, opened the door, and stepped out of the cab. Wary of a trick, he skirted wide around the trailer and approached it from the rear. One door was closed, while the other swung free. He stopped a few yards away and peered inside. At first he saw nothing.

"Get out, but keep away or I'll kill you."

Then he saw her move. She was sitting on the floor, leaning back against a heap of clothing, a dozen feet from the entrance. He stepped forward cautiously and flung open the other door. She turned her head to look at him peculiarly, but said nothing. He could see that she had donned some of the clothing, but one trouser-leg was rolled up, and she had tied a rag tightly about her ankle.

"Are you hurt?"

She nodded "Bullet . . ." She rolled her head dizzily and moaned.

Paul went back to the cab to search for a first-aid kit. He found one, together with a flashlight and spare batteries in the glove compartment. He made certain that the cells were not corroded and that the light would burn feebly. Then he returned to the trailer, chiding himself for a prize fool. A sensible human would haul the dermie out at the end of a towing chain and leave her sitting by the side of the road.

"If you try to touch me, I'll brain you!" he warned, as he clambered into the cab.

She looked up again. "Would you feel . . . like enjoying anything . . . if you were bleeding like this?" she muttered weakly. The flashing beam caught the glitter of pain in her eyes, and accentuated the pallor of her small face. She was a pretty girl—scarcely older than twenty—but Paul was in no mood to appreciate pretty women, especially dermies.

"So that's how you think of it, eh? Enjoying yourself!"

She said nothing. She dropped her forehead against her knee and rolled it slowly .

"Where are you hit? Just the foot?"

"Ankle . . ."

"All right, take the rag off. Let's see."

"The wound's in back."

"All right, lie down on your stomach, and keep your hands under your head."

She stretched out weakly, and he shone the light over her leg, to make certain its skin was clear of neuroderm. Then he looked at the ankle, and said nothing for a time. The bullet had missed the joint, but had neatly severed the Achilles-tendon just above the heel.

"You're a plucky kid," he grunted, wondering how she had endured the self-torture of getting the shoe off and clothing herself.

"It was cold back here—without clothes," she muttered.

Paul opened the first-aid packet and found an envelope of sulfa-powder. Without touching her, he emptied it into the wound, which was beginning to bleed again. There was nothing else he could do. The tendon had pulled apart and would require surgical stitching to bring it together until it could heal. Such attention was out of the question.

She broke the silence. "I . . . I'm going to be crippled, aren't I?"

"Oh, not crippled," he heard himself telling her. "If we can get you to a doctor, anyway. Tendons can be sutured with wire. He'll probably put your foot in cast, and you might get a stiff ankle from it."

She lay breathing quietly, denying his hopeful words by her silence.

"Here!" he said. "Here's a gauze pad and some tape. Can you manage it yourself."

She started to sit up. He placed the first aid pack beside her, and backed to the door. She fumbled in the kit, and whimpered while she taped the pad in place.

"There's a tourniquet in there, too. Use it if the bleeding's worse."

She looked up to watch his silhouette against the darkening evening sky. "Thanks . . . thanks a lot, mister. I'm grateful. I promise not to touch you. Not if you don't want me to."

Shivering, he moved back to the cab. Why did they always get that insane idea that they were doing their victims a favor by giving them the neural plague? *Not if you don't want me to.* He shuddered as he drove away. She felt that way now, while the pain robbed her of the craving, but later—unless he got rid of her quickly—she would come to feel that she owed it to him—as a favor. The disease perpetuated itself by arousing strange delusions in its bearer. The microorganisms' methods of survival were indeed highly specialized. Paul felt certain that such animalicules had not evolved on Earth.

A light gleamed here and there along the Alvin-Galveston highway— oil lamps, shining from lonely cottages whose occupants had not felt the pressing urgency of the crowded city. But he had no doubt that to approach one of the farmhouses would bring a rifle bullet as a welcome. Where could he find help for the girl? No one would touch

her but another dermie. Perhaps he could unhitch the trailer and leave
her in downtown Galveston, with a sign hung on the back—"Wounded
dermie inside." The plague-victims would care for their own—if they
found her.

He chided himself again for worrying about her. Saving her life
didn't make him responsible for her . . . did it? After all, if she lived,
and the leg healed, she would only prowl in search of healthy victims
again. She would never be rid of the disease, nor would she ever die
of it—so far as anyone knew. The death rate was high among dermies,
but the cause was usually a bullet.

Paul passed a fork in the highway and knew that the bridge was
just ahead. Beyond the channel lay Galveston Island, once brightly lit
and laughing in its role as sea-side resort—now immersed in darkness.
The wind whipped at the truck from the southwest as the road led
up onto the wide causeway. A faint glow in the east spoke of a moon
about to rise. He saw the side structure of the draw-bridge just
ahead.

Suddenly he clutched at the wheel, smashed furiously down on the
brake, and tugged the emergency back. The tires howled ahead on the
smooth concrete, and the force threw him forward over the wheel
Dusty water swirled far below where the upward folding gates of th
draw-bridge had once been. He skidded to a stop ten feet from th
end. When he climbed out, the girl was calling weakly from the trailer
but he walked to the edge and looked over. Someone had done a jo
with dynamite.

Why, he wondered. To keep islanders on the island, or to keep
mainlanders off? Had another Doctor Georgelle started his own small
nation in Galveston? It seemed more likely that the lower island dwellers had done the demolition.

He looked back at the truck. An experienced truckster might be
able to swing it around all right but Paul was doubtful. Nevertheless,
he climbed back in the cab and tried it. Half an hour later he was
hopelessly jammed with the trailer twisted aside and the cab wedged
near the sheer drop to the water. He gave it up and went back to
inspect his infected cargo.

She was asleep, but moaning faintly. He prodded her awake with
the jack-handle. "Can you crawl, kid? If you can, come back to the
door."

She nodded, and began dragging herself toward the flashlight. She
clenched her lip between her teeth to keep from whimpering, but her
breath came as a voiced murmur . . . *nnnng . . . nnnng . . .*

She sagged weakly when she reached the entrance, and for a moment he thought she had fainted. Then she looked up. "What next,
skipper?" she panted.

"I . . . I don't know. Can you let yourself down to the pavement?"
She glanced over the edge and shook her head. "With a rope, maybe.

There's one back there someplace. If you're scared of me, I'll try to crawl and get it."

"Hands to yourself?" he asked suspiciously; then he thanked the darkness for hiding the heat of shame that crawled to his face.

"I won't . . ."

He scrambled into the trailer quickly and brought back the rope. "I'll climb up on top and let it down in front of you. Grab hold and let yourself down."

A few minutes later she was sitting on the concrete causeway looking at the wrecked draw. "Oh!" she muttered as he scrambled down from atop the trailer. "I thought you just wanted to dump me here. We're stuck, huh?"

"Yeah! We might swim it, but doubt if you could make it."

"I'd try . . ." She paused, cocking her head slightly. "There's a boat moored under the bridge. Right over there."

"What makes you think so?"

"Water lapping against wood. Listen." Then she shook her head. "I forgot. You're not hyper."

"I'm not what?" Paul listened. The water sounds seemed homogeneous.

"Hyperacute. Sharp senses. You know, it's one of the symptoms."

He nodded, remembering vaguely that he'd heard something to that effect—but he'd chalked it up as a hallucinatory phenomenon. He walked to the rail and shone his light toward the water. The boat was there—tugging its rope taut from the mooring as the tide swirled about it. The bottom was still fairly dry, indicating that a recent rower had crossed from the island to the mainland.

"Think you can hold onto the rope if I let you down?" he called.

She gave him a quick glance, then picked up the end she had previously touched and tied a loop around her waist. She began crawling toward the rail. Paul fought down a crazy urge to pick her up and carry her; plague be damned. But he had already left himself dangerously open to contagion. Still, he felt the drumming charges of conscience . . . *depart from me, ye accursed, for I was sick and you visited me not . . .*

He turned quickly away, and began knotting the end of the rope about the rail. He reminded himself that any sane person would desert her at once, and swim on to safety. Yet, he could not. In the oversized clothing she looked like a child, hurt and helpless. Paul knew the demanding arrogance that could possess the wounded—*help me, you've got to help me, you damn merciless bastard . . . no, don't touch me there, damn you!* Too many times, he had heard the sick curse the physician, the injured curse the rescuer. Blind aggression, trying to strike back at pain.

But the girl made no complaint except for the involuntary hurt-sounds. She asked nothing, and accepted his aid with a wide-eyed gratitude that left him weak. He thought that it would be easier to leave her if she would only beg, or plead, or demand.

"Can you start me swinging a little?" she called as he lowered her toward the water.

Paul's eyes probed the darkness below, trying to sort the shadows, to make certain which was the boat. He used both hands to feed out the rope, and the light laid on the rail only seemed to blind him. She began swinging herself pendulum-wise somewhere beneath him.

"When I say 'ready,' let me go!" she shrilled.

"You're not going to drop!"

"Have to! Boat's out further. Got to swing for it. I can't swim, really."

"But you'll hurt your—"

"Ready!"

Paul still clung to the rope. "I'll let you down into the water and you can hang onto the rope. I'll dive, and then pull you into the boat."

"Uh-uh! You'd have to touch me. You don't want that, do you? Just a second now . . . one more swing . . . ready!"

He let the rope go. With a clatter and a thud, she hit the boat. Three sharp cries of pain clawed at him. Then—muffled sobbing.

"Are you all right?"

Sobs. She seemed not to hear him.

"Jeezis!" He sprinted for the brink of the draw-bridge and dived out over the deep channel. How far . . . down . . . down . . . Icy water stung his body with sharp whips, then opened to embrace him. He fought to the surface and swam toward the dark shadow of the boat. The sobbing had subsided. He grasped the prow and hauled himself dripping from the channel. She was lying curled in the bottom of the boat.

"Kid . . . you all right, kid?"

"Sorry . . . I'm such a baby," she gasped, and dragged herself back to the stern.

Paul found a paddle, but no oars. He cast off and began digging water toward the other side, but the tide tugged them relentlessly away from the bridge. He gave it up and paddled toward the distant shore. "You know anything about Galveston?" he called—mostly to reassure himself that she was not approaching him in the darkness with the death-gray hands.

"I used to come here for the summer. I know a little about it."

Paul urged her to talk while he plowed toward the island. Her name was Willie, and she insisted that it was for Willow, not for Wilhelmina. She came from Dallas, and claimed she was a salesman's daughter who was done in by a travelling farmer. The farmer, she explained, was just a wandering dermie who had caught her napping by the roadside.

He had stroked her arms until she awoke, then had run away, howling with glee.

"That was three weeks ago," she said. "If I'd had a gun, I'd have dropped him. Of course, I know better now."

Paul shuddered and paddled on. "Why did you head south?"

"I was coming here."

"Here? To Galveston?"

"Uh-huh. I heard someone say that a lot of nuns were coming to the island. I thought maybe they'd take me in."

The moon was high over the lightless city, and the tide had swept the small boat far east from the bridge by the time Paul's paddle dug into mud beneath the shallow water. He bounded out and dragged the boat through thin marsh grass onto the shore. Fifty yards away, a ramshackle fishing cottage lay sleeping in moonlight.

"Stay here, Willie," he grunted. "I'll find a couple of boards or something for crutches."

He rummaged about through a shed behind the cottage and brought back a wheel-barrow. Moaning and laughing at once, she struggled into it, and he wheeled her to the house, humming a verse of *Rickshaw Boy*.

"You're a funny guy, Paul. I'm sorry . . ." She jiggled her tousled head in the moonlight, as if she disapproved of her own words.

Paul tried the cottage door, kicked it open, then walked the wheel-barrow up three steps and into a musty room. He struck a match, found an oil lamp with a little kerosene, and lit it. Willie caught her breath.

He looked around. "Company," he grunted.

The company sat in a fragile rocker with a shawl about her shoulders and a shotgun between her knees. She had been dead at least a month. The charge of buckshot had sieved the ceiling and spattered it with bits of gray hair and brown blood.

"Stay here," he told the girl tonelessly, "I'll try to get a dermie somewhere—one who knows how to sew a tendon. Got any ideas?"

She was staring with a sick face at the old woman. "Here? With—"

"She won't bother you," he said as he gently disentangled the gun from the corpse. He moved to a cupboard and found a box of shells behind an ornate teapot. "I may not be back, but I'll send somebody."

She buried her face in her plague-stained hands, and he stood for a moment watching her shoulders shiver. "Don't worry . . . I will send somebody." He stepped to the porcelain sink and pocketed a wafer-thin sliver of dry soap.

"What's that for?" she muttered, looking up again.

He thought of a lie, then checked it. "To wash you off of me," he said truthfully. "I might have got too close. Soap won't do much good, but I'll feel better." He looked at the corpse coolly. "Didn't do her much good. Buckshot's the best antiseptic all right."

Willie moaned as he went out the door. He heard her crying as he walked down to the waterfront. She was still crying when he waded back to shore, after a thorough scrubbing. He was sorry he'd spoken cruelly, but it was such a damned relief to get rid of her . . .

With the shotgun cradled on his arm, he began putting distance between himself and the sobbing. But the sound worried his ears, even after he realized that he was no longer hearing her.

He strode a short distance inland past scattered fishing shanties, then took the highway toward the city whose outskirts he was entering. It would be at least an hour's trek to the end of the island where he would be most likely to encounter someone with medical training. The hospitals were down there, the medical school, and the most likely place for any charitable nuns—if Willie's rumor were true. Paul meant to capture a dermie doctor or nurse and force the amorous-handed maniac at gun-point to go to Willie's aid. Then he would be done with her. When she stopped hurting, she would start craving—and he had no doubt that he would be the object of her manual affections.

The bay was wind-chopped in the moonglow, no longer glittering from lights along 61st Street. The oleanders along Broadway were choked up with weeds. Cats or rabbits rustled in the tousled growth that had been a carefully tended parkway.

Paul wandered why the plague had chosen Man, and not the lower animals. It was true that an occasional dog or cow was seen with the plague, but the focus was upon humanity. And the craving to spread the disease was Man-directed, even in animals. It was as if the neural entity deliberately sought out the species with the most complex nervous system. Was its onslaught really connected with the meteorite swarm? Paul believed that it was.

In the first place, the meteorites had not been predicted. They were not a part of the regular cosmic bombardment. And then there was the strange report that they were *manufactured* projectiles, teeming with frozen micro-organisms which came alive upon thawing. In these days of tumult and confusion, however, it was hard. Nevertheless Paul believed it. Neuroderm had no first cousins among Earth-diseases.

What manner of beings, then, had sent such a curse? Potential invaders? If so, they were slow in coming. One thing was generally agreed upon by the scientists: the missiles had not been "sent" from another solar planet. Their direction upon entering the atmosphere was wrong. They could conceivably have been fired from an interplanetary launching ship, but their velocity was about equal to the theoretical velocity which a body would obtain in falling sunward from a near-infinite distance. This seemed to hint the projectiles had come from another star.

Paul was startled suddenly by the flare of a match from the shadow of a building. He stopped dead-still in the street. A man was leaning against the wall to light a cigarette. He flicked the match out, and Paul watched the cigarette-glow make an arc as the man waved at him.

"Nice night, isn't it? said the voice from the darkness.

Paul stood exposed in the moonlight, carrying the shotgun at the ready. The voice sounded like that of an adolescent, not fully changed to its adult timbre. If the youth wasn't a dermie, why wasn't he afraid that Paul might be one? And if he was a dermie, why wasn't he advancing in the hope that Paul might be as yet untouched?

"I said, 'Nice night, isn't it?' Watcha carrying the gun for? Been shooting rabbits?"

Paul moved a little closer and fumbled for his flashlight. Then he threw its beam on the slouching figure in the shadows. He saw a young man, perhaps sixteen, reclining against the wall. He saw the pearl-gray face that characterized the final and permanent stage of neuroderm! He stood frozen to the spot a dozen feet away from the youth, who blinked perplexedly in the light. The kid was assuming automatically that he was another dermie! Paul tried to keep him blinded while he played along with the fallacy.

"Yeah, it's a nice night. You got any idea where I can find a doctor?"

The boy frowned. "Doctor? You mean you don't know?"

"Know what? I'm new here."

"New? Oh . . . " the boy's nostrils began twitching slightly, as if he were sniffing at the night air. "Well, most of the priests down at Saint Mary's were missionaries. They're all doctors. Why? You sick?"

"No, there's a girl . . . But never mind. How do I get there? And are any of them dermies?"

The boys eyes wandered peculiarly, and his mouth fell open, as if he had been asked why a circle wasn't square. "You are new, aren't you? They're all dermies, if you want to call them that. Wh—" Again the nostrils were flaring. He flicked the cigarette away suddenly and inhaled a slow draught of the breeze. "I . . . I smell a non-hyper," he muttered.

Paul started to back away. His scalp bristled a warning. The boy advanced a step toward him. A slow beam of anticipation began to glow in his face. He bared his teeth in a wide grin of pleasure.

"You're not a hyper yet," he hissed moving forward. "I've never had a chance to touch a non-hyper . . ."

"Stay back, or I'll kill you!"

The lad giggled and came on, talking to himself. "The padre says it's wrong, but . . . you smell so . . . so . . . ugh . . ." He flung himself forward with a low throaty cry.

Paul sidestepped the charge and brought the gun-barrel down across the boy's head. The dermie sprawled howling in the street. Paul pushed the gun close to his face, but the youth started up again. Paul jabbed viciously with the barrel, and felt it strike and tear. "I don't want to have to blow your head off—"

The boy howled and fell back. He crouched panting on his hands and knees, head hung low, watching a dark puddle of blood gather on the pavement from a deep gash across his cheek. "Whatcha wanta do that for?" he whimpered. "I wasn't gonna hurt you." His tone was that of a wronged and rejected suitor.

"Now, where's St. Mary's? Is that one of the hospitals? How do I get there?" Paul had backed to a safe distance and was covering the youth with the gun.

"Straight down Broadway . . . to the Boulevard . . . you'll see it down that neighborhood. About fourth street, I think." The boy looked up, and Paul saw the extent of the gash. It was deep and ragged, and the kid was crying.

"Get up! You're going to lead me there."

Pain had blanketed the call of the craving. The boy struggled to his feet, pressed a handkerchief against the wound, and with an angry glance at Paul, he set out down the road. Paul followed ten yards behind.

"If you take me through any dermie traps, I'll kill you."

"There aren't any traps," the youth mumbled.

Paul snorted unbelief, but did not repeat the warning. "What made you think I was another dermie?" he snapped.

"Because there's no non-hypers in Galveston. This is a hyper colony. A non-hyper used to drift in occasionally, but the priests had the bridge dynamited. The non-hypers upset the colony. As long as there aren't any around to smell, nobody causes any trouble. During the day, there's a guard out on the causeway, and if any hypers come looking for a place to stay, the guard ferries them across. If non-hypers come, he tells them about the colony, and they go away."

Paul groaned. He had stumbled into a rat's nest. Was there no refuge from the gray curse? Now he would have to move on. It seemed a hopeless quest. Maybe the old man he met on his way to Houston had arrived at the only possible hope for peace: submission to the plague. But the thought sickened him somehow. He would have to find some barren island, find a healthy mate, and go to live a savage existence apart from all traces of civilization.

"Didn't the guard stop you at the bridge?" the boy asked. "He never came back today. He must be still out there."

Paul grunted "no" in a tone that warned against idle conversation. He guessed what had happened. The dermie guard had probably spotted some healthy wanderers; and instead of warning them away, he rowed across the draw-bridge and set out to chase them. His body probably lay along the highway somewhere, if the hypothetical wanderers were armed.

When they reached 23rd Street, a few blocks from the heart of the city, Paul hissed at the boy to stop. He heard someone laugh. Footsteps were wandering along the sidewalk, overhung by trees. He whispered to the boy to take refuge behind a hedge. They crouched in the shadows several yards apart while the voices draw nearer.

"Brother James has a nice tenor," someone said softly. "But he sings his Latin with a western drawl. It sounds . . . well . . . peculiar, to say the least. Brother John is a stickler for pronunciation. He won't let Fra James solo. Says it gives a burlesque effect to the choir. Says it makes the sisters giggle."

The other man chuckled quietly and started to reply. But his voice broke off suddenly. The footsteps stopped a dozen feet from Paul's hiding place. Paul, peering through the hedge, saw a pair of brown-robed monks standing on the sidewalk. They were looking around suspiciously.

"Brother Thomas, do you smell—"

"Aye, I smell it."

Paul changed his position slightly, so as to keep the gun pointed toward the pair of plague-stricken monastics. They stood in embarrassed silence, peering into the darkness, and shuffling their feet uneasily. One of them suddenly pinched his nose between thumb and forefinger. His companion followed suit.

"Blessed be God," quavered one.

"Blessed be His Holy Name," answered the other.

"Blessed be Jesus Christ, true God and true Man."

"Blessed be . . ."

Gathering their robes high about their shins, the two monks turned and scurried away, muttering the Litany of the Divine Praises as they went. Paul stood up and stared after them in amazement. The sight of dermies running from a potential victim was almost beyond belief. He questioned his young guide. Still holding the handkerchief against his bleeding face, the boy hung his head.

"Bishop made a ruling against touching non-hypers," he explained miserably. "Says it's a sin, unless the non-hyper submits of his own free will. Says even then it's wrong, except in the ordinary ways that people come in contact with each other. Calls it fleshly desire, and all that."

"Then why did you try to do it?"

"I ain't so religious."

"Well, sonny, you better get religious until we come to the hospital. Now, let's go."

They marched on down Broadway encountering no other pedestrians. Twenty minutes later, they were standing in the shadows before a hulking brick building, some of whose windows were yellow with lamplight. Moonlight bathed the statue of a woman standing on a ledge over the entrance, indicating to Paul that this was the hospital.

"All right, boy. You go in and send out a dermie doctor. Tell him somebody wants to see him, but if you say I'm not a dermie, I'll come in and kill you. Now move. And don't come back. Stay to get your face fixed."

The youth stumbled toward the entrance. Paul sat in the shadow of a tree, where he could see twenty yards in all directions and guard himself against approach. Soon a black-clad priest came out of the emergency entrance, stopped on the sidewalk, and glanced around.

"Over here!" Paul hissed from across the street.

The priest advanced uncertainly. In the center of the road he stopped again, and held his nose. "Y-you're a non-hyper," he said, almost accusingly.

"That's right, and I've got a gun, so don't try anything."

"What's wrong? Are you sick? The lad said—"

"There's a dermie girl down the island. She's been shot. Tendon behind her heel is cut clean through. You're going to help her."

"Of course, but . . .." The priest paused. "You? A non-hyper? Helping a so-called dermie?" His voice went high with amazement.

"So I'm a sucker!" Paul barked. "Now get what you need, and come on."

"The Lord bless you," the priest mumbled in embarrassment as he hurried away.

"Don't sic any of your maniacs on me!" Paul called after him. "I'm armed."

"I'll have to bring a surgeon," the cleric said over his shoulder.

Five minutes later, Paul heard the muffled grunt of a starter. Then an engine coughed to life. Startled, he scurried away from the tree and sought safety in a clump of shrubs. An ambulance backed out of the driveway and into the street. It parked at the curb by the tree, engine running. A pallid face glanced out curiously toward the shadows. "Where are you?" it called, but it was not the priest's voice.

Paul stood up and advanced a few steps.

"We'll have to wait on Father Mendelhaus," the driver called. "He'll be a few minutes."

"You a dermie?"

"Of course. But don't worry. I've plugged my nose and I'm wearing rubber gloves. I can't smell you. The sight of a non-hyper arouses some craving, of course. But it can be overcome with a little will-power. I won't infect you, although I don't understand why you non-hypers fight so hard. You're bound to catch it sooner or later. And the world can't get back to normal until everybody has it."

Paul avoided the startling thought. "You the surgeon?"

"Uh, yes. Father Williamson's the name. I'm not really a specialist, but I did some surgery in Korea. How's the girl's condition? Suffering shock?"

"I wouldn't know."

They fell silent until Father Mendelhaus returned. He came across the street carrying a bag in one hand and a brown bottle in the other. He held the bottle by the neck with a pair of tongs, and Paul could see the exterior of the bottle steaming slightly as the priest passed through the ambulance's headlights. He placed the flask on the curb without touching it, then spoke to the man in the shadows.

"Would you step behind the hedge and disrobe, young man? Then rub yourself thoroughly with this oil."

"I doubt it" Paul snapped. "What is it?"

"Don't worry, it's been in the sterilizer. That's what took me so long. It may be a little hot for you, however. It's only an antiseptic and deodorant. It'll kill your odor, and it'll also give you some protection against picking up stray micro-organisms."

After a few moments of anxious hesitation, Paul decided to trust the priest. He carried the hot flask into the brush, undressed, and bathed himself with the warm aromatic oil. Then he slipped back into his clothes and reapproached the ambulance.

"Ride in back," Mendelhaus told him. "And you won't be infected. No one's been in there for several weeks, and as you probably know, the micro-organisms die after a few hours exposure. They have to be transmitted from skin to skin, or else an object has to be rehandled very soon after a hyper has touched it."

Paul warily climbed inside. Mendelhaus opened a slide and spoke through it from the front seat. "You'll have to show us the way."

"Straight out Broadway. Say, where did you get the gasoline for this wagon."

The priest paused. "That has been something of a secret. Oh well . . . I'll tell you. There's a tanker out in the harbor. The people left town too quickly to think of it. Automobiles are scarcer than fuel in Galveston. Up north, you find them stalled everywhere. But since Galvestor didn't have any through-traffic, there were no cars running out of gas The ones we have are the ones that were left in the repair-shop. Something wrong with them. And we don't have any mechanics to fix them."

Paul neglected to mention that he was qualified for the job. The priest might get ideas. He fell into gloomy silence as the ambulance turned onto Broadway and headed down-island. He watched the back of the priests' heads, silhouetted against the head-lighted pavement. They seemed not at all concerned about their disease. Mendelhaus was a slender man, with a blond crew-cut and rather bushy eyebrows. He had a thin, aristocratic face—now plague-gray—but jovial enough. It might be the face of an ascetic but for the quick blue eyes that seemed full of lively interest rather than inward-turning mysticism. Williamson on the other hand was a rather plain man, with a stolid tweedy look, despite his black cassock.

"What do you think of our plan here?" asked Father Mendelhaus.

"What plan?" Paul grunted.

"Oh, didn't the boy tell you? We're trying to make the island a refuge for hypers who are willing to sublimate their craving and turn their attentions toward reconstruction. We're also trying to make an objective study of this neural condition. We have some good scientific minds, too—Doctor Relmone of Fordham, Father Seyes of Notre Dame, two biologists from Boston College . . ."

"Dermies trying to cure the plague?" Paul gasped.

Mendelhaus laughed merrily. "I didn't say cure it, son. I said 'study it.'"

"Why?"

"To learn how to live with it, of course. It's been pointed out by our philosophers that things become evil only through human misuse. Morphine, for instance, is a product of the Creator; it is therefore good when properly used for relief of pain. When mistreated by an addict, it becomes a monster. We bear this in mind as we study neuroderm."

Paul snorted contemptuously. "Leprosy is evil, I suppose, because Man mistreated bacteria?"

The priest laughed again. "You've got me there. I'm no philosopher. But you can't compare neuroderm with leprosy."

Paul shuddered. "The hell I can't! It's worse."

"Ah? Suppose you tell me what makes it worse? List the symptoms for me."

Paul hesitated, listing them mentally. They were: discoloration of the skin, low fever, hallucinations, and the insane craving to infect others. They seemed bad enough, so he listed them orally. "Of course, people don't die of it," he added. "But which is worse, insanity or death?"

The priest turned to smile back at him through the porthole. "Would you call me insane? It's true that victims have frequently lost their minds. But that's not a direct result of neuroderm. Tell me, how would you feel if everyone screamed and ran when they saw you coming, or hunted you down like a criminal? How long would your sanity last?"

Paul said nothing. Perhaps the anathema was a contributing factor . . .

"Unless you were of very sound mind to begin with, you probably couldn't endure it."

"But the craving . . . and the hallucinations . . ."

"True," murmured the priest thoughtfully. "The hallucinations. Tell me something else, if all the world was blind save one man, wouldn't the world be inclined to call that man's sight a hallucination? And the man with eyes might even come to agree with the world."

Again Paul was silent. There was no aruging with Mendelhaus, who probably suffered the strange delusions and thought them real.

"And the craving," the priest went on. "It's true that the craving can be a rather unpleasant symptom. It's the condition's way of perpetuating itself. Although we're not certain how it works, it seems able to stimulate erotic sensations in the hands. By some process in the brain, perhaps. We do know the micro-organisms get to the brain, but we're not yet sure what they do there."

"What facts have you discovered?" Paul asked cautiously.

Mendelhaus grinned at him. "Tut! I'm not going to tell you, because I don't want to be called a 'crazy dermie.' You wouldn't believe me, you see."

Paul glanced outside and saw that they were approaching the vicinity of the fishing cottage. He pointed out the lamplit window to the driver, and the ambulance turned onto a sideroad. Soon they were parked behind the shanty. The priests scrambled out and carried the stretcher toward the light, while Paul skulked to a safer distance and sat down in the grass to watch. When Willie was safe in the vehicle, he meant to walk back to the bridge, swim across the gap, and return to the mainland.

Soon Mendelhaus came out and walked toward him with a solemn stride, although Paul was sitting quietly in deepest shadow—invisible, he had thought. He arose quickly as the priest approached. Anxiety tightened his throat. "Is she . . . is Willie . . ."

"She's irrational," Mendelhaus murmured sadly. "Almost . . . less than sane. Some of it may be due to high fever, but . . ."

"Yes?"

"She tried to kill herself. With a knife. Said something about buckshot being the best way, or something . . ."

"Jeezis! Jeezis!" Paul sank weakly in the grass and covered his face with his hands.

"Blessed be His Holy Name," murmured the priest by way of turning the oath aside. "She didn't hurt herself badly, though. Wrist's cut a little. She was too weak to do a real job of it. Father Will's giving her a hypo and a tetanus shot and some sulfa. We're out of penicillin."

He stopped speaking and watched Paul's wretchedness for a moment. 'You love the girl, don't you?"

Paul stiffened. "Are you crazy? Love a little tramp dermie? Jeezis . . ."

"Blessed be—"

"Listen! Will she be all right? I'm getting out of here!" He climbed unsteadily to his feet.

"I don't know, son. Infection's the real threat, and shock. If we'd got to her sooner, she'd have been safer. And if she was in the ultimate stage of neuroderm, it would help."

"Why?"

"Oh, various reasons. You'll learn, someday. But listen, you look exhausted. Why don't you come back to the hospital with us? The third floor is entirely vacant. There's no danger of infection up there, and we keep a sterile room ready just in case we get a non-hyper case. You can lock the door inside, if you want to, but it wouldn't be necessary. Nuns are on the floor below. Our male staff lives in the basement. There aren't any laymen in the building. I'll guarantee that you won't be bothered."

"No, I've got to go," he growled, then softened his voice: "I appreciate it though, Father."

"Whatever you wish. I'm sorry, though. You might be able to provide yourself with some kind of transportation if you waited."

"Uh-uh! I don't mind telling you, your island makes me jumpy."

"Why?"

Paul glanced at the priest's gray hands. "Well . . . you still feel the craving, don't you?"

Mendelhaus touched his nose. "Cotton plugs, with a little camphor. I can't smell you." He hesitated. "No, I won't lie to you. The urge to touch is still there to some extent."

"And in a moment of weakness, somebody might—"

The priest straightened his shoulders. His eyes went chilly. "I have taken certain vows, young man. Sometimes when I see a beautiful woman, I feel desire. When I see a man eating a thick steak on a fast-day, I feel envy and hunger. When I see a doctor earning large fees, I chafe under the vow of poverty. But by denying desire's demands, desire learns to make itself useful in other ways. Sublimation, some call it. A priest can use it and do more useful work thereby. I am a priest."

He nodded curtly, turned on his heel and strode away. Halfway to the cottage, he paused. "She's calling for someone named Paul. Know who it might be? Family perhaps?"

Paul stood speechless. The priest shrugged and continued toward the lighted doorway.

"Father, wait . . ."

"Yes?"

"I—I am a little tired. The room . . . I mean, will you show me where to get transportation tomorrow?"

"Certainly."

Before midnight, the party had returned to the hospital. Paul lay on a comfortable mattress for the first time in weeks, sleepless, and staring at the moonlight on the sill. Somewhere downstairs, Willie was lying unconscious in an operating room, while the surgeon tried to repair the torn tendon. Paul had ridden back with them in the ambulance, sitting a few feet from the stretcher, avoiding her sometimes wandering arms, and listening to her delirious moaning.

Now he felt his skin crawling with belated hypochondria. What a fool he had been—touching the rope, the boat, the wheelbarrow, riding in the ambulance. There were a thousand ways he could have picked up a few stray microorganisms lingering from a dermie's touch. And now, he lay here in this nest of disease. . . .

But strange—it was the most peaceful, the sanest place he'd seen in months. The religious orders simply accepted the plague—with masochistic complacency perhaps—but calmly. A cross, or a penance, or something. But no, they seemed to accept it almost gladly. Nothing peculiar about that. All dermies went wild-eyed with happiness about the "lovely desire" they possessed. The priests weren't wild-eyed.

Neither was normal man equipped with socially shaped sexual desire. Sublimation?

"Peace," he muttered, and went to sleep.

A knocking at the door awoke him at dawn. He grunted at it disgustedly and sat up in bed. The door, which he had forgotten to lock, swung open. A chubby nun with a breakfast tray started into the room. She saw his face, then stopped. She closed her eyes, wrinkled her nose, and framed a silent prayer with her lips. Then she backed slowly out.

"I'm sorry, sir!" she quavered through the door. "I—I knew there was a patient in here, but I didn't know . . . you weren't a hyper. Forgive me."

He heard her scurrying away down the hall. Somehow, he began to feel safe. But wasn't that exactly what they wanted him to feel! He realized suddenly that he was trapped. He had left the shotgun in the emergency room. What was he—guest or captive? Months of fleeing from the gray terror had left him suspicious.

Soon he would find out. He arose and began dressing. Before he finished, Mendelhaus came. He did not enter, but stood in the hallway beyond the door. He smiled a faint greeting, and said, "So you're Paul?"

He felt heat rising in his face. "She's awake, then?" he asked gruffly.

The priest nodded. "Want to see her?"

"No, I've got to be going."

"It would do her good."

He coughed angrily. Why did the black-cassocked dermie have to put it that way? "Well, it wouldn't do me any good!" he snarled. "I've been around too many gray-leather hides already!"

Mendelhaus shrugged, but his eyes bore a hint of contempt. "As you wish. You may leave by the outside stairway—to avoid disturbing the sisters."

"To avoid being touched, you mean!"

"No one will touch you."

Paul finished dressing in silence. The reversal of attitudes disturbed him. He resented the seeming "tolerance" that was being extended him. It was like asylum inmates being "tolerant" of the psychiatrist.

"I'm ready!" he growled.

Mendelhaus led him down the corridor and out into a sunlit balcony. They descended a stone stairway while the priest talked over his shoulder.

"She's still not fully rational, and there's some fever. It wouldn't be anything to worry about two years ago, but now we're out of most of the latest drugs. If sulfa won't hold the infection, we'll have to amputate, of course. We should know in two or three days."

He paused and looked back at Paul, who had stopped on the stairway. "Coming?"

"Where is she?" Paul asked weakly. "I'll see her."

The priest frowned. "You don't have to, son. I'm sorry if I implied any obligation on your part. Really, you've done enough. I gather that you saved her life. Very few non-hypers would do a thing like that. I—"

"Where is she?" he snapped angrily.

The priest nodded. "Downstairs. Come on."

As they reentered the building on the ground floor, the priest cupped his hands to his mouth and called out, "Non-hyper coming! Plug your noses, or get out of the way! Avoid circumstances of temptation!"

When they moved along the corridor, it was Paul who felt like the leper. Mendelhaus led him into the third room.

Willie saw him enter and hid her gray hands beneath the sheet. She smiled faintly, tried to sit up, and failed. Williamson and a nun-nurse who had both been standing by the bedside turned to leave the room. Mendelhaus followed them out and closed the door.

There was a long, painful pause. Willie tried to grin. He shuffled his feet.

"They've got me in a cast," she said conversationally.

"You'll be all right," he said hastily. "It won't be long before you'll be up. Galveston's a good place for you. They're all dermies here."

She clenched her eyes tightly shut. "God! God! I hope I never hear that word again. After last night . . . that old woman in the rocking chair . . . I stayed there all alone . . . and the wind'd start the chair rocking. Ooh!" She looked at him with abnormally bright eyes. "I'd rather die than touch anybody now . . . after seeing that. Somebody touched her, didn't they, Paul? That's why she did it, wasn't it?"

He squirmed and backed toward the door. "Willie . . . I'm sorry for what I said. I mean—"

"Don't worry, Paul! I wouldn't touch you now." She clenched her hands and brought them up before her face, to stare at them with glittering hate. "I loathe myself!" she hissed.

What was it Mendelhaus had said, about the dermie going insane because of being an outcast rather than because of the plague? But she wouldn't be an outcast here. Only among non-hypers, like himself . . .

"Get well quick, Willie," he muttered, then hurriedly slipped out into the corridor. She called his name twice, then fell silent.

"That was quick," murmured Mendelhaus, glancing at his pale face.

"Where can I get a car?"

The priest rubbed his chin. "I was just speaking to Brother Matthew about that. Uh . . . how would you like to have a small yacht instead?"

Paul caught his breath. A yacht would mean access to the seas, and to an island. A yacht was the perfect solution. He stammered gratefully.

"Good," said Mendelhaus. "There's a small craft in dry-dock down at the basin. It was apparently left there because there weren't any dock crews around to get her afloat again. I took the liberty of asking Brother Matthew to find some men and get her in the water."

"Dermies?"

"Of course. The boat will be fumigated, but it isn't really necessary. The infection dies out in a few hours. It'll take a while, of course, to get the boat ready. Tomorrow . . . next day, maybe. Bottom's cracked; it'll need some patching."

Paul's smile weakened. More delay. Two more days of living in the gray shadow. Was the priest really to be trusted? Why should he even provide the boat? The jaws of an invisible trap, slowly closing.

Mendelhaus saw his doubt. "If you'd rather leave now, you're free to do so. We're really not going to as much trouble as it might seem. There are several yachts at the dock; Brother Matthew's been preparing to clean one or two up for our own use. And we might as well let you have one. They've been deserted by their owners. And . . . well . . . you helped the girl when nobody else would have done so. Consider the boat as our way of returning the favor, eh?"

A yacht. The open sea. A semi-tropical island, uninhabited, on the brink of the Carribbean. And a woman of course—chosen from among the many who would be willing to share such an escape. Peculiarly, he glanced at Willie's door. It was too bad about her. But she'd get along okay. The yacht . . . if he were only certain of Mendelhaus' intentions . . .

The priest began frowning at Paul's hesitation. "Well?"

"I don't want to put you to any trouble . . ."

"Nonsense! You're still afraid of us! Very well, come with me. There's someone I want you to see." Mendelhaus turned and started down the corridor.

Paul lingered. "Who . . . what—"

"Come on!" the priest snapped impatiently.

Reluctantly, Paul followed him to the stairway. They descended to a gloomy basement and entered a smelly laboratory through a double-door. Electric illumination startled him; then he heard the sound of a gasoline engine and knew that the power was generated locally.

"Germicidal lamps," murmured the priest, following his ceilingward gaze. "Some of them are. Don't worry about touching things. It's sterile in here."

"But it's not sterile for your convenience," growled an invisible voice. "And it won't be sterile at all if you don't stay out! Beat it, preacher."

Paul looked for the source of the voice, and saw a small, short-necked man bending his shaggy gray head over a microscope at the other end of the lab. He had spoken without glancing up at his visitors.

"This is Doctor Seevers, of Princeton, son," said the priest, unruffled by the scientist's ire. "Claims he's an atheist, but personally I think he's a puritan. Doctor, this is the young man I was telling you about. Will you tell him what you know about neuroderm?

Seevers jotted something on a pad, but kept his eye to the instrument. "Why don't we just give it to him, and let him find out for himself?" the scientist grumbled sadistically.

"Don't frighten him, you heretic! I brought him here to be illuminated."

"Illuminate him yourself. I'm busy. And stop calling me names. I'm not an atheist; I'm a bio-chemist."

"Yesterday you were a bio-physicist. Now, entertain my young man." Mendelhaus blocked the doorway with his body. Paul, with his jaw clenched angrily, had turned to leave.

"That's all I can do, preacher," Seevers grunted. "Entertain him. I know nothing. Absolutely nothing. I have some observed data. I have noticed some correlations. I have seen things happen. I have traced the patterns of the happenings and found some probable common denominators. And that is all! I know absolutely nothing, and I admit it. Why don't you preachers admit it in your racket?"

"Seevers, as you can see, is inordinately a product of his humility— if that's not a paradox," the priest said to Paul.

"Now, doctor, this young man—"

Seevers heaved a resigned sigh. His voice went sour-sweet. "All right, sit down, young man. I'll entertain you as soon as I get through counting free nerve-endings in this piece of skin."

Mendelhaus winked at his guest. "Seevers calls it masochism when we observe a fast-day or do penance. And there he sits, ripping off patches of his own hide to look at through his peeping glass. Masochism—heh!"

"Get out, preacher!" the scientist bellowed.

Mendelhaus laughed mockingly, nodded Paul toward a chair, and left the lab. Paul sat uneasily watching the back of Seever's lab jacket.

"Nice bunch of people really—these black-frocked yahoos," Seevers murmured conversationally. "If they'd just stop trying to convert me."

"Doctor Seevers, maybe I'd better—"

"Quiet! You bother me. And sit still, I can't stand to have people running in and out of here. You're in; now stay in."

Paul fell silent. He was uncertain whether or not Seevers was a dermie. The small man's lab jacket bunched up to hide the back of his neck, and the sleeves covered his arms. His hands were rubber-gloved, and a knot of white cord behind his head told Paul that he was wearing a gauze mask. His ears were bright pink, but their color was meaningless; it took several months for the gray coloring to seep to all areas of the skin. But Paul guessed he was a dermie—and wearing the gloves and mask to keep his equipment sterile.

He glanced idly around the large room. There were several glass cages of rats against the wall. They seemed airtight, with ducts for forced ventilation. About half the rats were afflicted with neuroderm in its various stages. A few wore shaved patches of skin where the disease had been freshly and forcibly inflicted. Paul caught the fleeting impression that several of the animals were staring at him fixedly. He shuddered and looked away.

He glanced casually at the usual maze of laboratory glassware, then turned his attention to a pair of hemispheres, suspended like a trophy on the wall. He recognized them as the twin halves of one of the meteorites, with the small jelly-pocket in the center. Beyond it hung a large picture frame containing several typewritten sheets. Another frame held four pictures of bearded scientists from another century, obviously clipped from magazine or textbook. There was nothing spectacular about the lab. It smelled of clean dust and sour things. Just a small respectable workshop.

Seevers' chair creaked suddenly. "It checks," he said to himself. "It checks again. Forty per cent increase." He threw down the stub pencil and whirled suddenly. Paul saw a pudgy round face with glittering eyes. A dark splotch of neuroderm had crept up from his chin to split his mouth and cover one cheek and an eye, giving him the appearance of a black and white bulldog with a mixed color muzzle.

"It checks," he barked at Paul, then smirked contentedly.

"What checks?"

The scientist rolled up a sleeve to display a patch of adhesive tape on a portion of his arm which had been discolored by the disease. "Here," he grunted. "Two weeks ago this area was normal. I took a centimeter of skin from right next to this one, and counted the nerve endings Since that time, the derm's crept down over the area. I took another square centimeter today, and recounted. Forty per cent increase."

Paul frowned with unbelief. It was generally known that neuroderm had a sensitizing effect, but new nerve endings . . . No. He didn't believe it.

"Third time I've checked it," Seevers said happily. "One place ran up to sixty-five per cent. Heh! Smart little bugs, aren't they? Inventing new somesthetic receptors that way!"

Paul swallowed with difficulty. "What did you say?" he gasped.

Seevers inspected him serenely. "So you're a non-hyper, are you? Yes, indeed. I can smell that you are. Vile, really. Can't understand why sensible hypers would want to paw you. But then, I've insured myself against such foolishness."

He said it so casually that Paul blinked before he caught the full impact of it. "Y-y-you've done what?"

"What I said. When I first caught it, I simply sat down with a velvet-tipped stylus and located the spots on my hands that gave rise to pleasureable sensations. Then I burned them out with an electric needle. There aren't many of them, really—one or two points per square centimeter." He tugged off his gloves and exhibited pock-marked palms to prove it. "I didn't want to be bothered with such silly urges. Waste of time, chasing non-hypers—for me it is. I never learned what it's like, so I've never missed it." He turned his hands over and stared at them. "Stubborn little critters keep growing new ones, and I keep burning them out."

Paul leaped to his feet. "Are you trying to tell me that the plague causes new nerve cells to grow?"

Seevers looked up coldly. "Ah, yes. You came here to be illoooomi-nated, as the padre put it. If you wish to be de-idiotized, please stop shouting. Otherwise, I'll ask you to leave."

Paul, who had felt like leaving a moment ago, now subsided quickly. "I'm sorry," he snapped, then softened his tone to repeat: "I'm sorry."

Seevers took a deep breath, stretched his short meaty arms in an unexpected yawn, then relaxed and grinned. "Sit down, sit down, m'boy. I'll tell you what you want to know, if you really want to know anything. Do you?"

"Of course!"

"You don't! You just want to know how you—whatever your name is—will be affected by events. You don't care about understanding for its own sake. Few people do. That's why we're in this mess. The padre now—he cares about understanding events—but not for their own sake. He cares—but for his flock's sake and for his God's sake—which is, I must admit, a better attitude than that of the common herd, whose only interest is in their own safety. But if people would just want to understand events for the understanding's sake—we wouldn't be in such a pickle."

Paul watched the professor's bright eyes and took the lecture quietly.

"And so, before I illuminate you, I want to make an impossible request."

"Yes, sir."

"I ask you to be completely objective," Seevers continued, rubbing the bridge of his nose and covering his eyes with his hand. "I want you to forget you ever heard of neuroderm while you listen to me. Rid yourself of all preconceptions, especially those connected with fear. Pretend these are purely hypothetical events that I'm going to discuss." He took his hands down from his eyes and grinned sheepishly. "It always embarrasses me to ask for that kind of cooperation when I know damn well I'll never get it."

"I'll try to be objective, sir."

"Bah!" Seevers slid down to sit on his spine, and hooked the base of his skull over the back of the chair. He blinked thoughtfully at the ceiling for a moment, then folded his hands across his small paunch and closed his eyes.

When he spoke again, he was speaking to himself: "Assume a planet, somewhat earthlike, but not quite. It has carboniferous life forms, but not human. Warm blooded, probably, and semi-intelligent. And the planet has something else—it has an overabundance of parasite forms. Actually, the various types of parasites are the dominant species. The warm-blooded animals are the parasites' vegetables, so to speak. Now, during two billion years, say, of survival contests between parasite species, some parasites are quite likely to develop some curious methods of adaptation. Methods of insuring the food supply—animals, who must have been taking a beating."

Seevers glanced down from the ceiling. "Tell me, youngster, what major activity did Man invent to secure his vegetable food supply?"

"Agriculture?"

"Certainly. Man is a parasite, as far as vegetables are concerned. But he learned to eat his cake and have it, too. He learned to perpetuate the species he was devouring. A very remarkable idea, if you stop to think about it. Very!"

"I don't see—"

"Hush! Now, let's suppose that one species of micro-parasites on our hypothetical planet learned, through long evolutionary processes, to stimulate regrowth in the animal tissue they devoured. Through exuding controlled amounts of growth hormone, I think. Quite an advancement, eh?"

Paul had begun leaning forward tensely.

"But it's only the first step. It let the host live longer, although not pleasantly, I imagine. The growth control would be clumsy at first. But soon, all parasite-species either learned to do it, or died out. Then came the contest for the best kind of control. The parasites who kept their hosts in the best physical condition naturally did a better job of survival—since the parasite-ascendency had cut down on the food supply, just as Man wastes his own resources. And since animals were contending among themselves for a place in the sun, it was to the parasite's advantage to help insure the survival of his host-species—through growth control."

Seevers winked solemnly.

"Now begins the downfall of the parasites—their decadence. They concentrated all their efforts along the lines of . . . uh . . . scientific farming, you might say. They began growing various sorts of defense and attack weapons for their hosts—weird biodevices, perhaps. Horns, swords, fangs, stingers, poison-throwers—we can only guess. But eventually, one group of parasites hit upon—what?"

Paul, who was beginning to stir uneasily, could only stammer. Where was Seevers getting all this?

"Say it!" the scientist demanded.

"The . . . nervous system?"

"That's right. You don't need to whisper it. The nervous system. It was probably an unsuccessful parasite at first, because nerve tissue grows slowly. And it's a long stretch of evolution between a micro-species which could stimulate nerve growth and one which could direct and utilize that growth for the host's advantage—and for its own. But at last, after a long struggle, our little species gets there. It begins sharpening the host's senses, building up complex senses from aggregates of old-style receptors, and increasing the host's intelligence within limits."

Seevers grinned mischievously. "Comes a planetary shake-up of the first magnitude. Such parasites naturally pick the host species with the highest intelligence to begin with. With the extra boost, this brainy animal quickly beats down its own enemies, and consequently the enemies of its micro-benefactor. It puts itself in much the same position that Man's in on Earth—lord it over the beasts, divine right to run the place, and all that. Now understand—it's the animal who's become intelligent, not the parasites. The parasites are operating on complex instinct patterns, like a hive of bees. They're wonderful neurological engineers—like bees are good structural engineers; blind instinct, accumulated through evolution."

He paused to light a cigarette. "If you feel ill, young man, there's drinking water in that bottle. You look ill."

"I'm all right!"

"Well, to continue: The intelligent animal became master of his planet. Threats to his existence were overcome—unless he was a threat to himself, like we are. But now, the parasites had found a safe home. No new threats to force readaptation. They sat back and sighed and became stagnant—as unchanging as horseshoe crabs or amoeba or other Earth ancients. They kept right on working in their neurological beehives, and now they became cultivated by the animal, who recognized their benefactors. The bugs didn't know it, but they were no longer the dominant species. They had insured their survival by leaning on their animal prop, who now took care of them with godlike charity—and selfishness. The parasites had achieved biological heaven. They kept on working, but they stopped fighting. The host was their welfare state, you might say. End of a sequence."

He blew a long breath of smoke and leaned forward to watch Paul with casual amusement. Paul suddenly realized that he was sitting on the edge of his chair and gaping. He forced a relaxation.

"Wild guesswork," he breathed uncertainly.

"Some of it's guesswork," Seevers admitted. "But none of it's wild. There is supporting evidence. It's in the form of a message."

"Message?"

"Sure. Come, I'll show you." Seevers arose and moved toward the wall. He stopped before the two hemispheres. "On second thought, you better show yourself. Take down that sliced meteorite, will you? It's sterile."

Paul crossed the room, climbed unsteadily upon a bench, and brought down the globular meteorite. It was the first time he had examined one of the things, and he inspected it curiously. It was a near-perfect sphere, about eight inches in diameter, with a four inch hollow in the center. The globe was made up of several concentric shells, tightly fitted, each apparently of a different metal. It was not seemingly heavier than aluminum, although the outer shell was obviously of tough steel.

"Set it face down," Seevers told him. Both halves. Give it a quick little twist. The shells will come apart. Take out the center shell— the hard, thin one between the soft protecting shells."

"How do you know their purposes?" Paul growled as he followed instructions. The shells came apart easily.

"Envelopes are to protect messages," snorted Seevers.

Paul sorted out the hemispheres, and found two mirror-polished shells of paper thin tough metal. They bore no inscription, either inside or out. He gave Seevers a puzzled frown.

"Handle them carefully while they're out of the protectors. They're already a little blurred . . ."

"I don't see any message."

"There's a small bottle of iron filings in that drawer by your knee. Sift them carefully over the outside of the shells. That powder isn't fine enough, really, but it's the best I could do. Felger had some better stuff up at Princeton, before we all got out. This business wasn't my discovery, incidentally."

Baffled, Paul found the iron filings and dusted the mirror-shells with the powder. Delicate patterns appeared—latitudinal circles, etched in iron dust and laced here and there with diagonal lines. He gasped. It looked like the map of a planet.

"I know what you're thinking," Seevers said. "That's what we thought too, at first. Then Felger came up with this very fine dust Fine as they are, those lines are rows of pictograph symbols. You can make them out vaguely with a good reading glass, even with this coarse stuff. It's magnetic printing—like two-dimensional wire-recording. Evidently, the animals that printed it had either very powerful eyes, or a magnetic sense."

"Anyone understand it?"

"Princeton staff was working on it when the world went crazy. They figured out enough to guess at what I've just told you. They found five different shell-messages among a dozen or so spheres. One of them was a sort of key. A symbol equated to a diagram of a carbon atom. Another symbol equated to pi in binary numbers. Things like that— about five hundred symbols, in fact. Some we couldn't figure. Then they defined other symbols by what amounted to blank-filling quizzes. Things like—'A star is . . .' and there would be the unknown symbol. We would try to decide whether it meant 'hot,' 'white,' 'huge,' and so forth."

"And you managed it?"

"In part. The ruthless way in which the missiles were opened destroyed some of the clarity. The senders were guilty of their own brand of anthropomorphism. They projected their own psychology on us. They expected us to open the things shell by shell, cautiously, and figure out the text before we went further. Heh! What happens. Some machinist grabs one, shakes it, weighs it, sticks it on a lathe, and—brrrrrrr! Our curiosity is still rather ape-like. Stick our arm in a gopher hole to see if there's a rattlesnake inside."

There was a long silence while Paul stood peering over the patterns on the shell. "Why haven't people heard about this?" he asked quietly.

"Heard about it!" Seevers roared. "And how do you propose to tell them about it?"

Paul shook his head. It was easy to forget that Man had scurried away from his presses and his broadcasting stations and his railroads, leaving his mechanical creatures to sleep in their own rust while he fled like a bee-stung bear before the strange terror.

"What, exactly, do the patterns say, doctor?"

"I've told you some of it—the evolutionary origin of the neuroderm parasites. We also pieced together their reasons for launching the missiles across space—several thousand years ago. Their sun was about to flare into a super-nova. They worked out a theoretical space-drive, but they couldn't fuel it—needed some element that was scarce in their system. They could get to their outer planet, but that wouldn't help much. So they just cultured up a batch of their parasite-benefactors, rolled them into these balls, and fired them like charges of buckshot at various stars. Interception-course, naturally. They meant to miss just a little, so that the projectiles would swing into long elliptical orbits around the suns—close enough in to intersect the radiational 'life-belt' and eventually cross paths with planets whose orbits were near-circular. Looks like they hit us on the first pass."

"You mean they weren't aiming at Earth in particular?"

"Evidently not. They couldn't know we were here. Not at a range like that. Hundreds of light years. They just took a chance on several stars. Shipping off their pets was sort of a last ditch stand against extinction—symbolic, to be sure—but a noble gesture, as far as they were concerned. A giving away of part of their souls. Like a man writing his will and leaving his last worldly possession to some unknown species beyond the stars. Imagine them standing there—watching the projectiles being fired out toward deep space. There goes their inheritance, to an unknown heir, or perhaps to no one. The little creatures that brought them up from beasthood."

Seevers paused, staring up at the sunlight beyond the high basement window. He was talking to himself again, quietly: "You can see them turn away and silently go back . . . to wait for their collapsing sun to reach the critical point, the detonating point. They've left their last mark—a dark and uncertain benediction to the cosmos."

"You're a fool, Seevers," Paul grunted suddenly.

Seevers whirled, whitening. His hand darted out forgetfully toward the young man's arm, but he drew it back as Paul sidestepped.

"You actually regard this thing as desirable, don't you?" Paul asked. "You can't see that you're under its effect. Why does it affect people that way? And you say I can't be objective."

The professor smiled coldly. "I didn't say it's desirable. I was simply pointing out that the beings who sent it saw it as desirable. They were making some unwarranted assumptions."

"Maybe they just didn't care."

"Of course they care. Their fallacy was that we would open it as they would have done—cautiously. Perhaps they couldn't see how a creature could be both brash and intelligent. They meant for us to read the warning on the shells before we went further."

"Warning . . . ?"

Seevers smiled bitterly. "Yes, warning. There was one group of oversized symbols on all the spheres. See that pattern on the top ring? It says, in effect—'Finder-creatures, you who destroy your own people —if you do this thing, then destroy this container without penetrating deeper. If you are self-destroyers, then the contents will only help to destroy you.'"

"But somebody would have opened one anyway," Paul protested.

Seevers turned his bitter smile on the window. "You couldn't be more right. The senders just didn't foresee our monkey-minded species. If they saw Man digging out the nuggets, braying over them, chortling over them, cracking them like walnuts, then turning tail to run howling for the forests—well, they'd think twice before they fired another round of their celestial buckshot."

"Doctor Seevers, what do you think will happen now? To the world, I mean."

Seevers shrugged. "I saw a baby born yesterday—to a woman down the island. It was fully covered with neuroderm at birth. It has some new sensory equipment—small pores in the finger tips, with taste buds and olfactory cells in them. Also a nodule above each eye sensitive to infra-red."

Paul groaned.

"It's not the first case. Those things are happening in adults, too, but you have to have the condition for quite a while. Brother Thomas has the finger pores already. Hasn't learned to use them yet, of course. He gets sensations from them, but the receptors aren't connected to olfactory and taste centers of the brain. They're still linked with the somesthetic interpretive centers. He can touch various substances and get different perceptive combinations of heat, pain, cold, pressure, and so forth. He says vinegar feels ice-cold, quinine sharp-hot, cologne warm-velvet-prickly, and . . . he blushes when he touches a musky perfume."

Paul laughed, and the hollow sound startled him.

"It may be several generations before we know all that will happen,"

Seevers went on. "I've examined sections of rat brain and found the microorganisms. They may be working at rerouting these new receptors to proper brain areas. Our grandchildren—if Man's still on Earth by then—can perhaps taste-analyze substances by touch, qualitatively determine the contents of a test tube by sticking a finger in it. See a warm radiator in a dark room—by infra-red. Perhaps there'll be some ultra-violet sensitization. My rats are sensitive to it."

Paul went to the rat cages and stared in at three grey-pelted animals that seemed larger than the others. They retreated against the back wall and watched him warily. They began squeaking and exchanging glances among themselves.

"Those are third-generation hypers," Severs told him. "They've developed a simple language. Not intelligent by human standards, but crafty. They've learned to use their sensory equipment. They know when I mean to feed them, and when I mean to take one out to kill and dissect. A slight change in my emotional odor, I imagine. Learning's the big hurdle, youngster. A hyper with finger pores gets sensations from them, but it takes a long time to attach meaning to the various sensations—through learning. A baby gets visual sensations from his untrained eyes—but the sensation is utterly without significance until he associates milk with white, mother with a face shape, and so forth."

"What will happen to the brain?" Paul breathed.

"Not too much, I imagine. I haven't observed much happening. The rats show an increase in intelligence, but not in brain size. The intellectual boost apparently comes from an ability to perceive things in terms of more senses. Ideas, concepts, precepts—are made of memory collections of past sensory experiences. An apple is red, fruity-smelling, sweet-acid flavored—that's your sensory idea of an apple. A blind man without a tongue couldn't form such a complete idea. A hyper, on the other hand, could add some new adjectives that you couldn't understand. The fully-developed hyper—I'm not one yet—has more sensory tools with which to grasp ideas. When he learns to use them, he'll be mentally more efficient. But there's apparently a hitch.

"The parasite's instinctive goal is to insure the host's survival—the individual host's survival. That's the substance of the warning. If Man has the capacity to work together, then the parasites will help him shape his environment. If Man intends to keep fighting with his fellows, the parasite will help him do a better job of that, too. Help him destroy himself more efficiently."

"Men have worked together—"

"In small tribes," Seevers interrupted. "Yes, we have group spirit. Ape-tribe spirit, not race spirit."

Paul moved restlessly toward the door. Seevers had turned to watch him with a cool smirk.

"Well, you're illuminated, youngster. Now what do you intend to do?"

Paul shook his head to scatter the confusion of ideas. "What can anyone do? Except run. To an island, perhaps?"

Seevers hoisted a cynical eyebrow. "Intend taking the condition with you? Or will you try to stay non-hyper?"

"Take . . . are you crazy? I mean to stay healthy!"

"That's what I thought. If your were objective about this, you'd give yourself the condition and get it over with. I did. You remind me of a monkey running away from a hypodermic needle. The hypo has serum health-insurance in it, but the needle looks sharp. The monkey chatters with fright."

Paul stalked angrily to the door, then paused. "There's a girl upstairs, a dermie. Would you—"

"Tell her all this? I always brief new hypers. It's one of my duties around this ecclesiastical leper-ranch. She's on the verge of insanity, I suppose. They all are, before they get rid of the idea that they're damned souls. What's she to you?"

Paul strode out into the corridor without answering. He felt physically ill. He hated Seevers' smug bulldog face with a violence that was unfamiliar to him. The man had given the plague to himself! So he said. But was it true? Was any of it true? To claim that the hallucinations were new sensory phenomena, to pose the plague as possibly desirable—Seevers had no patent on those ideas. Every dermie made such claims; it was a symptom. Seevers had simply invented clever rationalizations to support his delusions, and Paul had been nearly taken in. Seevers was clever. *Do you mean to take the condition with you when you go?* Wasn't that just another way of suggesting, "Why don't you allow me to touch you?" Paul was shivering as he returned to the third floor room to recoat himself with the pungent oil. Why not leave now? he thought.

But he spent the day wandering along the waterfront, stopping briefly at the docks to watch a crew of monks scrambling over the scaffolding that surrounded the hulls of two small sea-going vessels. The monks were caulking split seams and trotting along the platforms with buckets of tar and paint. Upon inquiry, Paul learned which of the vessels was intended for his own use. And he put aside all thoughts of immediate departure.

She was a fifty-footer, a slender craft with a weighted fin-keel that would cut too deep for bay-navigation. Paul guessed that the colony wanted only a flat-bottomed vessel for hauling passengers and cargo across from the mainland. They would have little use for the trim seaster with the lines of a baby destroyer. Upon closer examination, he guessed that it had been a police-boat, or Coast Guard craft. There was a gun-mounting on the forward deck, minus the gun. She was built for speed, and powered by diesels, and she could be provisioned for a nice long cruise.

Paul went to scrounge among the warehouses and locate a stock of supplies. He met an occasional monk or nun, but the gray-skinned monastics seemed only desirous of avoiding him. The dermie desire was keyed principally by smell, and the deodorant oil helped preserve him from their affections. Once he was approached by a wild-eyed layman who startled him amidst a heap of warehouse crates. The dermie was almost upon him before Paul heard the footfall. Caught without an escape route, and assailed by startled terror, he shattered the man's arm with a shot-gun blast, then fled from the warehouse to escape the dermie's screams.

Choking with shame, he found a dermie monk and sent him to care for the wounded creature. Paul had shot at other plague victims when there was no escape, but never with intent to kill. The man's life had been spared only by hasty aim.

"It was self-defense," he reminded himself.

But defense against what? Against the inevitable?

He hurried back to the hospital and found Mendelaus outside the small chapel. "I better not wait for your boat," he told the priest. "I just shot one of your people. I better leave before it happens again."

Mendclhaus' thin lips tightened. "You shot—"

"Didn't kill him," Paul explained hastily. "Broke his arm. One of the brothers is bringing him over. I'm sorry, Father, but he jumped me."

The priest glanced aside silently, apparently wrestling against anger. "I'm glad you told me," he said quietly. "I suppose you couldn't help it. But why did you leave the hospital? You're safe here. The yacht will be provisioned for you. I suggest you remain in your room until its ready. I won't vouch for your safety any farther than the building." There was a tone of command in his voice, and Paul nodded slowly. He started away.

"The young lady's been asking for you," the priest called after him.

Paul stopped. "How is she?"

"Over the crisis, I think. Infection's down. Nervous condition not so good. Deep depression. Sometimes she goes a little hysterical." He paused, then lowered his voice. "You're at the focus of it, young man. Sometimes she gets the idea that she touched you she raves about how she wouldn't do it."

Paul whirled angrily, forming a protest, but the priest continued: "Seevers talked to her, and then a psychologist—one of our sisters. It seemed to help some. She's asleep now. I don't know how much of Seever's talk she understood, however. She's dazed—combined effects of pain, shock, infection, guilt-feelings, fright, hysteria—and some other things. Morphine doesn't make her mind any clearer. Neither does the fact that she thinks you're avoiding her."

"It's the plague I'm avoiding!" Paul snapped. "Not her."

Mendelhaus chuckled mirthlessly. "You're talking to me, aren't you?" He turned and entered the chapel through a swinging door. As the door fanned back and forth, Paul caught a glimpse of a candle-lit altar and a stark wooden crucifix, and a sea of monk-robes flowing over the pews, waiting for the celebrant priest to enter the sanctuary and begin the Sacrifice of the Mass. He realized vaguely that it was Sunday.

Paul wandered back to the main corridor and found himself drifting toward Willie's room. The door was ajar, and he stopped short lest she see him. But after a moment he inched forward until he caught a glimpse of her dark mass of hair unfurled across the pillow. One of the sisters had combed it for her, and it spread in dark waves, gleaming in the candlelight. She was still asleep. The candle startled him for an instant—suggesting a deathbed and the sacrament of the dying. But a dog-eared magazine lay beneath it; someone had been reading to her.

He stood in the doorway, watching the slow rise of her breathing. Fresh, young, shapely—even in the crude cotton gown they had given her, even beneath the blue-white pallor of her skin—soon to become gray as a cloudy sky on a wintery twilight. Her lips moved slightly, and he backed a step away. They paused, parted moistly, showing thin white teeth. Her delicately carved face was thrown back slightly on the pillow. There was a sudden tightening of her jaw.

A weirdly pitched voice floated unexpectedly from down the hall, echoing the semi-singing of Gregorian chant: "*Asperges me, Domine, hyssopo, et mundabor. . . .*" The priest was beginning Mass.

As the sound came, the girl's hands clenched into rigid fists beneath the sheet. Her eyes flared open to stare wildly at the ceiling. Clutching the bedclothes, she pressed the fists up against her face and cried out: "No! Noooo! God, I won't!"

Paul backed out of sight and pressed himself against the wall. A knot of desolation tightened in his stomach. He looked around nervously. A nun, hearing the outcry, came scurrying down the hall, murmuring anxiously to herself. A plump mother hen in a dozen yards of starched white cloth. She gave him a quick challenging glance and waddled inside.

"Child, my child, what's wrong! Nightmares again?"

He heard Willie breathe a nervous moan of relief. Then her voice, weakly— "They . . . they made me touch . . . ooo, God! I want to cut off my hands!"

Paul fled, leaving the nun's sympathetic reassurance to fade into a murmur behind him.

He spent the rest of the day and the night in his room. On the following day, Mendelhaus came with word that the boat was not yet ready. They needed to finish caulking and stock it with provisions. But the priest assured him that it should be afloat within twenty-four hours. Paul could not bring himself to ask about the girl.

A monk brought his food—unopened cans, still steaming from the sterilizer, and on a covered tray. The monk wore gloves and mask, and he had oiled his own skin. There were moments when Paul felt as if he were the diseased and contagious patient from whom the others protected themselves. Like Omar, he thought, wondering—"which is the Potter, pray, and which the Pot?"

Was Man, as Seevers implied, a terrorized ape-tribe fleeing illogically from the gray hands that only wanted to offer a blessing? How narrow was the line dividing blessing from curse, god from demon! The parasites came in a devil's mask, the mask of disease. "Diseases have often killed me," said Man. "All disease is therefore evil." But was that necessarily true? Fire had often killed Man's club-bearing ancestors, but later came to serve him. Even diseases had been used to good advantage—artificially induced typhoid and malaria to fight venereal infections.

But the gray skin . . . tastebuds in the fingertips . . . alien micro-organisms tampering with the nerves and the brain. Such concepts caused his scalp to bristle. Man—made over to suit the tastes of a bunch of supposedly beneficent parasites—was he still Man, or something else? Little bacteriological farmers imbedded in the skin, raising a crop of nerve-cells—eat one, plant two, sow an olfactor in a new field reshuffle the feeder-fibers to the brain.

Monday brought a cold rain and stiff wind from the Gulf. He watched the water swirling through littered gutters in the street. Sitting in the window, he watched the gloom and waited, praying that the storm would not delay his departure. Mendelhaus smiled politely through his doorway once. "Willie's ankle seems healing nicely," he said. "Swelling's gone down so much we had to change casts. If only she would—"

"Thanks for the free report, padre," Paul growled irritably. The priest shrugged and went away.

It was still raining when the sky darkened with evening. The monastic dock-crew had certainly been unable to finish. Tomorrow . . . perhaps.

After nightfall, he lit a candle and lay awake watching its unflickering yellow tongue until drowsiness lolled his head aside. He snuffed it out and went to bed.

Dreams assailed him, tormented him, stroked him with dark hands while he lay back, submitting freely. Small hands, soft, cool, tender— touching his forehead and his cheeks, while a voice whispered caresses.

He awoke suddenly to blackness. The feel of the dreamhands was still on his face. What had aroused him? A sound in the hall, a creaking hinge? The darkness was impenetrable. The rain had stopped—

perhaps its cessation had disturbed him. He felt curiously tense as he lay listening to the humid, musty corridors. A . . . faint . . . rustle . . . and . . .

Breathing! The sound of soft breathing was in the room with him!

He let out a hoarse shriek that shattered the unearthly silence. A high-pitched scream of fright answered him! From a few feet away in the room. He groped toward it and fumbled against a bare wall. He roared curses, and tried to find first matches, then the shotgun. At last he found the gun, aimed at nothing across the room, and jerked the trigger. The explosion deafened him. The window shattered, and a sift of plaster rustled to the floor.

The brief flash had illuminated the room. It was empty. He stood frozen. Had he imagined it all? But no, the visitor's startled scream had been real enough.

A cool draft fanned his face. The door was open. Had he forgotten to lock it again? A tumult of sound was beginning to arise from the lower floors. His shot had aroused the sleepers. But there was a closer sound—sobbing in the corridor, and an irregular creaking noise.

At last he found a match and rushed to the door. But the tiny flame revealed nothing within its limited aura. He heard a doorknob rattle in the distance; his visitor was escaping via the outside stairway. He thought of pursuit and vengeance. But instead, he rushed to the washbasin and began scrubbing himself thoroughly with harsh brown soap. Had his visitor touched him—or had the hands been only dream-stuff? He was frightened and sickened.

Voices were filling the corridor.

The light of several candles was advancing toward his doorway. He turned to see monks' faces peering anxiously inside. Father Mendelhaus shouldered his way through the others, glanced at the window, the wall, then at Paul.

"What—"

"Safety, eh?" Paul hissed. "Well, I had a prowler! A woman! I think I've been touched."

The priest turned and spoke to a monk. "Go to the stairway and call for the Mother Superior. Ask her to make an immediate inspection of the sisters' quarters. If any nuns have been out of their rooms—"

A shrill voice called from down the hallway: "Father, Father! The girl with the injured ankle! She's not in her bed She's gone!"

"Willie!" Paul gasped.

A small nun with a candle scurried up and panted to recover her breath for a moment. "She's gone, Father. I was on night duty. I heard the shot, and I went to see if it disturbed her. She wasn't there!"

The priest grumbled incredulously. "How could she get out? She can't walk with that cast."

"Crutches, Father. We told her she could get up in a few days. While she was still irrational, she kept saying they were going to amputate her leg. We brought the crutches in to prove she'd be up soon. It's my fault, Father. I should have—"

"Never mind! Search the building for her."

Paul dried his wet skin and faced the priest angrily. "What can I do to disinfect myself?" he demanded.

Mendelhaus called out into the hallway where a crowd had gathered. "Someone please get Doctor Seevers."

"I'm here, preacher," grunted the scientist. The monastics parted ranks to make way for his short chubby body. He grinned amusedly at Paul. "So, you decided to make your home here after all, eh?"

Paul croaked an insult at him. "Have you got any effective—"

"Disinfectants? Afraid not. Nitric acid will do the trick on one or two local spots. Where were you touched?"

"I don't know. I was asleep."

Seevers' grin widened. "Well, you can't take a bath in nitric acid. We'll try something else, but I doubt if it'll work for a direct touch."

"That oil—"

"Uh-uh! That'll do for exposure-weakened parasites you might pick up by handling an object that's been touched. But with skin to skin contact, the bugs're pretty stout little rascals. Come on downstairs, though, we'll make a pass at it."

Paul followed him quickly down the corridor. Behind him, a soft voice was murmuring: "I just can't understand why non-hypers are so . . ." Mendelhaus said something to Seevers, blotting out the voice. Paul chafed at the thought that they might consider him cowardly.

But with the herds fleeing northward, cowardice was the social norm. And after a year's flight, Paul had accepted the norm as the only possible way to fight.

Seevers was emptying chemicals into a tub of water in the basement when a monk hurried in to tug at Mendelhaus' sleeve. "Father, the sisters report that the girl's not in the building."

"What? Well, she can't be far! Search the grounds. If she's not there, try the adjoining blocks."

Paul stopped unbuttoning his shirt. Willie had said some mournful things about what she would rather do than submit to the craving. And her startled scream when he had cried out in the darkness—the scream of someone suddenly awakening to reality—from a daze-world.

The monk left the room. Seevers sloshed more chemicals into the tub. Paul could hear the wind whipping about the basement windows and the growl of an angry surf not so far away. Paul rebuttoned his shirt.

"Which way's the ocean?" he asked suddenly. He backed toward the door.

"No, you fool!" roared Seevers. "You're not going to—*get him,* preacher!"

Paul sidestepped as the priest grabbed for him. He darted outside and began running for the stairs. Mendelhaus bellowed for him to stop.

"Not me!" Paul called back angrily. "Willie!"

Moments later, he was racing across the sodden lawn and into the street. He stopped on the corner to get his bearings. The wind brought the sound of the surf with it. He began running east and calling her name into the night.

The rain had ceased, but the pavement was wet and water gurgled in the gutters. Occasionally the moon peered through the thinning veil of clouds, but its light failed to furnish a view of the street ahead. After a minute's running, he found himself standing on the seawall. The breakers thundered a stone's throw across the sand. For a moment they became visible under the coy moon, then vanished again in blackness. He had not seen her.

"Willie!"

Only the breaker's growl responded. And a glimmer of phosphorescence from the waves.

"WILLIE!" He slipped down from the seawall and began feeling along the jagged rocks that lay beneath it. She could not have gotten down without falling. Then he remembered a rickety flight of steps just to the north, and he trotted quickly toward it.

The moon came out suddenly. He saw her, and stopped. She was sitting motionless on the bottom step, holding her face in her hands. The crutches were stacked neatly against the hand rail. Ten yards across the sand slope lay the hungry, devouring surf. Paul approached her slowly. The moon went out again. His feet sucked at the rain-soaked sand.

He stopped by the hand rail, peering at her motionless shadow. "Willie?"

A low moan, then a long silence. "I did it, Paul," she muttered miserably. "It was like a dream at first, but then . . . you shouted . . . and . . ."

He crouched in front of her, sitting on his heels. Then he took her wrists firmly and tugged her hands from her face.

"Don't . . ."

He pulled her close and kissed her. Her mouth was frightened. Then he lifted her—being cautious of the now-sodden cast. He climbed the steps and started back to the hospital. Willie, dazed and weary and still uncomprehending, fell asleep in his arms. Her hair blew about his face in the wind. It smelled warm and alive. He wondered what sensation it would produce to the finger-pore receptors. "Wait and see," he said to himself.

The priest met him with a growing grin when he brought her into the candlelit corridor. "Shall we forget the boat, son?"

Paul paused. "No . . . I'd like to borrow it anyway."

Mendelhaus looked puzzled.

Seevers snorted at him: "Preacher, don't you know any reasons for travelling besides running away?"

Paul carried her back to her room. He meant to have a long talk when she awoke. About an island—until the world sobered up.

Questions for Discussion and Review

1. This story seems to challenge our comfortable assumptions about sickness and health. To what end is this done?

2. The science that deals with alien life forms is *exobiology*. In exobiological terms, therefore, explain how it is possible for the parasites to adapt so readily to their new hosts. What does that signify?

3. The warning addressed to "you who destroy your own people" is both alike and different from the warning given Stark and Treon by the guardian of the underground laboratories in "Enchantress of Venus." Discuss the similarities and differences.

4. How would you feel about the sort of dark benediction that is the premise of Miller's story? What emotions or feelings are exercised by your experience of such an imagined transformation?

5. Would your reaction be different if you were of another race?

6. Compare the two social orders described in the story.

7. What reason do we have to believe that the alien benefactors possessec a higher standard of civilized thought and behavior than human beings?

8. What different kinds of love operate in this story, and how are they related?

Aliens

Strictly speaking, there is nothing about aliens that makes them the exclusive property of hard SF. Nevertheless, the associations of aliens with this type of SF is sufficiently well established to justify including alien stories with a connection to hard SF in this section.

One of the fondest wishes of post–Renaissance people has been to encounter alien creatures. In one sense, of course, that has happened as the world gradually has become a global village through European exploration and advances in travel and communication. The history of colonial expansion has been remarkable for its savagery, brutality, and exploitation. The truth is that neither the people of the West nor their unwilling hosts have shown up very well in their encounters. Despite everything bad that can be said about the confrontations of different races of the human family, there have been obvious benefits both materially and socially for both sides. Now that the frontiers of Earth have been at least tentatively explored, the expectations of human beings for alien contact have been turned outward to the stars.

Historically, stories about extraterrestrial beings (ETs) have been around for some time. The various space-travel stories noted earlier usually involved contact with ETs. Since the advent of SF, stories treating human-alien confrontations have become commonplace. Few may be as imposing as Voltaire's eight-mile-high Micromegas, but many have shown equally remarkable origins and powers. There seem to be two types of alien stories. One deals with aliens alone or with what amounts to an alien psychology or viewpoint. It tends to be utopian or dystopian, although there is no rule that can be applied usefully. Many of these stories, however, can be expected to fall into the soft type of SF. The aliens may come from "out there" and may be bizarre creatures like Micromegas, or they may be alienated human beings developing along new evolutionary paths, as in Heinlein's *The Moon Is a Harsh Mistress* (1967). Another alien figure is the primitive or prehistoric human being, of which Jack London's *Before Adam* (1907) provides an instance. Of course the alien viewpoint may not be human at all, as in James Tiptree's "Love Is the Plan, The Plan Is Death" (1973) or Samuel R. Delany's "Driftglass" (1967). Presumably such stories would fall into one of the types of fantasy SF, but a case could still be made for one of the soft sciences.

The second type of alien story involves alien-human contact and its many variations. Most stories deal with simple confrontations: They invade us, or we invade them. This is the staple of the space-opera plot. One of the more interesting variations is the story of first contact, because it poses a naturally dramatic incident. For the more credulous, there are newspaper accounts of unidentified flying objects (UFO's) and even of alien contact. Something clearly is going on, either in the human imagination or in human history, that accounts for our growing interest in such phenomena. The kind of alien-contact story will depend on the kind of alien and human being an author serves up, and on the sort of incident produced by their meeting. In Clarke's "Encounter in the Dawn," we are treated to the meeting of a philanthropic ancient astronaut with a type of primitive man. In the two stories in this section we are asked to imagine two rather different meetings. Each is more like the engagement of equals.

Perhaps the growing body of literature dealing with human-alien contact is a form of prophetic utterance. Perhaps it is a literary instance of the future casting shadows on the present. Everyone will agree, whatever view is taken, that if there are aliens in our future, we had better begin to think about how we should react to meeting them. First impressions are often lasting, and in the world of the future they may be fatal. The testimony of history should convince us that as a species, *sapientia* has not been such a distinctive behavior trait of *Homo sapiens*. Another thing: If there are aliens flying around out there looking for greener pastures, it is a fairly sure bet that they are not from paradise. Perhaps it is not too early to begin rehearsals for the first human-alien meeting. Will Emily Post see us through when two fallen species get together for the first time?

Berom

John Berryman

John Berryman was born in New York City in 1916. He took his undergraduate degree from Amherst and did graduate work at the University of Chicago. He worked in state and federal government service until he went into hardware supply in 1948. He is now the chief executive officer of the American Hardware Supply Company of Butler, Pennsylvania, where he makes his home.

Berryman revealed that he first got hooked on SF after reading E. E. "Doc" Smith's *Skylark of Space* (1928) in Gernsback's *Amazing Stories*. His first published story "Special Flight" was written for *Astounding Science Fiction* (May 1939). The story was a rewrite of an earlier version called "Flight 476," which Campbell rejected after giving several pages of detailed criticism and suggestions for improvement. Berryman took the suggestions and thus began a long and fruitful association with Campbell's *Astounding Science Fiction/Analog*. While in graduate school, Berryman wrote SF to pay the bills. Over the years since then, he has written more than fifty stories, some under the pseudonyms Joe Tinker and Walter Bupp. The Tinker-Bupp stories were regarded by Campbell as the best parapsychological stories he had ever printed. "Space Rating" (originally titled "Beyond the Stars," *Astounding*, October 1939) has been reprinted several times, as has "Modus Vivendi." Berryman's most recent story, "Something to Say," appeared in *Analog* (August 1966). "Berom" appeared in *Astounding Science Fiction* (January 1951).

Of the stories he has written, "Berom" is Berryman's own favorite. It was written in May 1950, while he was working on another tale, "The Solution," which had grown out of his reading of David Maurer's *The Big Con* (1940), the novel that inspired the movie *The Sting*. Berryman had been doing background research on codes for "The Solution" when he was interrupted by an inspiration for a new story. This is how the author described the experience to me in a letter: "The idea for 'Berom' came while I was in the shower. I wrapped a towel around me, called to my wife, whose shorthand was excellent, and dictated the yarn almost exactly as it was printed. I doubt I changed six hundred words from the dictation to the final." Later, John W. Campbell claimed that "Berom" was the inspiration for the government's Project Ozma during the 1950s, in which giant antennas were used to scan for radio transmissions from aliens in space.

The focus of this story is not so much on aliens as it is on human response to the promise that the sudden appearance of ETs seems to offer for new technological knowledge. The clichéd reactions of United States military and security forces to the opportunity for learning the secrets of alien technology seem, alas, entirely too plausible. A quarter-century has not dimmed, nor has use tarnished, this stereotype. The social criticism implied in attempts by political and military forces to gain a strategic advantage from the alien space drive anticipates the methods of social science fiction, which we will examine in the next section.

It seems clear that Berryman expects us to share Yancey's evaluation of the human capacity to make constructive use of any information the aliens wish to trade. Indeed, we may well be inspired to wonder what we could offer in exchange that the aliens might possibly need. The author is silent on this point, and maybe we have more to offer an alien culture than we might suppose.

In addition to its critique of social values, this story depends to a degree on the character of the protagonist, Professor Yancey of Amherst. A crusty intellectual who has lost his zest for living, he finds himself suddenly at the center of an adventure that seems to bring out the worst in almost everyone else. Yancey's sense of detachment is only increased by the bluster of General Smith and the arrogance of those who are managing affairs for the government.

Yancey's special qualifications are those of a linguist; specifically, he is a scholar of Sanskrit. More important, he has the sort of analytic mind that enables him to see the true nature of the problem before him; and, as the story illustrates, the problem is a complex one. Initially, it is one of communication. Yancey solves it by recognizing that the alien is using an artificial language, which he assumes his human counterparts will be able to interpret. However, the problem of communication in the larger sense also presents itself in the course of Yancey's understanding of all the likely consequences of successful exchange of ideas with aliens. The result is one of the more spectacular apotheoses of a university professor in literary history. It certainly beats Browning's "A Grammarian's Funeral.'

(EXCERPT FROM PROCEEDINGS IN THE COURT-MARTIAL OF BENJAMIN L. HARWOOD, COL., U.S.A., FORT MEYER, VA., JUNE 8, 2038.)

Judge Advocate: I have no further questions, colonel.

Defense Counsel: May it please the Court. Rather than recalling Colonel Harwood to the stand later, I would like to establish one point by cross-examination which properly should be made at this time.

J. A.: You may proceed.

D.C.: Colonel Harwood, going back to May 4th of this year, will you tell the Court how you received your orders from General Fairbank?

Defendant: How?

D. C.: In what manner were they communicated to you?

Def.: Verbally. There was no time, you understand, for any confirmation. I was told all General Fairbank knew about the ship in ten hurried sentences and given my orders.

D. C.: Can you recollect them?

Def.: Of course. Not *verbatim,* perhaps, but certainly their substance. Would you like me to repeat them?

D.C.: (*To the Court*) I should like the Court to understand this is merely to introduce in proper order the point we wish to make.

J.A.: On that understanding, the defendant may proceed.

Def.: I was ordered to find out who were the country's leading students of language and communication, considering the problem of the visitors as General Fairbank knew it; to find out where these students were; to get the necessary credentials from the Office of the Chief of Staff; and to bring the persons in question to the landing site immediately.

D. C.: In other words, colonel, your choice was to depend solely on the qualifications of these persons as students?

Def.: That's right.

D. C.: And nothing was said with reference to their emotional or political outlook?

Def.: I don't think Army regulations provide for either of those things.

(*Laughter*)

J. A.: Order! The colonel will restrain his mordant wit.

Def.: I beg the Court's pardon. No, sir, no mention was made of those factors.

D. C.: That is all, colonel. You may step down. (*To the Court*) This is the very nub of our defense. We contend that Colonel Harwood well and faithfully carried out his orders. No man can be accused of willful neglect simply because of the warped mentality of another. If it please the Court, I would like to—

When the dinner dishes were in the washer, Mrs. Johnson quickly made a round of the ashtrays in the professor's book-lined study, emptying them into her ever-present dust-pan. That was always her last act before leaving, Yancey reflected, rising from his easy-chair. By the time he had reached the door, his housekeeper had slipped on her coat and was bustling through the hall toward him.

She paused a moment for her wages, since it was Saturday night. "Good night, Professor Yancey," she said with mock crossness as he handed her the money. "Now, for pity's sake, don't stay up reading half the night!"

"Good night, Mrs. Johnson," he replied, coming as close to a smile as he ever did. He set the night-latch behind her and walked thoughtfully through the low-ceilinged old rooms to his side porch. The clock on the College chapel struck the half-hour.

Though the sun had set redly behind the Pelham hills some time before, there was still a luminosity in the spring sky that banned all but the brightest stars. The evening breeze soughed sadly through the perfumed blossoms of his apple orchard and rippled the grass of his large lawn, overdue for cutting.

Yancey sighed as he took his pipe away from his lips, better to savor the sweetness of the blooms. How Madge would have loved the orchard he thought. It was hard to believe that seventeen years had sped in their swift rounds since he had first turned the earth over their young roots, and so quickly had seen the same sod broken to receive his wife's shriveled body. The sad scent of the springtime always brought back her bitter-sweet memory. He sucked more life into his pipe. More and more, with the ripening blush of every spring, he felt that the world was leaving him behind. More and more he was out of place in a time where events rippled catastrophically about his head. With the despondent thought that he would be glad when life was through with him, he recalled the lines of David Morton, who had lived in that same house a hundred years before: "I like thee each day not more, but less."

A uniquely irritating sound drove him from his reverie. The unmistakable *hoooooooo* of a jet motor, coming from the direction of the campus, caused him to crane his scrawny neck around the old house's eaves. The sound drew loudly nearer. Then he saw the brilliant lance of the light through the arching trees. Although the craft was not clearly visible in the deepening dusk, it was directing a powerful beam toward the ground. It hung dangerously low, Yancey decided, hopping sprily over the porch railing and trotting to the picket fence. A ram-jet helicopter, he guessed, from its deliberate pace over the elms lining South Pleasant Street. The effulgent beam seared his eyes as it swept over him, and then returned, causing him to lower his head in pain.

Then the hooting was full upon him. He felt the wild downdraft of the blades and saw the scented blossoms vanish from his orchard in a blizzard of flying petals. His angry cries were scarcely swallowed by the sound of the jets before the helicopter had grounded on his lawn. The merciless brilliance of the light reddened and died. His dazzled eyes could barely see the uniformed figures that sprang from the 'copter and ran toward him. Rectangles of light sprang into being about the Common as doors swung open, silhouetting the curious in their frames.

"Professor Yancey?" one of the newcomers cried.

"Yes! Look what you've done to my orchard! You'll—"

"Yes! Of course! Quick, professor, you must get inside at once!" The voice was urgent, but there was no mistaking the genteel courtesy of the speaker. Yancey allowed himself to be urged back onto his porch. "Evans!" the newcomer ordered in a low tone. "Keep everybody out. Rocco," he went on, as he politely urged Yancey through his door into the study. "Get the professor packed!" The soldier named Rocco sprang vigorously up the stairs.

Yancey had no time to form his protest. "I extend you every apology," the officer giving the orders said with swift sincerity. "You are Professor George Yancey, the philologist?"

"Of course. See here—"

"Please, professor. I beg your indulgence. There is so little time. Believe me, sir," he went on with an urbanity not put out of joint by the strained circumstances. "I know this is an outrageous invasion of your privacy, but I have orders from the White House, professor. You must come with us at once." His clean-shaven, handsome features flashed a quick earnest smile that was clearly meant to tell Yancey how seriously he took it all.

"What the devil!" Yancey gasped. "What is this all about?" He heard the quick stamp of feet on his front steps. His front doorbell sounded insistently.

"Please don't answer it," Harwood asked, his hand gently restraining. "Professor, this is a matter of life and death for your country. We need your services urgently, this moment. I have authority to swear you into the Army, sir, with the rank of Lieutenant Colonel. Would you please raise your right hand?"

"Certainly not," Yancey said stubbornly. "I'm not used to having some smooth-talking public relations officer storm into my house and order me about. What in Tophet is going on?" The tough military tones of Evans came clearly through the door, ordering people to keep outside the picket fence. Yancey was about to protest the treatment of his neighbors when those at the front door despaired of the bell and took to thudding its heavy silver knocker. Students, he knew, young and impatient.

"Don't go," Harwood said breathlessly. "Professor, a spaceship from outside the Solar System has just landed in Kansas. We are trying desperately to communicate with the visitors. We need you. We *must* have you to help us."

It took a long moment for what Harwood told him to sink in. Yancey's sharp features narrowed farther as he digested the incredible fact. "You mean, you Army people are trying to talk to them?" he asked. He had a wry conception of a crew of narrow-minded militarists trying to make sense to an alien culture.

"Yes," Harwood said, not feeling the barb in Yancey's question. "Weird as it seems, they are reasonably human, and they seem convinced they can communicate with us. Pathetically convinced. It's a race against time."

"What's the rush?" Yancey demanded tartly.

"Partly that they insist. They've made hand signals, professor. Apparently something about their power. We think it deteriorates under a gravitational field. We can't understand exactly what they mean, but they keep pointing to the sun and—"

"Yes, I understand," Yancey said acidly, his mind making semantic sense of Harwood's overearnest babbling. "And they seem to think they can communicate with us? By which you mean that they seem to think they know how *we* communicate?" He paused while his mind went back over what the other had said. "You said 'partly.' What's the rest of the rush?"

"Really, professor," Harwood insisted deferentially. "I can tell you these things en route. The others are waiting for us at Westover Field."

Rocco trotted quickly down the stairs. Yancey saw that he was carrying his overnight case. "Ready, sir," the soldier called. He waited for no signal, but ran through the door to the yard, taking the bag toward the waiting 'copter.

"All right," Yancey said, intrigued by the thought of conversing with a completely foreign creature. "You'll get in touch with the College?" he asked, turning out the lights and setting the snap lock on his side door.

"Of course."

The starter's growl was whirling the blades up to starting speed before they were in the cabin. The jets belched fire, throbbed throatily, and whined quickly up to efficient velocity. Yancey gasped as the house fell swiftly away below them. He got a brief glimpse of the clock on Johnson Chapel before they swung off to the South. There was no talking possible with the eerie hooting of the ram-jets deafening them. Yancey collected his thoughts as they whirled over the Connecticut Valley toward the great Air Force base. All that he knew of language and semantics passed in well-ordered sequence through his scholarly mind. Always his circling thoughts came to rest on one fact. The visitors from outer space seemed convinced they could communicate. The idea titillated his rapier-sharp intellect.

A jet bomber waited squattily for them. Harwood seized the small suitcase himself as they grounded, and hurried Yancey toward the looming shape of the warplane. A small knot of people were bunched by it. Introductions were swift, mingled with the grunts of scholars straining their creaky frames through the bomber's small door.

"Professor Cottwold, the calligraphist," Harwood said hurriedly. "Meet—"

"Hello Cottwold," Yancey interrupted. "Glad to see you again." They shook hands briefly, and Cottwold turned away to climb in.

"And Professor Pratt," Harwood continued, pushing them up the ladder. "In your field, Professor Yancey."

"Yes," Yancey said acidly. "We've met, too."

Pratt laughed woodenly. "Indeed we have," he said with a heartiness that was not relish. He kept on talking as they strapped themselves in, until the cough of the starting turbines stopped. "How are things at Amherst these days, Yancey?"

"Quiet," the waspish little man replied. "You would hardly know we are waiting for the next Atomic War."

Pratt's stiff laugh was somehow condescending. "A little different at Yale," he confided. "We're somehow closer to life in New Haven. Don't see how you could spend time on a thing like that 'Sanskrit Revisited' you just published. We can't seem to ignore what's going on about us, the way you small-town people do."

Yancey's sharp retort was swallowed in the roar of sound. They taxied smoothly between the yellow rows of runway lights to the end of the long concrete ribbon, accelerated with neck-straining power, and hurtled into the black spring night. Red obstruction lights streaked into the distance behind them. Not until they felt the rippling passage of the bomber through the sonic barrier could they talk again. They could still feel the enormous power of the turbines surge through the hurtling ship, but they had left their screaming sound behind.

Harwood had wormed his way up forward with the pilots, using the radio. He crawled through the cramped passage back to them. "It's still there," he said breathlessly, his insignia glittering dully in the dimly lighted bomb bay.

"Where?" Yancey demanded.

"Near Emporia, Kansas," Harwood replied. "They've got the whole area sealed off. No aircraft. No oars. See here," he exclaimed, perching on a gunner's unoccupied stool. "You've all got to understand the need for utmost speed on this thing. I think all of you know the visitors have plainly signaled they can stay only five days."

"Now don't worry," Pratt boomed importantly. "The moment they realize a trained specialist in communication has been brought to them, they'll relax."

"I'm sorry," Harwood protested with that politeness Yancey found so ill-fitting. "But you can't think of it that way. There are other reasons for speed."

"Yes, what are they?" Yancey pursued him, recalling his remarks while still at his house.

Harwood gulped visibly in the dim light. "The Russians," he said unhappily. "They're raising the very devil about it."

"Well, just tell them to go to Hell," Pratt snapped. "They landed here, not in Russia, and showed uncommon good sense, if you ask me."

"Yes, I know," Harwood said. "But it's not that simple."

"How do the Russians know?" Yancey asked.

"Their radars must have tracked the ship, too. It was the strangest thing. It just suddenly appeared, with the greatest burst of radiant energies imaginable, about fifty million miles north of the ecliptic. It dropped down toward Earth without any hesitation. Didn't seem any question about which planet they were interested in. They took their time coming, only used about a quarter G acceleration, but they drove or braked the whole way. No drifting. They've obviously got an atomic drive of some kind. No rockets. Their power must be enormous. The electrical disturbance of their drive affected radars and other detectors all over the System."

"The atomic drive!" Pratt breathed. "At last!"

"Yes, I know," Harwood said miserably. "But of course the Russians are thinking exactly the same thing. The minute they knew the ship had landed here, we started to get demands that it be internationalized. They demand equal representation when we interview the visitors."

"Ha!" Pratt laughed bitterly. "Well, they know where that'll get them! Fat chance we'll share any atomic space drive with those blood-thirsty madmen!" Yancey shriveled with the implications of what the others had said. It was the same jingoistic talk that sooner or later guaranteed that the last two nations of the world would wipe each other out. They had come mighty close to it the last time, he recalled bitterly, thinking of his own wife, trapped in the dusting of New York.

Harwood was still talking persuasively, his tone low and tense. "They're not such fools," he explained. "They've told us they'll bomb and dust the area into extinction if we don't agree immediately. You can see the Russians would rather have the secret of the drive lost than see us get it before they do."

"What the devil!" Cottwold protested. "You mean we stand a good chance of being bombed while we're there! A fine time to tell us, young man! I consider this—"

"No, no," Harwood placated him. "We can stall them a day or so. They don't know, of course, that the visitors can't remain. By the time we get it all settled about how the thing will be internationalized, the ship will be gone. And we'll have the drive. I hope," he concluded. "It all depends on you."

Yancey's acid voice broke into laughter. "You fools," he told them bitterly. "And the moment the Russians think they've been tricked, they'll start their missiles toward us. They won't dare to wait until we have actually built and installed the drive. It will be now or never for them!"

"We can hold them," Harwood said tightly. "We haven't been sitting still. Our northern radar net—"

"Tophet!" Yancey exploded. "Then you admit we are starting the Second Atomic War. Well, I shall have nothing to do with it! See here, Pratt, you should be immune from the sordid appeals this sugar-tongued character is making! Cottwold!"

Pratt's sneer was plain in the gloom of the bomber's hurtling hull. "How you can defend an intellectualism that is not first concerned with its political freedom is beyond me," he said heavily. Cottwold was silent.

Yancey felt himself slump into his cramped seat with despair. The whole world was going mad, he knew. When the intellectuals buttressed the fatuous arguments of a constitutionally blind military, the place for his kind had vanished. But in spite of his hatred of the thought that he would contribute to the outbreak of war, his intellectual curiosity was too great for him to stay behind when the others were taken to the strangers from space.

There could be no doubt of the enormous scientific achievement of the visitors. Their huge vessel stretched its length a thousand feet across the green, sprouting wheat, and towered two hundred feet in diameter. A companionway of stairs, startling similar to the terrestrial equivalent, had been let down from a round lock or doorway low in the hull, so that the great ship bulged out above it. At its head there was a small landing or balcony, big enough to accommodate several persons.

The Army, with all the unpleasant things it represented to Yancey, was there in force. Bare, unpainted hutments already clustered around the foot of the companionway, huddling under the outward swelling curve of the giant, cylindrical hull. The tender shoots of wheat had been ground blackly into the muddy soil. The deep ruts of wheeled vehicles testified to its wetness, and explained why the ring of vehicles about the ship, holding the curious back, were now all provided with caterpillar tracks. Cameras were being confiscated on every hand, Yancey saw bitterly, reflecting on the military mind. No photographic negative could ever print the impression that every viewer of the monstrous ship was having burned indelibly into his memory. The Army might even try to confiscate that, he decided angrily.

Harwood struggled with them through the mud as far as the foot of the stairway. There was a squad of paratroops posted there, tommy-guns slung meaningfully over their shoulders, their faces grim and purposeful in spite of their youth. It was all hateful to Yancey. Soon to die, he reflected. Soon, and young!

A feverish young captain met them. The generals had stayed behind in their quarters, the way generals always do, Yancey observed silently.

"Call him out, captain," Harwood ordered.

The other officer turned to the open port. "Berom!" he called, his voice high and clear with excitement.

"What does that mean?" Cottwold asked.

"How do I know?" the captain asked. "That's the first thing he did when he stepped out of the ship. He showed us a sign with that word on it. We've already taught him how the alphabet is pronounced, but that's as far as we got. He won't let us in the ship. Acts as though he won't until we can talk to each other."

In spite of what Harwood had said about the visitor's being human. Yancey was unprepared for the appearance of the creature who stepped quickly onto the landing. Yancey's common sense told him it would be a miracle to find beings from the stars resembling humans even to the point of being erect and bifurcated. The visitor was a lot more than that. He wasn't much less like Yancey than an Australian fuzzy-wuzzy, but in the opposite direction. Pigmentation, while present, was light. He had hair on a head that bore two eyes, a nose, and an all-too-human mouth. His locks were platinum and fine to the point of suggesting a halo. He carried some kind of sign or placard and held a staff or wand in his tapering fingers, of which there seemed to be six rather than five.

"Berom!" he replied, his human features breaking into what was unmistakably a smile.

"Tell him 'Berom,'" the Captain said. "He likes that."

"Berom," Pratt called in his heavy voice. He led the three savants up the companionway to the landing. Yancey brought up the rear. For a long moment the beings of two worlds viewed each other at arms length, curiosity written in the same lines on all their faces.

"Berom," the visitor repeated, with an upward inflection, as if he were asking a question. The staff in his hand proved to be a stylus.

With it he wrote carefully on the placard in his hand. Its point was curiously fashioned, so that with a tiny lever on the shaft of the writing instrument he could control the width of the line it drew. His draughtsmanship was precise to the point of exciting Yancey's wonderment. The letters were a perfectly stylized typewriter font, albeit somewhat antique in their appearance. "BEROM" the visitor wrote, all in capital letters an inch or so high.

The three Terrestrials looked at it thoughtfully. "What is it?" Cottwold asked. "Does it make any sense to you?"

Yancey and Pratt exchanged glances. "Do you recognize the word?" Pratt asked the slighter man.

Yancey's eyebrows fluttered in the briefest shrug. "If it is a word," he said cautiously. "It is probably Hindustani. The root 'bero' in Sanskrit—"

"Oh, no," Pratt insisted heavily.

"Do you know the root?" Yancey asked icily.

"No. But, please, spare us Sanskrit. What would it be in Hindustani?"

"A 'berom' is a wedge, usually employed to hold a mattock on its shaft," Yancey said. "But I don't think that's important.'

Pratt grunted irritably. "See here, my friend," he said in English to the visitor. "You had better talk to us. Talk. Talk." He pointed vigorously to his lips. Comprehension was swift. With a soft smile the fine-haired creature broke into speech. His voice was soft and mellifluous, somewhat light in timbre, and in a girlish register. The phrases ran together in the formless torrent of any completely foreign language.

"Slower. Much slower," Pratt insisted, articulating his syllables with great deliberateness. "High degree of flexion," he noted over his shoulder to Yancey.

The result was surprising. A swift frown of disappointment crossed the visitor's face. He pointed excitedly to the word he had written on the placard. "Berom!" he exclaimed. "Berom!" He wrote it again, more quickly, his odd, adjustable stylus forming the expertly printed letters effortlessly.

"Look at those serifs!" Cottwold said. "An utterly novel approach toward calligraphy!"

Yancey pushed himself forward, around Pratt's lumbering bulk. He held his palms upward in what he hoped was a universal sign of friendship. To the surprise of all, not excluding the visitor, he encircled the stranger from space lightly in his arms and embraced him for a moment. A soft, unpracticed smile came and went on the philologist's features. Gently he removed the stylus from the other's slender hand. His flesh was as warm, firm and muscular and his bones as sturdy as Yancey's own. Using the visitor's hand, he placed it against his chest and said "Yancey," several times. The stranger caught on as quickly as before.

"Yancey," he repeated with excellent tone reproduction. Smilingly withdrawing his hand, he laid it against his own chest and said, "Gonish."

Yancey nodded, and supported the placard the other held with one hand while he wrote "BEROM" in simple Roman capitals, being unable to reproduce the other's skill at adding the cursive serifs of typewriter font. Then he printed his own name and, pointing to it, said it several times again. He followed by printing "Gonish," which he also spoke.

Gonish nodded quick understanding and retrieved the stylus. Still using the careful calligraphy that had so astonished Cottwold, he wrote a series of words on the placard:

"BEROM FANID ERPOT SIDAR YEVAH."

Pratt quickly copied them into his notebook, but all of them made it plain they did not understand the message. Gonish was plainly discouraged. He gestured toward the sun, and made several sweeping motions with his hand.

"Yes, yes," Yancey told him with the nod that was apparently a common signal of assent. "We understand. Only four more days." He turned and left the landing, leaving Platt and Cottwold to continue a fruitless attempt to establish better communication.

"Well?" Harwood demanded, when he had returned to the sticky mud.

"I can't tell yet," Yancey said, musingly. "I suppose there are all sorts of scientists here, are there not?"

"Of course."

"Get me an astronomer," he asked. "I think I can get farther than that fumbling old Pratt up there."

Pratt and Cottwold had left the landing after copying down a number of other messages that Gonish had written. Yancey led the astronomer up the companionway. "Smile when you meet him, Skinner," Yancey asked, scraping the gumbo from his shoes. "I think he can understand most of our gestures and conventions of unspoken communication."

Reaching the landing, he eschewed the cry of "Berom!" with which the captain had signaled the visitor. "Gonish," he called. "It is Yancey."

The white-haired visitor stepped through the open lock in a few moments. "Yancey!" he said with obvious pleasure. He stepped lightly to the professor's side, and repeated Yancey's previous embrace. The philologist smiled happily, returning the light, symbolic pressure of the other's arms.

He took the clock from the astronomer. It had a twenty-four hour military dial. Pointing to the sun, and making a gesture to suggest its full course around the Earth, he then pointed to the timepiece and showed one revolution of the hour hand. He reset the instrument, showing that the minute hand made one circuit for each of the twenty-four hourly movements of the smaller hand.

Gonish took the clock from him and twisted the set knob until he understood the linkage. By gesture he then repeated his understanding of the relationship between the course of the hour hand and the rotation of the planet.

"Sketch the Solar System, from north of the ecliptic," Yancey directed Skinner.

Gonish quickly nodded his assent as the representation of the sun, to which Skinner pointed, was surrounded by circles representing the elliptical orbits of the first three planets, with arrows flying in their direction of revolution. As he drew the third ring, he pointed significantly to the ground. Gonish nodded vigorously.

It took a little time to indicate the ten digits in the decimal numbering system, but eventually Gonish understood that nearly four hundred days were required for Earth to make one circuit about its parent.

At Yancey's continued direction, Skinner sketched wavy lines to indicate the vibratory pattern of light, and with the face of the clock showed that seven minutes were required for it to reach Earth from the sun. Gonish timed the sweep of the second hand of the clock with his own wrist instrument, and indicated sudden comprehension. He sketched a symbol.

"Undoubtedly the constant of the speed of light," Skinner said in awe.

"Yes," Yancey agreed. "Now, we must find how long light takes to go from here to his star." It was slow work in gesture, slow until the instant Gonish perceived what was wanted. He quickly understood that the period of revolution of Earth about the sun was the unit of time to be used as a measure. He made quick, crabbed calculations on the edge of the placard with a small pencillike stylus he took from his clothing, and, with careful copying of the arabic numerals, wrote the number "65."

"Sixty-five light years," Skinner said. "Yancey, this is terrific. Imagine that unthinkable distance. Find out how long it took them to get here."

"That doesn't matter," Yancey told him. He tapped his skull several times with his forefinger, nodding and smiling to Gonish. "I hope he gets that," he said to Skinner. "I want him to know that I understand." He pointed to the clock once again and showed two circuits of the hour hand. "Two days," he said, pointing to the arabic numeral "2" on the placard. Gonish nodded.

"Come on," Yancey said to Skinner.

"Why quit?" the astronomer protested. "We're just beginning to get somewhere."

"We are already there," Yancey said sourly. "We're wasting time. Come on." He trotted briskly down the companionway.

Harwood had left the trampled mud at its foot. "Where's the colonel?" Yancey asked the captain of the guard.

"They're all in General Swift's quarters, professor," he replied. "Something's up!"

Skinner tramped with him through the clinging mire. They had to step aside several times to avoid the lurching progress of light tanks, their whipping antennae barely skimming under the maze of telephone lines strung to hastily driven posts.

Harwood greeted them the instant they walked through the door. "Yancey!" he gasped. "The situation is deteriorating fast!"

"What happened?" Yancey asked, adding his muddy tracks to the hundreds of others that had soiled the rough wooden floor.

"The Russians apparently are wise to what's up. They've announced they are sending their representatives here Tuesday morning, under escort. They insist we permit them to land and join in communicating with Gonish and his crew."

"And if we don't?" Yancey said, knowing the answer beforehand.

"They will consider it an act of war. The 'escort' is obviously their full war fleet. They probably can't mobilize it any more quickly than that."

"Going to let them land?" Yancey asked irritably, sitting down to clean the muck from his oxfords.

"That depends on you and the others," Harwood told him feverishly. "Can you possibly get in communication with them before then?"

"This is Sunday," Yancey reminded him. "I have to go to Chicago for some references."

"References!" Pratt bellowed from the table at which General Swift and others in uniform were bent in earnest conversation with a number of scientists.

"That's what I said, Pratt," Yancey snapped.

"Don't be a fool!" General Swift rumbled. "We can't wait for a lot of bone-dry research. We've got to make those people understand."

"Understand what?" Yancey demanded acidly.

"That we want the secret of their drive, and that the Russians can't have it!" he growled ominously.

"And if they won't do that?" Yancey persisted.

"I have my orders," the general ground out pointedly.

"You wouldn't try to force your way into the ship?" Yancey marveled.

"They'll not leave here without our having the secret, or their being in no condition to pass it on," Swift snapped. "Didn't you get anywhere with them?"

"Nothing important," Yancey said. "But I have some ideas. I'll need to do some research, as I told you."

"What do you mean, nothing important?" Skinner protested excitedly. "Why, at the rate he was going, we'd have had anything we wanted in a couple hours!"

"Is that true?" Swift demanded.

"Not at all," Yancey said in a chill tone. "We merely exchanged references on our time system and found out that his star is about sixty-five light-years away."

General Swift was on his feet. "That's the stuff," he snapped. "Skinner, did you understand how he did it?"

"Yes, general. It's simple. Gonish wants to give information as hard as you can imagine."

"Well, come on," Swift roared, reaching for his cap.

"I've still got to go to Chicago," Yancey insisted. "Skinner can carry on, if that's what you care about. I'll be back tomorrow night or Tuesday."

"How can you consider leaving at a time like this?" Swift growled. "Haven't you got a scrap of patriotism in you?"

"I'm as old as you, if not as mentally ossified," Yancey seethed bitterly. "I have my own very strongly developed ideas of patriotism, undoubtedly arrived at after thought more cogent than you are capable of. I don't need you to tell me my duty! Are you trying to tell me I'm not free to go?"

All the military personnel froze into stiff silence in the electric tension. Swift slowly purpled, trembling with restrained fury. "Go ahead!" he gasped, with a furious swing of his arm. "But keep your idiotic mouth shut! And that's an order I can make stick!"

The Russians had arrived before Yancey's 'copter returned him from Chicago. A number of rotary-winged aircraft had alighted beside the looming bulk of the monster from space. Overhead, as far as the eye and ear could detect, a huge fleet of Soviet aircraft circled ominously.

Harwood met him as he eased himself from the 'copter's cabin, his shoes going over their tops in the slime.

"Have you got it?" he demanded hopelessly, his face lined and haggard.

"Yes," Yancey said impatiently, struggling through the heavy going. "Of course. That's why I'm back. Took longer than I thought to find it. Take me to General Swift."

"Professor," Harwood protested, as they trudged laboriously under the overhang of the huge spaceship, "he's in with the Russians. They're having the biggest fight you ever heard. The Russians have posted a guard at the companionway, too. They won't let anybody by. And we won't let them go in, either. They demand three days with Gonish before we see him again, on the theory that we have already had a three-day crack at him. It's awful!"

Yancey frowned, and they both stepped out of the way of a clanking, snorting tank. "That changes things a little," he said. "Still, you had better get Swift out of the meeting a minute."

The general brought Pratt with him. "Well?" he gasped. His red face ran with sweat. The tension of the day had told on them both.

"I can communicate with Gonish," Yancey told him.

"Not now," Swift said heavily.

"What?"

"You heard me. If you'd stayed here and done your duty—But no! Well, we're not doing any talking with that white-haired little idiot until we settle with the Russians. The Secretary of State will be here any minute."

"Gonish will leave before you settle anything," Yancey said sourly.

"No he won't. We'll either agree, or agree to disagree in the next hour," Swift snarled. "And I think war will start right in that room. Major, give me your sidearm." He gravely buckled the belt and holster over his uniform. "Those Russian generals are armed to the teeth," he swore, turning to leave.

"Wait, Yancey called. He handed him a sheet of typed paper. This is what I propose we should have told Gonish."

Swift glowered at the meaningless message. It was a short string of five-letter words, making no sense. "What does it say?" he demanded.

"It's in code," Yancey said, with a vindictive smile toward Pratt. "Bentley's Commercial Code, obsolete now, but in common use for fifty years in the last century. Look it up for yourself." He did not mention the copy of the code book in his pocket.

"What?" Pratt roared. "Inconceivable!"

"Who knows how many thousands of facsimile messages they received, how many labeled diagrams were transmitted? It may have taken years, but they did it. After all, code is still language."

"Ridiculous!" Pratt snapped, reddening at the thought he had missed the solution.

"Quite right," Yancey grinned acidly. "Of course you should have figured it out in a minute. Five-letter word groups. No flexion apparently present but, as you pointed out yourself, his speech has even more flexion than our own.

"And he thought we should understand. A complete stranger, he walked out of that ship printing words in our own letters that he thought we knew. And from sixty-five light-years away! It almost screamed that his race had been picking up facsimile transmissions. And of course, the transmissions had to have originated more than sixty-five years ago, the time it took them to travel through space to his planet.

"We don't use the system any more," he explained. "All commercial messages are now sent on keyed-variation pulses, to preserve their security. But for many years after 1954 or 1955 almost all commercial radiograms were broadcast as facsimiles, the way we still send radiophotos. The code was used to compress the message as much as possible and to keep the purely curious from reading it without effort. Many of the code words in Bentley's stand for whole sentences. Such as BEROM."

"What does it mean?" Pratt asked reluctantly, as Swift's eyebrows narrowed over his haggard face.

"It means, 'Suggest we pool our information,' a common commercial phrase," Yancey said blandly. "Something that was plain from Gonish's every action."

"That settles it!" Swift snapped.

"Settles what?"

"The Russians don't get to talk to Gonish," he said flatly. "That white-haired fool would as likely hand *them* the secret of the drive as not." He spun on his heel and re-entered the conference room, Pratt tagging across the muddy floor behind him.

Yancey walked disconsolately from the nerve-wracking atmosphere of the barrack. He felt rather than saw the rounded belly of the spaceship as he walked to where it curved into the great depression it had rammed in the mud of the prairie:

The squad at the foot of the companionway had been reinforced, as Harwood had told him. The Russian soldiery stood on one side, glaring at the equally grim group of paratroops on the other.

Yancey struggled slowly over to them. One of the Russians promptly raised his tommy-gun in an unmistakable gesture of threat. Yancey stopped and looked at the foreigners thoughtfully. Their broad Slavic faces and cropped blond hair marked them as elite troops of the Soviet. All but one of them. His flat Mongoloid nose and eye flaps marked him for a Tatar. Yancey grinned without humor.

With the unconsciously easy skill of the accomplished linguist, he produced the Tatar tongue he hadn't spoken for twenty years, since his student days in traveling over the highland steppes of northern Tibet.

"Greetings, my Tatar friend," he said in the difficult tongue. The soldier started with surprise. "Have no fear," the professor told him loudly. "It is only I, *Yancey*. Just *Yancey*, and I would do you no harm, my Soviet comrade."

The effect of his name was electric. Gonish appeared immediately on the landing, behind the back of the guard. Yancey raised his eyes. Four words he cried:

"BEROM BODAD VEMAN WEGOT."

Gonish stood transfixed. Slowly he re-entered the lock, making only an arresting gesture with his hand. Too late the Russian soldiery realized he had spoken with the ship. Consternation and fear crossed their regimented faces. Yancey stood stock still, waiting in fearful suspense. Had he over-estimated the capacities of the visitors?

He was not to be disappointed. The tractor beam seized him with a steely embrace that he recognized for deepest friendship. He heard the lock clang shut behind him. An enormous surge of acceleration threw him motionless to the floor of the lock. For many minutes it crushed him there, scarcely able to force a trickle of air into his straining lungs. When the crushing weight eased, he knew they were far beyond the stratosphere. The easing was only momentary. The whole structure *rippled* and his vision went wild, only to clear. He felt almost weightless. It was the interstellar drive, he told himself.

(CONTINUATION OF EXCERPT FROM PROCEEDINGS IN THE COURT-MARTIAL OF BENJAMIN L. HARWOOD, COL., U.S.A., FORT MEYER, VA., JUNE 8, 2038.)

Defense Counsel: . . . to introduce into evidence two documents which have an important bearing on this same point.

Judge Advocate: It seems to me that this is out of order, and that your exhibits should properly be presented when your direct examination of the defendant takes place.

D. C.: May it please the Court, the cross-examination I shall wish to make of General Swift who will, I understand, take the stand next, makes it desirable that these documents be introduced at this time.

J. A.: Very well. Proceed.

D.C.: Both these messages were originally in code. A copy of the book "Bentley's Commercial Codes," Seventeenth edition of 1961, has already been entered by the Court as Exhibit "C." It has been used to decode or translate the exhibits in question.

The first exhibit decodes what, to the best auditory recollection of several persons who stood near him when he was drawn or sucked into the ship, Professor Yancey cried out to Gonish, the visitor from space, namely "BEROM BODAD VEMAN WEGOT." Each of those words in Bentley's represents a standard sentence often used in commercial messages. This Exhibit decodes them to read, "Suggest we pool our information. You are in great danger. Leave at once. Take me with you." I offer it as Exhibit "L."

The second exhibit is a similar decoding of the suggested message to Gonish, given General Swift by Professor Yancey on his return from Chicago, where we now know he searched numerous old code books before discovering that Gonish was familiar only with Bentley's. This message, unlike the other, consists mostly of code words from Bentley's which represent only one word or simple phrase in English. It reads, "Visitors from space: We are flattered and pleased by your generous offer to pool information. Unfortunately our world has not reached the stage of political maturity where it can be trusted with the secrets of enormous power you obviously possess. We are still divided into warring tribes, each trying to wrest mastery of the planet from the other. The idea of cooperation between peoples separated by our seas is slow to take root. To prevent the immediate outbreak of a catastrophic conflict among our tribes you must leave at once." I offer it as Exhibit "M."

Now I wish the Court to understand that we make no point of the accuracy of Professor Yancey's belief that departure of the ship would prevent the outbreak of war. Only the superhuman efforts of General Swift, as we all know—

Questions for Discussion and Review

1. Why does Berryman begin his story with the court-martial scene?
2. What assumptions does Berryman make in the story about the aliens and alien psychology?

3. Should the government be training a task force to greet and communicate with alien visitors?

4. How should such a group be composed, and what procedures should it adopt for meeting such a contingency?

5. There are many satiric touches in the story, but the trump card is Yancey's message to Gonish marked "Exhibit 'M'." What purpose does this second message have?

First Contact
Murray Leinster

William Fitzgerald Jenkins, who wrote under the pseudonym Murray
Leinster, was born in Norfolk, Virginia, in 1896; he died in 1975. For a
quarter-century, he was considered the dean of SF writers. His first SF
story, "The Runaway Skyscraper," was published in the February 1919
issue of *Argosy* and was concerned with time travel. Leinster's career as a
writer was long and fruitful, with over a thousand short stories to his credit
and a dozen or so movie scripts. He wrote many SF stories that have
enriched the genre with new ideas, and introduced new concepts, and
explored new technology. His story "Sidewise in Time" (1934) was the
first of the parallel-universe stories to envision simultaneous tracks of time
capable of overlapping to produce startling results. That story has proved
a mine for later writers who have worked with ideas of parallel time tracks.
Leinster won a Hugo Award in 1956 for "Exploration Team." He is also
the author of such well-known titles as *The Forgotten Planet* (1950),
Creatures of the Abyss (1962), and *Time Tunnel* (1964). "First
Contact" first appeared in *Astounding Science Fiction* (May 1945).

This is an alien-human story that explores possible consequences of making
a first contact with an alien space ship in a distant part of our galaxy.
The difference in setting from the preceding story ("Berom") helps produce
the circumstances of a different kind of adventure. In Leinster's story, the
forces meet in neutral territory—the Crab nebula, both a likely and a
good choice. The problem in this story of alien contact is how to disengage
and return home with a profit from the momentous meeting. Actually,
the problem is one of logic, as the solution to the problem in "Berom" was
both logical and linguistic.

The expedition, which results in the meeting and the initial engagement
of the two space ships, gives the author an opportunity to create his
special effects of deep space exploration. He succeeds with an authority
matched by few writers who have attempted it. The elements derived from
romance and engineering are nicely balanced against the psychological
tension, and the awesome surroundings are neatly counterpointed to the
details of routine in the spacecraft. Following the alien contact, the visual
spectacle of deep space gains effectiveness as the setting for the duel of
wits testing the nerves of each side. But the contest is also a test of the
courage of each, as both sides probe to discover a common ground of trust.

Leinster is no idealist, and the resolution of the story is both ingenious
and practical. The heightening tension underlines the momentous character
of the meeting and the necessity of working out a satisfactory resolution.
Perhaps if the two species were more alike, there would have been only
the option of combat. The differences between alien and terrestrial
ecology count for a great deal, but not all. The extraordinary discipline
of the crews is, perhaps, of more immediate significance. Their military

codes are self-imposed restraints creating the framework necessary to hold together a society of human beings or humanlike aliens when they are under extreme stress. In a way, their cultural and military codes are liberating because they permit an orderly engagement of the two forces that gives them the time needed to work out a possible understanding. Conversely, these very codes are impediments to be overcome by the ingenuity of both parties. The challenge faced by the two crews requires a restraint that only rigid laws can maintain while it demands with an equal urgency that the imagination rise above conventional reaction patterns. The rule must be: "Adapt or perish"; and adaption is possible only as it is a function of a free intelligence. This story is a celebration of that rare combination of human attainments which turn out to be alien as well.

Tommy Dort went into the captain's room with his last pair of stereo-photos and said:

"I'm through, sir. These are the last two pictures I can take."

He handed over the photographs and looked with professional interest at the visiplates which showed all space outside the ship. Subdued, deep-red lighting indicated the controls and such instruments as the quartermaster on duty needed for navigation of the spaceship *Llanvabon*. There was a deeply cushioned control chair. There was the little gadget of oddly angled mirrors—remote descendant of the back-view mirrors of twentieth-century motorists—which allowed a view of all the visiplates without turning the head. And there were the huge plates which were so much more satisfactory for a direct view of space.

The *Llanvabon* was a long way from home. The plates, which showed every star of visual magnitude and could be stepped up to any desired magnification, portrayed stars of every imaginable degree of brilliance, in the startlingly different colors they show outside of atmosphere. But every one was unfamiliar. Only two constellations could be recognized as seen from Earth, and they were shrunken and distorted. The Milky Way seemed vaguely out of place. But even such oddities were minor compared to a sight in the forward plates.

There was a vast, vast mistiness ahead. A luminous mist. It seemed motionless. It took a long time for any appreciable nearing to appear in the vision plates, though the spaceship's velocity indicator showed an incredible speed. The mist was the Crab Nebula, six light-years long, three and a half light-years thick, and outward-reaching members that in the telescopes of Earth gave it some resemblance to the creature for which it was named. It was a cloud of gas, infinitely tenuous, reaching half again as far as from Sol to its nearest neighbor-sun. Deep within it burned two stars; a double star; one component the familiar yellow of the sun of Earth, the other an unholy white.

Tommy Dort said meditatively:

"We're heading into a deep, sir?"

The skipper studied the last two plates of Tommy's taking, and put them aside. He went back to his uneasy contemplation of the vision plates ahead. The *Llanvabon* was decelerating at full force. She was a bare half light-year from the nebula. Tommy's work was guiding the ship's course, now, but the work was done. During all the stay of the exploring ship in the nebula, Tommy Dort would loaf. But he'd more than paid his way so far.

He had just completed a quite unique first—a complete photographic record of the movement of a nebula during a period of four thousand years, taken by one individual with the same apparatus and with control exposures to detect and record any systematic errors. It was an achievement in itself worth the journey from Earth. But in addition, he had also recorded four thousand years of the history of a double star, and four thousand years of the history of a star in the act of degenerating into a white dwarf.

It was not that Tommy Dort was four thousand years old. He was, actually, in his twenties. But the Crab Nebula is four thousand light-years from Earth, and the last two pictures had been taken by light which would not reach Earth until the sixth millennium A.D. On the way here—at speeds incredible multiples of the speed of light— Tommy Dort had recorded each aspect of the nebula by the light which had left it from forty centuries since to a bare six months ago.

The *Llanvabon* bored on through space. Slowly, slowly, slowly, the incredible luminosity crept across the vision plates. It blotted out half the universe from view. Before was glowing mist, and behind was a star-studded emptiness. The mist shut off three-fourths of all the stars. Some few of the brightest shone dimly through it near its edge, but only a few. Then there was only an irregularly shaped patch of darkness astern against which stars shone unwinking. The *Llanvabon* dived into the nebula, and it seemed as if it bored into a tunnel of Darkness with walls of shining fog.

Which was exactly what the spaceship was doing. The most distant photographs of all had disclosed structural features in the nebula. It was not amorphous. It had form. As the *Llanvabon* drew nearer, indications of structure grew more distinct, and Tommy Dort had argued for a curved approach for photographic reasons. So the spaceship had come up to the nebula on a vast logarithmic curve, and Tommy had been able to take successive photographs from slightly different angles and get stereopairs which showed the nebula in three dimensions; which disclosed billowings and hollows and an actually complicated shape. In places, the nebula displayed convolutions like those of a human brain. It was into one of those hollows that the spaceship now plunged. They had been called "deeps" by analogy with crevasses in the ocean floor. And they promised to be useful.

The skipper relaxed. One of a skipper's functions, nowadays, is to think of things to worry about, and then worry about them. The skipper of the *Llanvabon* was conscientious. Only after a certain instrument remained definitely nonregistering did he ease himself back in his seat.

"It was just barely possible," he said heavily, "that those deeps might be nonluminous gas. But they're empty. So we'll be able to use overdrive as long as we're in them."

It was a light-year-and-a-half from the edge of the nebula to the neighborhood of the double star which was its heart. That was the problem. A nebula is a gas. It is so thin that a comet's tail is solid by comparison, but a ship traveling on overdrive—above the speed of light—does not want to hit even a merely hard vacuum. It needs pure emptiness, such as exists between the stars. But the *Llanvabon* could not do much in this expanse of mist if it was limited to speeds a merely hard vacuum will permit.

The luminosity seemed to close in behind the spaceship, which slowed and slowed and slowed. The overdrive went off with the sudden *pinging* sensation which goes all over a person when the overdrive field is released.

Then, almost instantly, bells burst into clanging, strident uproar all through the ship. Tommy was almost deafened by the alarm bell which rang in the captain's room before the quartermaster shut it off with a flip of his hand. But other bells could be heard ringing throughout the rest of the ship, to be cut off as automatic doors closed one by one.

Tommy Dort stared at the skipper. The skipper's hands clenched. He was up and staring over the quartermaster's shoulder. One indicator was apparently having convulsions. Others strained to record their findings. A spot on the diffusedly bright mistiness of a bow-quartering visiplate grew brighter as the automatic scanner focused on it. That was the direction of the object which had sounded collision-alarm. But the object locator itself—. According to its reading, there was one solid object some eighty thousand miles away—an object of no great size. But there was another object whose distance varied from extreme range to zero, and whose size shared its impossible advance and retreat.

"Step up the scanner," snapped the skipper.

The extra-bright spot on the scanner rolled outward, obliterating the undifferentiated image behind it. Magnification increased. But nothing appeared. Absolutely nothing. Yet the radio locator insisted that something monstrous and invisible made lunatic dashes toward the *Llanvabon*, at speeds which inevitably implied collision, and then fled coyly away at the same rate.

The visiplate went up to maximum magnification. Still nothing. The skipper ground his teeth. Tommy Dort said meditatively:

"D'you know, sir, I saw something like this on a liner on the Earth-Mars run once, when we were being located by another ship. Their locator beam was the same frequency as ours, and every time it hit, it registered like something monstrous, and solid."

"That," said the skipper savagely, "is just what's happening now.

There's something like a locator beam on us. We're getting that beam and our own echo besides. But the other ship's invisible! Who is out here in an invisible ship with locator devices? Not men, certainly!"

He pressed the button in his sleeve communicator and snapped:

"Action stations! Man all weapons! Condition of extreme alert in all departments immediately!"

His hands closed and unclosed. He stared again at the visiplate which showed nothing but a formless brightness.

"Not men?" Tommy Dort straightened sharply. "You mean—"

"How many solar systems in our galaxy?" demanded the skipper bitterly. "How many planets fit for life? And how many kinds of life could there be? If this ship isn't from Earth—and it isn't—it has a crew that isn't human. And things that aren't human but are up to the level of deep-space travel in their civilization could mean anything!"

The skipper's hands were actually shaking. He would not have talked so freely before a member of his own crew, but Tommy Dort was of the observation staff. And even a skipper whose duties include worrying may sometimes need desperately to unload his worries. Sometimes, too, it helps to think aloud.

"Something like this has been talked about and speculated about for years," he said softly. "Mathematically, it's been an odds-on bet that somewhere in our galaxy there'd be another race with a civilization equal to or further advanced than ours. Nobody could ever guess where or when we'd meet them. But it looks like we've done it now!"

Tommy's eyes were very bright.

"D'you suppose they'll be friendly, sir?"

The skipper glanced at the distance indicator. The phantom object still made its insane, nonexistent swoops toward and away from the *Llanvabon*. The secondary indication of an object at eighty thousand miles stirred ever so slightly.

"It's moving," he said curtly. "Heading for us. Just what we'd do if a strange spaceship appeared in our hunting grounds! Friendly? Maybe! We're going to try to contact them. We have to. But I suspect this is the end of this expedition. Thank God for the blasters!"

The blasters are those beams of ravening destruction which take care of recalcitrant meteorites in a spaceship's course when the deflectors can't handle them. They are not designed as weapons, but they can serve as pretty good ones. They can go into action at five thousand miles, and draw on the entire power output of a whole ship. With automatic aim and a traverse of five degrees, a ship like the *Llanvabon* can come very close to blasting a hole through a small-sized asteroid which gets in its way. But not on overdrive, of course.

Tommy Dort had approached the bow-quartering visiplate. Now he jerked his head around.

"Blasters, sir? What for?"

The skipper grimaced at the empty visiplate.

"Because we don't know what they're like and can't take a chance! I know!" he added bitterly. "We're going to make contacts and try to find out all we càn about them—especially where they come from. I suppose we'll try to make friends—but we haven't much chance. We can't trust them the fraction of an inch. We daren't! They've locators. Maybe they've tracers better than any we have. Maybe they could trace us all the way home without our knowing it! We can't risk a nonhuman race knowing where Earth is unless we're sure of them! And how can we be sure? They could come to trade, of course—or they could swoop down on overdrive with a battle fleet that could wipe us out before we knew what happened. We wouldn't know which to expect, or when!"

Tommy's face was startled.

"It's all been thrashed out over and over, in theory," said the skipper. "Nobody's ever been able to find a sound answer, even on paper. But you know, in all their theorizing, no one considered the crazy, rank impossibility of a deep-space contact, with neither side knowing the other's home world! But we've got to find an answer in fact! What are we going to do about them? Maybe these creatures will be aesthetic marvels, nice and friendly and polite—and underneath with the sneaking brutal ferocity of a Japanese. Or maybe they'll be crude and gruff as a Swedish farmer—and just as decent underneath. Maybe they're something in between. But am I going to risk the possible future of the human race on a guess that it's safe to trust them? God knows it would be worth while to make friends with a new civilization! It would be bound to stimulate our own, and maybe we'd gain enormously. But I can't take chances. The one thing I won't risk is having them know how to find Earth! Either I know they can't follow me, or I don't go home! And they'll probably feel the same way!"

He pressed the sleeve-communicator button again.

"Navigation officers, attention! Every star map on this ship is to be prepared for instant destruction. This includes photographs and diagrams from which our course or starting point could be deduced. I want all astronomical data gathered and arranged to be destroyed in a split second, on order. Make it fast and report when ready!"

He released the button. He looked suddenly old. The first contact of humanity with an alien race was a situation which had been forseen in many fashions, but never one quite so hopeless of solution as this. A solitary Earth-ship and a solitary alien, meeting in a nebula which must be remote from the home planet of each. They might wish peace, but the line of conduct which best prepared a treacherous attack was just the seeming of friendliness. Failure to be suspicious might doom the human race,—and a peaceful exchange of the fruits of civilization would be the greatest benefit imaginable. Any mistake would be irreparable, but a failure to be on guard would be fatal.

The captain's room was very, very quiet. The bow-quartering visiplate was filled with the image of a very small section of the nebula. A very small section indeed. It was all diffused, featureless, luminous mist. But suddenly Tommy Dort pointed.

"There, sir!"

There was a small shape in the mist. It was far away. It was a black shape, not polished to mirror-reflection like the hull of the *Llanvabon*. It was bulbous—roughly pear-shaped. There was much thin luminosity between, and no details could be observed, but it was surely no natural object. Then Tommy looked at the distance indicator and said quietly:

"It's headed for us at very high acceleration, sir. The odds are that they're thinking the same thing, sir, that neither of us will dare let the other go home. Do you think they'll try a contact with us, or let loose with their weapons as soon as they're in range?"

The *Llanvabon* was no longer in a crevasse of emptiness in the nebula's thin substance. She swam in luminescence. There were no stars save the two fierce glows in the nebula's heart. There was nothing but an all-enveloping light, curiously like one's imagining of underwater in the tropic of Earth.

The alien ship had made one sign of less than lethal intention. As it drew near the *Llanvabon,* it decelerated. The *Llanvabon* itself had advanced for a meeting and then come to a dead stop. Its movement had been a recognition of the nearness of the other ship. Its pausing was both a friendly sign and a precaution against attack. Relatively still, it could swivel on its own axis to present the least target to a slashing assault, and it would have a longer firing-time than if the two ships flashed past each other at their combined speeds.

The moment of actual approach, however, was tenseness itself. The *Llanvabon's* needle-pointed bow aimed unwaveringly at the alien bulk. A relay to the captain's room put a key under his hand which would fire the blasters with maximum power. Tommy Dort watched, his brow wrinkled. The aliens must be of a high degree of civilization if they had spaceships, and civilization does not develop without the development of foresight. These aliens must recognize all the implications of this first contact of two civilized races as fully as did the humans on the *Llanvabon*.

The possibility of an enormous spurt in the development of both, by peaceful contact and exchange of their separate technologies, would probably appeal to them as to the man. But when dissimilar human cultures are in contact, one must usually be subordinate or there is war. But subordination between races arising on separate planets could not be peacefully arranged. Men, at least, would never consent to subordination, nor was it likely that any highly developed race would agree. The benefits to be derived from commerce could never make up for a condition of inferiority. Some races—men, perhaps—would prefer commerce to conquest. Perhaps—perhaps!—these aliens would also. But some types even of human beings would have craved red war. If the alien ship now approaching the *Llanvabon* returned to its home base with news of humanity's existence and of ships like the *Llanvabon,* it would give its race the choice of trade or battle. They might want trade, or they might want war. But it takes two to make trade, and only one to make war. They could not be sure of men's peacefulness, nor could men be sure of theirs. The only safety for either civilization would lie in the destruction of one or both of the two ships here and now.

But even victory would not be really enough. Men would need to know where this alien race was to be found, for avoidance if not for battle. They would need to know its weapons, and its resources, and if it could be a menace and how it could be eliminated in case of need. The aliens would feel the same necessities concerning humanity.

So the skipper of the *Llanvabon* did not press the key which might possibly have blasted the other ship to nothingness. He dared not. But he dared not fire either. Sweat came out on his face.

A speaker muttered. Someone from the range room.

"The other ship's stopped, sir. Quite stationary. Blasters are centered on it, sir."

It was an urging to fire. But the skipper shook his head, to himself. The alien ship was no more than twenty miles away. It was dead-black. Every bit of its exterior was an abysmal, nonreflecting sable. No details could be seen except by minor variations in its outline against the misty nebula.

"It's stopped dead, sir," said another voice. "They've sent a modulated short wave at us, sir. Frequency modulated. Apparently a signal. Not enough power to do any harm."

The skipper said through tight-locked teeth:

"They're doing something now. There's movement on the outside of their hull. Watch what comes out. Put the auxiliary blasters on it."

Something small and round came smoothly out of the oval outline of the black ship. The bulbous hulk moved.

"Moving away, sir," said the speaker. "The object they let out is stationary in the place they've left."

Another voice cut in:

"More frequency modulated stuff, sir. Unintelligible."

Tommy Dort's eyes brightened. The skipper watched the visiplate, with sweat-droplets on his forehead.

"Rather pretty, sir," said Tommy, meditatively. "If they sent anything toward us, it might seem a projectile or a bomb. So they came close, let out a lifeboat, and went away again. They figure we can send a boat or a man to make contact without risking our ship. They must think pretty much as we do."

The skipper said, without moving his eyes from the plate:

"Mr. Dort, would you care to go out and look the thing over? I can't order you, but I need all my operating crew for emergencies. The observation staff—"

"Is expendable. Very well, sir," said Tommy briskly. "I won't take a lifeboat, sir. Just a suit with a drive in it. It's smaller and the arms and legs will look unsuitable for a bomb. I think I should carry a scanner, sir."

The alien ship continued to retreat. Forty, eighty, four hundred miles. It came to a stop and hung there, waiting. Climbing into his atomic-driven spacesuit just within the *Llanvabon's* air lock, Tommy heard the reports as they went over the speakers throughout the ship. That the other ship had stopped its retreat at four hundred miles was encouraging. It might not have weapons effective at a greater distance than that, and so felt safe. But just as the thought formed itself in his mind, the alien retreated precipitately still farther. Which, as Tommy reflected as he emerged from the lock, might be because the aliens had realized they were giving themselves away, or might be because they wanted to give the impression that they had done so.

He swooped away from the silvery-mirror *Llanvabon,* through a brightly glowing emptiness which was past any previous experience of the human race. Behind him, the *Llanvabon* swung about and darted away. The skipper's voice came in Tommy's helmet phones.

"We're pulling back, too, Mr. Dort. There is a bare possibility that they've some explosive atomic reaction they can't use from their own ship, but which might be destructive even as far as this. We'll draw back. Keep your scanner on the object."

The reasoning was sound, if not very comforting. An explosive which would destroy anything within twenty miles was theoretically possible, but humans didn't have it yet. It was decidedly safest for the *Llanvabon* to draw back.

But Tommy Dort felt very lonely. He sped through emptiness toward the tiny black speck which hung in incredible brightness. The *Llanvabon* vanished. Its polished hull would merge with the glowing mist at a relatively short distance, anyhow. The alien ship was not visible to the naked eye, either. Tommy swam in nothingness, four thousand light-years from home, toward a tiny black spot which was the only solid object to be seen in all of space.

It was a slightly distorted sphere, not much over six feet in diameter. It bounced away when Tommy landed on it, feet-first. There were small tentacles, or horns, which projected in every direction. They looked rather like the detonating horns of a submarine mine, but there was a glint of crystal at the tip-end of each.

"I'm here," said Tommy into his helmet phone.

He caught hold of a horn and drew himself to the object. It was all metal, dead-black. He could feel no texture through his space gloves, of course, but he went over and over it, trying to discover its purpose.

"Deadlock, sir, he said presently. "Nothing to report that the scanner hasn't shown you."

Then, through his suit, he felt vibrations. They translated themselves as clankings. A section of the rounded hull of the object opened

out. Two sections. He worked his way around to look in and see the
first nonhuman civilized beings that any man had ever looked upon.

But what he saw was simply a flat plate on which dim-red glows
crawled here and there in seeming aimlessness. His helmet phones
emitted a startled exclamation. The skipper's voice:

"Very good, Mr. Dort. Fix your scanner to look into the plate. They
dumped out a robot with an infrared visiplate for communication. Not
risking any personnel. Whatever we might do would damage only machinery. Maybe they expect us to bring it on board—and it may have a
bomb charge that can be detonated when they're ready to start for
home. I'll send a plate to face one of its scanners. You return to the
ship."

"Yes, sir," said Tommy. "But which way is the ship, sir?"

There were no stars. The nebula obscured them with its light. The
only thing visible from the robot was the double star at the nebula's
center. Tommy was no longer oriented. He had but one reference
point.

"Head straight away from the double star," came the order in his
helmet phone. "We'll pick you up."

He passed another lonely figure, a little later, headed for the alien
sphere with a vison plate to set up. The two spaceships, each knowing
that it dared not risk its own race by the slightest lack of caution, would
communicate with each other through this small round robot. Their
separate vision systems would enable them to exchange all the information they dared give, while they debated the most practical way of
making sure that their own civilization would not be endangered by
this first contact with another. The truly most practical method would
be the destruction of the other ship in a swift and deadly attack—in
self defense.

II

The *Llanvabon* thereafter, was a ship in which there were two separate
enterprises on hand at the same time. She had come out from Earth to
make close-range observations on the smaller component of the double
star at the nebula's center. The nebula itself was the result of the most
titanic explosion of which men have any knowledge. The explosion
took place sometime in the year 2946 B.C., before the first of the seven
cities of long-dead Ilium was even thought of. The light of that explosion reached Earth in the year 1054 A.D., and was duly recorded in
ecclesiastic annals and somewhat more reliably by Chinese court astronomers. It was bright enough to be seen in daylight for twenty-three
successive days. Its light—and it was four thousand light-years away—
was brighter than that of Venus.

From these facts, astronomers could calculate nine hundred years
later the violence of the detonation. Matter blown away from the center
of the explosion would have traveled outward at the rate of two million

three hundred thousand miles an hour; more than thirty-eight thousand miles a minute; something over six hundred thirty-eight miles per second. When twentieth-century telescopes were turned upon the scene of this vast explosion, only a double star remained—and the nebula. The brighter star of the doublet was almost unique in having so high a surface temperature that it showed no spectrum lines at all. It had a continuous spectrum. Sol's surface temperature is about 7,000° Absolute. That of the hot white star is 500,000 degrees. It has nearly the mass of the sun, but only one fifth its diameter, so that its density is one hundred seventy-three times that of water, sixteen times that of lead, and eight times that of iridium—the heaviest substance known on Earth. But even this density is not that of a dwarf white star like the companion of Sirius. The white star in the Crab Nebula is an incomplete dwarf; it is a star still in the act of collapsing. Examination—including the survey of a four-thousand-year column of its light—was worth while. The *Llanvabon* had come to make that examination. But the finding of an alien spaceship upon a similar errand had implications which overshadowed the original purpose of the expedition.

A tiny bulbous robot floated in the tenuous nebular gas. The normal operating crew of the *Llanvabon* stood at their posts with a sharp alertness which was productive of tense nerves. The observation staff divided itself, and a part went half-heartedly about the making of the observations for which the *Llanvabon* had come. The other half applied itself to the problem the spaceship offered.

It represented a culture which was up to space travel on an interstellar scale. The explosion of a mere five thousand years since must have blasted every trace of life out of existence in the area now filled by the nebula. So the aliens of the black spaceship came from another solar system. Their trip must have been, like that of the Earth ship, for purely scientific purposes. There was nothing to be extracted from the nebula.

They were, then, at least near the level of human civilization, which meant that they had or could develop arts and articles of commerce which men would want to trade for, in friendship. But they would necessarily realize that the existence and civilization of humanity was a potential menace to their own race. The two races could be friends, but also they could be deadly enemies. Each, even if unwillingly, was a monstrous menace to the other. And the only safe thing to do with a menace is to destroy it.

In the Crab Nebula the problem was acute and immediate. The future relationship of the two races would be settled here and now. If a process for friendship could be established, one race, otherwise doomed, would survive and both would benefit immensely. But that process had to be established, and confidence built up, without the most minute risk of danger from treachery. Confidence would need to be established upon a foundation of necessarily complete distrust. Neither dared return to its own base if the other could do harm to its race. Neither dared risk any of the necessities to trust. The only safe thing for either to do was destroy the other or be destroyed.

But even for war, more was needed than mere destruction of the other. With interstellar traffic, the aliens must have atomic power and some form of overdrive for travel above the speed of light. With radio location and visiplates and short-wave communication they had, of course, many other devices. What weapons did they have? How widely extended was their culture? What were their resources? Could there be a development of trade and friendship, or were the two races so unlike that only war could exist between them? If peace was possible, how could it be begun?

The men on the *Llanvabon* needed facts—and so did the crew of the other ship. They must take back every morsel of information they could. The most important information of all would be of the location of the other civilization, just in case of war. That one bit of information might be the decisive factor in an interstellar war. But other facts would be enormously valuable.

The tragic thing was that there could be no possible information which could lead to peace. Neither ship could stake its own race's existence upon any conviction of the good will or the honor of the other.

So there was a strange truce between the two ships. The alien went about its work of making observations, as did the *Llanvabon*. The tiny robot floated in bright emptiness. A scanner from the *Llanvabon* was focused upon a vision plate from the alien. A scanner from the alien regarded a vision plate from the *Llanvabon*. Communication began.

It progressed rapidly. Tommy Dort was one of those who made the first progress report. His special task on the expedition was over. He had now been assigned to work on the problem of communication with the alien entities. He went with the ship's solitary psychologist to the captain's room to convey the news of success. The captain's room, as usual, was a place of silence and dull-red indicator lights and the great bright visiplates on every wall and on the ceiling.

"We've established fairly satisfactory communication, sir," said the psychologist. He looked tired. His work on the trip was supposed to be that of measuring personal factors of error in the observation staff, for the reduction of all observations to the nearest possible decimal to the absolute. He had been pressed into service for which he was not especially fitted, and it told upon him. "That is, we can say almost anything we wish, to them, and can understand what they say in return. But of course we don't know how much of what they say is the truth."

The skipper's eyes turned to Tommy Dort.

"We've hooked up some machinery," said Tommy, "that amounts to a mechanical translator. We have vision plates, of course, and then short-wave beams direct. They use frequency-modulation plus what is probably variation in wave forms—like our vowel and consonant sounds in speech. We've never had any use for anything like that before, so our coils won't handle it, but we've developed a sort of code which isn't the language of either set of us. They shoot over short-wave stuff with frequency-modulation, and we record it as sound. When we shoot it back, it's reconverted into frequency-modulation."

The skipper said, frowning:

"Why wave-form changes in short waves? How do you know?"

"We showed them our recorder in the vision plates, and they showed us theirs. They record the frequency-modulation direct. I think," said Tommy carefully, "they don't use sound at all, even in speech. They've set up a communications room, and we've watched them in the act of communicating with us. They make no perceptible movement of anything that corresponds to a speech organ. Instead of a microphone, they simply stand near something that would work as a pick-up antenna. My guess, sir, is that they use microwaves for what you might call person-to-person conversation. I think they make short-wave trains as we make sounds."

The skipper stared at him:

"That means they have telepathy?"

"M-m-m. Yes, sir," said Tommy. "Also it means that we have telepathy too, as far as they are concerned. They're probably deaf. They've certainly no idea of using sound waves in air for communication. They simply don't use noises for any purpose."

The skipper stored the information away.

"What else?"

"Well, sir," said Tommy doubtfully, "I think we're all set. We agreed on arbitrary symbols for objects, sir, by way of the visiplates, and worked out relationships and verbs and so on with diagrams and pictures. We've a couple of thousand words that have mutual meanings. We set up an analyzer to sort out their short-wave groups, which we feed into a decoding machine. And then the coding end of the machine picks out recordings to make the wave groups we want to send back. When you're ready to talk to the skipper of the other ship, sir, I think we're ready."

"H-m-m. What's your impression of their psychology?" The skipper asked the question of the psychologist.

"I don't know, sir," said the psychologist harassedly. "They seem to be completely direct. But they haven't let slip even a hint of the tenseness we know exists. They act as if they were simply setting up a means of communication for friendly conversation. But there is . . . well . . . an overtone—"

The psychologist was a good man at psychological mensuration, which is a good and useful field. But he was not equipped to analyze a completely alien thought-pattern.

"If I may say so, sir—" said Tommy uncomfortably.

"What?"

"They're oxygen breathers," said Tommy, "and they're not too dissimilar to us in other ways. It seems to me, sir, that parallel evolution has been at work. Perhaps intelligence evolves in parallel lines, just as . . . well . . . basic bodily functions. I mean," he added conscientiously, "any living being of any sort must ingest, metabolize, and excrete. Perhaps any intelligent brain must perceive, apperceive, and find a personal reaction. I'm sure I've detected irony. That implies humor, too. In short, sir, I think they could be likable."

The skipper heaved himself to his feet.

"H-m-m." He said profoundly, "We'll see what they have to say."

He walked to the communications room. The scanner for the vision plate in the robot was in readiness. The skipper walked in front of it. Tommy Dort sat down at the coding machine and tapped at the keys. Highly improbable noises came from it, went into a microphone, and governed the frequency-modulation of a signal sent through space to the other spaceship. Almost instantly the vision screen which with one relay—in the robot—showed the interior of the other ship lighted up. An alien came before the scanner and seemed to look inquisitively out of the plate. He was extraordinarily manlike, but he was not human. The impression he gave was of extreme baldness and a somehow humorous frankness.

"I'd like to say," said the skipper heavily, "the appropriate things about this first contact of two dissimilar civilized races, and of my hopes that a friendly intercourse between the two peoples will result."

Tommy Dort hesitated. Then he shrugged and tapped expertly upon the coder. More improbable noises.

The alien skipper seemed to receive the message. He made a gesture which was wryly assenting. The decoder on the *Llanvabon* hummed to itself and word-cards dropped into the message frame. Tommy said dispassionately:

"He says, sir, 'That is all very well, but is there any way for us to let each other go home alive? I would be happy to hear of such a way if you can contrive one. At the moment it seems to me that one of us must be killed.' "

III

The atmosphere was of confusion. There were too many questions to be answered all at once. Nobody could answer any of them. And all of them had to be answered.

The *Llanvabon* could start for home. The alien ship might or might not be able to multiply the speed of light by one more unit than the Earth vessel. If it could, the *Llanvabon* would get close enough to Earth to reveal its destination—and then have to fight. It might or might not win. Even if it did win, the aliens might have a communication system by which the *Llanvabon's* destination might have been reported to the aliens' home planet before battle was joined. But the *Llanvabon* might lose in such a fight. If she was to be destroyed, it would be better to be destroyed here, without giving any clue to where human beings might be found by a forewarned, forearmed alien battle fleet.

The black ship was in exactly the same predicament. It, too, could start for home. But the *Llanvabon* might be faster, and an overdrive field can be trailed, if you set to work on it soon enough. The aliens, also, would not know whether the *Llanvabon* could report to its home base without returning. If the alien was to be destroyed, it also would prefer to fight it out here, so that it could not lead a probable enemy to its own civilization.

Neither ship, then, could think of flight. The course of the *Llanvabon* into the nebula might be known to the black ship, but it had been the end of a logarithmic curve, and the aliens could not know its properties. They could not tell from that from what direction the Earth ship had started. As of the moment, then, the two ships were even. But the question was and remained, "What now?"

There was no specific answer. The aliens traded information for information—and did not always realize what information they gave. The humans traded information for information—and Tommy Dort sweated blood in his anxiety not to give any clue to the whereabout of Earth.

The aliens saw by infrared light, and the vision plates and scanners in the robot communication-exchange had to adapt their respective images up and down an optical octave each, for them to have any meaning at all. It did not occur to the aliens that their eyesight told that their sun was a red dwarf, yielding light of greatest energy just below the part of the spectrum visible to human eyes. But after that fact was realized on the *Llanvabon,* it was realized that the aliens, also, should be able to deduce the Sun's spectral type by the light to which men's eyes were best adapted.

There was a gadget for the recording of short-wave trains which was as casually in use among the aliens as a sound-recorder is among men. The humans wanted that, badly. And the aliens were fascinated by the mystery of sound. They were able to perceive noise, of course, just as a man's palm will perceive infrared light by the sensation of heat it produces, but they could no more differentiate pitch or tone-quality than a man is able to distinguish between two frequencies of heat-radiation even half an octave apart. To them, the human science of sound was a remarkable discovery. They would find uses for noises which humans had never imagined—if they lived.

But that was another question. Neither ship could leave without first destroying the other. But while the flood of information was in passage, neither ship could afford to destroy the other. There was the matter of the outer coloring of the two ships. The *Llanvabon* was mirror-bright exteriorly. The alien ship was dead-black by visible light. It absorbed heat to perfection, and should radiate it away again as readily. But it did not. The black coating was not a "black body" color or lack of color. It was a perfect reflector of certain infrared wave lengths while simultaneously it fluoresced in just those wave bands. In practice, it absorbed the higher frequencies of heat, converted them to lower frequencies it did not radiate—and stayed at the desired temperature even in empty space.

Tommy Dort labored over his task of communications. He found the alien thought-processes not so alien that he could not follow them. The discussion of technics reached the matter of interstellar navigation. A star map was needed to illustrate the process. It would have been logical to use a star map from the chart room—but from a star map one could guess the point from which the map was projected. Tommy had a map made specially, with imaginary but convincing star images upon it. He translated direction for its use by the coder and decoder. In return, the aliens presented a star map of their own before the visiplate. Copied instantly by photograph, the Nav officers labored over it, trying to figure out from what spot in the galaxy the stars and Milky Way would show at such an angle. It baffled them.

It was Tommy who realized finally that the aliens had made a special star map for their demonstration too, and that it was a mirror-image of the faked map Tommy had shown them previously.

Tommy could grin, at that. He began to like these aliens. They were not human, but they had a very human sense of the ridiculous. In course of time Tommy essayed a mild joke. It had to be translated into code numerals, these into quite cryptic groups of short-wave, frequency-modulated impulses, and these went to the other ship and into heaven knew what to become intelligible. A joke which went through such formalities would not seem likely to be funny. But the aliens did see the point.

There was one of the aliens to whom communication became as normal a function as Tommy's own code-handlings. The two of them developed a quite insane friendship, conversing by coder, decoder and short-wave trains. When technicalities in the official messages grew too involved, that alien sometimes threw in strictly nontechnical interpolations akin to slang. Often, they cleared up the confusion. Tommy, for no reason whatever, had filed a code-name of "Buck" which the decoder picked out regularly when this particular operator signed his own symbol to a message.

In the third week of communication, the decoder suddenly presented Tommy with a message in the message frame.

You are a good guy. It is too bad we have to kill each other.—Buck.

Tommy had been thinking much the same thing. He tapped off the rueful reply:

We can't see any way out of it. Can you?

There was a pause, and the message frame filled up again.

If we could believe each other, yes, Our skipper would like it. But we can't believe you, and you can't believe us. We'd trail you home if we got a chance, and you'd trail us. But we feel sorry about it.—Buck.

Tommy Dort took the messages to the skipper.

"Look here, sir!" he said urgently. "These people are almost human, and they're likeable cusses."

The skipper was busy about his important task of thinking things to worry about, and worrying about them. He said tiredly:

"They're oxygen breathers. Their air is twenty-eight per cent oxygen instead of twenty, but they could do very well on Earth. It would be a highly desirable conquest for them. And we still don't know what weapons they've got or what they can develop. Would you tell them how to find Earth?"

"No-no," said Tommy, unhappily.

"They probably feel the same way," said the skipper dryly. "And if we did manage to make a friendly contact, how long would it stay friendly? If their weapons were inferior to ours, they'd feel that for their own safety they had to improve them. And we, knowing they were planning to revolt, would crush them while we could—for our own safety! If it happened to be the other way about, they'd have to smash us before we could catch up to them."

Tommy was silent, but he moved restlessly.

"If we smash this black ship and get home," said the skipper, "Earth Government will be annoyed if we don't tell them where it came from. But what can we do? We'll be lucky enough to get back alive with our warning. It isn't possible to get out of those creatures any more information than we give them, and we surely won't give them our address! We've run into them by accident. Maybe—if we smash this ship—there won't be another contact for thousands of years. And it's a pity, because trade could mean so much! But it takes two to make a peace, and we can't risk trusting them. The only answer is to kill them if we can, and if we can't, to make sure that when they kill us they'll find out nothing that will lead them to Earth. I don't like it," added the skipper tiredly, "but there simply isn't anything else to do!"

IV

On the *Llanvabon,* the technicians worked frantically in two divisions. One prepared for victory, and the other for defeat. The ones working for victory could do little. The main blasters were the only weapons with any promise. Their mountings were cautiously altered so that they were no longer fixed nearly dead ahead, with only a 5° traverse. Electronic controls which followed a radio-locator master-finder would keep them trained with absolute precision upon a given target regardless of its maneuverings. More; a hitherto unsung genius in the engine room devised a capacity-storage system by which the normal full-output of the ship's engines could be momentarily accumulated and released in surges of stored power far above normal. In theory, the range of the blasters should be multiplied and their destructive power considerably stepped up. But there was not much more that could be done.

The defeat crew had more leeway. Star charts, navigational instruments carrying telltale notations, the photographic record Tommy Dort had made on the six months' journey from Earth, and every other memorandum offering clues to Earth's position, were prepared for destruction. They were put in sealed files, and if any one of them was opened by one who did not know the exact complicated process, the contents of all the files would flash into ashes and the ashes be churned past any hope of restoration. Of course, if the *Llanvabon* should be victorious, a carefully not-indicated method of reopening them in safety would remain.

There were atomic bombs placed all over the hull of the ship. If its human crew should be killed without complete destruction of the ship, the atomic-power bombs should detonate if the *Llanvabon* were brought alongside the alien vessel. There were no ready-made atomic bombs on board, but there were small spare atomic-power units on board. It was not hard to trick them so that when they were turned on, instead of yielding a smooth flow of power they would explode. And four men of the earth ship's crew remained always in spacesuits with closed helmets, to fight the ship should it be punctured in many compartments by an unwarned attack.

Such an attack, however, would not be treacherous. The alien skipper had spoken frankly. His manner was that of one who wryly admits the uselessness of lies. The skipper and the *Llanvabon,* in turn, heavily admitted the virtue of frankness. Each insisted—perhaps truthfully—that he wished for friendship between the two races. But neither could trust the other not to make every conceivable effort to find out the one thing he needed most desperately to conceal—the location of his home planet. And neither dared believe that the other was unable to trail him and find out. Because each felt it his own duty to accomplish that unbearable—to the other—act, neither could risk the possible extinction of his race by trusting the other. They must fight because they could not do anything else.

They could raise the stakes of the battle by an exchange of information beforehand. But there was a limit to the stake either would put up. No information on weapons, population, or resources would be given by either. Not even the distance of their home bases from the Crab Nebula would be told. They exchanged information, to be sure, but they knew a battle to the death must follow, and each strove to represent his own civilization as powerful enough to give pause to the other's ideas of possible conquest—and thereby increased its appearance of menace to the other, and made battle more unavoidable.

It was curious how completely such alien brains could mesh, however. Tommy Dort, sweating over the coding and decoding machines, found a personal equation emerging from the at first stilted arrays of word-cards which arranged themselves. He had seen the aliens only in the vision screen, and then only in light at least one octave removed from the light they saw by. They, in turn, saw him very strangely, by transposed illumination from what to them would be the far ultraviolet. But their brains worked alike. Amazingly alike. Tommy Dort felt an actual sympathy and even something close to friendship for the gill-breathing, bald, and dryly ironic creatures of the black space vessel.

Because of that mental kinship he set up—though hopelessly—a sort of table of the aspects of the problem before them. He did not believe that the aliens had any instinctive desire to destroy man. In fact, the study of communications from the aliens had produced on the *Llanva-bon* a feeling of tolerance not unlike that between enemy soldiers during a truce on Earth. The men felt no enmity, and probably neither did the aliens. But they had to kill or be killed for strictly logical reasons.

Tommy's table was specific. He made a list of objectives the men must try to achieve, in the order of their importance. The first was the carrying back of news of the existence of the alien culture. The second was the location of that alien culture in the galaxy. The third was the carrying back of as much information as possible about that culture. The third was being worked on but the second was probably impossible. The first—and all—would depend on the result of the fight which must take place.

The aliens' objectives would be exactly similar, so that the men must prevent, first, news of the existence of Earth's culture from being taken back by the aliens, second, alien discovery of the location of Earth, and third, the acquiring by the aliens of information which would help them or encourage them to attack humanity. And again the third was in train, and the second was probably taken care of, and the first must await the battle.

There was no possible way to avoid the grim necessity of the destruction of the black ship. The aliens would see no solution to their problems but the destruction of the *Llanvabon*. But Tommy Dort, regarding his tabulation ruefully, realized that even complete victory would not be a perfect solution. The ideal would be for the *Llanvabon* to take back the alien ship for study. Nothing less would be a complete attainment of the third objective. But Tommy realized that he hated the idea of so complete a victory, even if it could be accomplished. He would hate the idea of killing even nonhuman creatures who understood a human joke. And beyond that, he would hate the idea of Earth fitting out a fleet of fighting ships to destroy an alien culture because its existence was dangerous. The pure accident of this encounter, between peoples who could like each other, had created a situation which could only result in wholesale destruction.

Tommy Dort soured on his own brain which could find no answer which would work. But there had to be an answer! The gamble was too big! It was too absurd that two spaceships should fight—neither one primarily designed for fighting—so that the survivor could carry back news which would set one side to frenzied preparation for war against the unwarned other.

If both races could be warned, though, and each knew that the other did not want to fight, and if they could communicate with each other but not locate each other until some grounds for mutual trust could be reached—

It was impossible. It was chimerical. It was a daydream. It was nonsense. But it was such luring nonsense that Tommy Dort ruefully put it into the coder to his gill-breathing friend Buck, then some hundred thousand miles off in the misty brightness of the nebula.

"Sure," said Buck, in the decoder's word-cards flicking into place in the message frame. "That is a good dream. But I like you and still won't believe you. If I said that first, you would like me but not believe me either. I tell you the truth more than you believe, and maybe you tell me the truth more than I believe. But there is no way to know. I am sorry."

Tommy Dort stared gloomily at the message. He felt a very horrible sense of responsibility. Everyone did, on the *Llanvabon*. If they failed in this encounter, the human race would run a very good chance of being exterminated in time to come. If they succeeded, the race of the aliens would be the one to face destruction, most likely. Millions or billions of lives hung upon the actions of a few men.

Then Tommy Dort saw the answer.

It would be amazing simple, if it worked. At worst it might give a partial victory to humanity and the *Llanvabon*. He sat quite still, not daring to move lest he break the chain of thought that followed the first tenuous idea. He went over and over it, excitedly finding objections here and meeting them, and overcoming impossibilities there. It was the answer! He felt sure of it.

He felt almost dizzy with relief when he found his way to the captain's room and asked leave to speak.

It is the function of a skipper, among others, to find things to worry about. But the *Llanvabon's* skipper did not have to look. In the three weeks and four days since the first contact with the alien black ship, the skipper's face had grown lined and old. He had not only the *Llanvabon* to worry about. He had all of humanity.

"Sir," said Tommy Dort, his mouth rather dry because of his enormous earnestness, "may I offer a method of attack on the black ship? I'll undertake it myself, sir, and if it doesn't work our ship won't be weakened."

The skipper looked at him unseeingly.

"The tactics are all worked out, Mr. Dort," he said heavily. "They're being cut on tape now, for the ship's handling. It's a terrible gamble, but it has to be done."

"I think," said Tommy carefully, "I've worked out a way to take the gamble out. Suppose, sir, we send a message to the other ship, offering—"

His voice went on in the utterly quiet captain's room, with the visiplates showing only a vast mistiness outside and the two fiercely burning stars in the nebula's heart.

V

The skipper himself went through the air lock with Tommy. For one reason, the action Tommy had suggested would need his authority behind it. For another, the skipper had worried more intensively than anybody else on the *Llanvabon*, and he was tired of it. If he went with Tommy, he would do the thing himself, and if he failed he would be the first one killed—and the tapes for the Earth ship's maneuvering were already fed into the control board and correlated with the mastertimer. If Tommy and the skipper were killed, a single control pushed home would throw the *Llanvabon* into the most furious possible all-out attack, which would end in the complete destruction of one ship or the other—or both. So the skipper was not deserting his post.

The outer airlock door swung wide. It opened upon that shining emptiness which was the nebula. Twenty miles away, the little round robot hung in space, drifting in an incredible orbit about the twin central suns, and floating ever nearer and nearer. It would never reach either of them, of course. The white star alone was so much hotter than Earth's sun that its heat-effect would produce Earth's temperature on an object five times as far from it as Neptune is from Sol. Even removed to the distance of Pluto, the little robot would be raised to cherry-red heat by the blazing white dwarf. And it could not possibly approach to the ninety-odd million miles which is the Earth's distance from the sun. So near, its metal would melt and boil away as vapor. But, half a light-year out, the bulbous object bobbed in emptiness.

The two spacesuited figures soared away from the *Llanvabon*. The small atomic drives which made them minute spaceships on their own had been subtly altered, but the change did not interfere with their functioning. They headed for the communication robot. The skipper, out in space, said gruffly:

"Mr. Dort, all my life I have longed for adventure. This is the first time I could ever justify it to myself."

His voice came through Tommy's space-phone receivers. Tommy wetted his lips and said:

"It doesn't seem like adventure to me, sir. I want terribly for the plan to go through. I thought adventure was when you didn't care."

"Oh, no," said the skipper. "Adventure is when you toss your life on the scales of chance and wait for the pointer to stop."

They reached the round object. They clung to its short, scannertipped horns.

"Intelligent, those creatures," said the skipper heavily. "They must want desperately to see more of our ship than the communications room, to agree to this exchange of visits before the fight."

"Yes sir," said Tommy. But privately, he suspected that Buck—his gill-breathing friend—would like to see him in the flesh before one or both of them died. And it seemed to him that between the two ships had grown up an odd tradition of courtesy, like that between two ancient knights before a tourney, when they admired each other wholeheartedly before hacking at each other with all the contents of their respective armories.

They waited.

Then, out of the mist, came two other figures. The alien spacesuits were also power-driven. The aliens themselves were shorter than men, and their helmet openings were coated with a filtering material to cut off visible and ultraviolet rays which to them would be lethal. It was not possible to see more than the outline of the heads within.

Tommy's helmet phone said, from the communications room on the *Llanvabon*:

"They say that their ship is waiting for you, sir. The airlock door will be open."

The skipper's voice said heavily:

"Mr. Dort, have you seen their spacesuits before? If so, are you sure they're not carrying anything extra, such as bombs?"

"Yes, sir," said Tommy. "We've showed each other our space equipment. They've nothing but regular stuff in view, sir."

The skipper made a gesture to the two aliens. He and Tommy Dort plunged on for the black vessel. They could not make out the ship very clearly with the naked eye, but directions for change of course came from the communication room.

The black ship loomed up. It was huge; as long as the *Llanvabon* and vastly thicker. The air lock did stand open. The two spacesuited men moved in and anchored themselves with magnetic-soled boots. The outer door closed. There was a rush of air and simultaneously the sharp quick tug of artificial gravity. Then the inner door opened.

All was darkness. Tommy switched on his helmet light at the same instant as the skipper. Since the aliens saw by infrared, a white light would have been intolerable to them. The men's helmet lights were, therefore, of the deep-red tint used to illuminate instrument panels so there would be no dazzling of eyes that must be able to detect the minutest specks of white light on a navigating vision plate. There were aliens waiting to receive them. They blinked at the brightness of the helmet lights. The space-phone receivers said in Tommy's ear:

"They say, sir, their skipper is waiting for you."

Tommy and the skipper were in a long corridor with a soft flooring underfoot. Their lights showed details of which every one was exotic.

"I think I'll crack my helmet, sir," said Tommy.

He did. The air was good. By analysis it was thirty percent oxygen instead of twenty for normal air on Earth, but the pressure was less. It felt just right. The artificial gravity, too, was less than that maintained on the *Llanvabon*. The home planet of the aliens would be smaller than Earth, and—by the infrared data—circling close to a nearly dead, dull-red sun. The air had smells in it. They were utterly strange, but not unpleasant.

An arched opening. A ramp with the same soft stuff underfoot. Lights which actually shed a dim, dull-red glow about. The aliens had stepped up some of their illuminating equipment as an act of courtesy. The light might hurt their eyes, but it was a gesture of consideration which made Tommy even more anxious for his plan to go through.

The alien skipper faced them, with what seemed to Tommy a gesture of wryly humorous deprecation. The helmet phones said:

"He says, sir, that he greets you with pleasure, but he has been able to think of only one way in which the problem created by the meeting of these two ships can be solved."

"He means a fight," said the skipper. "Tell him I'm here to offer another choice."

The *Llanvabon's* skipper and the skipper of the alien ship were face to face, but their communication was weirdly indirect. The aliens used no sound in communication. Their talk, in fact, took place on microwaves and approximated telepathy. But they could not hear, in any ordinary sense of the word, so the skipper's and Tommy's speech approached telepathy, too, as far as they were concerned. When the skipper spoke, his space phone sent his words back to the *Llanvabon*, where the words were fed into the coder and short-wave equivalents sent back to the black ship. The alien skipper's reply went to the *Llanvabon* and through the decoder, and was retransmitted by space phone in words read from the message frame. It was awkward, but it worked.

The short and stocky alien skipper paused. The helmet phones relayed his translated, soundless reply.

"He is anxious to hear, sir."

The skipper took off his helmet. He put his hands at his belt in a belligerent pose.

"Look here!" he said truculently to the bald, strange creature in the unearthly red glow before him. "It looks like we have to fight and one batch of us get killed. We're ready to do it if we have to. But if you win, we've got it fixed so you'll never find out where Earth is, and there's a good chance we'll get you anyhow! If we win, we'll be in the same fix. And if we win and go back home, our government will fit out a fleet and start hunting your planet. And if we find it we'll be ready to blast it to hell! If you win, the same thing will happen to us! And it's all foolishness! We've stayed here a month, and we've swapped information, and we don't hate each other. There's no reason for us to fight except for the rest of our respective races!"

The skipper stopped for breath, scowling. Tommy Dort inconspicuously put his own hands on the belt of his spacesuit. He waited, hoping desperately that the trick would work.

"He says, sir," reported the helmet phones, "that all you say is true. But that his race has to be protected, just as you feel that yours must be."

"Naturally!" said the skipper angrily, "but the sensible thing to do is to figure out how to protect it! Putting its future up as a gamble in a fight is not sensible. Our races have to be warned of each other's existence. That's true. But each should have proof that the other doesn't want to fight, but wants to be friendly. And we shouldn't be able to find each other, but we should be able to communicate with each other to work out grounds for a common trust. If our governments want to be fools, let them! But we should give them the chance to make friends, instead of starting a space war out of mutual funk!"

Briefly, the space phone said:

"He says that the difficulty is that of trusting each other now. With the possible existence of his race at stake, he cannot take any chance, and neither can you, of yielding an advantage."

"But my race," boomed the skipper, glaring at the alien captain, "my race has an advantage now. We came here to your ship in atom-powered spacesuits! Before we left, we altered the drives! We can set off ten pounds of sensitized fuel apiece, right here in this ship, or it can be set off by remote control from our ship! It will be rather remarkable if your fuel store doesn't blow up with us! In other words, if you don't accept my proposal for a commonsense approach to this predicament, Dort and I blow up in an atomic explosion, and your ship will be wrecked if not destroyed—and the *Llanvabon* will be attacking with everything its got within seconds after the blast goes off!"

The captain's room of the alien ship was a strange scene, with its dull-red illumination and the strange, bald, gill-breathing aliens watching the skipper and waiting for the inaudible translation of the harangue they could not hear. But a sudden tensity appeared in the air. A sharp, savage feeling of strain. The alien skipper made a gesture. The helmet phones hummed.

"He says, sir, what is your proposal?"

"Swap ships!" roared the skipper. "Swap ships and go on home! We can fix our instruments so they'll do no trailing, he can do the same with his. We'll each remove our star maps and records. We'll each dismantle our weapons. The air will serve, and we'll take their ship and they'll take ours, and neither one can harm or trail the other, and each will carry home more information than can be taken otherwise! We can agree on this same Crab Nebula as a rendezvous when the double-star has made another circuit, and if our people want to meet them they can do it, and if they are scared they can duck it! That's my proposal! And he'll take it, or Dort and I blow up their ship and the *Llanvabon* blasts what's left!"

He glared about him while he waited for the translation to reach the tense small stocky figures about him. He could tell when it came because the tenseness changed. The figures stirred. They made gestures. One of them made convulsive movements. It lay down on the soft floor and kicked. Others leaned against its walls and shook.

The voice in Tommy Dort's helmet phones had been strictly crisp and professional, before, but now it sounded blankly amazed.

"He says, sir, that it is a good joke. Because the two crew members he sent to our ship, and that you passed on the way, have their space-suits stuffed with atomic explosive too, sir, and he intended to make the very same offer and threat! Of course he accepts, sir. Your ship is worth more to him than his own, and his is worth more to you than the *Llanvabon*. It appears, sir, to be a deal."

Then Tommy Dort realized what the convulsive movements of the aliens were. They were laughter.

It wasn't quite as simple as the skipper had outlined it. The actual working-out of the proposal was complicated. For three days the crews of the two ships were intermingled, the aliens learning the workings of the *Llanvabon's* engines, and the men learning the controls of the black spaceship. It was a good joke—but it wasn't all a joke. There were men on the black ship, and aliens on the *Llanvabon,* ready at an instant's notice to blow up the vessels in question. And they would have done it in case of need, for which reason the need did not appear. But it was, actually, a better arrangement to have two expeditions return to two civilizations, under the current arrangement, than for either to return alone.

There were differences, though. There was some dispute about the removal of records. In most cases the dispute was settled by the destruction of the records. There was more trouble caused by the *Llanvabon's* books, and the alien equivalent of a ship's library, containing works which approximated the novels of Earth. But those items were valuable to possible friendship, because they would show the two cultures, each to the other, from the viewpoint of normal citizens and without propaganda.

But nerves were tense during those three days. Aliens unloaded and inspected the foodstuffs intended for the men on the black ship. Men transshipped the foodstuffs the aliens would need to return to their home. There were endless details, from the exchange of lighting equipment to suit the eyesight of the exchanging crews, to a final check-up of apparatus. A joint inspection party of both races verified that all detector devices had been smashed but not removed, so that they could not be used for trailing and had not been smuggled away. And of course, aliens were anxious not to leave any useful weapon on the black ship, nor the men upon the *Llanvabon*. It was a curious fact that each crew was best qualified to take exactly the measures which made an evasion of the agreement impossible.

There was a final conference before the two ships parted, back in the communication room of the *Llanvabon*.

"Tell the little runt," rumbled the *Llanvabon's* former skipper, "that he's got a good ship and he'd better treat her right."

The message frame flicked word-cards into position.

"I believe," it said on the alien skipper's behalf, "that your ship is just as good. I will hope to meet you here when the double star has turned one turn."

The last man left the *Llanvabon*. It moved away into the misty nebula before they had returned to the black ship. The vision plates in that vessel had been altered for human eye, and human crewmen watched jealously for any trace of their former ship as their new craft took a crazy, evading course to a remote part of the nebula. It came to a crevasse of nothingness, leading to the stars. It rose swiftly to clear space. There was the instant of breathlessness which the overdrive field produces as it goes on, and then the black ship whipped away into the void at many times the speed of light.

Many days later, the skipper saw Tommy Dort poring over one of the strange objects which were the equivalent of books. It was fascinating to puzzle over. The skipper was pleased with himself. The technicians of the *Llanvabon's* former crew were finding out desirable things about the ship almost momently. Doubtless the aliens were as pleased with their discoveries in the *Llanvabon*. But the black ship would be enormously worth while—and the solution that had been found was by any standard much superior even to a combat in which the Earthmen had been overwhelmingly victorious.

"Hm-m-m, Mr. Dort," said the skipper profoundly. "You've no equipment to make another photographic record on the way back. It was left on the *Llanvabon*. But fortunately, we have your record taken on the way out, and I shall report most favorably on your suggestion and your assistance in carrying it out. I think very well of you, sir."

"Thank you, sir," said Tommy Dort.

He waited. The skipper cleared his throat.

"You . . . ah . . . first realized the close similarity of mental processes between the aliens and ourselves," he observed. "What do you think of the prospects of a friendly arrangement if we keep a rendezvous with them at the nebula as agreed?"

"Oh, we'll get along all right, sir," said Tommy. "We've got a good start toward friendship. After all, since they see by infrared, the planets they'd want to make use of wouldn't suit us. There's no reason why we shouldn't get along. We're almost alike in psychology."

"Hm-m-m. Now just what do you mean by that?" demanded the skipper.

"Why, they're just like us, sir!" said Tommy. "Of course they breathe through gills and they see by heat waves, and their blood has a copper base instead of iron and a few little details like that. But otherwise we're just alike! There were only men in their crew, sir, but they have two sexes as we have, and they have families, and . . . er . . . their sense of humor—In fact—"

Tommy hesitated.

"Go on, sir," said the skipper.

"Well—There was the one I called Buck, sir, because he hasn't any name that goes into sound waves," said Tommy. "We got along very well. I'd really call him my friend, sir. And we were together for a couple of hours just before the two ships separated and we'd nothing in particular to do. So I became convinced that humans and aliens are bound to be good friends if they have only half a chance. You see, sir, we spent those two hours telling dirty jokes."

Questions for Discussion and Review

1. Compare and contrast this story and "Berom." What are the main points of similarity and difference, and what conclusions do you draw from them?

2. Why is the Crab nebula chosen for the story's setting?

3. What significance is there to the choice of the rotating stars within the nebula as a timepiece to set up a second meeting?

4. What purpose does the conclusion serve here? Is it effective and appropriate?

5. The potential for imagined wonder and awe seems especially pronounced in this story. What value do these elements have in this story?

6. Do you prefer Tommy Dort or Professor Yancey to Yaan, the pet humanoid of Clarke's "Encounter in the Dawn"? What do you suppose your preference may indicate about your own philosophy of the race?

Robots

Humanity's love affair with machines began with the wheel, a machine that performed work. The next step was the development of the water wheel and the windmill; engines that drive a machine by the application of natural forces. The development and use of machines may be considered an indicator of a sophisticated civilization. Most of the wonderful inventions of the Greeks and Romans were redeveloped after the Renaissance. Since then, a series of revolutions—scientific, industrial, and electronic—has increased the capacity to develop new machines. In turn, this stimulated the human imagination to think of machines that needed inventing.

Speculating about robots has a longer history than one might suppose. The mythic archetype may well be the story of Pygmalion and Galatea. The modern myth seems to have two forms. One is the creation of organic life as in *Frankenstein;* the other is the creation of mechanical, artificial life as in Karel Čapek's *R.U.R.* (*Rossum's Universal Robots,* 1921). The name "robot" comes from Čapek's play, and it is taken from the Czech word "robota," meaning forced labor. The key sciences involved in the two forms are biology, of course, in the creation, recreation, or control over organic life; and engineering, especially electrical engineering, which makes possible the mechanical servant, or robot. We will concentrate briefly on artificial, mechanical life.

The fascinating thing about robots is that they are machines made by human beings. They come to us perhaps out of the secret recesses of imagination, but they are also inventions of necessity. The mechanical Waldoes used in radiation laboratories were precursors of later more sophisticated robots. The mechanical servant was created to work beyond the range of human ability. If we ask ourselves what a robot should look like, we may think of *Star Wars'* R2D2 or perhaps some of the more tractorlike devices currently in use. But ideally, the model is the bilateral design of the manlike C3PO of *Star Wars.* As God created man in his image and likeness, so does man with his surrogate—the robot.

Robots may come in all shapes and sizes, but in fiction, at least, there are several familiar types. There are the mechanical, nonthinking servitor types seen in *Silent Running* (1972). There are the thinking robots of Irving Block's *Forbidden Planet* (1956) and Kurt Vonnegut's *The Sirens of Titan* (1950), whose powers are equal to or beyond those of human beings. There are even super robots, as in Harry Bates's story "Farewell to the Master" (1940), in which the robot turns out to be the master.

Another type that is related to robots is the *cyborg*—part human and part machine. Cyborgs are now living realities, and the prospects for the future are that human beings will acquire more and more mechanical parts to replace worn-out or defective organic ones. The recent popularity of the two television series "The Six Million Dollar Man" and "The Bionic Woman" emphasizes the great appeal that the idea holds for our culture. The possibilities for melodrama are especially attractive for a culture in which sports prowess and physical strength are so much admired. Imagine hitting a golf ball two miles! Nobody but the officials seems to be concerned that a two-mile drive would be definitely out of bounds, requiring one penalty stroke.

The next step up from robots is *androids,* synthetic human beings made from biological materials and possessing both intelligence and personality. Philip K. Dick's novel *Do Androids Dream of Electric Sheep?* (1968) offers one of the most satisfying treatments of the moral dimensions of android life. In practice, "robot" is the generic term for mechanically made, artificial creatures who are mobile and capable of performing a range of actions.

At this point, perhaps we should consult a psychologist to explain both the human desire to produce mechanical surrogates and the psychodynamics of the relationship between robots and masters. Come to think of it, though, most of the stories dealing with robots have speculated on one or both of these subjects and have gone on to explore the limitless application to those imagined versions of future life in which things are going to be different. The way the race relates to its mechanical offspring and the visions—nightmarish or utopian—which it associates with them tells us far more in the end about ourselves that it does about robots. But that is the way of SF. We discover ourselves in our science. We see ourselves in our machines. We come to know ourselves in our use of them and in our response to them. But even more than that, SF invites us to see with new eyes the pageants of past and future histories in which the destiny of the human race as a whole is involved. It tells us: "Look, for *this* is what you may make of yourselves as a species." Above all, it seems to be telling us that the human race has the choice and should exercise it knowingly and, we must hope, wisely.

Liar!

Isaac Asimov

Isaac Asimov was born January 2, 1920, in Petrovich, in the Soviet Union.
His family emigrated to America when he was three. He grew up in New
York City, where he earned graduate degrees in chemistry. After obtaining
his Ph.D. in 1948 from Columbia, he joined the faculty of Boston University Medical School. Meanwhile, as a young fan of SF, he joined the
faithful at the early prewar fan conventions. "Marooned Off Vesta" (1939)
was his first story, and it appeared in *Amazing Stories* (March 1939).
His association with John W. Campbell was to shape Asimov as a writer,
and his first story for *Astounding Science Fiction* appeared in July 1939.
Since then he has written countless short fiction and over two hundred
books of both fiction and nonfiction. Among the milestones in his career
have been the robot stories collected in *I, Robot* (1950) and *The Rest of
the Robots* (1964). He has won two Hugo Awards and a Nebula Award.
His *Foundation* trilogy (1951–1953) is highly regarded still after a
quarter-century. "Liar!" was first published in *Astounding Science Fiction*
(May 1941).

Asimov did not invent stories about robots—far from it—but he might as
well have. Even though Lester del Rey's "Helen O'Loy" (1938) had
appeared several years before Asimov published his first robot story, it
was the young Asimov who made his robots lovable (as opposed to love
objects) and created a future mythology to go along with the personality
of the friendly, eager-to-please "Robbies." Although Asimov himself has
revealed that John W. Campbell put the laws of robotics together, it was
Asimov who had written them into his stories. Since then, the Three Laws
of Robotics has become part of accepted SF robot lore.

The laws are especially important for this story, since the conclusion is
predicated on their operation. Here they are:

1. A robot may not injure a human being, or, through inaction, allow a
human being to come to harm.

2. A robot must obey the orders given it by human beings except where
such orders would conflict with the First Law.

3. A robot must protect its own existence as long as such protection does
not conflict with the First or Second Law.

"Liar!" is one of the early robot stories and does not fit the pattern
familiar to readers of the rest of the series. The customary plot has Dr.
Susan Calvin, a robot psychologist, investigating the apparent violation of
one of the inviolable three laws. Naturally, the puzzle is solved so as to
retain the integrity of the laws. In other stories, Dr. Calvin proves to be a
robotophile, finding in the Robbies qualities of loyalty and service that make
them a better species than their masters. Should we assume that the
doctor suffers from a guilt complex? In this story, Dr. Calvin proves that
she is more human being than scientist. She and the rest of the human
characters in the story also seem to prove the validity of Calvin's later

opinion of robots. As a case in point, this story shows us in a primarily comic vein the vanities and follies of certain members of genus *homo,* species *scientist.* Susan Calvin's revenge is supposed to be seen in the tradition of "Beware a woman scorned." But the men do not appear in any more flattering a light. As for the behavior of the robot, readers will have to make their own judgment. But remember: Although a robot can read thoughts, it does not foretell futures.

Alfred Lanning lit his cigar carefully, but the tips of his fingers were trembling slightly. His gray eyebrows hunched low as he spoke between puffs.

"It reads minds all right—damn little doubt about that! But why?" He looked at mathematician Peter Bogert. "Well?"

Bogert flattened his black hair down with both hands. "That was the thirty-fourth RB model we've turned out, Lanning. All the others were strictly orthodox."

The third man at the table frowned. Milton Ashe was the youngest officer of the U.S. Robot and Mechanical Men, Inc., and proud of his post.

"Listen, Bogert. There wasn't a hitch in the assembly from start to finish. I guarantee that."

Bogert's thick lips spread in a patronizing smile. "Do you? If you can answer for the entire assembly line, I recommend your promotion. By exact count, there are seventy-five thousand, two hundred and thirty-four operations necessary for the manufacture of a single positronic brain, each separate operation depending for successful completion upon any number of factors, from five to a hundred and five. If any one of them goes seriously wrong, the brain is ruined. I quote our own information folder, Ashe."

Milton Ashe flushed, but a fourth voice cut off his reply.

"If we're going to start by trying to fix the blame on one another, I'm leaving." Susan Calvin's hands were folded tightly in her lap, and the little lines about her thin, pale lips deepened. "We've got a mind-reading robot on our hands and it strikes me as rather important that we find out just why it reads minds. We're not going to do that by saying, 'Your fault! My fault!'"

Her cold gray eyes fastened upon Ashe and he grinned.

Lanning grinned too, and, as always at such times, his long white hair and shrewd little eyes made him the picture of a Biblical patriarch. "True for you, Dr. Calvin." His voice became suddenly crisp. "Here's everything in pill-concentrate form. We've produced a positronic brain of supposedly ordinary vintage that's got a remarkable property of being able to tune in on thought waves. It would mark the most important advance in robotics in decades if we knew how it happened. We don't, and we have to find out. Is that clear?"

"May I make a suggestion?" asked Bogert.

"Go ahead!"

"I'd say that until we do figure out the mess—and as a mathematician I expect it to be a very devil of a mess—we keep the existence of RB-34 a secret. I mean even from the other members of the staff. As heads of the departments, we ought not to find it an insoluble problem, and the fewer know about it . . ."

"Bogert is right," said Dr. Calvin. "Ever since the Interplanetary Code was modified to allow robot models to be tested in the plants before being shipped out to space, antirobot propaganda has increased. If any word leaks out about a robot being able to read minds before we can announce complete control of the phenomenon, pretty effective capital would be made out of it."

Lanning sucked at his cigar and nodded gravely. He turned to Ashe. "I think you said you were alone when you first stumbled on this thought-reading business."

"I'll say I was alone—I got the scare of my life. RB-34 had just been taken off the assembly table and they sent him down to me. Obermann was off somewheres, so I took him down to the testing rooms myself— at least I started to take him down." Ashe paused, and a tiny smile tugged at his lips. "Say, did any of you every carry on a thought conversation without knowing it?"

No one bothered to answer, and he continued. "You don't realize it at first, you know. He just spoke to me—as logically and sensibly as you can imagine—and it was only when I was most of the way down to the testing rooms that I realized that I hadn't said anything. Sure, I thought lots, but that isn't the same thing, is it? I locked that thing up and ran for Lanning. Having it walking beside me, calmly peering into my thoughts and picking and choosing among them, gave me the willies."

"I imagine it would," said Susan Calvin thoughtfully. Her eyes fixed themselves upon Ashe in an oddly intent manner. "We are so accustomed to considering our own thoughts private."

Lanning broke in impatiently. "Then only the four of us know. All right! We've got to go about this systematically. Ashe, I want you to check over the assembly line from beginning to end—everything. You're to eliminate all operations in which there was no possible chance of an error, and list all those where there were, together with its nature and possible magnitude."

"Tall order," grunted Ashe.

"Naturally! Of course you're to put the men under you to work on this—every single one if you have to, and I don't care if we go behind schedule, either. But they're not to know why, you understand."

"Hm-m-m, yes!" The young technician grinned wryly. "It's still a lulu of a job."

Lanning swiveled about in his chair and faced Calvin. "You'll have to tackle the job from the other direction. You're the robopsychologist of the plant, so you're to study the robot itself and work backward. Try to find out how he ticks. See what else is tied up with his telepathic powers, how far they extend, how they warp his outlook, and just exactly what harm it has done to his ordinary RB properties. You've got that?"

Lanning didn't wait for Dr. Calvin to answer. "I'll coordinate the work and interpret the findings mathematically." He puffed violently at his cigar and mumbled the rest through the smoke. "Bogert will help me there, of course."

Bogert polished the nails of one pudgy hand with the other and said blandly, "I daresay. I know a little in the line."

"Well! I'll get started." Ashe shoved his chair back and rose. His pleasantly youthful face crinkled in a grin. "I've got the darnedest job of any of us, so I'm getting out of here and to work." He left with a slurred "B' seein' ye!"

Susan Calvin answered with a barely perceptible nod, but her eyes followed him out of sight and she did not answer when Lanning grunted and said, "Do you want to go up and see RB-34 now, Dr. Calvin?"

RB-34's photoelectric eyes lifted from the book at the muffled sound of hinges turning, and he was upon his feet when Susan Calvin entered.

She paused to readjust the huge "No Entrance" sign upon the door and then approached the robot.

"I've brought you the texts upon hyperatomic motors, Herbie—a few, anyway. Would you care to look at them?"

RB-34—otherwise known as Herbie—lifted the three heavy books from her arms and opened to the title page of one.

"Hm-m-m! 'Theory of Hyperatomics.'" He mumbled inarticulately to himself as he flipped the pages, and then spoke with an abstracted air. "Sit down, Dr. Calvin! This will take me a few minutes."

The psychologist seated herself and watched Herbie narrowly as he took a chair at the other side of the table and went through the three books systematically.

At the end of half an hour he put them down. "Of course, I know why you brought these."

The corner of Dr. Calvin's lip twitched. "I was afraid you would. It's difficult to work with you, Herbie. You're always a step ahead of me."

"It's the same with these books, you know, as with the others. They just don't interest me. There's nothing to your textbooks. Your science is just a mass of collected data plastered together by makeshift theory— and all so incredibly simple that it's scarcely worth bothering about. It's your fiction that interests me. Your studies of the interplay of human motives and emotions . . ." His mighty hand gestured vaguely as he sought the proper words.

Dr. Calvin whispered, "I think I understand."

"I see into minds, you see," the robot continued, "and you have no idea how complicated they are. I can't begin to understand everything, because my own mind has so little in common with them—but I try, and your novels help."

"Yes, but I'm afraid that after going through some of the harrowing emotional experiences of our present-day sentimental novel"—there was a tinge of bitterness in her voice—"you find real minds like ours dull and colorless."

"But I don't!"

The sudden energy in the response brought the other to her feet. She felt herself reddening, and thought wildly, He must know!

Herbie subsided suddenly and muttered in a low voice from which the metallic timbre departed almost entirely, "But of course I know about it, Dr. Calvin. You think of it always, so how can I help but know?"

Her face was hard. "Have you—told anyone?"

"Of course not!" This with genuine surprise. "No one has asked me."

"Well, then," she flung out, "I suppose you think I am a fool."

"No! It is a normal emotion."

"Perhaps that is why it is so foolish." The wistfulness in her voice drowned out everything else. Some of the woman peered through the layer of doctorhood. "I am not what you would call—attractive."

"If you are referring to mere physical attraction, I couldn't judge. But I know, in any case, that there are other types of attraction."

"Nor young." Dr. Calvin had scarcely heard the robot.

"You are not yet forty." An anxious insistence had crept into Herbie's voice.

"Thirty-eight as you count the years; a shriveled sixty as far as my emotional outlook on life is concerned. Am I a psychologist or nothing?" She drove on with bitter breathlessness. "And he's barely thirty-five and looks and acts younger. Do you suppose he ever sees me as anything but . . . but what I am?"

"You are wrong!" Herbie's steel fist struck the plastic-topped table with a strident clang. "Listen to me—"

But Susan Calvin whirled on him now, and the hunted pain in her eyes became a blaze. "Why should I? What do you know about it all, anyway, you . . . you machine. I'm just a specimen to you; an interesting bug with a peculiar mind spread-eagled for inspection. It's a wonderful example of frustration, isn't it? Almost as good as your books." Her voice, emerging in dry sobs, choked into silence.

The robot cowered at the outburst. He shook his head pleadingly. "Won't you listen to me, please? I could help you if you would let me."

"How?" Her lips curled. "By giving me good advice?"

"No, not that. It's just that I know what other people think—Milton Ashe, for instance."

There was a long silence, and Susan Calvin's eyes dropped. "I don't want to know what he thinks," she gasped. "Keep quiet."

"I think you would want to know what he thinks."

Her head remained bent, but her breath came more quickly. "You are talking nonsense," she whispered.

"Why should I? I am trying to help. Milton Ashe's thought of you—" he paused.

And then the psychologist raised her head. "Well?"

The robot said quietly, "He loves you."

For a full minute Dr. Calvin did not speak. She merely stared. Then: "You are mistaken! You must be. Why should he?"

"But he does. A thing like that cannot be hidden, not from me."

"But I am so . . . so—" she stammered to a halt.

"He looks deeper than the skin, and admires intellect in others. Milton Ashe is not the type to marry a head of hair and a pair of eyes."

Susan Calvin found herself blinking rapidly and waited before speaking. Even then her voice trembled. "Yet he certainly never in any way indicated—"

"Have you ever given him a chance?"

"How could I? I never thought that—"

"Exactly!"

The psychologist paused in thought and then looked up suddenly. "A girl visited him here at the plant half a year ago. She was pretty, I suppose—blond and slim. And, of course, could scarcely add two and two. He spent all day puffing out his chest, trying to explain how a robot was put together." The hardness had returned. "Not that she understood! Who was she?"

Herbie answered without hesitation, "I know the person you are referring to. She is his first cousin, and there is no romantic interest there, I assure you."

Susan Calvin rose to her feet with a vivacity almost girlish. "Now, isn't that strange? That's exactly what I used to pretend to myself sometimes, though I never really thought so. Then it all must be true."

She ran to Herbie and seized his cold, heavy hand in both hers. "Thank you, Herbie." Her voice was an urgent, husky whisper. "Don't tell anyone about this. Let it be our secret—and thank you again." With that, and a convulsive squeeze of Herbie's unresponsive metal fingers, she left.

Herbie turned slowly to his neglected novel, but there was no one to read *his* thoughts.

Milton Ashe stretched slowly and magnificently, to the tune of cracking joints and a chorus of grunts, and then glared at Peter Bogert, Ph.D.

"Say," he said, "I've been at this for a week now with just about no sleep. How long do I have to keep it up? I thought you said the positronic bombardment in Vac Chamber D was the solution."

Bogert yawned delicately and regarded his white hands with interest. "It is. I'm on the track."

"I know what *that* means when a mathematician says it. How near the end are you?"

"It all depends."

"On what?" Ashe dropped into a chair and stretched his long legs out before him.

"On Lanning. The old fellow disagrees with me." He sighed. "A bit behind the times, that's the trouble with him. He clings to matrix mechanics as the all in all, and this problem calls for more powerful mathematical tools. He's so stubborn."

Ashe muttered sleepily, "Why not ask Herbie and settle the whole affair?"

"Ask the robot?" Bogert's eyebrows climbed.

"Why not? Didn't the old girl tell you?"

"You mean Calvin?"

"Yeah! Susie herself. That robot's a mathematical wiz. He knows all about everything plus a bit on the side. He does triple integrals in his head and eats up tensor analysis for dessert."

The mathematician stared skeptically, "Are you serious?"

"So help me! The catch is that the dope doesn't like math. He would rather read slushly novels. Honest! You should see the tripe Susie keeps feeding him: *Purple Passion* and *Love in Space*."

"Dr. Calvin hasn't said a word of this to us."

"Well, she hasn't finished studying him. You know how she is. She likes to have everything just so before letting out the big secret."

"She's told *you*."

"We sort of got to talking. I have been seeing a lot of her lately." He opened his eyes wide and frowned. "Say, Bogie, have you been noticing anything queer about the lady lately?"

Bogert relaxed into an undignified grin. "She's using lipstick, if that's what you mean."

"Hell, I know that. Rouge, powder and eye shadow too. She's a sight. But it's not that. I can't put my finger on it. It's the way she talks—as if she were happy about something." He thought a little and then shrugged.

The other allowed himself a leer, which, for a scientist past fifty, was not a bad job. "Maybe she's in love."

Ashe allowed his eyes to close again. "You're nuts, Bogie. You go speak to Herbie; I want to stay here and go to sleep."

"Right! Not that I particularly like having a robot tell me my job, nor that I think he can do it!"

A soft snore was his only answer.

Herbie listened carefully as Peter Bogert, hands in pockets, spoke with elaborate indifference.

"So there you are. I've been told you understand these things, and I am asking you more in curiosity than anything else. My line of reasoning, as I have outlined it, involves a few doubtful steps, I admit, which Dr. Lanning refuses to accept, and the picture is still rather incomplete."

The robot didn't answer, and Bogert said, "Well?"

"I see no mistake," Herbie studied the scribbled figures.

"I don't suppose you can go any further than that?"

"I daren't try. You are a better mathematician than I, and—well, I'd hate to commit myself."

There was a shade of complacency in Bogert's smile. "I rather thought that would be the case. It is deep. We'll forget it." He crumpled the sheets, tossed them down the waste shaft, turned to leave, and then thought better of it. "By the way . . ."

The robot waited.

Bogert seemed to have difficulty. "There is something—that is, perhaps you can—" He stopped.

Herbie spoke quietly. "Your thoughts are confused, but there is no doubt at all that they concern Dr. Lanning. It is silly to hesitate, for as soon as you compose yourself I'll know what it is you want to ask."

The mathematician's hand went to his sleek hair in the familiar smoothing gesture. "Lanning is nudging seventy," he said, as if that explained everything.

"I know that."

"And he's been director of the plant for almost thirty years."

Herbie nodded.

"Well, now—" Bogert's voice became ingratiating—"you would know whether . . . whether he's thinking of resigning. Health, perhaps, or some other—"

"Quite," said Herbie, and that was all.

"Well, do you know?"

"Certainly."

"Then—uh—could you tell me?"

"Since you ask, yes." The robot was quite matter-of-fact about it. "He has already resigned!"

"What!" The exclamation was an explosive, almost inarticulate sound. The scientist's large head hunched forward. "Say that again!"

"He has already resigned," came the quiet repetition, "but it has not yet taken effect. He is waiting, you see, to solve the problem of—er— myself. That finished, he is quite ready to turn the office of director over to his successor."

Bogert expelled his breath sharply. "And this successor? Who is he?" He was quite close to Herbie now, eyes fixed fascinatedly on those unreadable dull-red photoelectric cells that were the robot's eyes.

Words came slowly. "You are the next director."

And Bogert relaxed into a tight smile. "This is good to know. I've been hoping and waiting for this. Thanks, Herbie."

Peter Bogert was at his desk until five that morning, and he was back at nine. The shelf just over the desk emptied of its row of reference books and tables as he referred to one after the other. The pages of calculations before him increased microscopically, and the crumpled sheets at his feet mounted into a hill of scribbled paper.

At precisely noon he stared at the final page, rubbed a bloodshot eye, yawned and shrugged. "This is getting worse each minute. Damn!"

He turned at the sound of the opening door and nodded at Lanning, who entered, cracking the knuckles of one gnarled hand with the other.

The director took in the disorder of the room, and his eyebrows furrowed together.

"New lead?" he asked.

"No," came the defiant answer. "What's wrong with the old one?"

Lanning did not trouble to answer, nor to do more than bestow a single cursory glance at the top sheet upon Bogert's desk. He spoke through the flare of a match as he lit a cigar. "Has Calvin told you about the robot? It's a mathematical genius. Really remarkable."

The other snorted loudly. "So I've heard. But Calvin had better stick to robopsychology. I've checked Herbie on math, and he can scarcely struggle through calculus."

"Calvin didn't find it so."

"She's crazy."

"And I don't find it so." The director's eyes narrowed dangerously.

"You!" Bogert's voice hardened. "What are you talking about?"

"I've been putting Herbie through his paces all morning, and he can do tricks you never heard of."

"It that so?"

"You sound skeptical!" Lanning flipped a sheet of paper out of his vest pocket and unfolded it. "That's not my handwriting, is it?"

Bogert studied the large angular notation covering the sheet. "Herbie did this?"

"Right! And if you'll notice, he's been working on your time integration of Equation 22. It comes"—Lanning tapped a yellow fingernail upon the last step—"to the identical conclusion I did, and in a quarter the time. You had no right to neglect the Linger Effect in postronic bombardment."

"I didn't neglect it. For heaven's sake, Lanning, get it through your head that it would cancel out—"

"Oh, sure, you explained that. You used the Mitchell Translation Equation, didn't you? Well—it doesn't apply."

"Why not?"

"Because you've been using hyperimaginaries, for one thing."

"What's that to do with?"

"Mitchell's equation won't hold when—"

"Are you crazy? If you'll reread Mitchell's original paper in the *Transactions of the Far*—"

"I don't have to. I told you in the beginning that I didn't like his reasoning, and Herbie backs me in that."

"Well, then," Bogert shouted, "let that clockwork contraption solve the entire problem for you. Why bother with non-essentials?"

"That's exactly the point. Herbie can't solve the problem. And if he can't, we can't—alone. I'm submitting the entire question to the National Board. It's gotten beyond us."

Bogert's chair went over backward as he jumped up asnarl, face crimson. "You're doing nothing of the sort."

Lanning flushed in his turn. "Are you telling me what I can't do?"

"Exactly," was the gritted response. "I've got the problem beaten and you're not to take it out of my hands, understand? Don't think I don't see through you, you desiccated fossil. You'd cut your own nose off before you'd let me get the credit for solving robotic telepathy."

"You're a damned idiot, Bogert, and in one second I'll have you suspended for insubordination." Lanning's lower lip trembled with passion.

"Which is one thing you won't do, Lanning. You haven't any secrets with a mind-reading robot around so don't forget that I know all about your resignation."

The ash on Lanning's cigar trembled and fell and the cigar itself followed, "What . . . what—"

Bogert chuckled nastily. "And I'm the new director, be it understood. I'm very aware of that; don't think I'm not. Damn your eyes, Lanning, I'm going to give the orders about here or there will be the sweetest mess that you've ever been in."

Lanning found his voice and let it out with a roar. "You're suspended, d'ye hear? You're relieved of all duties. You're broken, do you understand?"

The smile on the other's face broadened. "Now, what's the use of that? You're getting nowhere. I'm holding the trumps. I know you've resigned. Herbie told me, and he got it straight from you."

Lanning forced himself to speak quietly. He looked an old, old man, with tired eyes peering from a face in which the red had disappeared, leaving the pasty yellow of age behind, "I want to speak to Herbie. He can't have told you anything of the sort. You're playing a deep game, Bogert, but I'm calling your bluff. Come with me."

Bogert shrugged. "To see Herbie? Good! Damned good!"

It was also precisely at noon that Milton Ashe looked up from his clumsy sketch and said, "You get the idea? I'm not too good at getting this down, but that's about how it looks. It's a honey of a house, and I can get it for next to nothing."

Susan Calvin gazed across at him with melting eyes. "It's really beautiful," she sighed. "I've often thought that I'd like to—" Her voice trailed away.

"Of course," Ashe continued briskly, putting away his pencil, "I've

got to wait for my vacation. Its only two weeks off, but this Herbie
business has everything up in the air." His eyes dropped to his fingernails. "Besides, there's another point—but it's a secret."

"Then don't tell me."

"Oh, I'd just as soon, I'm just busting to tell someone, and you're just
about the best—er—confidante I could find here." He grinned sheepishly.

Susan Calvin's heart bounded, but she did not trust herself to speak.

"Frankly"—Ashe scraped his chair closer and lowered his voice into
a confidential whisper—"the house isn't to be only for myself. I'm
getting married!" And then he jumped out of his seat. "What's the
matter?"

"Nothing!" The horrible spinning sensation had vanished, but it was
hard to get words out. "Married? You mean—"

"Why, sure! About time, isn't it? You remember that girl who was
here last summer. That's she! But you *are* sick. You—"

"Headache!" Susan Calvin motioned him away weakly. "I've . . . I've
been subject to them lately. I want to . . . to congratulate you, of
course. I'm very glad—" The inexpertly applied rouge made a pair
of nasty splotches upon her chalk-white face. Things had begun spinning again. "Pardon me—please—"

The words were a mumble, as she stumbled blindly out the door.
It had happened with the sudden castastrophe of a dream—and with
all the unreal horror of a dream.

But how could it be? Herbie had said—

And Herbie knew! He could see into minds!

She found herself leaning breathlessly against the door jamb, staring
into Herbie's metal face. She must have climbed the two flights of
stairs, but she had no memory of it. The distance had been covered in
an instant, as in a dream.

As in a dream!

And still Herbie's unblinking eyes stared into hers, and their dull
red seemed to expand into dimly shining nightmarish globes.

He was speaking, and she felt the cold glass pressing against her lips.
She swallowed and shuddered into a certain awareness of her surroundings.

Still Herbie spoke, and there was agitation in his voice—as if he were
hurt and frightened and pleading.

The words were beginning to make sense. "This is a dream," he
was saying, "and you mustn't believe in it. You'll wake into the real
world soon and laugh at yourself. He loves you, I tell you. He does,
he does! But not here! Not now! This is an illusion."

Susan Calvin nodded, her voice a whisper. "Yes! Yes!" She was
clutching Herbie's arm, clinging to it, repeating over and over, "It
isn't true, is it? It isn't, is it?"

Just how she came to her senses, she never knew—but it was like passing from a world of misty unreality to one of harsh sunlight. She pushed him away from her, pushed hard against that steely arm, and her eyes were wide.

"What are you trying to do?" Her voice rose to a harsh scream. "What are you trying to do?"

Herbie backed away. "I want to help."

The psychologist stared. "Help? By telling me this is a dream? By trying to push me into schizophrenia?" A hysterical tenseness seized her. "This is no dream! I wish it were!" She drew her breath sharply. "Wait! Why . . . why, I understand. Merciful heavens, it's so obvious."

There was horror in the robot's voice. "I had to!"

"And I believed you! I never thought—"

Loud voices outside the door brought her to a halt. She turned away, fists clenching spasmodically, and when Bogert and Lanning entered she was at the far window. Neither of the men paid her the slightest attention.

They approached Herbie simultaneously, Lanning angry and impatient, Bogert coolly sardonic. The director spoke first.

"Here, now, Herbie. Listen to me!"

The robot brought his eyes sharply down upon the aged director. "Yes, Dr. Lanning."

"Have you discussed me with Dr. Bogert?"

"No, sir." The answer came slowly, and the smile on Bogert's face flashed off.

"What's that?" Bogert shoved in ahead of his superior and straddled the ground before the robot. "Repeat what you told me yesterday."

"I said that—" Herbie fell silent. Deep within him his metallic diaphragm vibrated in soft discords.

"Didn't you say he had resigned?" roared Bogert. "Answer me!"

Bogert raised his arm frantically, but Lanning pushed him aside. "Are you trying to bully him into lying?"

"You heard him, Lanning. He began to say 'Yes' and stopped. Get out of my way! I want the truth out of him, understand!"

"I'll ask him!" Lanning turned to the robot. "All right, Herbie, take it easy. Have I resigned?"

Herbie stared, and Lanning repeated anxiously, "Have I resigned?" There was the faintest trace of a negative shake of the robot's head. A long wait produced nothing further.

The two men looked at each other, and the hostility in their eyes was all but tangible.

"What the devil," blurted Bogert, "has the robot gone mute? Can't you speak, you monstrosity?"

"I can speak," came the ready answer.

"Then answer the question. Didn't you tell me Lanning had resigned? Hasn't he resigned?"

And again there was nothing but dull silence, until from the end of the room, Susan Calvin's laugh rang out suddenly, high-pitched and semihysterical.

The two mathematicians jumped, and Bogert's eyes narrowed. "You here? What's so funny?"

"Nothing's funny." Her voice was not quite natural. "It's just that I'm not the only one that's been caught. There's irony in three of the greatest experts in robotics in the world falling into the same elementary trap, isn't there?" Her voice faded, and she put a pale hand to her forehead, "But it isn't funny!"

This time the look that passed between the two men was one of raised eyebrows. "What trap are you talking about?" asked Lanning stiffly. "Is something wrong with Herbie?"

"No." She approached them slowly. "Nothing is wrong with him— only with us." She whirled suddenly and shrieked at the robot, "Get away from me! Go to the other end of the room and don't let me look at you."

Herbie cringed before the fury of her eyes and stumbled away in a clattering trot.

Lanning's voice was hostile. "What is all this, Dr. Calvin?"

She faced them and spoke sarcastically. "Surely you know the fundamental First Law of Robotics."

The other two nodded together. "Certainly," said Bogert irritably. "A robot may not injure a human being or, through inaction, allow him to come to harm."

"How nicely put," sneered Calvin. "But what kind of harm?"

"Why—any kind."

"Exactly! Any kind! But what about hurt feelings? What about deflation of one's ego? What about the blasting of one's hopes? Is that injury?"

Lanning frowned. "What would a robot know about—" And then he caught himself with a gasp.

"You've caught on, have you? *This* robot reads minds. Do you suppose it doesn't know everything about mental injury? Do you suppose that if asked a question it wouldn't give exactly that answer that one wants to hear? Wouldn't any other answer hurt us, and wouldn't Herbie know that?"

"Good heavens!" muttered Bogert.

The psychologist cast a sardonic glance at him. "I take it you asked him whether Lanning had resigned. You wanted to hear that he had resigned and so that's what Herbie told you."

"And I suppose that is why," said Lanning tonelessly, "it would not answer a little while ago. It couldn't answer either way without hurting one of us."

There was a short pause in which the men looked thoughtfully across the room at the robot, crouching in the chair by the bookcase, head resting in one hand.

Susan Calvin stared steadfastly at the floor. "He knew of all this.

That . . . that devil knows everything—including what went wrong in his assembly." Her eyes were dark and brooding.

Lanning looked up. "You're wrong there, Dr. Calvin. He doesn't know what went wrong. I asked him."

"What does that mean?" cried Calvin. "Only that you didn't want him to give you the solution. It would puncture your ego to have a machine do what you couldn't. Did you ask him?" she shot at Bogert.

"In a way." Bogert coughed and reddened. "He told me he knew very little about mathematics."

Lanning laughed, not very loudly and the psychologist smiled caustically. She said, "I'll ask him! A solution by him won't hurt my ego." She raised her voice into a cold, imperative "Come here!"

Herbie rose and approached with hesitant steps.

"You know, I suppose," she continued, "just exactly at what point in the assembly an extraneous factor was introduced or an essential one left out."

"Yes," said Herbie, in tones barely heard.

"Hold on," broke in Bogert angrily. "That's not necessarily true. You want to hear that, that's all."

"Don't be a fool," replied Calvin. "He certainly knows as much math as you and Lanning together, since he can read minds. Give him his chance."

The mathematician subsided, and Calvin continued, "All right, then, Herbie, give! We're waiting." And in an aside, "Get pencils and paper, gentlemen."

But Herbie remained silent, and there was triumph in the psychologist's voice. "Why don't you answer, Herbie?"

The robot blurted out suddenly, "I cannot. You know I cannot! Dr. Bogert and Dr. Lanning don't want me to."

"They want the solution."

"But not from me."

Lanning broke in, speaking slowly and distinctly. "Don't be foolish, Herbie. We do want you to tell us."

Bogert nodded curtly.

Herbie's voice rose to wild heights. "What's the use of saying that? Don't you suppose that I can see past the superficial skin of your mind? Down below, you don't want me to. I'm a machine, given the imitation of life only by virtue of the positronic interplay in my brain—which is man's device. You can't lose face to me without being hurt. That is deep in your mind and won't be erased. I can't give the solution."

"We'll leave," said Dr. Lanning. "Tell Calvin."

"That would make no difference," cried Herbie, "since you would know anyway that it was I that was supplying the answer."

Calvin resumed, "But you understand, Herbie, that despite that, Doctors Lanning and Bogert want that solution."

"By their own efforts!" insisted Herbie.

"But they want it, and the fact that you have it and won't give it hurts them. You see that, don't you?"

"Yes! Yes!"

"And if you tell them that will hurt them, too."

"Yes! Yes!" Herbie was retreating slowly, and step by step Susan Calvin advanced. The two men watched in frozen bewilderment.

"You can't tell them," droned the psychologist slowly, "because that would hurt and you mustn't hurt. But if you don't tell them, you hurt, so you must tell them. And if you do, you will hurt and you musn't, so you can't tell them; but if you don't, you hurt, so you must; but if you do, you hurt, so you mustn't; but if you don't, you hurt, so you must; but if you do, you—"

Herbie was up against the wall, and here he dropped to his knees. "Stop!" he shrieked. "Close your mind! It is full of pain and frustration and hate! I didn't mean it, I tell you! I tried to help! I told you what you wanted to hear. I had to!"

The psychologist paid no attention. "You must tell them, but if you do, you hurt, so you musn't; but if you don't, you hurt, so you must; but—"

And Herbie screamed!

It was like the whistling of a piccolo many times magnified—shrill and shriller till it keened with the terror of a lost soul and filled the room with the piercingness of itself.

And when it died into nothingness, Herbie collapsed into a huddled heap of motionless metal.

Bogert's face was bloodless. "He's dead!"

"No!" Susan Calvin burst into body-racking gusts of wild laughter. "Not dead—merely insane. I confronted him with the insoluble dilemma, and he broke down. You can scrap him now—because he'll never speak again."

Lanning was on his knees beside the thing that had been Herbie. His fingers touched the cold, unresponsive metal face and he shuddered. "You did that on purpose." He rose and faced her, face contorted.

"What if I did? You can't help it now." And in a sudden access of bitterness: "He deserved it."

The director seized the paralyzed motionless Bogert by the wrist. "What's the difference. Come, Peter." He sighed. "A thinking robot of this type is worthless, anyway." His eyes were old and tired, and he repeated, "Come, Peter!"

It was minutes after the two scientists left that Dr. Susan Calvin regained part of her mental equilibrium. Slowly her eyes turned to the living-dead Herbie, and the tightness returned to her face. Long she stared while the triumph faded and the helpless frustration returned—and of all her turbulent thoughts only one infinitely bitter word passed her lips:

"*Liar!*"

Questions for Discussion and Review

1. If Robbie could have foretold the future, would that have made a difference in his actions?

2. How would you describe the comic element in this story?

3. Leaving aside the conclusion, what is wrong with the attitudes of the human beings toward the robot?

4. Is the title of this story aptly chosen? Explain.

Happy Ending

Henry Kuttner

Henry Kuttner (1914–1958) was born in Los Angeles. Except for a tour of duty in the military, he was a professional writer. He made his debut in *Weird Tales* in 1936 with "The Graveyard Rats," a story that showed the early influence of H. P. Lovecraft: Kuttner wrote both fantasy and SF with equal ease. During the 1930s and 1940s he experimented with a variety of fantasy and SF formulas, gradually developing a characteristic style and manner of treatment. The hallmark of his best stories seems to be a combination of inventiveness, ingenuity of plotting, and an ironic angle of vision as seen in stories like "Private Eye" (1949—as Lewis Padgett), "Don't Look Now" (1948), and "A Gnome There Was" (1940). As a writer, Kuttner brought urbanity and wit to the writing of SF, two qualities often in short supply. In 1940 he married Catherine L. Moore, also an SF writer, with whom he collaborated under the pseudonym Lawrence O'Donnell. *Robots Have No Tails* (1952) is a collection of the five stories in the Galloway Gallegher series that narrates the exploits of an eccentric robot with an independent mind. A two-volume collection of stories, *The Best of Henry Kuttner*, appeared in 1955–1956 and is the basis for a later, one-volume edition. "Happy Ending" first appeared in *Thrilling Wonder Stories* (August 1948).

This is not just another robot story. To the robot premise Kuttner adds elements of the time-travel story and the psi story (thought control and parapsychology) to create an ingenious pastiche. In this case, our author develops a point of view that is itself a kind of fiction, the fiction of James Kelvin, whose success story this is. Or is it? In any case, it makes an amusing contrast with Asimov's "Liar!"

For openers, we begin with an oddity of storytelling, because we start with the obligatory happy ending and conclude with the beginning. It is important that readers understand the consequences of this technique. Primarily it establishes the credibility of the narrator. It leads us to believe that the robot is a mind reader, as is Robbie in Asimov's story. This one is no fortuneteller either, although he pretends to be. As he says of astrology, it is a little out of his line. But he does offer a "logical, scientific method of attaining health, fame, and fortune." To that end, the robot produces the proverbial little black box that will supply Kelvin with the means of accomplishing the desired goal. The box is a decoy, but it permits Kelvin to communicate with the mind of a man, Quarra Vee, who lives in a distant future time. The disparity between the two worlds is such that the only form of successful telepathy between them is a sort of problem-solving inquiry on a subconscious level from present into future. It is not until the resolution that we learn the true identity of Quarra Vee and Tarn and just what sort of happy ending has had its beginning.

This is the way the story ended:

James Kelvin concentrated very hard on the thought of the chemist with the red moustache who had promised him a million dollars. It was simply a matter of tuning in on the man's brain, establishing a rapport. He had done it before. Now it was more important than ever that he do it this one last time. He pressed the button on the gadget the robot had given him, and thought hard.

Far off, across limitless distances, he found the rapport.

He clamped on the mental tight beam.

He rode it . . .

The red-mustached man looked up, gaped, and grinned delightedly.

"So there you are!" he said. "I didn't hear you come in. Good grief, I've been trying to find you for two weeks."

"Tell me one thing quick," Kelvin said. "What's your name?"

"George Bailey. Incidentally, what's yours?"

But Kelvin didn't answer. He had suddenly remembered the other thing the robot had told him about that gadget which established rapport when he pressed the button. He pressed it now—and nothing happened. The gadget had gone dead. Its task was finished, which obviously meant he had at last achieved health, fame and fortune. The robot had warned him, of course. The thing was set to do one specialized job. Once he got what he wanted, it would work no more.

So Kelvin got the million dollars.

And he lived happily ever after . . .

This is the middle of the story:

As he pushed aside the canvas curtain something—a carelessly hung rope—swung down at his face, knocking the horn-rimmed glasses askew. Simultaneously a vivid bluish light blazed into his unprotected eyes. He felt a curious, sharp sense of disorientation, a shifting motion that was almost instantly gone.

Things steadied before him. He let the curtain fall back into place, making legible again the painted inscription: HOROSCOPES—LEARN YOUR FUTURE—and he stood staring at the remarkable horomancer.

It was a—oh, impossible!

The robot said in a flat, precise voice, "You are James Kelvin. You are a reporter. You are thirty years old, unmarried, and you came to Los Angeles from Chicago today on the advice of your physician. Is that correct?"

In his astonishment Kelvin called on the Deity. Then he settled his glasses more firmly and tried to remember an expose of charlatans he had once written. There was some obvious way they worked things like this, miraculous as it sounded.

The robot looked at him impassively out of its faceted eye.

"On reading your mind," it continued in the pedantic voice, "I find this is the year Nineteen Forty-nine. My plans will have to be revised.

I had meant to arrive in the year Nineteen Seventy. I will ask you to assist me."

Kelvin put his hands in his pockets and grinned.

"With money, naturally," he said. "You had me going for a minute. How do you do it, anyhow? Mirrors? Or like Maelzel's chess player?"

"I am not a machine operated by a dwarf, nor am I an optical illusion," the robot assured him. "I am an artificially created living organism, originating at a period far in your future."

"And I'm not the sucker you take me for," Kelvin remarked pleasantly. "I came in here to—"

"You lost your baggage checks," the robot said. "While wondering what to do about it, you had a few drinks and took the Wilshire bus at exactly—exactly eight-thirty-five post meridian."

"Lay off the mind-reading," Kelvin said. "And don't tell me you've been running this joint very long with a line like that. The cops would be after you. *If* you're a real robot, ha, ha."

"I have been running this joint," the robot said, "for approximately five minutes. My predecessor is unconscious behind that chest in the corner. Your arrival here was sheer coincidence." It paused very briefly, and Kelvin had the curious impression that it was watching to see if the story so far had gone over well.

The impression was curious because Kelvin had no feeling at all that there was a man in the large, jointed figure before him. If such a thing as a robot were possible, he would have believed implicitly that he confronted a genuine specimen. Such things being impossible, he waited to see what the gimmick would be.

"My arrival here was also accidental," the robot informed him. "This being the case, my equipment will have to be altered slightly. I will require certain substitute mechanisms. For that, I gather as I read your mind, I will have to engage in your peculiar barter system of economics. In a word, coinage or gold or silver certificates will be necessary. Thus I am—temporarily—horomancer."

"Sure, sure," Kelvin said. "Why not a simple mugging? If you're a robot, you could do a super-mugging job with a quick twist of the gears."

"It would attract attention. Above all, I require secrecy. As a matter of fact, I am—"

The robot paused, searched Kelvin's brain for the right phrase, and said, "—on the lam. In my era, time-traveling is strictly forbidden, even by accident, unless government-sponsored."

There was a fallacy there somewhere, Kelvin thought, but he couldn't quite spot it. He blinked at the robot intently. It looked pretty unconvincing.

"What proof do you need?" the creature asked. "I read your brain the minute you came in, didn't I? You must have felt the temporary amnesia as I drew out the knowledge and then replaced it."

"So that's what happened," Kelvin said. He took a cautious step backward. "Well, I think I'll be getting along."

"Wait," the robot commanded. "I see you have begun to distrust me. Apparently you now regret having suggested a mugging job. You fear I may act on the suggestion. Allow me to reassure you. It is true that I could take your money and assure secrecy by killing you, but I am not permitted to kill humans. The alternative is to engage in the barter system. I can offer you something valuable in return for a small amount of gold. Let me see." The faceted gaze swept around the tent, dwelt piercingly for a moment on Kelvin. "A horoscope," the robot said. "It is supposed to help you achieve health, fame and fortune. Astrology, however, is out of my line. I can merely offer a logical scientific method of attaining the same results."

"Uh-hugh," Kelvin said skeptically. "How much? And why haven't *you* used that method?"

"I have other ambitions," the robot said in a cryptic manner. "Take this." There was a brief clicking. A panel opened in the metallic chest. The robot extracted a small, flat case and handed it to Kelvin, who automatically closed his fingers on the cold metal.

"Be careful. Don't push that button until—"

But Kelvin had pushed it. . . .

He was driving a figurative car that had got out of control. There was somebody else inside his head. There was a schizophrenic, double-tracked locomotive that was running wild and his hand on the throttle couldn't slow it down an instant. His mental steering-wheel had snapped.

Somebody else was thinking for him!

Not quite a human being. Not quite sane, probably, from Kelvin's standards. But awfully sane from his own. Sane enough to have mastered the most intricate principles of non-Euclidean geometry in the nursery.

The senses get synthesized in the brain into a sort of common language, a master-tongue. Part of it was auditory, part pictorial, and there were smells and tastes and tactile sensations that were sometimes familiar and sometimes spiced with the absolutely alien. And it was chaotic.

Something like this, perhaps. . . .

"—Big Lizards getting too numerous this season—tame threvvars have the same eyes not on Callisto though—vacation soon—preferably galactic—solar system claustroprobic—byanding tomorrow if square rootola and upsliding three—"

But that was merely the word-symbolism. Subjectively, it was far more detailed and very frightening. Luckily, reflex had lifted Kelvin's finger from the button almost instantly, and he stood there motionless, shivering slightly.

He was afraid now.

The robot said, "You should not have begun the rapport until I instructed you. Now there will be danger. Wait." His eye changed color. "Yes . . . there is . . . Tharn, yes. Beware of Tharn."

"I don't want any part of it," Kelvin said quickly. "Here, take this thing back."

"Then you will be unprotected against Tharn. Keep the device. It will, as I promised, ensure your health, fame and fortune, far more effectively than a—a horoscope."

"No thanks. I don't know how you managed that trick—sub-sonics, maybe, but I don't—"

"Wait," the robot said. "When you pressed that button, you were in the mind of someone who exists very far in the future. It created a temporal rapport. You can bring about that rapport any time you press the button."

"Heaven forfend," Kelvin said, still sweating a little.

"Consider the opportunities. Suppose a troglodyte of the far past had access to your brain? He could achieve anything he wanted."

It had become important, somehow, to find a logical rebuttal to the robot's arguments. "Like St. Anthony—or was it Luther?—arguing with the devil?" Kelvin thought dizzily. His headache was worse, and he suspected he had drunk more than was good for him. But he merely said:

"How could a troglodyte understand what's in my brain? He couldn't apply the knowledge without the same conditioning I've had."

"Have you ever had sudden and apparently illogical ideas? Compulsions? So that you seem forced to think of certain things, count up to certain numbers, work out particular problems? Well, the man in the future on whom my device is focused, doesn't know he's en rapport with you, Kelvin. But he's vulnerable to compulsions. All you have to do is concentrate on a problem and then press the button. Your rapport will be compelled—illogically, from his viewpoint—to solve that problem. And you'll be reading his brain. You'll find out how it works. There are limitations, you'll learn those too. And the device will ensure health, wealth and fame for you."

"It would ensure anything, if it really worked that way. I could do anything. That's why I'm not buying!"

"I said there were limitations. As soon as you've successfully achieved health, fame, and fortune, the device will become useless. I've taken care of that. But meanwhile you can use it to solve all your problems by tapping the brain of the more intelligent specimen in the future. The important point is to concentrate on your problems *before* you press the button. Otherwise you may get more than Tharn on your track."

"Tharn? What—"

"I think an—an android," the robot said, looking at nothing. "An artificial human . . . However, let us consider my own problem. I need a small amount of gold."

"So that's the kicker," Kelvin said, feeling oddly relieved. He said, "I haven't got any."

"Your watch."

Kelvin jerked his arm so that his wrist-watch showed. "Oh, no. That watch cost plenty."

"All I need is the gold-plating," the robot said, shooting out a reddish ray from its eye. "Thank you." The watch was now dull gray metal.

"Hey!" Kelvin cried.

"If you use the rapport device, your health, fame and fortune will be assured," the robot said rapidly. "You will be as happy as any man of this era can be. It will solve all your problems—including Tharn. Wait a minute." The creature took a backward step and disappeared behind a hanging Oriental rug that had never been east of Peoria.

There was silence.

Kelvin looked from his altered watch to the flat, enigmatic object in his palm. It was about two inches by two inches, and no thicker than a woman's vanity-case, and there was a sunken push-button on its side.

He dropped it into his pocket and took a few steps forward. He looked behind the pseudo-Oriental rug, to find nothing except emptiness and a flapping slit cut in the canvas wall of the booth. The robot, it seemed, had taken a powder. Kelvin peered out through the slit. There was the light and sound of Ocean Park amusement pier, that was all. And the silvered, moving blackness of the Pacific Ocean, stretching to where small lights showed Malibu far up the invisible curve of the coastal cliffs.

So he came back inside the booth and looked around. A fat man in a swami's costume was unconscious behind the carved chest the robot had indicated. His breath, plus a process of deduction, told Kelvin that the man had been drinking.

Not knowing what else to do, Kelvin called on the Deity again. He found suddenly that he was thinking about someone or something called Tharn, who was an android.

Horomancy . . . time . . . rapport . . . *no!* Protective disbelief slid like plate armor around his mind. A practical robot couldn't be made. He knew that. He'd have heard—he was a reporter, wasn't he?

Sure, he was.

Desiring noise and company, he went along to the shooting gallery and knocked down a few ducks. The flat case burned in his pocket. The dully burnished metal of his wrist-watch burned in his memory. The remembrance of that drainage from his brain, and the immediate replacement burned in his mind. Presently bar whiskey burned in his stomach.

He'd left Chicago because of sinusitis, recurrent and annoying. Ordinary sinusitis. Not schizophrenia or hallucinations or accusing voices coming from the walls. Not because he had been seeking bats or robots. That thing hadn't really been a robot. It all had a perfectly natural explanation. Oh, sure.

Health, fame and fortune. And if—

THARN!

The thought crashed with thunderbolt impact into his head.

And then another thought: I *am* going nuts!

A silent voice began to mutter insistently, over and over, "Tharn—Tharn—Tharn—Tharn—"

And another voice, the voice of sanity and safety, answered it and drowned it out. Half aloud, Kelvin muttered:

"I'm James Noel Kelvin. I'm a-reporter—special features, leg work, rewrite. I'm thirty years old, unmarried, and came to Los Angeles to-day and lost my baggage checks and—and I'm going to have another drink and find a hotel. Anyhow, the climate seems to be curing my sinusitis."

Tharn, the muffled drum-beat said almost below the threshold of realization. *Tharn, Tharn.*

Tharn.

He ordered another drink and reached in his pocket for a coin. His hand touched the metal case. And simultaneously he felt a light pressure on his shoulder.

Instinctively he glanced around. It was a seven-fingered, spidery hand tightening—hairless, without nails—and white as smooth ivory.

The one, overwhelming necessity that sprang into Kelvin's mind was a simple longing to place as much space as possible between himself and the owner of that disgusting hand. It was a vital requirement, but one difficult of fulfillment, a problem that excluded everything else from Kelvin's thoughts. He knew, vaguely, that he was gripping the flat case in his pocket as though that could save him, but all he was thinking was:

I've got to get away from here.

The monstrous, alien thoughts of someone in the future spun him insanely along their current. It could not have taken a moment while that skilled, competent, trained mind, wise in the lore of an unthinkable future, solved the random problem that had come so suddenly, with such curious compulsion.

Three methods of transportation were simultaneously clear to Kelvin. Two he discarded; motorplats were obviously inventions yet to come, and quirling—involving, as it did, a sensory coil-helmet—was beyond him. But the third method—

Already the memory was fading. And that hand was still tightening on his shoulder. He clutched at the vanished ideas and desperately made his brain and his muscles move along the unlikely direction the futureman had visualized.

And he was out in the open, a cold night wind blowing on him, still in a sitting position, but with nothing but empty air between his spine and the sidewalk.

He sat down suddenly.

Passersby on the corner of Hollywood Boulevard and Cahuenga were not much surprised at the sight of a dark, lanky man sitting by the curb. Only one woman had noticed Kelvin's actual arrival, and she knew when she was well off. She went right on home.

Kelvin got up laughing with soft hysteria. "Teleportation," he said. "How did I work it? It's gone. . . . Hard to remember afterward eh? I'll have to start carrying a notebook again."

And then—"But what about Tharn?"

He looked around, frightened. Reassurance came only after half an hour had passed without additional miracles. Kelvin walked along the Boulevard, keeping a sharp lookout. No Tharn, though.

Occasionally he slid a hand into his pocket and touched the cold metal of the case. Health, wealth and fortune. Why, he could—

But he did not press the button. Too vivid was the memory of that shocking, alien disorientation he had felt. The mind, the experiences, the habit-patterns of the far future were uncomfortably strong.

He would use the little case again—oh, yes. But there was no hurry. First, he'd have to work out a few angles.

His disbelief was completely gone. . . .

Tharn showed up the next night and scared the daylights out of Kelvin again. Prior to that, the reporter had failed to find his baggage tickets, and was only consoled by the two hundred bucks in his wallet. He took a room—paying in advance—at a medium-good hotel, and began wondering how he might apply his pipe-line to the future. Very sensibly, he decided to continue a normal life until something developed. At any rate, he'd have to make a few connections. He tried the *Times,* the *Examiner,* the *News,* and some others. But these things develop slowly except in the movies. That night Kelvin was in his hotel room when his unwelcome guest appeared.

It was, of course, Tharn.

He wore a very large white turban, and it was approximately twice the size of his head. He had a dapper black mustache, waxed downward at the tips like the mustache of a mandarin, or a catfish. He stared urgently at Kelvin out of the bathroom mirror.

Kelvin had been wondering whether or not he needed a shave before going out to dinner. He was rubbing his chin thoughtfully at the moment Tharn put in an appearance, and there was a perceptible mental lag between occurence and perception, so that to Kelvin it seemed that he himself had mysteriously sprouted a long mustache. He reached for his upper lip. It was smooth. But in the glass the black waxed hairs quivered as Tharn pushed his face up against the surface of the mirror.

It was so shockingly disorienting, somehow, that Kelvin was quite unable to think at all. He took a quick step backward. The edge of the bathtub caught him behind the knees and distracted him momentarily, fortunately for his sanity. When he looked again there was only his own appalled face reflected above the wash-bowl. But after a second or two the face seemed to develop a cloud of white turban, and mandarin-like whiskers began to form sketchily.

Kelvin clapped a hand to his eyes and spun away. In about fifteen seconds he spread his fingers enough to peep through them at the glass. He kept his palm pressed desperately to his upper lip, in some wild hope of inhibiting the sudden sprouting of a moustache. What peeped back at him from the mirror looked like himself. At least, it had no turban, and it did not wear horn-rimmed glasses. He risked snatching his hand away for a quick look, and clapped it in place again just in time to prevent Tharn from taking shape in the glass.

Still shielding his face, he went unsteadily into the bedroom and took the flat case out of his coat pocket. But he didn't press the button that would close a mental synapse between two incongruous eras. He didn't want to do that again, he realized. More horrible, somehow, than what was happening now was the thought of reentering that *alien* brain.

He was standing before the bureau, and in the mirror one eye looked out at him between reflected fingers. It was a wild eye behind the gleaming spectacle-lens, but it seemed to be his own. Tentatively he took his hand away. . . .

This mirror showed more of Tharn. Kelvin wished it hadn't. Tharn was wearing white knee-boots of some glittering plastic. Between them and the turban he wore nothing whatever except a minimum of loincloth, also glittering plastic. Tharn was very thin, but he looked active. He looked quite active enough to spring right into the hotel room. His skin was whiter than his turban, and his hands had seven fingers each, all right.

Kelvin abruptly turned away, but Tharn was resourceful. The dark window made enough of a reflecting surface to show a lean, loin-clothed figure. The feet showed bare, and they were less normal than Tharn's hands. And the polished brass of a lampbase gave back the picture of a small, distorted face not Kelvin's own.

Kelvin found a corner without reflecting surfaces and pushed into it, his hands shielding his face. He was still holding the flat case.

Oh fine, he thought bitterly. Everything's got a string on it. What good will this rapport gadget do me if Tharn's going to show up every day? Maybe I'm only crazy. I hope so.

Something would have to be done unless Kelvin was prepared to go through life with his face buried in his hands. The worst of it was that Tharn had a haunting look of familiarity. Kelvin discarded a dozen possibilities, from reincarnation to the *déjà vu* phenomenon, but—

He peeped through his hands, in time to see Tharn raising a cylindrical gadget of some sort and leveling it like a gun. That gesture formed Kelvin's decision. He'd *have* to do something, and fast. So, concentrating on the problem—*I want out!*—he pressed the button in the surface of the flat case.

And instantly the teleportation method he had forgotten was perfectly clear to him. Other matters, however, were obscure. The smells

—someone was thinking—were adding up to a—there was no word for that, only a shocking visio-auditory ideation that was simply dizzying. Someone named Three Million and Ninety Pink had written a new flatch. And there was the physical sensation of licking a twenty-four-dollar stamp and sticking it on a postcard.

But, most important, the man in the future had had—or would have —a compulsion to think about the teleportation method, and as Kelvin snapped back into his own mind and time, he instantly used that method. . . .

He was falling.

Icy water smacked him hard. Miraculously he kept his grip on the flat case. He had a whirling vision of stars in a night sky, and the phosphorescent sheen of silvery light on a dark sea. Then brine stung his nostrils.

Kelvin had never learned how to swim. As he went down for the last time, bubbling a scream, he literally clutched at the proverbial straw he was holding. His finger pushed the button down again. There was no need to concentrate on the problem; he couldn't think of anything else.

Mental chaos, fantastic images—and the answer.

It took concentration, and there wasn't much time left. Bubbles steamed up past his face. He felt them, but he couldn't see them. All around, pressing in avidly, was the horrible coldness of the salt water. . . .

But he did know the method now, and he knew how it worked. He thought along the lines the future mind had indicated. Something happened. Radiation—that was the nearest familiar term—poured out of his brain and did peculiar things to his lung tissue. His blood cells adapted themselves. . . .

He was breathing water, and it was no longer strangling him.

But Kelvin had also learned that this emergency adaptation could not be maintained for very long. Teleportation was the answer to that. And surely he could remember the method now. He had actually used it to escape from Tharn only a few minutes ago.

Yet he could not remember. The memory was expunged cleanly from his mind. So there was nothing else to do but press the button again, and Kelvin did that, most reluctantly.

Dripping wet, he was standing on an unfamiliar street. It was no street he knew, but apparently it was in his own time and on his own planet. Luckily, teleportation seemed to have limitations. The wind was cold. Kelvin stood in a puddle that grew rapidly around his feet. He stared around.

He picked out a sign up the street that offered Turkish Baths, and headed moistly in that direction. His thoughts were mostly profane. . . .

He was in New Orleans, of all places. Presently he was drunk in New Orleans. His thoughts kept going around in circles, and Scotch was a fine palliative, an excellent brake. He needed to get control again.

He had an almost miraculous power, and he wanted to be able to use it effectively before the unexpected happened again. Tharn. . . .

He sat in a hotel room and swigged Scotch. Gotta be logical!

He sneezed.

The trouble was, of course, that there were so few points of contact between his own mind and that of the futureman. Moreover, he'd got the rapport only in times of crisis. Like having access to the Alexandrian Library, five seconds a day. In five seconds you couldn't even start translating . . . .

Health, fame and fortune. He sneezed again. The robot had been a liar. His health seemed to be going fast. What about that robot? How had he got involved anyway? He said he'd fallen into this era from the future, but robots are notorious liars. Gotta be logical. . . .

Apparently the future was peopled by creatures not unlike the cast of a Frankenstein picture. Androids, robots, so-called men whose minds were shockingly different . . . *Sneeze.* Another drink.

The robot had said that the case would lose its power after Kelvin had achieved health, fame and fortune. Which was a distressing thought. Suppose he attained those enviable goals, found the little push-button useless, and *then* Tharn showed. Oh, no. That called for another shot.

Sobriety was the wrong condition in which to approach a matter that in itself was as wild as delirium tremens, even though Kelvin knew the science he had stumbled on was all theoretically quite possible. But not in this day and age. Sneeze.

The trick would be to pose the right problem and use the case at some time when you weren't drowning or being menaced by that be-whiskered android with his seven-fingered hands and his ominous rod-like weapon. Find the problem.

But that future-mind was hideous.

And suddenly, with drunken clarity, Kelvin realized that he was profoundly drawn to that dim, shadowy world of the future.

He could not see its complete pattern, but he sensed it somehow. He knew that it was *right,* a far better world and time than this. If he could be that unknown man who dwelt there, all would go well.

Man must needs love the highest, he thought wryly. Oh, well. He shook the bottle. How much had he absorbed? He felt fine.

Gotta be logical.

Outside the window street-lights blinked off and on. Neons traced goblin languages against the night. It seemed rather alien, too, but so did Kelvin's own body. He started to laugh, but a sneeze choked that off.

All I want, he thought, is health, fame and fortune. Then I'll settle down and live happily ever after, without a care or worry. I won't need this enchanted case after that. Happy ending.

On impulse he took out the box and examined it. He tried to pry it open and failed. His finger hovered over the button.

"How can I—" he thought, and his finger moved half an inch. . . .

It wasn't so alien now that he was drunk. The future man's name was Quarra Vee. Odd he had never realized that before, but how often does a man think of his own name? Quarra Vee was playing some sort of game vaguely reminiscent of chess, but his opponent was on a planet of Sirius, light-years away. The chessmen were all unfamiliar. Complicated, dizzying space-time gambits flashed through Quarra Vee's mind as Kelvin listened in. Then Kelvin's problem thrust though, the compulsion hit Quarra Vee, and—

It was all mixed up. There were two problems, really. How to cure a cold—coryza. And how to become healthy, rich and famous in a practically prehistoric era—for Quarra Vee.

A small problem, however, to Quarra Vee. He solved it and went back to his game with the Sirian.

Kelvin was back in the hotel room in New Orleans. He was very drunk or he wouldn't have risked it. The method involved using his brain to tune in on another brain in this present twentieth century that had exactly the wave-length he required. All sorts of factors would build up to the sum total of that wave-length—experience, opportunity, position, knowledge, imagination, honesty—but he found it at last, after hesitating among three totals that were all nearly right. Still one was righter, to three decimal points. Drunk as a lord, Kelvin clamped on a mental tight beam, turned on the teleportation, and rode the beam across America to a well-equipped laboratory where a man sat reading.

The man was bald and had a bristling red moustache. He looked up sharply at some sound Kelvin made.

"Hey!" he said. "How did you get in here?"

"Ask Quarra Vee," Kelvin said.

"Who? What?" The man put down his book.

Kelvin called on his memory. It seemed to be slipping. He used the rapport case for an instant, and refreshed his mind. Not so unpleasant this time, either. He was beginning to understand Quarra Vee's world a little. He liked it. However, he supposed he'd forget that too.

"An improvement on Woodward's protein analogues," he told the red-moustached man. "Simple synthesis will do it."

"Who the devil are you?"

"Call me Jim," Kelvin said simply. "And shut up and listen." He began to explain, as to a small, stupid child. (The man before him was one of America's foremost chemists.) "Proteins are made of amino acids. There are about thirty-three amino acids—"

"There aren't."

"There are. Shut up. Their molecules can be arranged in lots of ways. So we get an almost infinite variety of proteins. And all living things are forms of protein. The absolute synthesis involves a chain of amino acids long enough to recognize clearly as a protein molecule. That's been the trouble."

The man with the red moustache seemed quite interested. "Fischer assembled a chain of eighteen," he said, blinking. "Abderhalden got up to nineteen, and Woodward, of course, has made chains ten thousand units long. But as for testing—"

"The complete protein molecule consists of complete sets of sequences. But if you can test only one or two sections of an analogue you can't be sure of the others. Wait a minute." Kelvin used the rapport case again. "Now I know. Well, you can make almost anything out of synthesized protein. Silk, wool, hair—but the main thing, of course," he said, sneezing, "is a cure for coryza."

"Now look—" said the red-moustached man.

"Some of the viruses are chains of amino acids, aren't they? Well, modify their structure. Make 'em harmless. Bacteria too. And synthesize antibiotics."

"I wish I could. However, Mr.—"

"Just call me Jim."

"Yes. However, all this is old stuff."

"Grab your pencil," Kelvin said. "From now on it'll be solid, with riffs. The method of synthesizing and testing is as follows—"

He explained, very thoroughly and clearly. He had to use the rapport case only twice. And when he had finished, the man with the red moustache laid down his pencil and stared.

"This is incredible," he said. "If it works—"

"I want health, fame and fortune," Kelvin said stubbornly. "It'll work."

"Yes, but—my good man—"

However, Kelvin insisted. Luckily for himself, the mental testing of the red-moustached man had included briefing for honesty and opportunity, and it ended, with the chemist agreeing to sign partnership papers with Kelvin. The commercial possibilities of the process were unbounded. Dupont or GM would be glad to buy it.

"I want lots of money. A fortune."

"You'll make a million dollars," the red-moustached man said patiently.

"Then I want a receipt. Have to have this in black and white. Unless you want to give me my million now."

Frowning, the chemist shook his head. "Out of the question, I'm afraid. I'll have to run tests, open negotiations—but don't worry about that. Your discovery is certainly worth a million. You'll be famous, too."

"And healthy?"

"There won't be any more disease, after a while," the chemist said quietly. "That's the real miracle."

"Write it down," Kelvin clamored.

"All right. We can have partnership papers drawn up tomorrow.

This will do temporarily. Understand, the actual credit belongs to you."

"It's got to be in ink. A pencil won't do."

"Just a minute, then," the red-moustached man said, and went away in search of ink. Kelvin looked around the laboratory, beaming happily.

Tharn materialized three feet away. Tharn was holding the rod-weapon. He lifted it.

Kelvin instantly used the rapport case. Then he thumbed his nose at Tharn and teleported himself far away.

He was immediately in a cornfield, somewhere, but undistilled corn was not what Kelvin wanted. He tried again. This time, he reached Seattle.

That was the beginning of Kelvin's monumental two-week combination binge and chase.

His thoughts weren't pleasant.

He had a frightful hangover, ten cents in his pocket, and an overdue hotel bill. A fortnight of keeping one jump ahead of Tharn, via teleportation, had frazzled his nerves so unendurably that only liquor had kept him going. Now even that stimulus was failing. The drink died in him and left what felt like a corpse.

Kelvin groaned and blinked miserably. He took off his glasses and cleaned them, but that didn't help.

What a fool.

He didn't even know the name of that chemist!

There was health, wealth and fame waiting for him just around the corner, but what corner? Some day he'd find out, probably, when the news of the new protein synthesis was publicized, but when would that be? In the meantime, what about Tharn?

Moreover, the chemist couldn't locate him, either. The man knew Kelvin only as Jim. Which had somehow seemed a good idea at the time but not now.

Kelvin took out the rapport case and stared at it with red eyes. Quarra Vee, eh? He rather liked Quarra Vee now. Trouble was, a half hour after his rapport, at most, he would forget all the details.

This time he used the push-button almost as Tharn snapped into bodily existence a few feet away.

The teleportation angle again. He was sitting in the middle of a desert. Cactus and Joshua trees were all the scenery. There was a purple range of mountains far away.

No Tharn, though.

Kelvin began to be thirsty. Suppose the case stopped working now? Oh, this couldn't go on. A decision hanging fire for a week finally crystallized into a conclusion so obvious he felt like kicking himself. Perfectly obvious!

Why hadn't he thought of it at the very beginning?

He concentrated on the problem: How can I get rid of Tharn? He pushed the button. . . .

And a moment later, he knew the answer. It would be simple, really.

The pressing urgency was gone suddenly. That seemed to release a fresh flow of thought. Everything became quite clear.

He waited for Tharn.

He did not have to wait long. There was a tremor in the shimmering air, and the turbaned, pallid figure sprang into tangible reality.

The rod-weapon was poised.

Taking no chances, Kelvin posed his problem again, pressed the button, and instantly reassured himself as to the method. He simply thought in a very special and peculiar way—the way Quarra Vee had indicated.

Tharn was flung back a few feet. The moustached mouth gaped open as he uttered a cry.

"Don't!" the android cried. "I've been trying to—"

Kelvin focused harder on his thought. Mental energy, he felt, was pouring out toward the android.

Tharn croaked, "Trying—you didn't—give me—chance—"

And then Tharn was lying motionless on the hot sand staring blindly up. The seven-fingered hands twitched once and were still. The artificial life that had animated the android was gone. It would not return.

Kelvin turned his back and drew a long, shuddering breath. He was safe. He closed his mind to all thoughts but one, all problems but one.

How can I find the red-moustached man?

He pressed the button.

This is the way the story starts:

Quarra Vee sat in the temporal warp with his android Tharn, and made sure everything was under control.

"How do I look?" he asked.

"You'll pass," Tharn said. "Nobody will be suspicious in the era you're going to. It didn't take long to synthesize the equipment."

"Not long. Clothes—they look enough like real wool and linen, I suppose. Wrist watch, money—everything in order. Wrist watch—that's odd, isn't it? Imagine people who need machinery to tell time!"

"Don't forget the spectacles," Tharn said.

Quarra Vee put them on. "Ugh. But I suppose—"

"It'll be safer. The optical properties in the lenses are a guard you may need against dangerous mental radiations. Don't take them off, or the robot may try some tricks."

"He'd better not," Quarra Vee said. "That so-and-so runaway robot! What's he up to, anyway, I wonder? He always was a malcontent, but at least he knew his place. I'm sorry I ever had him made. No telling what he'll do, loose in a semi-prehistoric world, if we don't catch him and bring him home."

"He's in that horomancy booth," Tharn said, leaning out of the time-warp. "Just arrived. You'll have to catch him by surprise. And you'll need your wits about you, too. Try not to go off into any more of those deep-thought compulsions you've been having. They could be danger-ous. That robot will use some of his tricks if he gets the chance. I don't know what powers he's developed by himself, but I do know he's an expert at hypnosis and memory erasure already. If you aren't careful he'll snap your memory-track and substitute a false brain-pattern. Keep those glasses on. If anything should go wrong, I'll use the rehabilitation ray on you, eh?" And he held up a small rod-like projector.

Quarra Vee nodded.

"Don't worry. I'll be back before you know it. I have an appointment with that Sirian to finish our game this evening."

It was an appointment he never kept.

Quarra Vee stepped out of the temporal warp and strolled along the boardwalk toward the booth. The clothing he wore felt tight, uncom-fortable, rough. He wriggled a little in it. The booth stood before him now, with its painted sign.

He pushed aside the canvas curtain and something—a carelessly hung rope—swung down at his face, knocking the horn-rimmed glasses askew. Simultaneously a vivid bluish light blazed into his unprotected eyes. He felt a curious, sharp sensation of disorientation, a shifting motion that almost instantly was gone.

The robot said, "You are James Kelvin."

Questions for Discussion and Review

1. Why does the author reverse the beginning and ending? Is it merely a trick, or is it a legitimate technique of storytelling?

2. What is a "horomancer," and why is that occupation so important in this story?

3. Explain fully the true function of the box that the robot gives Kelvin.

4. What is an "O. Henry ending"? Compare the endings of "Happy Ending" and "Liar!"

5. What suggestions do you find here of satire and parody?

Part 4 Soft Science Fiction

Sometimes we forget in speaking of SF that the social sciences contribute their share of subjects and ideas, and even methods. Some so-called soft sciences are traditional ones: philosophy and history, for instance. Others—like sociology, psychology, and political science—are more modern. From the beginnings of the species, however, the impact of science on the moral and social life of the race has been of special interest to writers of SF. The traditions and perspectives of satire have also contributed their share to the development of soft SF literature.

Most commonly, soft SF works with images of the future, showing how people may experience imagined realities and how that experience may alter human perceptions and understanding. It asks us to consider how humanity will conceive itself in transformed circumstances in which science has altered the ways the race relates to its environment and to itself. Will such possible or even probable changes alter the quality or character of humanity's moral life? Of such questions and their hypothetical answers is soft SF made.

We should note at the beginning an apparent paradox in thinking about soft SF. Many stories of this class begin from a premise that was once the title of a Heinlein story—"if this goes on." That is, a writer will select a trend, a tendency, or simply an element of contemporary culture as the basis of a projected future and explore the implications of that idea in this fashion. It is a little like the sort of laboratory work H. G. Wells envisioned the writer of scientific romances performing as a way of testing existing values by opposing them to experimental ones. And this is where the apparent paradox comes in: Although the focus of readers' attention is on the character's future world, the point of reference (whether stated or implied) is always the present. This gives an author opportunities for social commentary and criticism by contrast—if this goes on. But the field is not limited to the critical or satirical, important though they may be.

One claim that supporters of SF have been making is that it permits writers to raise conceptual issues and moral questions which may not otherwise be treated in literature. In Philip K. Dick's *Do Androids Dream of Electric Sheep?* (1968), for instance, the questions raised about humanity's special moral obligation to androids put into a fresh perspective our conception of ethical values and the limits of their applicability. In the light of such possible futures in which humanity has created its own subspecies of intelligent, artificially conceived or manufactured beings, what does it mean to be human? Do the rights of humanity extend to all intelligent creatures whether they occur naturally or artificially? And so the questions go.

Such questions cannot even be stated in the realistic or psychological novel. Only SF has the capacity of bringing our imaginative or moral faculties to bear on possible futures in which human intelligence is called on to explore potential problems implicit equally in the technology of a scientific-industrial culture and in the nature of humanity.

The claim, therefore, that SF is a literature of ideas is supportable, and it is a key to one important trait of the species. However, we should remind ourselves that SF is also a literature of power. To the degree that aesthetic considerations are subordinated to ideas, however valuable, the story suffers as fiction. Authors must choose for themselves what the balance should be, and then readers and critics must judge the result. Too much matter may lead to allegory or to rhetoric disguised as fiction. Too little thought, on the other hand, may lead to SF that is dilettantish or weak-minded fantasy. The best examples are those which answer the claims of social thought and aesthetic pleasure with equal assurance.

Speculative Soft Science Fiction

Since speculative SF offers us imitations of ways we may theorize about the effects of science and technology on the nature and quality of human life, we may expect that speculative *soft* SF takes its materials and develops its methods from the soft sciences. In hard SF, we have seen that the chief interest in the story arises from problems created by science and technology which human beings must solve by like means. Soft SF focuses on the psychological, social, and moral implications of future science and technology and offers readers a way of confronting such ideas aesthetically, that is, through imitations.

As other types of speculative literature do, soft SF begins with ideas or ways of thinking about imagined futures. The ends to which this is done are not always the same, but they differ from those of, say, utopian-dystopian and social SF in at least one important sense: Social and utopian SF tends to be didactic, while speculative SF is not. Social SF is a literature that tells us how things should or should not be, while speculative SF tells us how they might be on a contemplative level that stresses the consequences of such being. We might say that speculative SF stresses a process, while social, utopian-dystopian SF stresses an end. The speculative soft SF story will rarely work out solutions to its problems or reach categorical conclusions about them. Its characteristic method is to work toward a resolution of the tensions produced by the complicating action of the story. As we have seen in the past two parts, speculative fiction helps create the potential for thinking about certain problems or circumstances in the future, and this contemplation leads to the distinctive pleasures of the SF class. If we want to think about what it means to possess a human personality, speculative SF offers means to that end. If we want to consider the dislocating effects of certain natural forces like population overgrowth, speculative SF furnishes models through which we may experience an imagined life in such an imagined world.

Nine Lives

Ursula K. Le Guin

Ursula Kroeber Le Guin was born in Berkeley, California, on October 21, 1929. She is the daughter of an anthropologist father and an author mother. Her husband is a historian. They live in Portland, Oregon, with their two children. By general consensus, she is ranked among the best writers of SF. Her *Wizard of Earthsea* trilogy has won awards in children's literature, including a Newberry Award for *The Tombs of Atuan* (1972) and a National Book Award for *The Farthest Shore* (1973). Among her novels, *The Left Hand of Darkness* (1969) and *The Dispossessed* (1974) have won both Hugo and Nebula awards. Of her short stories and novellas, the following have won awards: "The Ones Who Walk Away from Omelas" (Hugo, 1974); "The Word for World Is Forest" (Hugo, 1973); and "The Day Before the Revolution" (Nebula, 1974). "Nine Lives" first appeared in *Playboy* in 1969. The story printed here has been revised by the author.

This story had its beginnings, the author tells us, as the result of her reading Gordon Rattray Taylor's *The Biological Time Bomb* (1968). The chapter on the cloning process raised in her mind the most profound questions of human identity. If the person can be duplicated, then so can the personality. What does that mean? What is it like to be a multiple self, and what does that suggest about the identity of the self? What followed was the invention of a narrative structure that would compel readers to meet these issues in the guise of secondary experience.

The story, therefore, is concerned with certain moral and ethical constants of the human condition as they are disclosed by the interventions of science in human biology. The setting in an alien and hostile environment is an isolating device that allows the author to contrast the main character types of her story—Owen Pugh and the clone.

The clone raises all sorts of questions, biological and ethical, that contemporary readers will find challenging. We sense in the clone and in the author's handling of it the specter of unprecedented problems that science is forcing us to consider. Even so, the author is primarily interested in the way the unique, tragic dignity of humanity is revealed in contrasting types and uncommon relationships. The author finds, as she has in *The Left Hand of Darkness* and *The Dispossessed*, that danger, suffering, and even tragedy help define the enduring and ennobling values of human nature.

"Nine Lives" may be read in several ways. It is a story of the future in which we rediscover humanity's traditional existential dilemma. It is a story in which we are asked to recover our sense of ourselves. It is a story of the type once called the "fortunate fall," in which the glory of the human plight is revealed by tragedy. That tragedy, symbolized by the surviving clone, is the isolation and the solitude with which each human

being must come to terms and accept if life and growth are to be possible.
But neither is possible without love and the kind of openness that follows
from overcoming the illusion of self-sufficiency. The glory is dramatized
in the emergence of a new personality. The liberation of the true self
follows the recognition that friendship and love are sacred.

She was alive inside, but dead outside, her face a black and dun net of
wrinkles, tumors, cracks. She was bald and blind. The tremors that
crossed Libra's face were mere quiverings of corruption: underneath,
in the black corridors, the halls beneath the skin, there were crepita-
tions in darkness, ferments, chemical nightmares that went on for
centuries. "Oh the damned flatulent planet," Pugh murmured as the
dome shook and a boil burst a kilometer to the southwest, spraying silver
pus across the sunset. The sun had been setting for the last two days.
"I'll be glad to see a human face."

"Thanks," said Martin.

"Yours is human to be sure," said Pugh, "but I've seen it so long I
can't see it."

Radvid signals cluttered the communicator which Martin was operating, faded, returned as face and voice. The face filled the screen, the
nose of an Assyrian king, the eyes of a samurai, skin bronze, eyes the
color of iron: young, magnificent. "Is that what human beings look
like?" said Pugh with awe. "I'd forgotten."

"Shut up, Owen, we're on."

"Libra Exploratory Mission Base, come in please, this is *Passerine*
launch."

"Libra here. Beam fixed. Come on down, launch."

"Expulsion in seven E-seconds. Hold on." The screen blanked and
sparkled.

"Do they all look like that? Martin, you and I are uglier men than I
thought."

"Shut up, Owen. . . ."

For twenty-two minutes Martin followed the landing-craft down by
signal and then through the cleared dome they saw it, small star in the
blood-colored east, sinking. It came down neat and quiet, Libra's thin
atmosphere carrying little sound. Pugh and Martin closed the head-
pieces of their imsuits, zipped out of the dome airlocks, and ran with
soaring strides, Nijinsky and Nureyev, toward the boat. Three equipment modules came floating down at four-minute intervals from each
other and hundred-meter intervals east of the boat. "Come on out,"
Martin said on his suit radio, "we're waiting at the door."

"Come on in, the methane's fine," said Pugh.

The hatch opened. The young man they had seen on the screen came
out with one athletic twist and leaped down onto the shaky dust and

clinkers of Libra. Martin shook his hand, but Pugh was staring at the hatch, from which another young man emerged with the same neat twist and jump, followed by a young woman who emerged with the same neat twist, ornamented by a wriggle, and the jump. They were all tall, with bronze skin, black hair, high-bridged noses, epicanthic fold, the same face. They all had the same face. The fourth was emerging from the hatch with a neat twist and jump. "Martin bach," said Pugh, "we've got a clone."

"Right," said one of them, "we're a tenclone. John Chow's the name. You're Lieutenant Martin?"

"I'm Owen Pugh."

"Alvaro Guillen Martin," said Martin, formal, bowing slightly. Another girl was out, the same beautiful face; Martin stared at her and his eye rolled like a nervous pony's. Evidently he had never given any thought to cloning, and was suffering technological shock. "Steady," Pugh said in the Argentine dialect, "it's only excess twins." He stood close by Martin's elbow. He was glad himself of the contact.

It is hard to meet a stranger. Even the greatest extrovert meeting even the meekest stranger knows a certain dread, though he may not know he knows it. Will he make a fool of me wreck my image of myself invade me destroy me change me? Will he be different from me? Yes, that he will. There's the terrible thing: the strangeness of the stranger.

After two years on a dead planet, and the last half year isolated as a team of two, oneself and one other, after that it's even harder to meet a stranger, however welcome he may be. You're out of the habit of difference, you've lost the touch; and so the fear revives, the primitive anxiety, the old dread.

The clone, five males and five females, had got done in a couple of minutes what a man might have got done in twenty: greeted Pugh and Martin, had a glance at Libra, unloaded the boat, made ready to go. They went, and the dome filled with them, a hive of golden bees. They hummed and buzzed quietly, filled up all silences, all spaces with a honey-brown swarm of human presence. Martin looked bewilderedly at the long-limbed girls, and they smiled at him, three at once. Their smile was gentler than that of the boys, but no less radiantly self-possessed.

"Self-possessed," Owen Pugh murmured to his friend, "that's it. Think of it, to be oneself ten times over. Nine seconds for every motion, nine ayes on every vote. It would be glorious!" But Martin was asleep. And the John Chows had all gone to sleep at once. The dome was filled with their quiet breathing. They were young, they didn't snore. Martin sighed and snored, his hershey-bar-colored face relaxed in the dim afterglow of Libra's primary, set at last. Pugh had cleared the dome and stars looked in, Sol among them, a great company of lights, a clone of splendors. Pugh slept and dreamed of a one-eyed giant who chased him through the shaking halls of Hell.

From his sleeping-bag Pugh watched the clone's awakening. They all got up within one minute except for one pair, a boy and a girl, who lay snugly tangled and still sleeping in one bag. As Pugh saw this there was a shock like one of Libra's earthquakes inside him, a very deep tremor. He was not aware of this, and in fact thought he was pleased at the sight; there was no other such comfort on this dead hollow world, more power to them, who made love. One of the others stepped on the pair. They woke and the girl sat up flushed and sleepy, with bare golden breasts. One of her sisters murmured something to her; she shot a glance at Pugh and disappeared in the sleeping-bag, followed by a giant giggle, from another direction a fierce stare, from still another direction a voice: "Christ, we're used to having a room to ourselves. Hope you don't mind, Captain Pugh."

"It's a pleasure," Pugh said half-truthfully. He had to stand up then, wearing only the shorts he slept in, and he felt like a plucked rooster, all white scrawn and pimples. He had seldom envied Martin's compact brownness so much. The United Kingdom had come through the Great Famines well, losing less than half its population: a record achieved by rigorous food-control. Black-marketeers and hoarders had been executed. Crumbs had been shared. Where in richer lands most had died and a few had thriven, in Britain fewer died and none throve. They all got lean. Their sons were lean, their grandsons lean, small, brittle-boned, easily infected. When civilization became a matter of standing in lines, the British had kept queue, and so had replaced the survival of the fittest with the survival of the fair-minded. Owen Pugh was a scrawny little man. All the same, he was there.

At the moment he wished he wasn't.

At breakfast a John said, "Now if you'll brief us, Captain Pugh—"

"Owen, then."

"Owen, we can work out our schedule. Anything new on the mine since your last report to your Mission? We saw your reports when *Passerine* was orbiting Planet V, where they are now."

Martin did not answer, though the mine was his discovery and project, and Pugh had to do his best. It was hard to talk to them. The same faces, each with the same expression of intelligent interest, all leaned toward him across the table at almost the same angle. They all nodded together.

Over the Exploitation Corps insignia on their tunics each had a nameband, first name John and last name Chow of course, but the middle names different. The men were Aleph, Kaph, Yod, Gimel, and Samedh; the women Sadhe, Daleth, Zayin, Beth, and Resh. Pugh tried to use the names but gave it up at once; he could not even tell sometimes which one had spoken, for the voices were all alike.

Martin buttered and chewed his toast, and finally interrupted: "You're a team. Is that it?"

"Right," said two Johns.

"God, what a team! I hadn't seen the point. How much do you each know what the others are thinking?"

"Not at all, properly speaking," replied one of the girls, Zayin. The others watched her with the proprietary, approving look they had. "No ESP, nothing fancy. But we think alike. We have exactly the same equipment. Given the same stimulus, the same problem, we're likely to be coming up with the same reactions and solutions at the same time. Explanations are easy—don't even have to make them, usually. We seldom misunderstand each other. It does facilitate our working as a team."

"Christ yes," said Martin. "Pugh and I have spent seven hours out of ten for six months misunderstanding each other. Like most people. What about emergencies, are you as good at meeting the unexpected problem as a nor . . . an unrelated team?"

"Statistics so far indicate that we are," Zayin answered readily. Clones must be trained, Pugh thought, to meet questions, to reassure and reason. All they said had the slightly bland and stilted quality of answers furnished to the Public. "We can't brainstorm as singletons can, we as a team don't profit from the interplay of varied minds; but we have a compensatory advantage. Clones are drawn from the best human material, individuals of IIQ 99th percentile, Genetic Constitution alpha double A, and so on. We have more to draw on than most individuals do."

"And it's multiplied by a factor of ten. Who is—who was John Chow?"

"A genius surely," Pugh said politely. His interest in cloning was not so new and avid as Martin's.

"Leonardo Complex type," said Yod. "Biomath, also a cellist, and an undersea hunter, and interested in structural engineering problems, and so on. Died before he'd worked out his major theories."

"Then you each represent a different facet of his mind, his talents?"

"No," said Zayin, shaking her head in time with several others. "We share the basic equipment and tendencies, of course, but we're all engineers in Planetary Exploitation. A later clone can be trained to develop other aspects of the basic equipment. It's all training; the genetic substance is identical. We *are* John Chow. But we were differently trained."

Martin looked shell-shocked. "How old are you?"

"Twenty-three."

"You say he died young—Had they taken germ cells from him beforehand or something?"

Gimel took over: "He died at twenty-four in an aircar crash. They couldn't save the brain, so they took some intestinal cells and cultured them for cloning. Reproductive cells aren't used for cloning since they have only half the chromosomes. Intestinal cells happen to be easy to despecialize and reprogram for total growth."

"All chips off the old block," Martin said valiantly. "But how can . . . some of you be women . . . ?"

Beth took over: "It's easy to program half the clonal mass back to the female. Just delete the male gene from half the cells and they revert to the basic, that is, the female. It's trickier to go the other way, have to hook in artificial Y chromosomes. So they mostly clone from males, since clones function best bisexually."

Gimel again: "They've worked these matters of technique and function out carefully. The taxpayer wants the best for his money, and of course clones are expensive. With the cell-manipulations, and the incubation in Ngama Placentae, and the maintenance and training of the foster-parent groups, we end up costing about three million apiece."

"For your next generation," Martin said, still struggling, "I suppose you . . . you breed?"

"We females are sterile," said Beth with perfect equanimity; "you remember that the Y chromosome was deleted from our original cell. The males can interbreed with approved singletons, if they want to. But to get John Chow again as often as they want, they just reclone a cell from this clone."

Martin gave up the struggle. He nodded and chewed cold toast. "Well," said one of the Johns, and all changed mood, like a flock of starlings that change course in one wingflick, following a leader so fast that no eye can see which leads. They were ready to go. "How about a look at the mine? Then we'll unload the equipment. Some nice new models in the roboats; you'll want to see them. Right?" Had Pugh or Martin not agreed they might have found it hard to say so. The Johns were polite but unanimous; their decisions carried. Pugh, Commander of Libra Base 2, felt a qualm. Could he boss around this superman-woman-entity-of-ten? and a genius at that? He stuck close to Martin as they suited for outside. Neither said anything.

Four apiece in the three large jetsleds, they slipped off north from the dome, over Libra's dun rugose skin, in starlight.

"Desolate," one said.

It was a boy and girl with Pugh and Martin. Pugh wondered if these were the two that had shared a sleeping-bag last night. No doubt they wouldn't mind if he asked them. Sex must be as handy as breathing, to them. Did you two breathe last night?

"Yes," he said, "it is desolate."

"This is our first time Off, except training on Luna." The girl's voice was definitely a bit higher and softer.

"How did you take the big hop?"

"They doped us. I wanted to experience it." That was the boy; he sounded wistful. They seemed to have more personality, only two at a time. Did repetition of the individual negate individuality?

"Don't worry," said Martin, steering the sled, "you can't experience no-time because it isn't there."

"I'd just like to once," one of them said. "So we'd know."

The Mountains of Merioneth showed leprotic in starlight to the east, a plume of freezing gas trailed silvery from a vent-hole to the west, and the sled tilted groundward. The twins braced for the stop at one moment, each with a slight protective gesture to the other. Your skin is my skin, Pugh thought, but literally, no metaphor. What would it be like, then, to have someone as close to you as that? Always to be answered when you spoke, never to be in pain alone. Love your neighbor as you love yourself. . . . That hard old problem was solved. The neighbor was the self: the love was perfect.

And here was Hellmouth, the mine.

Pugh was the Exploratory Mission's ET geologist, and Martin his technician and cartographer; but when in the course of a local survey Martin had discovered the U-mine, Pugh had given him full credit, as well as the onus of prospecting the lode and planning the Exploitation Team's job. These kids had been sent out from Earth years before Martin's reports got there, and had not known what their job would be until they got here. The Exploitation Corps simply set out teams regularly and blindly as a dandelion sends out its seeds, knowing there would be a job for them on Libra or the next planet out or one they hadn't even heard about yet. The Government wanted uranium too urgently to wait while reports drifted home across the light-years. The stuff was like gold, old-fashioned but essential, worth mining extra-terrestrially and shipping interstellar. Worth its weight in people, Pugh thought sourly, watching the tall young men and women go one by one, glimmering in starlight, into the black hole Martin had named Hellmouth.

As they went in their homeostatic forehead-lamps brightened. Twelve nodding gleams ran along the moist, wrinkled walls. Pugh heard Martin's radiation counter peeping twenty to the dozen up ahead. "Here's the drop-off," said Martin's voice in the suit intercom, drowning out the peeping and the dead silence that was around them. "We're in a side-fissure; this is the main vertical vent in front of us." The black void gaped, its far side not visible in the headlamp beams. "Last vulcanism seems to have been a couple of thousand years ago. Nearest fault is twenty-eight kilos east, in the Trench. This region seems to be as safe seismically as anything in the area. The big basalt-flow overhead stabilizes all these substructures, so long as it remains stable itself. Your central lode is thirty-six meters down and runs in a series of five bubble-caverns northeast. It is a lode, a pipe of very high-grade ore. You saw the percentage figures, right? Extraction's going to be no problem. All you've got to do is get the bubbles topside."

"Take off the lid and let 'em float up." A chuckle. Voices began to talk, but they were all the same-voice and the suit radio gave them no location in space. "Open the thing right up. —Safer that way. —But it's a solid basalt roof, how thick, ten meters here? —Three to twenty, the report said. —Blow good ore all over the lot. —Use this access we're in, straighten it a bit and run slider-rails for the robos. —Import

burros. —Have we got enough propping material? —What's your estimate of total payload mass, Martin?"

"Say over five million kilos and under eight."

"Transport will be here in ten E-months. —It'll have to go pure.
—No, they'll have the mass problem in NAFAL shipping licked by
now; remember it's been sixteen years since we left Earth last Tuesday. —Right, they'll send the whole lot back and purify it in Earth
orbit. —Shall we go down, Martin?"

"Go on. I've been down."

The first one—Aleph? (Heb., the ox, the leader)—swung onto the
ladder and down; the rest followed. Pugh and Martin stood at the
chasm's edge. Pugh set his intercom to exchange only with Martin's
suit, and noticed Martin doing the same. It was a bit wearing, this listening to one person think aloud in ten voices, or was it one voice speaking the thoughts of ten minds?

"A great gut," Pugh said, looking down into the black pit, its veined
and warted walls catching stray gleams of headlamps far below. "A
cow's bowel. A bloody great constipated intestine."

Martin's counter peeped like a lost chicken. They stood inside the
epileptic planet, breathing oxygen from tanks, wearing suits imper-
meable to corrosives and harmful radiations, resistant to a two-hundred-
degree range of temperatures, tear-proof, and as shock-resistant as possible given the soft vulnerable stuff inside.

"Next hop," Martin said, "I'd like to find a planet that has nothing
whatever to exploit."

"You found this."

"Keep me home next time."

Pugh was pleased. He had hoped Martin would want to go on working with him, but neither of them was used to talking much about their
feelings, and he had hesitated to ask. "I'll try that," he said.

"I hate this plate. I like caves, you know. It's why I came in here.
Just spelunking. But this one's a bitch. Mean. You can't ever let down
in here. I guess this lot can handle it; though. They know their stuff."

"Wave of the future, whatever," said Pugh.

The wave of the future came swarming up the ladder, swept Martin
to the entrance, gabbled at and around him: "Have we got enough
material for supports? —If we convert one of the extractor-servos
to anneal, yes. —Sufficient if we miniblast? —Kaph can calculate
stress."

Pugh had switched his intercom back to receive them; he looked at
them, so many thoughts jabbering in an eager mind, and at Martin
standing silent among them, and at Hellmouth, and the wrinkled plain.
"Settled! How does that strike you as a preliminary schedule, Martin?"

"It's your baby," Martin said.

Within five E-days the Johns had all their material and equipment unloaded and operating, and were starting to open up the mine. They

worked with total efficiency. Pugh was fascinated and frightened by their effectiveness, their confidence, their independence. He was no use to them at all. A clone, he thought, might indeed be the first truly stable, self-reliant human being. Once adult it would need nobody's help. It would be sufficient to itself physically, sexually, emotionally, intellectually. Whatever he did, any member of it would always receive the support and approval of his peers, his other selves. Nobody else was needed.

Two of the clone stayed in the dome doing calculations and paper-work, with frequent sled-trips to the mine for measurements and tests. They were the mathematicians of the clone, Zayin and Kaph. That is, as Zayin explained, all ten had had thorough mathematical training from age three to twenty-one, but from twenty-one to twenty-three she and Kaph had gone on with math while the others intensified other specialties, geology, mining engineering, electronic engineering, equipment robotics, applied atomics, and so on. "Kaph and I feel," she said, "that we're the element of the clone closest to what John Chow was in his singleton lifetime. But of course he was principally in biomath, and they didn't take us far in that."

"They needed us most in this field," Kaph said, with the patriotic priggishness they sometimes evinced.

Pugh and Martin soon could distinguish this pair from the others, Zayin by gestalt, Kaph only by a discolored left fourth fingernail, got from an ill-aimed hammer at the age of six. No doubt there were many such differences, physical and psychological, among them; nature might be identical, nurture could not be. But the differences were hard to find. And part of the difficulty was that they really never talked to Pugh and Martin. They joked with them, were polite, got along fine. They gave nothing. It was nothing one could complain about; they were very pleasant, they had the standardized American friendliness. "Do you come from Ireland, Owen?"

"Nobody comes from Ireland, Zayin."

"There are lots of Irish-Americans."

"To be sure, but no more Irish. A couple of thousand in all the island, the last I knew. They didn't go in for birth-control, you know, so the food ran out. By the Third Famine there were no Irish left at all but the priesthood, and they were all celibate, or nearly all."

Zayin and Kaph smiled stiffly. They had no experience of either bigotry or irony. "What are you then, ethnically?" Kaph asked, and Pugh replied, "A Welshman."

"Is it Welsh that you and Martin speak together?"

None of your business, Pugh thought, but said, "No, it's his dialect, not mine: Argentinean. A descendant of Spanish."

"You learned it for private communication?"

"Whom had we here to be private from? It's just that sometimes a man likes to speak his native language."

"Ours is English," Kaph said unsympathetically. Why should they

have sympathy? That's one of the things you give because you need it
back.

"Is Wells quaint?" asked Zayin.

"Wells? Oh, Wales, it's called. Yes. Wales is quaint." Pugh
switched on his rock-cutter, which prevented further conversation by a
synapse-destroying whine, and while it whined he turned his back and
said a profane word in Welsh.

That night he used the Argentine dialect for private communication.
"Do they pair off in the same couples, or change every night?"

Martin looked surprised. A prudish expression, unsuited to his
features, appeared for a moment. It faded. He too was curious. "I
think it's random."

"Don't whisper, man, it sounds dirty. I think they rotate."

"On a schedule?"

"So nobody gets omitted."

Martin gave a vulgar laugh and smothered it. "What about us?
Aren't we omitted?"

"That doesn't occur to them."

"What if I proposition one of the girls?"

"She'd tell the others and they'd decide as a group."

"I am not a bull," Martin said, his dark, heavy face heating up. "I
will not be judged—"

"Down, down, *machismo*," said Pugh. "Do you mean to proposition
one?"

Martin shrugged, sullen. "Let 'em have their incest."

"Incest is it, or masturbation?"

"I don't care, if they'd do it out of earshot!"

The clone's early attempts at modesty had soon worn off, unmoti-
vated by any deep defensiveness of self or awareness of others. Pugh
and Martin were daily deeper swamped under the intimacies of its
constant emotional-sexual-mental interchange: swamped yet excluded.

"Two months to go," Martin said one evening.

"To what?" snapped Pugh. He was edgy lately and Martin's sullen-
ness got on his nerves.

"To relief."

In sixty days the full crew of their Exploratory Mission were due
back from their survey of the other planets of the system. Pugh was
aware of this.

"Crossing off the days on your calendar?" he jeered.

"Pull yourself together, Owen."

"What do you mean?"

"What I say."

They parted in contempt and resentment.

Pugh came in after a day alone on the Pampas, a vast lava-plain the
nearest edge of which was two hours south by jet. He was tired, but
refreshed by solitude. They were not supposed to take long trips alone,

but lately had often done so. Martin stooped under bright lights, drawing one of his elegant, masterly charts: this one was of the whole face of Libra, the cancerous face. The dome was otherwise empty, seeming dim and large as it had before the clone came. "Where's the golden horde?"

Martin grunted ignorance, crosshatching. He straightened his back to glance around at the sun, which squatted feebly like a great red toad on the eastern plain, and at the clock, which said 18:45. "Some big quakes today," he said, returning to his map. "Feel them down there? Lot of crates were falling around. Take a look at the seismo."

The needle jigged and wavered on the roll. It never stopped dancing here. The roll had recorded five quakes of major intensity back in midafternoon; twice the needle had hopped off the roll. The attached computer had been activated to emit a slip reading, "Epicenter 61' N by 4'24" E."

"Not in the Trench this time."

"I thought it felt a bit different from usual. Sharper."

"In Base one I used to lie awake all night feeling the ground jump. Queer how you get used to things."

"Go spla if you didn't. What's for dinner?"

"I thought you'd have cooked it."

"Waiting for the clone."

Feeling put upon, Pugh got out a dozen dinnerboxes, stuck two in the Instobake, pulled them out. "All right, here's dinner."

"Been thinking," Martin said, coming to the table. "What if some clone cloned itself? Illegally. Made a thousand duplicates—ten thousand. Whole army. They could make a tidy power-grab, couldn't they?"

"But how many millions did this lot cost to rear? Artificial placentae and all that. It would be hard to keep secret, unless they had a planet to themselves. . . . Back before the Famines when Earth had national governments, they talked about that: clone your best soldiers, have whole regiments of them. But the food ran out before they could play that game."

They talked amicably, as they used to do.

"Funny," Martin said, chewing. "They left early this morning, didn't they?"

"All but Kaph and Zayin. They thought they'd get the first payload aboveground today. What's up?"

"They weren't back for lunch."

"They won't starve, to be sure."

"They left at seven."

"So they did." Then Pugh saw it. The air-tanks held eight hours' supply.

"Kaph and Zayin carried out spare cans when they left. Or they've got a heap out there."

"They did, but they brought the whole lot in to recharge." Martin stood up, pointing to one of the stacks of stuff that cut the dome into rooms and alleys.

"There's an alarm signal on every imsuit."

"It's not automatic."

Pugh was tired and still hungry. "Sit down and eat, man. That lot can look after themselves."

Martin sat down, but did not eat. "There was a big quake, Owen. The first one. Big enough, it scared me."

After a pause Pugh sighed and said, "All right."

Unenthusiastically, they got out the two-man sled that was always left for them, and headed it north. The long sunrise covered everything in poisonous red jello. The horizontal light and shadow made it hard to see, raised walls of fake iron ahead of them through which they slid, turned the convex plain beyond Hellmouth into a great dimple full of bloody water. Around the tunnel entrance a wilderness of machinery stood, cranes and cables and servos and wheels and diggers and robocarts and sliders and control-huts, all slanting and bulking incoherently in the red light. Martin jumped from the sled, ran into the mine. He came out again, to Pugh. "Oh God, Owen, it's down," he said. Pugh went in and saw, five meters from the entrance, the shiny, moist, black wall that ended the tunnel. Newly exposed to air, it looked organic, like visceral tissue. The tunnel entrance, enlarged by blasting and double-tracked for robocarts, seemed unchanged until he noticed thousands of tiny spiderweb cracks in the walls. The floor was wet with some sluggish fluid.

"They were inside," Martin said.

"They may be still. They surely had extra air-cans—"

"Look, Owen, look at the basalt flow, at the roof; don't you see what the quake did, look at it."

The low hump of land that roofed the caves still had the unreal look of an optical illusion. It had reversed itself, sunk down, leaving a vast dimple or pit. When Pugh walked on it he saw that it too was cracked with many tiny fissures. From some a whitish gas was seeping, so that the sunlight on the surface of the gas-pool was shafted as if by the waters of a dim red lake.

"The mine's not on the fault. There's no fault here!"

Pugh came back to him quickly. "No, there's no fault, Martin. Look, they surely weren't all inside together."

Martin followed him and searched among the wrecked machines dully, then actively. He spotted the airsled. It had come down heading south, and stuck at an angle in a pothole of colloidal dust. It had carried two riders. One was half sunk in the dust, but his suit-meters registered normal functioning; the other hung strapped onto the tilted sled. Her imsuit had burst open on the broken legs, and the body was frozen hard as any rock. That was all they found. As both regulation and custom demanded, they cremated the dead at once with the laser-guns they carried by regulation and had never used before. Pugh, knowing he was going to be sick, wrestled the survivor onto the two-man sled and sent Martin off to the dome with him. Then he vomited, and flushed the waste out of his suit, and finding one four-man sled undamaged followed after Martin, shaking as if the cold of Libra had got through to him.

The survivor was Kaph. He was in deep shock. They found a swelling on the occiput that might mean concussion, but no fracture was visible.

Pugh brought two glasses of food-concentrate and two chasers of aquavit. "Come on," he said. Martin obeyed, drinking off the tonic. They sat down on crates near the cot and sipped the aquavit.

Kaph lay immobile, face like beeswax, hair bright black to the shoulders, lips stiffly parted for faintly gasping breaths.

"It must have been the first shock, the big one," Martin said. "It must have slid the whole structure sideways. Till it fell in on itself. There must be gas layers in the lateral rocks, like those formations in the Thirty-first Quadrant. But there wasn't any sign—" As he spoke the world slid out from under them. Things leaped and clattered, hopped and jigged, shouted Ha! Ha! Ha! "It was like this at fourteen hours," said Reason shakily in Martin's voice; amidst the unfastening and ruin of the world. But Unreason sat up, as the tumult lessened and things ceased dancing, and screamed aloud.

Pugh leaped across his spilled aquavit and held Kaph down. The muscular body flailed him off. Martin pinned the shoulders down. Kaph screamed, struggled, choked; his face blackened. "Oxy," Pugh said, and his hand found the right needle in the medical kit as if by homing instinct; while Martin held the mask he struck the needle home to the vagus nerve, restoring Kaph to life.

"Didn't know you knew that stunt," Martin said, breathing hard.

"The Lazarus Jab; my father was a doctor. It doesn't often work," Pugh said. "I want that drink I spilled. Is the quake over? I can't tell."

"Aftershocks. It's not just you shivering."

"Why did he suffocate?"

"I don't know, Owen. Look in the book."

Kaph was breathing normally and his color was restored, only the lips were still darkened. They poured a new shot of courage and sat down by him again with their medical guide. "Nothing about cyanosis or asphyxiation under 'shock' or 'concussion.' He can't have breathed in anything with his suit on. I don't know. We'd get as much good out of *Mother Mog's Home Herbalist*. . . . 'Anal Hemorrhoids,' fy!" Pugh pitched the book to a crate-table. It fell short, because either Pugh or the table was still unsteady.

"Why didn't he signal?"

"Sorry?"

"The eight inside the mine never had time. But he and the girl must have been outside. Maybe she was in the entrance, and got hit by the first slide. He must have been outside, in the control-hut maybe. He ran in, pulled her out, strapped her onto the sled, started for the dome. And all that time never pushed the panic button in his imsuit. Why not?"

"Well, he'd had that whack on his head. I doubt he ever realized the girl was dead. He wasn't in his senses. But if he had been I don't know if he'd have thought to signal us. They looked to one another for help."

Martin's face was like an Indian mask, grooves at the mouthcorners, eyes of dull coal. "That's so. What must he have felt, then, when the quake came and he was outside, alone—"

In answer Kaph screamed.

He came up off the cot in the heaving convulsions of one suffocating, knocking Pugh right down with his flailing arm, staggered into a stack of crates and fell to the floor, lips blue, eyes white. Martin dragged him back onto the cot and gave him a whiff of oxygen, then knelt by Pugh, who was just sitting up, and wiped at his cut cheekbone. "Owen, are you all right, are you going to be all right, Owen?"

"I think I am," Pugh said. "Why are you rubbing that on my face?"

It was a short length of computer-tape, now spotted with Pugh's blood. Martin dropped it. "Thought it was a towel. You clipped your cheek on that box there."

"Is he out of it?"

"Seems to be."

They stared down at Kaph lying stiff, his teeth a white line inside dark parted lips.

"Like epilepsy. Brain damage maybe?"

"What about shooting him full of meprobamate?"

Pugh shook his head. "I don't know what's in that shot I already gave him for shock. Don't want to overdose him."

"Maybe he'll sleep it off now."

"I'd like to myself. Between him and the earthquake I can't seem to keep on my feet."

"You got a nasty crack there. Go on, I'll sit up awhile."

Pugh cleaned his cut cheek and pulled off his shirt, then paused.

"Is there anything we ought to have done—have tried to do—"

"They're all dead," Martin said heavily, gently.

Pugh lay down on top of his sleeping-bag, and one instant later was wakened by a hideous, sucking, struggling noise. He staggered up, found the needle, tried three times to jab it in correctly and failed, began to massage over Kaph's heart. "Mouth-to-mouth," he said, and Martin obeyed. Presently Kaph drew a harsh breath, his heartbeat steadied, his rigid muscles began to relax.

"How long did I sleep?"

"Half an hour."

They stood up sweating. The ground shuddered, the fabric of the dome sagged and swayed. Libra was dancing her awful polka again, her Totentanz. The sun, though rising, seemed to have grown larger and redder; gas and dust must have been stirred up in the feeble atmosphere.

"What's wrong with him, Owen?"

"I think he's dying with them."

"Them—But they're dead, I tell you."

"Nine of them. They're all dead, they were crushed or suffocated. They were all him, he is all of them. They died, and now he's dying their deaths one by one."

"Oh pity of God," said Martin.

The next time was much the same. The fifth time was worse, for Kaph fought and raved, trying to speak but getting no words out, as if his mouth were stopped with rocks or clay. After that the attacks grew weaker, but so did he. The eighth seizure came at about four-thirty; Pugh and Martin worked till five-thirty doing all they could to keep life in the body that slid without protest into death. They kept him, but Martin said, "The next will finish him." And it did; but Pugh breathed his own breath into the inert lungs, until he himself passed out.

He woke. The dome was opaqued and no light on. He listened and heard the breathing of two sleeping men. He slept, and nothing woke him till hunger did.

The sun was well up over the dark plains, and the planet had stopped dancing. Kaph lay asleep. Pugh and Martin drank tea and looked at him with proprietary triumph.

When he woke Martin went to him: "How do you feel, old man?" There was no answer. Pugh took Martin's place and looked into the brown, dull eyes that gazed toward but not into his own. Like Martin he quickly turned away. He heated food-concentrate and brought it to Kaph. "Come on, drink."

He could see the muscles in Kaph's throat tighten. "Let me die," the young man said.

"You're not dying."

Kaph spoke with clarity and precision: "I am nine-tenths dead. There is not enough of me left alive."

That precision convinced Pugh, and he fought the conviction. "No," he said, peremptory. "They are dead. The others. Your brothers and sisters. You're not them, you're alive. You are John Chow. Your life is in your own hands."

The young man lay still, looking into a darkness that was not there.

Martin and Pugh took turns taking the Exploitation hauler and a spare set of robos over to Hellmouth to salvage equipment and protect it from Libra's sinister atmosphere, for the value of the stuff was, literally, astronomical. It was slow work for one man at a time, but they were unwilling to leave Kaph by himself. The one left in the dome did paperwork, while Kaph sat or lay and stared into his darkness, and never spoke. The days went by silent.

The radio spat and spoke: the Mission calling from ship. "We'll be down on Libra in five weeks, Owen. Thirty-four E-days nine hours I make it as of now. How's tricks in the old dome?"

"Not good, chief. The Exploit team were killed, all but one of them, in the mine. Earthquake. Six days ago."

The radio crackled and sang starsong. Sixteen seconds lag each way; the ship was out around Planet 11 now. "Killed, all but one? You and Martin were unhurt?"

"We're all right, chief."

Thirty-two seconds.

"*Passerine* left an Exploit team out here with us. I may put them on the Hellmouth project then, instead of the Quadrant Seven project. We'll settle that when we come down. In any case you and Martin will be relieved at Dome Two. Hold tight. Anything else?"

"Nothing else."

Thirty-two seconds.

"Right then. So long, Owen."

Kaph had heard all this, and later on Pugh said to him, "The chief may ask you to stay here with the other Exploit team. You know the ropes here." Knowing the exigencies of Far Out Life, he wanted to warn the young man. Kaph made no answer. Since he had said, "There is not enough of me left alive," he had not spoken a word.

"Owen," Martin said on suit intercom, "he's spla. Insane. Psycho."

"He's doing very well for a man who's died nine times."

"Well? Like a turned-off android is well? The only emotion he has left is hate. Look at his eyes."

"That's not hate, Martin. Listen, it's true that he has, in a sense, been dead. I cannot imagine what he feels. But it's not hatred. He can't even see us. It's too dark."

"Throats have been cut in the dark. He hates us because we're not Aleph and Yod and Zayin."

"Maybe. But I think he's alone. He doesn't see us or hear us, that's the truth. He never had to see anyone else before. He never was alone before. He had himself to see, talk with, live with, nine other selves all his life. He doesn't know how you go it alone. He must learn. Give him time."

Martin shook his heavy head. "Spla," he said. "Just remember when you're alone with him that he could break your neck one-handed."

"He could do that," said Pugh, a short, soft-voiced man with a scarred cheekbone; he smiled. They were just outside the dome airlock, programming one of the servos to repair a damaged hauler. They could see Kaph sitting inside the great half-egg of the dome like a fly in amber.

"Hand me the insert pack there. What makes you think he'll get any better?"

"He has a strong personality, to be sure."

"Strong? Crippled. Nine-tenths dead, as he put it."

"But he's not dead. He's a live man: John Kaph Chow. He had a jolly queer unbringing, but after all every boy has got to break free of his family. He will do it."

"I can't see it."

"Think a bit, Martin bach. What's this cloning for? To repair the human race. We're in a bad way. Look at me. My IIQ and GC are half this John Chow's. Yet they wanted me so badly for the Far Out Service that when I volunteered they took me and fitted me out with an artificial lung and corrected my myopia. Now if there were enough good sound lads about would they be taking one-lunged shortsighted Welshmen?"

"Didn't know you had an artificial lung."

"I do then. Not tin, you know. Human, grown in a tank from a bit of somebody; cloned, if you like. That's how they make replacement-organs, the same general idea as cloning, but bits and pieces instead of whole people. It's my own lung now, whatever. But what I am saying is this, there are too many like me these days, and not enough like John Chow. They're trying to raise the level of the human genetic pool, which is a mucky little puddle since the population crash. So then if a man is cloned, he's a strong and clever man. It's only logic, to be sure."

Martin grunted; the servo began to hum.

Kaph had been eating little; he had trouble swallowing his food, choking on it, so that he would give up trying after a few bites. He had lost eight or ten kilos. After three weeks or so, however, his appetite began to pick up, and one day he began to look through the clone's possessions, the sleeping-bags, kits, papers which Pugh had stacked neatly in a far angle of a packing-crate alley. He sorted, destroyed a heap of papers and oddments, made a small packet of what remained, then relapsed into his walking coma.

Two days later he spoke. Pugh was trying to correct a flutter in the tape-player, and failing; Martin had the jet out, checking their maps of the Pampas. "Hell and damnation!" Pugh said, and Kaph said in a toneless voice, "Do you want me to do that?"

Pugh jumped, controlled himself, and gave the machine to Kaph. The young man took it apart, put it back together, and left it on the table.

"Put on a tape," Pugh said with careful casualness, busy at another table.

Kaph put on the topmost tape, a chorale. He lay down on his cot. The sound of a hundred human voices singing together filled the dome. He lay still, his face blank.

In the next days he took over several routine jobs, unasked. He undertook nothing that wanted initiative, and if asked to do anything he made no response at all.

"He's doing well," Pugh said in the dialect of Argentina.

"He's not. He's turning himself into a machine. Does what he's programmed to do, no reaction to anything else. He's worse off than when he didn't function at all. He's not human any more."

Pugh sighed. "Well, good night," he said in English. "Good night, Kaph."

"Good night," Martin said; Kaph did not.

Next morning at breakfast Kaph reached across Martin's plate for the toast. "Why don't you ask for it," Martin said with the geniality of repressed exasperation. "I can pass it."

"I can reach it," Kaph said in his flat voice.

"Yes, but look. Asking to pass things, saying good night or hello, they're not important, but all the same when somebody says something a person ought to answer. . . ."

The young man looked indifferently in Martin's direction; his eyes still did not seem to see clear through to the person he looked toward. "Why should I answer?"

"Because somebody has said something to you."

"Why?"

Martin shrugged and laughed. Pugh jumped up and turned on the rock-cutter.

Later on he said, "Lay off that, please, Martin."

"Manners are essential in small isolated crews, some kind of manners, whatever you work out together. He's been taught that, everybody in Far Out knows it. Why does he deliberately flout it?"

"Do you tell yourself good night?"

"So?"

"Don't you see Kaph's never known anyone but himself?"

Martin brooded and then broke out, "Then by God this cloning business is all wrong. It won't do. What are a lot of duplicate geniuses going to do for us when they don't even know we exist?"

Pugh nodded. "It might be wiser to separate the clones and bring them up with others. But they make such a grand team this way."

"Do they? I don't know. If this lot had been ten average inefficient ET engineers, would they all have been in the same place at the same time? Would they all have got killed? What if, when the quake came and things started caving in, what if all those kids ran the same way, farther into the mine, maybe, to save the one that was farthest in? Even Kaph was outside and went in. . . . It's hypothetical. But I keep thinking, out of ten ordinary confused guys, more might have got out."

"I don't know. It's true that identical twins tend to die at about the same time, even when they have never seen each other. Identity and death, it is very strange. . . ."

The days went on, the red sun crawled across the dark sky, Kaph did not speak when spoken to, Pugh and Martin snapped at each other more frequently each day. Pugh complained of Martin's snoring. Offended, Martin moved his cot clear across the dome and also ceased speaking to Pugh for some while. Pugh whistled Welsh dirges until Martin complained, and then Pugh stopped speaking for a while.

The day before the Mission ship was due, Martin announced he was going over to Merioneth.

"I thought at least you'd be giving me a hand with the computer to finish the rock-analyses," Pugh said, aggrieved.

"Kaph can do that. I want one more look at the Trench. Have fun," Martin added in dialect, and laughed, and left.

"What is that language?"

"Argentinean. I told you that once, didn't I?"

"I don't know." After a while the young man added, "I have forgotten a lot of things, I think."

"It wasn't important, to be sure," Pugh said gently realizing all at once how important this conversation was. "Will you give me a hand running the computer, Kaph?"

He nodded.

Pugh had left a lot of loose ends, and the job took them all day. Kaph was a good co-worker, quick and systematic, much more so than Pugh himself. His flat voice, now that he was talking again, got on the nerves; but it didn't matter, there was only this one day left to get through and then the ship would come, the old crew, comrades and friends.

During tea-break Kaph said, "What will happen if the Explorer ship crashes?"

"They'd be killed."

"To you, I mean."

"To us? We'd radio SOS all signals, and live on half rations till the rescue cruiser from Area Three Base came. Four and a half E-years away it is. We have life-support here for three men for, let's see, maybe between four and five years. A bit tight, it would be."

"Would they send a cruiser for three men?"

"They would."

Kaph said no more.

"Enough cheerful speculations," Pugh said cheerfully, rising to get back to work. He slipped sideways and the chair avoided his hand; he did a sort of half-pirouette and fetched up hard against the dome-hide. "My goodness," he said, reverting to his native idiom, "what it is?"

"Quake," said Kaph.

The teacups bounced on the table with a plastic cackle, a litter of papers slid off a box, the skin of the dome swelled and sagged. Underfoot there was a huge noise, half sound half shaking, a subsonic boom.

Kaph sat unmoved. An earthquake does not frighten a man who died in an earthquake.

Pugh, white-faced, wiry black hair sticking out, a frightened man, said, "Martin is in the Trench."

"What trench?"

"The big fault line. The epicenter for the local quakes. Look at the seismograph." Pugh struggled with the stuck door of a still-jittering locker.

"Where are you going?"

"After him."

"Martin took the jet. Sleds aren't safe to use during quakes. They go out of control."

"For God's sake, man, shut up."

Kaph stood up, speaking in a flat voice as usual. "It's unnecessary to go out after him now. It's taking an unnecessary risk."

"If his alarm goes off, radio me," Pugh said, shut the headpiece of his suit, and ran to the lock. As he went out Libra picked up her ragged skirts and danced a belly-dance from under his feet clear to the red horizon.

Inside the dome, Kaph saw the sled go up, tremble like a meteor in the dull red daylight, and vanish to the northeast. The hide of the dome quivered; the earth coughed. A vent south of the dome belched up a slow-flowing bile of black gas.

A bell shrilled and a red light flashed on the central control board. The sign under the light read Suit Two and scribbled under that, A.G.M. Kaph did not turn the signal off. He tried to radio Martin, then Pugh, but got no reply from either.

When the aftershocks decreased he went back to work, and finished up Pugh's job. It took him about two hours. Every half hour he tried to contact Suit One, and got no reply, then Suit Two and got no reply. The red light had stopped flashing after an hour.

It was dinnertime. Kaph cooked dinner for one, and ate it. He lay down on his cot.

The aftershocks had ceased except for faint rolling tremors at long intervals. The sun hung in the west, oblate, pale-red, immense. It did not sink visibly. There was no sound at all.

Kaph got up and began to walk about the messy, half-packed-up, overcrowded, empty dome. The silence continued. He went to the player and put on the first tape that came to hand. It was pure music, electronic, without harmonies, without voices. It ended. The silence continued.

Pugh's uniform tunic, one button missing, hung over a stack of rock-samples. Kaph stared at it a while.

The silence continued.

The child's dream: There is no one else alive in the world but me. In all the world.

Low, north of the dome, a meteor flickered.

Kaph's mouth opened as if he were trying to say something, but no sound came. He went hastily to the north wall and peered out into the gelatinous red light.

The little star came in and sank. Two figures blurred the airlock. Kaph stood close behind the lock as they came in. Martin's imsuit was covered with some kind of dust so that he looked raddled and warty like the surface of Libra. Pugh had him by the arm.

"Is he hurt?"

Pugh shucked his suit, helped Martin peel off his. "Shaken up," he said, curt.

"A piece of cliff fell onto the jet," Martin said, sitting down at the table and waving his arms. "Not while I was in it, though. I was parked, see, and poking about that carbon-dust area when I felt things humping. So I went out onto a nice bit of early igneous I'd noticed from above, good footing and out from under the cliffs. Then I saw this bit of the planet fall off onto the flyer, quite a sight it was, and after a while it occurred to me the spare aircans were in the flyer, so I leaned on the panic button. But I didn't get any radio reception, that's always happening here during quakes, so I didn't know if the signal was getting through either. And things went on jumping around and pieces of the cliff coming off. Little rocks flying around, and so dusty you couldn't see a meter ahead. I was really beginning to wonder what I'd do for breathing in the small hours, you know, when I saw old Owen buzzing up the Trench in all that dust and junk like a big ugly bat—"

"Want to eat?" said Pugh.

"Of course I want to eat. How'd you come through the quake here, Kaph? No damage? It wasn't a big one actually, was it, what's the seismo say? My trouble was I was in the middle of it. Old Epicenter Alvaro. Felt like Richter Fifteen there—total destruction of planet—"

"Sit down," Pugh said. "Eat."

After Martin had eaten a little his spate of talk ran dry. He very soon went off to his cot, still in the remote angle where he had removed it when Pugh complained of his snoring. "Good night, you one-lunged Welshman," he said across the dome.

"Good night."

There was no more out of Martin. Pugh opaqued the dome, turned the lamp down to a yellow glow less than a candle's light, and sat doing nothing, saying nothing, withdrawn.

The silence continued.

"I finished the computations."

Pugh nodded thanks.

"The signal from Martin came through, but I couldn't contact you or him."

Pugh said with effort, "I should not have gone. He had two hours of air left even with only one can. He might have been heading home when I left. This way we were all out of touch with one another. I was scared."

The silence came back, punctuated now by Martin's long, soft snores.

"Do you love Martin?"

Pugh looked up with angry eyes: "Martin is my friend. We've worked together, he's a good man." He stopped. After a while he said, "Yes, I love him. Why did you ask that?"

Kaph said nothing, but he looked at the other man. His face was changed, as if he were glimpsing something he had not seen before; his voice too was changed. "How can you . . . ? How do you . . . ?"

But Pugh could not tell him. "I don't know," he said, "it's practice, partly. I don't know. We're each of us alone, to be sure. What can you do but hold your hand out in the dark?"

Kaph's strange gaze dropped, burned out by its own intensity.

"I'm tired," Pugh said. "That was ugly, looking for him in all that black dust and muck, and mouths opening and shutting in the ground. . . . I'm going to bed. The ship will be transmitting to us by six or so." He stood up and stretched.

"It's a clone," Kaph said. "The other Exploit team they're bringing with them."

"Is it, then?"

"A twelveclone. They came out with us on the *Passerine*."

Kaph sat in the small yellow aura of the lamp seeming to look past it at what he feared: the new clone, the multiple self of which he was not part. A lost piece of a broken set, a fragment, inexpert at solitude, not knowing even how you go about giving love to another individual, now he must face the absolute, closed self-sufficiency of the clone of twelve; that was a lot to ask of the poor fellow, to be sure. Pugh put a hand on his shoulder in passing. "The chief won't ask you to stay here with a clone. You can go home. Or since you're Far Out maybe you'll come on farther out with us. We could use you. No hurry deciding. You'll make out all right."

Pugh's quiet voice trailed off. He stood unbuttoning his coat, stooped a little with fatigue. Kaph looked at him and saw the thing he had never seen before: saw him: Owen Pugh, the other, the stranger who held his hand out in the dark.

"Good night," Pugh mumbled, crawling into his sleeping-bag and half asleep already, so that he did not hear Kaph reply after a pause, repeating, across darkness, benediction.

Questions for Discussion and Review

1. Compare and contrast the development of this story with that of "All You Zombies—" in Part Two.

2. "Think of it, to be oneself ten times over!" What importance does this statement have for the story?

3. One of Le Guin's interests as a writer is "the strangeness of the stranger." Explain the importance of this theme for the story.

4. In this story, SF elements make it possible for the author to redefine the meaning of loneliness and the necessity of love in human relationships. How is this done?

5. Compare and contrast the clone and its internal relationship with Martin and Pugh and their relationship.

6. What significance does the author's choice of setting (both physical and historical) have for the story?

The Sliced-Crosswise
Only-on-Tuesday World

Philip José Farmer

Philip José Farmer was born January 26, 1918, in North Terre Haute,
Indiana. After attending Bradley University, he worked in a steel mill for
eleven years as a military electronics technical writer, and then he was a
technical writer for Motorola. His introduction to SF came through the Oz
stories, and Gernsback, and Edgar Rice Burroughs. In 1953 he won a
Hugo Award as the most promising young SF writer. Some of Farmer's
work has achieved notoriety for breaking the sex taboos of SF. *Strange
Relations* (1960) is a collection of stories exploring unorthodox sexuality
and alien biology. *The Lovers* (1961) is an even more bizarre case of
interspecies housekeeping. Among his many novels, the Riverboat series,
beginning with *The Fabulous Riverboat* (1971), is noteworthy; and
To Your Scattered Bodies Go won a Hugo Award in 1972. Of the shorter
fiction, "Riders of the Purple Wage" won a Hugo for best novella in 1968.
"The Sliced-Crosswise Only-on-Tuesday World" was first published in
Robert Silverberg's *New Dimensions I* in 1971.

You might call this a story of time travel, but only in terms of the imagined
world created by Farmer. It is the world of Tuesday, created and maintained by Time Barriers and stoners, just as all the other days of the week
have their parallel worlds.

The story would read like a morality tale if the treatment of its materials
were different. In its perverse technology, new kinds of life control are
possible; and its inhabitants are obligingly docile and regimented. But
something goes wrong, as it often does in stories about such ant-colony
cultures. The protagonist, Tom Pym, falls in love with an unattainable
lady in Wednesday's world. With that complication in hand, the author sets
about the gulling of Tom Pym in the denouement of this perverse comedy.

Farmer's elaborately contrived Tuesday world probably represents the
idea behind the story, and it takes readers by surprise. The result is an
immediate sense of disorientation, until we accept Tuesday world with its
unique set of probabilities. Whether or not we are really being asked to
accept Tuesday as a secondary reality in which we share an imagined
belief with the characters is something else again. As it is, the world of
Tuesday must strike us as a deliberately exaggerated Rube Goldberg device
for solving the problem of world overpopulation. Technology amok,
however, appears to serve another purpose beside providing a certain comic
ambience. It also supports the subordinate theme of bureaucratic tyranny
over the lives of the people who are controlled.

Both themes have been the basis for dystopian stories and cautionary
tales universally familiar in Huxley's *Brave New World* (1932) and
Orwell's *1984* (1949). The difference here, of course, is one of tone,
and of the author's attitude toward his materials, particularly toward his

characters. Whereas Huxley, Orwell, and other social critics present us with heroes and heroines caught in the dehumanizing toils of a police-state society, Farmer gives us protagonists with clay feet. The discomforting of these characters, therefore, does not discomfort readers. It is not so much that Wednesday world is an ironic one; it is rather that in terms of morality it is just like this one. What day of the week is it in your world?

Getting into Wednesday was almost impossible.

Tom Pym had thought about living on other days of the week. Almost everybody with any imagination did. There were even TV shows speculating on this. Tom Pym had even acted in two of these. But he had no genuine desire to move out of his own world. Then his house burned down.

This was on the last day of the eight days of spring. He awoke to look out the door at the ashes and the firemen. A man in a white asbestos suit motioned for him to stay inside. After fifteen minutes, another man in a suit gestured that it was safe. He pressed the button by the door, and it swung open. He sank down in the ashes to his ankles; they were a trifle warm under the inch-thick coat of water-soaked crust.

There was no need to ask what had happened, but he did, anyway.

The fireman said, "A short-circuit, I suppose. Actually, we don't know. It started shortly after midnight, between the time that Monday quit and we took over."

Tom Pym thought that it must be strange to be a fireman or a policeman. Their hours were so different, even though they were still limited by the walls of midnight.

By then the others were stepping out of their stoners, or "coffins" as they were often called. That left sixty still occupied.

They were due for work at 08:00. The problem of getting new clothes and a place to live would have to be put off until off-hours, because the TV studio where they worked was behind in the big special it was due to put on in 144 days.

They ate breakfast at an emergency center. Tom Pym asked a grip if he knew of any place he could stay. Though the government would find one for him, it might not look very hard for a convenient place.

The grip told him about a house only six blocks from his former house. A makeup man had died, and as far as he knew the vacancy had not been filled. Tom got onto the phone at once, since he wasn't needed at that moment, but the office wouldn't be open until ten, as the recording informed him. The recording was a very pretty girl with red hair, tourmaline eyes, and a very sexy voice. Tom would have been more impressed if he had not known her. She had played in some small parts in two of his shows, and the maddening voice was not hers. Neither was the color of her eyes.

At noon he called again, got through after a ten-minute wait, and asked Mrs. Bellefield if she would put through a request for him. Mrs. Bellefield reprimanded him for not having phoned sooner; she was not sure that anything could be done today. He tried to tell her his circumstances and then gave up. Bureaucrats! That evening he went to a public emergency place, slept for the required four hours while the inductive field speeded up his dreaming, woke up, and got into the upright cylinder of eternium. He stood for ten seconds, gazing out through the transparent door at other cylinders with their still figures, and then he pressed the button. Approximately fifteen seconds later he became unconscious.

He had to spend three more nights in the public stoner. Three days of spring were gone; only five left. Not that that mattered in California so much. When he had lived in Chicago, winter was like a white blanket being shaken by a madwoman. Spring was a green explosion. Summer was a bright roar and a hot breath. Fall was the topple of a drunken jester in garish motley.

The fourth day, he received notice that he could move into the very house he had picked. This surprised and pleased him. He knew of a dozen who had spent a whole year—forty-eight days or so—in a public station while waiting. He moved in the fifth day with three days of spring to enjoy. But he would have to use up his two days off to shop for clothes, bring in groceries and other goods, and get acquainted with his housemates. Sometimes, he wished he had not been born with the compulsion to act. TV'ers worked five days at a stretch, sometimes six, while a plumber, for instance, only put in three days out of seven.

The house was as large as the other, and the six extra blocks to walk would be good for him. It held eight people per day, counting himself. He moved in that evening, introduced himself, and got Mabel Carta, who worked as a secretary for a producer, to fill him in on the household routine. After he made sure that his stoner had been moved into the stoner room, he could relax somewhat.

Mable Carta had accompanied him into the stoner room, since she had appointed herself his guide. She was a short, overly curved woman of about thirty-five (Tuesday time). She had been divorced three times, and marriage was no more for her, unless, of course, Mr. Right came along. Tom was between marriages himself, but he did not tell her so.

"We'll take a look at your bedroom," Mabel said. "It's small but it's soundproofed, thank God."

He started after her, then stopped. She looked back through the doorway and said, "What is it?"

"This girl . . ."

There were sixty-three of the tall gray eternium cylinders. He was looking through the door of the nearest at the girl within.

"Wow! Really beautiful!"

If Mabel felt any jealousy, she suppressed it.

"Yes, isn't she!"

The girl had long, black, slightly curly hair, a face that could have launched him a thousand times times a thousand times, a figure that had enough but not too much, and long legs. Her eyes were open; in the dim light they looked a purplish-blue. She wore a thin silvery dress.

The plate by the top of the door gave her vital data. Jennie Marlowe. Born A.D. 2031, San Marino, California. She would be twenty-four years old. Actress. Unmarried. Wednesday's child.

"What's the matter?" Mabel said.

"Nothing."

How could he tell her that he felt sick in his stomach from a desire that could never be satisfied? Sick from beauty?

For will in us is overruled by fate.
Who ever loved, that loved not at first sight?

"What?" Mabel said, and then, after laughing, "You must be kidding."

She wasn't angry. She realized that Jennie Marlowe was no more competition that if she were dead. She was right. Better for him to busy himself with the living of this world. Mabel wasn't too bad, cuddly, really, and, after a few drinks, rather stimulating.

They went downstairs afterward after 18:00 to the TV room. Most of the others were there, too. Some had their ear plugs in; some were looking at the screen but talking. The newscast was on, of course. Everybody was filling up on what had happened last Tuesday and today. The Speaker of the House was retiring after his term was up. His days of usefulness were over and his recent ill health showed no signs of disappearing. There was a shot of the family graveyard in Mississippi with the pedestal reserved for him. When science someday learned how to rejuvenate, he would come out of stonerment.

"That'll be the day!" Mabel said. She squirmed on his lap.

"Oh, I think they'll crack it," he said. "They're already on the track; they've succeeded in stopping the aging of rabbits."

"I don't mean that," she said. "Sure, they'll find out how to rejuvenate people. But then what? You think they're going to bring them all back? With all the people they got now and then they'll double, maybe triple, maybe quadruple, the population? You think they won't just leave them standing out there?" She giggled, and said, "What would the pigeons do without them?"

He squeezed her waist. At the same time, he had a vision of himself squeezing *that* girl's waist. Hers would be soft enough, but with no hint of fat.

Forget about her. Think of now. Watch the news.

A Mrs. Wilder had stabbed her husband and then herself with a kitchen knife. Both had been stonered immediately after the police arrived, and they had been taken to the hospital. An investigation of a work slowdown in the county government offices was taking place. The complaints were that Monday's people were not setting up the computers for Tuesday's. The case was being referred to the proper authorities of both days. The Ganymede base reported that the Great Red Spot of Jupiter was emitting weak but definite pulses that did not seem to be random.

The last five minutes of the program was a précis devoted to outstanding events of the other days. Mrs. Cuthmar, the house mother, turned the channel to a situation comedy with no protests from anybody.

Tom left the room, after telling Mabel that he was going to bed early—alone, and to sleep. He had a hard day tomorrow.

He tiptoed down the hall and the stairs and into the stoner room. The lights were soft, there were many shadows, and it was quiet. The sixty-three cylinders were like ancient granite columns of an underground chamber of a buried city. Fifty-five faces were white blurs behind the clear metal. Some had their eyes open; most had closed them while waiting for the field radiated from the machine in the base. He looked through Jennie Marlowe's door. He felt sick again. Out of his reach; never for him. Wednesday was only a day away. No, it was only a little less than four and half hours away.

He touched the door. It was slick and only a little cold. She stared at him. Her right forearm was bent to hold the strap of a large purse. When the door opened, she would step out, ready to go. Some people took their showers and fixed their faces as soon as they got up from their sleep and then went directly into the stoner. When the field was automatically radiated at 05:00, they stepped out a minute later, ready for the day.

He would like to step out of his "coffin," too, at the same time.

But he was barred by Wednesday.

He turned away. He was acting like a sixteen-year-old kid. He had been sixteen about one hundred and six years ago, not that that made any difference. Physiologically, he was thirty.

As he started up to the second floor, he almost turned around and went back for another look. But he took himself by his neck-collar and pulled himself up to his room. There he decided he would get to sleep at once. Perhaps he would dream about her. If dreams were wish fulfillments, they would bring her to him. It still had not been "proved" that dreams always expressed wishes, but it had been proved that man deprived of dreaming did go mad. And so the somniums radiated a field that put man into a state in which he got all the sleep, and all the dreams, that he needed within a four-hour period. Then he was awakened and a little later went into the stoner, where the field suspended all atomic and subatomic activity. He would remain in that state forever unless the activating field came on.

He slept, and Jennie Marlowe did not come to him. Or, if she did, he did not remember. He awoke, washed his face, went down eagerly to the stoner, where he found the entire household standing around, getting in one last smoke, talking, laughing. Then they would step into their cylinders, and a silence like that at the heart of a mountain would fall.

He had often wondered what would happen if he did not go into the stoner. How would he feel? Would he be panicked? All his life, he had known only Tuesdays. Would Wednesday rush at him, roaring, like a tidal wave? Pick him up and hurl him against the reefs of a strange time?

What if he made some excuse and went back upstairs and did not go back down until the field had come on? By then, he could not enter. The door to his cylinder would not open again until the proper time. He could still run down to the public emergency stoners only three blocks away. But if he stayed in his room, waiting for Wednesday?

Such things happened. If the breaker of the law did not have a reasonable excuse, he was put on trial. It was a felony second only to murder to "break time," and the unexcused were stonered. All felons, sane or insane, were stonered. Or *mañanaed,* as some said. The *mañanaed* criminal waited in immobility and unconsciousness, preserved unharmed until science had techniques to cure the insane, the neurotic, the criminal, the sick. *Mañana.*

"What was it like in Wednesday?" Tom had asked a man who had been unavoidably left behind because of an accident.

"How would I know? I was knocked out except for about fifteen minutes. I was in the same city, and I had never seen the faces of the ambulance men, of course, but then I've never seen them here. They stonered me and left me in the hospital for Tuesday to take care of."

He must have it bad, he thought. Bad. Even to think of such a thing was crazy. Getting into Wednesday was almost impossible. Almost. But it could be done. It would take time and patience, but it could be done.

He stood in front of his stoner for a moment. The others said, "See you! So long! Next Tuesday!" Mabel called, "Good night, lover!"

"Good night," he muttered.

"What?" she shouted.

"Good night!"

He glanced at the beautiful face behind the door. Then he smiled. He had been afraid that she might hear him say good night to a woman who called him "lover."

He had ten minutes left. The intercom alarms were whooping. Get going, everybody! Time to take the six-day trip! Run! Remember the penalties!

He remembered, but he wanted to leave a message. The recorder was on a table. He activated it, and said, "Dear *Miss* Jennie Marlowe. My name is Tom Pym, and my stoner is next to yours. I am an actor, too; in fact, I work at the same studio as you. I know this is presumptuous of me, but I have never seen anybody so beautiful. Do you have a talent to match your beauty? I would like to see some run-offs of your shows. Would you please leave some in room five? I'm sure the occupant won't mind. Yours, Tom Pym."

He ran it back. It was certainly bald enough, and that might be just what was needed. Too flowery or too pressing would have made her leery. He had commented on her beauty twice but not overstressed it. And the appeal to her pride in her acting would be difficult to resist. Nobody knew better than he about that.

He whistled a little on his way to the cylinder. Inside, he pressed the button and looked at his watch. Five minutes to midnight. The light on the huge screen above the computer in the police station would not be flashing for him. Ten minutes from now, Wednesday's police would step out of their stoners in the precinct station, and they would take over their duties.

There was a ten-minute hiatus between the two days in the police station. All hell could break loose in these few minutes, and it sometimes did. But a price had to be paid to maintain the walls of time.

He opened his eyes. His knees sagged a little and his head bent. The activation was a million microseconds fast—from eternium to flesh and blood almost instantaneously, and the heart never knew that it had been stopped for such a long time. Even so, there was a little delay in the muscles' response to a standing position.

He pressed the button, opened the door, and it was as if his button had launched the day. Mabel had made herself up last night so that she looked dawn-fresh. He complimented her, and she smiled happily. But he told her he would meet her for breakfast. Halfway up the staircase, he stopped, and waited until the hall was empty. Then he sneaked back down and into the stoner room. He turned on the recorder.

A voice, husky but also melodious, said, "Dear Mister Pym. I've had a few messages from other days. It was fun to talk back and forth across the abyss between the worlds, if you don't mind my exaggerating a little. But there is really no sense in it, once the novelty has worn off. If you become interested in the other person, you're frustrating yourself. That person can only be a voice in a recorder and a cold waxy face in a metal coffin. I wax poetic. Pardon me. If the person doesn't interest you, why continue to communicate? There is no sense in either case. And I *may* be beautiful. Anyway, I thank you for the compliment, but I am also sensible.

"I should have just not bothered to reply. But I want to be nice; I didn't want to hurt your feelings. So please don't leave any more messages."

He waited while silence was played. Maybe she was pausing for effect. Now would come a chuckle or a low honey-throated laugh, and she would say, "However, I don't like to disappoint my public. The run-offs are in your room."

The silence stretched out. He turned off the machine and went to the dining room for breakfast.

Siesta time at work was from 14:40 to 14:45. He lay down on the bunk and pressed the button. Within a minute he was asleep. He did dream of Jennie this time; she was a white shimmering figure solidifying out of the darkness and floating toward him. She was even more beautiful than she had been in her stoner.

The shooting ran overtime that afternoon so that he got home just in time for supper. Even the studio would not dare keep a man past his supper hour, especially since the studio was authorized to serve food only at noon.

He had time to look at Jennie for a minute before Mrs. Cuthmar's voice screeched over the intercom. As he walked down the hall, he thought, "I'm getting barnacled on her. It's ridiculous. I'm a grown man. Maybe . . . maybe I should see a psycher."

Sure, make your petition, and wait until a psycher has time for you. Say about three hundred days from now, if you are lucky. And if the psycher doesn't work out for you, then petition for another, and wait six hundred days.

Petition. He slowed down. Petition. What about a request, not to see a psycher, but to move? Why not? What did he have to lose? It would probably be turned down, but he could at least try.

Even obtaining a form for the request was not easy. He spent two nonwork days standing in line at the Center City Bureau before he got the proper forms. The first time, he was handed the wrong form and had to start all over again. There was no line set aside for those who wanted to change their days. There were not enough who wished to do this to justify such a line. So he had had to queue up before the Miscellaneous Office counter of the Mobility Section of the Vital Exchange Department of the Interchange and Cross Transfer Bureau. None of these titles had anything to do with emigration to another day.

When he got his form the second time, he refused to move from the office window until he had checked the number of the form and asked the clerk to double-check it. He ignored the cries and the mutterings behind him. Then he went to one side of the vast room and stood in line before the punch machines. After two hours, he got to sit down at a small rolltop desk-shaped machine, above which was a large screen. He inserted the form into the slot, looked at the projection of the form, and punched buttons to mark the proper spaces opposite the proper questions. After that, all he had to do was to drop the form into a slot and hope it did not get lost. Or hope he would not have to go through the same procedure because he had improperly punched the form.

That evening, he put his head against the hard metal and murmured to the rigid face behind the door, "I must really love you to go through all this. And you don't even know it. And, worse, if you did, you might not care one bit."

To prove to himself that he had kept his gray stuff, he went out with Mabel that evening to a party given by Sol Voremwolf, a producer. Voremwolf had just passed a civil-service examination giving him an

A-13 rating. This meant that, in time, with some luck and the proper pull, he would become an executive vice-president of the studio.

The party was a qualified success. Tom and Mabel returned about half an hour before stoner time. Tom had managed to refrain from too many blowminds and liquor, so he was not tempted by Mabel. Even so, he knew that when he became unstonered, he would be half-loaded and he'd have to take some dreadful counteractives. He would look and feel like hell at work, since he had missed his sleep.

He put Mabel off with an excuse, and went down to the stoner room ahead of the others. Not that that would do him any good if he wanted to get stonered early. The stoners only activated within narrow time limits.

He leaned against the cylinder and patted the door. "I tried not to think about you all evening, I wanted to be fair to Mabel; it's not fair to go out with her and think about you all the time."

All's fair in love . . .

He left another message for her, then wiped it out. What was the use? Besides, he knew that his speech was a little thick. He wanted to appear at his best for her.

Why should he? What did she care for him?

The answer was, he did care, and there was no reason or logic connect with it. He loved this forbidden, untouchable, far-away-in-time, yet-so-near woman.

Mable had come in silently. She said, "You're sick!"

Tom jumped away. Now, why had he done that? He had nothing to be ashamed of. Then why was he so angry with her? His embarrassment was understandable but his anger was not.

Mable laughed at him, and he was glad. Now he could snarl at her. He did so, and she turned away and walked out. But she was back in a few minutes with the others. It would soon be midnight.

By then he was standing inside the cylinder. A few seconds later, he left it, pushed Jennie's backward on its wheels, and pushed his around so that it faced hers. He went back in, pressed the button, and stood there. The double doors only slightly distorted his view. But she seemed even more removed in distance, in time, and in unattainability.

Three days later, well into winter, he received a letter. The box inside the entrance hall buzzed just as he entered the front door. He went back and waited until the letter was printed and had dropped out from the slot. It was the reply to his request to move to Wednesday.

Denied. Reason: he had no reasonable reason to move.

That was true. But he could not give his real motive. It would have been even less impressive than the one he had given. He had punched the box opposite No. 12. REASON: TO GET INTO AN ENVIRONMENT WHERE MY TALENTS WILL BE MORE LIKELY TO BE ENCOURAGED.

He cursed and he raged. It was his human, his civil right to move into any day he pleased. That is, it should be his right. What if a move did cause much effort? What if it required a transfer of his I.D. and all the records connected with him from the moment of his birth? What if . . . ?

He could rage all he wanted to, but it would not change a thing. He was stuck in the world of Tuesday.

Not yet, he muttered. Not yet. Fortunately, there is no limit to the number of requests I can make in my own day. I'll send out another. They think they can wear me out, huh? Well, I'll wear them out. Man against the machine. Man against the system. Man against the bureaucracy and the hard cold rules.

Winter's twenty days had sped by. Spring's eight days rocketed by. It was summer again. On the second day of the twelve days of summer, he received a reply to his second request.

It was neither a denial nor an acceptance. It stated that if he thought he would be better off psychologically in Wednesday because his astrologer said so, then he would have to get a psycher's critique of the astrologer's analysis. Tom Pym jumped into the air and clicked his sandaled heels together. Thank God that he lived in an age that did not classify astrologers as charlatans! The people—the masses—had protested that astrology was a necessity and that it should be legalized and honored. So laws were passed, and, because of that, Tom Pym had a chance.

He went down to the stoner room and kissed the door of the cylinder and told Jennie Marlowe the good news. She did not respond, though he thought he saw her eyes brighten just a little. That was, of course, only his imagination, but he liked his imagination.

Getting a psycher for a consultation and getting through the three sessions took another year, another forty-eight days. Dr. Sigmund Traurig was a friend of Dr. Stelhela, the astrologer, and so that made things easier for Tom.

"I've studied Dr. Stelhela's chart carefully and analyzed carefully your obsession for this woman," he said. "I agree with Dr. Stelhela that you will always be unhappy in Tuesday, but I don't quite agree with him that you will be happier in Wednesday. However, you have this thing going for this Miss Marlowe, so I think you should go to Wednesday. But only if you sign papers agreeing to see a psycher there for extended therapy."

Only later did Tom Pym realize that Dr. Traurig might have wanted to get rid of him because he had too many patients. But that was an uncharitable thought.

He had to wait while the proper papers were transmitted to Wednesday's authorities. His battle was only half-won. The other officials could turn him down. And if he did get to his goal, then what? She could reject him without giving him a second chance.

It was unthinkable, but she could.

He caressed the door and then pressed his lips against it.

"Pygmalion could at least touch Galatea," he said. "Surely, the gods —the big dumb bureaucrats—will take pity on me, who can't even touch you. Surely."

The psycher had said that he was incapable of a true and lasting bond with a woman, as so many men were in this world of easy-come-easy-go liaisons. He had fallen in love with Jennie Marlowe for several reasons. She may have resembled somebody he had loved when he was very young. His mother, perhaps? No? Well, never mind. He would find out in Wednesday—perhaps. The deep, the important, truth was that he loved Miss Marlowe because she could never reject him, kick him out, or become tiresome, complain, weep, yell, insult, and so forth. He loved her because she was unattainable and silent.

"I love her as Achilles must have loved Helen when he saw her on top of the walls of Troy," Tom said.

"I wasn't aware that Achilles was ever in love with Helen of Troy," Dr. Traurig said dryly.

"Homer never said so, but I *know* that he must have been! Who could see her and *not* love her?"

"How the hell would I know? I never saw her! If I had suspected these delusions would intensify . . ."

"I'm a poet!" Tom said.

"Overimaginative, you mean! Hmmm. She must be a douser! I don't have anything particular to do this evening. I'll tell you what . . . my curiosity is aroused . . . I'll come down to your place tonight and take a look at this fabulous beauty, your Helen of Troy."

Dr. Traurig appeared immediately after supper, and Tom Pym ushered him down the hall and into the stoner room at the rear of the big house as if he were a guide conducting a famous critic to a just-discovered Rembrandt.

The doctor stood for a long time in front of the cylinder. He hmmmed several times and checked her vital-data plate several times. Then he turned and said, "I see what you mean, Mr. Pym. Very well. I'll give the go-ahead."

"Ain't she something?" Tom said on the porch. "She's out of this world, literally and figuratively, of course."

"Very beautiful. But I believe that you are facing a great disappointment, perhaps heartbreak, perhaps, who knows, even madness, much as I hate to use that unscientific term."

"I'll take the chance," Tom said. "I know I sound nuts, but where would we be if it weren't for nuts? Look at the man who invented the wheel, at Columbus, at James Watt, at the Wright brothers, at Pasteur, you name them."

"You can scarcely compare these pioneers of science with their passion for truth with you and your desire to marry a woman. But, as I have observed, she is strikingly beautiful. Still, that makes me exceedingly cautious. Why isn't she married? What's wrong with her?"

"For all I know, she may have been married a dozen times!" Tom said. "The point is, she isn't now! Maybe she's disappointed and she's sworn to wait until the right man comes along. Maybe . . ."

"There's no maybe about it, you're neurotic," Traurig said. "But I actually believe that it would be more dangerous for you *not* to go to Wednesday than it would be *to* go."

"Then you'll say yes!" Tom said, grabbing the doctor's hand and shaking it.

"Perhaps. I have some doubts."

The doctor had a faraway look. Tom laughed and released the hand and slapped the doctor on the shoulder. "Admit it! You were really struck by her! You'd have to be dead not to!"

"She's all right," the doctor said. "But you must think this over. If you do go there and she turns you down, you might go off the deep end, much as I hate to use such a poetical term."

"No, I won't I wouldn't be a bit the worse off. Better off, in fact. I'll at least get to see her in the flesh."

Spring and summer zipped by. Then, a morning he would never forget, the letter of acceptance. With it, instructions on how to get to Wednesday. These were simple enough. He was to make sure that the technicians came to his stoner sometime during the day and readjusted the timer within the base. He could not figure out why he could not just stay out of the stoner and let Wednesday catch up to him, but by now he was past trying to fathom the bureaucratic mind.

He did not intend to tell anyone at the house, mainly because of Mabel. But Mabel found out from someone at the studio. She wept when she saw him at suppertime, and she ran upstairs to her room. He felt bad, but he did not follow to console her.

That evening, his heart beating hard, he opened the door to his stoner. The others had found out by then; he had been unable to keep the business to himself. Actually, he was glad that he had told them. They seemed happy for him, and they brought in drinks and had many rounds of toasts. Finally, Mabel came downstairs, wiping her eyes, and she said she wished him luck, too. She had known that he was not really in love with her. But she did wish someone would fall in love with her just by looking inside her stoner.

When she found out that he had gone to see Dr. Traurig, she said, "He's a very influential man. Sol Voremwolf had him for his analyst. He says he's even got influence on other days. He edits the *Psyche Crosscurrents*, you know, one of the few periodicals read by other people."

Other, of course, meant those who lived in Wednesdays through Mondays.

Tom said he was glad he had gotten Traurig. Perhaps he had used his influence to get the Wednesday authorities to push through his request so swiftly. The walls between the worlds were seldom broken, but it was suspected that the very influential did it when they pleased.

Now, quivering, he stood before Jennie's cylinder again. The last time, he thought, that I'll see her stonered. Next time, she'll be warm, colorful, touchable flesh.

"*Ave atque vale!*" he said aloud. The others cheered. Mable said, "How corny!" They thought he was addressing them, and perhaps he had included them.

He stepped inside the cylinder, closed the door, and pressed the button. He would keep his eyes open, so that . . .

And today was Wednesday. Though the view was exactly the same, it was like being on Mars.

He pushed open the door and stepped out. The seven people had faces he knew and names he had read on their plates. But he did not know them.

He started to say hello, and then he stopped.

Jennie Marlowe's cylinder was gone.

He seized the nearest man by the arm.

"Where's Jennie Marlowe?"

"Let go. You're hurting me. She's gone. To Tuesday."

"*Tuesday! Tuesday?*"

"Sure. She'd been trying to get out of here for a long time. She had something about this day being unlucky for her. She was unhappy, that's for sure. Just two days ago, she said her application had finally been accepted. Apparently, some Tuesday psycher had used his influence. He came down and saw her in her stoner, and that was it, brother."

The walls and the people and the stoners seemed to be distorted. Time was bending itself this way and that. He wasn't in Wednesday; he wasn't in Tuesday. He wasn't in *any* day. He was stuck inside himself at some crazy date that should never have existed.

"She can't do that!"

"Oh, no! She just did that!"

"But . . . you can't transfer more than once!"

"That's her problem."

It was his, too.

"I should never have brought him down to look at her!" Tom said. "The swine! The unethical swine!"

Tom Pym stood there for a long time, and then he went into the kitchen. It was the same environment, if you discounted the people. Later, he went to the studio and got a part in a situation play which was, really, just like all those in Tuesday. He watched the newscaster that night. The president of the U.S.A. had a different name and face, but the words of his speech could have been those of Tuesday's President. He was introduced to a secretary of a producer; her name wasn't Mabel, but it might as well have been.

The difference here was that Jennie was gone, and oh, what a world of difference it made to him.

Questions for Discussion and Review

1. What is the answer to the question Tom cannot answer about his instructions on how to get to Wednesday?
2. How does Farmer create the necessary distance between Tom's interests and those of the readers so that the denouement strikes us as other than tragic?
3. Describe as precisely as you can the effect this story is designed to produce.
4. There is an echo of what poem in the last sentence of the story? What is the connection?
5. Why does the title describe the Only-on-Tuesday World as "sliced crosswise"?

Utopias and Dystopias

The original utopia was the Garden of Eden. Most cultures and religions have versions of the idea of an earthly paradise from which things have since devolved. In one way or another, the Eden myth lies behind the many varieties of fantasy utopias. Perhaps we should consider them consolations for the disappointments of a world that rarely seems to make much of an effort to fulfill human expectations and desires.

Foremost among fantasy utopias is *faerie*. It is by no means either a perfect or a safe world for mortals to dwell in. Its varieties are many, and they are written about in ballads and romances, medieval and modern, from "Hind Horn" and *The Faerie Queene* to *The Wood Beyond the World* and *The Lord of the Rings*.

Closely related to faerie are pastoral utopias inhabited since Theocritus by poetic shepherds or philosophical swains piping native woodnotes wild. It is a world of leisure, rural courtship, poetry, and music that idealizes the simple virtues associated with country life and implicitly rejects the vanities and fleshpots of city life. It is Shangri-la.

A little further out on the scale of fantasy utopias is the land of the lotos-eaters, most recently revived by drug cultists. Beyond that is the land of Cockaine, a pleasure utopia where the sensualist finds gratification. At the outer limits is the dream utopia in which all expectations are fulfilled, however impossible they might be.

Another sort of utopia began with Plato's *Republic;* it offers a better world, an ideal world, that is attainable. Plato's is the first of the philosophical utopias, or utopias that have behind them a moral vision of the ideal culture. Thomas More's *Utopia* provided both the name and model for the social utopia, which proposes an ideal social order based on reason and natural law. Social utopias have appeared in Rousseau's *Social Contract*, Morris's *News from Nowhere*, and Austin T. Wright's *Islandia*. Finally we come to the scientific utopia, the main type since the Renaissance, which is created by the application of scientific principles enabling human beings to overcome their imperfections. Bacon's *New Atlantis* was the model of this type, and the best recent example is Aldous Huxley's *Island*.

Utopias originated before SF developed, and some of them are fantasies. However, since the scientific revolution, utopian and SF literatures have become identified more and more closely, particularly in the past three-quarters of a century. The reason for this is not that all recent utopias have been social or scientific ones; in fact, fantasy utopias probably have outnumbered rational ones during this period. Oddly enough, the association comes from the antiutopian and dystopian story.

The logic is inescapable. If one can imagine an ideal society, then one can also imagine its opposite. The aftereffects of the Industrial Revolution have taught Western culture a painful lesson. Misapplied, the very forces that are employed in the hope of making an earthly paradise also can make a hell. We know, because we have been there, in the trench and poison-gas warfare of World War I. And since then, a dozen times over, the nightmare has grown: Hitler's concentration camps, Stalin's purges, World War II beginning with Pearl Harbor and ending with Hiroshima and Nagasaki. But it is not just that warfare has become more savage and brutal; so also have the societies that have emerged from them. The totalitarian state found its image in Eugene Zamiatin's *We* and in more famous successors: Huxley's *Brave New World*, Orwell's *1984* and *Animal Farm*, and Ray Bradbury's *Fahrenheit 451*.

Although "dystopia" and "antiutopia" are used synonymously, they are different. Clearly the opposite of the utopia, in the antiutopia there is social disorder, repression, and the like. The dystopia is less absolute. Wells's vision of a future world inhabited by Eloi and Morlocks is a case in poir' That world is a decayed utopia. On the other hand, the social order may malfunction or becomes dysfunctional, as in Heinlein's *Stranger in a Strange Land* or Vonnegut's *Player Piano*, without ever achieving a utopian state.

The dystopian story (and I will use this term to include antiutopian for ease of reference) is almost exclusively in the realm of SF these days. Its roots are in the satires of Swift, Cyrano de Bergerac, and their predecessors. But with the new power that science has delivered into the hands of humanity, dystopias have taken on a new and more urgent importance as literature. The frame of reference that an author constructs for a story is rarely absolute. The usual moral of the dystopia is to imply that if certain trends of the present continue, the result may be a dysfunctioning social order or worse. In other words, in one way or another it is always the present that the author of a dystopia is asking us to examine. Pohl and Kornbluth's *The Space Merchants* illustrates a future commercial dystopia extrapolated from current trends in the capitalist economic and social structures.

It is worth noting that utopian and dystopian literature is more suited to longer than to shorter forms of fiction because the author must both create the other place and then show readers how it works. This usually requires a certain latitude in which to develop the argument of the narrative and to work out its application. Therefore, we can expect the single action of the short story to reveal but a part of the complex whole, leaving the rest suggested or implied in the main action. There are both advantages and disadvantages to these limitations, as the following two stories illustrate.

When the Vertical World Becomes Horizontal

Alexei Panshin

Alexei Panshin was born in 1940 in Michigan. He received his bachelor's
degree from Michigan State University and a master's from The University
of Chicago in 1966. He is known to the SF establishment as both an
author and a critic. His study *Heinlein in Dimension* (1968) is a highly
regarded assessment of Heinlein's work and influence. He has been at
work over the past several years on a history of SF. As author, he has
been publishing short fiction since 1960. His first novel, *Rite of Passage*,
won the Hugo Award for best novel of 1968. "When the Vertical World
Becomes Horizontal" was published first in 1974, in Terry Carr's anthology
of New Wave writers, *Universe 4*.

This story is a parable. As the title suggests, it tells of a change in the
social order from vertical to horizontal, from authoritarian and structured
to communal and open. The change in the social order is caused by forces
never specified; however, we may infer that they are of electromagnetic
origin associated with an unusual but natural phenomenon like an
alteration of the magnetic poles. H. G. Wells's novel *In the Days of the
Comet* (1906) describes a sudden and universal change of the social order
into a utopia as the result of a change in the gaseous composition of the
atmosphere caused by Earth's passage through the tail of a comet.

In a short story, where there is a limitation of length and effect, a writer
has to decide whether to work out the means by which the change takes
place, to concentrate upon the experience of the change itself, or to touch
upon the effects. Panshin chose the middle course. And while the other
interests are worthy intentions, they are peripheral in this story to the
narrator's relevation of what he calls a good moment—one of three since the
world began. What the others may have been, we are not told. This time
it is a change in the psychodynamics of social interaction, as social
scientists might explain it. Freudians might describe it as a victory of the
super ego over both the id and the ego.

Perhaps it is just as well, therefore, that the story is told as a *parable*,
a narrative with an attached moral; but here the moral is implied rather
than specified. In a sense, the story defines utopia in new terms—as the
realization of a new order in which the individual fulfills unique potentials
freely without the inhibiting restraints of either a social or a psychological
pecking order. The story relates in narrative form the disappearance of
that established order as experienced by one Woody Asenion, a retarded
thirty-seven-year-old. As someone not yet as high as the bottom rung of the
social ladder, Woody, in a mysterious fashion, is the key to the shift in
that order. Like all vertical orders, this one is supported from the bottom
largely through the insecurity and fear of those who are its victims.
Paradoxical as it may seem, it is those who are socially disadvantaged who
cling most resolutely to the established ways.

In this story, however, these matters are employed principally to heighten the contrast with the changing world. In the horizontal society people are liberated from restraints that have enslaved them. The social and economic disadvantages are the most obvious, but the personal inhibitions are the most important. If this parable has a moral, therefore, it is a familiar one: The kingdom of heaven lies within you!

The rain is coming closer, sending the heat running before it. I can see the rain, hanging like twists of smoke over the roofs. The city will be scrubbed clean.

This is an acute moment. The wind is raising gooseflesh on my arms. I can feel the thunder as electricity and the electricity as thunder. Down in the street I hear voices calling around the corner. I think I even hear the music.

This is the moment. I know it's here.

I've been waiting so long. I'll savor this last bit of waiting. The dark is so dark, so close-wrapped. The electricity is white. The streets are going to steam.

There has never been a better moment since the world began. This is it! It's here.

It's never happened since the last time, and it's going to happen now. The beginning of the world was a better moment. It was exalting. As nearly as I can tell, there have been two good moments since. I missed them both.

I'm going to be here for this one.

So are you.

I know the sun is baking the sidewalks. The heat is now. But listen with your skin. Rain is in the air.

It's going to be good. When you see the rain and steam and sun and people all mixed together in the afternoon, you'll know their tune is the one that's been in your head all along. Close your eyes. Feel the wind rising.

I'll tell you how good it's going to be. I'll tell you what it was like for someone who knew even less than you do about what is happening.

Woody Asenion was raised in the largest closet of an apartment at 206 W. 104th St. in Manhattan. Once there had been four—Papa, Granny, Mama and him—but now there were only two. There was room now for Woody to stretch out, but at night he still slept at Papa's feet, just like always, for the comfort of just like always.

Woody had never been out of the closet without permission. Well, once. When he was very small he had slipped out into the apartment one night and wandered the aisles alone until the blinking and bubbling became too frightening to bear and the robot found him, shook a finger at him and led him back home. He had never done it again.

But on this day, the vertical world was turning horizontal. People were no longer cringing and bullying. They were starting to think of other things.

It was already this close: When Woody's father, who was very vertical, flung the door of the closet open while in the grip of an intense excitement, Woody had his hand on the knob and the knob three quarters turned. That was a quarter-turn more than he usually dared when he toyed with strange thoughts of an afternoon.

Mr. Asenion broke Woody's grip on the knob with an automatic gesture. "You promised your papa," he said and rapped his knuckles with a demodulator he happened to have in his hand. But the moment was quickly forgotten in his excitement.

"I had it all backwards! I had it all backwards! It's the particular that represents the general."

That was part of the vertical world turning horizontal, too. Since he had flunked out of Columbia University in 1928, Mr. Asenion had been working on a Dimensional Redistributor. He had been seeking to open gateways to the many strange dimensions that exist around us. He had never been successful.

He had never been successful in the vertical world, either. He had fallen out of its bottom. He told himself that he did not fit because he hadn't yet found his place. He was very vertical. He knew the power that would be his if he ever invented the Dimensional Redistributor, and so labored all the harder through the many years of failure. It was his key to entry at the top of the pyramid.

But suddenly, on this day when the vertical world was turning horizontal, enough people being ready for that to happen, he had been struck with a crucial insight as he was standing with a demodulator in his hand. He suddenly saw that you could turn things around. The answer was *not* many gateways to many strange dimensions. It was *one* gateway, one gateway into this world.

He knew how to build it, too.

"I'll need a 28K-916 Hersh.," he said. That was a vacuum tube with special rhodomagnetic properties that had been out of stock for forty-two years.

There was only one place in New York, perhaps in all the world, where such a tube might be found, Stewart's Out-of-Stock Supply. Stewart's has *everything* that is out of stock, and Mr. Asenion had seen a 28K-916 Hersh. there in 1934. He had not needed it then, however.

Stewart's has everything out of stock that an out-of-date inventor might need, but they may not sell it to you if they disapprove of you. Mr. Asenion had not been welcome in Stewart's since the fall of 1937 when he had incautiously announced his ambitions under stern cross-questioning.

"Woodrow," Mr. Asenion said, "you must go to Stewart's in Brooklyn. They will have a 28K-916 Hersh. It's all I need to finish my machine. Then I will rule the world."

"Brooklyn?" said Woody. "I've never been to Brooklyn, Papa."

He had heard of Brooklyn from the lips of his dead mother. She said she had been to Brooklyn once.

Sometimes he had thought about Brooklyn when his father was experimenting and he was alone in the closet.

He had seen the Heights of Brooklyn once, the great towering wall of rock that conceals all but the spires of the land beyond. Or he believed that he had. Sometimes he thought that he must have imagined it when he was small. He would know if he should ever see it again. But to go to Brooklyn?

"It's farther that I've ever been. Why don't you go, Papa?"

"There are reasons," said Mr. Asenion with dignity. "At this special moment, I must stay with my machine. Further inspiration may come to me. I must be ready."

He had a point. Lack of success in the vertical world is no index of lack of skill in invention. He had something in the Dimensional Redistributor. What's more, his insight on this day when the vertical world was turning horizontal, was valid: with the particular representing the general, one reversed gateway, and a 28K-916 Hersh. in place, his Dimensional Redistributor would work. And there are even alternatives to the 28K-916 Hersh. which inspiration can reveal and ingenuity confirm.

Woody shook his head in fear and excitement. "I can't do it."

Mr. Asenion heard only the fear. "There's no need to be afraid, just because it's Brooklyn. I'll write out the way, just as I always do. And I'll send the robot along to keep you company. You will be safe as long as you stick to the path and carry your umbrella."

The robot nodded dumbly from behind Mr. Asenion. When Woody had run errands in the neighborhood, it had always kept him silent company.

"I don't want to," said Woody.

"I command you to go. You owe it to me, your father, for all the many years I've fed you and kept a roof over your head and let you sleep at my feet."

He was right if you look at things vertically.

"All right," said Woody. "I will go."

Mr. Asenion patted Woody on the head. "Good boy," he said.

When the Dimensional Redistributor was in operation, he meant to pat the whole world on the head when it did what he said. "Good boy," he would say.

As soon as Mr. Asenion turned away, Woody kicked the robot. It could not complain, but it did look reproachful.

So there you have Woody Asenion, raised in a closet, lower than the lowest in the vertical world, somebody who knows even less than you do about what is going on. He is even more limited than you know. Last birthday, Woody was thirty-seven years old.

Woody gave the robot one of his hands and held his map and directions tight in the other so as not to lose his way, said goodbye to his

father, who turned away to putter with his machine, and with one deep
breath cleared the first three thresholds—the door of the closet, the door
of the apartment, and the door of the building at 206 W. 104th St. in
Manhattan—and stood blinking in the sun, heat and sidewalk traffic.
There were threats, noise and distraction all about him. Cars clawed
and roared at each other, seeking advantage. Signs in bright colors
loomed at Woody yelling, "Number *1* in Quantity," and "Do As
You're Told, Son," and "Step Backward." It was confusing to Woody,
but he knew that if he did not panic, if he followed his instructions,
stayed on the path and did not lose his umbrella, he could pass through
the danger unscathed.

He let his breath out. The air in the street was wet and sticky. The
sunlight was oppressive. He seized the robot's hand all the tighter, and
they set off down the street. It was the robot who carried the rolled
umbrella.

The people they threaded through were these:

Three white men—one in a business suit, one an old man, one a
bum.

Two black men—one grateful, one not.

A student.

Three old women.

Five Puerto Ricans of both sexes and various ages.

Two young women—one bitter, one not.

A minister of the Church of God.

A group of snazzy black buccaneers talking bad.

And a little girl who also lived at 206 W. 104th St. in Manhattan.
"Hi, Woody," she said. "Hi, It."

Five of these twenty-five saw Woody Asenion walking along the street
with his hand in the hand of a tall skinny cuproberyl robot and knew
him immediately to be their inferior. All the others weren't sure or
didn't care about things like that any more.

That's how close the vertical world was to turning horizontal. But
it hadn't happened yet.

The map led Woody directly to the subway station. There was a
hooded green pit, an orange railing, and stairs leading down.

In his closet, when Woody was small, he could feel the force of the
subway train. When it prowled, the building would shudder. His
mother had told him not to be afraid.

Woody and the robot, on their errands in the neighborhood, had
twice walked past the stairpit into the subway. Once Woody had
stepped three steps down and then back up again quickly. That was
like a half-turn of the doorknob to the closet, but more daring. And
now their directions led them down the stairs. Woody looked to the
robot for assurance. The robot nodded, held Woody's hand and took
each stair first.

It was cooler in the dark cavern under the street. Only one light
was visible, a yellow light in a huddled booth. Woody and the robot

walked between dim pillars to the booth in the distance. Sitting on a stool in the booth was a blue extra-terrestrial. It looked something like a hound, something like Fred MacMurray. It was dressed in a blue Friends of the New York Subway System uniform.

Woody looked at his directions. "Four toll tokens," he said to the alien in the tollbooth.

The alien said, "Are you Woody Asenion?"

Woody stepped behind the robot. "How did you know me?"

The alien waved at him and turned away for the telephone. "Just forget I asked. It really isn't important, Woody." He dialed a number. While he waited for the ring, he said, "I'd only buy two tokens, if I were you. You'll only need two. Oh, hello, Clishnor. Listen, 'it's about to rain.' Right."

Woody looked at his directions. They said to buy four toll tokens. He set his jaw. "Four toll tokens, please," he said. "And how did you know me?"

"I was set here to ask," said the blue alien in the blue Friends of the New York Subway System uniform. "We're just observers here for the rain and we wanted to have warning."

"Rain?" said Woody.

"The weather forecast says that when Woody Asenion goes to Brooklyn it's going to rain." The alien passed four tokens under the grill of the booth. "See if it doesn't."

"Oh, is that how it is," said Woody, who wasn't sure how weather forecasts were made. He hadn't thought he was that important, though of course he was. Well, he was safe. The robot had the umbrella.

Woody and the robot turned away. There was a white electric sign on the other side of the booth. It had a black arrow and black letters that blinked and said, "To the Subway". They followed the arrow. Behind them, the tollbooth closed and the yellow light went off.

The directions and map mentioned the black arrow and the sign. Woody and the robot walked through the darkness between the metal pillars until they came to another stair. An automatic machine guarded the top of the stair. It held out a hand until Woody gave it two toll tokens and then it let them pass.

There was light at the bottom of the stairs and the stairs were very tall. Down they walked, down and down, until Woody was not at all sure that he wanted to go to Brooklyn at all, even to buy his father a 28K-916 Hersh. to finish his Dimensional Redistributor and control the world.

The station was a great vaulted catacomb. The walls were covered with grime-coated mosaics celebrating the muses of Science and Industry. Woody and the robot were all alone on the echoing platform.

Then suddenly a wind blew through the station, fluttering the map and directions in Woody's hand, a chill wind. Following the wind, the squealing, clashing and roaring of the great behemoth. Following the noise, the subway train itself. It hurtled into the station under the tight command of its pilot, whom Woody could see seated in the front window, and came to a stop with a tortured screech of metal. A voice more commanding than even Mr. Asenion's said, "Passengers will stand clear of the moving platform as trains enter and leave the station!" A shelf of metal moved silently out to the train as a pair of doors slammed open in front of them. Woody squeezed the robot's hand hard.

The robot nodded reassuringly and led Woody onto the metal shelf and aboard the train. One last look. The shelf began to withdraw and the doors closed like a trap, and Woody was committed.

Woody was afraid. He sat, uneasy as a cricket, on the seat next to the robot. Blackness hurtled by the window behind his head. There was great constantly modulating noise. All the passengers stared straight ahead.

But this was no ordinary subway train, even though it now ran on an obscure local line. There was a plaque on the wall across from Woody. It said, "This train, the *Lyman R. Long,* was dedicated at the New York World's Fair as the Subway Train of the Future, July 7, 1939." In no time at all, this great old train brought them into the gleaming Central Station of the New York Subway System.

They left the Subway Train of the Future then, and ventured out into the echoing bustle of this bright high-ceilinged underground world. The walls were alive with texture and color. High overhead, dominating Central Station, was a great stained glass window lit like a neon sign. It, too, celebrated the muses of Science and Industry, but it was much grander.

Woody took no notice of the wonder around him. He ignored the people. He ignored the color. He ignored the light. He ignored the shops that filled the caverns of the Central Station. He held tight to the robot's hand and looked resolutely straight ahead. All this around him was distraction. Woody was going to Brooklyn to buy his father a 28K-916 Hersh. so that he could finish his Dimensional Redistributor and control the world. If he lost his path, Woody would not dare to guess at his fate.

His directions said . . . but there it was, directly before him. The sign said, "To Brooklyn." Under it sat the plasteel form of a new modern train, doors open wide, waiting patiently. The *Lyman R. Long* was 1939's vision of the future, now relegated to a local line. This was the future made present. This was tomorrow now.

This smugly superior subway train was far more frightening somehow as it sat, quietly waiting. This open door was the last threshold. If Woody passed beyond it, he would be swallowed and carried to Brooklyn. He would not be able to help himself.

But he had no choice. He could not help himself now. He must stay on the path, and the path led to Brooklyn. Stepping aboard the train had the same disconcerting finality as the bursting of a soap bubble.

There were but two seats left together in the car, and Woody and his companion, the robot, sat down. As soon as they sat, as though by signal, the doors of the car slid shut automatically and silently, and automatically and silently the subway train slid out of the Central Station of the New York Subway System, bound for Brooklyn. It plunged immediately into the cold dark earth tunnel under the East River and down, down it went without consideration of what it might discover. Down. Noiselessly down. Relentlessly down.

One instant they were in the station. One instant there was still connection to the familiar world. One instant they were still in Manhattan. The next moment they were hurtling into an unknown nether world. It was all too sudden. Woody was paralyzed with fear.

It felt to him as though a hand were wringing his brain, and another hand were squeezing his throat, and another hand were tickling his heart, toying with his life and certainty. And the only hand that was really there was the strong cuproberyl hand of the robot Woody Asenion's father had made to keep Woody in the closet and safe from other harm. Woody held that familiar hand tight. He looked at the map and directions that he held. That was his talisman. He had not left the path. As long as he did not leave the path, he would be safe.

The train bumped a bottom bump and the lights in the car dimmed and then came up. The door between cars at Woody's left slammed open, allowing a brief snatch of the whirring whine of the rubberite wheels on the tracks, and three young people burst threateningly in. They were dangerous because no one in the subway car had ever seen anything like them. They were not apprentices. They were not secretaries. They were not management trainees. They were neither soldiers nor students. They were not hip, but then neither were they straight.

One was a boy, narrow, tall, ugly and graceful as a hatchet. He wore an extravagant white suit, dandy and neat, and carried a yellow chrysanthemum to play with. The other boy was short, dark, curly and cute. He wore a casual brown doublet over an orange shirt. He bounced and bubbled. The girl wore cheerfully vulgar purple to her ankle with a slit back up to the thigh. She was pale and her black hair was severe and dramatic.

The girl was the first into the car. She swung around and around the pole in front of Woody, laughing. The bouncy boy galloped in after her, swung her around the pole and then stopped her with a sudden kiss, even though an ad over his shoulder from Amy Vanderbilt suggested to him that public emotion is not good manners. The ugly one strolled in gracefully, shut the door to the car and blessed the two with his yellow mum, tapping them each on the head, saying nothing.

Then he turned and waved his flower menacingly at the rest of the car. He danced. This was too much for one vertical soul who leaped to his feet and said authoritatively, "We are all good citizens here on our way to Brooklyn. What do you mean by this intrusion?"

"Don't you feel it?" the bouncy one asked. "The world has changed.

The Great Common Dream is changing and so is the world. We're going to Brooklyn to dance in the rain and celebrate. Come on along."

The girl looked directly at the questioning man. "Listen with your skin," she said. "Don't you feel it? Don't you want to celebrate?"

The man looked puzzled. But he listened with his skin and you could tell he knew they were right, even if they were a little early. He was horizontal in his heart which is why he was so quick to seem vertical. He thought it might be noticed if he wasn't. But now he said, "I do feel it! I do feel it! You're right. You're right!" He howled a joyous howl of celebration.

And he began to dance in the aisles. "I feel it, too," someone else yelled. "I do." Who? It might have been any of the first six people to join him in the aisles.

Now that's how close the vertical world was to turning horizontal. All that was necessary was the suggestion. People were ready to go multiform as soon as they knew it was time.

Woody tugged at the sleeve of the tall boy in the extravagant white suit.

"Yes, sir, may I be of practical assistance?" said he, and winked.

"Is it raining now?" asked Woody. It seemed important that he should ask, since the strange blue toll-token seller had suggested that it was going to rain and he wanted to be prepared. The robot carried Woody's umbrella in his capable cuproberyl hand. He would be all right as long as he knew before he got wet.

"Raining," said the ugly one. "Raining? How would I know if it's raining? We're in a subway train under the East River."

"Oh, hey now, it's Woody," said the girl. "Go easy on Woody. It's going to rain, Woody. Don't you want to come along with us and dance in the rain?"

But she was too insistent for poor Woody. He didn't know enough of the world to be sure what it was that she intended, but he suspected the world too much to want to learn. She was a distraction. The whole car was a distraction, dancing, gadding and larking. He stared straight ahead of him at the subway ad for Amy Vanderbilt's new etiquette book. "Know Your Place in the Space Age," the ad whispered to him when it knew it had his full attention. And that was another distraction.

"Hey, dance with us, Woody," said the curly one in orange. "You can do any step you like. You can do a step no one else has ever done."

Woody explained, "I have this map and these directions." He pointed to them. "I'm very busy now. I'm running an errand for my father. I'm going to buy a 28K-916 Hersh. so that he can finish his Dimensional Redistributor and control the world."

The tall narrow boy said, "Why doesn't your father run his own errands? He's all grown up now." He said it impatiently. Woody didn't like him.

Woody stared straight ahead with all the best deafness he could muster. It was the deafness he used to do when he sat in the corner of the closet with his back to the world and wouldn't hear. He could shut out lots.

The other boy and the girl said, "Come on, Woody. The vertical world is turning horizontal. Come with us, Woody. We're in Brooklyn now. This is New Lots. This is our stop. This is our place. Take a chance, Woody. Be the first to celebrate. Dare. Dance. Dance in the rain."

And everybody in the car said,. "Come one, come all, Woody. There's room for you. There's room for everyone."

But Woody stared straight ahead, which made everything on either side blurry, and wouldn't hear. It was as good as shutting his eyes. He held onto his map and his directions with both hands so that he would not become lost.

Woody felt the subway come to a smooth stop. He wouldn't admit it, but he heard the doors slide gently open. He wouldn't admit it, but after a long moment he heard the doors slide gently shut again. He only unblinked his eyes when he felt the train begin to move again.

He was alone in the car. There was no one else there. The girl in the purple dress down to her ankle and up to her thigh was gone. The boy in the white suit was gone. The boy in the brown doublet and the orange shirt was gone. All the people in the car were gone. Even the robot was gone, and the umbrella was gone with him. You can imagine how that made Woody feel.

No hand to hold. No umbrella to keep him dry and safe if it did rain.

But still he had his map and directions. He wasn't completely lost.

He was driven to walk the length of the train. Every car was empty. Every car was as empty as his car when everyone had gone. He was alone. He walked from one end of the train to the other and he saw no one. When he got to the head of the train he looked in the window at the driver. But there was no pilot.

And still the train hurtled on. Woody was afraid.

He went back to his own seat. He sat there alone studying his map and directions. They said to get off at Rockaway Parkway.

And then the train came to a halt. An automatic voice said automatically, "Rockaway Parkway. End of the line." And the door slid open. Woody bolted through it and up the stairs.

There was another orange railing. The stairs ended between two great boulders with white lamps that said, "Subway." Woody was standing in a great rock park. And this was Brooklyn.

It was not raining, but the air was hot, damp, and heavy in Brooklyn, like a warm smothering washcloth. Woody wished he had his umbrella.

He looked at his directions. They said, "Follow the path to Stewart's."

So he followed the path and in a few minutes he came to the edge of the hill. He could see the flatlands below and on across the damp sand flats even to the palm-lined shores of Jamaica Bay itself. He could se the palms swaying sullenly under the threatening sky. He followed the path farther, never straying, and when he reached Flatlands Avenue he could suddenly see the great porcelain height of his landmark, white but marked by stains of rust. That was the Paerdegat Basin, and close by the Paerdegat Basin was Stewart's.

It was an easy walk. Woody had time to study his instructions. They were frightening, for they asked him to lie. He wasn't good at that. When he lied, his father always caught him out.

And then, almost before he knew, his feet had followed the true path to Stewart's Out-of-Stock Supply. It was a small block building. He hesitated and then he entered.

The small building was filled with many amazing machines, some of them a bit dusty, displayed to show the successes of the shop. All of them had been made of parts supplied by Stewart's. There were a four-dimensional roller-press, a positronic calculator, an in-gravity parachute —which seemed to be a metal harness with pads to protect the body— and a mobile can opener.

At the back of the building was a sharp-featured, crew-cut old man with a positive manner. He looked as though he had his mind made up about everything.

"Don't tell me. Don't tell me. I've got my theory." the old man said. He looked at Woody, measuring him with his eye. Then he punched authoritatively at a button console on the counter in front of him. The wall behind him dissolved as though it had forgotten to remember itself, and there were immense aisles with racks and bins and shelves filled with out-of-stock supplies. A sign overhead said, "1947–1957." And another sign said, "At Last. 4 Amazing *New* Scientific Discoveries Help to Make You Feel Like a *New Person* and *More Alive!*"

The old man put on a golf cap and said, "There. I'm right so far, aren't I? Now let me see. The rest of it should be easy. Yes, you're really quite simple, young man. I see to the bottom of you."

He pulled a series of buttons. A little robot rolled by, made a right turn down an aisle and then a left turn out of sight. The old man stood waiting with a sure-footed expression on his face. In a moment, the robot rolled back. It placed a flat plate in the old man's hand, and the old man placed the plate on the counter. Then he patted the robot on the head and it rolled away.

"There, you see. You're the right age. You're obviously a broad-headed Alpine. The half-life of strontium ninety is twenty-eight years. You're here to replace the tactile plate on your Erasmus Bean machine. Am I right?"

Woody shook his head.

"But of course I'm right."

Woody shook his head.

"Then what are you here for?"

Woody read from his paper, " 'I want a 28K-916 Hersh. It was discontinued in 1932.' "

"Don't tell me my business," the old man said, hanging up the golf cap reluctantly. "It's strange. You don't look like a 1932."

He punched again, and the configuration of aisles flickered and re-stabilized. The overhead sign now said, "1926–1935." And another sign said, "Are You Caught Behind the Bars of a 'Small-Time' Job? Learn Electricity! Earn $3000 a Year!" The old man slapped a straw skimmer on his head.

"We did have a 28K-916 Hersh.," he said. "Once. We don't have much call for one of those. I recollect seeing it along about 1934."

The little robot rolled out once again, made a right turn down an aisle and then a left turn out of sight.

The old man turned suddenly to Woody and said, "This tube isn't for your own invention, is it? You're not a 1932 at all. Who are you here for? Murray? Stanton? Hyatt?"

Woody lowered his eyes. He shook his head.

The robot rolled suddenly back into view. It placed an orange-and-black box, as shiny and new as though this were 1932 and it were fresh from the Hersh. factory, in the hand of the sharp-featured old man.

"This is a rare tube with special rhodomagnetic properties," the old man said. "Just how do you propose to put it to use?"

Woody looked down again. Below the counter top he looked again at his instructions and he read his lie. He read, " 'I am a collector. I mean to collect one of every vacuum tube in the world. When I own a 28K-916 Hersh., my collection will be complete.' "

But the old man looked over the counter and saw him reading and his suspicions were aroused. He snatched the map and directions from Woody's hands, and discovered their meaning with a single glance.

"Woodrow Asenion!" he said. "I barred your father from this store in 1937! You know what that man intends. He means to make a Dimensional Redistributor and control the world. Well, not with help from Stewart's. Power is to be used responsibly."

He threw the map and instructions behind him, seized Woody and hustled him through the showroom, past the four-dimensional roller-press, the positronic calculator, the in-gravity parachute, the mobile can opener and all the many other amazing inventions. He threw Woody onto the sand under the palm tree in front of the building.

"And never come back," he said. He straightened his skimmer. Then he looked up. Very slowly he said, "Why, I do believe it's going to rain."

The old man slammed the door and pulled down a curtain that said, "Closed on Account of Rain."

Woody looked around desperately. He looked at the sky. It *was* going to rain and he had no umbrella. He had not bought the tube. He had no map and directions. He was almost lost. He beat desperately on the door but it would not open. While he beat, all the lights within went out. The building was silent. Then thunder rumbled overhead.

In panic, Woody retreated along Flatlands Avenue. The sky was crackling and snarling. It was flaring and fleering. Woody wished desperately that he were safe at home in the comfort of his own familiar closet. He felt very vulnerable. He felt naked and alone in a strange country. What was he to do? What was he to do?

Woody thought that if he could only find the subway station in the rock park again, the green stairs with the orange railing under the lamps that said, "Subway," he might find his way home to 206 W. 104th St. in Manhattan. Home to his father and his own closet. Desperately, he began to run across the sand.

And then, suddenly, there they all were. There was the boy in the white suit. There was the boy in the brown doublet. There was the girl in the long purple dress. And behind them a pied piper's gathering of people, dancing, larking and gadding. And that was just anticipation, for the moment of shift when the old vertical world was forgotten and the new guiding dream was dreamed had not yet come. It had not yet begun to rain.

"Hi, Woody," said the boy in brown. "Are you ready to join us?"

"Hi, Woody," said the girl in purple. "Are you ready to dance in the rain?"

That was too frightening. Woody said to the tall ugly boy in white, "Where is my robot? It has my umbrella."

"He," said that one, and tapped Woody on the forehead with his yellow chrysanthemum. "He. And he isn't yours. And I have my doubts about the umbrella, too."

"Ha," everybody said. "Get wet."

"Ho," everybody said. "It will hardly hurt at all."

That was terrifying. Woody knew who he was now. He was the one at the bottom—and that was a secure position. If he left the path and joined this many, who would he be? He would be lost. He would not know himself.

"Who?" he said. "Who?"

"You," they said. "You."

They laughed. And they were singing, some of them. And doing other things. Celebrating beneath this final black threatening sky, this roiling heaven.

Woody could not bear it. "I have to find a 28K-916 Hersh.," he said. "I can't stay. I have to go."

"Goodbye. Goodbye." they called as he hurried away. He looked back from the hillside and some were looking up at the sky and waiting. Waiting for the clouds to open and the rain to pour down. Woody feared the rain. He ran.

No map. No directions. No map. No instructions. No umbrella. But he still had two toll tokens.

Down the path he ran into the rock park. Along the path. Still on the true path. And there before him were the twin boulders. Before him was the green stair with the orange railing. Before him was haven.

But there was a chain across the top of the stair. There was a locked gate across the bottom of the stair. And the lamps at the entrance were not lit. All said, "Closed." All said, "Try Other Entrance."

The other entrance. The other entrance. Where was the other entrance? There it was! It was visible on the other side of the rock park, marked by another pair of lamps set atop another pair of boulders.

Woody left the path and struck toward them. He ran in all his hope of home. He ran in all his fear of rain. His understanding was not profound, but he knew that if he were rained upon, nothing would be as it was.

He did not notice that in leaving the path his father had marked for him before Woody had ventured out of the closet, he had lost his last protection. First the robot, sturdy and comforting. Then the umbrella to shield him. Then he had lost his map and instructions. And finally he had left the true path.

Woody reached the other entrance. There was a chain across the top of the stairs. There was a gate across the bottom of the stairs. There were signs and the signs said, "Closed," and "Try Other Entrance."

The other entrance. The other entrance. Where was the other entrance? There it was! It was visible on the other side of the rock park.

Woody hurried toward it. But then halfway between the two he stopped. That was where he had already been. He looked confused. He began to spin. Around and around on his toe he went. He did not know what to do. Overhead the skies impended. Poor Woody. He really needed someone in charge to tell him what to do next.

Around and around he went. Suddenly an imposing figure flashed into being before him. It glowed lemon-yellow and it was very tall.

"Halt. Cease that," it said. It was an even stranger foreign creature than the blue alien in the Friends of the New York Subway System uniform. "Woody Asenion?"

Woody nodded. "Yes, sir."

"I know all about you. You're late. You're very late. It's time for the rain to start. It should have started by now."

"Is it going to rain?" Woody asked. "Is it truly going to rain?"

"Yes, it is."

"But I don't want it to rain," Woody said. "I want to be home safe in my own closet. Is it because I left the path?"

"Yes, it is," the strange creature said. "And now you're going to get wet."

"No," said Woody. "I won't. I'll run between the raindrops. I won't get wet."

And he started to run in fear and in trembling. The lightning lightened to see him run. Thunder clapped the stale air between its hands. The forefinger of the rain prodded after Woody.

Rain fell at Woody, but he dodged and ducked. He was slicker than a greased pig. He ran down Grapefruit Street, and the rain missed him. He ran up Joralemon and it spattered around him and never touched him. He ran past the infamous Red Hook of Brooklyn. He ran through the marketplaces and bazaars of Brooklyn. He ran through a quiet sleeping town of little brown houses, all like beehives. He ran through all the places of Brooklyn and the rain pursued him everywhere.

And he would not be touched. This was Woody Asenion, who was raised in a closet and who didn't dare to open the door by himself. Who would have thought he would be so daring? What would have thought he would be so nimble? Fear took him to heights he had never dreamed of. Fear made him magnificent.

Watching people paused and cheered as he passed. They had to admire him. Pigeons fled before him. Lightning circled his head. Thunder thundered. The skies rolled and tumbled blackly, but not a drop of rain could touch Woody Asenion.

Then at last as he ran up the long slow slope to Prospect Park, he began to tire. His breath was sharp in his throat. His steps grew labored. His dodges grew less canny. And then of a sudden lightning struck all around him. It struck before him. It struck behind him. It struck on his either hand. All at once. Woody was engulfed in thunder, drowned in thunder, rolled and tossed by thunder. He was washed to the ground. He was beached. He was helpless.

And as he lay there, unable to help himself, it rained on Woody. A single giant drop of water. The drop surrounded him and gently drenched him from head to toe, and after that Woody was not the same. That was a very strange drop of rain.

And now Woody was all wet. He stood and looked down at himself. He held his arms out and watched them drip. Then he laughed. He shook himself and laughed. He was really changed.

All the other multiforms, all the other people, came running up to Woody and surrounded him. They were all wet, too.

"Here," said the boy in the doublet. "Look what we found for you." It was an orange-and-black box, factory-new. It was a 28K–916 Hersh. It said so on the box. He gave it to Woody.

The girl said, "Woody. You made it, Woody." She kissed him and Woody could only smile and laugh some more. He was happy.

The boy in the white suit handed Woody his chrysanthemum. "We waited for you," he said. "We didn't get wet until you did."

It was such a great secret to be included in. It didn't matter to Woody that he was the very last to know. He was the first to get wet. How lucky he was.

Woody began to dance then. If fear had made him an inspired dodger, the promise of the new horizontal world made him an intoxicated dancer. His dance was brilliant. His dance was so brilliant that everybody danced Woody's dance for a time. But nobody danced it as well as Woody did.

Woody danced, and with him danced all the no-longer-verticals. With him danced three alien beings—two blue, one lemon-yellow. With him danced the two boys and the girl. With him danced all the people from the subway train. With him danced all the people from his neighborhood, including the little girl who also lived at 206 W. 104th St. in Manhattan. She danced between two robots, one tall, one short.

Then Woody saw his father. His father was dancing Woody's dance, too! There were three other men of his age dancing with him.

Woody danced over to his father and everybody danced after him. Mr. Asenion said, "These are my friends, Murray, Stanton and Hyatt. We are going to invent together."

Woody said, "I have your 28K–916 Hersh."

"No need," his father said, waving it away, never ceasing to dance. "No need. I made do without it." And everybody cheered for Woody's father.

Then the step changed and everybody danced his own way again. But Woody was still happy. Woody celebrated, too. And the horizontal world began.

Questions for Discussion and Review

1. What purpose does Woody's errand serve in this story?

2. What irony is there in the father's attitude toward his "Dimensional Redistributor"?

3. What kind of utopia is the horizontal?

4. This is also a parallel-world story. What evidence is there for that, and how does this affect our interpretation of the story?

5. Parables are allegorical. What kind of allegory is this? What are the main allegorical elements of the story?

6. Compare Panshin's use of his allegorical elements with that of Hawthorne in "The Birthmark" in Part One.

The Star Beast

Poul Anderson

Poul Anderson was born in Bristol, Pennsylvania, in 1926. He attended
college at the University of Minnesota and now resides in the Bay Area
near Berkeley, California. Despite an impressive number of awards, he may
be the most underrated American writer of the past decade. He is hardly
known outside the field of SF. Among his award-winning stories are "The
Longest Voyage" and "No Truce with Kings" (Hugo short story awards,
1961 and 1964); *The Sharing of Flesh* (Hugo novelette, 1969); *Queen
of Air and Darkness* (Hugo, 1972; and Nebula novella, 1971); and
Goat Song (Nebula, 1972; and Hugo novelette, 1973). "The Star Beast"
was first published in *Super Science Stories* (September 1950).

Prosperity doth best discover vice, but adversity doth best discover virtue.

Francis Bacon, "Of Adversity"

Anderson's story is a dystopia of a type we may call the decayed utopia.
It is the story of a decadent civilization at a distant future time. The
collapse of this earthly paradise, although long in coming, takes place with
the sudden impact of barbarous invasion. Perhaps it illustrates Voltaire's
old maxim about history being a record of hobnailed boots marching up
the stairs and satin slippers walking down the stairs.

While we may easily imagine the discomforts of the Spartan, militarist
world of Procyon, the focus of our attention is Earth. The millennium
long prophesied and dreamed of had arrived. People's greatest fears had
been overcome by the technology of the ultrawave. They possessed immortality; they had developed sources of practically unlimited power; they
had banished odious labor; they had the capability to create whatever was
needed or desired. The trammels of government had withered away
because, with robots and computers, society practically ran itself. A technological utopia, so it seems; but we learn soon enough that there are flaws.

Technology has solved the material and biological problems of life but
has created new problems of the spirit. A life devoted to satisfaction is
ultimately unsatisfying. Human beings have become parasites on their
machines. As a consequence, they have grown intellectually and spiritually
sterile. Nothing is left, as Harol says, "but a life of idleness and a round
of pleasure." Human society on Earth has become static and unproductive.
Worshiping youth and rebirth, humanity has grown old in spirit. In this
technological utopia, the one thing missing is incentive. In search of new
experiences and new pleasures, the Immortals have begun experimenting
with animal incarnations, a symbolic devolution.

The main action of the story involves both Harol's desire to be incarnated
a tiger as a therapy for neurosis and the consequences of Felgi's decision
to take over a defenseless Earth, plunging its people into barbarism by
destroying the machines that have maintained its culture. One action
reinforces the other. Ramacan's heroic sacrifice, preserving the power sta-

tion on Mercury, is the dark victory that saves Earth from Felgi's legions. But there will be a generation of darkness on Earth until the secrets of the technology are rediscovered. Harol's confrontation is not simply with barbarism but with the feral violence of the carnivore he has become. Gradually, human consciousness and identity are submerged in the instinctive life of the tiger. The parallel in the two plot lines is epitomized at the end in the confrontation of Avi and the tiger.

In a sense this is an unconventional dystopian story because it does not give us the expected direct vision of a repressive society. If anything, it does the reverse; but at the same time it shows us the truth of the big-brother paradox: "Freedom is slavery!" If this story may be said to have an intellectual content, it is an explication of the dilemma of an advanced society. Is it possible to have prolonged prosperity without decadence? Must a mature civilization of necessity decay? Are boredom and apathy the inevitable consequences of leisure? The questions have for our culture and for our time an importance—perhaps premature in the eyes of some, but already pressing. These are among the first inquiries political and social scientists would make upon meeting aliens who are further advanced than we. We need to understand how to make success succeed.

Chapter One
Therapy for Paradise

The rebirth technician thought he had heard everything in the course of some three centuries. But he was astonished now.

"My dear fellow—" he said. "Did you say a tiger—"

"That's right," said Harol. "You can do it, can't you?"

"Well—I suppose so. I'd have to study the problem first, of course. Nobody has ever wanted a rebirth that far from human. But offhand I'd say it was possible." The technician's eyes lit with a gleam which had not been there for many decades. "It would at least be—interesting!"

"I think you already have a record of a tiger," said Harol.

"Oh, we must have. We have records of every animal still extant when the technique was invented, and I'm sure there must still have been a few tigers around then. But it's a problem of modification. A human mind just can't exist in a nervous system that different. We'd have to change the record enough—larger brain with more convolutions, of course, and so on. . . . Even then it'd be far from perfect, but your basic mentality should be stable for a year or two, barring accidents. That's all the time you'd want anyway, isn't it?"

"I suppose so," said Harol.

"Rebirth in animal forms is getting fashionable these days," admitted the technician. "But so far they've only wanted animals with easily modified systems. Anthropoid apes, now you don't even have to change a chimpanzee's brain at all for it to hold a stable human mentality for

years. Elephants are good too. But—a tiger—" He shook his head.
"I suppose it can be done, after a fashion. But why not a gorilla?"

"I want a carnivore," said Harol.

"Your psychiatrist, I suppose—" hinted the technician.

Harol nodded curtly. The technician sighed and gave up the hope
of juicy confessions. A worker at Rebirth Station heard a lot of strange
stories, but this fellow wasn't giving. Oh, well, the mere fact of his
demand would furnish gossip for days.

"When can it be ready?" asked Harol.

The technician scratched his head thoughtfully. "It'll take a while,"
he said. "We have to get the record scanned, you know, and work out
a basic neural pattern that'll hold the human mind. It's more than a
simple memory-superimposition. The genes control an organism all
through its lifespan, dictating, within the limits of environment, even
the time and speed of aging. You can't have an animal with an
ontogeny entirely opposed to its basic phylogeny—it wouldn't be viable.
So we'll have to modify the very molecules of the cells, as well as the
gross anatomy of the nervous system."

"In short," smiled Harol, "this intelligent tiger will breed true."

"If it found a similar tigress," answered the technician. "Not a real
one—there aren't any left, and besides, the heredity would be too different. But maybe you want a female body for someone?"

"No, I only want a body for myself." Briefly, Harol thought of Avi
and tried to imagine her incarnated in the supple, deadly grace of the
huge cat. But no, she wasn't the type. And solitude was part of the
therapy anyway.

"Once we have the modified record, of course, there's nothing to
superimposing your memory patterns on it," said the technician. "That'll
be just the usual process, like any human rebirth. But to make up that
record—well, I can put the special scanning and computing units over
at Research on the problem. Nobody's working there. Say a week.
Will that do?"

"Fine," said Harol. "I'll be back in a week."

He turned with a brief good-by and went down the long slideway
toward the nearest transmitter. It was almost deserted now save for the
unhuman forms of mobile robots gliding on their errands. The faint,
deep hum of activity which filled Rebirth Station was almost entirely
that of machines, of electronic flows whispering through vacuum, the
silent cerebration of artificial intellects so far surpassing those of their
human creators that men could no longer follow their thoughts. A
human brain simply couldn't operate with that many simultaneous
factors.

The machines were the latter-day oracles. And the life-giving gods.
We're parasites on our machines, thought Harol. *We're little fleas
hopping around on the giants we created, once. There are no real
human scientists any more. How can there be, when the electronic
brains and the great machines which are their bodies can do it all so*

*much quicker and better—can do things we would never even have
dreamed of, things of which man's highest geniuses have only the
faintest glimmer of an understanding? That has paralyzed us, that and
the rebirth immortality. Now there's nothing left but a life of idleness
and a round of pleasure—and how much fun is anything after
centuries?*

It was no wonder that animal rebirth was all the rage. It offered
some prospect of novelty—for a while.

He passed a mirror and paused to look at himself. There was nothing unusual about him; he had the tall body and handsome features
that were uniform today. There was a little gray at his temples and
he was getting a bit bald on top, though his body was only thirty-five.
But then it always had aged early. In the old days he'd hardly have
reached a hundred.

*I am—let me see—four hundred and sixty-three years old. At least,
my memory is—and what am I, the essential I, but a memory track?*

Unlike most of the people in the building, he wore clothes, a light
tunic and cloak. He was a little sensitive about the flabbiness of his
body. He really should keep himself in better shape. But what was
the point of it, really, when his twenty-year-old record was so superb
a specimen?

He reached the transmitter booth and hesitated a moment, wondering where to go. He could go home—have to get his affairs in order
before undertaking the tiger phase—or he could drop in on Avi or—
His mind wandered away until he came to himself with an angry start.
After four and a half centuries, it was getting hard to coördinate all
his memories; he was becoming increasingly absent-minded. Have to
get the psychostaff at Rebirth to go over his record, one of these generations, and eliminate some of that useless clutter from his synapses.

He decided to visit Avi. As he spoke her name to the transmitter
and waited for it to hunt through the electronic files at Central for
her current residence, the thought came that in all his lifetime he had
only twice seen Rebirth Station from the outside. The place was immense, a featureless pile rearing skyward above the almost empty
European forests—as impressive a sight, in its way, as Tycho Crater
or the rings of Saturn. But when the transmitter sent you directly
from booth to booth, inside the buildings, you rarely had occasion to
look at their exteriors.

For a moment he toyed with the thought of having himself transmitted to some nearby house just to see the Station. But—oh, well,
any time in the next few millennia. The Station would last forever, and
so would he.

The transmitter field was generated. At the speed of light, Harold
flashed around the world to Avi's dwelling.

The occasion was ceremonial enough for Ramacan to put on his best
clothes, a red cloak over his tunic and the many jeweled ornaments

prescribed for formal wear. Then he sat down by his transmitter and waited.

The booth stood just inside the colonnaded verandah. From his seat, Ramacan could look through the open doors to the great slopes and peaks of the Caucasus, green now with returning summer save where the everlasting snows flashed under a bright sky. He had lived here for many centuries, contrary to the restlessness of most Earthlings. But he liked the place. It had a quiet immensity; it never changed. Most humans these days sought variety, a feverish quest for the new and untasted, old minds in young bodies trying to recapture a lost freshness. Ramacan was—they called him stodgy, probably. Stable or steady might be closer to the truth. Which made him ideal for his work. Most of what government remained on Earth was left to him.

Felgi was late, Ramacan didn't worry about it; he was never in a hurry himself. But when the Procyonite did arrive, the manner of it brought an amazed oath even from the Earthling.

He didn't come through the transmitter. He came in a boat from his ship, a lean metal shark drifting out of the sky and sighing to the lawn. Ramacan noticed the flat turrets and the ominous muzzles of guns projecting from them. Anachronism—Sol hadn't seen a warship for more centuries than he could remember. But—

Felgi came out of the airlock. He was followed by a squad of armed guards, who ground their blasters and stood to stiff attention. The Procyonite captain walked alone up to the house.

Ramacan had met him before, but he studied the man with a new attention. Like most in his fleet, Felgi was a little undersized by Earthly standards, and the rigidity of his face and posture were almost shocking. His severe, form-fitting black uniform differed little from those of his subordinates except for insignia of rank. His features were gaunt, dark with the protective pigmentation necessary under the terrible blaze of Procyon, and there was something in his eyes which Ramacan had never seen before.

The Procyonites looked human enough. But Ramacan wondered if there was any truth to those rumors which had been flying about Earth since their arrival, that mutation and selection during their long and cruel stay had changed the colonists into something that could never have been at home.

Certainly their social setup and their basic psychology seemed to be—foreign.

Felgi came up the short escalator to the verandah and bowed stiffly. The psychographs had taught him modern Terrestrial, but his voice still held an echo of the harsh colonial tongue and his phrasing was strange: "Greeting to you, Commander."

Ramacan returned the bow, but his was the elaborate sweeping gesture of Earth. "Be welcome, Gen—ah—General Felgi," Then, informally, "Please, come in."

"Thank you." The other man walked into the house.

"Your companions—?"

"My *men* will remain outside." Felgi sat down without being invited, a serious breach of etiquette—but after all, the mores of his home were different.

"As you wish." Ramacan dialed for drinks on the room creator.

"No," said Felgi.

"Pardon me?"

"We don't drink at Procyon. I thought you knew that."

"Pardon me. I had forgotten." Regretfully, Ramacan let the wine and glasses return to the matter bank and sat down.

Felgi sat with steely erectness, making the efforts of the seat to mold itself to his contours futile. Slowly, Ramacan recognized the emotion that crackled and smoldered behind the dark lean visage.

Anger.

"I trust you are finding your stay on Earth pleasant," he said into the silence.

"Let us not make meaningless words," snapped Felgi. "I am here on business."

"As you wish." Ramacan tried to relax, but he couldn't; his nerves and muscles were suddenly tight.

"As far as I can gather," said Felgi, "you head the government of Sol."

"I suppose you could say that. I have the title of Coördinator. But there isn't much to coördinate these days. Our social system practically runs itself."

"Insofar as you have one. But actually you are completely disorganized. Every individual seems to be sufficient to himself."

"Naturally. When everyone owns a matter creator which can supply all his ordinary needs, there is bound to be economic and thus a large degree of social independence. We have public services, of course—Rebirth Station, Power Station, Transmitter Central, and a few others. But there aren't many."

"I cannot see why you aren't overwhelmed by crime." The last word was necessarily Procyonian, and Ramacan raised his eyebrows puzzledly. "Anti-social behavior," explained Felgi irritably. "Theft, murder, destruction."

"What possible need has anyone to steal?" asked Ramacan, surprised. "And the present degree of independence virtually eliminates social friction. Actual psychoses have been removed from the neural components of the rebirth records long ago."

"At any rate, I assume you speak for Sol."

"How can I speak for almost a billion different people? I have little authority, you know. So little is needed. However, I'll do all I can if you'll only tell me—"

"The decadence of Sol is incredible," snapped Felgi.

"You may be right." Ramacan's tone was mild, but he bristled under the urbane surface. "I've sometimes thought so myself. However, what has that to do with the present subject of discussion— whatever it may be?"

"You left us in exile," said Felgi, and now the wrath and hate were edging his voice, glittering out of his eyes. "For nine hundred years, Earth lived in luxury while the humans on Procyon fought and suffered and died in the worst kind of hell."

"What reason was there for us to go to Procyon?" asked Ramacan. "After the first few ships had established a colony there—well, we had a whole galaxy before us. When no colonial ships came from your star, I suppose it was assumed the people there had died off. Somebody should perhaps have gone there to check up, but it took twenty years to get there and it was an inhospitable and unrewarding system and there were so many other stars. Then the matter creator came along and Sol no longer had a government to look after such things. Space travel became an individual business, and no individual was interested in Procyon." He shrugged. "I'm sorry."

"You're *sorry!*" Felgi spat the words out. "For nine hundred years our ancestors fought the bitterness of their planets, starved and died in misery, sank back almost to barbarism and had to slug their way every step back upwards, waged the cruelest war of history with the Czernigi—unending centuries of war until one race or the other should be exterminated. We died of old age, generation after generation of us—we wrung our needs out of planets never meant for humans—my ship spent twenty years getting back here, twenty years of short human lives—and you're sorry!"

He sprang up and paced the floor, his bitter voice lashing out. "You've had the stars, you've had immortality, you've had everything which can be made of matter. And *we* spent twenty years cramped up in metal walls to get here—wondering if perhaps Sol hadn't fallen on evil times and needed our help!"

"What would you have us do now?" demanded Ramacan. "All Earth has made you welcome—"

"We're a novelty!"

"—all Earth is ready to offer you all it can. What more do you want of us?"

For a moment the rage was still in Felgi's strange eyes. Then it faded, blinked out as if he had drawn a curtain across them, and he stood still and spoke with sudden quietness. "True. I—I should apologize, I suppose. The nervous strain—"

"Don't mention it," said Ramacan. But inwardly he wondered. Just how far could he trust the Procyonites? All those hard centuries of war and intrigue—and then they weren't really human any more, not the way Earth's dwellers were human—but what else could he do? "It's quite all right. I understand."

"Thank you." Felgi sat down again. "May I ask what you offer?"

"Duplicate matter creators, of course. And robots duplicated, to administer the more complex Rebirth techniques. Certain of the processes involved are beyond the understanding of the human mind."

"I'm not sure it would be a good thing for us," said Felgi. "Sol has gotten stagnant. There doesn't seem to have been any significant change in the last half millennium. Why, our spaceship drives are better than yours."

"What do you expect?" shrugged Ramacan. "What possible incentive have we for change? Progress, to use an archaic term, is a means to an end, and we have reached its goal."

"I still don't know—" Felgi rubbed his chin. "I'm not even sure how your duplicators work."

"I can't tell you much about them. But the greatest technical mind on Earth can't tell you everything. As I told you before, the whole thing is just too immense for real knowledge. Only the electronic brains can handle so much at once."

"Maybe you could give me a short résumé of it, and tell me just what your setup is. I'm especially interested in the actual means by which it's put to use."

"Well, let me see." Ramacan searched his memory. "The ultra-wave was discovered—oh, it must be a good seven or eight hundred years ago now. It carries energy, but it's not electromagnetic. The theory of it, as far as any human can follow it, ties in with wave mechanics.

"The first great application came with the discovery that ultra-waves transmit over distances of many astronomical units, unhindered by intervening matter, and with *no energy loss*. The theory of that has been interpreted as meaning that the wave is, well, I suppose you could say it's 'aware' of the receiver and only goes to it. There must be a receiver as well as a transmitter to generate the wave. Naturally, that led to a perfectly efficient power transmitter. Today all the Solar System gets its energy from the Sun—transmitted by the Power Station on the day side of Mercury. Everything from interplanetary spaceships to televisors and clocks run from that power source."

"Sounds dangerous to me," said Felgi. "Suppose the station fails?"

"It won't," said Ramacan confidently. "The Station has its own robots, no human technicians at all. Everything is recorded. If any one part goes wrong, it is automatically dissolved into the nearest matter bank and recreated. There are other safeguards too. The Station has never given trouble since it was first built.'"

"I see—" Felgi's tone was thoughtful.

"Soon thereafter," said Ramacan, "it was found that the ultra-wave could also transmit matter. Circuits could be built which would scan any body atom by atom, dissolve it to energy, and transmit this energy on the ultra-wave along with the scanning signal. At the receiver, of course, the process is reversed. I'm grossly oversimplifying, naturally. It's not a mere signal which is involved, but a fantastic complex of signals such as only the ultra-wave could carry. However, you get the general idea. Just about all transportation today is by this technique. Vehicles for air or space exist only for very special purposes and for pleasure trips."

"You have some kind of controlling center for this too, don't you?"

"Yes. Transmitter Station, on Earth, is in Brazil. It holds all the records of such things as addresses, and it coördinates the millions of units all over the planet. It's a huge, complicated affair, of course, but perfectly efficient. Since distance no longer means anything, it's most practical to centralize the public-service units.

"Well, from transmission it was but a step to recording the signal and reproducing it out of a bank of any other matter. So—the duplicator. The matter creator. You can imagine what that did to Sol's economy! Today everybody owns one, and if he doesn't have a record of what he wants he can have one duplicated and transmitted from Creator Station's great 'library'. Anything whatsoever in the way of material goods is his for the turning of a dial and the flicking of a switch.

"And this, in turn, soon led to the Rebirth technique. It's but an extension of all that has gone before. Your body is recorded at its prime of life, say around twenty years of age. Then you live for as much longer as you care to, say to thirty-five or forty or whenever you begin to get a little old. Then your neural pattern is recorded alone by special scanning units. Memory, as you surely know, is a matter of neural synapses and altered protein molecules, not too difficult to scan and record. This added pattern is superimposed electronically on the record of your twenty-year-old body. Then your own body is used as the matter bank for materializing the pattern in the altered record and—virtually instantaneously—your young body is created— but with all the memories of the old! You're—immortal!"

"In a way," said Felgi. "But it still doesn't seem right to me. The ego, the soul, whatever you want to call it—it seems as if you lose that. You create simply a perfect copy."

"When the copy is so perfect it cannot be told from the original," said Ramacan, "then what *is* the difference? The ego is essentially a matter of continuity. You, your essential self, are a constantly changing pattern of synapses bearing only a temporary relationship of the molecules that happen to carry the pattern at the moment. It is the design, not the structural material, that is important. And it is the design that we preserve."

"Do you?" asked Felgi. "I seemed to notice a strong likeness among Earthlings."

"Well, since the records can be altered there was no reason for us to carry around crippled or diseased or deformed bodies," said Ramacan. "Records could be made of perfect specimens and *all* ego-patterns wiped from them; then someone else's neural pattern could be superimposed. Rebirth—in a new body! Naturally, everyone would want to match the prevailing beauty standard, and so a certain uniformity has appeared. A different body would of course lead in time to a different personality, man being a psychosomatic unit. But the continuity which is the essential attribute of the ego would still be there."

"Ummm—I see. May I ask how old you are?"

"About seven hundred and fifty. I was middle-aged when Rebirth was established, but I had myself put into a young body."

Felgi's eyes went from Ramacan's smooth, youthful face to his own hands, with the knobby joints and prominent veins of his sixty years. Briefly, the fingers tightened, but his voice remained soft. "Don't you have trouble keeping your memories straight?"

"Yes, but every so often I have some of the useless and repetitious ones taken out of the record, and that helps. The robots know exactly what part of the pattern corresponds to a given memory and can erase it. After, say, another thousand years, I'll probably have big gaps. But they won't be important."

"How about the apparent acceleration of time with age?"

"That was bad after the first couple of centuries, but then it seemed to flatten out, the nervous system adapted to it. I must say, though," admitted Ramacan, "that it as well as lack of incentive is probably responsible for our present static society and general unproductiveness. There's a terrible tendency to procrastination, and a day seems too short a time to get anything done."

"The end of progress, then—of science, or art, of striving, of all which has made man human."

"Not so. We still have our arts and handicrafts and—hobbies, I suppose you could call them. Maybe we don't do so much any more, but—why should we?"

"I'm surprised at finding so much of Earth gone back to wilderness. I should think you'd be badly overcrowded."

"Not so. The creator and the transmitter make it possible for men to live far apart, in physical distance, and still be in as close touch as necessary. Communities are obsolete. As for the population problem, there isn't any. After a few children, not many people want more. It's sort of, well, unfashionable anyway."

"That's right," said Felgi quietly, "I've hardly seen a child on Earth."

"And of course there's a slow drift out to the stars as people seek novelty. You can send your recording in a robot ship, and a journey of centuries becomes nothing. I suppose that's another reason for the tranquility of Earth. The more restless and adventurous elements have moved away."

"Have you any communication with them?"

"None. Not when spaceships can only go at half the speed of light. Once in a while curious wanderers will drop in on us, but it's very rare. They seem to be developing some strange cultures out in the galaxy."

"Don't you do *any* work on Earth?"

"Oh, some public services must be maintained—psychiatry, human technicians to oversee various stations, and so on. And then there are any number of personal-service enterprises—entertainment, especially, and the creation of intricate handicrafts for the creators to duplicate. But there are enough people willing to work a few hours a month or week, if only to fill in their time or to get the credit-balance which will enable them to purchase such services for themselves if they desire.

"It's a perfectly stable culture, General Felgi. It's perhaps the only really stable society in all human history."

"I wonder—haven't you any precautions at all?" Any military forces, any defenses against invaders—*anything?*"

"Why in the cosmos should we fear that?" exclaimed Ramacan. "Who would come invading over light-years—at half the speed of light? Or if they did, *why?*"

"Plunder—"

Ramacan laughed. "We could duplicate anything they asked for and give it to them."

"Could you, now?" Suddenly Felgi stood up. "Could you?"

Ramacan rose too, with his nerves and muscles tightening again. There was a hard triumph in the Procyonite's face, vindictive, threatening.

Felgi signaled to his men through the door. They trotted up on the double, and their blasters were raised and something hard and ugly was in their eyes.

"Coördinator Ramacan," said Felgi, "you are under arrest."

"What—what—" The Earthling felt as if someone had struck him a physical blow. He clutched for support. Vaguely he heard the iron tones:

"You've confirmed what I thought. Earth is unarmed, unprepared, helplessly dependent on a few undefended key spots. And I captain a warship of space filled with soldiers.

"We're taking over!"

Chapter Two
"Tiger, Tiger"

Avi's current house lay in North America, on the middle Atlantic seaboard. Like most private homes these days, it was small and low-ceilinged, with adjustable interior walls and furnishings for easy variega-tion. She loved flowers, and great brilliant gardens bloomed around her dwelling, down toward the sea and landward to the edge of the immense forest which had returned with the end of agriculture.

They walked between the shrubs and trees and blossoms, she and Harol. Her unbound hair was long and bright in the sea breeze, her eighteen-year-old form was slim and graceful as a young deer's. Sud-denly he hated the thought of leaving her.

"I'll miss you, Harol," she said.

He smiled lopsidedly. "You'll get over that," he said. "There are others. I suppose you'll be looking up some of those spacemen they say arrived from Procyon a few days ago."

"Of course," she said innocently. "I'm surprised you don't stay around and try for some of the women they had along. It would be a change."

"Not much of a change," he answered. "Frankly, I'm at a loss to understand the modern passion for variety. One person seems very much the same as another in that regard."

"It's a matter of companionship," she said. "After not too many years of living with someone, you get to know him too well. You can tell exactly what he's going to do, what he'll say to you, what he'll have for dinner and what sort of show he'll want to go to in the evening. These colonists will be—new! They'll have other ways from ours, they'll be able to tell of a new, different planetary system, they'll—" She broke off. "But now so many women will be after the strangers, I doubt if I'll have a chance."

"But if it's conversation you want—oh, well." Harol shrugged. "Anyway, I understand the Procyonites still have family relationships. They'll be quite jealous of their women. And I need this change."

"A carnivore—!" Avi laughed, and Harol thought again what music it was. "You have an original mind, at least." Suddenly she was earnest. She held both his hands and looked close into his eyes. "That's always been what I liked about you, Harol. You've always been a thinker and adventurer, you've never let yourself grow mentally lazy like most of us. After we've been apart for a few years, you're always new again, you've gotten out of your rut and done something strange, you've learned something different, you've grown young again. We've always come back to each other, dear, and I've always been glad of it."

"And I," he said quietly. "Though I've regretted the separations too." He smiled, a wry smile with a tinge of sorrow behind it. "We could have been very happy in the old days, Avi. We would have been married and together for life."

"A few years, and then age and feebleness and death." She shuddered. "Death! Nothingness! Not even the world can exist when one is dead. Not when you've no brain left to know about it. Just— nothing. As if you had never been! Haven't you ever been afraid of the thought?"

"No," he said, and kissed her.

"That's another way you're different," she murmured. "I wonder why you never went out to the stars, Harol. All your children did."

"I asked you to go with me, once."

"Not I. I like it here. Life is fun, Harol. I don't seem to get bored as easily as most people. But that isn't answering my question."

"Yes, it is," he said, and then clamped his mouth shut.

He stood looking at her, wondering if he was the last man on Earth who loved a woman, wondering how she really felt about him. Perhaps, in her way, she loved him—they always came back to each other. But not in the way he cared for her, not so that being apart was a gnawing pain and reunion was— No matter.

"I'll still be around," he said. "I'll be wandering through the woods here; I'll have the Rebirth men transmit me back to your house and then I'll be in the neighborhood."

"My pet tiger," she smiled. "Come around to see me once in a while, Harol. Come with me to some of the parties."

A *nice spectacular ornament*— "No, thanks, But you can scratch my head and feed me big bloody steaks, and I'll arch my back and purr."

They walked hand in hand toward the beach. "What made you decide to be a tiger?" she asked.

"My psychiatrist recommended an animal rebirth," he replied. "I'm getting terribly neurotic, Avi. I can't sit still five minutes and I get gloomy spells where nothing seems worthwhile any more, life is a dreary farce and—well, it seems to be becoming a rather common disorder these days. Essentially it's boredom. When you have everything without working for it, life can become horribly flat. When you've lived for centuries, tried it all hundreds of times—no change, no real excitement, nothing to call forth all that's in you—Anyway, the doctor suggested I go to the stars. When I refused that, he suggested I change to animal for a while. But I didn't want to be like everyone else. Not an ape or an elephant."

"Same old contrary Harol," she murmured, and kissed him. He responded with unexpected violence.

"A year or two of wild life, in a new and unhuman body, will make all the difference," he said after a while. They lay on the sand, feeling the sunlight wash over them, hearing the lullaby of waves and smelling the clean, harsh tang of sea and salt and many windy kilometers. High overhead a gull circled, white against the blue.

"Won't you change?" she asked.

"Oh, yes. I won't even be able to remember a lot of things I now know. I doubt if even the most intelligent tiger could understand vector analysis. But that won't matter, I'll get it back when they restore my human form. When I feel the personality change has gone as far as is safe, I'll come here and you can send me back to Rebirth. The important thing is the therapy—a change of viewpoint, a new and challenging environment— Avi!" He sat up, on one elbow and looked down at her. "Avi, why don't you come along? Why don't we both become tigers?"

"And have lots of little tigers?" she smiled drowsily. "No, thanks, Harol. Maybe some day, but not now. I'm really not an adventurous person at all." She stretched, and snuggled back against the warm white dune. "I like it the way it is."

And there are those starmen— Sunfire, what's the matter with me?

*Next thing you know I'll commit an inurbanity against one of her
lovers. I need that therapy, all right.*

"And then you'll come back and tell me about it," said Avi.

"Maybe not," he teased her. "Maybe I'll find a beautiful tigress
somewhere and become so enamored of her I'll never want to change
back to human."

"There won't be any tigresses unless you persuade someone else to
go along," she answered. "But will you like a human body after having had such a lovely striped skin? Will we poor hairless people still
look good to you?"

"Darling," he smiled, "to me you'll always look good enough to eat."

Presently they went back into the house. The sea gull still dipped
and soared, high in the sky.

The forest was great and green and mysterious, with sunlight dap-
pling the shadows and a riot of ferns and flowers under the huge old
trees. There were brooks tinkling their darkling way between cool,
mossy banks, fish leaping like silver streaks in the bright shallows,
lonely pools where quiet hung like a mantle, open meadows of wind-
rippled grass, space and solitude and an unending pulse of life.

Tiger eyes saw less than human; the world seemed dim and flat
and colorless until he got used to it. After that he had increasing
difficulty remembering what color and perspective were like. And his
other senses came alive, he realized what a captive within his own
skull he had been—looking out at a world of which he had never
been so real a part as now.

He heard sounds and tones no man had ever perceived, the faint
hum and chirr of insects, the rustling of leaves in a light, warm breeze,
the vague whisper of an owl's wings, the scurrying of small, frightened
creatures through the long grass—it all blended into a rich symphony,
the heartbeat and breath of the forest. And his nostrils quivered to the
infinite variety of smells, the heady fragrance of crushed grass, the
pungency of fungus and decay, the sharp, wild odor of fur, the hot
drunkenness of newly spilled blood. And he felt with every hair, his
whiskers quivered to the smallest stirrings, he gloried in the deep, strong
play of his muscles—he had come alive, he thought; a man was half
dead compared to the vitality that throbbed—in the tiger.

At night, at night—there was no darkness for him now. Moonlight
was a white, cold blaze through which he stole on feathery feet; the
blackest gloom was light to him—shadows, wan patches of luminescence, a shifting, sliding fantasy of gray like an old and suddenly
remembered dream.

He laired in a cave he found, and his new body had no discomfort
from the damp earth. At night he would stalk out, a huge, dim ghost
with only the amber gleam of his eyes for light, and the forest would
speak to him with sound and scent and feeling, the taste of game on

the wind. He was master then, all the woods shivered and huddled away from him. He was death in black and gold.

Once an ancient poem ran through the human part of his mind, he let the words roll like ominous thunder in his brain and tried to speak them aloud. The forest shivered with the tiger's coughing roar.

> *Tiger, tiger, burning bright*
> *In the forest of the night,*
> *What immortal hand or eye*
> *Dared frame thy fearful symmetry?*

And the arrogant feline soul snarled response: *I did!*

Later he tried to recall the poem, but he couldn't.

At first he was not very successful, too much of his human awkwardness clung to him. He snarled his rage and bafflement when rabbits skittered aside, when a deer scented him lurking and bolted. He went to Avi's house and she fed him big chunks of raw meat and laughed and scratched him under the chin. She was delighted with her pet.

Avi, he thought, and remembered that he loved her. But that was with his human body. To the tiger, she had no esthetic or sexual value. But he liked to let her stroke him, he purred like a mighty engine and rubbed against her slim legs. She was still very dear to him, and when he became human again—

But the tiger's instincts fought their way back; the heritage of a million years was not to be denied no matter how much the technicians had tried to alter him. They had accomplished little more than to increase his intelligence, and the tiger nerves and glands were still there.

The night came when he saw a flock of rabbits dancing in the moonlight and pounced on them. One huge, steely-taloned paw swooped down, he felt the ripping flesh and snapping bone and then he was gulping the sweet, hot blood and peeling the meat from the frail ribs. He went wild, he roared and raged all night, shouting his exultance to the pale frosty moon. At dawn he slunk back to his cave, wearied, his human mind a little ashamed of it all. But the next night he was hunting again.

His first deer! He lay patiently on a branch overhanging a trail; only his nervous tail moved while the slow hours dragged by, and he waited. And when the doe passed underneath he was on her like a tawny lightning bolt. A great slapping paw, jaws like shears, a brief, terrible struggle, and she lay dead at his feet. He gorged himself, he ate till he could hardly crawl back to the cave, and then he slept like a drunken man until hunger woke him and he went back to the carcass. A pack of wild dogs were devouring it, he rushed on them and killed one and scattered the rest. Thereafter he continued his feast until only bones were left.

The forest was full of game; it was an easy life for a tiger. But not too easy. He never knew whether he would go back with full or empty belly, and that was part of the pleasure.

They had not removed all the tiger memories; fragments remained to puzzle him; sometimes he woke up whimpering with a dim wonder as to where he was and what had happened. He seemed to remember misty jungle dawns, a broad brown river shining under the sun, another cave and another striped form beside him. As time went on he grew confused, he thought vaguely that he must once have hunted sambar and seen the white rhinoceros go by like a moving mountain in the twilight. It was growing harder to keep things straight.

That was, of course, only to be expected. His feline brain could not possibly hold all the memories and concepts of the human, and with the passage of weeks and months he lost the earlier clarity of recollection. He still identified himself with a certain sound, "Harol," and he remembered other forms and scenes—but more and more dimly, as if they were the fading shards of a dream. And he kept firmly in mind that he had to go back to Avi and let her send—take—him somewhere else before he forgot who he was.

Well, there was time for that, thought the human component. He wouldn't lose that memory all at once, he'd know well in advance that the superimposed human personality was disintegrating in its strange house and that he ought to get back. Meanwhile he grew more and deeply into the forest life, his horizons narrowed until it seemed the whole of existence.

Now and then he wandered down to the sea and Avi's home, to get a meal and be made much of. But the visits grew more and more infrequent, the open country made him nervous and he couldn't stay indoors after dark.

Tiger, tiger—
And summer wore on.

He woke to a raw wet chill in the cave, rain outside and a mordant wind blowing through dripping dark trees. He shivered and growled, unsheathing his claws, but this was not an enemy he could destroy. The day and the night dragged by in misery.

Tigers had been adaptable beasts in the old days, he recalled; they had ranged as far north as Siberia. But his original had been from the tropics. *Hell!* he cursed, and the thunderous roar rattled through the woods.

But then came crisp, clear days with a wild wind hallooing through a high, pale sky, dead leaves whirling on the gusts and laughing in their thin, dry way. Geese honked in the heavens, southward bound, and the bellowing of stags filled the nights. There was a drunkenness in the air; the tiger rolled in the grass and purred like muted thunder and yowled at the huge orange moon as it rose. His fur thickened, he didn't feel the chill except as a keen tingling in his blood. All his

senses were sharpened now, he lived with a knife-edged alertness and
learned how to go through the fallen leaves like another shadow.

Indian summer, long lazy days like a resurrected springtime, enormous stars, the crisp smell of rotting vegetation, and his human mind
remembered that the leaves were like gold and bronze and flame. He
fished in the brooks, scooping up his prey with one hooked sweep; he
ranged the woods and roared on the high ridges under the moon.

Then the rains returned, gray and cold and sodden, the world
drowned in a wet woe. At night there was frost, numbing his feet and
glittering in the starlight, and through the chill silence he could hear
the distant beat of the sea. It grew harder to stalk game, he was often
hungry. By now he didn't mind that too much, but his reason worried
about winter. Maybe he'd better get back.

One night the first snow fell, and in the morning the world was
white and still. He plowed through it, growling his anger, and wondered about moving south. But cats aren't given to long journeys. He
remembered vaguely that Avi could give him food and shelter.

Avi—For a moment, when he tried to think of her, he thought of
a golden, dark-striped body and a harsh feline smell filling the cave
above the old wide river. He shook his massive head, angry with himself and the world, and tried to call up her image. The face was dim
in his mind, but the scent came back to him, and the low, lovely music
of her laughter. He would go to Avi.

He went through the bare forest with the haughty gait of its king,
and presently he stood on the beach. The sea was gray and cold and
enormous, roaring white-maned on the shore; flying spin-drift stung
his eyes. He padded along the strand until he saw her house.

It was oddly silent. He went in thourgh the garden. The door stood
open, but there was only desertion inside.

Maybe she was away. He curled up on the floor and went to sleep.

He woke much later, hunger gnawing in his guts, and still no one
had come. He recalled that she had been wont to go south for the
winter. But she wouldn't have forgotten him, she'd have been back
from time to time— But the house had little scent of her, she had
been away for a long while. And it was disordered. Had she left
hastily?

He went over to the creator. He couldn't remember how it worked,
but he did recall the process of dialing and switching. He pulled the
lever at random with a paw. Nothing happened.

Nothing! The creator was inert.

He roared his disappointment. Slow, puzzled fear came to him.
This wasn't as it should be.

But he was hungry. He'd have to try to get his own food, then, and
come back later in hopes of finding Avi. He went back into the
woods.

Presently he smelled life under the snow. Bear. Previously, he and
the bears had been in a state of watchful neutrality. But this one was

asleep, unwary, and his belly cried for food. He tore the shelter apart with a few powerful motions and flung himself on the animal.

It is dangerous to wake a hibernating bear. This one came to with a start, his heavy paw lashed out and the tiger sprang back with blood streaming down his muzzle.

Madness came, a berserk rage that sent him leaping forward. The bear snarled and braced himself. They closed, and suddenly the tiger was fighting for his very life.

He never remembered that battle save as a red whirl of shock and fury, tumbling in the snow and spilling blood to steam in the cold air. Strike, bite, rip, thundering blows, against his ribs and skull, the taste of blood hot in his mouth and the insanity of death shrieking and gibbering in his head!

In the end, he staggered bloodily and collapsed on the bear's ripped corpse. For a long time he lay there, and the wild dogs hovered near, waiting for him to die.

After a while he stirred weakly and ate of the bear's flesh. But he couldn't leave. His body was one of vast pain, his feet wobbled under him, one paw had been crushed by the great jaws. He lay by the dead bear under the tumbled shelter, and snow fell slowly on them.

The battle and the agony and the nearness of death brought his old instincts to the fore. All tiger, he licked his tattered form and gulped hunks of rotting meat, as the days went by and waited for a measure of health to return.

In the end, he limped back toward his cave. Dreamlike memories nagged him; there had been a house and someone who was good but—but—

He was cold and lame and hungry. Winter had come.

Chapter Three
Dark Victory

"We have no further use for you," said Felgi, "but in view of the help you've been you'll be allowed to live—at least till we get back to Procyon and the Council decides your case. Also, you probably have more valuable information about the Solar System than our other prisoners. They're mostly women."

Ramacon looked at the hard, exultant face and answered dully, "If I'd known what you were planning, I'd never have helped."

"Oh, yes, you would have," snorted Felgi. "I saw your reactions when we showed you some of our means of persuasion. You Earthlings are all alike. You've been hiding from death so long that the backbone has all gone out of you. That alone makes you unfit to hold your planet."

"You have the plans of the duplicators and the transmitters and power-beams—all our technology. I helped you get them from the Stations. What more do you want?"

"Earth."

"But why? With the creators and transmitters, you can make your planets like all the old dreams of paradise. Earth is more congenial, yes, but what does environment matter to you now?"

"Earth is still the true home of man," said Felgi. There was a fanaticism in his eyes such as Ramacan had never seen even in nightmare. "It should belong to the best race of man. Also—well, our culture couldn't stand that technology. Procyonite civilization grew up in adversity, it's been nothing but struggle and hardship, it's become part of our nature now. With the Czernigi destroyed, we *must* find another enemy."

Oh, yes, thought Ramacan. *It's happened before, in Earth's bloody old past. Nations that knew nothing but war and suffering, became molded by them, glorified the harsh virtues that had enabled them to survive. A militaristic state can't afford peace and leisure and prosperity; its people might begin to think for themselves. So the government looks for conquest outside the borders— Needful or not, there must be war to maintain the control of the military.*

How human are the Procyonites now? What's twisted them in the centuries of their terrible evolution? They're no longer men, they're fighting robots, beasts of prey, they have to have blood.

"You saw us shell the Stations from space," said Felgi. "Rebirth, Creator, Transmitter—they're radioactive craters now. Not a machine is running on Earth, not a tube is alight—nothing! And with the creators on which their lives depended inert, Earthlings will go back to utter savagery."

"Now what?" asked Ramacan wearily.

"We're standing off Mercury, refueling," said Felgi. "Then it's back to Procyon. We'll use our creator to record most of the crew, they can take turns being briefly recreated during the voyage to maintain the ship and correct the course. We'll be little older when we get home."

"Then, of course, the Council will send out a fleet with recorded crews. They'll take over Sol, eliminate the surviving population, and recolonize Earth. After that—" The mad fires blazed high in his eyes. "The stars! A galactic empire, ultimately."

"Just so you have war," said Ramacan tonelessly. "Just so you can keep your people stupid slaves."

"That's enough," snapped Felgi. "A decadent culture can't be expected to understand our motives."

Ramacan stood thinking. There would still be humans around when the Procyonites came back. There would be forty years to prepare. Men in spaceships, here and there throughout the System, would come home would see the ruin of Earth and know who must be guilty. With creators, they could rebuild quickly, they could arm themselves, duplicate vengeance-hungry men by the millions.

Unless Solarian man was so far gone in decay that he was only capable of blind panic. But Ramacan didn't think so. Earth had slipped, but not that far.

Felgi seemed to read his mind. There was cruel satisfaction in his tones: "Earth will have no chance to rearm. We're using the power from Mercury Station to run our own large duplicator, turning rock into osmium fuel for our engines. But when we're finished, we'll blow up the Station too. Spaceships will drift powerless, the colonists on the planets will die as their environmental regulators stop functioning, no wheel will turn in all the Solar System. That, I should think, will be the final touch!"

Indeed, indeed. Without power, without tools, without food or shelter, the final collapse would come. Nothing but a few starving savages would be left when the Procyonites returned. Ramacan felt an emptiness within himself.

Life had become madness and nightmare. The end. . . .

"You'll stay here till we get around to recording you," said Felgi. He turned on his heel and walked out.

Ramacan slumped back into a seat. His desperate eyes traveled around and around the bare little cabin that was his prison, around and around like the crazy whirl of his thoughts. He looked at the guard who stood in the doorway, leaning on his blaster, contemptuously bored with the captive. If—if—O almighty gods, if *that* was to inherit green Earth!

What to do, what to do? There must be some answer, some way, no problem was altogether without solution. Or was it? What guarantee did he have of cosmic justice? He buried his face in his hands.

I was a coward, he thought. *I was afraid of pain. So I rationalized, I told myself they probably didn't want much, I used my influence to help them get duplicators and plans. And the others were cowards too, they yielded, they were cravenly eager to help the conquerors—and this is our pay!*

What to do, what to do? If somehow the ship were lost, if it never came back—The Procyonites would wonder. They'd send another ship or two—no more—to investigate. And in forty years Sol could be ready to meet those ships—ready to carry the war to an unprepared enemy—if in the meantime they'd had a chance to rebuild, if Mercury Power Station were spared—

But the ship would blow the Station out of existence, and the ship would return with news of Sol's ruin, and the invaders would come swarming in—would go ravening out through an unsuspecting galaxy like a spreading plague—

How to stop the ship—*now*?

Ramacan grew aware of the thudding of his heart; it seemed to shake his whole body with its violence. And his hands were cold and clumsy, his mouth was parched, he was afraid.

He got up and walked over toward the guard. The Procyonite hefted his blaster, but there was no alertness in him, he had no fear of an unarmed member of the conquered race.

He'll shoot me down, thought Ramacan. *The death I've been running from all my life is on me now. But it's been a long life and a good one, and better to finish it now than drag out a few miserable years as their despised prisoner, and—and—I hate their guts!*

"What do you want?" asked the Procyonite.

"I feel sick," said Ramacan. His voice was almost a whisper in the dryness of his throat. "Let me out."

"Get back."

"It'll be messy. Let me to to the lavatory."

He stumbled, nearly falling. "Go ahead," said the guard curtly. "I'll be along, remember."

Ramacan swayed on his feet as he approached the man. His shaking hands closed on the blaster barrel and yanked the weapon loose. Before the guard could yell, Ramacan drove the butt into his face. A remote corner of his mind was shocked at the savagery that welled up in him when the bones crunched.

The guard toppled. Ramacan eased him to the floor, slugged him again to make sure he would lie quiet, and stripped him of his long outer coat, his boots, and helmet. His hands were really trembling now; he could hardly get the simple garments on.

If he was caught—well, it only made a few minutes' difference. But he was still afraid. Fear screamed inside him.

He forced himself to walk with nightmare slowness down the long corridor. Once he passed another man, but there was no discovery. When he had rounded the corner, he was violently sick.

He went down a ladder to the engine room. Thank the gods he'd been interested enough to inquire about the layout of the ship when they first arrived! The door stood open and he went in.

A couple of engineers were watching the giant creator at work. It pulsed and hummed and throbbed with power, energy from the sun and from dissolving atoms of rocks—atoms recreated as the osmium that would power the ship's engines on the long voyage back. Tons of fuel spilling down into the bins.

Ramacan closed the soundproof door and shot the engineers.

Then he went over to the creator and reset the controls. It began to manufacture plutonium.

He smiled then, with an immense relief, an incredulous realization that he had won. He sat down and cried with sheer joy.

The ship would not get back. Mercury Station would endure. And on that basis, a few determined men in the Solar System could rebuild. There would be horror on Earth, howling chaos, most of its population would plung into savagery and death. But enough would live, and remain civilized, and get ready for revenge.

Maybe it was for the best, he thought. Maybe Earth really had gone into a twilight of purposeless ease. True it was that there had been none of the old striving and hoping and gallantry which had made man what he was. No art, no science, no adventure—a smug self-satisfaction, an unreal immortality in a synthetic paradise. Maybe this shock and challenge was what Earth needed, to show the starward way again.

As for him, he had had many centuries of life, and he realized now what a deep inward weariness there had been in him. *Death,* he thought, *death is the longest voyage of all. Without death there is no evolution, no real meaning to life, the ultimate adventure has been snatched away.*

There had been a girl once, he remembered, and she had died before the rebirth machines became available. Odd—after all these centuries he could still remember how her hair had rippled in the wind, one day on a high summery hill. He wondered if he would see her.

He never felt the explosion as the plutonium reached critical mass.

Avi's feet were bleeding. Her shoes had finally given out, and rocks and twigs tore at her feet. The snow was dappled with blood.

Weariness clawed at her, she couldn't keep going—but she had to, she had to, she was afraid to stop in the wilderness.

She had never been alone in her life. There had always been the televisors and the transmitters, no place on Earth had been more than an instant away. But the world had expanded into immensity, the machines were dead, there was only cold and gloom and empty white distance. The world of warmth and music and laughter and casual enjoyment was as remote and unreal as a dream.

Was it a dream? Had she always stumbled sick and hungry through a nightmare world of leafless trees and drifting snow and wind that sheathed her in cold through the thin rags of her garments? Or was this the dream, a sudden madness of horror and death?

Death—no, no, no, she couldn't die, she was one of the immortals, she mustn't die!

The wind blew and blew.

Night was falling, winter night. A wild dog bayed, somewhere out in the gloom. She tried to scream, but her throat was raw with shrieking; only a dry croak would come out.

Help me, help me, help me.

Maybe she should have stayed with the man. He had devised traps, had caught an occasional rabbit or squirrel and flung her the leavings. But he looked at her so strangely when several days had gone by without a catch. He would have killed her and eaten her; she had to flee.

Run, run, run— She couldn't run, the forest reached on forever, she was caught in cold and night, hunger and death.

What had happened, what had happened, what had become of the world? What would become of her?

She had liked to pretend she was one of the ancient goddesses, creating what she willed out of nothingness, served by a huge and eternal world whose one purpose was to serve her. Where was that world now?

Hunger twisted in her like a knife. She tripped over a snow-buried log and lay there, trying feebly to rise.

We were too soft, too complacent, she thought dimly. *We lost all our powers, we were just little parasites on our machines. Now we're unfit—*

No! I won't have it! I was a goddess once—

Spoiled brat, jeered the demon in her mind. *Baby crying for its mother. You should be old enough to look after yourself—after all these centuries. You shouldn't be running in circles waiting for help that will never come, you should be helping yourself, making a shelter, finding nuts and roots, building a trap. But you can't. All the self-reliance has withered out of you.*

No—help, help, help—

Something moved in the gloom. She choked a scream. Yellow eyes glowed like twin fires, and the immense form stepped noiselessly forth.

For an instant she gibbered in a madness of fear, and then sudden realization came and left her gaping with unbelief—then instant eager acceptance.

There could only be one tiger in this forest.

"Harol," she whispered, and climbed to her feet. "Harol."

It was all right. The nightmare was over. Harol would look after her. He would hunt for her, protect her, bring her back to the world of machines that *must* still exist. "Harol," she cried. "Harol, my dear—"

The tiger stood motionless; only his twitching tail had life. Briefly, irrelevantly, remembered sounds trickled through his mind: *"Your basic mentality should be stable for a year or two, barring accidents. . . ."* But the noise was meaningless, it clipped through his brain into oblivion.

He was hungry. The crippled paw hadn't healed well, he couldn't catch game.

Hunger, the most elemental need of all, grinding within him, filling his tiger brain and tiger body until nothing else was left.

He stood looking at the thing that didn't run away. He had killed another a while back—he licked his mouth at the thought.

From somewhere long ago he remembered that the thing had once been—he had been—he couldn't remember—

He stalked forward.

"Harol," said Avi. There was fear rising horribly in her voice.

The tiger stopped. He knew that voice. He remembered—he remembered—

He had known her once. There was something about her that held him back.

But he was hungry. And his instincts were clamoring in him.

But if only he could remember, before it was too late—

Time stretched into a horrible eternity while they stood facing each other—the lady and the tiger.

Questions for Discussion and Review

1. In what ways are the cultures of Brackett's "Enchantress of Venus" similar to and different from those of the Immortals and the Procyonites of this story?

2. What are the parallels between Harol's tiger phase and the Proconite invasion? Why are they important in the story?

3. What is the dilemma of the lady and the tiger at the story's end?

4. To what degree are Felgi's arguments valid?

5. The temporary collapse of Earth's machine paradise is regarded by both Ramacan and Felgi as a purgative process. Assuming that Ramacan's hopes materialize, what is there beside revenge that would lead to a rebirth of Earth's civilization?

6. Could the utopia of the Immortals be saved from "a twilight of purposeless ease"? What is the remedy?

Social Science Fiction

Let us consider what differences there may be among the three types of soft SF considered in this section. They are all related, of course, but there are distinctions worth making. The chief differences between speculative and social SF are those of perspective and tone. Social SF tells us how things should or should not be, whereas speculative SF tells us how they may be at a more distant time and place. Social SF tends to treat attitudes and values in a polemical manner. Since social SF is almost always critical, there is no point in comparing it with utopias. If there is an important difference between dystopias and social SF, it is that the scope of the former tends to be more universal. Dystopias usually concern themselves with the whole social structure. Social SF is usually a more limited social criticism directed at more specific trends and ailments.

Social SF, therefore, is a literature of critical analysis examining social values and practice. Whereas dystopias are cautionary, social SF is admonitory. As SF, social criticism builds on a hard-science substructure, but its focus is on what we would normally call the setting of the story. If hard SF puts scientific process in the foreground, social SF gives the same emphasis to background. By background I mean the social environment in which the characters interact. As with all other fiction that makes an analysis of social values, social SF reminds us that society reflects the character of its citizens.

We may expect, therefore, that social SF is a literature that protests the abuse of technology and science. Or it may argue that the effects of either on human behavior or psychology have been destructive. Like the other types of soft SF, social SF aims at telling us something about the state of our society, or values, or even our souls. The historic affiliation of SF with satire has already been observed in several places, but nowhere is that relationship more direct, or the influence stronger, or the purposes more alike than in social SF. The seamier side of life becomes all the more potent in social SF as an indictment of human indifferences to suffering and injustice if we contemplate it not as something that we have seen in the sweatshops of nineteenth-century mill towns or in the concentration camps of the twentieth century but as a specter awaiting us in the future, like the ghost of Christmas yet to come, which we may be doomed to enact, unless. . . .

Baby, You Were Great!

Kate Wilhelm

Kate Wilhelm was born in Toledo, Ohio, in 1928. She is married to
Damon Knight, a noted SF author and editor. She has two children and is
now making her home in Oregon. Her novels include *More Bitter Than
Death* (1962), *The Clone* (1965, with Ted Thomas), *The Killer Thing*
(1967), and *Abyss* (1971); more recently she has written *Where Late the
Sweet Birds Sang* (1976). Her short-story collections are *The Mile-long
Space Ship* (1963), *The Downstairs Room* (1968), and *The Infinity Box*
(1975). Her short story "The Planners" won a Nebula Award in 1968.
"Baby, You Were Great!" was first published in Damon Knight's *Orbit II*
(Putnam, 1967).

SF has a way of discovering new symbols for old ideas. The education of
one's moral sense is not an exercise of mind alone, because morality is a
matter of conduct and disposition rather than of knowledge alone. Religions
and ethical teachers have long recognized this truth and have tried to reach
the emotions, the imagination, and the conscience of their followers so that
they would both know and feel the truth and thus be moved to take
appropriate action.

This story of the near future treats the oldest moral issues in terms that
bring them vividly to life for modern readers. Whether or not the particular
abuses of Wilhelm's tale ever come to us "Live from Burbank!" may depend
in no small measure on how well stories such as this help to sensitize our
moral awareness of what is happening "out there." If we think of people
as robots or as service personnel, then it is easy to remain detached and
disengaged from questions of wrong or right, evil or good. All the de-
personalizing and dehumanizing forces of modern life are daily at work to
mesmerize our moral sense. Happily, there are writers like Koestler,
Solzhenitsyn, and Vonnegut who are constantly repeating Huxley's imperative in *Island:* "Attention! Attention!" Of course we try to resist and—
like the moral sleepers we are—mumble, "Just a little while longer."

In Kate Wilhelm's story, Anne Beaumont is an electronically enhanced
sex symbol and television superstar. Gradually, she has been transformed
into a cyborg, the unwitting host for a form of parisitism that enslaves
both the actress and her audience. She leads a surrogate life for millions
of viewers. The women presumably enjoy the vicarious satisfaction of
sharing the emotions and sensations of Anne's life as an adventuress. The
men, in their turn, enjoy the fantasy of stimulating Anne's emotions and
directing her responses to each new adventure. As this relationship has
developed over the years, the actress and her audience have become each
other's prisoners.

The two heavies in the tale are John Lewisohn and Herb Javits. The
latter is motivated by greed and the desire to control or manipulate other
people. Lewisohn's is basically a nobler nature, but he suffers from egoism
and failure to perceive needs or moral claims beyond his own interests.

He has assumed the position of having abandoned moral responsibility for the consequences of his inventions. Instead, he permits Javits to degrade and humiliate the actresses he auditions, especially Anne, through the power given him by Lewisohn's technology. As an index of Lewisohn's moral and psychological decline, we find him at the end compelled to seek a vicarious relationship with Anne rather than the more real, human one he has chosen to abandon.

In the rhetoric of our times, we have here a story of sexism. The sexual exploitation of women by men is detailed in two related instances in the story. If anything, this brutality is worsened by the fact that it is done in the almost clinical spirit of commercial profit seeking. In a curiously unwholesome fashion, it is a descendant of the decayed puritanism traced by Hawthorne in the temperament of his characters more than a century ago. Sexism, however, is the basis for an anatomy of values and attitudes in which the dehumanization of people has become a technique of doing business. The scope of the exploitation is not restricted to women alone; it is universal.

John Lewisohn thought that if one more door slammed, or one more bell rang, or one more voice asked if he was all right, his head would explode. Leaving his laboratories, he walked through the carpeted hall to the elevator that slid wide to admit him noiselessly, was lowered, gently, two floors, where there were more carpeted halls. The door he shoved open bore a neat sign, AUDITIONING STUDIO. Inside, he was waved on through the reception room by three girls who knew better than to speak to him unless he spoke first. They were surprised to see him; it was his first visit there in seven or eight months. The inner room where he stopped was darkened, at first glance appearing empty, revealing another occupant only after his eyes had time to adjust to the dim lighting.

John sat in the chair next to Herb Javits, still without speaking. Herb was wearing the helmet and gazing at a wide screen that was actually a one-way glass panel permitting him to view the audition going on in the next room. John lowered a second helmet to his head. It fit snugly and immediately made contact with the eight prepared spots on his skull. As soon as he turned it on, the helmet itself was forgotten.

A girl had entered the other room. She was breathtakingly lovely, a long-legged honey blonde with slanting green eyes and apricot skin. The room was furnished as a sitting room with two couches, some chairs, end tables and a coffee table, all tasteful and lifeless, like an ad in a furniture trade publication. The girl stopped at the doorway and John felt her indecision, heavily tempered with nervousness and fear. Outwardly she appeared poised and expectant, her smooth face betraying none of her emotions. She took a hesitant step toward the couch, and a wire showed trailing behind her. It was attached to her head. At the same time a second door opened. A young man ran inside, slamming the door behind him; he looked wild and frantic. The girl registered surprise, mounting nervousness; she felt behind her for the door handle, found it and tried to open the door again. It was locked John could hear nothing that was being said in the room; he only felt the girl's reaction to the unexpected interruption. The wild-eyed man was approaching her, his hands slashing through the air, his eyes darting glances all about them constantly. Suddenly he pounced on her and pulled her to him, kissing her face and neck roughly. She seemed paralyzed with fear for several seconds, then there was something else, a bland nothing kind of feeling that accompanied boredom sometimes, or too-complete self-assurance. As the man's hands fastened on her blouse in the back and ripped it, she threw her arms about him, her face showing passion that was not felt anywhere in her mind or in her blood.

"Cut!" Herb Javits said quietly.

The man stepped back from the girl and left her without a word. She looked about blankly, her torn blouse hanging about her hips, one shoulder strap gone. She was very beautiful. The audition manager entered, followed by a dresser with a gown that he threw about her shoulders. She looked startled; waves of anger mounted to fury as she was drawn from the room, leaving it empty. The two watching men removed their helmets.

"Fourth one so far," Herb grunted. "Sixteen yesterday; twenty the day before . . . All nothing." He gave John a curious look. "What's got you stirred out of your lab?"

"Anne's had it this time," John said. "She's been on the phone all night and all morning."

"What now?"

"Those damn sharks! I told you that was too much on top of the airplane crash last week. She can't take much more of it."

"Hold it a minute, Johnny," Herb said. "Let's finish off the next three girls and then talk." He pressed a button on the arm of his chair and the room beyond the screen took their attention again.

This time the girl was slightly less beautiful, shorter, a dimply sort of brunette with laughing blue eyes and upturned nose. John liked her. He adjusted his helmet and felt with her.

She was excited; the audition always excited them. There was some fear and nervousness, not too much. Curious about how the audition would go, probably. The wild young man ran into the room, and her face paled. Nothing else changed. Her nervousness increased, not uncomfortably. When he grabbed her, the only emotion she registered was the nervousness.

"Cut," Herb said.

The next girl was also brunette, with gorgeously elongated legs. She was very cool, a real professional. Her mobile face reflected the range of emotions to be expected as the scene played through again, but nothing inside her was touched. She was a million miles away from it all.

The next one caught John with a slam. She entered the room slowly, looking about with curiosity, nervous, as they all were. She was younger than the other girls, less poised. She had pale gold hair piled in an elaborate mound of waves on top of her head. Her eyes were brown, her skin nicely tanned. When the man entered, her emotions changed quickly to fear, then to terror. John didn't know when he closed his eyes. He was the girl, filled with unspeakable terror; his heart pounded, adrenalin pumped into his system; he wanted to scream but could not. From the dim unreachable depths of his psyche there came something else, in waves, so mixed with terror that the two merged and became one emotion that pulsed and throbbed and demanded. With a jerk he opened his eyes and stared at the window. The girl had been thrown down to one of the couches, and the man was kneeling on the floor beside her, his hands playing over her bare body, his face pressed against her skin.

"Cut!" Herb said. His voice was shaken. "Hire her," he said. The man rose, glanced at the girl, sobbing now, and then quickly bent over and kissed her cheek. Her sobs increased. Her golden hair was down, framing her face; she looked like a child. John tore off the helmet. He was perspiring.

Herb got up, turned on the lights in the room, and the window blanked out, blending with the wall. He didn't look at John. When he wiped his face, his hand was shaking. He rammed it in his pocket.

"When did you start auditions like that?" John asked, after a few moments of silence.

"Couple of months ago. I told you about it. Hell, we had to, Johnny. That's the six hundred nineteenth girl we've tried out! Six hundred nineteen! All phonies but one! Dead from the neck up. Do you have any idea how long it was taking us to find that out! Hours for each one. Now it's a matter of minutes."

John Lewisohn sighed. He knew. He had suggested it, actually, when he had said, "Find a basic anxiety for the test." He hadn't wanted to know what Herb had come up with.

He said, "Okay, but she's only a kid. What about her parents, legal rights, all that?"

"We'll fix it. Don't worry. What about Anne?"

"She's called me five times since yesterday. The sharks were too much. She wants to see us, both of us, this afternoon."

"You're kidding! I can't leave here now!"

"Nope. Kidding I'm not. She says no plug-up if we don't show. She'll take pills and sleep until we get there."

"Good Lord! She wouldn't dare!"

"I've booked seats. We take off at twelve-thirty-five." They stared at one another silently for another moment, when Herb shrugged. He was a short man, not heavy but solid. John was over six feet, muscular,

with a temper that he knew he had to control. Others suspected that
when he did let it go, there would be bodies lying around afterward,
but he controlled it.

Once it had been a physical act, an effort of body and will to master
that temper; now it was done so automatically that he couldn't recall oc-
casions when it even threatened to flare anymore.

"Look, Johnny, when we see Anne, let me handle it. Right? I'll
make it short."

"What are you going to do?"

"Give her an earful. If she's going to start pulling temperament on
me, I'll slap her down so hard she'll bounce a week." He grinned.
"She's had it all her way up to now. She knew there wasn't a replacement if she got bitchy. Let her try it now. Just let her try." Herb was
pacing back and forth with quick, jerky steps.

John realized with a shock that he hated the stocky, red-faced man.
The feeling was new; it was almost as if he could taste the hatred he
felt, and the taste was unfamiliar and pleasant.

Herb stopped pacing and stared at him for a moment. "Why'd she
call you? Why does she want you down, too? She knows you're not
mixed up with this end of it."

"She knows I'm a full partner, anyway," John said.

"Yeah, but that's not it." Herb's face twisted in a grin. "She thinks
you're still hot for her, doesn't she? She knows you tumbled once, in the
beginning, when you were working on her, getting the gimmick working
right." The grin reflected no humor then. "Is she right, Johnny, baby?
Is that it?"

"We made a deal," John said. "You run your end, I run mine. She
wants me along because she doesn't trust you, or believe anything you
tell her anymore. She wants a witness."

"Yeah, Johnny. But you be sure you remember our agreement."
Suddenly Herb laughed. "You know what it was like, Johnny, seeing
you and her? Like a flame trying to snuggle up to an icicle."

At three-thirty they were in Anne's suite in the Skyline Hotel in
Grand Bahama. Herb had a reservation to fly back to New York on the
6 P.M. flight. Anne would not be off until four, so they made themselves comfortable in her rooms and waited. Herb turned her screen on,
offered a helmet to John, who shook his head, and they both seated
themselves. John watched the screen for several minutes; then he, too,
put on a helmet.

Anne was looking at the waves far out at sea where they were long,
green, undulating; then she brought her gaze in closer, to the blue-
green and quick seas, and finally in to where they stumbled on the sand-
bars, breaking into foam that looked solid enough to walk on. She was
peaceful, swaying with the motion of the boat, the sun hot on her back,
the fishing rod heavy in her hands. It was like being an indolent animal at peace with its world, at home in the world, being one with it.
After a few seconds she put down the rod and turned, looking at a tall

smiling man in swimming trunks. He held out his hand and she took it. They entered the cabin of the boat where drinks were waiting. Her mood of serenity and happiness ended abruptly, to be replaced by shocked disbelief, and a start of fear.

"What the hell . . . ?" John muttered, adjusting the audio. You seldom needed audio when Anne was on.

". . . Captain Brothers had to let them go. After all, they've done nothing yet—" the man was saying soberly.

"But why do you think they'll try to rob me?"

"Who else is here with a million dollars' worth of jewels?"

John turned it off and said, "You're a fool! You can't get away with something like that!"

Herb stood up and crossed to the window wall that was open to the stretch of glistening blue ocean beyond the brilliant white beaches. "You know what every woman wants? To own something worth stealing." He chuckled, a sound without mirth. "Among other things, that is. They want to be roughed up once or twice, and forced to kneel. . . . Our new psychologist is pretty good, you know? Hasn't steered us wrong yet. Anne might kick some, but it'll go over great."

"She won't stand for an actual robbery." Louder, emphatically, he added, "I won't stand for that."

"We can dub it," Herb said. "That's all we need, Johnny, plant the idea, and then dub the rest."

John stared at his back. He wanted to believe that. He needed to believe it. His voice was calm when he said, "It didn't start like this, Herb. What happened?"

Herb turned then. His face was dark against the glare of light behind him. "Okay, Johnny, it didn't start like this. Things accelerate, that's all. You thought of a gimmick, and the way we planned it, it sounded great, but it didn't last. We gave them the feeling of gambling, or learning to ski, of automobile racing, everything we could dream up, and it wasn't enough. How many times can you take the first ski jump of your life? After a while you want new thrills, you know? For you it's been great, hasn't it? You bought yourself a shiny new lab and closed the door. You bought yourself time and equipment and when things didn't go right, you could toss it out and start over, and nobody gave a damn. Think of what it's been like for me, kid! I gotta keep coming up with something new, something that'll give Anne a jolt and through her all those nice little people who aren't even alive unless they're plugged in. You think it's been easy? Anne was a green kid. For her everything was new and exciting, but it isn't like that now, boy. You better believe it is *not* like that now. You know what she told me last month? She's sick and tired of men. Our little hot-box Annie! Tired of men!"

John crossed to him and pulled him around toward the light. "Why didn't you tell me?"

"Why, Johnny? What would you have done that I didn't do? *I* looked harder for the right guy. What would you do for a new thrill for her? I worked for them, kid. Right from the start you said for me to leave you alone. Okay. I left you alone. You ever read any of the memos I sent? You initialed them, kiddo. Everything that's been done, we both signed. Don't give me any of that why didn't I tell you stuff. It won't work!" His face was ugly red and a vein bulged in his neck. John wondered if he had high blood pressure, if he would die of a stroke during one of his flash rages.

John left him at the window. He had read the memos. Herb was right; all he had wanted was to be left alone. It had been his idea; after twelve years of work in a laboratory on prototypes he had shown his—gimmick—to Herb Javits. Herb had been one of the biggest producers on television then; now he was the biggest producer in the world.

The gimmick was simple enough. A person fitted with electrodes in his brain could transmit his emotions, which in turn could be broadcast and picked up by the helmets to be felt by the audience. No words, or thoughts went out, only basic emotions—fear, love, anger, hatred . . . That, tied in with a camera showing what the person saw, with a voice dubbed in, and you were the person having the experience, with one important difference—you could turn it off if it got to be too much. The "actor" couldn't. A simple gimmick. You didn't really need the camera and the sound track; many users never turned them on at all, but let their own imaginations fill in the emotional broadcast.

The helmets were not sold, only leased or rented after a short, easy fitting session. A year's lease cost fifty dollars, and there were over thirty-seven million subscribers. Herb had created his own network when the demand for more hours squeezed him out of regular television. From a one-hour weekly show, it had gone to one hour nightly, and now it was on the air eight hours a day live, with another eight hours of taped programming.

What had started out as A DAY IN THE LIFE OF ANNE BEAUMONT was now a life in the life of Anne Beaumont and the audience was insatiable.

Anne came in then, surrounded by the throng of hangers-on that mobbed her daily—hairdressers, masseurs, fitters, script men . . . She looked tired. She waved the crowd out when she saw John and Herb were there. "Hello, John," she said, "Herb."

"Anne, baby, you're looking great!" Herb said. He took her in his arms and kissed her solidl; She stood still, her hands at her sides.

She was tall, very slender, with wheat-colored hair and gray eyes. Her cheekbones were wide and high, her mouth firm and almost too large. Against her deep red-gold suntan her teeth looked whiter than John remembered. Although too firm and strong ever to be thought of as pretty, she was a very beautiful woman. After Herb released her, she turned to John, hesitated only a moment, then extended a slim, sun-browned hand. It was cool and dry in his.

"How have you been, John?" It's been a long time."

He was very glad she didn't kiss him, or call him darling. She smiled only slightly and gently removed her hand from his. He moved to the bar as she turned to Herb.

"I'm through, Herb." Her voice was too quiet. She accepted a whiskey sour from John, but kept her gaze on Herb.

"What's the matter, honey? I was just watching you, baby. You were great today, like always. You've still got it, kid. It's coming through like always."

"What about this robbery? You must be out of your mind . . ."

"Yeah, that. Listen, Anne baby, I swear to you I don't know a thing about it. Laughton must have been giving you the straight goods on that. You know we agreed that the rest of this week you just have a good time, remember? That comes over too, baby. When you have a good time and relax, thirty-seven million people are enjoying life and relaxing. That's good. They can't be stimulated all the time. They like the variety." Wordlessly John held out a glass, scotch and water. Herb took it without looking.

Anne was watching him coldly. Suddenly she laughed. It was a cynical, bitter sound. "You're not a damn fool, Herb. Don't try to act like one." She sipped her drink again, staring at him over the rim of the glass. "I'm warning you, if anyone shows up here to rob me, I'm going to treat him like a real burglar. I bought a gun after today's broadcast, and I learned how to shoot when I was ten. I still know how. I'll kill him, Herb, whoever it is."

"Baby," Herb started, but she cut him short.

"And this is my last week. As of Saturday, I'm through."

"You can't do that, Anne," Herb said. John watched him closely, searching for a sign of weakness; he saw nothing. Herb exuded confidence. "Look around, Anne, at this room, your clothes, everything. . . . You are the richest woman in the world, having the time of your life, able to go anywhere, do anything . . ."

"While the whole world watches—"

"So what? It doesn't stop you, does it?" Herb started to pace, his steps jerky and quick. "You knew that when you signed the contract. You're a rare girl, Anne, beautiful, emotional, intelligent. Think of all those women who've got nothing but you. If you quit them, what do they do? Die? They might, you know For the first time in their lives they're able to feel like they're living. You're giving them what no one ever did before, what was only hinted at in books and films in the old days. Suddenly they know what it feels like to face excitement, to experience love, to feel contented and peaceful. Think of them, Anne, empty, with nothing in their lives but you, what you're able to give them. Thirty-seven million drabs, Anne, who never felt anything but boredom and frustration until you gave them life. What do they have? Work, kids, bills. You've given them the world, baby! Without you they wouldn't even want to live anymore."

She wasn't listening. Almost dreamily she said, "I talked to my lawyers, Herb, and the contract is meaningless. You've already broken it over and over. I agreed to learn a lot of new things. I did. My God! I've climbed mountains, hunted lions, learned to ski and water-ski, but now you want me to die a little bit each week . . . That airplane crash, not bad, just enough to terrify me. Then the sharks. I really do think it was having sharks brought in when I was skiing that did it, Herb. You see, you will kill me. It will happen, and you won't be able to top it, Herb. Not ever."

There was a hard, waiting silence following her words. *No!* John shouted soundlessly. He was looking at Herb. He had stopped pacing when she started to talk. Something flicked across his face—surprise, fear, something not readily identifiable. Then his face went blank and he raised his glass and finished the scotch and water, replacing the glass on the bar. When he turned again, he was smiling with disbelief.

"What's really bugging you, Anne? There have been plants before. You knew about them. Those lions didn't just happen by, you know. And the avalanche needed a nudge from someone. You know that. What else is bugging you?"

"I'm in love, Herb."

Herb waved that aside impatiently. "Have you ever watched your own show, Anne?" She shook her head. "I thought not. So you wouldn't know about the expansion that took place last month, after we planted that new transmitter in your head. Johnny boy's been busy, Anne. You know these scientist-types, never satisfied, always improving, changing. Where's the camera, Anne? Do you ever know where it is anymore? Have you ever seen a camera in the past couple of weeks, or a recorder of any sort? You have not, and you won't again. You're on now, honey." His voice was quite low, amused almost. "In fact the only time you aren't on is when you're sleeping. I know you're in love. I know who he is. I know how he makes you feel. I even know how much money he makes a week. I should know, Anne baby. I pay him." He had come closer to her with each word, finishing with his face only inches from hers. He didn't have a chance to duck the flashing slap that jerked his head around, and before either of them realized it, he had hit her back, knocking her into a chair.

The silence grew, became something ugly and heavy, as if words were being born and dying without utterance because they were too brutal for the human spirit to bear. There was a spot of blood on Herb's mouth where Anne's diamond ring had cut him. He touched it and looked at his finger. "It's all being taped now, honey, even this," he said. He turned his back on her and went to the bar.

There was a large red print on her cheek. Her gray eyes had turned black with rage.

"Honey, relax," Herb said after a moment. "It won't make any difference to you, in what you do, or anything like that. You know we can't use most of the stuff, but it gives the editors a bigger variety to pick from. It was getting to the point where most of the interesting stuff was going on after you were off. Like buying the gun. That's great stuff there, baby. You weren't blanketing a single thing, and it'll all come through like pure gold." He finished mixing his drink, tasted it, and then swallowed half of it. "How many women have to go out and buy a gun to protect themselves? Think of them all, feeling that gun, feeling the things you felt when you picked it up, looked at it . . ."

"How long have you been tuning in all the time?" she asked. John felt a stirring along his spine, a tingle of excitement. He knew what was going out over the miniature transmitter, the rising crests of emotion she was feeling. Only a trace of them showed on her smooth face, but the raging interior torment was being recorded faithfully. Her quiet voice and quiet body were lies; the tapes never lied.

Herb felt it too. He put his glass down and went to her, kneeling by the chair, taking her hand in both of his. "Anne, please, don't be that angry with me. I was desperate for new material. When Johnny got this last wrinkle out, and we knew we could record around the clock, we had to try it, and it wouldn't have been any good if you'd known. That's no way to test anything. You knew we were planting the transmitter . . ."

"How long?"

"Not quite a month."

"And Stuart? He's one of your men? He is transmitting also? You hired him to . . . to make love to me? Is that right?"

Herb nodded. She pulled her hand free and averted her face. He got up then and went to the window. "But what difference does it make?" he shouted. "If I introduced the two of you at a party, you wouldn't think anything of it. What difference if I did it this way? I knew you'd like each other. He's bright, like you, likes the same sort of things you do. Comes from a poor family, like yours . . . Everything said you'd get along."

"Oh, yes," she said almost absently. "We get along," She was feeling in her hair, her fingers searching for the scars.

"It's all healed by now," John said. She looked at him as if she had forgotten he was there.

"I'll find a surgeon," she said, standing up, her fingers white on her glass. "A brain surgeon—"

"It's a new process," John said slowly. "It would be dangerous to go in after them."

She looked at him for a long time. "Dangerous?"

He nodded.

"You could take it back out."

He remembered the beginning, how he had quieted her fear of the electrodes and wires. Her fear was that of a child for the unknown and the unknowable. Time and again he had proved to her that she could trust him, that he wouldn't lie to her. He hadn't lied to her, then. There was the same trust in her eyes, the same unshakable faith. She would believe him. She would accept without question whatever he said. Herb had called him an icicle, but that was wrong. An icicle would have melted in her fires. More like a stalactite, shaped by centuries of civilization, layer by layer he had been formed until he had forgotten how to bend, forgotten how to find release for the stirrings he felt somewhere in the hollow, rigid core of himself. She had tried and, frustrated, she had turned from him, hurt, but unable not to trust one she had loved. Now she waited. He could free her, and lose her again, this time irrevocably. Or he could hold her as long as she lived.

Her lovely gray eyes were shadowed with fear, and the trust that he had given to her. Slowly he shook his head.

"I can't," he said. "No one can."

"I see," she murmured, the black filling her eyes. "I'd die, wouldn't I? Then you'd have a lovely sequence, wouldn't you, Herb?" She swung around, away from John. "You'd have to fake the story line, of course, but you are so good at that. An accident, emergency brain surgery needed, everything I feel going out to the poor little drabs who never will have brain surgery done. It's very good," she said admiringly. Her eyes were black. "In fact, anything I do from now on, you'll use, won't you? If I kill you, that will simply be material for your editors to pick over. Trial, prison, very dramatic . . . On the other hand, if I kill myself . . ."

John felt chilled; a cold, hard weight seemed to be filling him. Herb laughed. "The story line will be something like this," he said. "Anne has fallen in love with a stranger, deeply, sincerely in love with him. Everyone knows how deep that love is, they've all felt it, too, you know. She finds him raping a child, a lovely little girl in her early teens. Stuart tells her they're through. He loves the little nymphet. In a passion she kills herself. You are broadcasting a real storm of passion, right now, aren't you, honey? Never mind, when I run through this scene, I'll find out." She hurled her glass at him, ice cubes and orange slices flying across the room. Herb ducked, grinning.

"That's awfully good, baby. Corny, but after all, they can't get too much corn, can they? They'll love it, after they get over the shock of losing you. And they will get over it, you know. They always do. Wonder if it's true about what happens to someone experiencing a violent death?" Anne's teeth bit down on her lip, and slowly she sat down again, her eyes closed tight. Herb watched her for a moment, then said, even more cheerfully, "We've got the kid already. If you give them a death, you've got to give them a new life. Finish one with a bang. Start one with a bang. We'll name the kid Cindy, a real Cinderella story after that. They'll love her, too."

Anne opened her eyes, black, dulled now; she was so full of tension that John felt his own muscles contract. He wondered if he would be able to stand the tape she was transmitting. A wave of excitement swept him and he knew he would play it all, feel it all, the incredibly contained rage, fear, the horror of giving a death to them to gloat over, and finally, anguish. He would know it all. Watching Anne, he wished she would break now. She didn't. She stood up stiffly, her back rigid, a muscle hard ridged in her jaw. Her voice was flat when she said, "Stuart is due in half an hour. I have to dress." She left them without looking back.

Herb winked at John and motioned toward the door. "Want to take me to the plane, kid?" In the cab he said, "Stick close to her for a couple of days, Johnny. There might be an even bigger reaction later when she really understands just how hooked she is." He chuckled again. "By God! It's a good thing she trusts you, Johnny boy!"

As they waited in the chrome and marble terminal for the liner to unload its passengers, John said, "Do you think she'll be any good after this?"

"She can't help herself. She's too life-oriented to deliberately choose to die. She's like a jungle inside, raw, wild, untouched by that smooth layer of civilization she shows on the outside. It's a thin layer, kid, real thin. She'll fight to stay alive. She'll become more wary, more alert to danger, more excited and exciting . . . She'll really go to pieces when he touches her tonight. She's primed real good. Might even have to do some editing, tone it down a little." His voice was very happy. "He touches her where she lives, and she reacts. A real wild one. She's one; the new kid's one; Stuart . . . They're few and far between, Johnny. It's up to us to find them. God knows we're going to need all of them we can get." His expression became thoughtful and withdrawn. "You know, that really wasn't such a bad idea of mine about rape and the kid. Who ever dreamed we'd get that kind of reaction from her? With the right sort of buildup . . ." He had to run to catch his plane.

John hurried back to the hotel, to be near Anne if she needed him. But he hoped she would leave him alone. His fingers shook as he turned on his screen; suddenly he had a clear memory of the child who had wept, and he hoped Stuart was on from six until twelve, and he already had missed almost an hour of the show. He adjusted the helmet and sank back into a deep chair. He left the audio off, letting his own words form, letting his own thoughts fill in the spaces.

Anne was leaning toward him, sparkling champagne raised to her lips, her eyes large and soft. She was speaking, talking to him, John, calling him by name. He felt a tingle start somewhere deep inside him, and his glance was lowered to rest on her tanned hand in his, sending electricity through him. Her hand trembled when he ran his fingers up her palm, to her wrist where a blue vein throbbed. The slight throb became a pounding that grew and when he looked into her eyes, they were dark and very deep. They danced and he felt her body against his, yielding, pleading. The room darkened and she was an outline against the window, her gown floating down about her. The darkness grew denser, or he closed his eyes, and this time when her body pressed against his, there was nothing between them, and the pounding was everywhere.

In the deep chair, with the helmet on his head, John's hand clenched, opened, clenched, again and again.

Questions for Discussion and Review

1. Of what significance is the title of this story?
2. Compare this story to "The Mindworm." What are the chief similarities and differences?
3. To what extent is Anne Beaumont a culpable party in this story? Does this affect our interpretation of the story's critical perspective?
4. Why does the story begin and end as it does?
5. Which soft sciences are involved in this story?

Coming Attraction

Fritz Leiber

Fritz Leiber was born on Christmas Day, 1910, in Chicago. Both parents—
his father, Fritz, and his mother, Virginia Bronson—were Shakespearean
actors. For many years Leiber was married to Jonquil Stephens, the writer,
until her death in 1969; they had one child, a son.

Leiber received his bachelor's degree at the University of Chicago, and
he attended Episcopal General Theological Seminary. He served as an
Episcopal minister in New Jersey in the early 1930s and then followed his
parents onto the stage as a Shakespearean actor. He later worked as an
editor and as a college literature instructor before turning to writing as a
full-time profession. Among his many novels, *Conjure Wife* (1953) and
A Specter Is Haunting Texas (1969) stand out, along with his award-
winning novels and stories. He won the Hugo Award for *The Big Time*
(1958), *The Wanderer* (1965), and "Ship of Shadows" (1970). Both
Hugo and Nebula awards went to "Gonna Roll the Bones" (1968) and
"Ill Met in Lankhmar" (1971). The last story is part of the famous
sword-and-sorcery series, Fafhrd and the Grey Mouser. "Coming Attraction" appeared in one of the first issues of *Galaxy Magazine* (November
1950).

Visits into the future, like excursions into faerie, are perilous because we
are likely to meet there reflections of our other selves. We may see in
those imitations a self we have wished to bury or forget but which the
writer has conjured into life as a grim reminder of our capacity for evil.
One would think that of all the generations since Adam, this one would not
require such recollections. But that is one of the traditional functions of
prophecy.

Like the modified turbine-powered coupe, this is a story with fishhooks;
and by the time it is finished with us, our best Sunday goin'-to-meetin'
clothes are not much to look at any more, and there are a few pieces of
flesh missing from our collective hindquarters.

Leiber's *Dorian Gray* portrait of New York after World War III carries
with it the nightmarish potential of self-discovery. As all skillful satirists
of society, the author cheerfully leads us into the hooks of recognition.
It is not simply that he is showing us images of possible futures. That
would be disturbing enough, what with the remains of New York as disorderly as the society that has emerged after the holocaust. Bad enough,
indeed. What is worse is the social and moral decay. Worst of all is the
fact that the author forces on us an awareness of a pattern of deteriorating
values which fits today's culture. It does not help to realize that this story
was written more than a quarter-century ago and grows more modern at
each anniversary.

The author has some fun at the expense of our fashion mores, past and
future, and the tendency to confuse haberdashery with morality. However,
just as we are chuckling to ourselves with a sense of cultural superiority,

along come the fishhooks again, and this time we have swallowed the bait. In Leiber's postwar culture, such a confusion of values would be a relief, compared with the real depravity we discover lying beneath the masks of the women. We have enjoyed lady wrestlers for some time, of course, and women boxers are here at last. We are halfway to Leiber's future world already! If we are lucky, it may not even take another world war to do the trick. A few more experiences like Vietnam should be enough to reduce us to the level of barbarism in which "Coming Attraction" will qualify as a nursery tale.

The coupe with the fishhooks welded to the fender shouldered up over the curb like the nose of a nightmare. The girl in its path stood frozen, her face probably stiff with fright under her mask. For once my reflexes weren't shy. I took a fast step toward her, grabbed her elbow, yanked her back. Her black skirt swirled out.

The big coupe shot by, its turbine humming. I glimpsed three faces. Something ripped. I felt the hot exhaust on my ankles as the big coupe swerved back into the street. A thick cloud like a black flower blossomed from its jouncing rear end, while from the fishhooks flew a black shimmering rag.

"Did they get you?" I asked the girl.

She had twisted around to look where the side of her skirt was torn away. She was wearing nylon tights.

"The hooks didn't touch me," she said shakily. "I guess I'm lucky."

I heard voices around us:

"Those kids! What'll they think up next?"

"They're a menace. They ought to be arrested."

Sirens screamed at a rising pitch as two motor-police, their rocket-assist jets full on, came whizzing toward us after the coupe. But the black flower had become an inky fog obscuring the whole street. The motor-police switched from rocket assists to rocket brakes and swerved to a stop near the smoke cloud.

"Are you English?" the girl asked me. "You have an English accent."

Her voice came shudderingly from behind the sleek black satin mask. I fancied her teeth must be chattering. Eyes that were perhaps blue searched my face from behind the black gauze covering the eyeholes of the mask. I told her she'd guessed right. She stood close to me. "Will you come to my place tonight?" she asked rapidly. "I can't thank you now. And there's something else you can help me about."

My arm, still lightly circling her waist, felt her body trembling. I was answering the plea in that as much as in her voice when I said, "Certainly." She gave me an address south of Inferno, an apartment number and a time. She asked my name and I told her.

"Hey, you!"

I turned obediently to the policeman's shout. He shooed away the small clucking crowd of masked women and barefaced men. Coughing from the smoke that the black coupe had thrown out, he asked for my papers. I handed him the essential ones.

He looked at them and then at me. "British Barter? How long will you be in New York?"

Suppressing the urge to say, "For as short a time as possible," I told him I'd be here for a week or so.

"May need you as a witness," he explained. "Those kids can't use smoke on us. When they do that, we pull them in."

He seemed to think the smoke was the bad thing. "They tried to kill the lady," I pointed out.

He shook his head wisely. "They always pretend they're going to, but actually they just want to snag skirts. I've picked up rippers with as many as fifty skirt-snags tacked up in their rooms. Of course, sometimes they come a little too close."

I explained that if I hadn't yanked her out of the way, she'd have been hit by more than hooks. But he interrupted, "If she'd thought it was a real murder attempt, she'd have stayed here."

I looked around. It was true. She was gone.

"She was fearfully frightened," I told him.

"Who wouldn't be? Those kids would have scared old Stalin himself."

"I mean frightened of more than 'kids.' They didn't look like 'kids.' "

"What did they look like?"

I tried without much success to describe the three faces. A vague impression of viciousness and effeminacy doesn't mean much.

"Well, I could be wrong," he said finally. "Do you know the girl? Where she lives?"

"No," I half lied.

The other policeman hung up his radiophone and ambled toward us, kicking at the tendrils of dissipating smoke. The black cloud no longer hid the dingy facades with their five-year-old radiation flash-burns, and I could begin to make out the distant stump of the Empire State Building, thrusting up out of Inferno like a mangled finger.

"They haven't been picked up so far," the approaching policeman grumbled. "Left smoke for five blocks, from what Ryan says."

The first policeman shook his head. "That's bad," he observed solemnly.

I was feeling a bit uneasy and ashamed. An Englishman shouldn't lie, at least not on impulse.

"They sound like nasty customers," the first policeman continued in the same grim tone. "We'll need witnesses. Looks as if you may have to stay in New York longer than you expect."

I got the point. I said, "I forgot to show you all my papers," and handed him a few others, making sure there was a five dollar bill in among them.

When he handed them back a bit later, his voice was no longer ominous. My feelings of guilt vanished. To cement our relationship, I chatted with the two of them about their job.

"I suppose the masks give you some trouble," I observed. "Over in England we've been reading about your new crop of masked female bandits."

"Those things get exaggerated," the first policeman assured me. "It's the men masking as women that really mix us up. But, brother, when we nab them, we jump on them with both feet."

"And you get so you can spot women almost as well as if they had naked faces," the second policeman volunteered. "You know, hands and all that."

"Especially all that," the first agreed with a chuckle. "Say, is it true that some girls don't mask over in England?"

"A number of them have picked up the fashion," I told him. "Only a few, though—the ones who always adopt the latest style, however extreme."

"They're usually masked in the British newscasts."

"I imagine it's arranged that way out of deference to American taste," I confessed. "Actually, not very many do mask."

The second policeman considered that. "Girls going down the street bare from the neck up." It was not clear whether he viewed the prospect with relish or moral distaste. Likely both.

"A few members keep trying to persuade Parliament to enact a law forbidding all masking," I continued, talking perhaps a bit too much.

The second policeman shook his head. "What an idea. You know, masks are a pretty good thing, brother. Couple of years more and I'm going to make my wife wear hers around the house."

The first policeman shrugged. "If women were to stop wearing masks, in six weeks you wouldn't know the difference. You get used to anything, if enough people do or don't do it."

I agreed, rather regretfully, and left them. I turned north on Broadway (old Tenth Avenue, I believe) and walked rapidly until I was beyond Inferno. Passing such an area undecontaminated radioactivity always makes a person queasy. I thanked God there weren't any such in England, as yet.

The street was almost empty, though I was accosted by a couple of beggars with faces tunneled by H-bomb scars, whether real or of makeup putty, I couldn't tell. A fat woman held out a baby with webbed fingers and toes. I told myself it would have been deformed anyway and that she was only capitalizing on our fear of bomb-induced mutations. Still, I gave her a seven-and-a-half-cent piece. Her mask made me feel I was paying tribute to an African fetish.

"May all your children be blessed with one head and two eyes, sir."

"Thanks," I said, shuddering, and hurried past her.

". . . There's only trash behind the mask, so turn your head, stick to your task: Stay away, stay away—from—the—girls!"

This last was the end of an anti-sex song being sung by some religionists half a block from the circle-and-cross insignia of a femalist temple. They reminded me only faintly of our small tribe of British monastics. Above their heads was a jumble of billboards advertising predigested foods, wrestling instruction, radio handies and the like.

I stared at the hysterical slogans with disagreeable fascination. Since the female face and form have been banned on American signs, the very letters of the advertiser's alphabet have begun to crawl with sex— the fat-bellied, big-breasted capital B, the lascivious double O. However, I reminded myself, it is chiefly the mask that so strangely accents sex in America.

A British anthropologist has pointed out, that, while it took more than 5,000 years to shift the chief point of sexual interest from the hips to the breasts, the next transition to the face has taken less than 50 years. Comparing the American style with Moslem tradition is not valid; Moslem women are compelled to wear veils, the purpose of which is to make a husband's property private, while American women have only the compulsion of fashion and use masks to create mystery.

Theory aside, the actual origins of the trend are to be found in the anti-radiation clothing of World War III, which led to masked wrestling, now a fantastically popular sport, and that in turn led to the current female fashion. Only a wild style at first, masks quickly became as necessary as brassieres and lipsticks had been earlier in the century.

I finally realized that I was not speculating about masks in general, but about what lay behind one in particular. That's the devil of the things; you're never sure whether a girl is heightening loveliness or hiding ugliness. I pictured a cool, pretty face in which fear showed only in widened eyes. Then I remembered her blonde hair, rich against the blackness of the satin mask. She'd told me to come at the twenty-second hour—ten p.m.

I climbed to my apartment near the British Consulate; the elevator shaft had been shoved out of plumb by an old blast, a nuisance in these tall New York buildings. Before it occurred to me that I would be going out again, I automatically tore a tab from the film strip under my shirt. I developed it just to be sure. It showed that the total radiation I'd taken that day was still within the safety limit. I'm no phobic about it, as so many people are these days, but there's no point in taking chances.

I flopped down on the day bed and stared at the silent speaker and the dark screen of the video set. As always, they made me think, somewhat bitterly, of the two great nations of the world. Mutilated by each other, yet still strong, they were crippled giants poisoning the planet with their respective dreams of an impossible equality and as impossible success.

I fretfully switched on the speaker. By luck, the newscaster was talking excitedly of the prospects of a bumper wheat crop, sown by planes across a dust bowl moistened by seeded rains. I listened carefully to the rest of the program (it was remarkably clear of Russian telejamming) but there was no further news of interest to me. And, of course, no mention of the Moon, though everyone knows that America and Russia are racing to develop their primary bases into fortresses capable of mutual assault and the launching of alphabet-bombs toward Earth. I myself knew perfectly well that the British electronic equipment I was helping trade for American wheat was destined for use in spaceships.

I switched off the newscast. It was growing dark and once again I pictured a tender, frightened face behind a mask. I hadn't had a date since England. It's exceedingly difficult to become acquainted with a girl in America, where as little as a smile, often, can set one of them yelping for the police—to say nothing of the increasingly puritanical morality and the roving gangs that keep most women indoors after dark. And naturally, the masks which are definitely not, as the Soviets claim, a last invention of capitalist degeneracy, but a sign of great psychological insecurity. The Russians have no masks, but they have their own signs of stress.

I went to the window and impatiently watched the darkness gather. I was getting very restless. After a while a ghostly violet cloud appeared to the south. My hair rose. Then I laughed. I had momentarily fancied it a radiation from the crater of the Hell-bomb, though I should instantly have known it was only the radio-induced glow in the sky over the amusement and residential area south of Inferno.

Promptly at twenty-two hours I stood before the door of my unknown girl friend's apartment. The electronic say-who-please said just that. I answered clearly, "Wysten Turner," wondering if she'd given my name to the mechanism. She evidently had, for the door opened. I walked into a small empty living room, my heart pounding a bit.

The room was expensively furnished with the latest pneumatic hassocks and sprawlers. There were some midgie books on the table. The one I picked up was the standard hard-boiled detective story in which two female murderers go gunning for each other.

The television was on. A masked girl in green was crooning a love song. Her right hand held something that blurred off into the foreground. I saw the set had a handie, which we haven't in England as yet, and curiously thrust my hand into the handie orifice beside the screen. Contrary to my expectations, it was not like slipping into a pulsing rubber glove, but rather as if the girl on the screen actually held my hand.

A door opened behind me. I jerked out my hand with as guilty a reaction as if I'd been caught peering through a keyhole.

She stood in the bedroom doorway. I think she was trembling. She was wearing a gray fur coat, white-speckled, and a gray velvet evening mask with shirred gray lace around the eyes and mouth. Her fingernails twinkled like silver.

It hadn't occurred to me that she'd expect us to go out.

"I should have told you," she said softly. Her mask veered nervously toward the books and the screen and the room's dark corners. "But I can't possibly talk to you here."

I said doubtfully, "There's a place near the Consulate. . . ."

"I know where we can be together and talk," she said rapidly. "If you don't mind."

As we entered the elevator I said, "I'm afraid I dismissed the cab."

But the cab driver hadn't gone for some reason of his own. He jumped out and smirkingly held the front door open for us. I told him we preferred to sit in back. He sulkily opened the rear door, slammed it after us, jumped in front and slammed the door behind him.

My companion leaned forward. "Heaven," she said.

The driver switched on the turbine and televisor.

"Why did you ask if I were a British subject?" I said, to start the conversation.

She leaned away from me, tilting her mask close to the window. "See the Moon," she said in a quick, dreamy voice.

"But why, really?" I pressed, conscious of an irritation that had nothing to do with her.

"It's edging up into the purple of the sky."

"And what's your name?"

"The purple makes it look yellower."

Just then I became aware of the source of my irritation. It lay in the square of writhing light in the front of the cab beside the driver.

I don't object to ordinary wrestling matches, though they bore me, but I simply detest watching a man wrestle a woman. The fact that the bouts are generally "on the level," with the man greatly outclassed in weight and reach and the masked females young and personable, only makes them seem worse to me.

"Please turn off the screen," I requested the driver.

He shook his head without looking around. "Uh-uh, man," he said. "They've been grooming that babe for weeks for this bout with Little Zirk."

Infuriated, I reached forward, but my companion caught my arm. "Please," she whispered frightenedly, shaking her head.

I settled back, frustrated. She was closer to me now, but silent and for a few moments I watched the heaves and contortions of the powerful masked girl and her wiry masked opponent on the screen. His frantic scrambling at her reminded me of a male spider.

I jerked around, facing my companion. "Why did those three men want to kill you?" I asked sharply.

The eyeholes of her mask faced the screen. "Because they're jealous of me," she whispered.

"Why are they jealous?"

She still didn't look at me. "Because of him."

"Who?"

She didn't answer.

I asked. "What *is* the matter?"

She still didn't look my way. She smelled nice.

"See here," I said laughingly, changing my tactics, "you really should tell me something about yourself. I don't even know what you look like."

I half playfully lifted my hand to the band of her neck. She gave it an astonishingly swift slap. I pulled it away in sudden pain. There were four tiny indentations on the back. From one of them a tiny bead of blood welled out as I watched. I looked at her silver fingernails and saw they were actually delicate and pointed metal caps.

"I'm dreadfully sorry," I heard her say, "But you frightened me. I thought for a moment you were going to . . ."

At last she turned to me. Her coat had fallen open. Her evening dress was Cretan Revival, a bodice of lace beneath and supporting the breasts without covering them.

"Don't be angry," she said, putting her arms around my neck. "You were wonderful this afternoon."

The soft gray velvet of her mask, molding itself to her cheek, pressed mine. Through the mask's face the wet warm tip of her tongue touched my chin.

"I'm not angry," I said. "Just puzzled and anxious to help."

The cab stopped. To either side were black windows bordered by spears of broken glass. The sickly purple light showed a few ragged figures slowly moving toward us.

The driver muttered, "It's the turbine, man. We're grounded." He sat there hunched and motionless. "Wish it had happened somewhere else."

My companion whispered, "Five dollars is the usual amount."

She looked out so shudderingly at the congregating figures that I suppressed my indignation and did as she suggested. The driver took the bill without a word. As he started up, he put his hand out the window and I heard a few coins clink on the pavement.

My companion came back into my arms, but her mask faced the television screen, where the tall girl just pinned the convulsively kicking Little Zirk.

"I'm so frightened," she breathed.

Heaven turned out to be an equally ruinous neighborhood, but it had a club with an awning and a huge doorman uniformed like a spaceman, but in gaudy colors. In my sensuous daze I rather liked it all. We stepped out of the cab just as a drunken old woman came down the sidewalk, her mask awry. A couple ahead of us turned their heads from the half revealed face, as if from an ugly body at the beach. As we followed them in I heard the doorman say, "Get along, grandma, and cover yourself."

Inside, everything was dimness and blue glows. She had said we could talk here, but I didn't see how. Besides the inevitable chorus of sneezes and coughs (they say America is fifty per cent allergic these days), there was a band going full blast in the latest robop style, in which an electronic composing machine selects an arbitrary sequence of tones into which the musicians weave their raucous little individualities.

Most of the people were in booths. The band was behind the bar. On a small platform beside them, a girl was dancing, stripped of her mask. The little cluster of men at the shadowy far end of the bar weren't looking at her.

We inspected the menu in gold script on the wall and pushed the buttons for breast of chicken, fried shrimps and two scotches. Moments later, the serving bell tinkled. I opened the gleaming panel and took out our drinks.

The cluster of men at the bar filed off toward the door, but first they stared around the room. My companion had just thrown back her coat. Their look lingered on our booth. I noticed that there were three of them.

The band chased off the dancing girl with growls. I handed my companion a straw and we sipped our drinks.

"You wanted me to help you about something," I said. "Incidentally, I think you're lovely."

She nodded quick thanks, looked around, leaned forward. "Would it be hard for me to get to England?"

"No," I replied, a bit taken aback. "Provided you have an American passport."

"Are they difficult to get?"

"Rather," I said, surprised at her lack of information. "Your country doesn't like its nationals to travel, though it isn't quite as stringent as Russia."

"Could the British Consulate help me get a passport?"

"It's hardly their. . . ."

"Could you?"

I realized we were being inspected. A man and two girls had paused opposite our table. The girls were tall and wolfish-looking, with spangled masks. The man stood jauntily between them like a fox on its hind legs.

My companion didn't glance at them, but she sat back. I noticed that one of the girls had a big yellow bruise on her forearm. After a moment they walked to a booth in the deep shadows.

"Know them?" I asked. She didn't reply. I finished my drink. "I'm not sure you'd like England," I said. "The austerity's altogether different from your American brand of misery."

She leaned forward again. "But I must get away," she whispered.

"Why?" I was getting impatient.

"Because I'm so frightened."

There were chimes. I opened the panel and handed her the fried shrimps. The sauce on my breast of chicken was a delicious steaming compound of almonds, soy and ginger. But something must have been wrong with the radionic oven that had thawed and heated it, for at the first bite I crunched a kernel of ice in the meat. These delicate mechanisms need constant repair and there aren't enough mechanics.

I put down my fork. "What are you really scared of?" I asked her.

For once her mask didn't waver away from my face. As I waited I could feel the fears gathering without her naming them, tiny dark shapes swarming through the curved night outside, converging on the radioactive pest spot of New York, dipping into the margins of the purple. I felt a sudden rush of sympathy, a desire to protect the girl opposite me. The warm feeling added itself to the infatuation engendered in the cab.

"Everything," she said finally.

I nodded and touched her hand.

"Im afraid of the Moon," she began, her voice going dreamy and brittle as it had in the cab. "You can't look at it and not think of guided bombs."

"It's the same Moon over England," I reminded her.

"But it's not England's Moon any more. It's ours and Russia's. You're not responsible."

"Oh, and then," she said with a tilt of her mask, "I'm afraid of the cars and the gangs and the loneliness and Inferno. I'm afraid of the lust that undresses your face. And—" her voice hushed— "I'm afraid of the wrestlers."

"Yes?" I prompted softly after a moment.

Her mask came forward. "Do you know something about the wrestlers?" she asked rapidly. "The ones that wrestle women, I mean. They often lose, you know. And then they have to have a girl to take their frustration out on. A girl who's soft and weak and terribly frightened. They need that, to keep them men. Other men don't want them to have a girl. Other men want them just to fight women and be heroes. But they must have a girl. It's horrible for her."

I squeezed her fingers tighter, as if courage could be transmitted— granting I had any. "I think I can get you to England," I said.

Shadows crawled onto the table and stayed there. I looked up at the three men who had been at the end of the bar. They were the men I had seen in the big coupe. They wore black sweaters and close-fitting black trousers. Their faces were as expressionless as dopers. Two of them stood about me. The other loomed over the girl.

"Drift off, man," I was told. I heard the other inform the girl: "We'll wrestle a fall, sister. What shall it be? Judo, slapsie or kill-who-can?"

I stood up. There are times when an Englishman simply must be maltreated. But just then the foxlike man came gliding in like the star of a ballet. The reaction of the other three startled me. They were acutely embarrassed.

He smiled at them thinly. "You won't win my favor by tricks like this," he said.

"Don't get the wrong idea, Zirk," one of them pleaded.

"I will if it's right," he said. "She told me what you tried to do this afternoon. That won't endear you to me, either. Drift."

They backed off awkwardly. "Let's get out of here," one of them said loudly, as they turned. "I know a place where they fight naked with knives."

Little Zirk laughed musically and slipped into the seat beside my companion. She shrank from him, just a little. I pushed my feet back, leaned forward.

"Who's your friend, baby?" he asked, not looking at her.

She passed the question to me with a little gesture. I told him.

"British," he observed. "She's been asking you about getting out of the country? About passports?" He smiled pleasantly. "She likes to start running away. Don't you, baby?" His small hand began to stroke her wrist, the fingers bent a little, the tendons ridged, as if he were about to grab and twist.

"Look here," I said sharply. "I have to be grateful to you for ordering off those bullies, but—"

"Think nothing of it," he told me. "They're no harm except when they're behind steering wheels. A well-trained fourteen-year-old girl could cripple any one of them. Why, even Theda here, if she went in for that sort of thing. . . ." He turned to her, shifting his hand from her wrist to her hair. He stroked it, letting the strands slip slowly through his fingers. "You know I lost tonight, baby, don't you?" he said softly.

I stood up. "Come along," I said to her. "Let's leave."

She just sat there, I couldn't even tell if she was trembling. I tried to read a message in her eyes through the mask.

"I'll take you away," I said to her. "I can do it. I really will."

He smiled at me. "She'd like to go with you," he said. "Wouldn't you, baby?"

"Will you or won't you?" I said to her. She still just sat there.

He slowly knotted his fingers in her hair.

"Listen, you little vermin," I snapped at him. "Take your hands off her."

He came up from the seat like a snake. I'm no fighter. I just know that the more scared I am, the harder and straighter I hit. This time I was lucky. But as he crumbled back, I felt a slap and four stabs of pain in my cheek. I clapped my hand to it. I could feel the four gashes made by her dagger finger caps, and the warm blood oozing out from them.

She didn't look at me. She was bending over little Zirk and cuddling her mask to his cheek and crooning: "There, there, don't feel bad, you'll be able to hurt me afterward."

There were sounds around us, but they didn't come close. I leaned forward and ripped the mask from her face.

I really don't know why I should have expected her face to be anything else. It was very pale, of course, and there weren't any cosmetics. I suppose there's no point in wearing any under a mask. The eyebrows were untidy and the lips chapped. But as for the general expression, as for the feelings crawling and wriggling across it—

Have you ever lifted a rock from damp soil? Have you ever watched the slimy white grubs?

I looked down at her, she up at me. "Yes, you're so frightened, aren't you?" I said sarcastically. "You dread this little nightly drama, don't you? You're scared to death."

And I walked right out into the purple night, still holding my hand to my bleeding cheek. No one stopped me, not even the girl wrestlers. I wished I could tear a tab from under my shirt, and test it then and there, and find I'd taken too much radiation, and so be able to ask to cross the Hudson and go down New Jersey, past the lingering radiance of the Narrows Bomb, and so on to Sandy Hook to wait for the rusty ship that would take me back over the seas to England.

Questions for Discussion and Review

1. Consider and discuss the appropriateness of this story's title.
2. Why is the narrator British?
3. Describe the attitude of the police and its significance for the story.
4. Compare and contrast the ideas of decadence in this story with "Enchantress of Venus" and "Star Beast." What are the differences, and what accounts for them?
5. What relationship is there between the war and the behavior of the surviving New Yorkers?
6. If women are the victims in Wilhelm's story, they seem to be getting even in this one. Still, why does the moral stigma fall so heavily on women in this story?

The blending of SF with other kinds or genres is a minor art form in itself. SF seems to go well with almost everything, as so many modern writers have discovered. We could call it a universal mixer. This quality is so pronounced as to be nearly a distinguishing trait of the species. If readers will recall some of the stories already read in this anthology, they will be reminded that different types of SF combine just as naturally with one another to produce blended types. In this part, however, we are concerned with combinations in which SF is used with another genre, like comedy, or with another species of romance, like the mystery.

The possible combinations of SF with other kinds of literature seem almost limitless, as the company of players in *Hamlet* who proclaim themselves "the best actors in the world either for tragedy, comedy, history, pastoral, pastoral-comical, historical-pastoral, tragical-historical, tragical-comical-historical-pastoral" (Act 2, Scene 2, lines 415–418). So it is with SF. The only limits that exist are those of a writer's imagination.

When SF is combined with other literary forms, it is almost always in the same way. The materials, themes, conventions, or devices of SF are employed by writers for the ends of comedy, mystery, or horror. I chose these three particular combinations because of all mixtures they are the most important and the most familiar. They also illustrate admirably the range of alliances SF has made with other types of mainstream, elite, and popular literature.

Mystery and Horror
Science Fiction

Mystery and horror seem often to go together, perhaps because each touches on fear of the unknown. Yet, although often associated, as in the story to follow, they are yet distinct enough to be different, at least in theory.

Although mystery stories are old hat in literary history, the modern mystery story—the "whodunit," particularly—is a middle-class variation that first caught the popular imagination in the last century. The founding father of the detective story is none other than Edgar Allan Poe. In terms of literary pedigrees, the mystery seems to be most at home as a relation to the romance, that is, to the adventure story. On stage, it would be considered a form of melodrama.

The basic appeal of mystery lies in its effectiveness as a problem-solving narrative. The problem is usually a puzzle involving the commission of some crime, either in its prevention or detection. The protagonist, the detective, plays the familiar role of sleuth, sifting evidence, weighing probabilities, and assessing motives. The working out of the solution itself is, of course, the theme of each mystery. Usually, though, the solution depends upon the investigator's special knowledge, or an exceptional ability to state and analyze the enigma, or an understanding of human psychology. The essential conflict of the mystery is often a dual of wits, a cat-and-mouse game for people who enjoy thinking.

The horror story, on the other hand, need not employ mystery, although it usually does. The key to the horror story is the generation of imagined terror. It is the purpose of the tale of horror to stimulate and exercise that elemental emotion in a secondary way. Ghost stories are a familiar type of horror story, which, like the mystery, is related to the adventure romance. Older stories featuring "ghoulies and ghosties, long leggitie beasties, and things that go bump in the night," played upon humanity's long-standing fear of the unknown. Many a horror-story bogie came out of mythology and the occult; others were probably of decayed racial memories or defunct religious talismans. Mary Shelley wrote the granddaddy of all SF horror stories in *Frankenstein*. Some other favorite monsters of modern mythology are products of fantasy rather than of SF, such as Bram Stoker's *Dracula*. The movies have exploited just about every type of monster, werewolf to worm, because horror movies are very popular. The overwhelming majority of them are badly made and poorly acted, but the people who flock to see them seem content with the anticipation that a story will give them an experience of terror which they will both feel and yet walk away from.

Since the Industrial Revolution, machines have played an increasingly prominent role in horror stories, gradually eclipsing most other sources of mayhem and destruction. The supernatural remains, perhaps, the most potent source of frightful creatures; but SF has developed a formidable assembly of its own from Frankenstein's monster to Fred Saberhagen's Berserkers. SF horror stories seem to have a prophetic character about their horrors and their mysteries. Perhaps it is simply that they take place in an imagined future—at least, we all hope it is imagined.

Who Goes There?

Don A. Stuart (John W. Campbell, Jr.)

John W. Campbell, Jr. (1910–1961), was born in Newark, New Jersey, and spent most of his life in the New York City area. His first story, "When Atoms Failed," appeared in Gernsback's *Amazing Stories* when he was still an undergraduate at Massachusetts Institute of Technology. The early influences on his writing came from Edgar Rice Burroughs and E. E. "Doc" Smith, and he first established himself as a writer of intergalactic potboilers. By the mid-1930s, Campbell was busy moving SF in the direction of more serious subjects while keeping the emphasis on new ideas. Under the pseudonym Don A. Stuart (his wife's maiden name was Donna Stuart), Campbell began writing a series of stories, beginning with the famous "Twilight" in 1934, in which ideas from the hard sciences were used to dramatize problems with implications for sociclogy, psychology, political science, and the like.

In 1937 Campbell began a second career, when he became editor of *Astounding Science Fiction*, later *Analog* (1960). He remained in that post until his untimely death in 1971. Under his direction, SF began to mature as a literature. He helped develop some of the young writers of the 1930s into the major talents of the 1940s and 1950s. His enthusiasms ranged from the mysterious "Dean Drive" and L. Ron Hubbard's "Dianetics" to psi power, but he stimulated his writers by constantly challenging them with new ideas.

"Who Goes There?" appeared in the August 1938 edition of *Astounding Science Fiction* and marks the climax of Campbell's career as a writer.

Mysteries come in all types and combinations. This one by John W. Campbell, Jr., is a mixture of hard science (biology), mystery (detection problem solving), and terror (of individual and racial extinction by an alien menace). Readers of SF have their personal choices for best this and that (it's that kind of literature), and this one is *my* favorite mystery-horror story.

The story shares a common quality with Campbell's early future-invention tales in that the main action centers on the solution of a scientific question. In "Who Goes There?" the problem is nearly as much a logical one as it is biological. Campbell's answer is one that meets the requirements of all good crime-prevention mysteries: It challenges readers' wits while satisfying their expectations about the ultimate solution of the problem.

As a terror story, this one knows few peers. Its effect builds on several related kinds of anxiety at once. The fear of the alien is both psychological and physical. This alien is a blue terror, an implacably hostile force that asks and gives no quarter. To be overcome by the alien is to be possessed to the degree that one loses identity and one's very nature. As Campbell knew, there may be nothing modern human beings fear more than that. The stakes in this match of wits and power become progressively higher, until

nothing less than the future survival of humanity hangs in the balance.
The story was made into one of those "sci-fi" movies in the 1950s—its
title was changed to *The Thing*, and the rest of the story was similarly
emasculated to go along with the new title. Happily, the story has survived
the vicissitudes of both thirty years and Hollywood, and it is here to
dramatize the effect that a really close call with annihilation produces on
the human nervous system.

The place stank. A queer, mingled stench that only the ice-buried
cabins of an Antarctic camp know, compounded of reeking human
sweat, and the heavy, fish-oil stench of melted seal blubber. An overtone of liniment combated the musty smell of sweat-and-snow-drenched
furs. The acrid odor of burnt cooking fat, and the animal, not-
unpleasant smell of dogs, diluted by time, hung in the air.

Lingering odors of machine oil contrasted sharply with the taint of
harness dressing and leather. Yet, somehow, through all that reek of
human beings and their associates—dogs, machines and cooking—
came another taint. It was a queer, neck-ruffling thing, a faintest suggestion of an odor alien among the smells of industry and life. And
it was a life-smell. But it came from the thing that lay bound with
cord and tarpaulin on the table, dripping slowly, methodically onto the
heavy planks, dank and gaunt under the unshielded glare of the electric
light.

Blair, the little bald-pated biologist of the expedition, twitched nervously at the wrappings, exposing clear, dark ice beneath and then
pulling the tarpaulin back into place restlessly. His little birdlike motions of suppressed eagerness danced his shadow across the fringe of
dingy gray underwear hanging from the low ceiling, the equatorial
fringe of stiff, graying hair around his naked skull a comical halo about
the shadow's head.

Commander Garry brushed aside the lax legs of a suit of underwear,
and stepped toward the table. Slowly his eyes traced around the rings
of men sardined into the Administration Building. His tall, stiff body
straightened finally, and he nodded. "Thirty-seven. All here." His
voice was low, yet carried the clear authority of the commander by
nature, as well as by title.

"You know the outline of the story back of that find of the Secondary
Pole Expedition. I have been conferring with Second-in-Command
McReady, and Norris, as well as Blair and Dr. Copper. There is a
difference of opinion, and because it involves the entire group, it is only
just that the entire Expedition personnel act on it.

"I am going to ask McReady to give you the details of the story, because each of you has been too busy with his own work to follow closely
the endeavors of the others. McReady?"

Moving from the smoke-blued background, McReady was a figure from some forgotten myth, a looming, bronze statue that held life, and walked. Six-feet-four inches he stood as he halted beside the table, and, with a characteristic glance upward to assure himself of room under the low ceiling beams, straightened. His rough, clashingly orange windproof jacket he still had on, yet on his huge frame it did not seem misplaced. Even here, four feet beneath the driftwind that droned across the antarctic waste above the ceiling, the cold of the frozen continent leaked in, and gave meaning to the harshness of the man. And he was bronze—his great red-bronze beard, the heavy hair that matched it. The gnarled, corded hands gripping, relaxing, gripping and relaxing on the table planks were bronze. Even the deep-sunken eyes beneath heavy brows were bronzed.

Age-resisting endurance of the metal spoke in the cragged heavy outlines of his face, and the mellow tones of the heavy voice. "Norris and Blair agree on one thing; that animal we found was not—terrestrial in origin. Norris fears there may be danger in that; Blair says there is none.

"But I'll go back to how, and why, we found it. To all that was known before we came here, it appeared that this point was exactly over the South Magnetic Pole of Earth. The compass does point straight down here, as you all know. The more delicate instruments of the physicists, instruments especially designed for this expedition and its study of the magnetic pole, detected a secondary effect, a secondary, less powerful magnetic influence about 80 miles southwest of here.

"The Secondary Magnetic Expedition went out to investigate it. There is no need for details. We found it, but it was not the huge meteorite or magnetic mountain Norris had expected to find. Iron ore is magnetic, of course; iron more so—and certain special steels even more magnetic. From the surface indications, the secondary pole we found was small, so small that the magnetic effect it had was preposterous. No magnetic material conceivable could have that effect. Soundings through the ice indicated it was within one hundred feet of the glacier surface.

"I think you should know the structure of the place. There is a broad plateau, a level sweep that runs more than 150 miles due south from the Secondary station, Van Wall says. He didn't have time or fuel to fly farther, but it was running smoothly due south then. Right there, where that buried thing was, there is an ice-drowned mountain ridge, a granite wall of unshakable strength that has dammed back the ice creeping from the south.

"And four hundred miles due south is the South Polar Plateau. You have asked me at various times why it gets warmer here when the wind rises, and most of you know. As a meteorologist I'd have staked my word that no wind could blow at −70 degrees—that no more than a

5-mile wind could blow at −50—without causing warming due to friction with ground, snow and ice and the air itself.

"We camped there on the lip of that ice-drowned mountain range for twelve days. We dug our camp into the blue ice that formed the surface, and escaped most of it. But for twelve consecutive days the wind blew at 45 miles an hour. It went as high as 48, and fell to 41 at times. The temperature was −63 degrees. It rose to −60 and fell to −68. It was meteorologically impossible, and it went on uninterruptedly for twelve days and twelve nights.

"Somewhere to the south, the frozen air of the South Polar Plateau slides down from that 18,000 foot bowl, down a mountain pass, over a glacier, and starts north. There must be a funneling mountain chain that directs it, and sweeps it away for four hundred miles to hit that bald plateau where we found the secondary pole, and 350 miles farther north reaches the Antarctic Ocean.

"It's been frozen there since Antarctica froze twenty million years ago. There never has been a thaw there.

"Twenty million years ago Antarctica was beginning to freeze. We've investigated, thought and built speculations. What we believe happened was about like this.

"Something came down out of space, a ship. We saw it there in the blue ice, a thing like a submarine without a conning tower or directive vanes, 280 feet long and 45 feet in diameter at its thickest.

"Eh, Van Wall? Space? Yes, but I'll explain that better later." McReady's steady voice went on.

"It came down from space, driven and lifted by forces men haven't discovered yet, and somehow—perhaps something went wrong then—it tangled with Earth's magnetic field. It came south here, out of control probably, circling the magnetic pole. That's a savage country there, but when Antarctica was still freezing it must have been a thousand times more savage. There must have been blizzard snow, as well as drift, new snow falling as the continent glaciated. The swirl there must have been particularly bad, the wind hurling a solid blanket of white over the lip of that now-buried mountain.

"The ship struck solid granite head-on, and cracked up. Not every one of the passengers in it was killed, but the ship must have been ruined, her driving mechanism locked. It tangled with Earth's field, Norris believes. No thing made by intelligent beings can tangle with the dead immensity of a planet's natural forces and survive.

"One of its passengers stepped out. The wind we saw there never fell below −41, and the temperature never rose above −60. Then— the wind must have been stronger. And there was drift falling in a solid sheet. The *thing* was lost completely in ten paces." He paused for a moment, the deep, steady voice giving way to the drone of wind overhead, and the uneasy, malicious gurgling in the pipe of the galley-stove.

Drift—a drift-wind was sweeping by overhead. Right now the snow picked up by the mumbling wind fled in level, blinding lines across the face of the buried camp. If a man stepped out of the tunnels that connected each of the camp buildings beneath the surface, he'd be lost in ten paces. Out there, the slim, black finger of the radio mast lifted 300 feet into the air, and at its peak was the clear night sky. A sky of thin, whining wind rushing steadily from beyond to another beyond under the licking, curling mantle of the aurora. And off north, the horizon flamed with queer, angry colors of the midnight twilight. That was spring 300 feet above Antarctica.

At the surface—it was white death. Death of a needle-fingered cold driven before the wind, sucking heat from any warm thing. Cold —and white mist of endless, everlasting drift, the fine, fine particles of licking snow that obscured all things.

Kinner, the little, scar-faced cook, winced. Five days ago he had stepped out to the surface to reach a cache of frozen beef. He had reached it, started back—and the drift-wind leapt out of the south. Cold, white death that streamed across the ground blinded him in twenty seconds. He stumbled on wildly in circles. It was half an hour before rope-guided men from below found him in the impenetrable murk.

It was easy for man—or *thing*—to get lost in ten paces.

"And the drift-wind then was probably more impenetrable than we know." McReady's voice snapped Kinner's mind back. Back to welcome, dank warmth of the Ad Building. "The passenger of the ship wasn't prepared either, it appears. It froze within ten feet of the ship.

"We dug down to find the ship, and our tunnel happened to find the frozen—animal. Barclay's ice-ax struck its skull.

"When we saw what it was, Barclay went back to the tractor, started the fire up and when the steam pressure built, sent a call for Blair and Dr. Copper. Barclay himself was sick then. Stayed sick for three days, as a matter of fact.

"When Blair and Copper came, we cut out the animal in a block of ice, as you see, wrapped it and loaded it on the tractor for return here. We wanted to get into that ship.

"We reached the side and found the metal was something we didn't know. Our beryllium-bronze, non-magnetic tools wouldn't touch it. Barclay had some tool-steel on the tractor, and that wouldn't scratch it either. We made reasonable tests—even tried acid from the batteries with no results.

"They must have had a passivating process to make magnesium metal resist acid that way, and the alloy must have been at least 95% magnesium. But we had no way of guessing that, so when we spotted the barely opened lock door, we cut around it. There was clear, hard ice inside the lock, where we couldn't reach it. Through the little crack we could look in and see that only metal and tools were in there, so we decided to loosen the ice with a bomb.

"We had decanite bombs and thermite. Thermite is the ice-softener; decanite might have shattered valuable things, where the thermite's heat would just loosen the ice. Dr. Copper, Norris and I placed a 25-pound thermite bomb, wired it, and took the connector up the tunnel to the surface, where Blair had the steam tractor waiting. A hundred yards the other side of that granite wall we set off the thermite bomb.

"The magnesium metal of the ship caught, of course. The glow of the bomb flared and died, then it began to flare again. We ran back to the tractor, and gradually the glare built up. From where we were we could see the whole ice-field illuminated from beneath with an unbearable light; the ship's shadow was a great, dark cone reaching off toward the north, where the twilight was just about gone. For a moment it lasted, and we counted three other shadow-things that might have been other—passengers—frozen there. Then the ice was crashing down and against the ship.

"That's why I told you about that place. The wind sweeping down from the Pole was at our backs. Steam and hydrogen flame were torn away in white ice-fog; the flaming heat under the ice there was yanked away toward the Antarctic Ocean before it touched us. Otherwise we wouldn't have come back, even with the shelter of that granite ridge that stopped the light.

"Somehow in the blinding inferno we could see great hunched things, black bulks glowing, even so. They shed even the furious incandescence of the magnesium for a time. Those must have been the engines, we knew. Secrets going in blazing glory—secrets that might have given Man the planets. Mysterious things that could lift and hurl that ship— and had soaked in the force of the Earth's magnetic field. I saw Norris' mouth move, and ducked. I couldn't hear him.

"Insulation—something—gave way. All Earth's field they'd soaked up twenty million years before broke lose. The aurora in the sky above licked down, and the whole plateau there was bathed in cold fire that blanketed vision. The ice-ax in my hand got red hot, and hissed on the ice. Metal buttons on my clothes burned into me. And a flash of electric blue seared upward from beyond the granite wall.

"Then the walls of ice crashed down on it. For an instant it squealed the way dry-ice does when it's pressed between metal.

"We were blind and groping in the dark for hours while our eyes recovered. We found every coil within a mile was fused rubbish, the dynamo and every radio set, the earphones and speakers. If we hadn't had the steam tractor, we wouldn't have gotten over to the Secondary Camp.

"Van Wall flew in from Big Magnet at sun-up, as you know. We

came home as soon as possible. That is the history of—that."
McReady's great bronze beard gestured toward the thing on the table.

II

Blair stirred uneasily, his little, bony fingers wriggling under the harsh
light. Little brown freckles on his knuckles slid back and forth as the
tendons under the skin twitched. He pulled aside a bit of the tarpaulin
and looked impatiently at the dark ice-bound thing inside,

McReady's big body straightened somewhat. He'd ridden the rocking,
jarring steam tractor forty miles that day, pushing on to Big Magnet
here. Even his calm will had been pressed by the anxiety to mix again
with humans. It was lone and quiet out there in Secondary Camp,
where a wolf-wind howled down from the Pole. Wolf-wind howling
in his sleep—winds droning and the evil, unspeakable face of that
monster leering up as he'd first seen it through clear, blue ice, with a
bronze ice-ax buried in its skull.

The giant meteorologist spoke again. "The problem is this. Blair
wants to examine the thing. Thaw it out and make micro slides of its
tissues and so forth. Norris doesn't believe that is safe, and Blair does.
Dr. Copper agrees pretty much with Blair. Norris is a physicist, of
course, not a biologist. But he makes a point I think we should all hear.
Blair has described the microscopic life-forms biologists find living,
even in this cold and inhospitable place. They freeze every winter, and
thaw every summer—for three months—and live.

"The point Norris makes is—they thaw, and live again. There must
have been microscopic life associated with this creature. There is with
every living thing we know. And Norris is afraid that we may release
a plague—some germ disease unknown to Earth—if we thaw those
microscopic things that have been frozen there for twenty million
years.

"Blair admits that such micro life might retain the power of living.
Such unorganized things as individual cells can retain life for unknown
periods, when solidly frozen. The beast itself is as dead as those frozen
mammoths they find in Siberia. Organized, highly developed life-forms
can't stand that treatment.

"But micro-life could. Norris suggests that we may release some
disease-form that man, never having met it before, will be utterly defenseless against.

Blair's answer is that there may be such still-living germs, but that
Norris has the case reversed. They are utterly non-immune to man.
Our life-chemistry probably—"

"Probably!" The little biologist's head lifted in a quick, birdlike
motion. The halo of gray hair about his bald head ruffled as though
angry. "Heh. One look—"

"I know," McReady acknowledged. "The thing is not Earthly. It
does not seem likely that it can have a life-chemistry sufficiently like

ours to make cross-infection remotely possible. I would say that there is no danger."

McReady looked toward Dr. Copper. The physician shook his head slowly. "None whatever," he asserted confidently. "Man cannot infect or be infected by germs that live in such comparatively close relatives as the snakes. And they are, I assure you," his clean-shaven face grimaced uneasily, "*much* nearer to us than—*that.*"

Vance Norris moved angrily. He was comparatively short in this gathering of big men, some five-feet-eight, and his stocky, powerful build tended to make him seem shorter. His black hair was crisp and hard, like short, steel wires, and his eyes were the gray of fractured steel. If McReady was a man of bronze, Norris was all steel. His movements, his thoughts, his whole bearing had the quick, hard impulse of a steel spring. His nerves were steel—hard, quick-acting—swift corroding.

He was decided on his point now, and he lashed out in its defense with a characteristic quick, clipped flow of words. "Different chemistry be damned. That thing may be dead—or, by God, it may not— but I don't like it. Damn it, Blair, let them see the monstrosity you are petting over there. Let them see the foul thing and decide for themselves whether they want that thing thawed out in this camp.

"Thawed out, by the way. That's got to be thawed out in one of the shacks to-night, if it is thawed out. Somebody—who's watchman to-night? Magnetic—oh, Connant. Cosmic rays to-night. Well, you get to sit up with that twenty-million-year-old mummy of his.

"Unwrap it, Blair. How the hell can they tell what they are buying, if they can't see it? It may have a different chemistry. I don't care what else it has, but I know it has something I don't want. If you can judge by the look on its face—it isn't human so maybe you can't—it was annoyed when it froze. Annoyed, in fact, is just about as close an approximation of the way it felt as crazy, mad, insane hatred. Neither one touches the subject.

"How the hell can these birds tell what they are voting on? They haven't seen those three red eyes, and that blue hair like crawling worms. Crawling—damn, it's crawling there in the ice right now!

"Nothing Earth ever spawned had the unutterable sublimation of devastating wrath that thing let loose in its face when it looked around his frozen desolation twenty million years ago. Mad? It was mad clear through—searing, blistering mad!

"Hell, I've had bad dreams ever since I looked at those three red eyes. Nightmares. Dreaming the thing thawed out and came to life— that it wasn't dead, or even wholly unconscious all those twenty million years, but just slowed, waiting—waiting. You'll dream, too, while that damned thing that Earth wouldn't own is dripping, dripping in the Cosmos House tonight.

"And, Connant," Norris whipped toward the cosmic ray specialist, "won't you have fun sitting up all night in the quiet. Wind whining above—and that thing dripping—" He stopped for a moment, and looked around.

"I know. That's not science. But this is, it's psychology. You'll have nightmares for a year to come. Every night since I looked at that thing I've had 'em. That's why I hate it—sure I do—and don't want it around. Put it back where it came from and let it freeze for another twenty million years. I had some swell nightmares—that it wasn't made like we are—which is obvious—but of a different kind of flesh that it can really control. That it can change its shape, and look like a man—and wait to kill and eat—

"That's not a logical argument. I know it isn't. The thing isn't Earth-logic anyway.

"Maybe it has an alien body-chemistry, and maybe its bugs do have a different body-chemistry. A germ might not stand that, but, Blair and Cooper, how about a virus? That's just an enzyme molecule, you've said. That wouldn't need anything but a protein molecule of any body to work on.

"And how are you so sure that, of the million varieties of microscopic life it may have, none of them are dangerous? How about diseases like hydrophobia—rabies—that attacks any warm-blooded creature, whatever its body-chemistry may be? And parrot fever? Have you a body like a parrot, Blair? And plain rot—gangrene—necrosis if you want? *That* isn't choosy about body chemistry!"

Blair looked up from his puttering long enough to meet Norris' angry, gray eyes for an instant. "So far the only thing you have said this thing gave off that was catching was dreams. I'll go so far as to admit that." An impish, slightly malignant grin crossed the little man's seamed face. "I had some, too. So. It's dream-infectious. No doubt an exceedingly dangerous malady.

"So far as your other things go, you have a badly mistaken idea about viruses. In the first place, nobody has shown that the enzyme-molecule theory, and that alone, explains them. And in the second place, when you catch tobacco mosaic or wheat rust, let me know. A wheat plant is a lot nearer your body-chemistry than this other-world creature is.

"And your rabies is limited, strictly limited. You can't get it from, nor give it to, a wheat plant or a fish—which is a collateral descendant of a common ancestor of yours. Which this, Norris, is not." Blair nodded pleasantly toward the tarpaulined bulk on the table.

"Well, thaw the damned thing in a tub of formalin if you must thaw it. I've suggested that—"

"And I've said there would be no sense in it. You can't compromise. Why did you and Commander Garry come down here to study magnetism? Why weren't you content to stay at home? There's magnetic force enough in New York. I could no more study the life this thing once had from a formalin-pickled sample than you could get the information you wanted back in New York. And—if this one is so treated, *never in all time to come can there be a duplicate!* The race it came from must have passed away in the twenty million years it lay frozen, so that even if it came from Mars then, we'd never find its like. And— the ship is gone.

"There's only one way to do this—and that is the best possible way. It must be thawed slowly, carefully, and not in formalin."

Commander Garry stood forward again, and Norris stepped back muttering angrily. "I think Blair is right, gentlemen. What do you say?"

Connant grunted. "It sounds right to us, I think—only perhaps he ought to stand watch over it while it's thawing." He grinned ruefully, brushing a stray lock of ripe-cherry hair back from his forehead. "Swell idea, in fact—if he sits up with his jolly little corpse."

Garry smiled slightly. A general chuckle of agreement rippled over the group. "I should think any ghost it may have had would have starved to death if it hung around here that long, Connant," Garry suggested. "And you look capable of taking care of it. 'Ironman' Connant ought to be able to take out any opposing players, still."

Connant shook himself uneasily. "I'm not worrying about ghosts. Let's see that thing. I—"

Eagerly Blair was stripping back the ropes. A single throw of the tarpaulin revealed the thing. The ice had melted somewhat in the heat of the room, and it was clear and blue as thick, good glass. It shone wet and sleek under the harsh light of the unshielded globe above.

The room stiffened abruptly. It was face up there on the plain, greasy planks of the table. The broken half of the bronze ice-ax was still buried in the queer skull. Three mad, hate-filled eyes blazed up with a living fire, bright as fresh-spilled blood, from a face ringed with a writhing, loathsome nest of worms, blue, mobile worms that crawled where hair should grow—

Van Wall, six feet and 200 pounds of ice-nerved pilot, gave a queer, strangled gasp and butted, stumbled his way out to the corridor. Half the company broke for the doors. The others stumbled away from the table.

McReady stood at one end of the table watching them, his great body planted solid on his powerful legs. Norris from the opposite end glowered at the thing with smouldering hate. Outside the door, Garry was talking with half a dozen of the men at once.

Blair had a tack hammer. The ice that cased the thing *schluffed* crisply under its steel claw as it peeled from the thing it had cased for twenty thousand thousand years—

III

"I know you don't like the thing, Connant, but it just has to be thawed out right. You say leave it as it is till we get back to civilization. All right, I'll admit your argument that we could do a better and more complete job there is sound. But—how are we going to get this across the Line? We have to take this through one temperate zone, the equatorial zone, and half way through the other temperate zone before we get it to New York. You don't want to sit with it one night, but you suggest, then, that I hang its corpse in the freezer with the beef?" Blair looked up from his cautious chipping, his bald, freckled skull nodding triumphantly.

Kinner, the stocky, scar-faced cook, saved Connant the trouble of answering. "Hey, you listen, mister. You put that thing in the box with the meat, and by all the gods there ever were, I'll put you in to keep it company. You birds have brought everything movable in this camp in onto my mess tables here already, and I had to stand for that. But you go putting things like that in my meat box or even my meat cache here, and you cook your own damn grub."

"But, Kinner, this is the only table in Big Magnet that's big enough to work on," Blair objected. "Everybody's explained that."

"Yeah, and everybody's brought everything in here. Clark brings his dogs every time there's a fight and sews them up on that table. Ralsen brings in his sledges. Hell, the only thing you haven't had on that table is the Boeing. And you'd 'a' had that in if you coulda figured a way to get it through the tunnels."

Commander Garry chuckled and grinned at Van Wall, the huge Chief Pilot. Van Wall's great blond beard twitched suspiciously as he nodded gravely to Kinner. "You're right, Kinner. The aviation department is the only one that treats you right."

"It does get crowded, Kinner," Garry acknowledged. "But I'm afraid we all find it that way at times. Not much privacy in an antarctic camp."

"Privacy? What the hell's that? You know, the thing that really made me weep, was when I saw Barclay marchin' through here chantin' 'The last lumber in the camp! The last lumber in the camp!' and carryin' it out to build that house on his tractor. Damn it, I missed that moon cut in the door he carried out more'n I missed the sun when it set. That wasn't just the last lumber Barclay was walkin' off with. He was carrying' off the last bit of privacy in this blasted place."

A grin rode even on Connant's heavy face as Kinner's perennial, good-natured grouch came up again. But it died away quickly as his dark, deep-set eyes turned again to the red-eyed thing Blair was chipping from its cocoon of ice. A big hand ruffed his shoulder-length hair, and tugged at a twisted lock that fell behind his ear in a familiar gesture. "I know that cosmic ray shack's going to be too crowded if I have to sit up with that thing," he growled. "Why can't you go on chipping the ice away from around it—you can do that without anybody butting in, I assure you—and then hang the thing up over the power-plant boiler? That's warm enough. It'll thaw out a chicken, even a whole side of beef, in a few hours."

"I know," Blair protested, dropping the tack hammer to gesture more effectively with his bony, freckled fingers, his small body tense with eagerness, "but this is too important to take any chances. There never was a find like this; there never can be again. It's the only chance men will ever have, and it has to be done exactly right.

"Look, you know how the fish we caught down near the Ross Sea would freeze almost as soon as we got them on deck, and come to life again if we thawed them gently? Low forms of life aren't killed by quick freezing and slow thawing. We have—"

"Hey, for the love of Heaven—you mean that damned thing will come to life!" Connant yelled. "You get the damned thing—Let me at it! That's going to be in so many pieces—"

"NO! *No*, you fool—" Blair jumped in front of Connant to protect his precious find. "No. Just *low* forms of life. For Pete's sake let me finish. You can't thaw higher forms of life and have them come to. Wait a moment now—hold it! A fish can come to after freezing because it's so low a form of life that the individual cells of its body can revive, and that alone is enough to reëstablish life. Any higher forms thawed out that way are dead. Though the individual cells revive, they die because there must be organization and coöperative effort to live. That coöperation cannot be reëstablished. There is a sort of potential life in any uninjured, quick-frozen animal. But it can't—can't under any circumstances—become active life in higher animals. The higher animals are too complex, too delicate. This is an intelligent creature as high in its evolution as we are in ours. Perhaps higher. It is as dead as a frozen man would be."

"How do you know?" demanded Connant, hefting the ice-ax he had seized a moment before.

Commander Garry laid a restraining hand on his heavy shoulder. "Wait a minute, Connant. I want to get this straight. I agree that there is going to be no thawing of this thing if there is the remotest chance of its revival. I quite agree it is much too unpleasant to have alive, but I had no idea there was the remotest possibility."

Dr. Copper pulled his pipe from between his teeth and heaved his stocky, dark body from the bunk he had been sitting in. "Blair's being technical. That's dead. As dead as the mammoths they find frozen in Siberia. Potential life is like atomic energy—there, but nobody can get it out, and it certainly won't release itself except in rare cases, as rare as radium in the chemical analogy. We have all sorts of proof that things don't live after being frozen—not even fish, generally speaking —and no proof that higher animal life can under any circumstances. What's the point, Blair?"

The little biologist shook himself. The little ruff of hair standing out around his bald pate waved in righteous anger. "The point is," he said in an injured tone, "that the individual cells might show the characteristics they had in life, if it is properly thawed. A man's muscle cells

live many hours after he has died. Just because they live, and a few
things like hair and fingernail cells still live, you wouldn't accuse a
corpse of being a Zombie, or something.

"Now if I thaw this right, I may have a chance to determine what
sort of world it's native to. We don't, and can't know by any other
means, whether it came from Earth or Mars or Venus or from beyond
the stars.

"And just because it looks unlike men, you don't have to accuse it
of being evil, or vicious or something. Maybe that expression on its
face is its equivalent to a resignation to fate. White is the color of
mourning to the Chinese. If men can have different customs, why
can't a so-different race have different understandings of facial ex-
pressions?"

Connant laughed softly, mirthlessly. "Peaceful resignation! If that is
the best it could do in the way of resignation, I should exceedingly dislike seeing it when it was looking mad. That face was never designed
to express peace. It just didn't have any philosophical thoughts like
peace in its make-up.

"I know it's your pet—but be sane about it. That thing grew up
on evil, adolesced slowly roasting alive the local equivalent of kittens,
and amused itself through maturity on new and ingenious torture."

"You haven't the slightest right to say that," snapped Blair. "How
do you know the first thing about the meaning of a facial expression
inherently inhuman? It may well have no human equivalent whatever. That is just a different development of Nature, another example
of Nature's wonderful adaptability. Growing on another, perhaps
harsher world, it has different form and features. But it is just as much
a legitimate child of Nature as you are. You are displaying that childish
human weakness of hating the different. On its own world it would
probably class you as a fish-belly, white monstrosity with an insufficient
number of eyes and a fungoid body pale and bloated with gas.

"Just because its nature is different, you haven't any right to say it's
necessarily evil."

Norris burst out a single, explosive, "Haw!" He looked down at the
thing. "May be that things from other worlds don't *have* to be evil just
because they're different. But that thing *was!* Child of Nature, eh?
Well, it was a hell of an evil Nature."

"Aw, will you mugs cut crabbing at each other and get the damned
thing off my table?" Kinner growled. "And put a canvas over it. It
looks indecent."

"Kinner's gone modest," jeered Connant.

Kinner slanted his eyes up to the big physicist. The scarred cheek
twisted to join the line of his tight lips in a twisted grin. "All right,
big boy, and what were you grousing about a minute ago? We can
set the thing in a chair next to you tonight, if you want."

"I'm not afraid of its face," Connant snapped. "I don't like keeping a wake over its corpse particularly, but I'm going to do it."

Kinner's grin spread. "Uh-huh." He went off to the galley stove and shook down ashes vigorously, drowning the brittle chipping of the ice as Blair fell to work again.

IV

"*Cluck,*" reported the cosmic ray counter, "*cluck-brrrp-cluck.*" Connant started and dropped his pencil.

"Damnation." The physicist looked toward the far corner, back at the Gieger counter on the table near that corner, and crawled under the desk at which he had been working to retrieve the pencil. He sat down at his work again, trying to make his writing more even. It tended to have jerks and quavers in it, in time with the abrupt proud-hen noises of the Gieger counter. The muted whoosh of the pressure lamp he was using for illumination, the mingled gargles and bugle calls of a dozen men sleeping down the corridor in Paradise House formed the background sounds for the irregular, clucking noises of the counter, the occasional rustle of falling coal in the copper-bellied stove. And a soft, steady *drip-drip-drip* from the thing in the corner.

Connant jerked a pack of cigarettes from his pocket, snapped it so that a cigarette protruded and jabbed the cylinder into his mouth. The lighter failed to function, and he pawed angrily through the pile of papers in search of a match. He scratched the wheel of the lighter several times, dropped it with a curse and got up to pluck a hot coal from the stove with the coal-tongs.

The lighter functioned instantly when he tried it on returning to the desk. The counter ripped out a series of chucking guffaws as a burst of cosmic rays struck through to it. Connant turned to glower at it, and tried to concentrate on the interpretation of data collected during the past week. The weekly summary—

He gave up and yielded to curiosity, or nervousness. He lifted the pressure lamp from the desk and carried it over to the table in the corner. Then he returned to the stove and picked up the coal tongs. The beast had been thawing for nearly 18 hours now. He poked at it with an unconscious caution; the flesh was no longer hard as armor plate, but had assumed a rubbery texture. It looked like wet, blue rubber glistening under droplets of water like little round jewels in the glare of the gasoline pressure lantern. Connant felt an unreasoning desire to pour the contents of the lamp's reservoir over the thing in its box and drop the cigarette into it. The three red eyes glared up at him sightlessly, the ruby eyeballs reflecting murky, smoky rays of light.

He realized vaguely that he had been looking at them for a very long time, even vaguely understood that they were no longer sightless. But it did not seem of importance, of no more importance than the labored, slow motion of the tentacular things that sprouted from the base of the scrawny, slowly pulsing neck.

Connant picked up the pressure lamp and returned to his chair. He sat down, starting at the pages of mathematics before him. The clucking of the counter was strangely less disturbing, the rustle of the coals in the stove no longer distracting.

The creak of the floorboards behind him didn't interrupt his thoughts as he went about his weekly report in an automatic manner, filling in columns of data and making brief, summarizing notes.

The creak of the floorboards sounded nearer.

V

Blair came up from the nightmare-haunted depths of sleep abruptly. Connant's face floated vaguely above him; for a moment it seemed a continuance of the wild horror of the dream. But Connant's face was angry, and a little frightened. "Blair—Blair you damned log, wake up."

"Uh-eh?" the little biologist rubbed his eyes, his bony, freckled fingers crooked to a mutilated child-fist. From surrounding bunks other faces lifted to stare down at them

Connant straightened up. "Get up—and get a lift on. Your damned animal's escaped."

"Escaped—what!" Chief Pilot Van Wall's bull voice roared out with a volume that shook the walls. Down the communication tunnels other voices yelled suddenly. The dozen inhabitants of Paradise House tumbled in abruptly, Barclay, stocky and bulbous in long woolen underwear, carrying a fire extinguisher.

"What the hell's the matter?" Barclay demanded.

"Your damned beast got loose. I fell asleep about twenty minutes ago, and when I woke up, the thing was gone. Hey, Doc, the hell you say those things can't come to life. Blair's blasted potential life developed a hell of a lot of potential and walked out on us."

Copper stared blankly. "It wasn't—Earthly," he sighed suddenly. "I—I guess Earthly laws don't apply."

"Well, it applied for leave of absence and took it. We've got to find it and capture it somehow." Connant swore bitterly, his deep-set black eyes sullen and angry. "It's a wonder the hellish creature didn't eat me in my sleep."

Blair started back, his pale eyes suddenly fear-struck. "Maybe it di—er—uh—we'll have to find it."

"You find it. It's your pet. I've had all I want to do with it, sitting there for seven hours with the counter clucking every few seconds, and you birds in here singing night-music. It's a wonder I got to sleep. I'm going through to the Ad Building."

Commander Garry ducked through the doorway, pulling his belt tight. "You won't have to. Van's roar sounded like the Boeing taking off down wind. So it wasn't dead?"

"I didn't carry it off in my arms, I assure you," Connant snapped. "The last I saw, that split skull was oozing green goo, like a squashed caterpillar. Doc just said our laws don't work—it's unearthly. Well, it's an unearthly monster, with an unearthly disposition, judging by the face, wandering around with a split skull and brains oozing out."

Norris and McReady appeared in the doorway, a doorway filling with other shivering men. "Has anybody seen it coming over here?" Norris asked innocently. "About four feet tall—three red eyes—brains oozing out—Hey, has anybody checked to make sure this isn't a cracked idea of humor? If it is, I think we'll unite in tying Blair's pet around Connant's neck like the Ancient Mariner's albatross."

"It's no humor," Connant shivered. "Lord, I wish it were. I'd rather wear—" He stopped. A wild, weird howl shrieked through the corridors. The men stiffened abruptly, and half turned.

"I think it's been located," Connant finished. His dark eyes shifted with a queer unease. He darted back to his bunk in Paradise House, to return almost immediately with a heavy .45 revolver and an ice-ax. He hefted both gently as he started for the corridor toward Dogtown. "It blundered down the wrong corridor—and landed among the huskies. Listen—the dogs have broken their chains—"

The half-terrorized howl of the dog pack had changed to a wild hunting melee. The voices of the dogs thundered in the narrow corridors, and through them came a low rippling snarl of distilled hate. A shrill of pain, a dozen snarling yelps.

Connant broke for the door. Close behind him, McReady, then Barclay and Commander Garry came. Other men broke for the Ad Building, and weapons—the sledge house. Pomroy, in charge of Big Magnet's five cows, started down the corridor in the opposite direction—he had a six-foot-handled, long-tined pitchfork in mind.

Barclay slid to a halt, as McReady's giant bulk turned abruptly away from the tunnel leading to Dogtown, and vanished off at an angle. Uncertainly, the mechanician wavered a moment, the fire extinguisher in his hands, hesitating from one side to the other. Then he was racing after Connant's broad back. Whatever McReady had in mind, he could be trusted to make it work.

Connant stopped at the bend in the corridor. His breath hissed suddenly through his throat. "Great God—" The revolver exploded thunderously; three numbing, palpable waves of sound crashed through the confined corridors. Two more. The revolver dropped to the hard-packed snow of the trail, and Barclay saw the ice-ax shift into defensive position. Connant's powerful body blocked his vision, but beyond he heard something mewing, and, insanely, chuckling. The dogs were quieter; there was a deadly seriousness in their low snarls. Taloned feet scratched at hard-packed snow, broken chains were clinking and tangling.

Connant shifted abruptly, and Barclay could see what lay beyond.

For a second he stood frozen, then his breath went out in a gusty curse. The Thing launched itself at Connant, the powerful arms of the man swung the ice-ax flatside first at what might have been a head. It scrunched horribly, and the tattered flesh, ripped by a half-dozen savage huskies, leapt to its feet again. The red eyes blazed with an unearthly hatred, an unearthly, unkillable vitality.

Barclay turned the fire extinguisher on it; the blinding, blistering stream of chemical spray confused it, baffled it, together with the savage attacks of the huskies, not for long afraid of anything that did, or could live, held it at bay.

McReady wedged men out of his way and drove down the narrow corridor packed with men unable to reach the scene. There was a sure fore-planned drive to McReady's attack. One of the giant blowtorches used in warming the plane's engines was in his bronzed hands. It roared gustily as he turned the corner and opened the valve. The mad mewing hissed louder. The dogs scrambled back from the three-foot lance of blue-hot flame.

"Bar, get a power cable, run it in somehow. And a handle. We can electrocute this—monster, if I don't incinerate it." McReady spoke with an authority of planned action. Barclay turned down the long corridor to the power plant, but already before him Norris and Van Wall were racing down.

Barclay found the cable in the electrical cache in the tunnel wall. In a half-minute he was hacking at it, walking back. Van Wall's voice rang out in warning shout of "Power!" as the emergency gasoline-powered dynamo thudded into action. Half a dozen other men were down there now; the coal, kindling were going into the firebox of the steam power plant. Norris, cursing in a low, deadly monotone, was working with quick, sure fingers on the other end of Barclay's cable, splicing in a contactor in one of the power leads.

The dogs had fallen back when Barclay reached the corridor bend, fallen back before a furious monstrosity that glared from baleful red eyes, mewing in trapped hatred. The dogs were a semi-circle of red-dipped muzzles with a fringe of glistening white teeth, whining with a vicious eagerness that near matched the fury of the red eyes. McReady stood confidently alert at the corridor bend, the gustily muttering torch held loose and ready for action in his hands. He stepped aside without moving his eyes from the beast as Barclay came up. There was a slight, tight smile on his lean, bronzed face.

Norris' voice called down the corridor, and Barclay stepped forward. The cable was taped to the long handle of a snow-shovel, the two conductors split, and held 18 inches apart by a scrap of lumber lashed at right angles across the far end of the handle. Bare copper conductors, charged with 220 volts, glinted in the light of pressure lamps. The Thing mewed and halted and dodged. McReady advanced to

Barclay's side. The dogs beyond sensed the plan with the almost-telepathic intelligence of trained huskies. Their whining grew shriller, softer, their mincing steps carried them nearer. Abruptly, a huge, night-black Alaskan leapt onto the trapped thing. It turned squalling, saber-clawed feet slashing.

Barclay leapt forward and jabbed. A weird, shrill scream rose and choked out. The smell of burnt flesh in the corridor intensified; greasy smoke curled up. The echoing pound of a gas-electric dynamo down the corridor became a slogging thud.

The red eyes clouded over in a stiffening, jerking travesty of a face. Armlike, leglike members quivered and jerked. The dogs leapt forward, and Barclay yanked back his shovel-handled weapon. The thing on the snow did not move as gleaming teeth ripped it open.

VI

Garry looked about the crowded room. Thirty-two men, some tensed nervously standing against the wall, some uneasily relaxed, some sitting, most perforce standing, as intimate as sardines. Thirty-two, plus the five engaged in sewing up wounded dogs, made thirty-seven, the total personnel.

Garry started speaking. "All right, I guess we're here. Some of you —three or four at most—saw what happened. All of you have seen that thing on the table, and can get a general idea. Anyone hasn't, I'll lift—" His hand strayed to the tarpaulin bulking over the thing on the table. There was an acrid odor of singed flesh seeping out of it. The men stirred restlessly, hasty denials.

"It looks rather as though Charnauk isn't going to lead any more teams," Garry went on. "Blair wants to get at this thing, and make some more detailed examination. We want to know what happened, and make sure right now that this is permanently, totally dead. Right?"

Connant grinned. "Anybody that doesn't agree can sit up with it to-night."

"All right then, Blair, what can you say about it? What was it?" Garry turned to the little biologist.

"I wonder if we ever saw its natural form," Blair looked at the covered mass. "It may have been imitating the beings that built that ship—but I don't think it was. I think that was its true form. Those of us who were up near the bend saw the thing in action; the thing on the table is the result. When it got loose, apparently, it started looking around. Antarctica still frozen as it was ages ago when the creature first saw it—and froze. From my observations while it was thawing out, and the bits of tissue I cut and hardened then, I think it was native to a hotter planet than Earth. It couldn't, in its natural form, stand the temperature. There is no life-form on Earth that can live in Antarctica during the winter, but the best compromise is the dog. It found the dogs, and somehow got near enough to Charnauk to get him. The others smelled it—heard it—I don't know—anyway they went wild, and broke chains, and attacked it before it was finished. The thing we found was part Charnauk, queerly only half-dead, part Charnauk half-digested by the jellylike protoplasm of that creature, and part the remains of the thing we originally found, sort of melted down to the basic protoplasm.

"When the dogs attacked it, it turned into the best fighting thing it could think of. Some other-world beast apparently."

"Turned," snapped Garry. "How?"

"Every living thing is made up of jelly—protoplasm and minute, submicroscopic things called nuclei, which control the bulk, the protoplasm. This thing was just a modification of that same worldwide plan of Nature; cells made up of protoplasm, controlled by infinitely tinier nuclei. You physicists might compare it—an individual cell of any living thing—with an atom; the bulk of the atom, the space-filling part, is made up of the electron orbits, but the character of the thing is determined by the atomic nucleus.

"This isn't wildly beyond what we already know. It's just a modification we haven't seen before. It's as natural, as logical, as any other manifestation of life. It obeys exactly the same laws. The cells are made of protoplasm, their character determined by the nucleus.

"Only in this creature, the cell-nuclei can control those cells *at will.* It digested Charnauk, and as it digested, studied every cell of his tissue, and shaped its own cells to imitate them exactly. Parts of it—parts that had time to finish changing—are dog-cells. But they don't have dog-cell nuclei." Blair lifted a fraction of tarpaulin. A torn dog's leg with stiff gray fur protruded. "That, for instance, isn't dog at all; it's imitation. Some parts I'm uncertain about; the nucleus was hiding itself, covering up with dog-cell imitation nucleus. In time, not even a microscope would have shown the difference."

"Suppose," asked Norris bitterly, "it had had lots of time?"

"Then it would have been a dog. The other dogs would have accepted it. We would have accepted it. I don't think anything would have distinguished it, not microscope, nor X-ray, nor any other means. This is a member of a supremely intelligent race, a race that has learned the deepest secrets of biology, and turned them to its use."

"What was it planning to do?" Barclay looked at the humped tarpaulin.

Blair grinned unpleasantly. The wavering halo of thin hair round his bald pate wavered in a stir of air. "Take over the world, I imagine."

"Take over the world! Just it, all by itself?" Connant gasped. "Set itself up as a lone dictator?"

"No," Blair shook his head. The scalpel he had been fumbling in his bony fingers dropped; he bent to pick it up, so that his face was hidden as he spoke. "It would become the population of the world."

"Become—populate the world? Does it reproduce asexually?"

Blair shook his hand and gulped. "It's—it doesn't have to. It weighed 85 pounds. Charnauk weighed about 90. It would have become Charnauk, and had 85 pounds left, to become—oh, Jack for instance, or Chinook. It can imitate anything—that is, become anything. If it had reached the Antarctic Sea, it would have become a seal, maybe two seals. They might have attacked a killer whale, and become either killers, or a herd of seals. Or maybe it would have caught an albatross, or a skua gull, and flown to South America."

Norris cursed softly. "And every time it digested something, and imitated it—"

"It would have had its original bulk left, to start again," Blair finished. "Nothing would kill it. It has no natural enemies, because it becomes whatever it wants to. If a killer whale attacked it, it would become a killer whale. If it was an albatross, and an eagle attacked it, it would become an eagle. Lord, it might become a female eagle. Go back—build a nest and lay eggs!"

"Are you sure that thing from hell is dead?" Dr. Copper asked softly.

"Yes, thank Heaven," the little biologist gasped. "After they drove the dogs off, I stood there poking Bar's electrocution thing into it for five minutes. "It's dead and—cooked."

"Then we can only give thanks that this is Antarctica, where there is not one, single, solitary, living thing for it to imitate, except these animals in camp."

"Us," Blair giggled. "It can imitate us. Dogs can't make 400 miles to the sea; there's no food. There aren't any skua gulls to imitate at this season. There aren't any penguins this far inland. There's nothing that can reach the sea from this point—except us. We've got brains. We can do it. Don't you see—*it's got to imitate us—it's got to be one of us—that's the only way it can fly an airplane—fly a plane for two hours, and rule—be—all Earth's inhabitants.* A world for the taking—*if it imitates us!*

"It didn't know yet. It hadn't had a chance to learn. It was rushed —hurried—took the thing nearest its own size. Look—I'm Pandora! I opened the box! And the only hope that can come out is—that nothing can come out. You didn't see me. I did it. I fixed it. I smashed every magneto. Not a plane can fly. Nothing can fly." Blair giggled and lay down on the floor crying.

Chief Pilot Van Wall made a dive for the door. His feet were fading echoes in the corridors as Dr. Copper bent unhurriedly over the little man on the floor. From his office at the end of the room he brought something, and injected a solution into Blair's arm, "He might come out of it when he wakes up," he sighed rising. McReady helped him lift the biologist onto a near-by bunk. "It all depends on whether we can convince him that thing is dead."

Van Wall ducked into the shack brushing his heavy blond beard absently. "I didn't think a biologist would do a thing like that up thoroughly. He missed the spares in the second cache. It's all right. I smashed them."

Commander Garry nodded. "I was wondering about the radio."

Dr. Copper snorted. "You don't think it can leak out on a radio wave, do you? You'd have five rescue attempts in the next three months if you stop the broadcasts. The thing to do is talk loud and not make a sound. Now I wonder—"

McReady looked speculatively at the doctor. "It might be like an infectious disease. Everything that drank any of its blood—"

Copper shook his head. "Blair missed something. Imitate it may, but it has, to a certain extent, its own body chemistry, its own metabolism. If it didn't, it would become a dog—and be a dog and nothing more. It has to be an imitation dog. Therefore you can detect it by serum tests. And its chemistry, since it comes from another world, must be so wholly, radically different that a few cells, such as gained by drops of blood, would be treated as disease germs by the dog, or human body."

"Blood—would one of those imitations bleed?" Norris demanded.

"Surely. Nothing mystic about blood. Muscle is about 90% water; blood differs only in having a couple per cent more water, and less connective tissue. They'd bleed all right," Copper assured him.

Blair sat up in his bunk suddenly. "Connant—where's Connant?"

The physicist moved over toward the little biologist. "Here I am. What do you want?"

"Are you?" giggled Blair. He lapsed back into the bunk contorted with silent laughter.

Connant looked at him blankly. "Huh? Am I what?"

"*Are* you there?" Blair burst into gales of laughter. "*Are* you Connant? The beast wanted to be *a man*—not a dog—"

VII

Dr. Copper rose wearily from the bunk, and washed the hypodermic carefully. The little tinkles it made seemed loud in the packed room, now that Blair's gurgling laughter had finally quieted. Copper looked toward Garry and shook his head slowly. "Hopeless, I'm afraid. I don't think we can ever convince him the thing is dead now."

Norris laughed uncertainly. "I'm not sure you can convince me. Oh, damn you, McReady."

"McReady?" Commander Garry turned to look from Norris to McReady curiously.

"The nightmares," Norris explained. "He had a theory about the nightmares we had at the Secondary Station after finding that thing."

"And that was?" Garry looked at McReady levelly.

Norris answered for him, jerkily, uneasily. "That the creature wasn't dead, had a sort of enormously slowed existence, an existence that permitted it, none the less, to be vaguely aware of the passing of time, of our coming, after endless years. I had a dream it could imitate things."

"Well," Copper grunted, "it can."

"Don't be an ass," Norris snapped. "That's not what's bothering me. In the dream it could read minds, read thoughts and ideas and mannerisms."

"What's so bad about that? It seems to be worrying you more than the thought of the joy we're going to have with a mad man in an Antarctic camp." Copper nodded toward Blair's sleeping form.

McReady shook his great head slowly. "You know that Connant is Connant, because he not merely looks like Connant—which we're beginning to believe that beast might be able to do—but he thinks like Connant, talks like Connant, moves himself around as Connant does. That takes more than merely a body that looks like him; that takes Connant's own mind, and thoughts and mannerisms. Therefore, though you know that the thing might make itself look like Connant, you aren't much bothered, because you know it has a mind from another world, a totally unhuman mind, that couldn't possibly react and think and talk like a man we know, and do it so well as to fool us for a moment. The idea of the creature imitating one of us is fascinating, but unreal because it is too completely unhuman to deceive us. It doesn't have a human mind."

"As I said before," Norris repeated, looking steadily at McReady, "you can say the damnedest things at the damnedest times. Will you be so good as to finish that thought—one way or the other?"

Kinner, the scar-faced expedition cook, had been standing near Connant. Suddenly he moved down the length of the crowded room toward his familiar galley. He shook the ashes from the galley stove noisily.

"It would do it no good," said Dr. Copper, softly as though thinking out loud, "to merely look like something it was trying to imitate; it would have to understand its feelings, its reactions. It *is* unhuman; it has powers of imitation beyond any conception of man. A good actor, by training himself, can imitate another man, another man's mannerisms, well enough to fool most people. Of course no actor could imitate so perfectly as to deceive men who had been living with the imitated one in the complete lack of privacy of an Antarctic camp. That would take a super-human skill."

"Oh, you've got the bug too?" Norris cursed softly.

Connant, standing alone at one end of the room, looked about him wildly, his face white. A gentle eddying of the men had crowded them slowly down toward the other end of the room, so that he stood quite alone. "My God, will you two Jeremiahs shut up?" Connant's voice shook. "What am I? Some kind of a microscopic specimen you're dissecting? Some unpleasant worm you're discussing in the third person?"

McReady looked up at him; his slowly twisting hands stopped for a moment. "Having a lovely time. Wish you were here. Signed: Everybody.

"Connant, if you think you're having a hell of a time, just move over on the other end for a while. You've got one thing we haven't; you know what the answer is. I'll tell you this, right now you're the most feared and respected man in Big Magnet."

"Lord, I wish you could see your eyes," Connant gasped. "Stop staring, will you! What the hell are you going to do?"

"Have you any suggestions, Dr. Copper?" Commander Garry asked steadily. "The present situation is impossible."

"Oh, is it?" Connant snapped. "Come over here and look at that crowd. By Heaven, they look exactly like that gang of huskies around the corridor bend. Benning, will you stop hefting that damned ice-ax?"

The coppery blade rang on the floor as the aviation mechanic nervously dropped it. He bent over and picked it up instantly, hefting it slowly, turning it in his hands, his brown eyes moving jerkily about the room.

Copper sat down on the bunk beside Blair. The wood creaked noisily in the room. Far down a corridor, a dog yelped in pain, and the dog-drivers' tense voices floated softly back. "Microscopic examination," said the doctor thoughtfully, "would be useless, as Blair pointed out. Considerable time has passed. However, serum tests would be definitive."

"Serum tests? What do you mean exactly?" Commander Garry asked.

"If I had a rabbit that had been injected with human blood—a poison to rabbits, of course, as is the blood of any animal save that of another rabbit—and the injections continued in increasing doses for some time, the rabbit would be human-immune. If a small quantity of its blood were drawn off, allowed to separate in a test-tube, and to the clear serum, a bit of human blood were added, there would be a visible reaction, proving the blood was human. If cow, or dog blood were added —or any protein material other than that one thing, human blood—no reaction would take place. That would prove definitely."

"Can you suggest where I might catch a rabbit for you, Doc?" Norris asked. "That is, nearer than Australia; we don't want to waste time going that far."

"I know there aren't any rabbits in Antarctica," Copper nodded, "but that is simply the usual animal. Any animal except man will do. A dog for instance. But it will take several days, and due to the greater size of the animal, considerable blood. Two of us will have to contribute."

"Would I do?" Garry asked.

"That will make two," Copper nodded. "I'll get to work on it right away."

"What about Connant in the meantime?" Kinner demanded. "I'm going out that door and head off for the Ross Sea before I cook for him."

"He may be human—" Copper started.

Connant burst out in a flood of curses. "Human! *May* be human, you damned saw-bones! What in hell do you think I am?"

"A monster," Copper snapped sharply. "Now shut up and listen." Connant's face drained of color and he sat down heavily as the indictment was put in words. "Until we know—you know as well as we do that we have reason to question the fact, and only you know how that question is to be answered—we may reasonably be expected to lock you up. If you are—unhuman—you're a lot more dangerous than poor Blair there, and I'm going to see that he's locked up thoroughly. I expect that his next stage will be a violent desire to kill you, all the dogs, and probably all of us. When he wakes, he will be convinced we're all unhuman, and nothing on the planet will ever change his conviction. It would be kinder to let him die, but we can't do that, of course. He's going in one shack, and you can stay in Cosmos House with your cosmic ray apparatus. Which is about what you'd do anyway. I've got to fix up a couple of dogs."

Connant nodded bitterly. "I'm human. Hurry that test. Your eyes —Lord, I wish you could see your eyes staring—"

Commander Garry watched anxiously as Clark, the dog-handler, held the big brown Alaskan husky, while Copper began the injection treatment. The dog was not anxious to coöperate; the needle was painful, and already he'd experienced considerable needle work that morning. Five stitches held closed a slash that ran from his shoulder across the ribs half way down his body. One long fang was broken off short; the missing part was to be found half-buried in the shoulder bone of the monstrous thing on the table in the Ad Building.

"How long will that take?" Garry asked pressing his arm gently. It was sore from the prick of the needle Dr. Copper had used to withdraw blood.

Copper shrugged. "I don't know, to be frank. I know the general method, I've used it on rabbits. But I haven't experimented with dogs. They're big, clumsy animals to work with; naturally rabbits are preferable, and serve ordinarily. In civilized places you can buy a stock of human-immune rabbits from suppliers, and not many investigators take the trouble to prepare their own."

"What do they want with them back there?" Clark asked.

"Criminology is one large field. A says he didn't murder B, but that the blood on his shirt came from killing a chicken. The State makes a test, then it's up to A to explain how it is the blood reacts on human-immune rabbits, but not on chicken-immunes."

"What are we going to do with Blair in the meantime?" Garry asked wearily. "It's all right to let him sleep where he is for a while, but when he wakes up—"

"Barclay and Benning are fitting some bolts on the door of Cosmos House," Copper replied grimly. "Connant's acting like a gentleman. I think perhaps the way the other men look at him makes him rather want privacy. Lord knows, heretofore we've all of us individually prayed for a little privacy."

Clark laughed brittlely. "Not any more, thank you. The more the merrier."

"Blair," Copper went on, "will also have to have privacy—and locks. He's going to have a pretty definite plan in mind when he wakes up. Ever hear the old story of how to stop hoof-and-mouth disease in cattle?"

Clark and Garry shook their heads silently.

"If there isn't any hoof-and-mouth disease, there won't be any hoof-and-mouth disease," Copper explained. "You get rid of it by killing every animal that exhibits it, and every animal that's been near the diseased animal. Blair's a biologist, and knows that story. He's afraid of this thing we loosed. The answer is probably pretty clear in his mind now. Kill everybody and everything in this camp before a skua gull or a wandering albatross coming in with the spring chances out this way and—catches the disease."

Clark's lips curled in a twisted grin. "Sounds logical to me. If things get too bad—maybe we'd better let Blair get loose. It would save us committing suicide. We might also make something of a vow that if things get bad, we see that that does happen."

Copper laughed softly. "The last man alive in Big Magnet—wouldn't be a man," he pointed out. "Somebody's got to kill those—creatures that don't desire to kill themselves, you know. We don't have enough thermite to do it all at once, and the decanite explosive wouldn't help much. I have an idea that even small pieces of one of those beings would be self-sufficient."

"If," said Garry thoughtfully, "they can modify their protoplasm at will, won't they simply modify themselves to birds and fly away? They can read all about birds, and imitate their structure without even meeting them. Or imitate, perhaps, birds of their home planet."

Copper shook his head, and helped Clark to free the dog. "Man studied birds for centuries, trying to learn how to make a machine to fly like them. He never did do the trick; his final success came when he broke away entirely and tried new methods. Knowing the general idea, and knowing the detailed structure of wing and bone and nerve-tissue is something far, far different. And as for other-world birds, perhaps, in fact very probably, the atmospheric conditions here are so vastly different that their birds couldn't fly. Perhaps, even, the being came from a planet like Mars with such a thin atmosphere that there were no birds."

Barclay came into the building, trailing a length of airplane control cable. "It's finished, Doc. Cosmos House can't be opened from the inside. Now where do we put Blair?"

Copper looked toward Garry. "There wasn't any biology building. I don't know where we can isolate him."

"How about East Cache?" Garry said after a moment's thought. "Will Blair be able to look after himself—or need attention?"

"He'll be capable enough. We'll be the ones to watch out," Copper assured him grimly. "Take a stove, a couple of bags of coal, necessary supplies and a few tools to fix it up. Nobody's been out there since last fall, have they?"

Garry shook his head. "If he gets noisy—I thought that might be a good idea."

Barclay hefted the tools he was carrying and looked up at Garry. "If the muttering he's doing now is any sign, he's going to sing away the night hours. And we won't like his song."

"What's he saying?" Copper asked.

Barclay shook his head. "I didn't care to listen much. You can if you want to. But I gathered that the blasted idiot had all the dreams McReady had, and a few more. He slept beside the thing when we stopped on the trail coming in from Secondary Magnetic, remember. He dreamt the thing was alive, and dreamt more details. And—damn his soul—knew it wasn't all dream or had reason to. He knew it had telepathic powers that were stirring vaguely, and that it could not only read minds, but project thoughts. They weren't dreams, you see. They were stray thoughts that thing was broadcasting, the way Blair's broadcasting his thoughts now—a sort of telepathic muttering in its sleep. That's why he knew so much about its powers. I guess you and I, Doc, weren't so sensitive—if you want to believe in telepathy."

"I have to," Copper sighed. "Dr. Rhine of Duke University has shown that it exists, shown that some are much more sensitive than others."

"Well, if you want to learn a lot of details, go listen in on Blair's broadcast. He's driven most of the boys out of the Ad Building; Kinner's rattling pans like coal going down a chute. When he can't rattle a pan, he shakes ashes.

"By the way, Commander, what are we going to do this spring, now the planes are out of it?"

Garry sighed. "I'm afraid our expedition is going to be a loss. We cannot divide our strength now."

"It won't be a loss—if we continue to live, and come out of this," Copper promised him. "The find we've made, if we can get it under control, is important enough. The cosmic ray data, magnetic work, and atmospheric work won't be greatly hindered."

Garry laughed mirthlessly. "I was just thinking of the radio broadcasts. Telling half the world about the wonderful results of our exploration flights, trying to fool men like Byrd and Ellsworth back home there that we're doing something."

Copper nodded gravely. "They'll know something's wrong. But men like that have judgment enough to know we wouldn't do tricks without some sort of reason, and will wait for our return to judge us. I think it comes to this: men who know enough to recognize our deception will wait for our return. Men who haven't discretion and faith enough to wait will not have the experience to detect any fraud. We know enough of the conditions here to put through a good bluff."

"Just so they don't send 'rescue' expeditions," Garry prayed. "When —if—we're ever ready to come out, we'll have to send word to Captain Forsythe to bring a stock of magnetos with him when he comes down. But—never mind that."

"You mean if we don't come out?" asked Barclay. "I was wondering if a nice running account of an eruption or an earthquake via radio— with a swell windup by using a stick of decanite under the microphone —would help. Nothing, of course, will entirely keep people out. One of those swell, melodramatic 'last-man-alive-scenes' might make 'em go easy though."

Garry smiled with genuine humor. "Is everybody in camp trying to figure that out too?"

Copper laughed. "What do you think, Garry? We're confident we can win out. But not too easy about it, I guess."

Clark grinned up from the dog he was petting into calmness. "Confident, did you say, Doc?"

VIII

Blair moved restlessly around the small shack. His eyes jerked and quivered in vague, fleeting glances at the four men with him; Barclay, six feet tall and weighing over 190 pounds; McReady, a bronze giant of a man; Dr. Copper, short, squatly powerful; and Benning, five-feet-ten of wiry strength.

Blair was huddled up against the far wall of the East Cache cabin, his gear piled in the middle of the floor beside the heating stove, forming an island between him and the four men. His bony hands clenched and fluttered, terrified. His pale eyes wavered uneasily as his bald, freckled head darted about in birdlike motion.

"I don't want anybody coming here. I'll cook my own food," he snapped nervously. "Kinner may be human now, but I don't believe it. I'm going to get out of here, but I'm not going to eat any food you send me. I want cans. Sealed cans."

"O.K., Blair, we'll bring 'em tonight," Barclay promised. "You've got coal, and the fire's started. I'll make a last—" Barclay started forward.

Blair instantly scurried to the farthest corner. "Get out! Keep away from me, you monster!" the little biologist shrieked, and tried to claw his way through the wall of the shack. "Keep away from me—keep away—I won't be absorbed—I won't be—"

Barclay relaxed and moved back. Dr. Copper shook his head. "Leave him alone, Bar. It's easier for him to fix the thing himself. We'll have to fix the door, I think—"

The four men let themselves out. Efficiently, Benning and Barclay fell to work. There were no locks in Antarctica; there wasn't enough privacy to make them needed. But powerful screws had been driven in each side of the door frame, and the spare aviation control cable, immensely strong, woven steel wire, was rapidly caught between them and drawn taut. Barclay went to work with a drill and a key-hole saw. Presently he had a trap cut in the door through which goods could be passed without unlashing the entrance. Three powerful hinges from a stock-crate, two hasps and a pair of three-inch cotterpins made it proof against opening from the other side.

Blair moved about restlessly inside. He was dragging something over to the door with panting gasps and muttering, frantic curses. Barclay opened the hatch and glanced in, Dr. Copper peering over his shoulder. Blair had moved the heavy bunk against the door. It could not be opened without his coöperation now.

"Don't know but what the poor man's right at that," McReady sighed. "If he gets loose, it is his avowed intention to kill each and all of us as quickly as possible, which is something we don't agree with. But we've something on our side of that door that is worse than a homicidal maniac. If one or the other has to get loose, I think I'll come up and undo those lashings here."

Barclay grinned. "You let me know, and I'll show you how to get these off fast. Let's go back."

The sun was painting the northern horizon in multi-colored rainbows still, though it was two hours below the horizon. The field of drift swept off to the north, sparkling under its flaming colors in a million reflected glories. Low mounds of rounded white on the northern horizon showed the Magnet Range was barely awash above the sweeping drift. Little eddies of wind-lifted snow swirled away from their skis as they set out toward the main encampment two miles away. The spidery finger of the broadcast radiator lifted a gaunt black needle against the white of the Antarctic continent. The snow under their skies was like fine sand, hard and gritty.

"Spring," said Benning bitterly, "is came. Ain't we got fun! I've been looking forward to getting away from this blasted hole in the ice."

"I wouldn't try it now, if I were you." Barclay grunted. "Guys that set out from here in the next few days are going to be marvelously unpopular."

"How is your dog getting along, Dr. Copper?" McReady asked. "Any results yet?"

"In 30 hours? I wish there were. I gave him an injection of my blood today. But I imagine another five days will be needed. I don't know certainly enough to stop sooner."

"I've been wondering—if Connant were—changed, would he have warned us so soon after the animal escaped? Wouldn't he have waited long enough for it to have a real chance to fix itself? Until we woke up naturally?" McReady asked slowly.

"The thing is selfish. You don't think it looked as though it were possessed of a store of the higher justices, did you?" Dr. Copper pointed out. "Every part of it is all of it, every part of it is all for itself, I imagine. If Connant were changed, to save his skin, he'd have to—but Connant's feelings aren't changed; they're imitated perfectly, or they're his own. Naturally, the imitation, imitating perfectly Connant's feelings, would do exactly what Connant would do."

"Say, couldn't Norris or Vane give Connant some kind of a test? If the thing is brighter than men, it might know more physics than Connant should, and they'd catch it out," Barclay suggested.

Copper shook his head wearily. "Not if it reads minds. You can't plan a trap for it. Vane suggested that last night. He hoped it would answer some of the questions of physics he'd like to know answers to."

"This expedition-of-four idea is going to make life happy." Benning looked at his companions. "Each of us with an eye on the others to make sure he doesn't do something—peculiar. Man, aren't we going to be a trusting bunch! Each man eyeing his neighbors with the grandest exhibition of faith and trust— I'm beginning to know what Connant meant by 'I wish you could see your eyes'. Every now and then we all have it, I guess. One of you looks around with a sort of 'I-wonder-if-the-other-*three*-are-look.' Incidentally, I'm not excepting myself."

"So far as we know, the animal is dead, with a slight question as to Connant. No other is suspected," McReady stated slowly. "The 'always-four' order is merely a precautionary measure."

"I'm waiting for Garry to make it four-in-a-bunk," Barclay sighed. "I thought I didn't have any privacy before, but since that order—"

None watched more tensely than Connant. A little sterile glass test-tube, half-filled with straw-colored fluid. One—two—three—four—five drops of the clear solution Dr. Copper had prepared from the drops of blood from Connant's arm. The tube was shaken carefully, then set in a beaker of clear warm water. The thermometer read blood heat, a little thermostat clicked noisily, and the electric hotplate began to glow as the lights flickered slightly.

Then—little white flecks of precipitation were forming, snowing down in the clear straw-colored fluid. "Lord," said Connant. He dropped heavily into a bunk, crying like a baby. "Six days—" Connant sobbed, "six days in there—wondering if that damned test would lie—"

Garry moved over silently, and slipped his arm across the physicist's back.

"It couldn't lie," Dr. Copper said, "The dog was human-immune—and the serum reacted."

"He's—all right?" Norris gasped. "Then—the animal is dead—dead forever?"

"He is human," Copper spoke definitely, "and the animal is dead."

Kinner burst out laughing, laughing hysterically. McReady turned toward him and slapped his face with a methodical one-two, one-two action. The cook laughed, gulped, cried a moment, and sat up rubbing his cheeks, mumbling his thanks vaguely. "I was scared. Lord, I was scared—"

Norris laughed brittlely. "You think we weren't, you ape? You think maybe Connant wasn't?"

The Ad Building stirred with a sudden rejuvenation. Voices laughed, the men clustering around Connant spoke with unnecessarily loud voices, jittery, nervous voices relievedly friendly again. Somebody called out a suggestion and a dozen started for their skis. Blair. Blair might recover— Dr. Copper fussed with his test-tubes in nervous relief, trying solutions. The party of relief for Blair's shack started out the door, skis clapping noisily. Down the corridor, the dogs set up a quick yelping howl as the air of excited relief reached them.

Dr. Copper fussed with his tubes. McReady noticed him first, sitting on the edge of the bunk, with two precipitin-whitened test-tubes of straw-colored fluid, his face whiter than the stuff in the tubes, silent tears slipping down from horror-widened eyes.

McReady felt a cold knife of fear pierce through his heart and freeze in his breast. Dr. Copper looked up.

"Garry," he called hoarsely. "Garry, for God's sake, come here."

Commander Garry walked toward him sharply. Silence clapped down on the Ad Building. Connant looked up, rose stiffly from his seat.

"Garry—tissue from the monster—precipitates too. It proves nothing. Nothing but—but the dog was monster-immune too. That *one of the two contributing blood—one of us two,* you and I, Garry— *one of us is a monster.*"

IX

"Bar, call back those men before they tell Blair." McReady said quietly. Barclay went to the door; faintly his shouts came back to the tensely silent men in the room. Then he was back.

"They're coming," he said. "I didn't tell them why. Just that Dr. Copper said not to go."

"McReady," Garry sighed, "you're in command now. May God help you. I cannot."

The bronzed giant nodded slowly, his deep eyes on Commander Garry.

"I may be the one," Garry added. "I know I'm not, but I cannot prove it to you in any way. Dr. Copper's test has broken down. The fact that he showed it was useless, when it was to the advantage of the monster to have that uselessness not known, would seem to prove he was human."

Copper rocked back and forth slowly on the bunk. "I know I'm human. I can't prove it either. One of us two is a liar, for that test cannot lie, and it says one of us is. I gave proof that the test was wrong, which seems to prove I'm human, and now Garry has given that argument which proves me human—which he, as the monster, should not do. Round and round and round and round and—"

Dr. Copper's head, then his neck and shoulders began circling slowly in time to the words. Suddenly he was lying back on the bunk, roaring with laughter. "It doesn't have to prove one of us is a monster! It doesn't have to prove that at all! Ho-ho. If we're *all* monsters it works the same! We're all monsters—all of us—Connant and Garry and I— and all of you."

"McReady," Van Wall, the blond-bearded Chief Pilot, called softly, "you were on the way to an M.D. when you took up meteorology, weren't you? Can you make some kind of test?"

McReady went over to Copper slowly, took the hypodermic from his hand, and washed it carefully in 95% alcohol. Garry sat on the bunk-edge with wooden face, watching Copper and McReady expression-lessly. "What Copper said is possible," McReady sighed. "Van, will you help here? Thanks." The filled needle jabbed into Copper's thigh. The man's laughter did not stop, but slowly faded into sobs, then sound sleep as the morphia took hold.

McReady turned again. The men who had started for Blair stood at the far end of the room, skis dripping snow their faces as white as their skis. Connant had a lighted cigarette on each hand; one he was puffing absently, and staring at the floor. The heat of the one in his left hand attracted him and he stared at it, and the one in the other hand stupidly for a moment. He dropped one and crushed it under his heel slowly.

"Dr. Copper," McReady repeated, "could be right. I know I'm human—but of course can't prove it. I'll repeat the test for my own information. Any of you others who wish to may do the same."

Two minutes later, McReady held a test-tube with white precipitin settling slowly from straw-colored serum. "It reacts to human blood too, so they aren't both monsters."

"I didn't think they were," Van Wall sighed. "That wouldn't suit the monster either; we could have destroyed them if we knew. Why, hasn't the monster destroyed us, do you suppose? It seems to be loose."

McReady snorted. Then laughed softly. "Elementary, my dear Watson. The monster wants to have life forms available. It cannot animate a dead body, apparently. It is just waiting—waiting until the best opportunities come. We who remain human, it is holding in reserve."

Kinner shuddered violently. "Hey. Hey, Mac. Mac, would I know if I was a monster? Would I know if the monster had already got me? Oh Lord, I may be a monster already."

"You'd know," McReady answered.

"But we wouldn't," Norris laughed shortly, half-hysterically.

McReady looked at the vial of serum remaining. "There's one thing this damned stuff is good for, at that," he said thoughtfully. "Clark, will you and Van help me? The rest of the gang better stick together here. Keep an eye on each other," he said bitterly. "See that you don't get into mischief, shall we say?"

McReady started down the tunnel toward Dog Town, with Clark and Van Wall behind him. "You need more serum?" Clark asked.

McReady shook his head. "Tests. There's four cows and a bull, and nearly seventy dogs down there. This stuff reacts only to human blood and—monsters."

McReady came back to the Ad Building and went silently to the wash stand. Clark and Van Wall joined him a moment later. Clark's lips had developed a tic, jerking into sudden, unexpected sneers.

"What did you do?" Connant exploded suddenly. "More immunizing?"

Clark snickered, and stopped with a hiccough. "Immunizing. Haw! Immune all right."

"That monster," said Van Wall steadily, "is quite logical. Our immune dog was quite all right, and we drew a little more serum for the tests. But we won't make any more."

"Can't—can't you use one man's blood on another dog—" Norris began.

"There aren't," said McReady softly, "any more dogs. Nor cattle, I might add."

"No more dogs?" Benning sat down slowly.

"They're very nasty when they start changing," Van Wall said precisely, "but slow. That electrocution iron you made up, Barclay, is very fast. There is only one dog left—our immune. The monster left that for us, so we could play with our little test. The rest—" He shrugged and dried his hands.

"The cattle—" gulped Kinner.

"Also. Reacted very nicely. They look funny as hell when they start melting. The beast hasn't any quick escape, when it's tied in dog chains, or halters, and it had to be to imitate."

Kinner stood up slowly. His eyes darted around the room, and came to rest horribly quivering on a tin bucket in the galley. Slowly, step by step, he retreated toward the door, his mouth opening and closing silently, like a fish out of water.

"The milk—" he gasped. "I milked 'em an hour ago—" His voice broke into a scream as he dived through the door. He was out on the ice cap without windproof or heavy clothing.

Van Wall looked after him for a moment thoughtfully. "He's probably hopelessly mad," he said at length, "but he might be a monster escaping. He hasn't skis. Take a blow-torch—in case."

The physical motion of the chase helped them; something that needed doing. Three of the other men were quietly being sick. Norris was lying flat on his back, his face greenish, looking steadily at the bottom of the bunk above him.

"Mac, how long have the—cows been not-cows—"

McReady shrugged his shoulders hopelessly. He went over to the milk bucket, and with his little tube of serum went to work on it. The milk clouded it, making certainty difficult. Finally he dropped the test-tube in the stand and shook his head. "It tests negatively. Which means either they were cows then, or that, being perfect imitations, they gave perfectly good milk."

Copper stirred restlessly in his sleep and gave a gurgling cross between a snore and a laugh. Silent eyes fastened on him. "Would morphia—a monster—" somebody started to ask.

"Lord knows," McReady shrugged. "It affects every Earthly animal I know of."

Connant suddenly raised his head. "Mac! The dogs must have swallowed pieces of the monster, and the pieces destroyed them! The dogs were where the monster resided. I was locked up. Doesn't that prove—"

Van Wall shook his head. "Sorry. Proves nothing about what you are, only proves what you didn't do."

"It doesn't do that," McReady sighed. "We are helpless because we don't know enough, and so jittery we don't think straight. Locked up! Ever watch a white corpuscle of the blood go through the wall of a blood vessel? No? It sticks out a pseudopod. And there it is—on the far side of the wall."

"Oh," said Van Wall unhappily. "The cattle tried to melt down, didn't they? They could have melted down—become just a thread of stuff and leaked under a door to re-collect on the other side. Ropes—no —no, that wouldn't do it. They couldn't live in a sealed tank or—"

"If," said McReady, "you shoot it through the heart, and it doesn't die, it's a monster. That's the best test I can think of, offhand."

"No dogs," said Garry quietly, "and no cattle. It has to imitate men now. And locking up doesn't do any good. Your test might work, Mac, but I'm afraid it would be hard on the men."

X

Clark looked up from the galley stove as Van Wall, Barclay, McReady and Benning came in, brushing the drift from their clothes. The other men jammed into the Ad Building continued studiously to do as they were doing, playing chess, poker, reading. Ralsen was fixing a sledge on the table; Vane and Norris had their heads together over magnetic data, while Harvey read tables in a low voice.

Dr. Copper snored softly on the bunk. Garry was working with Dutton over a sheaf of radio messages on the corner of Dutton's bunk and a small fraction of the radio table. Connant was using most of the table for Cosmic Ray sheets.

Quite plainly through the corridor, despite two closed doors, they could hear Kinner's voice. Clark banged a kettle onto the galley stove and beckoned McReady silently. The meteorologist went over to him.

"I don't mind the cooking so damn much," Clark said nervously, "but isn't there some way to stop that bird? We all agreed that it would be safe to move him into Cosmos House."

"Kinner?" McReady nodded toward the door. "I'm afraid not. I can dope him, I suppose, but we don't have an unlimited supply of morphia, and he's not in danger of losing his mind. Just hysterical."

"Well, we're in danger of losing ours. You've been out for an hour and a half. That's been going on steadily ever since, and it was going for two hours before. There's a limit, you know."

Garry wandered over slowly, apologetically. For an instant, Mc-Ready caught the feral spark of fear—horror—in Clark's eyes, and knew at the same instant it was in his own. Garry—Garry or Copper—was certainly a monster.

"If you could stop that, I think it would be a sound policy, Mac," Garry spoke quietly. "There are—tensions enough in this room. We agreed that it would be safe for Kinner in there, because everyone else in camp is under constant eyeing." Garry shivered slightly. "And try, try in God's name, to find some test that will work."

McReady sighed. "Watched or unwatched, everyone's tense. Blair's jammed the trap so it won't open now. Says he's got food enough, and keeps screaming 'Go away, go away—you're monsters. I won't be absorbed. I won't. I'll tell men when they come. Go away.' So—we went away."

"There's no other test?" Garry pleaded.

McReady shrugged his shoulders. "Copper was perfectly right. The serum test could be absolutely definitive if it hadn't been—contaminated. But that's the only dog left, and he's fixed now."

"Chemicals? Chemical tests?"

McReady shook his head. "Our chemistry isn't that good. I tried the microscope, you know."

Garry nodded. "Monster-dog and real dog were identical. But—you've got to go on. What are we going to do after dinner?"

Van Wall had joined them quietly. "Rotation sleeping. Half the crowd sleep; half awake. I wonder how many of us are monsters? All the dogs were. We thought we were safe, but somehow it got Copper—or you." Van Wall's eyes flashed uneasily. "It may have gotten every one of you—all of you but myself may be wondering, looking. No, that's not possible. You'd just spring then. I'd be helpless. We humans must somehow have the greater numbers now. But—" he stopped.

McReady laughed shortly. "You're doing what Norris complained of in me. Leaving it hanging. 'But if one more is changed—that may shift the balance of power.' It doesn't fight. I don't think it ever fights. It must be a peaceable thing, in its own—inimitable—way. It never had to, because it always gained its end—otherwise."

Van Wall's mouth twisted in a sickly grin. "You're suggesting then, that perhaps it already *has* the greater numbers, but is just waiting—waiting, all of them—all of you, for all I know—waiting till I, the last human, drop my wariness in sleep. Mac, did you notice their eyes, all looking at us?"

Garry sighed. "You haven't been sitting here for four straight hours, while all their eyes silently weighed the information that one of us two, Copper or I, is a monster certainly—perhaps both of us."

Clark repeated his request. "Will you stop that bird's noise? He's driving me nuts. Make him tone down, anyway."

"Still praying?" McReady asked.

"Still praying," Clark groaned. "He hasn't stopped for a second. I don't mind his praying if it relieves him, but he yells, he sings psalms and hymns and shouts prayers. He thinks God can't hear well way down here."

"Maybe he can't," Barclay grunted. "Or he'd have done something about this thing loosed from hell."

"Somebody's going to try that test you mentioned, if you don't stop him," Clark stated grimly. "I think a cleaver in the head would be as positive a test as a bullet in the heart."

"Go ahead with the food. I'll see what I can do. There may be something in the cabinets." McReady moved wearily toward the corner Copper had used as his dispensary. Three tall cabinets of rough boards, two locked, were the repositories of the camp's medical supplies. Twelve years ago McReady had graduated, had started for an internship, and been diverted to meteorology. Copper was a picked man, a man who knew his profession thoroughly and modernly. More than half the drugs available were totally unfamiliar to McReady; many of the others he had forgotten. There was no huge medical library here, no series of journals available to learn the things he had forgotten, the elementary, simple things to Copper, things that did not merit inclusion in the small library he had been forced to content himself with. Books are heavy, and every ounce of supplies had been freighted in by air.

McReady picked a barbiturate hopefully. Barclay and Van Wall went with him. One man never went anywhere alone in Big Magnet.

Ralsen had his sledge put away, and the physicists had moved off the table, the poker game broken up when they got back. Clark was putting out the food. The click of spoons and the muffled sounds of eating were the only sign of life in the room. There were no words spoken as the three returned; simply all eyes focused on them questioningly, while the jaws moved methodically.

McReady stiffened suddenly. Kinner was screeching out a hymn in a hoarse, cracked voice. He looked wearily at Van Wall with a twisted grin and shook his head. "Hu-uh."

Van Wall cursed bitterly, and sat down at the table. "We'll just plumb have to take that till his voice wears out. He can't yell like that forever."

"He's got a brass throat and a cast-iron larynx," Norris declared savagely. "Then we could be hopeful, and suggest he's one of our friends. In that case he could go on renewing his throat till doomsday."

Silence clamped down. For twenty minutes they ate without a word. Then Connant jumped up with an angry violence. "You sit as still as a bunch of graven images. You don't say a word, but oh, Lord, what expressive eyes you've got. They roll around like a bunch of glass marbles spilling down a table. They wink and blink and stare—and whisper things. Can you guys look somewhere else for a change, please?

"Listen, Mac, you're in charge here. Let's run movies for the rest of the night. We've been saving those reels to make 'em last. Last for what? Who is it's going to see those last reels, eh? Let's see 'em while we can, and look at something other than each other."

"Sound idea, Connant. I, for one, am quite willing to change this in any way I can."

"Turn the sound up loud, Dutton. Maybe you can drown out the hymns," Clark suggested.

"But don't," Norris said softly, "don't turn off the lights altogether."

"The lights will be out." McReady shook his head. "We'll show all the cartoon movies we have. You won't mind seeing the old cartoons, will you?"

"Goody, goody—a moom pitcher show. I'm just in the mood." McReady turned to look at the speaker, a lean, lanky New Englander, by the name of Caldwell. Caldwell was stuffing his pipe slowly, a sour eye cocked up to McReady.

The bronze giant was forced to laugh. "O.K., Bart, you win. Maybe we aren't quite in the mood for Popeye and trick ducks, but it's something."

"Let's play Classifications," Caldwell suggested slowly. "Or maybe you call it Guggenheim. You draw lines on a piece of paper, and put down classes of things—like animals, you know. One for 'H' and one for 'U' and so on. Like 'Human' and 'Unknown' for instance. I think that would be a hell of a lot better game. Classification, I sort of figure, is what we need right now a lot more than movies. Maybe somebody's got a pencil that he can draw lines with, draw lines between the 'U' animals and the 'H' animals for instance."

"McReady's trying to find that kind of a pencil," Van Wall answered quietly, "but we've got three kinds of animals here, you know. One that begins with 'M'. We don't want any more."

"Mad ones, you mean. Uh-huh. Clark, I'll help you with those pots so we can get our little peep-show going." Caldwell got up slowly.

Dutton and Barclay and Benning, in charge of the projector and sound mechanism arrangements, went about their job silently, while the Ad Building was cleared and the dishes and pans disposed of. McReady drifted over toward Van Wall slowly, and leaned back in the bunk beside him. "I've been wondering, Van," he said with a wry grin, "whether or not to report my ideas in advance. I forgot the 'U animals' as Caldwell named it, could read minds. I've a vague idea of something that might work. It's too vague to bother with though. Go ahead with your show, while I try to figure out the logic of the thing. I'll take this bunk."

Van Wall glanced up, and nodded. The movie screen would be

practically on a line with his bunk, hence making the pictures least distracting here, because least intelligible. "Perhaps you should tell us what you have in mind. As it is, only the unknowns know what you plan. You might be—unknown before you got it into operation."

"Won't take long, if I get it figured out right. But I don't want any more all-but-the-test-dog-monsters things. We better move Copper into this bunk directly above me. He won't be watching the screen either." McReady nodded toward Copper's gently snoring bulk. Garry helped them lift and move the doctor.

McReady leaned back against the bunk, and sank into a trance, almost, of concentration, trying to calculate chances, operations, methods. He was scarcely aware as the others distributed themselves silently, and the screen lit up. Vaguely Kinner's hectic, shouted prayers and his rasping hymn-singing annoyed him till the sound accompaniment started. The lights were turned out, but the large, light-colored areas of the screen reflected enough light for ready visibility. It made men's eyes sparkle as they moved restlessly. Kinner was still praying, shouting, his voice a raucous accompaniment to the mechanical sound. Dutton stepped up the amplification.

So long had the voice been going on, that only vaguely at first was McReady aware that something seemed missing. Lying as he was, just across the narrow room from the corridor leading to Cosmos House, Kinner's voice had reached him fairly clearly, despite the sound accompaniment of the pictures. It struck him abruptly that it had stopped.

"Dutton, cut that sound," McReady called as he sat up abruptly. The pictures flickered a moment, soundless and strangely futile in the sudden, deep silence. The rising wind on the surface above bubbled melancholy tears of sound down the stove pipes. "Kinner's stopped," McReady said softly.

"For God's sake start that sound then, he may have stopped to listen," Norris snapped.

McReady rose and went down the corridor. Barclay and Van Wall left their places at the far end of the room to follow him. The flickers bulged and twisted on the back of Barclay's gray underwear as he crossed the still-functioning beam of the projector. Dutton snapped on the lights, and the pictures vanished.

Norris stood at the door as McReady had asked. Garry sat down quietly in the bunk nearest the door, forcing Clark to make room for him. Most of the others had stayed exactly where they were. Only Connant walked slowly up and down the room, in steady, unvarying rhythm.

"If you're going to do that, Connant," Clark spat, "we can get along without you altogether, whether you're human or not. Will you stop that damned rhythm?"

"Sorry." The physicist sat down in a bunk, and watched his toes thoughtfully. It was almost five minutes, five ages while the wind made the only sound, before McReady appeared at the door.

"We," he announced, "haven't got enough grief here already. Somebody's tried to help us out. Kinner has a knife in his throat, which was why he stopped singing, probably. We've got monsters, madmen and murderers. Any more 'M's' you can think of, Caldwell? If there are, we'll probably have 'em before long."

<h1 style="text-align:center">XI</h1>

"Is Blair loose?" someone asked.

"Blair is not loose. Or he flew in. If there's any doubt about where our gentle helper came from—this may clear it up." Van Wall held a foot-long, thin-bladed knife in a cloth. The wooden handle was half-burnt, charred with the peculiar pattern of the top of the galley stove.

Clark stared at it. "I did that this afternoon. I forgot the damn thing and left it on the stove."

Van Wall nodded. "I smelled it, if you remember. I knew the knife came from the galley."

"I wonder," said Benning, looking around at the party warily, "how many more monsters have we? If somebody could slip out of his place, go back of the screen to the galley, and then down to the Cosmos House and back—he did come back, didn't he? Yes—everybody's here. Well, if one of the gang could do all that—"

"Maybe a monster did it," Garry suggested quietly. "There's that possibility."

"The monster, as you pointed out today, has only men left to imitate. Would he decrease his—supply, shall we say?" Van Wall pointed out. "No, we just have a plain, ordinary louse, a murderer to deal with. Ordinarily we'd call him an 'inhuman murderer' I suppose, but we have to distinguish now. We have inhuman murderers, and now we have human murderers. Or one at least."

"There's one less human," Norris said softly. "Maybe the monsters have the balance of power now."

"Never mind that," McReady sighed and turned to Barclay. "Bar, will you get your electric gadget? I'm going to make certain—"

Barclay turned down the corridor to get the pronged electrocuter, while McReady and Van Wall went back toward Cosmos House. Barclay followed them in some thirty seconds.

The corridor to Cosmos House twisted, as did nearly all corridors in Big Magnet, and Norris stood at the entrance again. But they heard, rather muffled, McReady's sudden shout. There was a savage flurry of blows, dull *ch-thunk, shluff* sounds. "Bar—Bar—" And a curious, savage mewing scream, silenced before even quick-moving Norris had reached the bend.

Kinner—or what had been Kinner—lay on the floor, cut half in two by the great knife McReady had had. The meteorologist stood against the wall, the knife dripping red in his hand. Van Wall was stirring vaguely on the floor, moaning, his hand half-consciously rubbing at his jaw. Barclay, an unutterably savage gleam in his eyes, was methodically leaning on the pronged weapon in his hand, jabbing—jabbing, jabbing.

Kinner's arms had developed a queer, scaly fur, and the flesh had twisted. The fingers had shortened, the hand rounded, the finger nails become three-inch long things of dull red horn, keened to steel-hard razor-sharp talons.

McReady raised his head, looked at the knife in his hand and dropped it. "Well, whoever did it can speak up now. He was an inhuman murderer at that—in that he murdered an inhuman. I swear by all that's holy, Kinner was a lifeless corpse on the floor here when we arrived. But when It found we were going to jab it with the power—It changed."

Norris stared unsteadily. "Oh, Lord, those things can act. Ye gods—sitting in here for hours, mouthing prayers to a God it hated! Shouting hymns in a cracked voice—hymns about a Church it never knew. Driving us mad with its ceaseless howling—

"Well. Speak up, whoever did it. You didn't know it, but you did the camp a favor. And I want to know how in blazes you got out of that room without anyone seeing you. It might help in guarding ourselves."

"His screaming—his singing. Even the sound projector couldn't drown it." Clark shivered. "It was a monster."

"Oh," said Van Wall in sudden comprehension. "You were sitting right next to the door, weren't you! And almost behind the projection screen already."

Clark nodded dumbly. "He—it's quiet now. It's a dead—Mac, your test's no damn good. It was dead anyway, monster or man, it was dead."

McReady chuckled softly. "Boys, meet Clark, the only one we know is human! Meet Clark, the one who proves he's human by trying to commit murder—and failing. Will the rest of you please refrain from trying to prove you're human for a while? I think we may have another test."

"A test!" Connant snapped joyfully, then his face sagged in disappointment. "I suppose it's another either-way-you-want-it."

"No," said McReady steadily. "Look sharp and be careful. Come into the Ad Building. Barclay, bring your electrocuter. And somebody—Dutton—stand with Barclay to make sure he does it. Watch every neighbor, for by the Hell these monsters came from, I've got something, and they know it. They're going to get dangerous!"

The group tensed abruptly. An air of crushing menace entered into every man's body, sharply they looked at each other. More keenly than ever before—*is that man next to me an inhuman monster?*

"What is it?" Garry asked, as they stood again in the main room. "How long will it take?"

"I don't know, exactly," said McReady, his voice brittle with angry determination. "But I *know* it will work, and no two ways about it.

It depends on a basic quality of the *monsters,* not on us. 'Kinner' just convinced me." He stood heavy and solid in bronzed immobility, completely sure of himself again at last.

"This," said Barclay, hefting the wooden-handled weapon, tipped with its two sharp-pointed, charged conductors, "is going to be rather necessary, I take it. Is the power plant assured?"

Dutton nodded sharply. "The automatic stoker bin is full. The gas power plant is on stand-by. Van Wall and I set it for the movie operation and—we've checked it over rather carefully several times, you know. Anything those wires touch, dies," he assured them grimly. "*I* know that."

Dr. Copper stirred vaguely in his bunk, rubbed his eyes with fumbling hand. He sat up slowly, blinked his eyes blurred with sleep and drugs, widened with an unutterable horror of drug-ridden nightmares. "Garry," he mumbled, "Garry—listen. Selfish—from hell they came, and hellish shellfish—I mean self—Do I? What do I mean?" he sank back in his bunk, and snored softly.

McReady looked at him thoughtfully. "We'll know presently," he nodded slowly. "But selfish is what you mean all right. You may have thought of that, half-sleeping, dreaming there. I didn't stop to think what dreams you might be having. But that's all right. Selfish is the word. They must be, you see." He turned to the men in the cabin, tense, silent men staring with wolfish eyes each at his neighbor. "Selfish, and as Dr. Copper said—*every part is a whole.* Every piece is self-sufficient, an animal in itself.

"That, and one other thing, tell the story. There's nothing mysterious about blood; it's just as normal a body tissue as a piece of muscle, or a piece of liver. But it hasn't so much connective tissue, though it has millions, billions of life-cells."

McReady's great bronze beard ruffled in a grim smile. "This is satisfying, in a way. I'm pretty sure we humans still outnumber you—others. Others standing here. And we have what you, your other-world race, evidently doesn't. Not an imitated, but a bred-in-the-bone instinct, a driving, unquenchable fire that's genuine. We'll fight, fight with a ferocity you may attempt to imitate, but you'll never equal! We're human. We're real. You're imitations, false to the core of your every cell.

"All right. It's a showdown now. You know. You, with your mind reading. You've lifted the idea from my brain. You can't do a thing about it.

"Standing here—

"Let it pass. Blood is tissue. They have to bleed, if they don't bleed when cut, then, by Heaven, they're phony! Phony from hell! If they bleed—then that blood, separated from them, is an individual—*a newly formed individual in its own right, just as they, split, all of them, from one original, are individuals!*

"Get it, Van? See the answer Bar?"

Van Wall laughed very softly. "The blood—the blood will not obey. It's a new individual, with all the desire to protect its own life that the original—the main mass from which it was split—has. The *blood* will live—and try to crawl away from a hot needle, say!"

McReady picked up the scalpel from the table. From the cabinet, he took a rack of test tubes, a tiny alcohol lamp, and a length of platinum wire set in a little glass rod. A smile of grim satisfaction rode his lips. For a moment he glanced up at those around him. Barclay and Dutton moved toward him slowly, the wooden-handled electric instrument alert.

"Dutton," said McReady, "suppose you stand over by the splice there where you've connected that in. Just make sure no—thing pulls it loose."

Dutton moved away. "Now, Van, suppose you be first on this."

White-faced, Van Wall stepped forward. With a delicate precision, McReady cut a vein in the base of his thumb. Van Wall winced slightly, then held steady as a half inch of bright blood collected in the tube. McReady put the tube in the rack, gave Van Wall a bit of alum, and indicated the iodine bottle.

Van Wall stood motionlessly watching. McReady heated the platinum wire in the alcohol lamp flame, then dipped it into the tube. It hissed softly. Five times he repeated the test. "Human, I'd say." McReady sighed, and straightened "As yet, my theory hasn't been actually proven—but I have hopes. I have hopes.

"Don't, by the way, get too interested in this. We have with us some unwelcome ones, no doubt. Van, will you relieve Barclay at the switch? Thanks. O.K., Barclay, and may I say I hope you stay with us? You're a damned good guy."

Barclay grinned uncertainly; winced under the keen edge of the scalpel. Presently, smiling widely, he retrived his long-handled weapon.

"Mr. Samuel Dutt—*Bar!*"

The tensity was released in that second. Whatever of hell the monsters may have had within them, the men in that instant matched it. Barclay had no chance to move his weapon as a score of men poured down on that thing that had seemed Dutton. It mewed, and spat, and tried to grow fangs—and was a hundred broken torn pieces. Without knives, or any weapon save the brute-given strength of a staff of picked men, the thing was crushed, rent.

Slowly they picked themselves up, their eyes smouldering, very quiet in their emotions. A curious wrinkling of their lips betrayed a species of nervousness.

Barclay went over with the electric weapon. Things smouldered and stank. The caustic acid Van Wall dropped on each spilled drop of blood gave off tickling, cough-provoking fumes.

McReady grinned, his deep-set eyes alight and dancing. "Maybe," he said softly, "I underrated man's abilities when I said nothing human could have the ferocity in the eyes of that thing we found. I wish we could have the opportunity to treat in a more befitting manner these things. Something with boiling oil, or melted lead in it, or maybe slow roasting in the power boiler. When I think what a man Dutton was—

"Never mind. My theory is confirmed by—by one who knew? Well, Van Wall and Barclay are proven. I think, then, that I'll try to show you what I already know. That I too am human." McReady swished the scalpel in absolute alcohol, burned it off the metal blade, and cut the base of his thumb expertly.

Twenty seconds later he looked up from the desk at the waiting men. There were more grins out there now, friendly grins, yet withal, something else in the eyes.

"Connant," McReady laughed softly, "was right. The huskies watching that thing in the corridor bend had nothing on you. Wonder why we think only the wolf blood has the right to ferocity? Maybe on spontaneous viciousness a wolf takes tops, but after these seven days—abandon all hope, ye wolves who enter here!

"Maybe we can save time. Connant, would you step for—"

Again Barclay was too slow. There were more grins, less tensity still, when Barclay and Van Wall finished their work.

Garry spoke in a low, bitter voice. "Connant was one of the finest men we had here—and five minutes ago I'd have sworn he was a man. Those damnable things are more than imitation." Garry shuddered and sat back in his bunk.

And thirty seconds later, Garry's blood shrank from the hot platinum wire, and struggled to escape the tube, struggled as frantically as a suddenly feral, red-eyed, dissolving imitation of Garry struggled to dodge the snake-tongue weapon Barclay advanced at him, white-faced and sweating. The Thing in the test-tube screamed with a tiny, tinny voice as McReady dropped it into the glowing coal of the galley stove.

XII

"The last of it?" Dr. Copper looked down from his bunk with bloodshot, saddened eyes. "Fourteen of them—"

McReady nodded shortly. "In some ways—if only we could have permanently prevented their spreading—I'd like to have even the imitations back. Commander Garry—Connant—Dutton—Clark—"

"Where are they taking those things?" Copper nodded to the stretcher Barclay and Norris were carrying out.

"Outside. Outside on the ice, where they've got fifteen smashed· crates, half a ton of coal, and presently will add 10 gallons of kerosene. We've dumped acid on every spilled drop, every torn fragment. We're going to incinerate those."

"Sounds like a good plan." Copper nodded wearily. "I wonder, you haven't said whether Blair—"

McReady started. "We forgot him! We had so much else! I wonder—do you suppose we can cure him now?"

"If—" began Dr. Copper, and stopped meaningly.

McReady started a second time. "Even a madman. It imitated Kinner and his praying hysteria—" McReady turned toward Van Wall at the long table. "Van, we've got to make an expedition to Blair's shack."

Van looked up sharply, the frown of worry faded for an instant in surprised remembrance. Then he rose, nodded. "Barclay better go along. He applied the lashings, and may figure how to get in without frightening Blair too much."

Three quarters of an hour, through −37° cold, while the Aurora curtain bellied overhead. The twilight was nearly 12 hours long, flaming in the north on snow like white, crystalline sand under their skis. A 5-mile wind piled it in drift-lines pointing off to the northwest. Three quarters of an hour to reach the snow-buried shack. No smoke came from the little shack, and the men hastened.

"Blair!" Barclay roared into the wind when he was still a hundred yards away. "Blair!"

"Shut up," said McReady softly. "And hurry. He may be trying a lone hike. If we have to go after him—no planes, the tractors disabled—"

"Would a monster have the stamina a man has?"

"A broken leg wouldn't stop it for more than a minute," McReady pointed out.

Barclay gasped suddenly and pointed aloft. Dim in the twilit sky, a winged thing circled in curves of indescribable grace and ease. Great white wings tipped gently, and the bird swept over them in silent curiosity. "Albatross—" Barclay said softly. "First of the season, and wandering way inland for some reason. If a monster's loose—"

Norris bent down on the ice, and tore hurriedly at his heavy, windproof clothing. He straightened, his coat flapping open, a grim blue-metaled weapon in his hand. It roared a challenge to the white silence of Antarctica.

The thing in the air screamed hoarsely. Its great wings worked frantically as a dozen feathers floated down from its tail. Norris fired again. The bird was moving swiftly now, but in an almost straight line of retreat. It screamed again, more feathers dropped and with beating wings it soared behind a ridge of pressure ice, to vanish.

Norris hurried after the others. "It won't come back," he panted.

Barclay cautioned him to silence, pointing. A curiously, fiercely blue light beat out from the cracks of the shack's door. A very low, soft humming sounded inside, a low, soft humming and a clink and click of tools, the very sounds somehow bearing a message of frantic haste.

McReady's face paled. "Lord help us if that thing has—" He grabbed Barclay's shoulder, and made snipping motions with his fingers, pointing toward the lacing of control-cables that held the door.

Barclay drew the wire-cutters from his pocket, and kneeled soundlessly at the door. The snap and twang of cut wires made an unbearable racket in the utter quiet of the Antarctic hush. There was only that strange, sweetly soft hum from within the shack, and the queerly, hecticly clipped clicking and rattling of tools to drown their noises.

McReady peered through a crack in the door. His breath sucked in huskily and his great fingers clamped cruelly on Barclay's shoulder. The meteorologist backed down. "It isn't," he explained very softly, "Blair. It's kneeling on something on the bunk—something that keeps lifting. Whatever it's working on is a thing like a knapsack—and it lifts."

"All at once," Barclay said grimly. "No. Norris, hang back, and get that iron of yours out. It may have—weapons."

Together, Barclay's powerful body and McReady's giant strength struck the door. Inside, the bunk jammed against the door screeched madly and crackled into kindling. The door flung down from broken hinges, the patched lumber of the doorpost dropping inward.

Like a blue-rubber ball, a Thing bounced up. One of its four tentaclelike arms looped out like a striking snake. In a seven-tentacled hand a six-inch pencil of winking, shining metal glinted and swung upward to face them. Its line-thin lips twitched back from snakefangs in a grin of hate, red eyes blazing.

Norris' revolver thundered in the confined space. The hate-washed face twitched in agony, the looping tentacle snatched back. The silvery thing in its hand a smashed ruin of metal, the seven-tentacled hand became a mass of mangled flesh oozing greenish-yellow ichor. The revolver thundered three times more. Dark holes drilled each of the three eyes before Norris hurled the empty weapon against its face.

The thing screamed in feral hate, a lashing tentacle wiping at blinded eyes. For a moment it crawled on the floor, savage tentacles lashing out, the body twitching. Then it staggered up again, blinded eyes working, boiling hideously, the crushed flesh sloughing away in sodden gobbets.

Barclay lurched to his feet and dove forward with an ice-ax. The flat of the weighty thing crushed against the side of the head. Again the unkillable monster went down. The tentacles lashed out, and suddenly Barclay fell to his feet in the grip of a living, livid rope. The thing dissolved as he held it, a white-hot band that ate into the flesh of his hands like living fire. Frantically he tore the stuff from him, held his hands where they could not be reached. The blind Thing felt and ripped at the tough, heavy, wind-proof cloth, seeking flesh—flesh it could convert—

The huge blow-torch McReady had brought coughed solemnly. Abruptly it rumbled disapproval throatily. Then it laughed gurglingly, and thrust out a blue-white, three-foot tongue. The Thing on the floor shrieked, flailed out blindly with tentacles that writhed and withered in the bubbling wrath of the blow-torch. It crawled and turned on the floor, it shrieked and hobbled madly, but always McReady held the blow-torch on the face, the dead eyes burning and bubbling uselessly. Frantically the Thing crawled and howled.

A tentacle sprouted a savage talon—and crisped in the flame. Steadily McReady moved with a planned, grim campaign. Helpless, maddened, the Thing retreated from the grunting torch, the caressing, licking tongue. For a moment it rebelled, squalling in inhuman hatred at the touch of the icy snow. Then it fell back before the charring breath of the torch, the stench of its flesh bathing it. Hopelessly it retreated—on and on across the Antarctic snow. The bitter wind swept over it twisting the torch-tongue; vainly it flopped, a trail of oily, stinking smoke bubbling away from it—

McReady walked back toward the shack silently. Barclay met him at the door. "No more?" the giant meteorologist asked grimly.

Barclay shook his head. "No more. It didn't split?"

"It had other things to think about," McReady assured him. "When I left it, it was a glowing coal. What was it doing?"

Norris laughed shortly. "Wise boys, we are. Smash magnetos, so planes won't work. Rip the boiler tubing out of the tractors. And leave that Thing alone for a week in this shack. Alone and undisturbed."

McReady looked in at the shack more carefully. The air, despite the ripped door, was hot and humid. On a table at the far end of the room rested a thing of coiled wires and small magnets, glass tubing and radio tubes. At the center a block of rough stone rested. From the center of the block came the light that flooded the place, the fiercely blue light bluer than the glare of an electric arc, and from it came the sweetly soft hum. Off to one side was another mechanism of crystal glass, blown with an incredible neatness and delicacy, metal plates and a queer, shimmery sphere of insubstantiality.

"What is that?" McReady moved nearer.

Norris grunted, "Leave it for investigation. But I can guess pretty well. That's atomic power. That stuff to the left—that's a neat little thing for doing what men have been trying to do with 100-ton cyclotrons and so forth. It separates neutrons from heavy water, which he was getting from the surrounding ice."

"Where did he get all—oh. Of course. A monster couldn't be locked in—or out. He's been through the apparatus caches." McReady stared at the apparatus. "Lord, what minds that race must have—"

"The shimmery sphere—I think it's a sphere of pure force. Neutrons can pass through any matter, and he wanted a supply reservoir of neutrons. Just project neutrons against silica—calcium—beryllium—almost anything, and the atomic energy is released. That thing is the atomic generator."

McReady plucked a thermometer from his coat. "It's 120° in here, despite the open door. Our clothes have kept the heat out to an extent, but I'm sweating now."

Norris nodded. "The light's cold. I found that. But it gives off heat to warm the place through that coil. He had all the power in the world. He could keep it warm and pleasant, as his face thought of warmth and pleasantness. Did you notice the light, the color of it?"

McReady nodded. "Beyond the stars is the answer. From beyond the stars. From a hotter planet that circled a brighter, bluer sun they came."

McReady glanced out the door toward the blasted, smoke-stained trail that flopped and wandered blindly off across the drift. "There won't be any more coming, I guess. Sheer accident it landed here, and that was twenty million years ago. What did it do all that for?" He nodded toward the apparatus.

Barclay laughed softly. "Did you notice what it was working on when we came? Look." He pointed toward the ceiling of the shack.

Like a knapsack made of flattened coffee-tins, with dangling cloth straps and leather belts, the mechanism clung to the ceiling. A tiny, glaring heart of supernal flame burned in it, yet burned through the ceiling's wood without scorching it. Barclay walked over to it, grasped two of the dangling straps in his hands, and pulled it down with an effort. He strapped it about his body. A slight jump carried him in a weirdly slow arc across the room.

"Anti-gravity," said McReady softly.

"Anti-gravity," Norris nodded. "Yes, we had 'em stopped, with no planes, and no birds. The birds hadn't come—but they had coffee-tins and radio parts, and glass and the machine shop at night. And a week—a whole week—all to itself. America in a single jump—with anti-gravity powered by the atomic energy of matter.

"We had 'em stopped. Another half hour—it was just tightening these straps on the device so it could wear it—and we'd have stayed in Antarctica, and shot down any moving thing that came from the rest of the world."

"The albatross—" McReady said softly. "Do you suppose—"

"With this thing almost finished? With that death weapon it held in its hand?

"No, by the grace of God, who evidently does hear very well, even down here, and the margin of half an hour, we keep our world, and the planets of the system too. Anti-gravity, you know, and atomic power. Because *They* came from another sun, a star beyond the stars. *They* came from a world with a bluer sun."

Questions for Discussion and Review

1. Why is this story set in the Antarctic?
2. Does the author offer any explanation or suggest a reason for the alien's savage aggressiveness?
3. To what degree are the various ends of SF, the mystery, and the terror story realized in "Who Goes There?" Explain your view.
4. Is there another solution to the problem of detecting those possessed by the alien?

Comic Science Fiction

Rarely do we associate SF and comedy, perhaps because the former usually takes itself so seriously. However, the two have been joined together from the early beginnings of SF. A glance at the Time Capsule reminds us that Godwin's *Man in the Moon* (1638), Cyrano's *Comic Histories* (1657), and the later comic satires of Swift and Voltaire had established the comic-SF marriage as a tradition before Mary Shelley wrote *Frankenstein.* You will recall from Part One that Edgar Allen Poe wrote comic SF fantasies, as did Washington Irving before him and Jules Verne after him. In many of these early comic SF tales, the comedy or satire is generally directed at the pride and presumption of science and scientists. This sort of critical comedy has remained a staple of comic SF ever since, as we are reminded by Asimov's "Liar!"

The varieties and forms of comedy are numerous and plentiful, enough certainly to fill out a collection devoted solely to comic SF stories. Beside the following story, some stories in Parts One through Four have elements of the comic in them. Poe's "Some Words with a Mummy" illustrates farce, or low comedy. Walter Miller's "Dark Benediction" might be classified as serious or even romantic comedy, and there are comic elements in both Berryman's "Berom" and Leinster's "First Contact." And the irony of Kuttner's "Happy Ending" is an ingenious variation of the sentimental comic formula.

One of the most notable and venerable forms of the comic is parody, which can be gentle and delightful or vicious and remorseless, depending on whether an author is out for fun or blood. Parody exaggerates selectively, as caricature does. The parody may be verbal, stylistic, or thematic, and its effectiveness is rooted deeply in our delight of the

543

ridiculous. Especially are we amused when pretentions are deflated and extremes are revealed as absurd.

We end this section and the text with a comic parody by Robert Sheckley that brings us humorously to grips with some of the follies of SF. Sheckley's SF *Dunciad* is directed mainly at the space opera, but it finishes off whole types with its broadside. In the next few pages, our author performs one of the most amusing and economical literary demolitions since the salad days of Robert Benchley and George S. Kaufman.

Zirn Left Unguarded, the Jenghik Palace in Flames, Jon Westerley Dead

Robert Sheckley

Robert Sheckley was born in July 1928, in New York City. He served in the army from 1946 to 1948 and received a Bachelor of Arts from New York University in 1951. He writes both straight and comic SF stories, but he is best known for the comic ones. His comedy is often of the type called "zany," which usually means intelligent farce as opposed to the punning, slapstick variety we found in Poe's "Some Words with a Mummy." Among Sheckley's works are *Untouched by Human Hands* (1953), *Citizen in Space* (1955), *Immortality Inc.* (1958), *Journey beyond Tomorrow* (1962), and *Can You Feel Anything When I Do This?* (1974). "Zirn Left Unguarded" first appeared in 1972 in *Nova II*, edited by Harry Harrison.

This last story, Robert Sheckley's parody of space opera, is an appropriate conclusion to our study of SF. After this, there remains nothing left to study. Sheckley's undoing of all this mighty world is complete, absolute, and final. The story is not so much a narrative as a pastiche of the conventions and clichés of heroic SF. Sheckley's comic inventory is the prelude to a literary going-out-of-business sale.

The techniques of comedy in this story are many, but the most obvious and effective is a kind of burlesque that combines parody and travesty. Parody has to do with the ludicrous imitation of style, and travesty treats its subjects with an exaggerated intemperance. The most exquisite absurdity of them all is reached when President Edgars of Earth calls God on the heavenly hotline to advise the Diety of the impending destruction of both planet and race and to ask Him to effect the obligatory intervention. Instead, his call is intercepted by the officious Paradise receptionist, Miss Ophelia, who puts Edgars off with the studied politeness of an efficient secretary protecting the boss from crank calls. And so, we must fortify ourselves to face the worst. What comfort there is we must take from the fact that it has all happened before and will all happen again.

> Our revels now are ended. These our actors,
> As I foretold you, were all spirits and
> Are melted into air, into thin air:
> And, like the baseless fabric of this vision,
> The cloud-capped towers, the gorgeous palaces,
> The solemn temples, the great globe itself
> Yea, all which it inherit shall dissolve
> And, like this insubstantial pageant faded

Leave not a rack behind. We are such stuff
As dreams are made on, and our little life
Is rounded with a sleep.

> (*The Tempest*, Act 4, Scene 1, lines 147–158)

The bulletin came through blurred with fear. "Somebody is dancing on our graves," said Charleroi. His gaze lifted to include the entire Earth. "This will make a fine mausoleum."

"Your words are strange," she said. "Yet there is that in your manner which I find pleasing . . . Come closer, stranger, and explain yourself."

I stepped back and withdrew my sword from its scabbard. Beside me, I heard a metallic hiss; Ocpetis Marn had drawn his sword, too, and now he stood with me, back to back, as the Megenth horde approached.

"Now shall we sell our lives dearly, Jon Westerley," said Ocpetis Marn in the peculiar guttural hiss of the Mnerian race.

"Indeed we shall," I replied. "And there will be some more than one widow to dance the Passagekeen before this day is through."

He nodded. "And some disconsolate fathers will make the lonely sacrifice to the God of Deteriorations."

We smiled at each other's staunch words. Yet it was no laughing matter. The Megenth bucks advanced slowly, implacably, across the green and purple moss-sward. They had drawn their *raftii*—those long, curved, double-pointed dirks that had struck terror in the innermost recesses of the civilized galaxy. We waited.

The first blade crossed mine. I parried and thrust, catching the big fellow full in the throat. He reeled back, and I set myself for my next antagonist.

Two of them came at me this time. I could hear the sharp intake of Ocpetis's breath as he hacked and hewed with his sword. The situation was utterly hopeless.

I thought of the unprecedented combination of circumstances that had brought me to this situation. I thought of the Cities of the Terran Plurality, whose very existence depended upon the foredoomed outcome of this present impasse. I thought of autumn in Carcassone, hazy mornings in Saskatoon, steel-colored rain falling on the Black Hills. Was all this to pass? Surely not. And yet—why not?

We said to the computer: "These are the factors, this is our predicament. Do us the favor of solving our problem and saving our lives and the lives of all Earth."

The computer computed. It said: "The problem cannot be solved."

"Then how are we to go about saving Earth from destruction?"

"You don't," the computer told us.

We left sadly. But then Jenkins said, "What the hell—that was only one computer's opinion."

That cheered us up. We held our heads high. We decided to take further consultations.

The gypsy turned the card. It came up Final Judgement. We left sadly. Then Myers said, "What the hell—that's only one gypsy's opinion."

That cheered us up. We held our heads high. We decided to take further consultations.

You said to yourself: " 'A bright blossom of blood on his forehead.' You looked at me with strange eyes. Must I love you?"

It all began so suddenly. The reptilian forces of Megenth, long quiescent, suddenly began to expand due to the serum given them by Charles Engstrom, the power-crazed telepath. Jon Westerly was hastily recalled from his secret mission to Augos II. Westerley had the supreme misfortune of materializing within a ring of Black Force, due to the inadvertent treachery of Ocpetis Marn, his faithful Mnerian companion, who had, unknown to Westerley, been trapped in the Hall of Floating Mirrors, and his mind taken over by the renegade Santhis, leader of the Entropy Guild. That was the end for Westerley, and the beginning of the end for us.

The old man was in a stupor. I unstrapped him from the smouldering control chair and caught the characteristic sweet-salty-sour odor of manginee—that insidious narcotic grown only in the caverns of Ingidor —whose insidious influence had subverted our guardposts along the Wall Star Belt.

I shook him roughly. "Preston!" I cried. "For the sake of Earth, for Magda, for everything you hold dear—tell me what happened."

His eyes rolled. His mouth twitched. With vast effort he said, "Zirn! Zirn is lost, is lost, is lost!"

His head lolled forward. Death rearranged his face.

Zirn lost! My brain worked furiously. That meant that the High Star Pass was open, the negative accumulators no longer functioning, the drone soldiers overwhelmed. Zirn was a wound through which our lifeblood would pour. But surely there was a way out?

President Edgars looked at the cerulean telephone. He had been warned never to use it except in the direst emergency, and perhaps not even then. But surely the present situation justified? . . . He lifted the telephone.

"Paradise Reception, Miss Ophelia speaking."

"This is President Edgars of Earth. I must speak to God immediately."

"God is out of his office just now and cannot be reached. May I be of service?"

"Well, you see," Edgars said, "I have this really bad emergency on my hands. I mean, it looks like the end of everything."

"Everything?" Miss Ophelia asked.

"Well, not *literally* everything. But it does mean the destruction of us. Of Earth and all that. If you could just bring this to God's attention—"

"Since God is omniscient, I'm sure he knows all about it."

"I'm sure he does. But I thought that if I could just speak to him personally—"

"I'm afraid that is not possible at this time. But you could leave a message. God is very good and very fair, and I'm sure he will consider your problem and do what is right and godly. He's wonderful, you know. I love God."

"We all do," Edgars said sadly.

"Is there anything else?"

"No. Yes! May I speak with Mr. Joseph J. Edgars, please?"

"Who is that?"

"My father. He died ten years ago."

"I'm sorry, sir. That is not permitted."

"Can you at least tell me if he's up there with you people?"

"Sorry, we are not allowed to give out that information."

"Well, can you tell me if *anybody* is up there? I mean, is there really an afterlife? Or is it maybe only you and God up there? Or maybe only you?"

"For information concerning the afterlife," Miss Ophelia said, "kindly contact your nearest priest, minister, rabbi, mullah, or anyone else on the accredited list of God representatives. Thank you for calling."

There was a sweet tinkle of chimes. Then the line went dead.

"What did the Big Fellow say?" asked General Muller.

"All I got was double-talk from his secretary."

"Personally, I don't believe in superstitions like God," General Muller said. "Even if they happen to be true, I find it healthier not to believe. Shall we get on with it?"

They got on with it.

Testimony of the robot who might have been Dr. Zach:

"My true identity is a mystery to me, and one which, under the circumstances, I do not expect to be resolved. But I was at the Jenghik Palace. I saw the Megenth warriors swarm over the crimson balustrades, overturn the candelabra, smash, kill, destroy. The governor died with a sword in his hand. The Terran Guard made their last stand in the Dolorous Keep, and perished to a man after mighty blows given and received. The ladies of the court defended themselves with daggers so small as to appear symbolic. They were granted quick passage. I saw the great fire consume the bronze eagles of Earth. The subject peoples had long fled. I watched the Jenghik Palace—that great pile, marking the furthest extent of Earth's suzerainty, topple soundlessly into the dust from which it sprung. And I knew then that all was lost, and that the fate of Terra—of which planet I consider myself a loyal son, despite the fact that I was (presumably) crafted rather than created, produced rather than born—the fate of divine Terra, I say, was to be annihilated utterly, until not even the ghost of a memory remained.

"You said it yourself: 'A star exploded in his eye.' This last day I must love you. The rumors are heavy tonight, and the sky is red. I love it when you turn your head just so. Perhaps it is true that we are chaff between the iron jaws of life and death. Still, I prefer to keep time by my own watch. So I fly in the face of the evidence. I fly with you.

"It is the end, I love you, it is the end."

Questions for Discussion and Review

1. What elements of space opera are burlesqued here? Make special reference to "Enchantress of Venus" where possible.

2. What other aspects of SF are burlesqued? Once again, try illustrating your answer with specific references to stories in this collection.

3. Compare and contrast the comic subjects and treatment of this story with Poe's "Some Words with a Mummy."

4. Compare and contrast the comic elements of Byron's "Darkness" with those in this story.

5. Write an additional concluding paragraph, saving everything, in the style and spirit of the original.

6. Now, justify your new ending.

Selected Bibliography

The following bibliography is selected rather than complete. It is intended as a reference list for students and general readers who would like to become more familiar with SF and the critical and reference materials available for further study. The best and most complete bibliographic guide to the field is Neil Barron's *Anatomy of Wonder* (New York: R. R. Bowker Co., 1976). I have included in the references only works that I have used and know and that I believe can be used with profit and understanding by students and general readers. The list of novels is intended to be a guide—a purely personal one—to many standard titles in the literature. A balanced selection from among the titles listed will provide a complementary offering to this text. To keep the reference list within reasonable limits, titles of short stories are not included; however, collections of short stories are marked with an asterisk(*).

Pulps (*currently in print*)

Amazing Stories
Analog Science Fiction/Science Fact
Galaxy Magazine
The Magazine of Fantasy and Science Fiction

Magazines and Journals

DeLap's Fantasy and Science Fiction Review
Extrapolation
Locus
Luna Monthly
Newsletter, Science Fiction Research Association
Science Fiction Studies

Bibliographies and Reference

Barron, Neil. *Anatomy of Wonder: Science Fiction.* New York: R. R. Bowker, 1976.
Tuck, Donald H. *Encyclopedia of Science Fiction and Fantasy,* vol. 1. Chicago: Advent, 1974.

SF Histories

Aldiss, Brian. *Billion Year Spree: The True History of Science Fiction.* Garden City, N.Y.: Doubleday, 1973.
Gunn, James. *Alternate Worlds: An Illustrated History of Science Fiction.* Englewood Cliffs, N.J.: Prentice-Hall, 1976.

Critical Studies

Allen, L. David. *Ballantine's Teacher's Guide to Science Fiction.* New York: Ballantine, 1976.
Amis, Kingsley. *New Maps of Hell: A Survey of Science Fiction.* New York: Harcourt Brace Jovanovich, 1960.
Clareson, Thomas D., ed. *Science Fiction: The Other Side of Realism.* Bowling Green, Ohio: Bowling Green University Press, 1972.
Hillegas, Mark. *The Future as Nightmare: H. G. Wells and the Anti-Utopians.* New York: Oxford University Press, 1967.
Lewis, C. S. *Of Other Worlds.* New York: Harcourt Brace Jovanovich, 1966.
Philmus, Robert M. *Into the Unknown: The Evolution of Science Fiction from Francis Godwin to H. G. Wells.* Berkeley: University of California Press, 1970.
Scholes, Robert, and Rabkin, Eric S. *Science Fiction: History, Science, Vision.* New York: Oxford University Press, 1977.

Anthologies

Asimov, Isaac. *Before the Golden Age: A Science Fiction Anthology of the 1930s.* 3 vols. Garden City, N.Y.: Doubleday, 1974.
————. *The Hugo Winners.* 2 vols. Garden City, N.Y.: Doubleday, 1971.
Boucher, Anthony. *A Treasury of Great Science Fiction.* 2 vols. Garden City, N.Y.: Doubleday, 1959.
Bova, Ben. *The Science Fiction Hall of Fame.* 2 vols. Garden City, N.Y.: Doubleday, 1973.
Clareson, Thomas D. *A Spectrum of Worlds.* Garden City, N.Y.: Doubleday, 1972.
Ellison, Harlan. *Dangerous Visions.* Garden City, N.Y.: Doubleday, 1967.
————. *Again, Dangerous Visions.* Garden City, N.Y.: Doubleday, 1972.
Healy, Raymond J., and McComas, J. Francis. *Adventures in Time and Space.* New York: Random House, 1946.
Silverberg, Robert. *The Mirror of Infinity.* New York: Harper & Row, 1970.
————. *The Science Fiction Hall of Fame,* vol. 1. Garden City, N.Y.: Doubleday, 1970.
Spinrad, Norman. *Modern Science Fiction.* New York: Anchor, 1974.

SF Novels and Collected Stories

Anderson, Poul. *Brain Wave*. New York: Ballantine, 1954.

————. *Tau Zero*. Garden City, N.Y.: Doubleday, 1970.

Asimov, Isaac. *The Caves of Steel*. Garden City, N.Y.: Doubleday, 1954.

————. *Foundation* trilogy. Garden City, N.Y.: Doubleday, 1951–1953.

————. *The End of Eternity*. Garden City, N.Y.: Doubleday, 1955.

————. *The Naked Sun*. Garden City, N.Y.: Doubleday, 1957.

————. *The Gods Themselves*. Garden City, N.Y.: Doubleday, 1972.

Ballard, James G. *Chronopolis and Other Stories*. New York: Putnam, 1971.*

Bester, Alfred. *The Demolished Man*. New York: Shasta, 1953.

————. *The Stars My Destination*. New York: Signet, 1956.

Blish, James. *A Case of Conscience*. New York: Ballantine, 1958.

————. *Cities in Flight*. New York: Avon, 1970.

Borges, Jorge L. *Ficciones*. New York: Grove, 1962.*

Bradbury, Ray. *Fahrenheit 451*. New York: Ballantine, 1953.

————. *The Martian Chronicles*. Garden City, N.Y.: Doubleday, 1950.*

————. *The Illustrated Man*. Garden City, N.Y.: Doubleday, 1951.*

Brunner, John. *Stand on Zanzibar*. Garden City, N.Y.: Doubleday, 1968.

————. *The Sheep Look Up*. New York: Harper & Row, 1972.

————. *The Shockwave Rider*. New York: Harper & Row, 1975.

Calvino, Italo. *Invisible Cities*. New York: Harcourt Brace Jovanovich, 1974.

Clarke, Arthur C. *Childhood's End*. Boston: Houghton Mifflin Co., 1953.

————. *2001: A Space Odyssey*. New York: New American Library, 1968.

————. *Tales from the White Hart*. New York: Ballantine, 1957.*

————. *The Nine Billion Names of God*. New York: Harcourt Brace Jovanovich, 1967.*

Clement, Hal. *Mission of Gravity*. Garden City, N.Y.: Doubleday, 1954.

Davidson, Avram. *Or All the Seas with Oysters*. New York: Berkley, 1962.*

De Camp, L. Sprague. *Lest Darkness Fall*. New York: Holt, Rinehart and Winston, 1949 (rev.).

Delany, Samuel. *The Einstein Intersection*. New York: Ace, 1967.

————. *Driftglass*. Garden City, N.Y.: Doubleday, 1971.*

Dick, Philip K. *The Man in the High Castle*. New York: Putnam, 1962.

————. *Do Androids Dream of Electric Sheep?* Garden City, N.Y.: Doubleday, 1968.

Ellison, Harlan. *I Have No Mouth and I Must Scream*. New York: Pyramid, 1967.*

Farmer, Philip José. *To Your Scattered Bodies Go*. New York: Putnam, 1971.

Gerrold, David. *The Man Who Folded Himself*. New York: Random House, 1973.

Haldeman, Joe. *The Forever War*. New York: St. Martin's Press, 1974.

Harrison, Harry. *Deathworld*. New York: Bantam, 1960.

Harrison, M. John. *The Pastel City.* Garden City, N.Y.: Doubleday, 1971.

Heinlein, Robert A. *Door into Summer.* Garden City, N.Y.: Doubleday, 1957.

————. *Stranger in a Strange Land.* New York: Putnam, 1961.

————. *The Moon Is a Harsh Mistress.* New York: Putnam, 1966.

————. *The Past Through Tomorrow.* New York: Putnam, 1967.*

Herbert, Frank. *Dune.* Radnor, Pa.: Chilton, 1965.

Huxley, Aldous. *Brave New World.* Garden City, N.Y.: Doubleday, 1932.

————. *Island.* New York: Harper & Row, 1962.

Kuttner, Henry. *The Best of Henry Kuttner.* New York: Ballantine, 1975.*

Le Guin, Ursula K. *The Left Hand of Darkness.* New York: Ace, 1969.

————. *The Dispossessed.* New York: Harper & Row, 1974.

————. *The Wind's Twelve Quarters.* New York: Harper & Row, 1975.*

Leiber, Fritz. *A Specter Is Haunting Texas.* New York: Walker, 1969.

Lem, Stanislaw. *Solaris.* New York: Walker, 1970.

Lewis, C. S. *Out of the Silent Planet.* New York: Collier, 1938.

————. *Perelandra.* New York: Collier, 1943.

————. *That Hideous Strength.* New York: Collier, 1945.

Lovecraft, H. P. *At the Mountains of Madness.* Sauk City, Wisc.: Arkham House, 1964.

Miller, Walter M. *A Canticle for Leibowitz.* Philadelphia: Lippincott, 1960.

————. *Conditionally Human.* New York: Ballantine, 1962.*

Moore, Ward. *Bring the Jubilee.* Garden City, N.Y.: Farrar, 1953.

Niven, Larry. *Ringworld.* New York: Ballantine, 1970.

————. *Neutron Star.* New York: Ballantine, 1968.*

Orwell, George. *1984.* New York: Harcourt Brace Jovanovich, 1949.

Panshin, Alexei. *Rite of Passage.* New York: Ace, 1968.

Pohl, Frederick, and Kornbluth, Cyril. *The Space Merchants.* New York: Ballantine, 1953.

Sheckley, Robert. *Can You Feel Anything When I Do This?* Garden City, N.Y.: Doubleday, 1971.*

Simak, Clifford. *City.* New York: Ace, 1952.

————. *Way Station.* Garden City, N.Y.: Doubleday, 1963.

Stapledon, Olaf. *Last and First Men.* London: Methuen, 1930.

————. *Star Maker.* London: Methuen, 1937.

Stewart, George. *Earth Abides.* New York: Random House, 1949.

Sturgeon, Theodore. *More Than Human.* Garden City, N.Y.: Farrar, 1953.

Vonnegut, Kurt. *Player Piano.* New York: Holt, Rinehart and Winston, 1952.

————. *The Sirens of Titan.* New York: Dell, 1959.

————. *Slaughterhouse-Five.* New York: Delacorte, 1969.

Weinbaum, Stanley. *A Martian Odyssey and Other Science Fiction Tales.* Westport, Conn.: Hyperion Press, 1975.*

Wells, H. G. *The Time Machine.* London: Heinemann, 1895.

————. *The Island of Dr. Moreau.* London: Heinemann, 1896.

————. *The Invisible Man.* London: Pearson, 1897.

————. *The War of the Worlds.* London: Heinemann, 1898.

Wilhelm, Kate. *Where Late the Sweet Birds Sang.* New York: Harper & Row, 1976.

Wyndham, John. *The Day of the Triffids.* Garden City, N.Y.: Doubleday, 1951.

Zamiatin, Eugene. *We.* New York: Dutton, 1924.

Zelazny, Roger. *The Dream Master.* New York: Ace, 1966.

————. *The Doors of His Face, the Lamps of His Mouth and Other Stories.* Garden City, N.Y.: Doubleday, 1971.*

Index

Aliens, 299–300, 319, 496–497

Alternate history, 205, 218

Amazing Stories, 17, 253, 301, 496

Anderson, Poul, 184, 441
  "Delenda Est," 205
  "Star Beast," 22, 441–464

Androids, 347

Arnold, Matthew, 1

Asimov, Isaac, 2, 100, 348
  "Liar!," 348–363, 543
  Three Laws of Robotics, 348

Astounding Science Fiction / Analog,
  18, 206, 231, 301, 319, 348,
  596

Awe, imagined, 19, 20–23, 24, 26,
  185, 228

Bacon, Francis, "The New Atlantis,"
  423

Bailey, J. O., 231

Bates, Harry, "Farewell to the
  Master," 347

Belief, imagined, 26, 408

Bellamy, Edward, *Looking Backward,*
  205

Bergson, Henri, 204

Berryman, John, 25, 301
  "Berom," 301–317, 543

Bierce, Ambrose, 184

"The Bionic Woman," 347

Bleiler, E. F., 204

Bloch, Robert, 184

Boucher, Anthony, 192

Brackett, Leigh, 100–101
  "Enchantress of Venus", 101–153

Bradbury, Ray, 156, 184
  Fahrenheit 451, 423
  "Mars Is Heaven!," 23–24, 156–
  171

Brown, Fredric, "The Answer,"
  22–23

Brunner, John, *Stand on Zanzibar,*
  19, 25

Burroughs, Edgar Rice, 100, 101,
  408, 496

Byron, Lord (George Gordon),
  30–31

"Darkness," 32–35

Campbell, John W., Jr., 18, 25, 184,
  206, 227, 231, 348, 496
  "Who Goes There?," 496–542

Čapek, Karl, 17, 346

Cartmill, Clive, "Deadline," 231

Cautionary tale, 22, 73, 408

Chandler, Raymond, 206

Chesney, Sir George Tomkyns, "The
  Battle of Dorking," 205

Clarke, Arthur C., 100, 172, 185,
  231
  "Encounter in the Dawn," 22, 25,
  172–182, 300
  "The Nine Billion Names of God,"
  185–191
  Profiles of the Future, 173

Clement, Hal, *Mission of Gravity,*
  231

Clones, 385

Comic science fiction, 26, 58–59,
  493, 543–545
  parody, 543–545

Cyborgs, 347, 467

Cyrano de Bergerac, 98, 423, 543

Darwinism, 253

De Camp, L. Sprague, 184

Defoe, Daniel, *Robinson Crusoe,* 16

Delany, Samuel R., 300

del Rey, Lester
  "Helen O'Loy," 348
  "Nerves," 231

De Quincey, Thomas, 1

Derleth, August, 184

Dick, Philip K., 184
  *Do Androids Dream of Electric
  Sheep?,* 347, 382
  The Man in the High Castle, 205

Dunsany, Lord (Edward Plunkett),
  184

Dystopia, 14, 299, 408, 422–424,
  441, 465

Einstein, Albert, 204, 205

Ellison, Harlan, 154

Emotions
  primary, 20–21
  secondary, 1, 19–26, 156, 183,
    494–495
Epic, 99, 100
Extrapolation, 206, 227, 230

Fantasy, 98, 99, 100, 101, 183, 422
Fantasy science fiction, 97–98, 183
  parallel worlds, 18, 204–205, 218
  space opera, 18, 99–100, 101–
    102, 300, 544, 545
  speculative, 154–155, 172–173,
    185
  time travel, 98, 204–205, 207,
    319, 408
  weird, 183–185, 192–193
Farmer, Philip José, 184, 408–409
  "The Sliced Crosswise Only-on-
    Tuesday World," 408–421
Future history, 206

Gadget story, 17, 227
Galaxy Magazine, 18, 480
Gernsback, Hugo, 17, 229, 231, 409
  Ralph 124C41 +, 229
Godwin, Tom, 232
  "The Cold Equations," 232–252
Godwin, William, 30, 204, 543
Goldberg, Rube, 408
Gothic, 14, 17, 57, 100, 101, 184
Gregor, Lee, "Heavy Planet," 231

Haggard, H. Rider, 100
Hale, Edward Everett, "The Brick
  Moon," 228
Hammett, Dashiell, 206
Hard science fiction, 14, 15, 59, 86,
    206, 227–228, 299–300, 383,
    465, 496
  gadget story, 17, 227
Hawthorne, Nathaniel, 30, 31,
    72–73, 184, 468
  "The Birthmark," 72–85
Heinlein, Robert A., 15, 25, 184,
    206, 231, 381
  "All You Zombies—," 206–217
  future history, 206
  The Moon Is a Harsh Mistress,
    300
  Stranger in a Strange Land, 423
Horror story, 1, 4, 15, 18, 20, 26,
    494–495, 496–497
Hubbard, L. Ron, 496
Huxley, Aldous
  Brave New World, 17, 423
  Island, 19, 25, 408, 423, 467

Irving, Washington, 543

Kline, Otis Adelbert, 101
Koestler, Arthur, 467
Kornbluth, Cyril, 192
  "The Mindworm," 192–203
Kuttner, Henry, 364
  "Happy Ending," 364–380, 543

Le Fanu, J. Sheridan, 184
Le Guin, Ursula K., 15, 385
  The Dispossessed, 385
  "Nine Lives," 385–407
  The Left Hand of Darkness, 385
Leiber, Fritz, 101, 184, 192, 480
  "Catch That Zeppelin!," 205
  "Coming Attraction," 480–491
Leinster, Murray, 25, 319
  "First Contact," 22, 23, 319–345,
    543
  "The Runaway Skyscraper," 319
  "Sidewise in Time," 205, 319
Lewis, C. S., 17, 100
London, Jack, *Before Adam,* 300
Lovecraft, H. P., 184
  Supernatural Horror in Literature,
    20
Lucian, *True History,* 99

Madden, Samuel, *The Reign of
    George VI 1900–1925,* 204
*The Magazine of Fantasy and Science
    Fiction,* 18, 184
Malzberg, Barry, 184
Maurer, David, *The Big Con,* 301
McIntyre, Vonda, 184
Merritt, Abraham, 184
Miller, R. DeWitt, 172
Miller, Walter M., Jr., 15, 253
  "Dark Benediction," 253–298, 543
Mixed genres, 15, 26, 493–495,
    543–544
Moorcock, Michael, 184
Moore, Thomas, 422
Moore, Ward, *Bring the Jubilee,* 205
Morris, William
  News from Nowhere, 423
  The Wood Beyond the World, 422
Mystery and horror science fiction, 1,
    4, 15, 18, 20, 26, 494–495,
    496–497
Myth, 100, 192, 495

New Wave, 18, 154, 184
Niven, Larry, 98, 218, 231
  "All the Myriad Ways," 218–225

Oates, Joyce Carol, 26
Orwell, George, 408
  Animal Farm, 423
  1984, 17, 423

Panshin, Alexei, 425
  "When the Vertical World Becomes Horizontal," 425–440
Parallel worlds, 18, 204–205, 218
Poe, Edgar Allan, 17, 30, 58, 184, 192, 218, 229, 230, 494, 543
  "Some Words with A Mummy," 58–71, 543
Pohl, Frederick and Kornbluth, Cyril, *The Space Merchants,* 423–424
Power, literature of, 1–2, 101
Pratt, Fletcher, 184
Pulps, 17

Realism, 15–16
Robots, 346–347, 348–349, 364, 467
  Three Laws of Robotics, 348
Romance, 14–15, 72, 97, 204, 319, 493, 494
Rousseau, Jean Jacques, *The Social Contract,* 423

Saberhagen, Fred, 495
Sheckley, Robert, 544–545
  "Zirn Left Unguarded, the Jenghik Palace in Flames, Jon Westerley Dead," 545–549
Science fiction
  and allegory, 73, 207
  backgrounds, 29–31, *see also* Time Capsule
  characterization in, 15, 17, 205
  comic, 26, 58–59, 493, 543–545
  defined, 19
  fantasy, 97–98, 183
  history, 13–19
  horror, 1, 4, 15, 18, 20, 26, 494–495, 496–497
  as a literature of ideas, 1, 14–15, 16, 25–26, 97, 154–155, 382, 385, 442, 465–466, 496
  mystery, 1, 4, 15, 18, 20, 26, 494–495, 496–497
  pleasure, 1, 19–20, 382–383
  and popular culture, 19, 100, 184, 493
  pulps, 17
  romance, 12, 14, 15, 16, 72–73, 86, 97
  and satire, 12, 14, 15, 16, 301, 466, 480–481

  and science treatise, 12–14, 16
  and tragedy, 232, 385
  utopias, 15
Serling, Rod, 184
Shelley, Mary, 17, 31, 36
  Frankenstein, 16–17, 19, 26, 30, 36–57, 346, 495
Silverberg, Robert, 408
  "Translation Error," 218, 408
Silent Running, 347
Sir Gawain and the Green Knight, 99
"The Six Million Dollar Man," 347
Smith, Clark Ashton, 184
Smith, E. E. "Doc," 100, 301, 496
Social science fiction, 206, 301–302, 381, 382, 425–426, 442, 465–466, 480–481
Soft science fiction, 18, 300, 302, 381–384, 465–466
  social science fiction, 206, 301–302, 381, 382, 425–426, 442, 465–466, 480–481
  speculative, 230, 347, 465
  utopias, 299, 347, 422–424, 425, 441
Solzhenitsyn, Alexander, 467
Space opera, 18, 99–100, 101–102, 300, 544, 545
Speculative, 25–26, 230, 347, 465
  fantasy science fiction, 154–155, 172–173, 185
  hard science fiction, 227, 230–231
  soft science fiction, 383–384
Spenser, Edmund, *The Faerie Queen,* 422
Spinrad, Norman, 154
Stapledon, Olaf, 17; 100
The Sting, 301
Stoker, Bram, 495
Stuart, Don A. (pseud.), *see* Campbell, John W. Jr.
Sturgeon, Theodore, 184
Supernatural, 183, 184, 185
  terror, 20, 192
Super Science Fiction Stories, 441
Swift, Jonathan, 98, 100, 423
  Gulliver's Travels, 30
Sword and sorcery, 101

Taylor, Gordon Rattray, *The Biological Time Bomb,* 395
The Thing, 497
Thrilling Wonder Stories, 364
Time Capsule, 2–13, 227
Time travel, 98, 204–205, 207, 319, 408

Tiptree, James, 184, 300
Tolkien, J. R. R., *Lord of the Rings,*
   422
Unknown, 184
Utopias, 299, 347, 422–424, 425,
   441
   fantasy, 422–423
   pastoral, 422
   philosophical, 422
   scientific, 423
   social, 423

Vampire (vampirism), 36, 192–193
Von Daniken, Erich, 172
Verne, Jules, 30, 100, 231, 543
   The Mysterious Island, 30
   20,000 Leagues Under the Sea,
      228
Voltaire, 30, 98, 300, 441
Vonnegut, Kurt, 100, 347
   Player Piano, 423

Weird science fiction, 183–185, 192–
   193
Weird Tales, 184, 364
Wells, H. G., 17, 30, 32, 86–87, 98,
   381
   In the Days of the Comet, 425
   "The Star," 86–95, 100, 230
   The Time Machine, 204–205,
      423
Wilhelm,. Kate, 1,5, 467
   "Baby, You Were Great!," 467–
      479
Wonder, imagined, 19, 20–21,
   23–25, 26, 156, 173, 185, 228
Wright, Austin T., 423

Zamiatin, Eugene, 17
   We, 423